Home is

Rancher Trent Cre... ...r
and plans to keep... ...
matchmaking uncles arrange to give him a
Christmas—and a woman—to remember....

Rodeo cowboy Abe Cockburn
isn't the settling-down type—
until he's confronted by a lover he can't
forget...and a child he didn't know existed....

Relive the romance
By Request
Two complete novels by your favorite authors

HEATHER MacALLISTER

lives with her electrical-engineer husband
and two live-wire sons whose antics inspire
her humorous approach to love and life.
And they're doing a good job! Heather is a
three-time finalist for the prestigious RITA
Award and is a *USA Today* bestselling author!
Heather has written for both the Harlequin
Romance and Harlequin Temptation lines,
finding the main difference between her stories
for each is that her Harlequin Romance heroines
find love, but love always has to go out and catch
her Temptation heroines. In the end, of course,
they all live happily ever after.

MARGOT EARLY

says she's written romance fiction since she
was twelve. (Her first hero and heroine were
kids as well, solving a mystery together.) She's
been writing ever since—humor, features,
scripts, as well as fiction. In fact, Margot met her
husband at a murder mystery for which he wrote
the script. He played an undertaker, she played a
nun. And in a matter of hours he told her he was
falling in love. Margot lives in Colorado with her
husband and son.

HEATHER MacALLISTER
MARGOT EARLY

Home on the Range

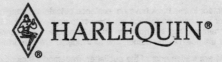

HARLEQUIN®

TORONTO • NEW YORK • LONDON
AMSTERDAM • PARIS • SYDNEY • HAMBURG
STOCKHOLM • ATHENS • TOKYO • MILAN • MADRID
PRAGUE • WARSAW • BUDAPEST • AUCKLAND

HARLEQUIN BOOKS

by Request—HOME ON THE RANGE

Copyright © 2001 by Harlequin Books S.A.

ISBN 0-373-21723-4

The publisher acknowledges the copyright holders
of the individual works as follows:
CHRISTMAS MALE
Copyright © 1996 by Heather W. MacAllister
THE TRUTH ABOUT COWBOYS
Copyright © 1997 by Margot Early

This edition published by arrangement with Harlequin Books S.A.

CONTENTS

Matchmaking doesn't get any better than this...

CHRISTMAS MALE
Heather MacAllister

"TRENT, MY BOY, it's high time you got yourself hitched."

Although he'd been expecting such a comment, Trent Davis Creighton had hoped to escape from this weekend visit to the Triple D Ranch without discussing his future matrimonial prospects with his uncles.

He finished countersigning the papers authorizing him to buy certificates of deposit with the ranch's quarterly oil royalties, then met his uncle Clarence's shrewd brown eyes. "Does this mean you like Miranda?" As Trent spoke, he gazed out the ranch office window where a tall blonde, wearing a wrinkled linen outfit, stood next to his car and waited impatiently for him to drive her back to Dallas.

"Whether or not I like her isn't the point." The leather chair creaked as Clarence shifted his weight, easing his arthritic hip. "The point is that you should be looking for a wife. You're not going to find one in that direction."

Trent had no intention of looking for a wife in any direction, but he'd hoped bringing Miranda with him for the weekend would appease his uncles. "Miranda would make any man a fine wife," Trent found himself saying. And she would—when she was ready for marriage. However, she wasn't, and Trent was honest enough to admit that her disinterest in a permanent commitment was a large part of her attraction for him.

"And so she will," Clarence agreed. "But she's not the type of woman you want for a wife."

"And why not?" Actually, if he was to consider marriage right now—and he most assuredly was not—Trent considered Miranda exactly the sort of wife he'd want. She managed to look classy and sexy at the same time, which appealed to him. He couldn't imagine what his uncles objected to—because he knew if Clarence objected, then Harvey and Doc, Trent's other uncles, objected as well.

"She's a high-maintenance quarter horse. Lots of flash, fast out of the gate, but no stamina."

Trent burst out laughing.

Clarence leveled a look at him. "We've talked to you before about your blondes."

Boot heels striking a wooden floor announced the approach of another one of the uncles. Trent glanced toward the doorway as Doc entered the office.

"What can I say?" Still chuckling, Trent turned to face the most taciturn of his uncles, holding out another set of papers. "I like blondes. Tall blondes." He pointed to the signature line and watched as Doc signed. "And *she*—" he hooked a thumb toward the window "—is a mighty fine blonde."

After scrawling his name, Doc snorted and walked over to the window. "She's got long flanks but a narrow pelvis. Not much breeding room."

Trent was *very* glad Miranda could not hear this conversation.

Doc finished his assessment. "You'll not get more than one or two kids out of her."

Trent grimaced. "You're assuming I want more than one or two children. Besides, you're a vet, not an obstetrician." Why did he let himself get drawn into these discussions?

"A narrow pelvis is a narrow pelvis," Doc stated.

"You have to consider these things, Trent," added Clarence, complacently folding his hands across his ample stomach. "Along with the fact that you'd better get started growing young 'uns before you're too old to enjoy them."

"Point taken." Arguing was fruitless. "Where's Uncle Harvey? I still need his signature on these transfer papers."

"He's looking for a pen," Clarence responded.

"I *have* a pen," Trent said. "Several pens, as I'm sure he knows." He walked to the office door. "Uncle Harvey? It's time Miranda and I left for Dallas. We want to avoid the Sunday afternoon traffic."

From somewhere inside the ranch house, he heard a faint response, but couldn't make it out.

Clarence appeared lost in thought. Doc continued to gaze out the window, probably assessing one of Miranda's other physical traits.

He confirmed this momentarily. "Broad shoulders. I couldn't tell at first because the narrow pelvis skewed the ratio, but with your shoulders, Trent, and hers, your sons— few though there'll likely be—" he glanced at Trent "—should have a good set of shoulders. I'll be able to tell you more after meeting her parents."

No one was going to meet anyone's parents. Trent did not feel any pressing need to get married. He had the Triple D's assets to manage as well as other financial irons in the fire. He was, in fact, on the verge of making his mark in the Dallas financial world and he'd be doing it without Triple D funds, a distinction becoming increasingly important to him.

A wife didn't fit into his plans.

Unfortunately, his uncles didn't agree.

"Uncle Harvey!" Trent called again, wincing as he recognized the impatience in his voice. He loved his uncles and all their endearing quirks. However a man had his limits.

"Might have girls," Clarence said, still pondering Trent's future progeny.

"A possibility," Doc agreed somberly.

Trent was saved from a lecture on the exact mathematical probability by the breathless arrival of Harvey, the remaining Davis brother.

"I found it!" Triumphantly, he held up an angular silver pen. "Trent, this is the same kind of pen used by the NASA astronauts in space. It will write in any direction with or without gravity."

Trent smiled and tapped the third set of papers.

"I thought you ordered one of those last year." Clarence examined the pen.

"Oh, yes, but I gave it to the Miller boy when he graduated. I never got the chance to try it, so I reordered."

"Uncle Harvey, if you would sign your name right here?" Trent prompted.

Harvey retrieved his pen and grabbed for the papers. "It really works. Let me show you." Bending over, he placed the papers against the front of the desk and turned so that he was writing upside down. "There you go, Trent. The ink flows without interruption. Want to try it?"

Trent, already countersigning, shook his head. "Thanks, but I'm using the Executive Compass Pen you got for me the Christmas before last."

Harvey's face lit up. "How has that one performed? As I recall, it was guaranteed for a full year or my money back."

"Fine. It's worked just fine." Or at least it had through the Trent D. Creig part of his name. He pressed harder, but the Ultimate Executive Compass Pen, with tweezers and toothpick, had run out of ink. Irritated, he shook it.

"Been over a year since you bought it?" Clarence asked.

"Yes, but a high-quality product would have lasted

longer." Harvey frowned. "A year should have been the minimum."

"It's okay," Trent broke into the discussion, which he knew from experience could last for some time. "I write more than the average person."

"Use the NASA pen." Harvey thrust it at him. "Astronauts depend on them, you know."

"Now that'll be a quality product," Clarence added.

Trent accepted the NASA pen and finished signing his name, quickly packing away the papers before another discussion could boil over. And from the way his uncles were looking at him, he could sense one simmering now.

"I'll, uh, be back in September, if I don't see you all before then." Trent felt unaccountably guilty as three pairs of identical brown eyes, topped by graying bushy eyebrows, gazed at him. Why were they so set on his marrying? He picked up his briefcase and walked from behind the huge wooden desk that had served as the hub of Triple D Ranch business since his grandfather's time.

Clarence leaned forward, and the leather chair creaked. Trent offered a hand to help him stand. Usually Clarence refused, but today he accepted the help.

They're getting older, Trent thought, even as he suspected Clarence was exaggerating his infirmities to lend a sense of urgency to Trent's search for a wife. Still, he thought he smelled horse liniment, which he suspected Doc had prescribed for Clarence's joints. "It's time for me to leave. I've kept Miranda waiting for too long as it is."

"Oh, yes. She appears quite put out," Harvey informed him from the window.

Trent stepped forward, but Clarence held on to his hand. "Keep looking, boy, she isn't the right one."

Trent intended to smile and make some innocuous remark. He *should* have let the comment pass. Instead he blurted, "How do you know she isn't the right one? Other than her narrow pelvis," he added before Doc could.

"She's not a comfortable sort of woman."

"Bony," elaborated Doc.

"That, too," Clarence acknowledged before continuing his lecture. The strength of his grip belied his earlier struggle to stand. "But she wouldn't be happy here at the Triple D."

"We'd live in Dallas," Trent reminded him. He meant his future wife, not necessarily Miranda, but knew it was useless to point that out.

"You won't always live in Dallas. We're getting on in years." Clarence squeezed Trent's arm before releasing it.

"But we're taking good care of ourselves," Harvey broke in. "We take a multivitamin with one hundred percent of the minimum daily requirements for adults over age fifty-five. We exercise on Dr. Pritchard's Healthcycle to raise our heart rates for twenty minutes three times—"

"The boy knows that, Harvey."

Harvey broke off immediately. Clarence rarely interrupted him.

"What we're trying to say is that it's time you looked for a wife. Seriously looked. She should be a willing life partner who isn't afraid of a little work. Someone who'll be a good mother to your children, should you be blessed with them. Feed 'em right, raise 'em straight and keep the home fires burning while you're out supporting your family."

"And she should do it wearing high heels and pearls, right?" As soon as the words were out, Trent regretted them. His uncles meant well, but his marital status was becoming a sore point. "I mean, you've described a housewife from those old television shows."

"And what's wrong with that?"

"It was nearly forty years ago. Modern women aren't like that."

"Not the women you keep company with. You need to find someone like your aunt Emma, may she rest in peace."

Now how was a man supposed to argue with that? Though they'd never had children of their own, Clarence's wife, Emma, had been a mother to Trent since he'd come to live at the Triple D when he was seven years old. Neither Doc nor Harvey had ever married and Emma Davis had taken care of all of them.

"Aunt Emma was one of a kind," Trent said quietly.

"That she was," Clarence said, with murmured agreements from Doc and Harvey. "But that doesn't let you off the hook."

"What do you expect me to do—order a wife from one of your catalogs?"

Doc scratched his chin. "Why not? You can order livestock."

"And I have a catalog." Harvey dashed from the room.

"Why am I not surprised?" Trent muttered to himself.

"I'm glad you brought the subject up." Clarence put on his reading glasses and reached into his pocket just as Harvey galloped back into the room.

"That was quick," Trent said dryly, suspecting he'd been set up.

"Because I'm wearing ultra-gripper track shoes." Harvey raised his foot to reveal a pale gridded sole. "They grip the pavement sixty-seven percent more than the bestselling store brand."

Trent knew better than to point out the lack of pavement at the Triple D Ranch. He was more concerned with the magazine Harvey held. *"Texas Men?* What is this?" Flipping through the glossy publication, he groaned. "It's a giant personals ad. You aren't seriously suggesting that I—"

"'Rancher seeks traditional wife,'" Clarence read from a creased paper.

"What rancher?" Trent asked, suspecting he didn't want to know.

"You, Trent."

"You've got to be kidding."

Clarence peered over his half-glasses.

"I'm not a rancher," Trent insisted.

"It's in your blood, boy." Clearing his throat, Clarence proceeded. "'Although I currently live in Dallas, my heart is in the Texas Hill Country where I'm the only heir to the Triple D Ranch.'"

"Oh, please. You're not—"

Clarence held up his hand and continued reading. "'Living in the city has taught me what's important in life—family, the land and the love of a good woman. Not just any woman, but that one special woman who'll share my life's vision of hearth and home. I'm a simple man who values honesty and hard work. The woman with whom I'd like to share my life should be willing to work right along beside me, raising our children and keeping our home happy and healthy.'"

"You're describing pioneers!" Not only that, Trent hardly considered himself a simple man who loved the land.

Doc pointed. "Read the next bit."

"'I'm aware that this way of life has fallen into disfavor, but I believe that people today are working too hard for too little. Parents are letting others raise their children, resulting in unhappy families. That's why I want to return to the natural order of a male providing and a female nurturing.'"

"What if I don't *want* to be nurtured? What if I don't

want to provide so some woman can twiddle her thumbs all day?"

Undeterred, Clarence continued. "'My wife won't have to exhaust herself trying to do my job as well as hers. If you agree and are between the ages of eighteen—'"

"Uncle Clarence, I wouldn't even consider dating an eighteen-year-old!" Trent protested that point, though why, he didn't know. His uncle had just described a politically incorrect nightmare.

Harvey handed Clarence the NASA pen. Clarence made a note. "'Between the ages of twenty-one and thirty...What do you think, Doc? Can we bump that up to thirty-five?"

Doc rubbed the back of his head. "Prime childbearing years are somewhat younger, but with today's medicine..." He shrugged. "Go ahead—and add that it's okay if she has some meat on her bones."

Even given his fond tolerance for his uncles, Trent was speechless. As he listened, Clarence outlined qualities that might describe the daughter of Betty Crocker and Norman Rockwell, concluding with, "'Help me capture the spirit of an old-fashioned country Christmas with all the trimmings here at the Triple D.'"

"Wait a minute—"

"That was my idea," a pleased Harvey inserted.

"'Come prepared to cook up a storm and hang the cholesterol.'"

Doc harumphed.

"That was Clarence's idea," Harvey said.

"'Piano players will be given preference.'"

"For the love of—"

"'The Triple D has a modern, fully equipped kitchen—'"

"With cupochino machine. Don't forget to tell them about my cupochino machine." Harvey pointed to where Clarence should add that information.

"Cappuccino," Trent corrected under his breath.

"Mention the satellite television, too," Harvey instructed.

"That'll be a real draw," Trent muttered.

Clarence made a note. "How does that sound to you, Trent?"

No woman in her right mind will answer that ad. The only responses he was likely to get would be hate mail from feminist groups.

On the other hand, this could be just the answer. The search for a woman who met their outdated criteria would keep his uncles occupied and convince them they were making progress toward getting him married off. When they failed to interest any woman in returning to the Dark Ages, they'd ease up on Trent. In the meantime, he'd be able to concentrate on his business.

A white blur caught his eye. Miranda was stalking back into the house and he didn't blame her. He'd promised her he'd only be a few minutes longer and he didn't want her to overhear them. "I think you've covered just about everything. Look, I've got to leave now." He started for the door. "Take care."

"What about the responses?"

"I'll meet one woman of your choice." Assuming there would be one.

"Now, Trent, son—"

"One." He held up a finger.

Clarence, an old horse trader, knew when to back off. "And you'll promise to come and meet her?"

"Yes."

"For Christmas?" Harvey asked. For all his dithering, Harvey wasn't a bad negotiator, either.

"Yes, for Christmas," Trent promised.

"Two weeks?"

"Uncle Harvey, I can't spare two weeks at the end of the year."

Harvey looked stubborn.

"Not much time to get acquainted with your future wife." Clarence rubbed his hip. Trent refrained from rolling his eyes.

"All right, all right! Two weeks at Christmas." He actually felt guilty since that was one promise he knew he wouldn't have to keep.

RUSTY ROMERO inhaled gratefully as she unlocked the door to her Chicago apartment. Food. She smelled food.

"Gran? Is that you?" Rusty dumped her purse and jacket on the sideboard and kicked off her pumps.

A trim woman with an attractive silver bob stepped to the door of the kitchen. "And who else would be warming a casserole in your kitchen?"

"A *casserole*? How domestic. Did you make it yourself?"

"Certainly." Agnes Romero smiled triumphantly before disappearing inside the kitchen.

"This I've got to see." Rusty followed her grandmother, dropping her portfolio onto the couch on the way.

"Where have you been?" Agnes asked. "It's nine-thirty."

"Working." Rusty slumped against the doorjamb.

Her grandmother shot her a you've-been-working-too-hard look. "I brought the dish over a couple of hours ago, but when you didn't call and *rave* over it, I naturally assumed you could barely stomach it."

"Gran!" Laughing, Rusty shook her head. "What is it this time?"

Wearing cow oven mitts, Agnes removed the rectangular dish. "Tuna noodle casserole."

"For Thanksgiving?" Rusty's grandmother had been testing potential Thanksgiving menus for weeks. It would be the first home-cooked turkey dinner the two had ever shared.

"Of course not. This is a small deviation. Go get comfortable and I'll bring you a plate."

Too tired to protest her grandmother's waiting on her, Rusty collapsed onto her living room sofa.

From in the kitchen came the sound of the silverware drawer being opened. "How's the campaign going?"

"I'm reviewing magazines for the print ads."

"Is this still the shaving lotion?"

"Gran, *please*," Rusty said in mock indignation. "This is much more than mere shaving lotion. This is a complete line of men's grooming essentials based on all-natural ingredients."

"How complete a line can it be?" Agnes Romero stuck her head out the kitchen door. "A man doesn't need anything more than shaving lotion, deodorant and hair dressing."

"They don't call it 'dressing' anymore. It's bio-fixative."

Rusty heard smothered laughter. "Let me guess, there's tinted moisturizer and bronzing gel."

"No bronzing gel. Men have caught on to that. It's 'tan evener.' And there's a cellular eye treatment, as well."

"Tinted?"

"Pine, oak and walnut. Guaranteed to freshen your expression." Rusty flipped open her portfolio and withdrew a stack of publications.

Agnes appeared with a tray. "Put those away and relax for a bit." Setting her burden down on the coffee table in front of the sofa, Rusty's grandmother pushed aside the magazines and sat beside her.

"Thanks, Gran." Rusty reached for the plate. A beige gelatinous lump wiggled in the center.

Agnes frowned. "I've probably seen a hundred recipes,

all virtually alike, touting tuna noodle casserole as though it's some nutritional elixir. I thought I'd see what all the fuss is about."

"Have you eaten any yet?" From previous experience Rusty knew that Agnes's culinary efforts were uneven at best.

"Yes." Agnes watched as Rusty propped her feet on the table and scooped a forkful of the casserole. "It lacks a certain visual appeal. Though it was more appealing two hours ago."

"Sorry. If I'd known you were experimenting today, I would have called." She tasted it. "Hmm."

"That's what I thought." Agnes reached for the plate.

"No, no." Rusty held it out of the way. "I'll eat it. It's not bad." Especially since she was starving.

"But it's nothing you feel you lacked in your youth, is it?"

Rusty exhaled. Underneath her grandmother's teasing was a genuine concern. Since Agnes Romero had sold her real estate business and retired a couple of years ago, she'd tried to turn herself into some sort of domestic goddess, apparently feeling the need to atone for not being one during Rusty's childhood. "No. I don't feel I was deprived of *anything* in my youth." She gripped her grandmother's hand for emphasis.

"Well, that's a relief. I'll never have to make this dish again."

They both laughed.

"What happened to all the Thanksgiving experiments?" Rusty fondly remembered the two glorious weeks her grandmother learned to make pies.

"Oh, I'm still working on the ultimate menu, but I found references to tuna fish in the 'family favorites' section of

Holiday Hearth and Home and I just..." She trailed off with a shrug.

"And you just felt guilty because you didn't give me an apple-pie childhood in the suburbs." Rusty set the plate down and hugged her grandmother. "I had a *great* childhood. You taught me survival skills for the big city. How many seven-year-olds can order a complete, nutritionally balanced meal for two? *And* calculate the tip?"

Agnes chuckled. "How many seven-year-olds have to?" She leaned back. "I suppose that since I retired, I've had time to think about my life. And I'll admit that I have a few regrets. When I see you and the kind of life you lead now, I see myself."

Rusty knew what was bothering her grandmother. "And you don't want me to have regrets, too, is that it?"

Agnes nodded.

"Hey, no problem. I love my life. It's *perfect* for me right now. I'm at my ideal weight and have no wrinkles. How many people can say that?"

"But you work so hard."

"So did you! At least I'm not out showing houses on weekends." Rusty retrieved the plate and continued eating the casserole. "Now look, this isn't bad, but do you really think it's a substitute for having my own dessert named after me at a four-star restaurant?"

Agnes groaned. "I should have been home more for you. I've made the same mistakes with you that I did with your mother."

"Oh, I disagree. You made completely different mistakes with me."

At her grandmother's startled expression, Rusty burst out laughing. "I don't think you made mistakes with either one of us," she said firmly. "You made choices."

Agnes looked pensive. "But sometimes I wonder if I should have made other choices."

"Nonsense." Rusty had finished inhaling the casserole. "I'm going to make some coffee. Want some?"

"This late you'd better make decaf."

Rusty walked into the kitchen. She'd planned to put in a few more hours of work before bed and definitely needed the caffeine. She'd have to make a new pot after her grandmother left. "Decaf it is," she called.

Pulling open the refrigerator door to get out the coffee beans, she discovered a foreign plastic container. "What's this in the fridge?"

"I tried to make a pecan pie and it didn't set," her grandmother called out. "But the filling tastes great over ice cream."

It looked like it would, too. "I don't have any ice cream."

"Yes, you do."

Rusty yanked open the freezer to find a carton of the most expensive brand of vanilla ice cream. She sighed in bliss. "Now, how can a woman of such perception and insight feel regrets about anything?"

"You always could be swayed with food," her grandmother replied.

"All too true."

When Rusty returned with the coffee and two bowls of pecan-topped ice cream, she found her grandmother flipping through the pages of one of the men's magazines Rusty had brought home.

"These are quite enlightening," her grandmother said.

"Any one in particular?" Rusty asked, taking a heavenly mouthful of ice cream.

"*This* one." Agnes held up a copy of *Texas Men.*

"Ah, the beefcake mag. Can you believe it? Men actually advertising for dates?" Rusty snickered.

"Oh, I don't know..." Trailing off, her grandmother studied some of the profiles. "Rusty, darling, have you ever considered writing to one of these men?"

"Oh, Gran, please!"

"Don't be hasty...I see a six-foot-four, brown-eyed brunet—"

"What's the matter with him?"

"*Nothing.* It says that he's built a construction business and hasn't had time to meet women."

"Yeah, right."

"Seriously, doesn't he attract you at all?" Agnes held out the picture.

"Nope."

"All your hard work is suppressing your hormones. This one's five-eight, but he's really cute."

"Gran, ask yourself what kind of man has to advertise to meet women?"

"It appears that busy, vibrant and successful men do. Look." She pointed to a photograph of an admittedly attractive man.

His picture was a typical businessman's studio pose and yet something about his eyes caught Rusty's attention. "I look like this because it's expected, but this isn't the real me," they said. And, she had to admit, there was a definite invitation to "meet the real me" there. In fact, she wondered where the "real me" lived.

"See?" Her grandmother smiled slyly.

"Okay, he's cute." Quite attractive. Definitely worth a second look. "What's the matter with him?"

"Rusty!"

Rusty set down her bowl and grabbed for the magazine. After a brief struggle, Agnes let go.

"Aha! 'Rancher seeks *traditional* wife.' He doesn't look like a rancher to me." Not that she knew any ranchers.

However, Rusty's eyes widened as she read the biographical profile. "Did you see this? He's a Neanderthal! The missing link!"

"Rusty, darling—"

Rusty waved her grandmother into silence. "Listen to this—'That's why I want to return to the natural order of a *male providing and a female nurturing.*' No wonder this guy isn't married. Can you say 'domestic slavery'?" Rusty tossed the magazine back to her grandmother and cleared away their dishes.

"All right, I'll admit his ideas are unilluminated—"

"Ha! He's setting women's rights back a hundred years! Two hundred, even."

"But read the part about going to his ranch and having an old-fashioned Christmas."

"'Old-fashioned' meaning women do all the work."

With half an ear, Rusty listened as her grandmother read about cutting a Christmas tree, sleigh rides and caroling. "Oh, and he wants someone who can play the piano."

"When would she have time?" Rusty grumbled on her way back to the living room.

"And—" Agnes glanced toward Rusty "—a woman with meat on her bones."

What patronizing nerve! Rusty's mouth opened and closed. Finally she shook her head. "I *pity* the poor woman who hooks up with that guy!" Incensed, she paced in front of her grandmother. "In fact, Mr. King of the Neanderthals should be reported to somebody in human rights. There's got to be a committee somewhere. Can you believe him?" She stared down at the man's picture. He couldn't be an *unattractive* jerk, oh, no. A shame those eyes had to be wasted on him. "Any woman responding to that profile needs therapy."

2

"YOU RESPONDED to the chauvinistic rancher?" Rusty stared at her grandmother over a golden brown but over-cooked Thanksgiving turkey. "How funny. Why didn't you tell me? I would've loved to have been in on the joke."

"It wasn't a joke." Her grandmother's serious blue eyes met hers.

Rusty waited, but Agnes didn't crack a smile. "Come on, Gran, you're scaring me."

"And I wasn't the only respondent. There are plenty of women ready to forsake the rat race. But I, or rather, we—you, actually—are the one the Davis brothers have invited for Christmas. Naturally, I'd come with you to chaperone."

Spend Christmas on a ranch with strangers who wanted to check her out as housewife material? Her grandmother *had* to be joking. "You turned them down, right?"

Agnes shook her head. "I don't want to turn them down."

Rusty's silverware clattered in the silence. "Let me get this straight. You answered a personals ad *in my name* and now you want me to meet this man?"

Agnes stared at her plate. "Yes, but I knew that I'd need to talk to you first."

"Darn right!" Rusty was so agitated she helped herself to another glob of stuffing. It was warm, soft and full of fat—just what she needed at the moment.

"The Triple D Ranch is owned by the three Davis brothers. There's Clarence, Harvey and William, but everybody calls him Doc."

"I don't want to hear this."

"Trent is their nephew."

"Send them my condolences."

"Rusty."

Rusty abandoned the stuffing. "I'm sorry, Gran. This isn't like you and I don't understand."

Agnes began clearing away the remains of an opulent Thanksgiving feast. She'd prepared far too much food for just the two of them, and Rusty had been happily looking forward to leftovers. "Their description of Christmas on the ranch sounded like my girlhood on the farm."

"You couldn't wait to leave the farm," Rusty reminded her. She looked around her grandmother's elegantly contemporary apartment. "I can't even imagine you on a farm."

"Oh, but there were good things about the country. And we'd have the same things on the ranch—a *real* Christmas tree that we'd cut ourselves. Popcorn and cranberry strings, carols, hot chocolate...and family." Smiling, her grandmother looked off into the distance.

"Hold it. We are not related to those people."

To Rusty's shock, her grandmother's eyes grew moist. "I want to go, Rusty. I *want* an old-fashioned Christmas. I want *you* to have an old-fashioned Christmas at least once."

This suddenly sentimental woman was not the grandmother who had raised her. Rusty managed a shaky laugh. "I'm going to take away all your home and craft magazines. They're an evil influence."

Agnes ignored her. "Couldn't you spare a couple of weeks?"

Said that way, it sounded like such a small request. But it wasn't. "You're not asking for just any two weeks. That's when Dearsing is reviewing the Next to Nature campaigns." Rusty gestured helplessly. "I've got to be there and make sure mine is the most dynamic presentation that Dearsing has ever seen. This campaign could go national and I want it so bad, Gran. I just can't take those two weeks off."

The light went out of Agnes's eyes. "Of course you can't. I was foolish to suggest it."

Rusty felt awful. Worse than awful. She owed her grandmother for the years Agnes had spent raising her. Now her grandmother had retired, and Rusty had vowed to see that she would be financially secure for the rest of her life. Landing the Next to Nature campaign would mean a promotion and a salary increase. She couldn't jeopardize this opportunity. "Not foolish—just unrealistic. I mean, I can't cook."

"He doesn't have to know that."

"It'd be obvious fairly quickly."

Agnes gestured to the table. "*I've* learned to cook. I could teach you—or do all the cooking for you."

She was completely sincere. Rusty could see it in her eyes. "That's deceitful."

"A grandmother helping her granddaughter in the kitchen? I don't think so."

"Even if you did, I'm not anything like the woman he describes, thank heavens."

"How do you know you aren't if you've never given it a try?" Agnes headed for the kitchen.

"Because I have my own career and don't feel like giving it all up to wait hand and foot on some man." Shuddering, Rusty picked up the turkey and followed her. "Gran, we don't need to go play house at this ranch. The two of us will have a great Christmas together, just like always."

"Of course we will." Her smile tight-lipped, Agnes began scraping the plates.

Rusty couldn't stand it. For some unfathomable reason, her grandmother had her heart set on spending Christmas at the Triple D Ranch and she couldn't go unless Rusty agreed to go, too.

How unappealing.

On the other hand, it would be an opportunity to strike a blow for womankind by enlightening a certain Texas rancher to the realities of modern life. And, too, her grandmother was bound to lose interest in cooking three meals a day for all those men. Rusty predicted a four-day stay, tops. By then, her grandmother would have gotten over this domestic nonsense.

Four days. Hmm. Rusty could steal four days, if she took her laptop computer with fax modem and her printer with her. It would be worth the time away to have her grandmother back to normal, though Rusty'd miss sampling the cooking experiments.

"Oh, all right, Gran," she said as if granting a great concession. "If you want to go, we'll give it a shot. But we're only going because *you* want to. Don't get any ideas about me hooking up with this relic from the Dark Ages."

STUNNED, Trent hung up the telephone after talking to his gleefully euphoric uncles. There were some pretty desperate women out there, judging by the letters they said they'd received. And now he had to meet one of them. *And* her grandmother. At the worst possible time.

Leaning his chair back on two legs, Trent gazed out from the window in his twenty-second-floor corner office onto the Dallas skyline.

His uncles expected him for two weeks at Christmas. Two weeks. And he'd promised. It didn't matter that he'd never expected to have to keep it, he'd given his word.

Just to his left was an easel with an artist's rendering of

the proposed Ridge Haven Retirement Village—Trent's personal project. He'd invested everything into it—both time and money. The entire package of bids and financing had to be in place by December thirty-first. To be away for two weeks at this crucial time was impossible.

And breaking a promise to his uncles was unthinkable.

Perhaps he could still manage to satisfy everybody by meeting this woman and failing to be impressed by either her or her domestic talents. That's the tack he'd take. Polite indifference. He would not seek her out or otherwise encourage her. A few days of hard work on an isolated ranch with no husband in sight would send Miss Suzy Homemaker running back to—he checked his notes—Chicago before they could say "Jingle Bells." By the end of the week he'd be back in Dallas.

Now all he'd have to do was find a way to stay in touch with his office...people telecommuted all the time. There was no reason he couldn't do it, too. He'd have to.

"THEY'RE COMING! I can see them through my aluminum, ten-magnification binoculars!"

Harvey's excitement was mirrored by Trent's other uncles. He'd never seen them like this. Even Doc smiled, and Trent, though still skeptical of this entire scheme, was glad he'd come.

"Harvey, those binoculars beat the Junior Astronomer telescope." Clarence patted the tripod next to him. "Better make a note."

Harvey's face fell. "Can't I meet the Romero ladies first?"

"Only proper," Doc growled.

"Of course, of course. We'll all greet the ladies. Won't we, Trent?"

"Sure, Uncle Clarence."

Teeth gritted, Trent smiled and followed them as they

went to stand on the front porch. He'd decided to play his polite though indifferent role to the hilt. No matter how enthusiastic his uncles were, these poor women had been lured here under false pretenses and the sooner they left, the sooner Trent could get back to work. He'd return for Christmas Day—maybe even manage Christmas Eve, too, if all went well.

Trent watched a small, nondescript blue car trail a cloud of dust into the ranch yard. Conscious that he was about to meet a species of female with whom he had no adult experience—the kind who aspired to drive a minivan full of children—he pondered his approach to her. He couldn't make himself be deliberately rude. That wasn't his way and it wasn't this poor woman's fault that he'd been misrepresented. This situation was entirely his own doing and he was annoyed with himself for allowing it to happen.

The car stopped. "Go open their doors for them, Trent."

Trent almost laughed. For all their talk about it being time for him to marry, his uncles still dispensed instructions as though he were a boy.

Trent deliberately approached the passenger side, guessing that the grandmother would not be the driver.

Opening the door, he reached down expecting to grasp a gnarled hand and help a gray-haired lady wearing an apron and support hose to stand.

Slim legs encased in designer jeans swung toward him and one ankle-booted foot collided with his shin. "Sorry."

Not only didn't the voice quiver with age, it didn't sound sorry at all. Trent refrained from rubbing his leg and gazed down at the car's occupant instead.

A chestnut-haired woman, head cocked to one side, stared back. Raising an eyebrow, she asked, "Going to let me out of the car, or don't I pass inspection?"

Trent backed away. Obviously this wasn't the woman

who'd responded to the *Texas Men* profile. The thought actually crossed his mind that some feminist group had come to stage a protest.

The woman stood. Trent noted immediately that she was a fair height. Since he was six-three himself, he liked tall women and never understood men of his height who liked tiny ones. A guy could strain his neck looking down all the time. Even kissing was more effort than it was worth. As for sleeping with them, forget it.

She wore a vest over a blouse with big sleeves, but as far as Trent could tell, she was possessed of at least an adequate figure.

She slammed the car door with enough force to let him know she was put out with him. There might be some justification there, he acknowledged. He wasn't normally so obvious about checking out a woman, but this wasn't a normal situation.

Before he could atone for his rudeness, she stuck out her hand. "Hi, I'm Rusty Romero."

Romero. These were the women who'd been corresponding with his uncles, all right. "Trent Creighton," he replied as he attempted to adjust his mental picture with a surprisingly pleasant reality.

Her hand shook his firmly. It was the handshake of a woman used to shaking hands. He tested his theory by turning his wrist slightly so he would have the superior position.

Rusty resisted and maintained the handshake as one between equals. Her eyes never left his.

Her reaction disoriented him. He'd met women like her. Women who'd had to fight for respect in the construction contracting industry, a field dominated by men. Trent dealt with these women very well, because he didn't consider them women. They were business adversaries or allies. Gender neutral.

But this woman was here in a domestic capacity. Home and hearth. Raising children. Nurturing. Very gender specific.

Housewives had certainly changed since those fifties television shows.

"Shall we call it a draw, or adjourn to the hood of the car where we can arm wrestle?" she asked.

Trent released her hand immediately. "The offer's tempting, but I'll pass."

"You're sure?" That eyebrow of hers was still raised. It had a high arch that lent itself to raising. "I wouldn't want to violate any local greeting customs."

"Around here, we generally don't arm wrestle until the second meeting."

"And what do you wrestle on the third meeting?"

This was no meek Betty Crocker wannabe. Had his uncles been conned? Trent glanced over to see how they were faring and received a second shock.

A well-dressed woman, looking just like any corporate executive's wife Trent had ever seen, chatted with the three men.

He glanced back to Rusty and found her watching him, her lips curved in a superior smile. "My grandmother, Agnes."

"Really?" He looked at the woman again. "She doesn't look the way I pictured." He meant it as a compliment. Rusty didn't take it that way.

"Probably because she left her apron and rolling pin in the car."

"With yours?" he replied, goaded.

"I assumed you'd have one I could borrow," she said after a pause.

"Of course," Trent assured her, though he honestly had no idea whether the Triple D kitchen boasted a rolling pin or not.

It was apparent that Rusty Romero had disliked him on sight. This should have cheered him, but inexplicably, it didn't. He hadn't been at his best during this critical first meeting, however Trent had not reached the age of thirty-three without being unaware of how to charm a woman, even one as prickly as Rusty.

Putting a little extra into his smile, he managed a belated, "Welcome to the Triple D." *That was lame.* Surely he could have done better.

Apparently Rusty thought so, too. "Thanks." She reached back inside the car and retrieved her purse and the keys.

Trent was annoyed with both himself and her. She was supposed to be some meek and mousy homebody who would be dazzled by him and by her good fortune in being selected to visit the Triple D. He'd expected a tenacious husband-hunter and had planned to very carefully, yet firmly, discourage her.

It appeared that this Rusty Romero would need no discouraging at all. That fact chafed at him a bit.

"Shall we unload the luggage?" Trent held out his hand for the keys to the trunk.

After a brief hesitation, Rusty surrendered them. "I'd better warn you that we didn't travel light this trip."

"I've never known a woman to travel light," Trent said without thinking. He popped open the trunk lid to reveal a crammed interior.

"I travel light when it's called for," Rusty snapped. "However, complying with your requirements for an old-fashioned Christmas and a two-week stay resulted in extra baggage."

This was not going to work. Trent had known that, but presumably this woman had been hoping to find a soul mate and life partner. Her attitude was incomprehensible.

Trent propped his hand on the open trunk lid and leveled his gaze at her. "If you didn't want to 'comply with my requirements,' then why are you here?"

"I—" She broke off abruptly, her eyes darting toward her grandmother. When she spoke again, her tone was entirely different. Softer. Conciliatory.

Suspicious.

"I've found that men are eager to appreciate a woman's efforts, yet have no idea of the tools, if you will, required to do the job."

Her big brown eyes challenged him to understand. "We received...conflicting instructions from your uncles."

Oh, no. Trent could only imagine, not that he wanted to. No wonder she'd arrived annoyed.

"My uncles get a bit enthusiastic at times." He looked at them and couldn't help smiling. Harvey was showing his NASA pen to the grandmother. She studied it carefully, pleasing both Harvey and Trent.

"So does my grandmother," Rusty said unexpectedly.

Trent grinned down at her just as she smiled up at him. It was a perfect moment of mutual understanding.

It was also the moment Trent realized that Rusty Romero had a dangerous smile. Her full lips stretched widely, revealing her top teeth in a flawless white crescent. The smile spoke of uninhibited pleasure and her lips...

Trent had never considered himself a lip man before. No, he was more an everything else man. But there was something about Rusty Romero's lips that invited further study—preferably at much closer quarters.

As her smile faded, Trent was reminded of the circumstances. "I'm sorry for the crack about your luggage," he said.

"It's okay. You were just buying into a stereotype."

She made him sound as though he were incapable of thinking for himself. The perfect moment of understanding evaporated. Trent lifted out the top suitcase.

"I'll get this one." Rusty reached for a flat case.

It looked for all the world like— "Is that a laptop?"

Clutching it to her, Rusty regarded him warily. "Yes."

"What do you need that for?"

"Recipes," she answered quickly.

"What happened to three-by-five cards in a plastic box?"

Rusty blinked and her eyebrows drew together. "You mean, diskettes?"

"No, I..." Shaking his head, Trent reached for another suitcase. "I didn't realize domestic science had entered the computer age."

"I imagine there are a lot of things you don't realize," Rusty responded, and turned toward the house.

THAT WENT WELL, Rusty thought. She'd established that she was no meek domestic slave to be ordered around and had even embarked on a little enlightening.

By apologizing, Trent had proved he was trainable. He might even be salvageable, and Rusty wouldn't mind claiming salvage rights.

She hadn't realized he was so tall. Of course she'd read his profile and description in *Texas Men*, memorized them in fact, but had expected some exaggeration. No, this man was every bit six-three and didn't need to exaggerate anything. Reality was enough to make a woman catch her breath—but not enough to sign up for the lifestyle he wanted.

No, Rusty shouldn't forget her primary mission here was

to enlighten—both her grandmother and these men. She had no doubt the uncles shared their nephew's views of women.

She glanced at them as she headed toward the ranch house, then changed course. Might as well meet them now.

"Here's my granddaughter." Agnes beamed at her.

Maintaining a pleasant expression, Rusty shifted her laptop to her left hand and held out her right to the nearest uncle, prepared to engage in the same maneuvering she'd done with Trent.

"This is Clarence." Her grandmother indicated a portly gentleman with a fair quantity of nearly white hair.

Rusty smiled up into a pair of eyes that looked exactly like Trent's, or the way Trent's would look in thirty or forty years. They were friendly, but shrewd. Glancing quickly at the other men, Rusty surmised that Clarence was in charge.

"Welcome to the Triple D." Clarence spoke with a lot more sincerity than his nephew had. His grip was warm, strong and cordial.

"Thank you." Rusty responded with an abundance of pleasantry and wondered if behavior modification techniques would have any effect on Trent.

"I'll run your bags into the house." Trent's look told her he'd heard her gushing thanks and didn't care one way or the other.

Clarence took over the introductions. "This is Doc." He indicated the man on the other side of Agnes. Because the ratio of gray to white in his hair was in favor of gray, Rusty guessed that this uncle was younger. When she met his eyes, she was prepared for the family resemblance, but Doc barely shook her hand or met her gaze before stepping back.

"And this is my brother, Harvey."

The third Davis brother skipped shaking Rusty's hand

altogether. "Is that a laptop?" He pointed to the computer, his eyes bright and childlike.

"Uh." Rusty looked down as though surprised to find herself holding it. "Yes."

"How fast is it?" he asked.

"It's a one hundred thirty-three megahertz Pentium." Let him put that in his pipe and smoke it.

He nodded. "How many megs of RAM?"

"Sixteen, expandable to sixty-four." Rusty had no idea if any of this meant anything to Harvey or not. Her laptop was her pride and joy.

"And the hard disk?"

"Uh, it's a one point three gig." A quick glance around revealed that everybody was smiling, so Rusty described her computer and discussed the assorted peripherals with Harvey.

To her amazement, he was quite knowledgeable. "I have some computer catalogs. Would you mind if we looked up this model?"

"I—sure." What an odd request. "Are you in the market for a computer?"

"I'm always in the market." Harvey dashed off, nearly colliding with Trent, who was carrying another load of their luggage.

"Oh, dear. We should help him," Agnes fluttered, though Rusty had never heard her flutter before.

"Nonsense," Clarence said. "Exercise will do the boy good. Sits behind a desk too much as it is."

"I thought he lived here," Rusty said.

"We'd like for him to live here, but he insists on staying in Dallas."

"Because he works in Dallas," Trent muttered as he walked past. Rusty heard him, but she wasn't certain the others had. "And this is the last of the luggage."

The group turned and followed him to the ranch house.

And that had been another surprise. Rusty had expected some modest homestead, but instead she found herself facing a two-story, columned, brick and white-painted wood house that could have been in any well-to-do Chicago neighborhood. Within sight, but not too close, was a barn and two more buildings she didn't know the purpose of. A few cows grazed in a nearby pasture, but there wasn't a sign of the thundering herds of longhorns Rusty had been expecting.

Dusty plains with cactus and tumbleweeds were missing, too. Instead, the house was surrounded by gently rolling hills and a thicket of trees. The weather was mild enough that Rusty hadn't bothered to put on her jacket. It was a refreshing change from this time of year in Chicago.

She threw back her head and breathed deeply. She'd been working hard and actually could use a break. A long weekend here wouldn't be so bad.

Rusty climbed the steps and crossed the porch, entering the front door in time to hear Harvey's voice.

"And they adjust vertically, as well."

Harvey was demonstrating a forest green leather recliner, one of three. The others were in black and burgundy. "Let me show you." As Rusty watched, her grandmother sat in the chair. Harvey flipped open a panel in the arm and began pressing buttons.

The back dipped and the front extended, supporting Agnes's feet.

"Feel that lumbar support," he said as he pressed another button.

"Oh-hh." Her grandmother sighed and closed her eyes. "Wonderful."

"Do you want to try, Miss Rusty?"

Miss Rusty. Charmed, Rusty sat in the burgundy recliner.

Within seconds, Harvey had manipulated the chair into an admittedly comfortable position.

Rusty relaxed her neck—and found that she was staring directly at a big-screen TV turned to a home shopping channel. At the moment, a woman with red fingernails modeled cubic zirconia dinner rings at only $99 and going fast.

"Uncle Harvey, perhaps Rusty and her grandmother would like to see their rooms," Trent prompted, stepping into her line of sight.

As he spoke, Rusty watched his gaze sweep the length of her body. He probably wasn't even aware he was doing it. However, Rusty had to admit that being in a reclining position in front of an admittedly handsome rancher who had just given her the once-over was awakening her hibernating libido.

She sat up and fluffed the back of her hair. Trent's eyes followed the movement of her arms.

Interesting. She swung her legs down and stood.

"Here, I'll lower the footrest for you." Trent reached for the control panel on the chair.

Rusty deliberately leaned toward him so that he'd brush against her. She was testing the chemistry, just for the record.

For the record, the chemistry was combustible. His chest brushed her cheek and shoulder and sent tingles of awareness throughout her upper body.

"Sorry, didn't mean to crowd you there." He smiled down at her and moved away.

Rusty wanted to move with him.

Wasn't this a pleasant surprise? Or maybe not. She remembered staring at his picture and the way his ad had managed to provoke such heightened emotions in her. True, those emotions had been primarily outrage, but she'd always known indifference was the relationship-killing emotion.

She wasn't indifferent to Trent and suspected that he wasn't indifferent to her, either.

"Shall I show you your room now?"

"That would be great. Are we sharing?"

Trent cleared his throat. "No. I put your grandmother in the guest room. Harvey will be testing orthopedic mattresses in the storage barn, so you'll get his room."

"I wouldn't feel right about making your uncle sleep in the barn," Rusty said pointedly. If anybody should be sleeping in the barn, it should be Trent.

Trent chuckled. "It's not what you're thinking. When this ranch was bigger, extra hands used to bunk out there. Unless the weather turns nasty, he'll be fine."

"Are you sure?"

"Let's put it this way. He'd be testing those mattresses whether you were here or not."

"Okay. And where will you be?" she asked casually.

Trent's gaze flicked over her face and lingered on her mouth. "Down the hall from you." He gestured toward the door on the other side of the den, allowing her grandmother to precede them. The uncles remained.

He's being nice now, but don't forget what he really thinks about women, Rusty reminded herself as "not indifferent" slipped into "definitely interested." *Your mission is to enlighten.*

But couldn't she enlighten by demonstrating how a modern woman took charge of her own sexuality? A little short-term dalliance might be beneficial for all concerned. As long as she was away for these few days, shouldn't she make the most of this break? She'd return to Chicago rested and refreshed and with certain tensions eased.

As she walked past him, Rusty wondered if Trent was

42   *Christmas Male*

tense. Conscious of his presence directly behind her, Rusty put a little extra sway in her hips as she followed her grandmother across the room.

Just before she walked through the doorway, she heard Doc's voice.

"Nice, wide pelvis."

"THIS KNIFE is so sharp you can cut a tomato thin enough to read a newspaper through it." Harvey turned to pick up another gadget in a never-ending display of kitchen gadgetry that should be a shoo-in for the infomercial hall of fame.

"When are they going to leave us alone?" Rusty muttered to Agnes. She couldn't believe that just an hour after their arrival, she and her grandmother were apparently expected to produce the evening meal.

Agnes saw nothing wrong with this thinking and had come prepared with homemade goodies she'd perfected in the weeks after Thanksgiving.

Harvey was giving them the grand tour of the kitchen, eye-boggling in its selection of modern appliances, though he was getting a bit too detailed for Rusty.

"And this is the Radish Rosetter," he continued, showing them a metal contraption that looked like a Medieval instrument of torture.

If they wanted their radishes rosetted, they could do it themselves, Rusty grumbled silently.

Clarence and Doc watched from the sidelines, chiming in only for major appliances. Trent, his arms crossed, kept a watchful eye from the butcher block island.

During a demonstration of the vegetable curler, which cut potatoes, carrots and the like into spirals for no practical reason Rusty could discern, she stole a look at him.

A small line appeared between his eyebrows and he seemed ready to intervene at any moment.

When his eyes caught hers, they held that same look of wary concern. He was probably afraid she'd insult his eccentric but endearing uncle.

Detaching herself from the gadgetfest that held her grandmother entranced, Rusty wandered over to stand by Trent. "Don't look so worried," she said in an undertone. "I won't hurt his feelings."

"Or run screaming into the night?"

Rusty almost laughed out loud. "Hey, anybody who knows as much about computers as he does can be allowed certain idiosyncrasies."

The rigid set of Trent's shoulders softened and he uncrossed his arms. "I don't think he actually understands how to operate one. But if something is made for sale, Harvey knows about it."

"And has already purchased it, no doubt."

"Being a consumer is his hobby." Trent grinned, revealing shallow dimples on either side of his mouth. Rusty had never considered dimples particularly masculine—until now. They disappeared quickly as Trent's face relaxed into a pleasant expression.

"So, when do you expect your dinner to be ready?" Rusty changed the subject, mainly to remind herself why she was currently standing in a strange kitchen hundreds of miles from home.

"How long will it take you to cook it?"

Tripped up already. "I have no idea," she said truthfully.

"What are you cooking?"

Rusty wished she'd paid more attention to the goodies her grandmother had packed. As she watched, the little group abandoned the gadget drawer. Doc was demonstrating the cappuccino machine. At least Rusty was assured of decent coffee while she was here. But she still didn't know what was on tonight's menu. "Dinner," she said, "will be a surprise."

"Have you looked in the refrigerator yet? I think Harvey stocked it." Trent pushed away from the butcher block and yanked open the door of the biggest refrigerator Rusty had seen outside of a restaurant kitchen.

A large foil-wrapped lump gleamed at her with golden familiarity. "A spiral-sliced ham! Is that for Christmas dinner?"

"I haven't a clue." Trent poked through the shelves. "There's a turkey in here, as well. Take your pick."

Rusty murmured a heartfelt thank-you to the kitchen gods. "I vote for the ham." Very difficult to ruin something already cooked.

Trent obligingly hauled it out. "It must weigh thirty-five pounds."

"At least. It's as big as the one we get for the office Christmas party." Rusty was uncrinkling the wrapper so she could read the heating instructions and had spoken without thinking.

"Office? You work?"

She hesitated. Well, why not admit it? "Yes."

"As what? A secretary?"

It was the way he said it, as though he couldn't imagine a woman being anything else. Not that being a secretary was anything to be ashamed of—Rusty had worked as a secretary during the summers between college terms. It was just that a secretary was one of the three occupations—teaching and nursing being the other two—that had, until recently, been considered the only suitable work for women.

She knew her grandmother had struggled for acceptance in the real estate business, scraping out a living with commissions on the smaller properties while the larger listings—and commissions—went to men who needed the income to support their families. But Agnes had been supporting a family, too.

Trent's comment brought it all back to Rusty. She, herself, had not had to struggle because women like her grandmother had blazed the trail for her. Obviously her grandmother's work wasn't finished, though for some reason she was in regression at the moment.

It was up to Rusty to carry on.

Trent had turned away and was looking into a cabinet, obviously not even interested in Rusty's response. *The only work that's important is man's work.* He might as well have shouted the words aloud.

"This ought to hold it." He pulled out a roasting pan and smiled at her, the creases dimpling attractively.

Rusty's breath caught before she hardened her heart.

Dimples or not, Trent had a lot to learn.

"KISS THE COOK?" Rusty looked down at the apron she wore. "I hope they don't take this as a suggestion."

"We don't have time for subtlety, dear." Agnes, with her cow oven mitts and matching apron that said Udder Delight, breezed past carrying a green bean casserole.

"*Subtlety?* What are you talking about?"

"Trent Creighton, Rusty. I can't believe some smart cookie hasn't snapped up such a handsome young man."

"I can," Rusty muttered. She'd agreed to come here so her grandmother could get all this domestic nostalgia out of her system. Granted, ostensibly, the purpose of their visit was so Rusty and Trent could get to know each other. But her grandmother couldn't *seriously* believe Rusty would consider leading the kind of life Trent wanted to live. She'd *told* her so. Repeatedly.

But obviously, ineffectively.

"Rachel Marie Romero, you have the opportunity of a lifetime here and I intend to see that you make the most of it!" Agnes punctuated her words by slapping her oven mitts on the counter. "You have to be prepared to use all the feminine ammunition you've got."

Rusty intended to use feminine ammo, all right. But she and her grandmother had different targets in mind. Her grandmother would assume she was aiming for Trent's heart. Instead, Rusty was trying to shoot holes in his over-inflated ego.

Eyeing her grandmother's outfit—the ruffled pinafore top was really too much—Rusty decided the Kiss-the-Cook apron wasn't so bad after all. "Hey, look." She pointed to the casserole. "I cooked something!"

A buzzer sounded and Agnes whizzed past. "Canned green beans, canned cream of mushroom soup and canned fried onions mixed together *barely* counts."

Rusty made a sound of protest. "Didn't I open those cans all by myself?"

Her grandmother pulled open the oven door and withdrew cornbread muffins that she'd baked back in Chicago and had just warmed in the oven with the ham. "Oh, I hope this will do for our first dinner," she fretted. "We should have cooked something really impressive instead of using the ham." Shooting Rusty an accusing look, she shut the oven door.

"They should have given us more notice. And the ham was just sitting there." Rusty returned to cutting tomatoes for the salad. "If they hadn't wanted us to serve it, then why was it in the refrigerator?"

"Maybe they were saving it for Christmas dinner. Or maybe it was a gift for somebody else."

"Trent *said* we could use it."

The mention of Trent's name mollified Agnes somewhat.

"There's a turkey in there, too. We won't have to go to the grocery store for a while." Rusty laid a slice of tomato on the green bean can label and tried to read through it. By golly, Harvey was right. She could see dark lines, but the words were blurry. The tomato slice was limp, though, and disintegrated before she could get it into the salad bowl. She was concentrating so completely, her grandmother's silence didn't register immediately. When it did, she glanced back over her shoulder and caught her grandmother's stare.

Agnes immediately looked away.

"What?" Rusty asked, suspicious.

"Nothing." Her grandmother spread a cloth in the bread basket.

"There's something." Rusty carried the salad bowl over to the butcher block island. "Something about grocery shopping?"

Agnes turned around and peered into the oven.

"You can't see through foil. What gives?"

"Well, Rusty." Agnes straightened and wiped her hands on the terry cow-trimmed hand towel attached to her pocket. "This *is* a rural area."

"So we'll have to drive a few miles and do all our shopping at once. We can do that. It's a matter of step-by-step planning." Rusty excelled at planning.

"This is a ranch. They grow their own food."

"They didn't grow that spiral-sliced ham."

"No, but I did see chickens."

"Did you? Were they in the freezer?"

"Not yet."

"What do you—oh! That's awful! No way." Holding out her hands, Rusty backed up. "There is no way I'm touching one of those chickens. A live chicken—clucking. I couldn't—and the feathers, what happens to those?" She waved her hands. "No. Don't tell me. I can't think about it."

"Rusty..." Agnes advanced toward her.

"No! Absolutely not!"

"Absolutely not what?" Rusty heard just before backing into someone. Trent, of course.

Strong arms clasped around her, a sensation she might have enjoyed if she hadn't been so revolted by the thought of murdering chickens.

"Steady there."

Rusty whirled around and launched into an immediate attack. "If there's to be any chicken necks wrung, they'll have to be wrung by somebody else. I prefer mine wrapped in plastic."

"You smother your chickens then?" Trent grinned.

"Ye-ees," Rusty drew out the word. "In a lovely Marsala sauce, as they nestle in a bed of wild rice."

"Sounds good."

"I can give you the phone number—"

"Rusty!" Agnes immediately moderated her voice. "As long as Trent is here, perhaps he could wrestle that heavy old ham out of the oven for us."

"Certainly, Mrs. Romero."

As Trent crossed the kitchen, Rusty mimicked, "Certainly, Mrs. Romero," behind his back.

Her grandmother glared.

Trent removed the ham. "I guess this means we'll be eating soon? I need to make a couple of telephone calls and wanted to check your timetable."

"Dinner will be served soon," Agnes trilled. "But please, do take your time. The ham should sit for a few minutes anyway."

Rusty would have mimicked her grandmother, too, but she wasn't that brave.

Trent's remark reminded Rusty that she needed to make a couple of calls to see how things had gone in the office today, too. Looking around the mess in the kitchen, she knew it would be several hours before she could steal away to find a telephone with some privacy.

"What were you so hot about when I came in here just now?" Trent asked as Rusty's grandmother carried the cornbread and salad into the dining room.

"Gran was wondering when we should put chicken on the menu. She mentioned seeing some running around outside."

"Not those!" Trent blanched. "Those are Cochin chickens, Doc's pride and joy. He raises them for show."

"You mean, they're like pets?" This was great. They wouldn't be expected to cook pets.

"Very special pets. If you want chickens to eat, check the deep-freeze." He opened the walk-in pantry door and flipped on the light. At the back sat a large white chest. "Doc experiments with special feed and food supplements on several different animals. It's his hobby now that he's sold his veterinary practice."

"Good. I'll tell Gran to bury the hatchet—so to speak."

Trent chuckled and lifted the heavy freezer lid. White vapors clouded the top. Waving them away, Trent revealed a well-stocked freezer.

Rusty sighed in relief. That was more like it. She stepped inside the pantry, then stopped. "Look at all this stuff!" She pulled out a box of tissue-wrapped grapefruit. Each one was an unblemished yellow. "Are these real?"

Trent nodded. "Fruit of the Month Club. Each of my uncles belongs to a different one. Uncle Harvey may belong to several."

"No kidding. Can we eat these?"

"Yes, in fact, he was concerned about some pears that

came several days ago. He thought they weren't ripe." Trent peered into several decorative crates and boxes. "Here they are." He carried a domed bowl into the kitchen. "This is a fruit ripener," he explained.

"Of course it is." And from the appearance of the pears, it worked quite well. "I think we'll have these for dinner." She hefted one glorious pear in each hand.

"It looks like you've got everything under control. Call me when you're ready to serve dinner." Trent's gaze flicked down to her Kiss-the-Cook-emblazoned chest. He stared for a moment, then said, "I'll take a rain check." Grinning, he left the kitchen.

Rusty hated aprons, especially aprons that invited smart-aleck remarks from dictatorial ranchers.

DINNER PROVED TO BE...interesting. Trent found the food uninspired but tolerable—except for the green bean mess. Weren't the onion rings supposed to be crispy?

But he shouldn't be too quick to judge since the women had only just arrived.

And his uncles seemed satisfied. Yet Trent didn't want them becoming too satisfied. He could only spare a few more days on their find-Trent-a-wife project.

"Yes, I've found the Worthington hams to be superior. They trim to leave only the smallest layer of fat before baking." Harvey helped himself to another slice.

"Trent tells us you raise show chickens, Dr. Davis," Agnes said.

"Doc'll do, ma'am." He blotted his mouth with the napkin and proceeded to give a lecture on his prize Cochins.

Normally, Trent would have found a way to shorten the monologue, but Rusty's grandmother was listening with apparent interest. And with Doc talking, Trent didn't have to come up with anything to say. He looked across the table to see Rusty's reaction.

Rusty was staring at her plate.

Her hair was a pretty color in the subdued lighting of the dining room. Not quite red, yet more than a plain brown, it was definitely the rust color of her nickname.

She wasn't at all the sort of person Trent had expected to answer his uncles' profile. From the little they'd spoken, Trent knew she definitely had strong opinions that she wasn't afraid to express and seemed a modern sort of city girl. So what appealed to her about living on the Triple D?

The rat race must have gotten to her. Two couples Trent knew had quit their jobs, sold everything, moved into the country and home-schooled their children. They called it "simplifying their lives." Another couple was considering it.

Trent couldn't understand them. Didn't they get bored?

He studied Rusty's downcast head.

She flinched, then glared at her grandmother.

"*Isn't* the house lovely, dear?" Agnes prompted.

"Yes." Trent could see Rusty gather herself. "I love the fireplace. I hope the weather turns cold enough to have a fire," she said.

And Trent suddenly visualized her in front of the fireplace, the golden glow turning her hair into molten copper.

No. Wrong. Dangerous image. He liked blondes with a yen for honeymoons and an allergy to weddings.

He cleared his throat. "There's plenty of wood out back. Any time you want a fire, just grab an ax."

"Now, boy," his uncle Clarence warned.

Trent didn't listen because he knew what Clarence was about to say.

However, Rusty...Rusty slowly turned her head and raised an eyebrow. That disdainful arch said it all. Trent knew exactly what she thought of his comment and of him for making it. She remained silent because of his uncles and her grandmother.

This was almost too easy. At this rate Rusty and her grandmother would be gone by the end of the weekend and Trent could hasten their departure without his uncles ever knowing exactly what he'd done.

Trent succumbed to the urge to bait Rusty. "That was a mighty fine supper," he said, patting his stomach. "Though dessert demonstrates a woman's true cooking talent, and I know you've been—" What was Clarence's phrase? "Cooking up a storm in there to impress me."

The other eyebrow arched to join the first.

"So what's for dessert?" Trent was enjoying himself.

"Brownies and chocolate chip cookies," Agnes supplied when her granddaughter remained silent. "It was Rusty's suggestion."

"My favorite," Trent said. If he could have belched on command, he would have done so.

"Which one?" Rusty asked.

"I like 'em both so much, I think we ought to have them at every meal." He grinned wolfishly.

From the look on her face, he knew that brownies and chocolate chip cookies would not make another appearance at the Triple D table while she was here.

Too bad. He did like brownies.

"It's time to clear the table," Agnes prompted Rusty. "Would anyone like coffee?"

Everyone murmured their assent and the two women took away the dishes.

As soon as Rusty disappeared with the last plate, Clarence began speaking. "Trent, you are doing nothing to fix that girl's interest."

"I've been talking to her," Trent protested.

"Not the way you talked to Miranda," Harvey countered.

He shouldn't underestimate Harvey's powers of observation, Trent reminded himself. "She's different than Miranda."

Doc nodded. "Wider pelvis and a bit stockier. Doesn't have the shoulders, but you do. Looks strong and has good teeth. And you can tell by the grandmother that she's from a good bloodline."

"Don't be too quick to judge by this dinner, Trent. I know you like your fancy food, but this is wholesome farm food and never hurt a body." Clarence patted his stomach the way Trent had earlier.

"She'll want romance, Trent. Flowers—I've got several catalogs and when the time is right—" Harvey glanced toward the kitchen door and lowered his voice "—I've got a new Victoria's Secret catalog."

"You didn't tell us the new one came." Clarence sounded aggrieved.

"I know how to court a woman," Trent broke in when he could. "I just haven't decided if this is one I wish to court."

The three Davis brothers opened their mouths to protest just as Agnes entered, carrying a tray of coffee cups.

From then on, Trent was prompted, usually by a nudge from Harvey's sneaker-clad foot, into engaging Rusty in conversation.

"Tell me how you managed to come across the issue of *Texas Men*," Trent said as his opening gambit.

Rusty flinched, glanced briefly at her grandmother, and then met Trent's eyes. "Someone brought it to the office."

Harvey leaned forward eagerly. "And when you saw Trent's picture you knew he was the one, right?"

"I knew he was something, all right," Rusty agreed.

"Ow." Harvey frowned at Clarence.

A rustling sounded and Rusty glared at her grandmother.

"You said you work in Dallas but you want to give up your job and move here, is that right?" Rusty's expression was pleasant, but strained.

"No, I—"

Harvey's foot connected with his shin.

"Eventually." Trent leveled a look at Harvey.

"What exactly do you do?"

"I manage investments and assemble financing packages."

"He takes good care of us," Harvey said.

Interest appeared in Rusty's eyes.

Great, thought Trent. Mention money and they're all interested.

"So what kind of deals do you have cooking now?" Rusty swiveled, presumably out of her grandmother's reach.

"Now, Rusty, dear, this business talk is all so complicated."

"But I want to hear—"

"Why don't we just enjoy our coffee. Cookie, Trent? Rusty baked these herself."

"Gran!"

Trent took one and bit into it. "Very good." Burned on the bottom.

Agnes tittered. "I tried to help her and left some in the oven a wee bit too long."

"But, Gran, I didn't—"

"Rusty, the gentlemen need their coffee warmed." Agnes smiled around the table. "Now, Doc, do you only show chickens, or are there other prize-winning animals here on the ranch?"

Rusty glowered and left the room.

"Trent." Harvey rubbed his arms. "I'm cold."

Pushing back his chair, Trent stood. "I'll adjust the thermostat."

"*Trent*, I'm *cold*." Harvey raised his eyebrows and jerked his head toward the fireplace. "I imagine Miss Rusty and Miss Agnes are cold, too."

The fireplace yawned blackly. Harvey wanted a fire and he wanted a fire because Rusty had mentioned it.

"Then a fire is just what we need to take the chill off," Trent offered with false cheer.

Harvey smiled happily.

"How lovely," said Agnes.

Trudging toward the kitchen, Trent walked through the doorway in time to see Rusty bang the cappuccino machine with her fist.

"What are you doing?"

She whirled around, guilt written on her features. "Eventually, I hope to extract coffee from this machine."

"That'll teach you to play hooky during the demo." Trent checked to see that she'd loaded the coffee grounds properly. After reseating the basket, he flipped a switch and within moments a hissing sound announced the arrival of hot water.

"Thanks," she said. "Where are you going?"

"To split some logs for firewood. Harvey thought you might be cold."

A delighted grin spread over her face. "Oh, I am." She stamped her feet and rubbed her hands together. "Brrr. I'm freezing."

Trent slipped his jacket off the peg by the back door. "Somehow, I thought you would be."

"You're not angry, are you, Trent? This is man's work, just the way you wanted it. You remember, men providing, women nurturing?" She smiled smugly.

"Ah, yes, nurturing." He paused, his hand on the door-knob. "I can guarantee that when I finish splitting those logs for your fire, I'm going to need serious nurturing—and I'll expect more than burned chocolate chip cookies."

Before he went out the door, Trent had the satisfaction of watching Rusty Romero's smug smile disappear.

4

"RUSTY, wake up."

Rusty opened her eyes to find her grandmother standing over her in the gray predawn light. "What's the matter?"

"You've got to hurry and get into the kitchen."

Dragging herself into a sitting position, Rusty tried to wake up. "You smell like bacon."

"Things got a trifle smoky."

"Nothing's on fire, is it?"

Her grandmother shook her head. "Nothing important."

"Then I'll just go back to sleep." Rusty slid down the headboard.

"No, you have to get dressed." Agnes rummaged through the pile of clothes on the chair. "There isn't much time."

"Are we sneaking away?" Rusty threw aside the covers. The day was shaping up nicely after all.

"This *can't* be your robe." Agnes held out a velour robe with velourless patches at the elbows.

"I promise not to wear it on the plane." Rusty tied her favorite garment around her.

"We're not leaving. I want you to get dressed in something pretty. Did you bring pink?"

"Pink?" Rusty made a gagging motion.

"Yes." Agnes pushed Rusty's bangs off her forehead and examined her. "It'll complement that rosy color in your eyes."

"If you'd let me go back to sleep, that rosy color will go away."

Agnes was unsympathetic. "If you hadn't stayed awake so long last night, you wouldn't be sleepy this morning."

Rusty yawned. "I had work to do and we didn't get out of that kitchen until ten-thirty. Did you have to offer them bedtime snacks?"

"It was the least we could do after dear Trent chopped all that wood."

Dear Trent had been moving kind of slow after hauling in the firewood last night, Rusty remembered. She smiled. It almost made her forget that her own back was sore from standing up so long. How could her grandmother function so early in the morning?

Agnes was pushing Rusty toward the bathroom. "Put on your makeup and hurry out to the kitchen. Breakfast is nearly ready."

"You've already cooked breakfast?" The thought of food so early was definitely unappetizing.

"The men eat early and often here in the country," Agnes informed her.

"I would've helped you," Rusty grumbled. Or tried to talk her into waiting an hour.

"It doesn't matter now. Hurry, or you'll spoil everything." Agnes gave her a final push.

It was more the thought of a mug of coffee than her grandmother's urging that sent Rusty shuffling out to the kitchen after throwing on jeans and a baggy sweater.

"Rusty, couldn't you have put on some lipstick?" Agnes asked when she saw her. "Well, never mind. Trent probably prefers the wholesome country girl look."

Rusty did an about-face. "I've got some Chanel Vamp in my purse."

"Not that ghastly color." Agnes grabbed her arm. "Halloween was weeks ago, dear."

Then why were they masquerading as happy homemakers? Rusty wondered. "Is the coffee ready?"

"Not yet. We want it to be fresh."

"Don't worry. The first pot's for me." With single-minded determination, Rusty headed for the cappuccino machine. She wanted plain, unadorned coffee. That shouldn't be too much to ask, should it?

Tiny vacuumed-packed foil pouches of various flavored coffees stood at attention in the cabinet above the machine. "I had no idea there were coffee bean clubs. Oh, hazelnut crème." Flavored coffee suddenly sounded just right.

She put the machine on Drip and turned around, blinking as the condition of the kitchen finally registered. "How much food did you cook?"

Agnes hurried over. "Here put this on."

"Oh, Gran, not the cow apron."

"You'll look cute in it."

Rusty winced at the word "cute." Her grandmother pulled her arms through as though she were a little girl, spun her around and tied the apron behind her back. "Bulky over that sweater, but functional. Hold this."

Rusty found herself with a spatula in her hand as her grandmother propelled her toward the stove.

Something was burning.

"Drat and double drat." Agnes jerked the skillet off the stove and dumped out the contents. "This is a gas stove and the one in my apartment is an electric one."

Rusty followed her over to the sink and noticed several other burnt offerings. "Pancakes?"

"It's awful." Agnes sounded desperate. "There's hardly any batter left. You try to cook one." The oven timer buzzed and she hurried off.

Rusty dipped batter into the iron skillet. It hissed and smoked. She turned the flame lower.

"At least these came out." Agnes carried a pan of biscuits to the butcher block. They joined bacon, sausage and ham.

"Gran...that's a lot of food. Who's going to eat it all?"

"Appetites are bigger on the farm."

Farm. Her grandmother must be reliving her girlhood when she and the other women had had to cook for all the farm workers. Though how she could mistake the three egg-shaped Davis brothers for lean cowhands was beyond Rusty.

She decided not to say anything more. Her grandmother obviously felt a huge breakfast was called for on their first morning. Fine. They'd have a huge breakfast and then see who ate what and how much. Tomorrow, there'd be changes.

Sneaking across the kitchen, Rusty maneuvered a mug under the still-brewing coffee and only splashed a little getting the pot back onto the burner.

Agnes looked up at the hissing sound. "Rusty! You abandoned your post."

"A momentary lapse, ma'am." Saluting, Rusty returned to the stove and tried to flip her pancake. It was burnt on the bottom and runny on the top. She tried turning it anyway, but it fell apart. Eventually, she scraped the mess into the sink.

Agnes sighed. "I've put toast in the oven to broil since we apparently won't be having many pancakes."

"Toast? You've got biscuits."

"Someone might want toast. Be sure and watch it. And I've put out eggs. Ask them how they want their eggs cooked."

"There's more than one way?"

"Rusty, *try* and cooperate!" Agnes hurried from the room.

"Where are you going?" Rusty called, but didn't get a response.

Toast was ridiculous and she couldn't do two things at once. Rusty turned off the broiler and concentrated on her next pancake attempt. Eggs. Nobody should be eating eggs. And if they did, Rusty would scramble them because that's the only way she knew how to fix them.

There was a pot on the stove. Peering into it, Rusty saw a lumpy gray mass. Oatmeal. She poked it with a wooden spoon. The spoon bounced off the surface, so she stabbed it. The spoon stood at attention. No oatmeal today.

"Poor Gran." Shaking her head, Rusty sipped at her coffee and checked the bottom of the pancake.

"Well, good morning!" Trent's uncle Clarence poked his head into the kitchen. "What have we here?"

Rusty straightened. "Breakfast."

"So I see—and smell." Closing his eyes, Clarence inhaled. "Biscuits." He wandered over to the butcher block. "My Emma made the best biscuits."

"Good morning!"

At her grandmother's voice, Rusty turned, then stared.

Agnes, her hair mussed, was dressed in a robe—and not one of her satin peignoirs, either. This was a quilted yellow print. Calico. Her grandmother was wearing calico.

"I must have overslept. Rusty, you should have called me." Agnes gave her open-mouthed granddaughter a hug.

"What are you doing?" Rusty whispered. "You look like an extra in a spaghetti Western."

"Flip your pancake," Agnes replied, and wandered over to marvel at the bounty on the butcher block, as though seeing the food for the first time.

Obviously, she intended for her granddaughter to get

sole credit for the morning meal. Rusty toyed with the idea of exposing her grandmother and would have, if Trent hadn't chosen that moment to walk in. "Now this is a serious breakfast." He met her eyes. "I'm impressed."

Her grandmother shot her a triumphant look to which Rusty responded by flipping her pancake with a resounding splat. To her utter surprise, the top was a golden brown. "Oh! Gran, come look!"

Agnes rushed over. "Don't act so surprised," she whispered. "They're always supposed to look like that." In a louder voice, she sang, "Anyone want eggs?"

"Two, sunny-side up," Trent said on his way to the coffeepot.

Rusty glared after him. "That would be the unbroken kind, right?"

Agnes laughed shrilly. "Oh, Rusty, such a sense of humor. Do you like a woman with a sense of humor in the mornings, Trent?"

His eyes gleamed. "Occasionally."

Rusty took in his unshaven face—and the fact that he'd emptied the coffeepot. "He probably has to take what he can get."

Trent saluted her with his coffee mug.

Just then Doc and Harvey came in through the back door. Their entry provided sufficient distraction for Agnes to break the eggs into a small skillet without anyone noticing. The yolks remained whole.

"How'd you do that?" Rusty murmured.

Doc stopped short when he saw Agnes at the stove. His gaze went from Agnes to Rusty, then back to Agnes, whose cheeks were pink.

"Did you feed all your animals?" she asked, not meeting his eyes.

"Yes, ma'am." Nodding, he passed by them.

"I encountered Doc this morning when I came to the kitchen for...something to drink," Agnes explained to Rusty in tones loud enough for everyone to hear. "I didn't expect to find anyone out and about so early." She finished with a forced chuckle.

I'll bet you didn't. Her grandmother was blushing. A good thing, too. She needed the color to counteract the yellow calico.

Rusty wondered just how much of her grandmother's activities good old Doc had witnessed in the kitchen.

"Did the Back-Saver 92A sleep good?" Clarence grabbed a biscuit as Harvey wandered by.

"Not as superior as the 92B model, but I need two more nights on it for an accurate comparison." Deep in thought, Harvey was oblivious to the food.

"Breakfast is ready," Clarence informed him. "Don't spend too long making notes."

"I won't," was the vague response as Harvey drifted from the room.

Doc followed him, making a muttered remark about cleaning up.

Silence followed as Clarence snitched another biscuit and Agnes stared at the eggs.

"Coffee's all gone," Trent told Rusty.

"I can *see* that," she snapped.

Agnes poked her. "I can watch Trent's eggs while you make more coffee."

Couldn't he make his own coffee? For her grandmother's sake, Rusty swallowed her annoyance and made another pot. Trent watched her measure the grounds, then set his empty mug beside the pot. "I'll be in the dining room."

Where he obviously expected to be served, Rusty fumed. Imagine waking up to this work every morning for the rest of her life.

Forget it. She'd stay single.

Rusty spent the next hour carrying plates in and out of the dining room, refilling coffee, juice and milk, and rewarming meats that had gone cold because they'd been cooked too far in advance.

Agnes, her color heightened, frantically made more pancake batter when Rusty's lonely pancake was praised by Harvey. Rusty's "Let them eat toast" comment had no effect, especially since she'd turned off the broiler before toasting the other side of the bread.

Trent read the *Wall Street Journal* and ate his food without comment, leaving before Rusty even sat down. She found she was so resentful she couldn't eat, so she excused herself to do the dishes, leaving an exhausted Agnes drinking coffee with the uncles.

Trent had some nerve. Her grandmother must have spent hours cooking. In fact, as soon as the uncles went off to do whatever they did, Rusty would insist that Agnes go back to bed. The uncles, especially Clarence, had been highly complimentary. Trent had barely said a word. Would a little praise kill him?

Rusty loaded the dishwasher, but there were so many dishes left over, she resigned herself to washing the rest by hand.

She wrestled with the heavy cast-iron skillets, scrubbing them with steel wool. It was taking forever and she was desperate to hook up her modem and contact her office. Her assistant, Alisa, had express instructions to E-mail Rusty daily with any news of her competition for the campaign. She sighed, wishing she could be at the office to oversee the final details of her presentation. She couldn't believe she was scrubbing pots and pans while the opportunity of her professional life was within grasp.

"Any more coffee?" A freshly shaven Trent padded across the black-and-white tiled floor.

"Whatever's left in the pot," Rusty said through gritted teeth. Because of him, she was hundreds of miles from home instead of fine-tuning her advertising campaign. And he didn't even seem to appreciate her efforts, well technically, her grandmother's efforts, but still.

"There's a little." He emptied the rest into his mug and looked at her questioningly.

"Why, yes, thank you. I *would* like some." Forearm-deep in sudsy water, Rusty pushed her bangs out of her eyes with her shoulder.

Trent stood there, holding the empty pot in one hand and his mug in the other. "There wasn't much left."

"Well, the coffee fairy is busy, so I guess you'll have to make more," Rusty snapped.

"I didn't realize you wanted coffee." Trent spoke very carefully, which only angered Rusty more. "I thought you were ready to wash the pot."

Of course. "Sure, just add it to the mountain of dirty dishes over there."

"I can make more coffee—"

"Can you?"

Trent's lips pressed together. "What is the matter with you?"

Rusty was mad and her grandmother wasn't in the room to stop her from saying what she felt. "You sat at that table, read a newspaper and ate without saying a word. Don't you have any idea how long it took to fix all that food?" Rusty conveniently ignored the fact that she didn't have any idea, either.

Trent set the coffeepot down. "The food was great." He hesitated. "But I'm not really a big breakfast person. Dry cereal would have been fine."

It was all Rusty could do to keep from using the skillet as a weapon. He could have told them. "Dry cereal? What happened to 'cook up a storm and hang the cholesterol'?"

"What?" He appeared genuinely puzzled.

"Your profile in *Texas Men*."

"Oh, that."

"Yes, *that*."

"Well..." Trent rubbed his forehead. "I guess I was tired of dry cereal then." He offered a smile.

They stared at each other for a few seconds.

Trent looked away first. "I think we have a plain old drip coffee maker somewhere around here." He started opening and closing cabinet doors. "It's got a bigger pot so you won't have to remake coffee so often." He pulled out a white model just like the one Rusty had in her apartment and set it on the counter. "I'll make a pot as soon as I find the filters," he offered.

"Don't bother. I don't really want any more coffee." Rusty rinsed the skillet and set it on the sideboard.

Trent stood there a moment longer. "Okay, then I guess I'll see you at lunch." With a brief, impersonal smile, he left Rusty to her dishes.

He could have offered to dry, she grumbled to herself. At this rate, when she finished, it would be time to start fixing lunch.

She banged another skillet into the sink. Dry cereal. That was unexpected. In fact, come to think of it, Trent's behavior was unexpected. The only time he'd paid any attention to her was at his uncles' urging. He hardly seemed to be checking her out as a potential helpmate and nurturer.

Rusty brightened. Maybe she'd already flunked his wife test.

HE DID NOT understand this woman. If he'd known she'd wanted the dregs of the coffee, he would have made himself a cup of instant.

She certainly didn't have a sweetly compliant disposition and he ought to be relieved that she wasn't the clingy type. He'd get more work done and he didn't want to endear himself to her, since there was no future for her here.

But she wasn't trying to attract him *at all*.

Honestly, it appeared as though she'd just rolled out of bed. The back of her hair was fluffed up from where she'd slept on it. Having seen her yesterday, Trent knew Rusty wasn't wearing makeup to enhance those brown eyes, so her brows must be naturally dark. She was swimming in a baggy sweater with a neckline that had a tendency to shift to the right, revealing a beige, lace-free bra strap.

She actually looked kind of cute, in a slovenly sort of way. He hadn't realized before that slovenly could look cute. Obviously, he'd been dating too many blond fashion plates.

And her attitude was so prickly, especially about breakfast. He supposed he should have raved over the food, but frankly, the sausage was cold, the biscuits weren't warm enough to melt the butter and the eggs were overdone.

He probably should have said something anyway. Maybe that *was* the reason for her antagonism. He'd be sure and praise her efforts at lunch so she'd feel appreciated.

But not encouraged. The last thing he wanted to do was offer any encouragement to Rusty Romero and her grandmother. But it was becoming increasingly difficult to tread the line between rudeness and indifference.

Sighing to himself, Trent sat in front of his computer. All the bids for building supplies were coming in and he would have to select one prior to the end of the year. It meant keeping abreast of the price of the raw materials along with a hundred other details.

Dialing the number of a stock quote service, he waited for his modem to connect. Nothing. Picking up the phone, he heard Harvey ordering fresh balsam fir wreaths.

Quietly replacing the phone, Trent took a long, slow breath. How was he going to get anything done?

RUSTY FIGURED she had half an hour of free time before she had to start preparing lunch. The dishes were dried and put away, Agnes was resting, the three men were parked in their loungers in front of the big-screen TV and Trent was who knew—and who cared—where. She could check her E-mail.

All she needed was a phone jack. Neither bedroom had a telephone, so she slipped down the hall, carrying her laptop with her. She passed the master suite, where King Trent was probably ensconced, and kept going. At the end of the hall, she saw a closed door. Another bedroom. She tapped, and when there was no answer, she opened the door.

Trent sat in front of a computer, holding his head in his hands. He looked up before Rusty could retreat.

"I, uh, sorry."

"Did you need something?" His look was wary.

He probably thought she was tracking him down in his lair. What an ego.

"A telephone outlet."

His gaze dropped to the laptop in her arms.

"I...wanted to check my E-mail." Frankly, at this point, Rusty didn't care what Trent thought about her or the type of woman she was supposed to be. She was desperate to contact her office.

Trent leaned his head back and stared at the ceiling. "There's a jack in here, but Harvey is tying up the line. Even if you could get through, he constantly picks up and breaks the connection."

"Oh." Curious, Rusty wandered further into the room. "What are you doing?"

Without lifting his head from the back of the chair, he turned and looked at her. "A project with an end-of-the-year timeline."

"I hear that." Rusty sat on a trunk at the foot of the bed. "Would your Uncle Harvey mind if we just asked to use the phone?"

"Probably not for you, but I'm supposed to be on vacation. He'd lecture me about not relaxing." Trent sighed and got to his feet. "Tell you what, I'll go distract him and you can get, oh, maybe, five minutes of phone time. Will that help?"

"Yes." Rusty hesitated, then offered, "Maybe I can do the same for you."

Trent smiled. "Deal."

He could really be quite attractive, Rusty thought, watching Trent walk from the room. The rear view wasn't bad, either.

And he didn't seem to be the slightest bit interested in her.

Earlier, when she'd thought that, she'd been satisfied. Things could have become so sticky and awkward when she'd be forced to tell him that her future was not on some ranch. He would have been devastated, naturally, because he was unlikely to see a woman of Rusty's caliber answering his silly ad, if she did say so herself.

Now she wasn't so sure. Having an attractive and relationship-free man express complete disinterest was not good for her feminine ego. She'd think about that some other time. Right now, she had to connect her computer.

Trent was as good as his word and within moments Rusty had retrieved her E-mail and captured it in a file to read later. She didn't want to chance taking up too much time.

With a few minutes left before Trent's return, Rusty checked out his setup. He had a nifty laser printer—better than the portable inkjet she'd brought. Maybe he'd let her use it. Her laptop was better than his computer, though, she noticed with satisfaction.

Next to the bed, against the wall, were boxes of papers and file folders. Good grief, it looked like the man had brought his entire office. He obviously hadn't intended to take any sort of vacation. Now, that didn't matter to her, but hadn't he planned to spend any time getting to know the woman who'd responded to his *Texas Men* profile? Or perhaps he hadn't anticipated such a heavy end-of-the-year workload when he'd sent in his ad.

"See anything you like?" Trent walked through the doorway, his expression stern.

"Yeah, your laser printer." Rusty hooked a thumb over her shoulder. "Mind if I borrow it sometime?"

He gazed at her, unblinking. "You've got nerve, I'll give you that."

"Why?"

"I do you a favor, catch you snooping through my stuff, and you ask to borrow my printer." He advanced until he was close enough to invade her personal space.

Rusty kind of liked having him stand so close. Little prickles of awareness raised the hairs on the back of her neck. "Hey, if I were snooping, you'd never know it. By the way, thanks for the phone time."

"No problem." Still stern-faced, he hadn't moved.

A power play. Well, *she* wasn't going to yield. In fact...Rusty looked up at him and leaned a fraction of an inch closer to increase the stakes. He retained his position, though something flashed deep in the back of those choco-late brown eyes.

Just to see what would happen, Rusty sent him one of those if-you-try-and-kiss-me-I-might-just-let-you looks.

His eyes narrowed. Obviously he knew the look. His gaze darted around the room and Rusty could almost hear his internal male alarm sound. *Warning. You are alone in a bedroom with a marriageable female. Proceed with caution.*

Holding up a finger, Trent said, "I don't know what your game is, but I don't want to play." Taking her shoulders and spinning her around, he walked her to the door.

She'd gotten to him. He'd tried to intimidate her and hadn't. Rusty felt daring. "Why do you think it's a game?"

"Life is a game."

"And all the men and women merely players. Playing sounds like fun, huh?"

"Not to me."

Rusty turned around in the doorway and stopped so he ran into her. "Well, it does to me."

He looked down at her. "That's exactly what I'm afraid of." A pulse throbbed in his temple.

"Afraid?" Rusty held their chest-to-chest position.

He didn't blink. "Uninterested."

She raised her eyebrow. "Uninterested in women in general?"

His gaze left her eyes and swept the length of her. "You in particular."

Ouch. She'd given him the opening, but hadn't expected him to use it so effectively. Teasing him had lost its allure. She backed off.

If he wasn't interested, he wasn't interested. Fine. His loss. His sort didn't appeal to her anyway. "Okay, I under-stand," she said with forced cheerfulness, stepping back-ward into the hall.

With a clear conscience, Rusty could now report to her grandmother that Trent was off the list and her matchmaking should cease at once. In fact, there was no reason for them to remain at the Triple D. They could go home. Soon. It had been a productive morning.

"See you at lunch." She smiled, unable to resist one last shot. "No hard feelings—so to speak."

Rusty had already turned to leave. In one movement Trent grabbed her arm and hauled her against him.

"Wha—"

Cupping her head with his hand, he swooped down and captured her open mouth with his.

Shock held her immobile as Trent demonstrated that he was one of the world's all time great kissers. Absolutely masterful, yet at no time did she feel the slightest bit threatened. Instinctively, Rusty knew that at the first sign of resistance, Trent would release her.

So she was careful not to resist.

Unfortunately, before she could actively participate, he broke the kiss. For a few more seconds his lips remained just an inch above hers as he gazed into her eyes.

"*Now* you can leave," he said, releasing her.

And then he shut the door.

5

THAT WAS NOT uninterested. That was definitely interested. Even though he'd just been responding to that crack she'd made, there was definite interest in that kiss.

Rusty stared at the closed door for longer than she would have liked. She didn't want to admit that she half hoped—okay, fully hoped—Trent would open the door and kiss her again. A girl didn't encounter Olympic gold medal kissers often enough to ignore one when she did.

Alas, the door remained closed.

Perhaps she ought to rethink her timetable for leaving the Triple D, Rusty reflected as she took a step and found that her knees wobbled.

HEAD PRESSING on the closed door, Trent held his breath until he heard Rusty's footfalls retreat down the hallway.

What had he been thinking? Well, he knew what he'd been thinking, but *how* could he have thought it? Or done it?

He deliberately bumped his forehead against the doorjamb. *Stupid, stupid.*

Prior to this little slip, he'd done everything but hang a sign saying, I'm Not Interested. He'd even told her he wasn't interested. Then he had to go and kiss her, which she'd interpret as him being interested.

And he was, but not in the whole marriage scenario that came with her. Unfortunately, marriage was the ultimate purpose of her visit here. She'd brought her *grandmother*, for pity's sake. How much more proper could she get? And she expected him to be looking for a wife to live with him on the ranch. Trent wasn't ready to live on the ranch yet, so he couldn't, in good conscience, encourage her. Or take advantage of her.

True, she'd been surprisingly aggressive. True, he'd liked it. But he was supposed to be discouraging her, and now any hope of Rusty Romero and her grandmother throwing in the towel and leaving the Triple D early was gone. He'd given her hope.

A marriage-minded woman with hope was a formidable opponent.

Like Clarence on one of his bad days, Trent slowly made his way across the room to the computer, slumped onto the chair and stared at the screen. The situation was not unsalvageable *if* he exhibited no further interest in her, which meant remaining cordially remote and no kissing.

Trent thought again of her mouth and the pleasantly stunned look on her face, the teasing look in her eyes...how she'd felt in his arms...the way she insisted on making each meeting a confrontation...and the way he was beginning to look forward to those meetings...

Showing complete apathy toward Rusty Romero was going to be harder than he thought.

IT WAS A TESTAMENT to Trent's kissing expertise that Rusty dropped off her laptop and headed for the kitchen without reading her E-mail. By the time she remembered, she and Agnes were in the middle of making soup and sandwiches.

"We'll have a light lunch and cook something special for supper," Agnes said. She had dressed and when Rusty had wandered, dazed, through the den with the loungers and big-screen TV, she'd been chatting happily with the uncles.

"We're planning decorations for the house. And tomorrow, we'll cut down a Christmas tree! Can you imagine?"

"Sounds like fun." Sounded like work, but her grandmother was so excited, Rusty tried to muster some enthusiasm.

"This afternoon, we can look for cookie recipes and try one."

She'd better grab some time for herself before her entire stay was planned. "Uh, Gran? I may have to let you choose the recipe. There was a message from Alisa that I haven't had time to read yet."

"But how will I know what cookies appeal to you?"

Slathering mayonnaise on bread, Rusty thought quickly. "We've never had time to make those really fancy Christmas cookies. You know, the decorated kind? How about those?"

Agnes beamed. "That'll be so much fun!"

And time-consuming. While her grandmother fooled around with all that colored icing, Rusty should have hours to herself.

By the time lunch was ready, Rusty had decided that she would treat Trent very matter-of-factly. After all, nothing had really changed, she told herself. She'd teased him and he'd called her bluff. The balance of power was equal once more.

As long as Trent kept his lips to himself.

So when he beckoned to her right before they sat down to eat, Rusty took her time before responding. "Did you retrieve your E-mail okay?" he asked under his breath.

Apparently, Rusty wasn't the only one to decide that it was business as usual. How unfortunate for her peace of mind that it took this query from Trent to remind her that she hadn't even read Alisa's message.

"Yes. In fact, I need to act on it."

"If Harvey's eating, he isn't dialing," Trent commented, sitting in his seat.

Rusty took the hint, scarfed down her sandwich and escaped from the table, ignoring Agnes's raised eyebrows.

There were three separate messages from Alisa, which immediately alarmed Rusty. The first one assured her that all was well. The second mentioned that George Kaylee, Rusty's chief rival for the Next to Nature campaign bid, was also out of the office for the rest of the week. Rusty breathed a little easier. Maybe since she was gone, he'd also decided to take a break from the long hours that pulling together an ad campaign demanded.

But the third message made Rusty queasy. Alisa reported that she'd run into George's assistant in the supply room where she'd requisitioned materials for mounting photos. *Mounting photos?*

Rusty had a bad feeling about that. George was spending all his time on his Next to Nature presentation, as was she, so why did he need to mount photos? She'd planned to illustrate storyboards with sketches and knew George was doing so, as well. That was the way they worked. Cost prohibited them from hiring models and photographers for an in-house proposal—unless George was paying for a professional shoot out of his own pocket. Which he very well could be.

After typing a message imploring Alisa to find out what was going on, Rusty raced into Trent's room and sent the E-mail.

He arrived just as she was hooking the phone line back to his computer.

"Hey, are you coming or going?"

"Going." Rusty got to her feet, her thoughts back in Chicago. What was George up to? She should *be* there at this crucial time to keep an eye on him and her own project. Sighing, she closed her laptop.

"Bad news?" Trent asked.

She'd forgotten he was standing there.

"I don't know yet." Rusty frowned, then remembered she owed Trent some free phone time. "Do you need me to stall Harvey for you?" She looked directly at him for the first time since he'd entered the room.

Mistake. Trent was staring at her mouth.

"Hmm?"

She wished he wouldn't do that. "Phone time?"

He drew a deep breath. "Yeah." His gaze left her mouth and met her eyes.

They gazed at each other. Rusty knew what *she* was thinking and had a fairly good idea that Trent was thinking the same thing. He was remembering kissing her. And she was remembering being kissed.

And neither one of them planned to act on those memories.

Trent stood aside and Rusty walked past, holding herself carefully so she wouldn't touch him.

She made it all the way to the door before Trent spoke.

"If you can, give me some notice when you plan to pry my uncles away from the telephone."

"Gran said something about cookies." Rusty paused in the doorway. "I bet we'll have a midafternoon snack. In fact, I'll suggest it. That would be a good time."

Trent grinned. "Thanks."

Rusty then proceeded to spend all afternoon in the kitchen trying to learn enough to fake a lifetime of baking expertise. So much for free time. Well, she really couldn't do anything until she heard from Alisa, anyway, and baking cookies with her grandmother was a novel experience.

Mixing up batches of cookie dough wasn't so bad, she found. It almost kept her mind off George's activities.

Periodically, Harvey would gallop into the kitchen and alert Agnes to some product being sold on television. Rusty usually remained in the kitchen and iced cookies while Agnes went to look, but raised voices drew her into the den on one occasion. It was a mistake, because she found herself embroiled in an incident involving lighted pine garland.

"White lights? Have you no imagination, Clarence? Can't you see this room all full of color?" Harvey waved his arms about.

Clarence, the phone to his ear, shushed him.

"Oh, oh!" Harvey hopped up and down and pointed to the screen. "Hand-tied red velvet bows! At only four ninety-nine. It's a steal! A steal, I tell you! And you're on the telephone." He groaned. "Hurry!"

Clarence covered the mouthpiece. "I can order both at the same time, Harvey. How many did you want?"

"You haven't decided on whether you're ordering colored or white lights," declared Doc.

"Colored!" Harvey screeched.

Agnes made ineffective soothing noises. Rusty tried to melt back into the kitchen before her presence registered.

"I won't have the ranch house tarted up—" began Clarence.

"Why don't you let the Romero ladies decide?" suggested a deep voice. Trent walked into the room, crossed his arms and grinned.

Rusty sent him a look of complete disgust. "That's right. Put *us* on the spot."

"The bows, the bows!" Harvey whimpered. "There are only three dozen left!" On the TV screen, in a box announcing the number of items available for purchase, the number of bows declined at an alarming rate, then suddenly dropped to zero.

"Oh, no." Crushed, Harvey collapsed in his recliner. "We'll never see them at that price for that quality ever again."

"White lights or colored lights?" Clarence looked at Agnes.

Agnes looked at Rusty.

Rusty glared at Trent. "White lights, greenery and red velvet bows is one of my favorite looks," she said. "But since we don't have the bows—"

"Oh, we got 'em," Clarence said. "Yes, ma'am," he said into the phone. "That'll be on my American Express card."

"How many?" Harvey clutched the side of the recliner.

Clarence held up two fingers and Harvey's face fell. "*Two?* That's all?"

Clarence shook his head. "Dozen. Give me some credit— no, ma'am, I wasn't speaking to you. You just put the bows and a hundred yards of the *white*-lighted garland on my card."

"Have 'em sent Express Mail service," Doc reminded Clarence.

Clarence nodded.

Closing his eyes, Harvey sighed in relief.

"Harvey, you're missing the cashmere scarves." Doc gestured to the screen. "And look—matching socks."

Harvey sat bolt upright, the contretemps over the lights apparently forgotten. "Cashmere socks sacrifice durability for comfort."

"Your point?" Doc, who had successfully remained neutral during the colored-versus-white-light controversy, was obviously a man who picked his battles.

"Well," Rusty said brightly. "I think we should celebrate with some cocoa and warm cookies." She raised her eyebrows at Trent, who gave her the thumbs-up sign and retreated.

He didn't deserve the favor after putting her in the middle of the light mess, but she *had* promised.

"Rusty, I'm so proud of you," her grandmother whispered. "This is just the sort of afternoon I'd imagined when we decided to come here."

Rather than pointing out that most of their activities had revolved around either the television shopping network or the kitchen, she just hugged her pink-cheeked grandmother.

Rusty turned off the television while the brothers ate cookies and drank cocoa. They didn't seem to miss the TV, turning their attention to the ubiquitous catalogs.

Or most of their attention.

"Trent isn't here," Harvey announced the obvious in the middle of a discussion concerning the taste differences between Texas pecans and Georgia pecans. "And Trent is partial to pecans." The brothers exchanged a look with Agnes.

The natives were getting restless. "I'll get him." Rusty jumped up, grabbing a napkin and two cookies. "Just a sample to lure him out here for more."

Ignoring four satisfied smiles, she hurried down the hall and tapped on Trent's door.

"Come in," he called.

She walked in to find him talking on the telephone. He gestured for her to stay, so she did.

"I'll have it by the thirtieth," he was saying. "That way, we can sign before the end of the business day on the thirty-first."

He sounded so confidently professional he could have been ensconced in a plush executive suite instead of a small back bedroom in a ranch house. This was a man who intended to conduct business, not a man who was trying to catch up on a few things during the holidays.

After a few sign-off pleasantries, he hung up the telephone. "Of course, that was a complete lie on my part." Tension lines creased his forehead.

"Have a cookie." Rusty handed him the napkin, surprised he'd admitted such a thing in front of her.

"And how did you know I needed a cookie?" He gave her a weary smile and bit into a crumbly powdered-sugar-dusted lump.

"The world is a better place when you're eating warm cookies." She wished she'd nabbed a couple for herself.

His dimples appeared briefly. "These are great."

"Aren't they?" Feeling dangerously pleased, Rusty sat on the chest at the foot of the bed again and Trent swiveled in his chair until he faced her. "It's amazing how such a simple cookie can taste so good." Especially when it wasn't burned on the bottom. Harvey's insulated cookie sheets had made all the difference. "We used real butter," she added, in case Trent was avoiding butter. She had no idea what state had provided the pecans.

"Good decision." Trent ate the second cookie.

Rusty grappled with unexpected emotions. Trent's obvious pleasure made her feel warmly satisfied in a feminine, nurturing way. Just the sort of nurturing way she was avoiding. She didn't want to feel as though she'd fulfilled some womanly destiny after waiting on a man. And yet, if Trent had been gruff or unappreciative, she would have been furious. Go figure.

"I didn't get a chance to bring you cocoa," Rusty said. Really, two cookies hardly justified a nesting attack. "Your absence was noted by the group."

"Thanks for the tip." He smiled such an obviously forced smile that Rusty took pity on him. "Problems?"

"Hmm?"

"What are you *not* going to have ready on the thirtieth?" she asked, referring to his earlier comment.

Trent stared at her and Rusty thought she'd never seen such indecision on a man's face before.

He was tempted to talk, yet he was reluctant. Or didn't he feel she was capable of understanding his business woes?

"I don't want to bore you," he said.

"Is that man talk for 'don't worry your little head about it'?" She'd forgotten that he was hung up on separating men's work and women's work.

"It's man talk for once I get started I might not stop." Trent held her gaze in silent rebuke, making Rusty feel ashamed.

"I'm sorry. That was a nasty crack." She pulled her knees to her chest and wrapped her arms around them. "So, what's going on?"

TRENT WANTED to tell her. In fact, he wanted to tell her everything and drop this damn charade.

But he couldn't, and she sat there, ready to listen, looking sincerely interested at a time when he desperately needed feedback from somebody—anybody. Even the nettlesome woman in front of him.

The thing was, he was beginning to like her. He didn't want to like her. He didn't want to think about her at all.

Take the kiss. She could have become all huffy about it, but she'd been a good sport. And he noticed how she'd extended the amused fondness with which she regarded her grandmother to his uncles. She didn't patronize any of them and that counted for a lot in his book.

"A contract," he said, at last answering her question. "I don't think I can have the contract cut by the thirtieth."

"And if you don't?"

Trent brought his fingers together, then opened them wide. "My loan goes poof."

"Is that all? Not that losing a loan isn't enough."

"Actually, no it isn't all. The bids expire, building permits expire, my option on the property I want to buy expires." People's confidence in a Trent not backed by Triple D money would evaporate. He'd probably never get another chance to prove himself.

But he didn't say that to Rusty. He wasn't about to confide *everything* to her.

She was chewing her thumbnail in a classic thoughtful pose. "What's the holdup?"

Only that he was here instead of in Dallas. Only that all the bids were going to his office first before being sent here. Only that he didn't have vital information he needed at his fingertips and had to call his secretary—assuming he could get through. Only that he wished he'd never agreed to his uncles' scheme for meeting a "suitable" woman. But all he said was, "The bids aren't coming in as fast as I'd like."

"What are the bids for?"

Now there was a topic he could discuss without any qualms. "A retirement village. And not one of those places where the elderly just go to wait out their lives. I want a place where they can *live*—with their families nearby, if they want to." He shifted in his chair. "You see, most of these planned communities are family oriented, but they're forgetting the older family members."

He paused to allow her to escape if she wanted to. But he hoped she wouldn't.

"And?" She impatiently gestured with her hand for him to continue.

Pleased, he did. "And since developers have largely ignored this segment of the population, I'm building a community geared for people who've raised their children and are looking forward to an active retirement."

"People have been retiring to these sorts of places in Florida and Arizona for years. How is your plan different?"

Trent was nodding before she finished speaking. "I'm trying to incorporate the whole community, rather than isolate one age group. My plan is to start building the retirement housing and amenities, then add more assisted-living housing, building the houses for families last, since homes for them are more prevalent now. What I really hope is that some other developer will build family housing within the village."

Rusty was gazing at him with a blank look. She was bored. Disappointment stabbed him, the wound deeper than he'd expected. For reasons unknown to him, he'd felt Rusty would be interested. After all, she was obviously close to her grandmother. The time might come when Agnes couldn't live alone anymore.

"You're talking about transition housing, aren't you?"

She'd been paying attention after all. Pleased, he continued, "Not in the traditional sense. Probably a level before that."

Rusty gestured toward the computer and the surrounding debris. "And it all has to come together before the thirtieth?"

Trent nodded.

She eyed him. "You've been very involved with all this since I got here, haven't you?"

He hesitated, nodding again. "Sorry. I lost track of the afternoon." Not to mention the morning.

Rusty and her grandmother were guests here and he'd abandoned them to be entertained by his uncles. He fully expected Clarence to point that out in the very near future along with an admonition to give Rusty a fair chance. It *was* too early to convincingly announce that he and Rusty hadn't hit it off since he hadn't spent any time with her.

True, he'd kissed her, but he'd been annoyed with her when he'd done so. Afterward, he'd been annoyed with himself. He *certainly* didn't think Clarence would be pleased to hear about it.

"Since you're obviously in a time crunch, *why* did you advertise for someone to come and celebrate Christmas with you?" Rusty asked. "You have plenty going on in your life right now."

She deserved an answer but Trent wasn't entirely certain what response to give her.

The trouble was that he'd been expecting a completely different sort of woman to respond to the profile—one who wouldn't have questioned him. One who'd quietly throw in the towel and go home when he indicated no interest in her. Not one who challenged him and provoked him into kissing her.

"I'd hoped to be finished with the contracts by now." True. "And my uncles were looking forward to your visit. They were thrilled when you asked to bring your grandmother. I didn't want to disappoint them just because my timing was off."

He wondered if he should apologize. Rusty held herself very still, looking at him with an expression he couldn't read.

Then her brown eyes softened and the side of her mouth pulled upward. "You're a decent guy, Trent. And I understand—better than you might expect. You see—"

Rusty's comment was interrupted by a tapping on the open door. Agnes walked in. "These came for you, Trent." She handed him three overnight delivery envelopes.

"Thanks." More files from his office. He tossed the cardboard envelopes onto the floor beside all the other papers he needed to review later.

"Doc thought you might be back here working." Agnes leveled a stern look at the computer. "It's a lovely afternoon and you two shouldn't be cooped up here in the *bedroom*." She raised her eyebrows at Rusty, who promptly rolled her eyes. "Rusty, we used those Georgia pecans from the pantry in our cookies."

"Is that bad?"

"No, but Harvey claims he can tell the difference between those nuts and the ones they pick here at the ranch. He insists that Triple D pecans would be best for our Christmas cooking. We need more. Now, if you two will gather pecans, I'll make a pecan pie for tonight. What do you say?"

Taking a break suddenly appealed to Trent. "I like pecan pie."

"Have you ever had pecan ice cream sauce?" asked Rusty with a look at her grandmother.

"No, can't say that I have."

She laughed. "You just might get the chance."

The weather was cool enough to wear jackets, but not really cold. Armed with sacks, Trent and Rusty walked toward the pecan trees behind the ranch house.

"The time to pick pecans was in November," Trent said. "Harvey knows that. I'm surprised he didn't pick this year."

"News flash," Rusty said. "They were trying to get us out of your bedroom."

Oh. "We're not a couple of teenagers. Nothing improper is going to happen in there," Trent protested.

"Too bad. You're a great kisser." Tossing an impish grin over her shoulder, Rusty started jogging.

She liked the way he kissed. Trent grinned, ignoring all

his internal alarms. He was supposed to be alienating her. The trouble was, he hadn't expected to *like* any woman his uncles found with that ad. Never would he have picked Rusty for the type of woman to respond to it.

But something about the profile had appealed to her or she wouldn't be here. Therefore, she not only assumed he was the man described, she wanted that sort of man.

And he was not that sort of man.

What a mess. He should turn around now and head back to his bedroom. Alone.

"Come on, Creighton, get the lead out!" Laughter peppered Rusty's voice.

Trent wasn't a jogger. Running after her and not catching her would be humiliating. Catching her might be worse. He started jogging.

He was going to regret this.

Trent gave a halfhearted chase, but Rusty was sidetracked by something she saw or heard near the big old barn on the way to the grove of trees.

"Does Doc keep his animals in here?" She wasn't even breathing hard.

Trent nearly passed out trying to pretend he wasn't breathing hard, either. "No." He pointed to the low, metal building and pen east of the barn. "That's where they are. He wanted a modern facility and added on to his old vet clinic four years ago."

"Then what's in here?"

Trent shrugged. "Not much. Harvey uses it for storage."

"I thought I heard something." She looked up at him in that way women have when they expect you to do something.

"You want me to check?"

"Don't *you* want to?"

"Not particularly. I want to find plenty of pecans for your grandmother to make a pie."

"Yeah, we'll have to get extra in case she ne—wants to make more than one," Rusty muttered. She tugged at the wooden bar holding the door closed.

Resigned, Trent helped her.

Creaking, the big double doors swung toward them a few feet. Trent pulled one side open and stared into the black interior.

"It's dark in there. Is there a light switch?" Rusty felt along the sides of the inner wall.

"It *is* dark." Trent couldn't shake the feeling that something was off. "Too dark. Usually light shines through the cracks and seams in the wooden siding."

Just then Rusty's hand connected with a switch. Scattered bare light bulbs valiantly attempted to relieve the gloom.

Stunned, Trent gazed around him. Boxes, cartons and crates were stacked floor to rafter, blocking out any daylight that would have normally seeped inside the barn.

"Look at all this junk!" Rusty wandered to the nearest brown column, which appeared to have been recently shoved inside. One of the boxes was upside down and must have fallen, causing the sound Rusty had heard.

"'L.L. Bean, Sharper Image, DAK...' This is a monument to mail order." She turned to face him. "Your uncles are power shoppers."

"This place is a warehouse." Tracing his fingers over the cartons, Trent walked to the end of the row. What he found there brought a reluctant chuckle.

"What?" Rusty joined him.

Trent pointed to three beds. "Harvey's mattress-testing facility."

Rusty bounced on one. "This bed's too hard," she said in

a little girl voice and moved to the next mattress. "This bed's too soft." Moving to the third, she sighed and stretched out on it. "And this bed's just right." Scooting over, she patted the space beside her. "Care to try it out for yourself?"

"I'll take your word for it." Seeing a warehouseful of unopened packages alarmed Trent. Normal people didn't stockpile massive quantities of...stuff like this.

"You were more fun to tease back in your bedroom." Rusty sat up and stuck out her lower lip.

"Sorry. I'm just surprised to see all this." Trent squeezed around the column of boxes to the bigger crates in back.

Rusty dropped the Goldilocks routine. "Didn't you know about it?"

"No." Farming equipment. New farming equipment. But the Davis brothers hadn't grown anything more than a vegetable garden in years.

The boxes around him shook as Rusty went exploring on her own.

"Careful," he called.

"Yeah. I'd be a little concerned about one of these towers falling on Harvey."

"Oh, I'm concerned all right."

"Trent."

The tone of her voice drew him. He found her standing next to a waist-level crate. "What did you find?"

"Medical equipment." She pointed. "Unless this is mislabeled, that's an ultrasound machine."

And a stand for it, too. Trent was speechless.

Rusty nudged him with her elbow. "When was the last time you checked their credit card limit?"

Trent leaned against the crate and rubbed his temple. "Because of their *excellent* credit rating, they don't have a limit."

"If they keep charging at this rate, they won't have that nasty excellent rating problem for much longer."

In spite of himself, Trent burst out laughing, then shook his head. "I don't know why I put up with my uncles."

"Because you love them," Rusty answered simply. "I know men don't like to say that word, but I can tell you love them by the way you act and watch out for them." There was a short silence before she continued grudgingly, "Don't get conceited, but it's one of your more appealing qualities."

"Thanks," he managed to choke out as emotions bombarded him. Not one woman he'd brought to the Triple D had ever understood how important his uncles were to him. Not one woman would have truly cared.

"They raised me," he told her. "My mother was their only sister."

"What happened?" Rusty circled back to Harvey's mattresses.

Trent followed her. "When I was seven, my parents were killed in a tour bus accident. I was visiting the Triple D at the time and I just stayed on. Emma, Clarence's wife, was alive then and they took me in."

"You didn't have cousins?"

"No."

Rusty nodded as though mentally fitting a piece to a puzzle. "So Clarence must think of you as his son."

"Probably. He put me right to work, which kept me from moping around. That was back when the ranch was operating and before they struck it rich. I was a teenager when the well came in and nobody knew how to handle that amount of money."

Rusty started to laugh. "And now they do?"

Trent joined her. "No, but now they've got me to handle it for them."

"And a fine job you're doing, too."

"Hey, I'll have you know that I just turned down a request for a raise in their allowance."

"You're such a Scrooge," she said dryly.

As their laughter died away, he asked, "So, how about you? When did you lose your parents?"

"I never had any to lose," she answered promptly, and, as far as Trent could tell, without any bitterness. "You see, I understand how you feel about your uncles because I feel the same way about my grandmother. She raised me, so she's the one I consider to be my mother. My biological mother is Dr. Ellen Romero. The botanist?"

"Sorry, I haven't heard of her."

Rusty lifted a shoulder, then tugged the sweater back into place. "You'd have to be interested in that field. Her lifelong work has been to develop strains of agricultural plants that will thrive in arid conditions. She lives in Africa somewhere."

Rusty tossed out the last bit of information a bit too casually. She did care, no matter how much she tried to pretend otherwise.

"As I understand the story, she and my father, whom I've never met, were grad students living together. They applied for research grants and were told it would look better if they were married. So they got married and it worked. In fact, they were offered two grants. My father wanted one and my mother wanted the other. No problem—they divorced. Then Ellen discovered she was pregnant. Babies weren't allowed in whatever remote area she was going to be living in, so she decided to give me up for adoption. Gran insisted on raising me."

Trent was appalled by Rusty's parents. "Your grandmother sounds like a very special person."

"She is."

By the way she said it, Trent knew Rusty was just as protective of her grandmother as he was of his uncles.

"Gran was a single mother back when there weren't many single mothers and then she had to turn around and do it all over again with me. I know she thought Ellen would come back for me after a couple of years and be grateful, but Ellen's maternal feelings are directed toward her plants."

She was trying to be so tough, yet she was showing him a vulnerability that he found disturbingly appealing. "Do you ever see your mother?"

"Rarely. And I don't think of her as my 'mother.' I know it sounds strange, but she's more like an older sister or a distant cousin or something."

"So it's been just you and your grandmother?"

Rusty nodded.

Trent thought he now understood why Rusty had answered that profile his uncles had written. She'd never had a traditional family, so naturally, she was seeking one.

After what she'd just told him, he felt like scum. He should never have agreed to go along with his uncles' scheme.

6

AFTER THEY LEFT the warehouse, Rusty pretty much forgot about the pecans until she and Trent walked into the kitchen and encountered Agnes's expectant gaze. His mind obviously elsewhere, Trent hung his jacket on the coatrack by the door and stalked toward the den. Rusty thrust her empty sack behind her back and edged toward the pantry. Maybe she could steal some of those Georgia pecans from the cellophane wrapping. She doubted anyone would notice the difference.

"That was quick," commented Agnes with a speculative arch to her eyebrow.

"Mmm." Rusty quickly disappeared behind the pantry door.

"You two aren't squabbling, are you?"

Squabbling? Rusty made faces from inside the pantry. "I don't know Trent well enough to squabble with him," she said. Squabbling implied a relationship of some duration. Her grandmother was still living the home-and-hearth fantasy. Just goes to show what fresh, country air will do to a person.

"Well, good. Men don't like it at all."

"That's because they've usually done something wrong."

Rusty heard a sigh.

Searching the pantry, she discovered brown grocery bags filled with unshelled pecans. By the lack of the usual commercial packaging, she surmised that Harvey, indeed, had gone pecan picking. Her recent excursion with Trent had been a clumsy matchmaking ploy, which she should have anticipated. She needed to have a little talk with her grandmother. No matchmaking.

After all, she thought smugly, within hours of their arrival, Trent had kissed her. Okay, so it didn't mean anything, but technically, he *had* kissed her.

And technically, the kiss was great. There could be some serious perks to being a domestic slave.

Rusty was on her way to solicit nutcracking help from the uncles when she saw that Trent had reached them first. From their expressions, Rusty guessed that he was having a financial chat with them. Harvey looked stubborn, Clarence, indulgent, and Doc, bored. They hadn't lowered the footrests on their recliners, but Trent had taken control of the television remote and held it in crossed arms.

And no one was currently using the telephone.

What a glorious opportunity. Still carrying a sack of pecans, Rusty hurried to her room, grabbed her computer and within moments was sitting in Trent's desk chair reading alarming E-mail from Alisa.

"We need to talk," Alisa had written. No kidding.

Rusty pushed the unshelled pecans and Trent's shopaholic uncles out of her mind.

That rotten George Kaylee had commissioned photo illustrations of his proposal for the Next to Nature campaign. According to Alisa, they were top-notch professional.

George must feel the bonus he'd earn if he were successful was worth the personal financial investment. He'd also seen Rusty's trip out of town as the perfect opportunity to punch up his proposal without giving her time to counter with a little punching of her own.

This was serious. Rusty sat back and stared at her computer screen. She was using sketches that would be mounted on storyboards. By comparison, her campaign proposal wouldn't look as impressive, even if her ideas were better. Clients were funny that way. She's seen entire campaigns decided on something as trivial as the background color used for the presentation folders.

Checking her watch, Rusty decided to try to call Alisa even though it was after work hours in Chicago.

"Dearsing Agency. Rusty Romero's office."

"Alisa? You're still there on a Friday night? What a pro."

"Rusty! I've been about to go out of my mind! Why haven't you called?"

Rusty briefly explained the telephone situation at the Triple D. "I'm lucky I caught you."

"Lucky, nothing! I want you to get this account because then you'll be promoted. And if you're promoted, then *I'll* be promoted. But right now, it doesn't look good for the home team."

The phone line clicked and Rusty heard Harvey call, "What's that order number?" before piercing tones blasted her ear.

"Excuse me? Mr. Davis?"

"I'd like two dozen wire deer, dear."

"No, it's Rusty."

"At that price they shouldn't rust. Isn't the wire coated with white vinyl?"

"Mr. Davis—it's Rusty Romero. I'm on the extension."

"Oh, Miss Rusty. Are you ordering the wire deer, too?"

"No, I'm speaking to a friend of mine."

"Is she taking orders for the deer?"

"No...yes. Yes, she is." Truly, it was easier this way. "Go ahead and give her your order." Now Rusty'd have to remember to order the stupid deer herself.

After Harvey ordered his herd of deer from a bemused

Alisa and got off the telephone, Rusty sighed. "You see? Listen, do you suppose you could get a closer look at George's campaign? I don't want you to do anything to jeopardize your job, but—"

"I'm ahead of you. As we speak, I'm holding photographs in my hot little hand."

Rusty's heart picked up speed. Alisa was the best. "How did you get them?"

"Out of George's garbage. They're outtakes, but ought to give you the general idea."

"You're kidding." What a break. "Why didn't he shred them?"

"He told Tammy to, but she had a date, so I offered to shred the garbage for her."

"Aren't you a pal." Rusty gave a low whistle. "She won't make that mistake again."

"I know." Alisa sighed. "You can only use the garbage bit with newbies once before they catch on. Shall I send the pictures to you, or are you coming back soon?"

Rusty closed her eyes. Originally she'd assumed her grandmother would quickly tire of cooking for strangers and want to leave well before Christmas. Unfortunately it appeared that just the opposite had happened. Agnes was in homemaker heaven and was reveling in the uncles' company. Rusty couldn't remember the last time she'd seen her grandmother so animated.

Dragging her back to Chicago now would be cruel. And had Agnes ever asked her for anything before? It was time for Rusty to be unselfish.

"Better overnight the pictures," she said to Alisa.

"Okay, except the mail's gone out for the day and there's no overnight delivery in the hinterlands. It'll be Monday before you get them."

"Nuts. Hey, can you fax me copies tonight, so I can get a

general idea of what he's doing?" There was no way Rusty could wait until Monday to see George's pictures. Even though the copies would be awful, it was better than nothing.

"Fax now?"

"Uh..." Harvey would undoubtedly interrupt the transmission. This single telephone line was the pits. "It'll have to be later tonight."

"What time?"

Good question. After everyone had gone to bed would be best, but that would be imposing on Trent. What choice did she have? "Midnight?"

"I'll put the fax on automatic," Alisa responded.

"Oh, and, Alisa? Since you've got all the information, will you please order the deer?"

AS SHE WORKED on her laptop that night, Rusty vowed to find a way to install another phone line. Why Trent hadn't done so before now was beyond her. Unless he thought that by keeping the uncles limited to one telephone line he'd cut back on their ordering.

Like that had really worked. She thought of the barn and shook her head. She didn't envy Trent *that* problem. Besides, she had her own difficulties. Agnes had been annoyed that Rusty hadn't joined her in the kitchen—not because of the extra work, but because there wasn't any way Rusty could take credit for cooking dinner.

In spite of her grandmother's promise not to make it again, dinner had been tuna noodle casserole, and frankly, Rusty had been happy to give full credit to Agnes for that dish. Still, Agnes was concerned that Rusty wasn't acting the part of Supreme Domestic Goddess. Rusty wasn't worried. Trent had been so preoccupied, he hadn't even noticed her culinary talents. Or lack of.

Rusty shifted in the bed so she could see the clock. It was eleven forty-five. Pulling on her robe, she closed her laptop and slid her stocking feet carefully across the wooden floor, hoping to avoid telltale creaking. Pulling open her door, she peered into the hallway.

Unless Trent had fallen asleep with the light on in his room, he was still awake. One problem averted.

Unfortunately, his light wasn't the only one on. Either Clarence or Doc must be the night owl, since Harvey was still testing mattresses in the barn.

She crept toward Trent's room, conscious of the irony in the situation. Here she was, sneaking into an attractive bachelor's room in the middle of the night to receive a fax. Perhaps her priorities *could* stand an overhaul.

Reaching Trent's closed door, Rusty hesitated before tapping. Sounds carried at night and she didn't want to be discovered by whichever uncle was still awake.

She tapped lightly and winced. No response. Leaning her ear against the door, she heard shuffling and pulled back just as Trent opened the door.

"Hi, can I—" It was at that point that Rusty noticed Trent wasn't wearing a shirt.

All the air left her lungs.

Gray sweatpants rode low on his hips, his feet were encased in thick white socks and he was wearing black wire-rimmed glasses.

He looked great. He looked more than great—he looked casual manly great. And since he hadn't been expecting company, this was his natural manly state. And his natural manly state was...great. Really, really great.

His natural manly state was affecting her vocabulary. There were no words left in her oxygen-starved brain.

"Can you what?"

He'd spoken. Rusty knew she should respond but she

seemed incapable of it. Besides, she'd forgotten why she'd come to his room anyway. The original reason didn't matter. There was the issue of a shirtless Trent to be dealt with. Delightful possibilities arrayed themselves before her, all of them involving ways to come in contact with Trent and his chest. Any other incidental body contact would be welcome, too.

Where had he been hiding those muscles? Rusty's mental image of the perfect male physique rapidly morphed into Trent.

He had strong shoulders and subtly defined pectorals, with just enough chest hair to enhance rather than detract. Rusty wasn't a hairy chest aficionado, and while Trent's chest wasn't exactly *hairy*, neither was it entirely smooth. Just right, as a matter of fact. Why hadn't she realized how utterly *male* chest hair was before?

Especially the dark patch in the center. Rusty's gaze fastened upon it as she mentally buried her fingers in the curls.

"Rusty?" Trent spoke to the top of her head, since Rusty was staring at his chest.

"Mmm?"

"It's the middle of the night and you're standing in my doorway."

"Yes." She let her eyes travel upward. It was his neck. That was it. He had a lovely long neck that disguised his scrumptious muscles. In fact, his neck was almost as good as his chest. What an unexpected delight. Necks as an erogenous zone. Who'd have thought it?

"Are you coming in?" He stepped aside.

"Yes, please." She took a few steps forward, then stopped. There was an interesting hollow at the side of his neck where the shoulder sloped up to meet it. A little indentation just waiting to be filled with kisses. Rusty would have sighed if she'd had any air in her lungs to sigh with.

Trent raised his eyebrows.

She should say something. "You have a neck." Hmm. Perhaps she should have said something else.

He drew his hands to his waist, the movement deepening the indentation that so fascinated her. "Most people do."

"Well...some men don't have much of a neck. You do, though. It's...nice. A nice neck." *Shut up!*

"Thank you," he said gravely.

In the silence that followed, the corner of his mouth quivered. "You brought your computer." He pointed to the forgotten weight in her arms. "Therefore, I'm assuming this is *not* a midnight seduction attempt."

"It didn't start out that way," Rusty murmured.

"And now?"

She sighed regretfully. "Probably not."

"In that case, I should put on my shirt." He reached for the garment hanging on the closet doorknob.

Cover up his chest? "Don't go to any trouble on my account."

He paused in the act of shrugging into his shirt, blinked twice and grinned the smug grin a man gets when he knows a woman is attracted to him. "You're sure this isn't a seduction?"

Teeth. Dimples. The chest and neck she'd so admired. "No..."

His grin widened. "How about I just leave the shirt unbuttoned while you decide?"

"Okay." Rusty took a deep breath, followed by another to jump-start her brain.

Her brain remembered the fax. "My fax! What time is it?"

"Almost midnight."

Yelping, Rusty dived for the phone jack. "Can I hook up my modem?" She jerked out Trent's modem line. Oops. His computer wasn't on, was it?

"Go ahead." Trent sat on the bed.

Rusty couldn't believe she'd been sidetracked by Trent's chest. Okay, his neck, too, but necks, she saw all the time. She shouldn't have been sidetracked by a mere neck. And she was an intelligent, ambitious woman who was not normally overcome by the sight of a bare male chest, either.

Which meant that there was something about *this* male chest that was different.

The fact that it belonged to Trent?

From under the desk, Rusty peered at him. Bespectacled, he sat on the bed and stared at a paper. Then he put it down and picked up another one, rubbed his forehead and picked up the first again.

No, she decided from her crouched position, it wasn't Trent. It couldn't be Trent. He happened to be in the vicinity, that's all. It must be the effect fresh, country air had on her. That fresh air was lethal. It turned her grandmother into a domestic zombie and attacked Rusty's hormones.

She should cut down on breathing. But look what had happened when she'd tried that moments ago. No, maybe she should go find some pollution to breathe and counteract all that fresh air.

Backing out from under the desk, Rusty stood and brushed at her knees. She was wearing the robe her grandmother hated. Agnes had a point that Rusty only now fully appreciated. Nope. She sighed a regretful sigh. No seduction possible at this time. "I'm receiving several pages, so it'll be a few minutes. Should I come back later or..."

Without looking up from the papers, Trent waved vaguely. "Have a seat."

Gingerly, Rusty moved a small paper pile and sat on the trunk.

Exactly at midnight, the telephone rang and her modem picked it up. Rusty bounded over to watch until she saw that the connection had been made. Now all she had to do was wait.

"You don't think the phone woke up anyone, do you?"

Trent shook his head. Tossing a file folder onto the bed, he removed his glasses and rubbed the bridge of his nose. He looked tired.

"I didn't know you wore glasses," Rusty said. Wasn't she the witty conversationalist.

"I took out my contacts."

Of course he had. Any normal person would have been able to figure that out. It was just that she couldn't stop staring at him and figured she'd better say something to have an excuse to keep looking at him.

"What did your uncles have to say about all the stuff in the barn?"

Trent gave her a doleful look. "Christmas presents."

Rusty's eyes widened. "Whoa."

"They were very cagey. Tried the old don't-ask-too-many-questions-around-Christmas routine. But since I haven't asked for any farm equipment under my tree, I mentioned the unusual quantity and *variety* of items in the barn."

"And?"

He sighed. "They told me to mind my own business. I pointed out that their financial well-being *was* my business and once we established that they could afford this little shopping spree, they wrestled me for the TV remote and sent me out of the room."

Rusty burst into laughter. The thought of those three

couch potatoes wrestling their muscular nephew was too much.

"I'm glad you're amused."

Trying to stifle her laughter, Rusty asked, "They really *can* afford all that?"

Trent nodded.

"Wow." Then they ought to be able to afford a second— or even third telephone line. She wondered how to broach the subject.

"Rusty?"

"Yes?"

She could see him choose his words.

"As an outsider, you...uh, you haven't noticed anything mentally off-kilter with them, have you?"

Rusty sobered immediately. She could tell Trent was seriously concerned. "No," she answered with equal seriousness. "Now, Harvey is a little unusual..."

"That's just Harvey."

"I thought so. And my grandmother would have said something to me if she thought anything was wrong. She worked in real estate before she retired and learned to size up people quickly."

"Good." Trent closed his eyes in relief. "I'll have to assume my uncles have their reasons for stockpiling all that stuff."

His obvious concern for his uncles added points in the "good guy" column. Trent was racking up a lot of positive points lately, Rusty noted. Almost enough to counter the negative ones he'd started with.

How had that happened? Dragging her eyes away from him, Rusty searched for another topic of conversation.

"Are those your bids?" She indicated the folders spread over the bedspread.

"Yes." Changing the subject seemed to suit him. "I hope

more will come in, but I thought I'd start comparing and eliminating now."

"Hey." Rusty recognized a familiar logo. "I know this company." Without considering that she might be looking at material Trent would rather not share with her, Rusty picked up a folder that had been set away from the others.

"Lance Construction." She shook her head. "I can't believe they're still in business."

"You know that company?" He spoke sharply.

Nodding, Rusty decided it didn't really matter if she told Trent about her work. He probably wondered why she was receiving faxes in the middle of the night, anyway. "I work for the Dearsing Ad Agency in Chicago." She hooked a thumb over her shoulder. "That's what the faxes are about."

Trent lifted his hand, palm outward. "You don't have to explain."

No, but I thought you'd at least be curious. His disinterest was probably just as well. "Anyway, back when I was very green, Lance Construction offered Dearsing their account. The dollar figure they threw around meant a huge budget for the lucky account exec." Rusty shrugged. "Naturally, I thought I'd take a crack at it, along with everybody else. So they sat and looked at all the presentations, nodded their heads and offered a contract for a fraction of the original budget they'd mentioned. Dearsing couldn't do the campaign they'd selected for that amount. The deal was off and Lance Construction proceeded to use in-house staff—with our ideas."

"You had no recourse?"

Rusty grimaced. "Oh, they changed everything just enough to avoid a lawsuit. Believe me, I'm certain Dearsing explored the options." She picked up the folder and pointed to the logo. "See the knight on horseback with the lance? That was my idea. Not that I was ever going to get the credit, but still."

"Why wouldn't you get credit if your idea was used?"

Rusty looked up at him. "Because that wasn't my job. I was just a general project assistant—a glorified errand girl. I was in on the brainstorming and showed my sketch to one of the account executives."

"And he stole it?"

Rusty waved her hands. Trent was beginning to look outraged on her behalf and she hastened to set him straight. "No, I was thrilled he used it, because I wanted him to request me for a staff position if he got the project. That's how people work their way up at Dearsing."

Trent's forehead smoothed. "So you have to pay your dues first."

"Right. But I got off track about Lance Construction. Bait and switch is their modus operandi. They lowball a bid—they did, didn't they?"

Slowly, Trent nodded.

"They get the job and midway through, they need more money. In fact, there was some government building in Chicago they were supposed to build and the situation was so bad, it was in the papers for weeks. Taxpayer money and all that. I guess that's where you heard about them." Rusty handed him the folder. "They've got a *major* PR problem."

Trent looked at the folder, then back at her. "I—you're sure this is the same company?"

"Based in a little town in Illinois?"

"Yes."

Standing, Rusty spread her hands. "How many other firms like that can there be?" She stepped over to the computer and saw that it was still receiving. Alisa must have recovered a ton of pictures. Returning to the trunk at the foot of the bed, Rusty saw that Trent was staring at the Lance Construction folder.

It was a great-looking folder, if she did say so herself. Along with her knight idea, they'd appropriated the black and silver-blue color scheme that had been George Kaylee's idea. Probably his last good one, she thought disparagingly. He'd been an account executive then and she'd been eager to have him select her for a project. George was very good at selecting and using the best ideas.

Unfortunately, he wasn't good at generating them and after several months, Rusty chafed at the lack of recognition.

Those were the days. She sighed and wondered whose ideas he'd used for his Next to Nature campaign.

"Rusty?"

Trent recaptured her attention. He'd put his glasses back on. Honestly, the man looked like a commercial for loungewear. That chest of his was something.

"I had *not* heard anything adverse about Lance Construction and I was seriously considering going with them."

It took a moment for Trent's words to register. "I assumed if *I* knew about them, everybody in the construction industry knew about them." She concentrated on trying to remember when the big flap over the public building had occurred. "Check the Chicago papers about four or five years ago. I can't remember exactly when it was, but I do remember gloating over their troubles." She grinned.

"I'll have my assistant check it out." He pressed his lips together. "As she should have done before forwarding this bid to me." He chucked the folder against the wall. It slid down and disappeared behind the bed.

"Thanks for the heads-up," he said. "You saved me considerable time."

Rusty waved off his compliment, though it pleased her. "You wouldn't have contracted with them without investigating."

"No, but I might not have had time to investigate anyone else after I found out they weren't suitable. I owe you."

An incredibly good-looking man with a great chest and lovely neck was indebted to her. Life didn't get much better than this.

As Trent gathered up the various papers and files spread over the bed, Rusty spent several pleasurable moments fantasizing about ways he might repay his debt.

He stacked the folders on the floor beside the bed and leaned against the headboard, lacing his fingers over his stomach.

This pose drew attention to his chest, which was already prominently featured in Rusty's repayment fantasies.

"You know, you're not anything like I expected." His eyes drifted over her, making Rusty acutely conscious of her unmade-up face and ratty robe.

She should have listened to her grandmother, but she'd never expected to find herself wearing the robe in front of Trent, or the Trent who'd placed that "traditional wife" profile.

"What were you expecting?" she asked cautiously.

"Someone more—" he gestured "—aggressively domestic."

"What, like hitting you on the head with a rolling pin? I considered it a time or two."

Laughing, Trent took off his glasses and set them on the bedside table. Rearranging the pillows, he said, "Yes, we've both avoided mentioning that time I was out of line. I apologize."

She'd been referring to his views on women's roles.

"Please don't. Then I'll have to apologize for that crack I made and...I don't want to."

Trent blinked.

Rusty smiled benignly.

Trent cleared his throat. "Clarence really chewed me out about not spending more time with you." His expression warmed. "I'm beginning to think he had a good point."

Uh-oh. Just when she needed to spend more time at the computer herself. "It's okay. I know you've got this deal in the works and you're busy."

"Even so—"

"No, really. Take as much time as you need."

His eyes narrowed thoughtfully. "You're very understanding for someone who traveled all this way to spend her Christmas holiday with strangers."

"That's the way the cookie crumbles." She laughed weakly. All these food references—she'd better quit it before he really thought about how much "help" her grandmother had given her in the kitchen. Taken over for her, was more the case.

Her computer beeped, signaling the end of Alisa's transmission. Rusty jumped up. "Well, looks like I'm finished here," she announced brightly, and scuttled over to disconnect her computer.

"Tell me something," Trent said as she ducked beneath the desk. "You're obviously intelligent and you have a job that requires you to stay in contact with your office. Why do you want to give that all up and move to the country?"

His question caught her so off guard that Rusty froze in her crouched position. What on earth could she say?

Rusty wished she could just confess that she wasn't interested in the position of "traditional wife" as advertised but was willing to negotiate anything else Trent had in mind. He'd probably be shocked and kick her out. Wouldn't her grandmother be pleased if Rusty was asked to leave over matters of moral turpitude?

She emerged from under the desk, to find Trent standing there, just inches away, regarding her closely.

Rusty smiled, perhaps a bit too widely. "I think change can be good for people." *Like you changing your views about women.* From what he'd told her, his poor aunt Emma had cooked and cleaned for everybody. No wonder he expected the same from Rusty.

"And you think this is a good change?"

Hardly. "Well, there was just something about your profile." *An irritating something.* "I don't meet too many men who are so up front about marriage and children."

Trent studied her. "You liked that part?"

Are you kidding? "You'd obviously put a lot of thought into your future and laid it right out there." Rusty slid her arm sideways. "No woman could possibly misunderstand what you want in a wife."

Trent said nothing.

She probably hadn't sounded very positive. "Actually, I do find it refreshing to know a man's views on marriage and family before I become involved with him." *Especially if I don't agree with them.* "It...saves time." Rusty let her words trail off, wondering if she should keep talking or quit now.

She could see Trent mulling over what she'd said, which she hoped sounded like a fair explanation.

Involved with him. Inwardly sighing, Rusty wished she hadn't spoken that last part out loud, especially with Trent's chest inches in front of her.

After her little speech, any physical overtures on her part would certainly indicate her acceptance of Trent's archaic views of family life. What rotten luck. Unless...

Unless Trent made the first physical overture. That might work. Just when things were heating up, she could drop little hints about having second thoughts concerning the whole kids-in-the-country bit. He'd murmur away her objections, as men are known to do when in the throes of passion, and things could proceed nicely. Then later, it wouldn't be a complete surprise when Rusty told him being a ranch wife wasn't for her.

Sounded like a plan.

Now, for the plan to work, she would have to subtly encourage him. Perhaps she'd arrange for some additional midnight faxes and arrive to receive them dressed in more alluring attire.

"Yes, it does help to know exactly what a person expects from a relationship," Trent was saying. "That way, no one's disappointed."

She watched as his gaze traveled over her face, coming to rest on her lips. Rusty was reminded of the kiss they'd shared, and shivered.

"You're cold. I should let you get back to your room." With a hand at the small of her back, he guided her to the door.

Rusty scoured her mind for an excuse to stay.

"Oh, and don't worry about a repeat of my earlier behavior." He rubbed his temple and smiled disarmingly. "I promise it won't happen again."

No! "I'm not worried, in fact—"

"It's okay, Rusty. Chalk it up to an uncharacteristic impulse." Smiling platonically, he stuck out his hand. "Good night."

That chest. That neck. Those lips. With a silent whimper of regret, Rusty shook his hand good-night.

7

WHEN THE ALARM went off the next morning, Rusty had slept only a few hours. Between unwelcome thoughts of Trent and trying to decipher the details in the faxed pictures, she didn't get to sleep until nearly three o'clock.

It was now five-thirty, as her alarm persisted in reminding her. Rusty batted at it and groaned. This morning she was determined to get up and fix breakfast all by herself. Last night it had seemed vitally important that she do so, if only to prove that she could, but in the predawn darkness, she was much less enthusiastic.

Rusty reached for her robe, reconsidered, dropped it back onto the chair and got dressed. There was no way her eyes would tolerate makeup just now, so she avoided looking in the mirror as she stumbled past it on the way into the cold kitchen.

A light was already on and when she looked out the back door she could see lights burning in Doc's animal shed. He was up and she guessed he'd been up early yesterday, too, and had caught her grandmother cooking. Well, this morning he'd catch Rusty cooking.

Now, what to cook? she wondered, rubbing her arms.

Biscuits seemed to be a big hit and she'd just about gotten the hang of pancakes. That was two breads. Perhaps something from another food group.

Pulling open the refrigerator, Rusty took out buttermilk and the ham. Then she put back the ham. She was tired of ham. Besides, if she ingested any more salt, she'd stay bloated until Christmas.

Bacon. Another fatty, salty meat. Oh, well. She didn't have to eat it. Eggs seemed to be expected, so she pulled out those, as well. Brightening, she remembered Harvey's fruit and checked the ripening bowl. Two more pears. She decided to eat one all by herself right now.

Humming, Rusty bit into the pear and went to make coffee. While it brewed, she studied the cookbooks her grandmother had brought with her. The kitchen boasted several others, but Rusty didn't feel experienced enough to stray from anything with which she was acquainted, no matter how superficially.

Okay, where was the biscuit recipe? Rusty flipped through the bread section. There, biscuits. And more biscuits. She turned the page. Yet more biscuits. Drop biscuits, whole wheat, rolled, buttermilk, yeast, soda and cheese. Rich biscuits, egg biscuits, sour cream biscuits, corn meal...Rusty panicked. Other than popping open a can, how was she to have known that there was more than one way to make biscuits?

Which recipe had her grandmother made? Which one should she tackle? Rusty was not about to make such a momentous decision without coffee. As soon as she could pour a cup from the still-brewing pot, she did so and took a swallow.

That was better. While the caffeine kicked in, Rusty looked up pancakes. Buttermilk, whole wheat...good grief. She knocked back the entire cup of coffee before a replacement cup had dripped into the pot.

She would make her selection logically and choose the recipe with the least ingredients.

Fortified with another cup of coffee, Rusty began assembling the ingredients for buttermilk biscuits. This wasn't so hard, she thought, stirring the dough and feeling competently domestic for the first time in her life.

The feeling didn't last. She dumped the dough onto the butcher block and *then* read that she should have floured the surface first. Fine. Scraping runaway dough back into the bowl, Rusty cleaned off the counter, in the process discovering the tenacious sticking properties of wet flour, dried the countertop, spread flour over it and plopped the dough on top.

A white cloud poofed out and settled all over her black jeans. She, of course, was not wearing the infamous cow apron, but now wished she was.

Never mind. Rusty grabbed a rolling pin and started rolling. All she managed to accomplish was to coat the pin with sticky dough.

She cleaned it off and tried again with the same results. The dough was too sticky. Rusty added more flour and mixed everything with her hands until she had a nice stiff lump. Perhaps a bit *too* stiff, but by pounding instead of rolling, she was finally able to flatten the dough enough to cut out several circles of varying thicknesses.

Nearly an hour had passed since she'd entered the kitchen and this was all she'd accomplished. But it was a start, she told herself as she pushed the biscuits into the oven.

Rusty decided to tackle bacon and eggs next. Maybe she'd skip pancakes this morning.

Leaving the mess on the butcher block for later, Rusty grabbed for the iron skillets she'd washed yesterday. Slamming them on the stove, she lit the burners and ripped open the package of bacon, then stared.

The skillets were coated in rust. What had happened? She couldn't cook in rusty skillets. She might not be experienced, but she knew that much.

Dawn pinked the sky by the time Rusty had scoured the skillets and returned to the stove. She dumped the entire package of bacon into the skillet and went to set the table.

She returned to a smoking mass, grabbed the handle of the skillet and burned herself. Retrieving the stupid cow oven mitts, she raced to the back door and held the smoking pan outside. Wouldn't it be charming to awaken the household with the smoke alarm? Rusty held the door wider, hoping for a draft to dissipate the smoke. When she thought it was safe, she brought the pan back inside.

Okay, too much heat on the bacon. Next time she'd know. But that didn't save the bacon this time. Rusty tried in vain to separate the strips, but they were burned to the bottom of the pan. She salvaged the parts not directly in contact with the skillet, but it made for some strange-looking strips of bacon.

Eggs. She'd simply arrange a mound of fluffy, yellow scrambled eggs over the bacon and maybe no one would notice.

Rusty cracked a whole dozen eggs into a bowl, beat as much air into them as she could and poured them into a fresh skillet over more moderate heat.

While she watched the eggs, she arranged pieces of bacon on a platter. This could work. It wasn't so bad.

She could still smell the burned bacon, which meant everyone else would smell it, too. Rusty propped open the kitchen door and searched for an aerosol room freshener under the sink. When she didn't find one, she considered running back to her room for her perfume and shooting a few squirts of that around.

But first, the eggs. Rusty stirred them and discovered that in spite of the low flame, they were sticking to the pan. She stirred harder and dislodged bits of egg and ominous black particles, which reminded her that she hadn't added pepper. She did so now, hoping for the best.

As the eggs scrambled, they turned from the yellow she'd expected to a black-flecked gray. And they were still sticking to the pan.

What was the matter? She pulled the eggs off the heat. Until she figured out what had gone wrong, it didn't make sense to waste more.

The scorched smell was as strong as ever. Rusty fanned her oven mitts at the stove. Well, at least she still had the biscuits. And coffee. And the bacon wasn't too bad. She tried a lump of the scrambled eggs. They tasted fine, except for the crunchy black things that appeared to be pieces of the cast-iron skillet. She wished the eggs had stayed yellow.

As she stared at the unappetizing mass, an idea formed. Food coloring. Well, why not? Everyone had eaten it in cookie icing yesterday and eggs were food. Or they had been until she'd messed with them.

Rusty trotted over to the cabinet where spices and baking supplies were stored, found the yellow food coloring and, with a guilty look around the kitchen and out to Doc's shed, she squirted a yellow stream onto the eggs. By smashing the eggs with a fork, she managed to incorporate enough yellow dye to offset the gray. The result, while not entirely natural-looking, was better than it had been. She'd keep the curtains drawn, the lights low and hope for the best.

Rusty decided to celebrate with more coffee. On the way to the pot, she opened the oven door to check on the biscuits.

A blast of heat was accompanied by an overwhelming scorched odor. Frantically, Rusty removed the pan and stared at a dozen misshapen dark brown lumps. She'd forgotten to set the timer.

Disgusted with herself, Rusty slammed the baking tray on top of the mess on the butcher block and refilled her coffee cup. Leaning against the counter, she surveyed the disastrous results of her cooking attempts. Realistically, what could she salvage?

Not much.

She wouldn't panic; situations had appeared bleak before. After all, she shouldn't have expected culinary perfection on her first attempt.

But she *had* expected better than this. What was wrong with her? Cooking couldn't be that hard. People in every culture around the world had cooked since the discovery of fire. Some of that ability had to be encoded in the genes. Obviously a recessive gene in her case.

Walking over to the butcher block, she poked at the biscuits and pried one off the baking sheet. Rock hard. Her failure was complete.

Rusty hurled the biscuit out the kitchen door. All she'd had to do was cook a simple breakfast so she could get back to her real work. Important work. Not stupid, mindless cooking. Not spending hours in the stupid kitchen, stuck on a stupid ranch, miles away from a decent carryout restaurant, trying to impress some stupid man.

Sniffing back frustrated tears, Rusty grabbed a wad of paper napkins and buried her face in them. Crying was stupid. Everything was stupid.

George Kaylee was stupid.

No, George Kaylee was *not* stupid, unfortunately. George was no doubt thrilled that his closest competitor had inexplicably chosen to take these critical days off. He'd be dancing in the streets if he learned that her stay was supposed to stretch as long as two weeks.

Of course, there was no chance of that now. Rusty was just moments away from being unmasked as the domestic impostor that she was, at which point she and her grand-mother would be sent back to Chicago in humiliating defeat.

Yesterday that would have thrilled her. Yet today, incomprehensibly and irrationally, Rusty didn't want to leave in defeat. She wanted to be the one who chose to leave—preferably after everyone had enjoyed a gourmet breakfast she'd prepared with her own two hands.

After a few minutes of blubbering self-pity, she felt better. She rarely cried, but when she felt like it, Rusty discovered it was best to give in and get it over with, then fix whatever problem had upset her in the first place. The problem now was the lack of food and lack of time to fix it. Sighing, she decided to start over anyway.

She'd just blown her nose when she realized she wasn't alone.

Jerking her head up, she caught Trent sneaking into the kitchen.

He looked guilty. "I smelled...uh, I could tell you were cooking and thought I might grab a cup of coffee?"

Rusty wadded the napkins and wished she'd thrown *all* the biscuits out the door.

Silently she watched Trent concentrate on the coffeepot and avoid her eyes.

A blue haze shrouded the kitchen, even though cold air flooded the room. Rusty said nothing. She did, however, stare at the food coloring on the stove in hopes she could levitate it into a cabinet before Trent discovered it.

He cleared his throat. "You, uh, need some help?"

"Does it *look* like I need help?"

Trent's gaze flicked around the room as he sipped his coffee. "Yes."

Rusty felt tears threaten again and closed her eyes. Never had she imagined becoming so overwrought about, of all things, a cooking failure. Obviously the lack of sleep and the stress of her work was playing a big part in her weepiness. Whatever, she wished Trent would say what he was going to say and be done with it.

She felt, rather than heard, him approach her.

"You know, you make a *great* cup of coffee," he said, leaning against the counter next to her.

Rusty gave a watery chuckle. "Apparently that is the *only* thing I can make."

"No, you..." He glanced behind them. "Okay, the biscuits are a little brown."

"They're burned." Which, judging by the density of the one she'd thrown out the door, was a good thing. "I forgot to set the oven timer."

"That can happen to anybody. Just make toast this morning. I see you've got...bacon?" Trent sounded doubtful.

"Stuck to the pan." She watched as he poked at the pink and charred bits on the platter.

"So it's extra crispy...in places." He held up one of the only whole strips. "Look, you even managed crispy and limp on the same strip in case anyone prefers both."

She sighed. "Give it up, Trent."

He tossed the bacon back onto the platter. "I'm going to have to, since I have *no* idea what's in the other pan."

"Scrambled eggs." Rusty moved to block his view of the food coloring.

"From what animal?"

"Very funny. They taste fine." She picked up the skillet. "I'm not trying to make excuses, but something is wrong with these skillets. This morning, they were coated with rust and all the food sticks."

"Sounds like you didn't reseason them."

"What?"

"These are made of cast iron." He hefted one. "They have to be seasoned with oil before you use them."

"You mean all the food has to be fried in oil?" She made a face.

"No, just after the pans have been scrubbed." He carefully set the skillet with the blackened bacon grease back onto the stove. "I figured you knew what you were doing when you attacked them with the steel wool yesterday."

The fact that she'd appeared competent enough to fool him yesterday momentarily mollified her. "Well, black gunk kept coming off and I figured they needed a good cleaning." Rusty remembered all the burned pancakes. Trent didn't mention them.

"You need to coat cast iron with some vegetable oil and bake it in the oven for a few hours to let the oil soak in. The oil keeps the iron from rusting and the food from sticking when you cook it."

How did he know all this? "You do that after every use? Give me stainless steel any day."

Trent laughed and shook his head. "No, only when you reseason the pans. In between times, don't scrub quite so hard when you're cleaning."

"Oh, ick." Rusty was no longer hungry.

Unfortunately, the others would be. "Well, I suppose I better mix up some more biscuits." She gazed unenthusiastically at the flour-encrusted butcher block and hoped everyone would want to skip breakfast today.

"'Morning." Wiping his feet on the mat outside the door, Doc nodded at them and stepped into the kitchen.

With a sinking feeling, Rusty watched the middle Davis brother's face as he took in the kitchen. Without changing expression, he paused at the stove, blinked at the eggs, glanced toward Trent, then Rusty, then back to Trent again.

"Stove can be cantankerous at times," he said, then nodded once more and kept walking.

TRENT REALLY FELT for Rusty, though he tried not to.

Her face whitened and she bit her lip as Doc walked into the other room. So she'd messed up a panful of biscuits. Big deal. Probably overseasoned the eggs, but that could be attributed to differences in taste. He wasn't going to attribute the bacon to anything.

But what was with Doc? The stove was never cantankerous. Harvey didn't allow cantankerous objects anywhere in the house. Besides, the stove was relatively new and the cast-iron skillets were from a line of cookware some chef had touted on television and were supposed to be of superior quality.

Or they had been until the Romero women had gotten hold of them. Trent doubted the skillets would ever be the same.

"Perhaps now that the oven is warmed up, the next batch of biscuits will turn out better." With a tight smile, Rusty collected the debris and carried it over to the sink. Jamming her foot on the metal flip-top trash can, she scraped the burned biscuits off the baking sheet. They clanged against the trash can like hail falling on a tin roof.

As the metal lid crashed back into place, Rusty shot Trent a defiant glance and snatched up the cookbook.

"Hey, don't worry about making more. I'll just have cereal this morning." He started for the pantry.

"There are four other people besides you and me who have to eat." She slammed down the cookbook and began scrubbing the butcher block. "They'll be awake any minute."

Trent paused, his hand on a box of sugared cereal that he'd slipped past Harvey and hidden behind the oatmeal.

He had work to do. He should just pour a bowl of cereal and carry it back to the bedroom. "There's plenty of cereal back here—"

"I am *not* going to feed your uncles cereal!"

"Why not?" Trent found two boxes of something resembling shredded tree bark.

"Because my grandmother and I are supposed to be cooking, not pouring!"

Trent hesitated, put back the cereal and heard himself say, "Then let me help you."

"*You?*"

The astonished expression on her face was truly annoying, but he'd offered to help and help he would. "Yes. May I have the cookbook?"

She surrendered it with a laugh. "This, I've got to see."

"Stick around and you might learn something." He could tell that jab really got to her.

Rusty started banging the skillets around as she washed the dishes. Trent was aware of her watching him and especially aware when she thunked the freshly washed rolling pin on the counter, barely missing his fingers.

"Sorry." Not looking sorry at all, she carried the skillets over to the stove.

"Come here." Trent hooked her arm and pulled her back to the counter. "The dough is ready to be rolled out."

She peered into the bowl. "So it is. Carry on."

"Not so fast." Trent handed her the rolling pin and went to wash his hands.

When he turned around, a pink-cheeked Rusty was glaring at a dough-covered rolling pin. "Why does it keep doing that?"

"Beats me." Drying his hands, Trent came to stand beside her. "The dough looks like it could use more flour."

"Then why didn't you put more in?"

"I followed the recipe."

"Well, so did I." Visibly exasperated, Rusty cleaned white glops off the rolling pin, dumped flour everywhere and attacked the biscuit dough.

Trent watched her frustrated struggles. "I thought baking was supposed to be soothing."

"Yeah, right." Rusty swiped at her bangs, leaving dough and flour smeared across her forehead.

Careful not to smile, Trent held out a towel, realized her hands were all doughy, and wiped her forehead off himself.

"Thanks," she said grudgingly.

"You're trying too hard at this. Here." Standing behind her, Trent placed his hands over hers on the rolling pin handles. She held herself stiffly. "Relax." Rusty dropped her shoulders. "Now, roll slowly." He demonstrated. "Back and forth."

Trent had intended to back off at this point—what did he know about rolling out dough?—but her hair was right under his nose and he could smell the shampoo she used, along with the smoke from her earlier cooking efforts. Her back pressed against his chest and he liked the way she fit against him when the movements of rolling out the dough brought her body in contact with his.

Back and forth. Back and forth.

Trent became aware of the suggestive rhythm and the fact that he was unconsciously echoing it. By now the dough was so thin they'd have the world's flattest biscuits, but he wasn't about to stop.

When Rusty's tongue crept to the corner of her mouth as she concentrated on the edges, Trent wanted to fling away the rolling pin and ravish her on the spot. Instead he dipped his head and grazed the back of her neck, hoping she'd think his touch was the unavoidable result of her reaching to the edges of the ever-widening circle.

"Is that enough?" She turned her head to look at him, bringing her mouth to within a millimeter of his.

"No. Not at all," he whispered.

Rusty's gaze fastened on his lips. She didn't move.

He remembered the feel of her mouth on his. But he'd promised her it would never happen again.

So help him, he was going to break that promise. Rusty's eyes fluttered shut as he moved toward her.

Footsteps sounded outside the kitchen. "Rusty, I can't believe I overslept. We've got—"

Skidding to a halt, Agnes stopped in the act of tying a belt around a satiny white robe and stared at them.

No one said anything, unless dual sighs from Rusty and Trent counted.

He straightened, careful to keep his movements slow, so Rusty's grandmother wouldn't think anything fishy was going on even though Trent knew there had been.

"Trent was helping me roll out the biscuit dough," Rusty said brightly.

Agnes finished tying her robe and grabbed the lapels, pulling them together over some lace thing she wore. She looked a lot different than she had yesterday morning, Trent thought.

"Trent...good morning." She patted at her hair and sent a wary look toward the stove.

"Good morning." Both women darted looks at each other and Trent decided to make his exit. "Let me know when the biscuits are done." He grabbed his coffee cup and headed out the door, regretfully glad Agnes had chosen that particular moment to enter the kitchen.

"WHAT'S GOING ON?" Agnes asked the minute Trent left. "It smells like you're burning the place down." She passed by the platter of bacon, picked up a piece and nodded. "Not bad, though."

"Oh, come on, Gran. It's awful."

"Bacon is inherently awful. The Davis brothers should be discouraged from eating it."

"I know *I'm* discouraged." Rusty turned to the biscuit dough.

"What is that?" Agnes pointed to the huge circle.

"My second batch of biscuits. Or, rather, Trent's batch."

"What happened to yours?"

Rusty pointed to the trash can.

"It's no wonder if you rolled the dough this thin. What were you trying to make, crackers?" Agnes folded the dough into quarters and mashed it together. "Try cutting them out now."

Rusty checked her watch and sighed. "Gran, why bother? Trent told me there's cereal in the pantry."

"Bite your tongue!" Agnes began to cut the biscuits herself. "We owe these men a hearty breakfast."

"Gran." Rusty stilled her hand. "The jig is up, as they say. I can't fake being able to cook any longer. Doc's already been by this morning. And you saw Trent—"

"Doc's been by already?" Agnes interrupted.

"Yes." Rusty eyed her grandmother's pinkening cheeks. "Is that why you're wearing your peignoir instead of your Homestead Hattie calico?"

"I—" Agnes looked down at herself. "That was an accident."

"Sure it was." Rusty grinned. Her grandmother and Doc? Stranger things had happened.

"Rachel Marie, have some respect for your grandmother. At least *I* didn't have some man 'helping' me roll out biscuits, of all things."

"It was *his* idea!" Rusty protested.

"*Was* it?" Agnes looked thoughtful.

Rusty didn't want her having those thoughts. "He was just being *nice*. Something I didn't think he was capable of." That wasn't really true. Rusty didn't know why she felt compelled to hide from her grandmother the fact that she found Trent not entirely repulsive. She only knew she did.

He'd helped her and hadn't said one word about her not being able to cook.

He wasn't such a bad guy, after all.

And he had a really great chest.

8

"Rusty, dear, we're ready to go cut down the Christmas tree," Agnes called from the doorway to Rusty's room.

Rusty winced. She'd forgotten. "Gran, why don't you go along with them and I'll help decorate the tree this evening."

Agnes eyed her granddaughter.

Rusty sat cross-legged in the middle of her bed, her computer in front of her.

"Trent's coming," Agnes said.

Poor Trent. He hadn't been able to get out of the tree-cutting excursion, either. "Gran...Alisa sent me a fax last night, and George—you remember me talking about him?"

Agnes nodded.

"Well, George is up to something with the Next to Nature campaign and I really need to study these pictures." She'd printed them out and they were arranged in a semicircle around her.

Agnes glanced at them. "There's nothing to study. They look like inkblots."

"Sort of, but I can see what George has in mind and it's a good idea. Too good. I need time to counter. Can't I skip—"

"Not after this morning's fiasco in the kitchen."

"Nobody complained."

"They were being polite. Now put on something pretty." Agnes opened Rusty's closet and inspected the slim contents. "This is your chance to make up lost ground."

"But I'd planned to work this morning!"

Agnes tossed a disparaging look at Rusty's computer and plucked an orange sweater from its hanger. "Wear this, it'll give you some color. You're looking peaked."

"I'm looking peaked because I only got two hours of sleep last night!" Giving up, Rusty tugged the sweater on over her shirt.

"I knew I shouldn't have let you bring that computer with you."

"It's a good thing I did!" Exhaling, Rusty turned off her computer and pulled on her boots. "Alisa found out that George is using photography for his Next to Nature presentation. I'm only using sketches. Now I've got to use pictures, too, or my presentation won't look as good."

"So take your camera along today!" Agnes threw up her arms. "Good heavens, Rusty. We're going into the woods to cut down a tree. You don't get much closer to nature than that."

EVERYTHING HE OWNED in the world was at stake on this construction project, yet Trent found himself jouncing along in the back of a horse-drawn cart on the way to cut down a Christmas tree. Clarence and Harvey were driving, he, Doc and the Romero women were sitting on hay bales in the back.

He wasn't certain how he'd been maneuvered into the tree-cutting expedition, but something Harvey had said—and Doc hadn't—and the way Clarence had looked, suggested that they were going to curtail Trent's work time completely if he didn't come along.

Okay, then he'd stay up nights and start sleeping in.

"How about another round of 'Jingle Bells'?" Harvey suggested before launching into the song. "Dashing through..." he trailed off. "Snow. You know what we need?

Snow for a genuine white Christmas." Harvey abandoned "Jingle Bells" and started singing "White Christmas," his thin tenor augmented by Clarence's growling bass.

Trent and the others joined in. It was difficult to remain unmoved after thirty minutes of Harvey's spirited caroling. Even Doc had smiled a time or two.

Rusty had lost the tight expression she'd worn when Trent had helped her into the cart and was looking around at the scenery as they rolled down one of the many old cow paths crisscrossing this area of the Triple D.

Her lips naturally turned up at the corners, telling him she was basically a happy person. He'd noticed she was easy to be around. Silences with her were never uncomfortable. She didn't sulk, she didn't cling, and she didn't demand his attention all the time.

Feeling vaguely guilty, Trent mentally compared her to the women he dated. They were usually longer, leaner, blonder, and not the type to ride in a hay wagon. Since he didn't plan to use this form of transportation often, that quality wasn't important to him.

The way a woman looked standing next to him was. He liked watching the envious expressions on other men's faces when they saw his latest date. If he'd had to put up with an occasional pout, that was a price he'd willingly paid.

Although she'd never be with him back in Dallas, Trent imagined Rusty standing beside him and was surprised at how easily the picture came to him. She had a city sophistication about her and looks that would be dramatic, rather than merely pretty. She could actually carry on a conversation, too. He imagined her charming his friends.

The thought so unnerved him, he actually shuddered.

"Hot chocolate, Trent?" Agnes Romero offered him a cup from the thermos she'd brought.

"Sure, why not?" The temperature outside wasn't that cold, but it wasn't a summer day, either. "Would you like some?" he asked, holding out the thermos to Rusty.

"Thanks—but don't fill it too full," she cautioned as the cart lurched to one side.

The chocolate was rich and hot. Trent exhaled and let his mind wander—away from women and numbers and bids and legalese. Instead he allowed his body to sway with the movement of the cart.

"How much longer?" Rusty asked, grabbing at the side of the cart when it shifted.

"Hard to tell at this pace. The trip's usually about fifteen minutes by car."

"Where are we going?"

"We're headed to the edge of a piece of grazing land. Years ago, Clarence planted firs there as a windbreak and my uncles have been cutting them for Christmas trees ever since."

"So you've got your own private grove." Smiling as though the idea appealed to her, Rusty sipped her hot chocolate. "I've been looking at all these pines—" she gestured to the towering trees that lined the path "—and I wondered how on earth you thought you were going to get one inside the house."

Trent laughed and started to reply when he noticed three pairs of eyes scrutinizing them. Clarence was still watching the road, but Trent knew he was straining to hear what they said. Great. Every move he and Rusty made today was going to be examined for romance potential. He wondered if she was aware of it.

Instead of keeping the conversation going, Trent leaned back and pretended to drink hot chocolate from his empty cup. He wished he could just forget why Rusty was here and talk with her like a normal person. He had a feeling—

okay, more than a feeling—that he could get to like her if the circumstances and timing were different.

"We're here!" Clarence announced sometime later. He drove the horse into a small clearing and stopped beside a wooden trough by an old-fashioned pump.

"It's a little house all alone in the woods." Rusty sounded intrigued.

"An old line shack for hands to sleep in when they were out working cattle," Trent told her as he lowered the back of the cart.

"Does anyone live there?" she asked, turning to him.

"Oh, no. It's too primitive. No more than minimum temporary shelter." Trent jumped down and held out his arms, but Rusty was already in mid-leap.

She landed beside him. "How primitive?"

"Take a look. Uncle Clarence, hang on and I'll be there in a minute." Trent helped Agnes out and offered a hand to Doc, who looked as though he wanted to refuse it.

Agnes, whether deliberately or not, turned away to exclaim over the cluster of firs in varying heights. Since she wasn't watching, Doc accepted Trent's help.

Harvey, clad in his running shoes, bounded out and tended to the horse. Trent saw that Rusty was rubbing at a window and peering inside the old shack, so he approached Clarence.

"I'm getting old, boy." Clarence hefted his weight to the edge of the driver's seat and handed Trent a step stool. After Trent positioned it, Clarence held on to his shoulders and maneuvered himself to the ground, where he stood and wheezed.

"Now don't be telling me I need more exercise," he said when he saw Trent's face. "I get enough of that from Doc and Harvey."

"You should listen to them," Trent replied, more concerned than he let on.

"The only reason I'd need to stay in shape would be if I had grandnieces and nephews to chase after." Clarence arched a gray eyebrow in Rusty's direction.

Trent gritted his teeth. "She can't cook, you know."

As both men watched, Rusty walked to another window and bent to peer inside. A breeze lifted her sweater a few inches above her middle, revealing form-fitting jeans and a trim waist.

"Maybe not," Clarence said. "But who cares?"

"TRENT?" Rusty called. "Is it okay to go inside? I don't think the door's locked." With its weathered gray wood, this place looked like a relic from the Old West.

"It shouldn't be." Trent left his uncle and walked toward her. Clarence grinned and waved at her from behind Trent's back. "However, some uninvited guests from the animal kingdom might be inside."

"I didn't see anything moving," Rusty said as Trent reached the shack and pushed the door handle.

The rough wood screeched before the door gave. No scurrying or rustling sounded, so Rusty followed him cautiously inside. The two outside windows let in just enough light to illuminate the functional interior.

"Not much in here." Trent flipped a light switch. Nothing happened. "There's a generator out back for electricity—"

"This place is wired for electricity?" Rusty asked sharply, an idea beginning to form.

"To a certain extent."

Rusty gazed around the one-room shack. Triple-decker bunk beds with grimy mattresses lined two walls at one end. Never mind. At the other end, a black cook stove straight out of a museum sat beneath simple wooden cabinets secured with hooks and eyes. A water pump curved over a stained porcelain sink. A stone fireplace with all the character one could wish for dominated the rest of the room. What a find.

Trent gazed out the uncurtained window, apparently lost in thought.

Rusty's mind whirled. This shack, though neglected and obviously well-used, was picturesque and she desperately needed picturesque right now. A little cleaning—not much, she wasn't into that—but with some judicious props... Rusty opened her camera and with shaking fingers attached the flash. Alisa had to see this.

Agnes had been right. This abandoned shack screamed Next to Nature. Drape some plaids...light a fire in the fireplace...maybe a bearskin rug...and a discreet display of Next to Nature products in the foreground.

Rusty snapped off two pictures.

"What are you doing?"

"Taking pictures." She zoomed in on the black woodburning stove.

"Why?"

"I like the way the place looks." Rusty lowered her camera. Judging by Trent's suspicious expression, confession time had arrived. The campaign proposal was too important to jeopardize by continuing to play the Happy Homemaker.

At the thought of admitting that she was not here on a husband hunt, Rusty felt both relief and trepidation. She'd need a photo release to use Triple D property in her presentation, but more than that, she'd need time—the time she was spending keeping up the kitchen charade. It was probably pointless now, anyway.

Yet, if she told Trent she had no interest in the life-style he sought, what was the point of her remaining at the ranch? He'd be justified in asking both Rusty and her grandmother to leave. She'd lose her chance to photograph his property.

Rusty was well aware of the irony in her situation. She'd arrived wanting to leave as soon as possible. Now she was seeking a way to remain.

Before she could figure out how to state her case, Trent spoke.

"You like rustic and abandoned?"

"I think this place is great," Rusty was able to say in all sincerity. "Antiques like these would go for big bucks in the city. And the view..." She gestured out the windows. Even the grime couldn't detract from the pines and the sloping field beyond. Her grandmother and his uncles looked like storybook characters as they wandered in and out of a small grove of living Christmas trees. "It looks like the backdrop of a painting." Or an ad campaign.

Trent stared hard at her, making Rusty nervous. Perhaps her confession should wait.

He shoved his hands into the back pockets of his jeans, shot another look out the window and appeared to come to a decision. "Have a seat." With a scraping sound, he pulled out one of the ladder-back chairs surrounding a plain, four-legged wooden table.

Uh-oh. Rusty sat.

He took the chair across from her, leaving the table between them as though they were in negotiations. "You come from Chicago, right?"

Rusty nodded.

"Lived all your life in the big city?"

"Yes."

"House or apartment?"

"Apartment. What are you getting at?"

Shifting, Trent rested his forearms on the table and leaned forward. "You know...this rugged outdoors environment is new and different to you."

"I'll say."

A corner of his mouth tilted upward. "I always enjoy spending a few days here myself after being surrounded by the concrete and noise of a big city. To you, getting away from it all may seem—" he gestured as he sought for the right words "—romantically appealing, but living here day after day could get boring. It's isolated—"

Rusty held up a hand. "Wait a minute. What makes you think I want to live here? Because I took pictures?"

"Not *here*." Trent drew a breath. "At the Triple D."

"Excuse me, but weren't you looking for someone to live with you at the Triple D?"

Trent sent a glance heavenward. "I can certainly understand how you came to think that." He swallowed. "But, no. And you need to be aware of my feelings before you become too attached to..."

"To *you*?" The nerve!

"To the idea of ranch life," Trent finished heavily. "To the 'romantic cabin in the woods' scenario."

Wait a minute. *He* was rejecting *her*. Rusty stared. He was trying to tell her she wasn't the one for him and his domestic fantasies. Well, she knew that. She'd been expecting a talk like this ever since breakfast. How mortifying to realize she couldn't fake domesticity for even a weekend. But she had other appealing qualities, didn't she?

"It's because I can't cook, isn't it?"

Trent gripped his forehead and sighed. "I don't care whether you can cook or not."

"Then it's me." She didn't appeal to him. Rusty absorbed this blow to her femininity with mixed feelings. "Well, you did tell me you weren't interested in me, so I suppose I shouldn't be surprised." *After that kiss, I just didn't believe you.*

"That's not true—" Trent groaned. "Rusty, I'm sorry, but I can't keep pretending any longer. You responded to the *Texas Men* profile in good faith, but the man it described isn't me."

"Who is it? Your evil twin?"

Trent's laugh was subdued. "You're going to get a kick out of this—at least I hope you will—but my uncles placed that ad." He grinned a hopeful let's-laugh-about-it-together grin.

"And you didn't know about it?" Pieces were beginning to fall into place.

"I knew about it," Trent admitted with a rueful grimace. "But I didn't think any woman, any *normal* woman, would respond. But I have to tell you, there are a *lot* of desperate women out there. I couldn't believe it, I mean, that write-up was about as feudal as you can get. Can you imagine any—" He caught himself, his eyes widening.

"Yes?" Rusty arched an eyebrow, enjoying his discomfort.

"I don't mean to imply that *you* were anything other than an unexpected surprise," he said in a game attempt to salvage things.

"I'll bet." If she weren't so relieved to learn Trent wasn't the Neanderthal she'd thought he was, Rusty would be angry. In fact, she might be angry after all.

Trent ran a hand through his brown hair. "I've really screwed this up, haven't I?"

"Maybe not. Let me recap. This was a joke?"

"No! Not a joke. My uncles are completely serious. They've been after me to get married and they haven't liked any of the women I've brought to meet them."

"Have there been a lot of women?" Rusty slid the question in.

"Oh, y—no." Trent shook his head. "Not many. One or two." He cleared his throat and hurriedly went on. "My uncles wanted me to find a real homebody. I told them that women weren't like that anymore and they asked if they could find one, would I meet her, I said yes, never dreaming—anyway, here you are." He stopped, took a breath and said, "I'm sorry, but I'm not ready to settle down at the Triple D or anywhere else and it's not fair to you for me to continue to pretend that I am."

Trent looked her right in the eye as he spoke, she'd give him that.

Rusty let out the breath she'd been holding. "Oh, I am so torn. On one hand, it would be wonderful to have you groveling at my feet, begging forgiveness, but I am a decent human being..." She stopped. Better not push it. "Who needs a favor."

"Anything." He exhaled in patent relief.

"Hey, really?" Things were *definitely* looking up.

Trent narrowed his eyes. "It occurs to me that I've left myself open to blackmail."

Rusty shrugged. "A favor, blackmail, it's all the same."

"I might argue the point with you, but go ahead." His chuckle had a harsh edge.

Rusty toyed with the idea of retaining the upper hand. He'd just told her his profile was a fake, but he didn't know Rusty was a fake, as well. But that would mean she'd have to keep pretending and all this pretending was time-consuming. For both of them. "Will it set your mind at ease if I tell you that Gran answered your uncles, not me? I never had any intention of giving up my career to play house on a ranch."

"You mean...?"

"I'm *not* husband hunting."

Trent blinked twice, then settled back in his chair, a slow smile spreading over his face. "Go on."

"For reasons unknown to me, my grandmother became obsessed with spending Christmas here, and since she couldn't come without me, I said I'd come with her. But I never planned to stick it out for the full two weeks."

"That's cheating."

"Hey, look who's talking."

They grinned at each other.

"So you aren't the homemaker type?" Trent asked.

"What was your first clue?"

"I think it might have been the arm wrestling invitation."

"It's still open."

"I'm still passing." Trent tilted his head to one side. "So, what type are you?"

The desperate corporate type. Perhaps there was a way to mention that she was also a member of the Olympic gold medal kissers fan club. "I'm a not-ready-to-settle-down type."

"My favorite." Trent gave her a frank look that made her insides quiver.

"What a coincidence." A happy, stupendously, wonderful coincidence.

Trent sent a breathtaking smile her way. "You mentioned a favor?"

"Ah, yes." Rusty told him all about the Next to Nature campaign and how she wanted to use the shack as a backdrop for photographs. "So, I would much appreciate it if my grandmother and I could stay a few more days."

"I wasn't going to make you leave," Trent said, surprise in his voice.

"But I assumed that's why you told me the truth about your profile. If we're gone, you can work."

Trent shook his head. "Didn't you see them watching us on the way out here?"

"Sort of."

"It's going to get worse. They expect us to spend time together and I just don't have that time."

"But if we left, you would." Rusty had hoped to acquire professional photography equipment, but it appeared the camera she had with her now was going to have to do the job. There would be no opportunity to get another or to add the props she wanted.

"If you leave, my uncles will just bring in someone else, and I might not be so lucky next time."

"How gallant."

"It's true. The next woman might want to spend all her days cooking and catering to my every whim," he said in a dry voice. "What a horrible thought."

Rusty raised her eyebrow. "Let's not forget bearing your children. Lots and lots of children. You'll spend your nights and weekends lovingly surrounded by diapers, baby bottles and plastic toys in bright primary colors."

"I'm doomed, aren't I?" Trent held his chin in his hand.

"Not necessarily. Maybe we could work together." Real close together. "We could pretend to be spending time with each other, but you could work on your project and I could work on mine."

Trent nodded. "We'd have to get out of the house. I fully expect them to confiscate my computer as it is."

"Have laptop, will travel," Rusty said. "Some place in town, then?"

"Too far away." He thought for a minute, then assessed their surroundings. "How about right here? Once we run the generator, we'd have electricity and privacy. Rudimentary plumbing, but it is indoor."

"Swell." Rusty looked around. "But no telephone."

"I've got a cell phone."

She gaped at him. "You've had a cellular phone all this time? Then why were you putting up with Harvey's interruptions?"

"Because cellular transmissions aren't secure. They can be overheard and I don't want any of my competitors knowing details of my business negotiations."

That made sense to Rusty. "But I need E-mail and fax."

"You can do all that through my cell phone," he informed her offhandedly.

"You can?" There was light at the end of the tunnel.

"My phone has jacks. Reception might be a bit iffy at times, but, yes."

Technology was wonderful. "And you'd let me use your phone? I'll pay you back."

Waving away her offer, Trent stood. "Don't worry about it." He gestured to the window where their relatives were huddled together, sending glances toward the shack. "We can talk more later. Right now, we'd better go look at Christmas trees."

Rusty was euphoric. After this morning's breakfast failure, things had looked pretty grim. Now not only did she have a chance to augment her presentation with dynamite pictures, she'd discovered that she and Trent were on the same wavelength.

Things were going to get very interesting at the Triple D in the next few days.

"I THINK that tree is the one." Agnes had dithered back and forth between two gorgeous firs while Harvey had collected pinecones to grow seedlings and replant. Everyone else was still seated on the ground after lunch.

"Trent." Clarence gestured to the tree. "Start sawing."

Trent popped the last bit of cookie into his mouth,

brushed his hands on his jeans, then took a red chain saw out of the cart.

While Rusty cleared away the remains of their picnic lunch, Trent yanked the starter rope on the saw. With a loud roar the motor leapt to life, the noise making it impossible to talk or even to think.

The whining screech the saw made as it bit into the tree trunk hurt Rusty's teeth, so she wasn't sorry when an ominous clanking sounded moments before blessed quiet reigned once more.

"The chain broke," Trent said, his voice deceptively mild.

"That's impossible," Harvey protested. "The parts are guaranteed for thirty-six months!"

Trent jerked off his safety glasses and set the saw aside. "Make a note not to buy that brand next time."

"But they have a warranty."

"Which I'm sure they'll honor," Clarence said. "In the meantime, see if there's an ax in the shack and we'll cut this tree down the old-fashioned way."

Rusty knew Trent was thinking about how much time chopping the tree with an ax was going to take. She half hoped there wouldn't be an ax, but Harvey had disappeared inside and was now brandishing an old, but probably still useful ax.

"Gran, did you bring anything else to drink?" Rusty called. Agnes and Doc were off trimming branches from the rejected trees for decoration. Had they forgotten about the lighted pine garland Clarence had ordered?

"Look in the cooler," Agnes replied on her way to the cart, her arms full of branches.

Rusty couldn't find any drink cans. "Nothing in here. What about the ice chest in the cart?"

"I'll check." Her grandmother took two steps forward, caught her foot on a tree root and went sprawling.

"Gran!" Rusty raced to her grandmother's side, but Trent reached her first. Doc shoved him aside.

"Agnes?" Dropping to his knees, Doc rolled her over, cradling her against him.

"Stand back, I know CPR!" Harvey yelled.

Huffing and puffing, Clarence ambled toward them. "The woman's still breathing," he affirmed, sounding in need of some resuscitation himself.

"Nothing's hurt but my pride." Agnes tried to sit up and grimaced.

"Gran, you *are* hurt!" Rusty knelt down.

"No—"

"Now, Miss Rusty, you just let Doc have a look," Clarence instructed.

"He's a vet!" Rusty protested as the middle Davis brother ran his hands over her grandmother's limbs.

"It'll be all right," said a voice in her ear. "Doc knows what he's doing." Trent rubbed her shoulders and Rusty relaxed in spite of herself.

"An ankle's an ankle," Doc said. "And this one's sprained."

"Nonsense." Agnes tried to stand, but failed.

"Oh, Gran!" Rusty had never seen her grandmother suffer from anything other than a cold. She looked so frail surrounded by the hefty Davis brothers.

"We're going to take you back to the house now," Doc announced, his tone precluding argument.

Supported by Doc on one side and Trent on the other, Agnes limped to the cart. Doc tucked a blanket around her.

"But the Christmas tree!" Agnes protested, waving at it.

"Don't worry about that, Mrs. Romero." Trent helped his

uncle Clarence into the driver's seat. "We can cut it down tomorrow."

"No need for that. I'll just drive them back, then I'll turn around and pick up you two and the tree," Clarence offered.

"I'm going with my grandmother," Rusty said firmly. How could anyone think she'd abandon her grandmother to chop down a Christmas tree?

"Oh, no!" Harvey pulled himself up beside Clarence. "I'm going, so you don't have to. I know CPR," he reassured her again.

"You keep your lips off my grandmother!"

Mouth twitching, Trent took Rusty's arm and pulled her away from the cart. "Calm down."

"I *am* calm!" Rusty searched the clearing for her camera and found it next to the cooler.

"They'll take good care of her." Trent didn't appear unduly alarmed, which set Rusty off again.

"But she's *my* grandmother! I should be with her." She marched toward the cart.

Clarence flicked the reins. "You two just stay here and have fun!" Grinning, he waved.

"Wait!" Rusty ran after them.

"I'll be fine, dear," Agnes called as the cart lurched out of the clearing.

Appalled, Rusty turned to Trent. "Do something!"

He waved.

Rusty watched as the cart rolled away at a brisk pace. "I don't believe this."

Trent retrieved the ax. "I do. Didn't you hear what Clarence said? 'I'll be back for you *two*.' And that was before Harvey got in the cart."

What was he saying? "They couldn't have planned this. My grandmother was really hurt."

"I don't think they planned that part." He toed the cut branches Agnes had been carrying. "But wasn't it fortunate that these cushioned her fall?"

Of all the.... Rusty sighed. She and Trent were alone together—without their computers. It made horrible sense. "So what do we do now?"

Trent hefted the ax. "I guess we're going to chop down a Christmas tree."

9

"HEY, HARVEY, how's it going?" The UPS driver opened the back of his van.

Harvey, barely able to contain his excitement, examined the return address of each box as it was unloaded.

"The deer! Clarence, the deer have arrived!"

Rusty had been in the kitchen with Agnes, whose ankle was much better, bagging Christmas cookies for the parade of delivery men. She knew many by name now and Harvey treated the regulars like members of his extended family.

She walked out onto the porch in time to see the FedEx van pull up. Harvey was delirious with excitement.

Rusty waved to both drivers—honestly, she'd met more eligible men out here in the middle of nowhere than she'd met in the past several months in the city.

"Miss Rusty," Harvey called. "There's a package for you!"

Props for the line shack, she hoped. She'd only sent the film off yesterday and though Alisa hadn't seen the pictures yet, she'd been wild about Rusty's idea to photograph the Next to Nature products there. Still, this time lag was a killer.

Rusty was also worried. According to Alisa, Mr. Dearsing had been asking if she'd been in contact with Rusty, and making some vague reference about moving up the presentations a week.

That was George Kaylee's doing, she knew. He wanted her to be rushed and not fully prepared.

Or maybe he suspected Alisa had discovered his use of photographs and this was his way of retaliating. Whatever, Rusty needed to produce the Next to Nature product pictures immediately.

It had been three days since the tree-cutting excursion. Rusty almost felt guilty that being stranded with Trent had produced exactly the opposite effect her grandmother and his uncles had been hoping for.

Instead of a blossoming romance, the afternoon had resulted in an alliance against meddling relatives.

After Trent had chopped down the Christmas tree, they'd used the time until Clarence returned preparing the shack as an office hideaway.

Now the problem was finding time to use the place. Rusty hadn't been able to get away since Agnes's sprained ankle had kept her off her feet, so Rusty, horror of horrors, had been cooking. Actually, what she'd done was make a huge dent in Harvey's stores of frozen prepared food, but nobody complained.

Agnes and the uncles had done a superb job of keeping Rusty and Trent occupied with garland hanging, light stringing and tree decorating. But today, after lunch, she and Trent planned to go horseback riding. Alone.

Rusty didn't let the fact that she wasn't a horsewoman dissuade her. She needed to take more pictures and work on that ad copy.

As she signed for her package, Trent and Clarence emerged from the house and joined Harvey and his deer.

Picking up two of the white-lighted wire forms, Trent approached her. "Can you be ready to leave at one o'clock today?" he asked under his breath.

"More than ready. Did you get the generator working?"

"Yes." He gazed at her. "Smile, or they'll think we're quarreling."

Smiling through gritted teeth, Rusty wiggled her fingers at Trent's watching uncles.

"I WILL NEVER WALK again." Rusty slid off her horse and into Trent's arms. If she weren't so sore, she would have made more of the situation. But not much more. "I have no idea how I'll ride back to the ranch house, either."

"You can do it," Trent said in a buck-up-old-girl voice. "Remember, we don't have as much time here as I'd like. The trip out took longer than I thought it would."

"I told you I didn't ride," Rusty complained. "Did you think I was going to gallop?"

"I'd hoped for an occasional canter." Trent tied the horses.

"Now I know why cowboys are bowlegged." Rusty limped toward the shack. "Will you please untie the picnic basket?"

"Sure."

There was no food in the basket, just Rusty's computer and supplies, but she'd been trying to avoid suspicion.

Trent handed the basket to her. "If you'll carry this inside, I'll fire up the generator."

Nodding, Rusty took the basket and shouldered her way into the shack.

The generator motor pounded into life, shattering the silence. Rusty sighed. Not the best working conditions, but better than nothing. She should be grateful.

"The place looks surprisingly decent," she complimented Trent when he came inside. She had to raise her voice to be heard over the motor.

"Thanks." His gaze met hers, dipped to her mouth, then slid on past.

For her part, Rusty looked away from his chest, about which she'd had nightly fantasies. "I guess I'll get to work, then."

"Work." He nodded tightly.

They sat at opposite ends of the wooden table, the generator chugging in the background. Rusty wouldn't be surprised if they could hear it back at the ranch house.

She glanced up at Trent to comment about it and caught him looking at her.

A heartbeat later he turned his attention to his laptop screen with such renewed determination, Rusty didn't say anything at all.

He was thinking about her.

She was thinking about him.

She tried not to think about him. Often. Now that they'd established the new ground rules, she shouldn't be thinking about him at all. He had his goals and she had hers. Neither needed a romance muddying the waters.

Unfortunately, Rusty found it difficult to ignore the handsome, ambitious, single *decent* man who sat at the other end of the rickety table.

Decent. Honorable. Solid traits without flash. Traits missing in many of the men she'd met.

She shifted on the hard wooden chair. The fact that all Trent's decentness came packaged so nicely kept him in her thoughts. Instead of the words on her screen, she saw a shirtless Trent answering his bedroom door. She saw his mouth angling toward hers. She felt...

Rusty slammed the computer closed.

"What's wrong?"

As if she'd really tell him. "I can't concentrate." Rusty gestured feebly toward the sound of the generator.

He blinked at her, then rose from the table. "Let me check my briefcase. I might have an extra set of earplugs."

"In your briefcase?"

The locks snapped as Trent flipped them open. "Sometimes the noise on construction sites exceeds the government safety maximums."

Rusty smiled at his words.

He withdrew a pouch and unzipped it. "Great for airplane flights, too." Trent leaned over and dropped two yellow cylinders into her palm.

The tips of his fingers brushed her skin and Rusty felt the touch zing all the way to her elbow. Her hand jerked and one of the earplugs bounced to the floor.

"Careful." Trent stooped to retrieve it and replaced it in her open palm.

"Th-thanks." Rusty was horrified to hear herself stutter.

Trent returned to his computer and Rusty stuffed the plugs into her ears.

Tolerable. Definitely better. She gave a watching Trent a thumbs-up and opened her computer.

Thirty minutes later she'd typed nothing but gibberish. Pure gibberish just so Trent would think she was so unaffected by his presence that she was actually coming up with brilliant new ad slogans incorporating the pictures she'd taken instead of fantasizing about him.

He was so close, yet so far. If she ever wrote that for ad copy she would be shot. Yet, it was true.

Rusty knew her legs were only a foot or two away from Trent's legs. She imagined she could feel the heat from his skin. She wanted to touch him and be touched by him.

Her fingertips tingled. Her lips tingled. Other places really tingled. She was *not* going to get any work done.

She closed her computer.

Trent looked up at the movement.

"I'm going to take some pictures, if that's okay with you?"

"Am I in your way?" he asked.

I wish. "No, I'm going to shoot toward the kitchen and fireplace. Let me know if I bother you."

YOU BOTHER ME.

Trent gave up his work on spreadsheets and watched Rusty drape plaid fabric here and there. She added fake daisies to an old teakettle and stapled fabric at the kitchen windows.

She spent the most time positioning empty boxes and bottles of the product she was advertising. Stepping around the chair seat she was using as a stand, she bent over. Trent caught his breath as her sweater gaped away from her chest and exposed her cleavage.

Adolescent though it was, Trent looked and kept looking. The creamy expanse of her neck and throat continued, unmarred by any tan lines. The image that evoked made him sweat. The tanned blond look he'd previously been drawn to seemed common and overexposed. Rusty's creamy-peach skin was that color because it wasn't exposed to the sun—and other men's eyes.

His mouth was dry. He'd been breathing—rapidly— through parted lips.

Rusty straightened, then grabbed her camera and started photographing the products from every angle, contorting herself into interesting poses that did nothing for Trent's equilibrium.

She was incredibly flexible and he gave up all pretense of working at the computer and stared at her.

She didn't look his way once, but rearranged the products and went through all the angles again.

Trent's favorite pose was the one where Rusty was on her knees leaning backward as though she was doing the limbo.

Or maybe it was the one where she bent forward and arched her back to shoot from below the products.

Occasionally, she'd rake her hair back from her face or shimmy her shoulders to relax them.

Weak with longing, Trent slid down in his seat.

This was torture. Working together wasn't...working. He couldn't stand it. Abruptly slamming his computer screen down, he jerked a thumb toward the door. "I'm going to check on the horses."

Rusty, looking flushed and tousled, nodded.

Trent waited until she'd brought the camera up to her eye before standing and carefully walking out of the shack.

WITH A SLOW, feminine smile, Rusty sat back on her heels. That had gone surprisingly well.

Especially since there'd only been six exposures left on the roll of film.

"*BEFORE* CHRISTMAS? George got Dearsing to agree that the proposals should be presented *before* Christmas?"

"Yes."

"He can't *do* that!"

"Well, he did." From long experience, Alisa knew the routine—deliver the bad news, then wait for Rusty to yell about it.

This time was no different and Rusty appreciated Alisa's perception.

"I'm on *vacation* and he knows it!" Rusty sat on a fallen log. She and Trent were back at the shack, but Rusty had gone outside to put some distance between her and that infernal generator. The stupid thing chugged incessantly and interfered with both phone and fax transmissions.

And besides, being in a state of suspended lust made her cranky. Agnes and the uncles had thrown her together with

Trent in an orgy of Christmas preparations. As much as Rusty wanted to work, being alone with him was too distracting, so she usually took the phone outside and walked around.

"Can't Dearsing see that this is one of George's sneaky tactics?" Rusty leapt from the log and tromped back and forth over the dry leaves and pine needles. They crunched with a satisfying crackle. "Doesn't the man know I'm on vacation?" she repeated.

"Uh, George did bring that to his attention," Alisa said.

"Don't tell me...something like, 'I can't imagine why Rusty chose to take these crucial days off,' intimating that I was letting Dearsing down?"

Silence.

"Well?"

"You told me not to tell you."

Rusty lowered the phone and let out a howl of frustration that echoed through the forest. It felt good.

"Rusty?"

She brought the phone back to her ear. "What?" she snapped.

"The pictures turned out great. Who's the guy with the ax?"

She smiled, remembering the tree cutting excursion. "Trent."

Alisa inhaled. "No *wonder* you haven't come back."

Rusty whimpered.

"SKIING? Can you believe it?" Trent pounded the steering wheel as he and Rusty drove away from the shack. "I tell the man he's got the bid and he tells me he's going skiing over Christmas and won't be back until after the first of the year. I told him I wouldn't have the paperwork ready until the last week of the year and all he says is sorry, he's leaving. Sorry!"

Rusty had been quiet. She'd ranted at Alisa and had felt better, so she figured Trent would feel better after ranting a little, too. Besides, she didn't feel like talking.

Eventually, Trent was reduced to muttering, pounding the steering wheel and shaking his head.

"Trent."

He exhaled. "Rusty, look, I know I've been running on—"

"Hey, *believe* me, I understand. Dearsing has set the Next to Nature presentation for the morning of the twenty-fourth."

Trent shot a startled look at her. "That's—"

"Christmas Eve," Rusty finished. "He thinks he'll see the presentations in the morning, have the office Christmas luncheon, and then send everybody home a little early."

Silence filled the four-wheel-drive vehicle all the way to the ranch house. The tires crunched on the gravel drive as Trent drove around to the back and parked.

Rusty didn't know how long they sat there before Trent's quiet question broke the silence.

"What are you going to do?"

Rusty shook her head. "I don't know. How about you?"

Trent flexed his fingers on the steering wheel. "I'm going to run some numbers and see where I stand. Which reminds me, tomorrow's Sunday."

"Church and the snow party." Rusty sighed. "I had no idea there were machines that made snow." Or why anyone would want to make it. Rusty hadn't missed the white stuff at all.

"If a product's made, Harvey finds it. But actually, my uncles have been throwing snow parties on the front lawn of the church for several years. It's always the Sunday afternoon before Christmas. The kids love it. There's hot chocolate and funnel cake and the choir sings Christmas carols. Clarence judges the snowman building contest."

"And snowball fights?"

"Of course." Trent smiled. "We hardly ever get much snow in these parts."

Rusty was amused as Trent's tone took on a rural flavoring.

"I was thinking," he continued, "one of us could go to church and the other could put in an appearance at the snow party in the afternoon. That way, we could each have some time alone to work."

Rusty nodded in agreement. She needed to think without having the distraction of Trent sitting across the table. "Sounds like you enjoy the snow party."

"I do," he confirmed lightly.

Rusty imagined him out in the thick of the snowball fights and grinned. "Okay, though I still think snow is highly overrated."

Trent nodded to the kitchen door where Agnes was silhouetted. "This is the third time she's come to the door." He turned back to her. "A good-night kiss might give them something to talk about." His voice was casually nonchalant.

Though her heart threatened to pound through her chest, Rusty tried to match that nonchalance. "Oh, definitely. Definitely," she agreed. "They'll be so pleased, they won't even notice that we're not spending any time together tomorrow."

"It'll be insurance," he said, moving closer.

"A realistic touch," she said, leaning toward him.

Rusty had no idea how realistic Trent intended his kiss to be but seconds after their lips fused together, he abruptly wrenched himself away from her and drew a deep breath.

"That's enough realism for now."

Still recovering, Rusty could only nod.

"WHAT ARE YOU DOING here?"

Trent stood in the doorway of the shack. He couldn't believe it when he'd driven up to find Rusty's blue rental car parked in the clearing.

"Printing out the millionth draft of my presentation." She was standing by his laser printer, which she'd balanced on a chair so the cord would reach the power source. "What are *you* doing here? I thought you were going to church so you could skip the snow party."

"I thought *you* were going to church. You said you didn't like snow."

"Well, I don't particularly."

"Great." Trent slammed the door and stalked over to the table. "What was your excuse for missing church?" He shrugged off his suit jacket.

"Headache. And yours?"

Trent draped his jacket over the back of the chair. "I ran late and was supposedly following them. I'd planned to plead car trouble."

Her gaze swept over him. "That would explain the suit. You can still have car trouble. Smear a little grease on that shirt and everything will be fine."

"I hope so." Trent ripped off his tie and unbuttoned his collar and cuffs.

Rusty was looking at him. Really looking at him. Looking at his body with the type of raw hunger he had never seen on a woman's face. And he felt the same unfamiliar hunger of desire long denied.

Unfortunately, Trent planned to continue to deny that desire. Though he was known for his Teflon-coated heart, after the brief kiss last night, he knew Rusty Romero wasn't a woman he could easily walk away from. Since that was precisely what he was going to do in not so very many days, it was best for him to avoid touching her. Or her touching him.

Or being alone with her the way he was now.

The laser printer had finished, but Rusty hadn't noticed.

Trent's fingers fumbled. He wished she wouldn't look at him that way.

RUSTY HAD A THING for men in expensive suits and laundry-crisp shirts.

Trent rolled up his shirtsleeves as he stared at his computer, clearly oblivious to the fact that Rusty had lost all power of speech and was probably drooling, as well.

He'd looked good in plaid, great in the flesh, but commanding in a suit.

Could she help it if deep down she wanted a man to be stronger and more powerful than she was? She wasn't proud of her secret, but that's the way it was.

Long ago, she'd even had a crush on George Kaylee, which had lasted until the first time one of her ideas was chosen over his. Then he was no longer powerful to her and his attraction for her ended.

But Trent... She'd grown to like Trent even without seeing him in a suit and now that she had—

"Are you finished printing?"

Rusty blinked at the printer. "Uh, yes."

He looked at her expectantly, so she disconnected her computer.

"I—I brought some canned drinks," she said, backing toward the door. "I'll just get them out of the car."

Without glancing up from the screen, he nodded, and Rusty fled, chanting to herself.

Calm down. Visualize. Take deep breaths and focus on the Next to Nature campaign.

Rusty opened the car door and brought out the six-pack of sodas. Although cloudy and cool, the weather wasn't unpleasant. She could proof her work outside—away from Trent. Yes, that's what she'd do. Out of sight really could be out of mind.

"MISS RUSTY, you took the new-and-improved, caffeine-free Anderson pain powders for your headache, didn't you?"

"Yes, thank you, Harvey."

Harvey peered at her closely. "You still look pale. Maybe you shouldn't come with us this afternoon."

"And miss the snow festival?" Clarence boomed. "Nonsense. She just needs some fresh air and distraction."

Rusty put her hand to her temple where a true headache throbbed. In spite of her best efforts, she hadn't accomplished nearly what had to be done this morning. A Christmas Eve presentation. That was low, even for George. And Rusty still hadn't decided if she was going to fly back to Chicago, or let Alisa handle the presentation.

Agnes and Doc were whispering together and sending glances her way. Her grandmother approached and took her arm, leading her away from the others.

"Rachel Marie, I've never known you to succumb to a headache."

"Gran, I'm under a lot of stress—"

"I haven't said much about you spending all your time at your computer—"

"I *haven't* spent all my time at the computer! I practically live in the kitchen!"

"So you should be spending every spare moment with Trent." Her grandmother leaned forward. "I saw that little peck he gave you last night." She clucked her tongue. "Pitiful."

If her grandmother only knew. "Gran, we're here because *you* wanted to come here. Have you forgotten?"

"I have forgotten nothing, but I see a young woman throwing away her chance of a lifetime."

Rusty stared at her grandmother. "You've got that right."

"Don't sass me, Rachel Marie." Agnes obviously knew Rusty had been referring to her work. "Whenever we've planned any activities for you two, it's not long before one or the other of you disappears. And now you claim that you can't come to the snow festival."

"Gran..." Rusty winced. Harvey's pain powder hadn't kicked in yet.

Agnes's face softened and she felt Rusty's forehead with the back of her hand. "All right, Rusty. Stay here and rest. Perhaps tonight you can carol with us."

Rusty nodded and looked across the drive to see how Trent had fared.

Surrounded by his uncles, Trent tinkered under the hood of his car, embellishing on his car-trouble story. "I'll stay here and keep Rusty company," he offered, wiping his hands on a rag.

This mollified their relatives and they soon departed.

Rusty and Trent watched them go.

"Good work," he said.

"Except that I really *do* have a headache."

"Oh, hey." He looked down at her in concern. "Do you want to stay here, then?"

Rusty thought for a minute. "I left my laptop at the line shack, so I'll have to come with you. Maybe I'll feel better by then."

But she didn't feel better, especially after Trent started

the generator. Rusty hated the generator. She hated George Kaylee. She hated snow. She hated the thought of spending one more minute on a campaign she'd had to redo.

She hated feeling guilty.

Still, Rusty took her place at the table and opened her computer.

Trent signaled her and she removed her ear plugs. "I've got to use the phone," he said.

The generator never seemed to bother him. He just shouted over it. Her head pounded at the thought of trying to think with the additional noise. Rusty closed the computer. "You know what? I'm going to stretch out on the couch and see if I can take a nap. Wake me when you're off the phone."

Nodding, Trent had already begun punching numbers.

Carefully spreading Alisa's plaid blankets over the ancient fabric covering, Rusty put in her ear plugs and closed her eyes, never expecting to fall asleep.

A high-pitched grinding roar woke her. Disoriented, Rusty thought at first that her earplugs had fallen out. She sat up and dug at her ears to find Trent at the table doing the same thing.

"What is that?" she shouted. Thuds sounded against the cabin door. A second later, the generator chugged to a halt.

Shaking his head, Trent stepped to the window. "Hey! What are you doing?"

Rusty scrambled off the couch as Trent ran to the door and jerked it open.

A wall of white greeted them. Snow?

"Rusty, climb out the window. Now!" Trent shut the door, straining to latch it again.

Too startled to argue, Rusty ran around the table to the window. The front of the uncles' red pickup pointed away from the clearing. What was going on?

She lost a few seconds while she figured out that the window pushed out instead of lifting up. Unfortunately, years of weathering and disuse had lodged it firmly in place. She pushed, then jumped back when a wad of white spattered against the grimy glass.

Trent ran past her to the kitchen. "Come try this one!" He climbed onto the counter as the light in the room grew dim.

Rusty saw two figures standing in the back of the pickup truck aim the spout of a strange machine. "That's your uncle Clarence and Doc!" Rusty shouted as white obscured the view. Just before the window was completely covered, Rusty caught a glimpse of her grandmother and a gleeful Harvey standing by.

"I know. Get over here!" Trent strained to open the kitchen window, the only one left. "Got it!" The window squeaked outward just as white sprayed it. Too late.

"The bathroom?"

Trent shook his head. "The window's too small and high. Very funny, Uncle Clarence," he shouted through the partially open window. "Now let us out!"

Only the roar of the snow machine answered him.

"Trent!" Rusty had to shout to make herself heard. "It's getting dark in here. Do you have a flashlight? Matches? Candles?"

Trent yanked open cabinets and drawers as the light slowly but thoroughly faded. Giving up, he stalked over to the door and pounded on it. "Let us out!"

Rusty could hear the machine as it moved around to the back and eventually blotted out the thin strip of light that glowed from the bathroom.

And then there was a sudden and eerie quiet. Except for Trent pounding on the door.

"Are you crazy? Let us out!"

"...time together." Rusty made out a muffled response.

"Okay," Trent called, his voice taking a tone obviously meant to be conciliatory. "You made your point. We should have come this afternoon."

"If you don't let us out we can't go caroling tonight," Rusty shouted.

In response, there was the faint sound of a pickup truck driving out of the clearing.

Rusty heard a violent bump and an inhaled curse.

"Trent?"

"Over here."

Where was here? "I can't see anything. It's totally black. You okay?"

"Yes." There was a wealth of suppressed anger and frustration in the word. "How about you?"

"I don't know, am I okay?"

She heard a heartfelt sigh. "I hope so, because it appears that my uncles and your grandmother have snowed us in."

10

"MAYBE THEY DIDN'T KNOW we were in here."

"My car's right out front. They knew."

"Then, why?" Rusty's question hung in the black silence.

"For starters, I'd guess they're ticked at us." Trent's disembodied voice was no closer and Rusty assumed he was still by the door.

She wasn't exactly sure where she was. "Good grief, Trent, why didn't you tell me that frolicking in fake snow was so important to them?"

She heard muttering. "I think it's the fact that we lied so we could sneak off to work."

"Excuse me, but *I* really had a headache."

"You didn't this morning."

The point wasn't worth arguing. It was apparent that Rusty's grandmother and Trent's uncles had figured out that what they'd fondly hoped was a budding romance was just Rusty and Trent carrying on business as usual. And their relatives were angry. "How could they have found us?"

"I don't know. Does it matter?" Resignation sounded in his voice.

She supposed not. "How long are they going to leave us here?"

"Until they feel we've spent enough quality time together, I suppose. Why do you keep asking me these questions?"

"Because they're *your* uncles. For all I know, trapping women for you is standard operating procedure for them."

"Not until they met *your* grandmother."

Rusty squeaked in outrage. "You can't blame this on her!"

"Why not?" Rusty heard something soft smack against something not so soft, followed by a loud and clear curse.

Served him right.

"It's okay. I'll live," he said, his voice subdued.

"What a pity."

After that, the conversation lagged as each dealt with the ramifications of the situation.

Rusty was inclined to blame the influence of Trent's uncles on her grandmother, but then Agnes had been exhibiting latent streaks of romance lately. Snowbound with a handsome man in a remote cabin sounded romantic—especially if they'd been serving something stronger than milk in the hot chocolate at the snow party.

Rusty heard shuffling. "Where are you going?"

"Forward. I'm aiming for the couch where you spent the afternoon snoring," he grumbled.

"I did not snore."

"How do you know?"

"No, the question is, how would you know? The generator was going and you had earplugs in," she noted with smug satisfaction.

"And I could still hear you snore," he maintained.

Rusty smothered a laugh. "That was the snow machine, which brings up an interesting question. I was asleep. How did four people sneak a pickup truck and a snow machine past you?"

Silence answered her. Though he tried to hide it, she knew Trent was blazingly angry at his uncles and frustrated at being trapped. She also knew that quarreling was one way to avoid thinking about the fact that they were alone together.

"My eyes were bothering me and I may have dozed off myself," Trent finally admitted. "I was waiting for a call—"

"The cell phone!" The same thought occurred to both of them.

"Where did you leave it?" Rusty asked.

"On the table."

"I think I'm closer." Rusty reached out in a wide circle and encountered nothing. She took a step, then another. She smelled the musty couch before she touched it. "Here's the couch." Feeling her way along the cushions, she reached the edge. "I'm in the clear. There's nothing between me and the table."

Confidently stepping forward, arms outstretched, Rusty felt a tug against her knees a split second before she remembered that the cord of the laser printer stretched directly across her path.

Her momentum propelled her forward and she tripped over the cord, hearing the sickening crack of expensive plastic breaking as the printer fell off the chair and hit the floor.

"Rusty!"

She heard Trent's cry as she fell into the darkness, arms flailing wildly. She caught the corner of the table, tilting it as she broke her fall.

Trent knocked into the table. Something slid. "Grab the computers!"

Rusty groped toward the slithering sound but missed.

The two laptop computers, followed by a smaller object, joined the laser printer on the floor. "I think I found your phone," she said, trying not to think of the demise of her computer.

"Are you okay?" Trent asked in the quiet.

Physically, yes, but when was the last time she backed up the hard drive on her laptop? "Just bruised." Was all her brilliant new ad copy lost?

"This is no longer funny," he said.

"Was it ever?"

"I suppose there will come a time when we'll look back on this and laugh."

"Yes, after we lure your uncles and my grandmother in here and give them a taste of their own medicine."

Trent made a sound that sounded like a cross between a chuckle and a groan. "They probably thought we'd light a fire or that we had flashlights. I don't think they realized how dark it would be."

"I don't think they thought at all." Rusty didn't feel like being charitable. She searched the floor around her and found the overturned chair and the laser printer. Something slick coated her fingers. "Trent, I think your printer is bleeding."

He actually laughed and she felt better. "Stay still. I'm going to try to find the phone," he said.

She reached out in a circle. "It's not near me."

"Okay, I'll go the other way."

Rusty heard him cautiously sliding around the table. "I suppose the laptops are history."

"You've got that right."

"This is not good." The loss of her laptop at this critical time was a disaster of such magnitude that Rusty couldn't fully absorb it.

"Don't think about that now."

Good idea, but then what were they supposed to think about?

Plastic crunched. "Found a laptop." Trent's knees cracked as he bent down. "The phone couldn't have fallen far...got it."

Rusty heard the breath hiss between his teeth and then several small objects hit various electronic carcasses before rolling across the floor.

"What was that?"

There was a silence before Trent answered. "The phone cracked open. I didn't step on a laptop, I stepped on the battery pack. Those were the batteries."

And the batteries had just scattered to the four corners of the room.

"I don't suppose finding the batteries would do any good?"

"No."

"So we're stuck here?"

"Until the snow melts or they come back and dig us out."

Rusty stopped herself from asking when that would be. "I do not believe this is happening."

"It's already happened." Trent's voice changed direction and Rusty guessed that he'd stood. "Let's push the debris to the edges of the room so we won't keep tripping over it."

"Good idea."

Together they pushed thousands of dollars worth of ruined electronic equipment against the wall, along with the chairs and table.

"Something slickish is all over my hands," she said.

"Slickish?"

"You know, smooth but not wet."

"No, I didn't know, but it sounds promising." His voice was tinged with the barest thread of humor.

"I can't believe you're making jokes."

"What else is there to do?"

Rusty tried for a flip comeback, but the truth was, she had spent the week avoiding being alone with Trent. And now, here they were. Together. No elderly relatives chaperoning. No computers. No light. No distractions. No work they could do. Just plenty of time alone with the man who currently had the starring role in her nightly fantasies.

Not only didn't she feel flip, she could think of quite a lot to do.

HE SHOULD KEEP moving around. Then he could bang into more furniture. Maybe the resulting bruises would distract him from the constant ache Rusty's presence generated.

Quite simply, he wanted to touch her and hold her and explore the body he dreamed about. And just as simply, he knew he couldn't and then just walk away after Christmas. But how could he endure the next few hours with her and not acknowledge the attraction between them?

Blast his uncles and their stupid plan. In the most unorthodox way, they'd found a woman who was dangerously close to being his ideal. And Trent hadn't even known what his ideal was. He smiled in the darkness. Rusty wasn't his uncles' ideal, but they obviously didn't care at this point.

His smile faded. Fighting fate wasn't an option any longer. He was doomed.

He heard her move. "Where are you headed?"

"The couch."

The couch. He gritted his teeth, then came to a decision. "Mind if I join you?" His voice sounded almost normal.

"If you can find me." The couch's ancient cushions puffed.

"Oh, I'll find you." Cautiously, he moved until he felt the cushion at the back of his legs. How far away was she?

He sent his hand on an exploratory foray and found hers on a similar journey. They both pulled back and laughed awkwardly.

"Are you cold?" The temperature was pleasant, with the snow acting as insulation, but one could hope.

"A little," she answered.

"Scoot closer and I'll put my arm around you." His stage directions sounded stilted when he was trying for matter-of-fact, but Rusty moved closer nonetheless.

Trent lifted his arm and aimed up and around in the dark, bouncing against the back of the couch and settling heavily with his hand curving around Rusty's soft shoulder. Her soft, boneless shoulder.

They both sat very still. Trent, for one, was grateful for the dark, because, as his body was screaming to him, his hand was not curving around her shoulder after all, it was curving around her breast. Her creamy-skinned, full, lacily upholstered breast.

What were the chances? What were the odds?

Should he pretend he didn't notice? Casually move his hand? Apologize or not? Wait for her to say something?

It was difficult to think. This was serious and he shouldn't act hastily. Whatever he said now would most assuredly set the tone for the rest of the evening.

"Rusty?"

"Ye-ees?" She'd noticed.

"Uh, sorry." He moved his hand to her shoulder. "My aim was off."

"Oh, I think you hit your target."

He couldn't tell if she was angry or not. "Rusty, it's dark. I can't see."

"You don't need to see. Men's hands have sonar—like bats."

She was mad. Trent reluctantly removed his arm from around her shoulders. "It was an accident."

"Sure it was." She shifted. "The same way I could just reach out like this and *accidentally* grab—"

They both gasped as her hand closed around him.

"Well, what do you know?"

He froze. "Rusty." His fingers dug into the ancient cushions and his mouth went dry. *Don't move and maybe she won't, either.*

Not only didn't she let go, she adjusted her grip.

His heart stopped. His brain stopped. His lungs stopped.

"How long have you been like this?"

"Days," he groaned, then gritted his teeth as her fingers outlined him.

"I'm impressed."

Involuntarily, Trent surged against her and he bit back a moan. "Since I have no secrets left, you should know that you've got about three seconds to move or deal with the consequences."

He heard a soft giggle and her other hand joined the first. "Promises, promises."

Where was her mouth? "Keep talking, Rusty."

"Is that all you want me to keep doing?"

Trent adjusted his descent to the left, touched her shoulder—her real shoulder—then held her head still until his lips found hers.

Usually, he began with a series of light teasing kisses he'd found made women melt and part their lips, eager for more. There was no need to rush the early sensual exploration. Warming the motor made the car run more smoothly.

But Rusty's mouth was open and ready.

And Trent plunged his tongue inside, shocked that she'd aroused him to the point where he'd think of his own gratification before hers.

Rusty didn't seem to mind. Trent tried to pull back to throw in a little light nibbling but she drew on his tongue, keeping the kiss hot and deep.

Fine with him, especially when she matched the movements of his tongue with her hands.

He could kiss this woman all day. All night.

Forever.

He stilled as the word drifted by his lust-soaked brain. He'd known this would happen. Forever. He tested the word again. Yes, he'd meant forever, as in Forever forever.

And ever...ever... ever... His tongue stroked in rhythm with the cadence and Rusty echoed it with her hands.

And then one of those hands found his and moved it to her breast.

"I was getting there," he murmured.

"Yeah, but I figured you were lost in the dark again."

Chuckling softly, he trailed a path down the side of her neck, enjoying the little panting gasps she made, especially since each gasp was accompanied by a spasmodic gripping that nearly drove him over the edge.

They both shuddered when his hand finally covered her other breast.

He felt the lace of her bra beneath the silky fabric of her blouse and the warmth of her beneath it all, sensations he'd never noticed before. He lightly traced the lace through her blouse, imagining the way it looked.

Rusty squirmed and sighed against his mouth.

Trent was on fire.

And they were both still fully clothed in the erotic darkness, where neither could predict when or where the other would touch.

He felt her hands at his throat. "What are you doing?" He heard his voice crack and didn't care. He was surprised he'd been able to speak at all.

"Unbuttoning your shirt. Losing patience with the buttons. Thinking of ripping."

"Rusty." Trent stilled her hands.

"Good idea. You do yours and I'll do mine."

He fought against the mental image of Rusty unbuttoning her blouse. "You can't."

"I don't need to be able to see—"

"Rusty, we're adults. We both know where we're headed. We have to...be adult."

He heard a swish—her blouse being removed from her body. He could smell her perfume. He heard a groan. His.

"You don't have to make that speech. I already know it. We're headed in different directions, we have no future, we'll regret this in the morning. Well, guess what? I'd rather regret a night of passion than a night of frustration. Did I cover everything?"

"With one exception."

"What?"

Trent swallowed. "Rusty, I don't have anything with me."

All movement stopped. As the silence lengthened, Trent's hope that Rusty would say, "No problem. Help me find my purse," faded.

What she did say was, "I don't suppose your uncles dropped any condoms down the chimney before they snowed us in?"

"Are you kidding? They *want* babies. Or rather, they want *me* to have babies."

"How do you feel about having babies?" Rusty asked in a small voice.

"I want babies, but...not now."

"Me, either."

They sat in the silence and Trent listened to her breathe. "We do have certain alternatives here."

He heard her shake her head. "No. Too high-schoolish."

Trent cleared his throat and inched closer. "I don't mean to brag, but I can assure you that you won't be reminded of high school."

She sighed. "I'll only feel worse than I do now."

"But not until you've felt a lot better."

"I don't think so." It was a whisper.

Rusty was right. They should cool it.

He leaned his head against the back of the couch and imagined her doing the same.

He listened to her breathe in the dark and forced himself to focus on all the reasons why a relationship wouldn't work. The more he thought, the less important those reasons seemed. Maybe they could have a future.

"Rusty, I've been thinking."

"Don't think."

Her words stopped him momentarily. "We feel something for each other."

"Lust."

"It's more than that and you know it."

She was quiet for a moment. Then she said, "It can't be more because I'm not leaving my grandmother. Everyone in her life left her. She's been there for me and I'm going to be there for her. After Christmas, you'll go back to Dallas and I'll go back to Chicago and by the end of the first day at work, we'll each be relieved we didn't do anything stupid." She groaned. "In fact, with my computer gone, I'll have to leave as soon as we get out of here."

Trent was silent. Broken computer or not, he'd known she wouldn't be content to let her assistant handle the presentation, just as he'd known he'd be returning to Dallas to meet with the owner of the construction company prior to Christmas.

She was right.

But he still felt lousy. Resolutely, he pushed aside all carnal thoughts of Rusty. "So, seen any good movies lately?"

RUSTY HAD NO IDEA how long she and Trent talked. Hours, she supposed. Hours spent in the dark learning his hopes and dreams, appreciating his sense of humor, criticizing his hideous taste in movies, and vowing to cancel his vote in all future elections.

Hours when the darkness freed her to confide thoughts she hadn't shared with anyone else.

Hours in which she refused to fall in love with him or think about a future life where they could spend similar evenings talking.

Or making love.

Desire was there in the darkness, thrumming between them like the lowest of musical notes, more felt than heard.

Rusty wanted to touch him. Several times she'd extend her hand until she could feel the heat from his body. But she'd move away before he discovered what she was doing.

After a while, they remembered the bags of munchies and sodas in the kitchen and ate a highly unnutritious dinner, getting crumbs all over. Then Rusty planned a fantasy advertising campaign for Trent's retirement village and he created a financing package for her own advertising agency.

Owning her own agency had been her secret goal, but until she'd talked with Trent, she'd never thought it could be a reality.

Maybe she could use the financing as an excuse to call him after the holidays.

And then what? asked the voice inside her. *You and your grandmother live in Chicago. He lives in Dallas. A relationship between you will never work.*

Which brought her thoughts full circle. She massaged her temple.

"Is your headache back?"

"Sort of. How could you tell?"

"I heard your fingers rub against your hair."

"I don't know what time it is, but Harvey's pain powders have worn off."

"I've got aspirin in my briefcase. Shall I embark on a search mission?"

"Aye, aye, soldier."

Chuckling, Trent left the couch, his footsteps loud in the silence.

Rusty tried to imagine his progress across the shack. "Where are you now?"

"Heading toward the windows. That's where we pushed the table and I'd set the case next to it."

Rusty heard chairs moving.

"Here's the case. That slick stuff got on it, too," he said as he brushed at the leather.

Something occurred to her. "Are aspirin the only pills you have? I want to know what I'm swallowing."

She felt the couch shift with his weight as he sat down and flipped open the case.

"I've got a few antihistamines, but they're in a bubble pack. Here's the toiletry case." He unzipped it. "I've got antacids in a roll, breath mints...this is toothpaste, shaving cream...moist towelettes."

"Good grief."

"I told you, it's my emergency travel kit. Okay, here's the aspirin bottle. Where's your hand?"

Rusty waved it toward him and banged into his. He placed a small container into her palm.

"Good luck with the childproof cap." He continued digging in his bag.

Rusty was trying to line up the arrows on the cap by touch when she heard Trent inhale sharply.

"What is it?"

Something crackled as he withdrew it from the bag. "I, uh...found a condom."

Rusty blinked in the darkness, wishing she could see his expression. He was probably wishing the same thing. "You keep condoms in your *briefcase?*"

"No—I keep a small toiletry bag in my briefcase. The condom—singular—happened to be in the bag." He seemed to feel the distinction was important.

They sat very still, except for a muffled crackle that told Rusty that Trent was turning the package over and over in his fingers.

"This changes things, I suppose." She was thinking aloud.

"It doesn't have to." Trent exhaled. "I think we decided it would be easier if we didn't know what we were missing."

"That's what we decided, all right." At every crackle, Rusty reconsidered that decision.

"I mean, now, I can only imagine how your skin would feel as I ran my hands over your body. That's better than knowing exactly how soft and silky smooth it is."

Rusty swallowed.

"Or knowing how you would taste," he continued, his voice seductively mesmerizing. "Or where you're ticklish."

Rusty knew and those places tingled.

"Or whether you're a screamer or a moaner."

"A screamer? I think not."

"You've got the potential." He gave a mock sigh. "But I'll never know."

"I'm *not* a screamer. There. Now you know." Rusty fanned her face.

"*I* could make you scream." He spoke just above a whisper, wrapping his words around her, using them as a sensual noose.

She gave a shaky laugh. "You're very sure of yourself."

"I'm very sure of you."

She was damp with desire and he hadn't even touched her.

Rusty pressed her knuckles against her mouth. Regrets. This was all about regrets.

She closed her eyes and relived Trent's kisses and his touch. Would she truly rather regret a night of passion than a night of frustration?

Yes.

The instant she made her decision, something warm uncoiled within her, loosening her tense muscles, reducing the pounding in her temples.

"Okay. Make me scream." She tossed the aspirin bottle over her shoulder. "But it only counts if I scream loud enough to start an avalanche."

She heard the briefcase hit the floor. "You're a difficult woman to please."

She inched sideways. "I can give you hints."

"Hints are good." He inched sideways. "Though I'd rather have light."

"But the dark can be full of surprises." Her voice was husky.

"Or hide the location of this wonderful little package during certain crucial moments." His voice was equally husky.

"I'm sure you'll manage to keep track of it," she murmured as his thigh touched hers. She braced herself for his touch, every nerve in her body straining because she didn't know where to expect it.

Trent skimmed his hand along her thigh, over her hip and toward her waist.

Rusty held her breath just as his fingers reached the bare skin above her jeans.

He paused, then explored a few more inches. "You've

been sitting there all this time without your blouse and I didn't even know it?"

She giggled. "Surprise."

The discovery seemed to unleash something in Trent. "So you like surprises."

"Don't you?"

Chuckling deep in his throat, he maneuvered her into a reclining position on the couch while he knelt on the floor. Lacing their fingers together, he positioned her arms above her head and whispered, "You have no idea where I'll kiss you next."

Rusty's breathing quickened. She felt a stream of air cool her skin as he blew across her stomach, her neck and her arms. Gooseflesh rose as she tried to anticipate where she'd feel the coolness next.

He kissed her on the side, just beneath her ribs. From there, he set a meandering course of kisses, licks and nibbles that had Rusty straining against his hands.

"Trent, let—"

"No."

"No?"

"Not now."

But she wanted to touch him, wanted to kiss him. Instead she gasped as Trent used his teeth to pull the snap to her jeans apart and edge down the zipper. "Surprise."

Kissing the newly exposed skin, he began a journey upward until he encountered her bra. "Front hook?"

"No," she panted. "Though if I'd known..."

"No problem."

Trent continued his unhurried trail of nibbling kisses, distracting her so much that she was barely aware of him catching both her hands in one of his.

"You're goo-ood," she breathed as her bra fell away and he laced their fingers together once more.

"I wish I could see you," he murmured. "I'm imagining creamy white..." Catching the lacy fabric in his teeth, he pulled it gently over her chest, then down her ribs.

Rusty heard the tiny sound as her bra slithered to the floor.

Except for breathing—his slow and deep, hers fast and shallow—there was silence.

Every inch of her skin was sensitized and waiting for his touch. She wanted, needed that touch. She began to move, clutching at his fingers and straining to bring the rest of him closer.

"Trent?" she whispered, and heard the pleading in her voice.

"Right here," he breathed next to her collarbone. He kissed her there and along the side of her neck.

Rusty jerked her head, trying to kiss him, too, but he laughed softly and moved out of her reach.

"Trent, *please.*" She was begging. Rusty couldn't believe she was actually begging. Usually she was the one in control.

Even tonight, she'd sat in the dark without her blouse waiting for the right moment to taunt him with the knowledge.

But she was playing the game with a grand master.

"*Trent.*" She couldn't stand the suspense.

With a suddenness that caused the air to leave her lungs, Trent drew his tongue from her throat to her waist in one broad stroke.

Rusty quivered.

Trent traced a series of languid circles that inched northward.

Rusty broke out in a sweat.

"I can feel the texture of your skin with my tongue. I can feel your heat."

It was as though his words summoned that very heat. Rusty felt the warmth begin deep within her and spread to her exposed skin. She was on fire and his tongue did nothing to quench the burning.

She stilled, concentrating on forming her words. "If you do not touch my breasts *right this instant*, I will die."

"Or scream?" And Trent's mouth reached her breast— right that instant.

Rusty thought she might die anyway.

She buried her fingers in his hair, realizing for the first time that her hands were free. She clutched at his back and became annoyed that he was still wearing his shirt. "Take this off!"

She pushed herself to a sitting position and fumbled for the buttons, shaking so badly she could barely work them through the buttonholes.

"I'll help." His hands covered hers and she found they were shaking, too.

Rusty pulled his shirt out of his waistband and tackled the bottom buttons, nearly weeping when she couldn't work them fast enough.

Forget it, just forget it. She sought and found the open part and spread her hands over his chest, feeling the hair curl over her fingers. "I've been lusting after your chest for days."

"I know exactly what you mean." There was a ripping sound as Trent obviously gave in to his impatience.

Nothing was slow after that.

They tore off the rest of their clothes, not caring where they landed.

Rusty ran her hands over Trent's body. "I'm trying to imagine how you look."

"I'm concentrating on how you feel," he replied, and

proceeded to explore hollows and crevices that made her moan.

At last she sank back onto the couch and he covered her with his body, drugging her with kisses. Soon, even Trent's magical kisses weren't enough.

"I...can't...wait—"

"Neither can I."

The instant he joined with her, they both gasped and stilled.

Rusty felt profoundly humbled by the sweet rightness of it all.

"Rusty." He breathed her name on a sigh.

"I know," she said.

His kiss held a promise she didn't want to acknowledge. She couldn't acknowledge it. She *refused* to acknowledge it.

And then he began to move, stroking her in the overpowering age-old rhythm of love.

Love.

No.

But just before she lost her mind to the pleasure, her last conscious thought was *yes*.

And then she screamed.

11

A ROARING woke them.

"What's that?" Rusty, entwined in Trent's arms, blinked in the darkness.

"Sounds like a motor. A big motor," Trent replied.

"More snow?"

She felt him shake his head. "They must be digging us out."

"Oh, my gosh! We don't have any clothes on!" She scrambled off the couch.

"Don't panic. We've got a few minutes." Trent sounded calm.

Well, of course. He didn't have to find as many clothes as she did. "Where did you throw my jeans?"

"Hell, I don't know. Not far."

The motor sounded closer. A lot closer. "Trent!" she wailed.

"Here's something." He handed her a wad of cloth.

"That's *your* shirt!"

"Put it on if you can't find anything else."

"Oh, sure. Why don't we just announce to everyone what we've been doing?"

"They won't necessarily assume we've been doing anything." His voice dipped and she guessed he was searching the floor.

She found her blouse draped on the arm of the couch. "Oh, great, we slept on my blouse!"

"Big deal. We've been here all night, they'll expect us to look rumpled."

"Rumpled, not naked!"

"Here, these jeans are yours. Now you won't be naked."

"I haven't found my panties, yet." She had to shout over the noise.

"Maybe you should skip them for now."

Rusty knelt and searched the floor anyway. She found her bra, which was better than nothing. She put it on, along with her jeans. "Trent, are you still naked?"

"No, I found everything."

She heard him step into his jeans. "Even your underwear?"

"Yes."

"Great, you found your underwear, but mine is who knows where?"

"Will you stop going on about your underwear? I've got to get my pants zipped here."

"Need help, big boy?"

She heard a snap. "Very funny."

Gray light began to show around the door.

"All buttoned up?" Trent shouted. "I think we're about to be rescued."

The engine cranked to a stop. "Trent? Rusty? You two all right in there?" Clarence called.

"You mean, other than being mad as hell?" Trent called back.

Shovels scraped against the wood. "We thought the snow would melt real fast." Harvey's voice was full of apology. "We didn't know a cold front would come in."

Great. Everybody was probably out there. Rusty didn't even know if she'd buttoned her blouse correctly and somehow, she knew they'd be able to tell she wasn't wearing underwear. She finger-combed her hair and hoped her makeup hadn't smeared too badly.

Moments later, with Trent pulling and one of his uncles pushing, the door gave and bright sunlight blinded Rusty's eyes.

"Hey, there you go. Come on out, you two." Clarence's joviality grated on Rusty's nerves.

Stumbling toward the doorway, she shivered and shaded her eyes. Doing the same, Trent grabbed her hand and urged her through the doorway. Glistening white was piled high on either side of an escape tunnel. Doc sat in the driver's seat of a yellow digging machine of some kind.

"Now, boy, I know you're mad—" Clarence broke off abruptly.

"Rachel Marie!"

Agnes had used her full name. Not a good sign. "Gran?" Standing in the doorway, surrounded by leftover snow, Rusty blinked against the sun and searched for her grandmother.

At the end of the snow tunnel, Agnes stared at her with a horrified expression, echoed in varying degrees by Trent's uncles.

Puzzled, she turned to look at Trent at the same instant he looked down at her.

Her eyes widened, as did his.

Black ringed his mouth, smudged his face, his neck and disappeared under his shirt. Fingerprints marked where Rusty had fumbled with the buttons. Two were missing.

"Laser printer toner," she whispered as Trent turned his back and shielded her.

She stared at her blackened hands and arms and could guess what the rest of her looked like.

The silky slickness that she'd forgotten all about now graphically displayed exactly how Trent and Rusty had stayed warm last night.

"We look like sexual road maps," he murmured. "X marks the spot."

She looked down and felt her face flame when she saw the dark area between his legs where her fingers had explored. An impressively large dark area, she had to admit.

Then she looked at her blouse where two handprints clearly covered her breasts. If she'd kept her blouse on, the prints would have smudged, but no, she'd taken it off and thus preserved the outline of Trent's hands for all to see.

And see they had.

"Let me handle this," Trent whispered.

"I think you already have."

He grinned just as Clarence cleared his throat.

They turned to look at him.

"Rusty, dear." He approached, arms outstretched, a determined smile on his face. "Welcome to the family."

One look at her grandmother's face and Rusty made the only possible response. "Thank you."

THE TONER on her body was a vivid reminder of Trent's lovemaking. Rusty wished she could scrub away the memories as she'd scrubbed away the toner.

Though she and Trent had tried to play down the situation, Agnes and the uncles had been impossible with their pointed comments. They seated a freshly scrubbed Trent and Rusty next to each other at a stunningly uncomfortable breakfast where they were plied with mountains of food while the others sat at the table, drank coffee and watched the two of them. Each time they spoke, even when it was only, "Pass the salt," all conversation ceased and the two were regarded with expectant smiles.

Trent looked as uncomfortable as Rusty felt. In a display of shutting-the-barn-door-after-the-horse-has-left, the two hadn't had a chance to be alone.

And it didn't look like they ever would be.

When Harvey brought out his bridal supply catalogs, Rusty couldn't stand it any longer and escaped to her room. She dragged her suitcase onto the bed and began haphazardly folding clothes.

"What are you doing?" Agnes had followed her.

"Packing. Under the circumstances, I think it would be best if we left immediately."

"Under what circumstances?"

Rusty started pulling clothes off the hangers in the closet. It was time to be blunt. "Trent and I have no intention of marrying."

"But...but you..."

"What? Slept with him?" She laughed harshly. "We were bored. It's hardly the basis for marriage." Maybe if Agnes believed the words, Rusty could, too.

"Bored? Haven't you ever heard of Scrabble?"

"It was dark!" Rusty slapped a sweater into the suitcase. "Completely dark! There was no way out. You should be glad one of us wasn't hurt stumbling around. Our computers are broken and, obviously, the laser printer. What were you thinking?"

A subdued Agnes sat on the corner of the bed. "I thought

it would be romantic. I figured after your computer batteries went out, you two would be forced to talk and get to know one another."

"We talked. We got to know one another." She folded another sweater. "We're not marrying."

"Rusty!" Agnes bit her lip. "I don't believe that you two don't feel something for each other."

"Because it's obvious we felt something last night, right? It was a fling. It's over." Saying the words hurt.

Agnes pushed Rusty's bangs out of her eyes. "You're in love with him, aren't you?"

Her heart pounded. No. Wrong. She was not in love with him. Not. She was simply having a natural hormonal response to...laser printer toner.

She ignored the question. "You'd better go pack. There's a flight leaving just after midnight and I booked two seats. I know the middle of the night is inconvenient, but I was lucky to get anything this time of year."

"I'm not going back with you."

"What?" Stunned, Rusty dropped the sweatshirt she was folding.

"I'm not going back before Christmas. There's still so much to do here. And Harvey ordered costumes for us."

"*What* are you talking about?"

"For delivering presents. And the baking isn't nearly done. We promised."

Something had gone wrong with her grandmother. Rusty had simply thought this domestic nonsense was a phase, but it appeared her grandmother was delusional.

"We came here because you wanted me to check out Trent. I checked him out."

"Perhaps too thoroughly."

Okay, that remark meant her grandmother wasn't totally off her rocker. "At any rate, there's no need for us to stay any longer."

"You promised me!"

Rusty folded the sweatshirt and set it in the suitcase. Taking her grandmother's hands, she said, "I said I'd give it a shot, and I did. But my computer is trashed and Dearsing moved the presentations to Christmas Eve. I don't have a choice." She returned to packing.

"We always have a choice, Rusty." Her grandmother stood. "But you're making the wrong one."

"YOU BETTER BE PLANNING to do right by that little gal, Trent."

Clarence sat behind the big desk in the Triple D office. Doc leaned against the window frame and Harvey sat on the sofa, thumbing through catalogs. Trent, as he had when he was a boy, stood in front of the desk to face Clarence.

It had been years since he'd received a dressing down. He'd decided to let them have their say in hopes that it would defuse the situation.

"Has Miss Rusty said what her colors will be, Trent?"

"Colors?"

"For the wedding."

"No," Trent answered shortly.

"But there will be a wedding," Clarence said. It wasn't a question.

"Good breeding stock," was Doc's contribution.

The situation wasn't diffusing. Trent had had enough. "Whether or not there is a wedding is an issue to be decided by Rusty and me. Thank you all for your concern." He turned and strode toward the door.

"Now, boy—"

"Trent!"

Harvey scuttled over to him and thrust a slim catalog into his hands. "This is for while you're deciding," he whispered.

Trent was halfway down the hall before he looked at Harvey's offering.

It was a condom catalog.

IN THE END, Trent drove Rusty to the airport. He was continuing on to Dallas.

"If you change your mind, you can come back anytime!" Harvey had called.

But Rusty wasn't going to change her mind.

"This is the first chance we've had to talk," Trent said as they waved goodbye to four somber-faced people and drove off into the night.

"There isn't much to talk about, is there?" Rusty had been dreading this conversation. Over and over she'd rearranged the pieces of her life, hoping they'd all fit together. But Trent just didn't fit into her life, no matter how much she might wish otherwise.

He slid a sideways glance at her. "I feel we have unfinished business."

"And I feel that a clean break is best." She stared straight ahead.

"Damn it, Rusty, I want to see you again!"

Rusty closed her eyes. For some reason, she found it easier to talk with him when she couldn't see him. "We both know that the only way we can continue to have a relationship is if I give up everything."

"I'm not asking you to give up anything!"

"Oh? So you're saying you plan to resign from your business, forget your retirement project, abandon your uncles and move to Chicago?"

"You're being unnecessarily extreme."

"Maybe for now, but that's what's down the road, isn't it? How else would we be together?"

He was silent long enough for her to know that he'd never considered changing anything at all about his life. "We could work something out."

Men were always saying that "things would work out." And they did because women took care of the details.

Not this time. "I have a responsibility to my grandmother. She sacrificed years of freedom to raise me and I'm not going to abandon her." Rusty ignored the fact that Agnes had elected to remain at the Triple D for Christmas. "And to be able to fulfill that responsibility, I've got to give this presentation my best shot. If I don't get this campaign, then I'll have to try for another one."

"In a few weeks, when things settle down—"

"Nothing will have changed," Rusty broke in harshly. "You'll be here and I'll be there."

"Rusty…"

"This isn't easy for me." Her voice broke. "You—making l-love with you—" A sob escaped. "Darn it! The thought of leaving you is tearing me apart. I can't go through this again and again, Trent, I just can't. It's better that we break it off now. Please."

He stopped at an interchange and looked away from the road to stare at her, his eyes dark with emotion. "Is that what you really want? A clean break?"

"Yes." She made her voice strong. "It's what I want."

ON DECEMBER twenty-fourth at 10:30 a.m., Rusty presented her Next to Nature campaign, illustrated with eight-by-ten glossy photos of a flannel-shirted Trent and the line shack. The clients were impressed by the emotion they heard in her voice and decided that someone who felt so passionately about their product was the person they wanted handling their account.

Rusty went home to celebrate Christmas Eve alone in her undecorated apartment.

On December twenty-fourth at 2:37 p.m., Trent signed a contract with the owner of the construction company just as the man was leaving town for his skiing trip.

Trent went home to celebrate Christmas Eve alone in his undecorated apartment.

SHE HAD TO SHARE the news with somebody. Digging Trent's business card out of her purse, Rusty called his office. When there was no answer, she called his home. His answering machine picked up and she burst into tears.

She was alone. Alone on Christmas Eve. She'd achieved the vice presidency she'd sought ever since she'd joined the Dearsing Ad Agency. She was going to be in charge of a huge national advertising campaign. She should be happy. She should celebrate. Instead, Rusty headed for the bathroom and took a shower.

WHERE WAS SHE? Trent slammed down the telephone as Rusty's answering machine picked up. Had she landed the account? Was she happy?

Wasn't she interested in whether or not he'd been able to get the contracts ready to be signed?

He'd done it. He'd put together a major deal and hadn't

used one penny of Triple D money to do it. Someday his uncles might live at the Ridge Haven Retirement Village. And from now on, the investment community would see that Trent didn't have to depend on Triple D money to swing a deal.

Life was good. He should be happy. Satisfied. He should celebrate.

And he did want to celebrate. With Rusty.

Trent collapsed on his leather and chrome couch. Though new and expensive, it wasn't as comfortable as a certain broken down piece of furniture in a deserted line shack.

He closed his eyes. What had he been thinking? He shouldn't have let her go. He certainly shouldn't have agreed to this "clean break" she wanted.

When two people love each other, they try to work out the logistics. And he loved her. So why hadn't he told her?

No wonder she wanted a clean break. He hadn't given her any reason to want to see him again. He'd been so wrapped up in his project and she'd been so determined to land that ad campaign that they both had lost sight of what was important: how they felt about each other.

With renewed purpose, Trent picked up the telephone.

TOWELING DRY her hair, Rusty walked through her apartment and paused by the answering machine. Someone had called while she was in the shower, but when she listened for the message, she heard only a dial tone. On a whim, she called the Triple D, but the line was busy. Naturally, what had she expected?

She trudged into the kitchen and yanked open the

freezer. Great. Christmas Eve dinner was going to be frozen leftover Chinese take-out.

This was horrible. Awful. How could Agnes have done this to her? They *always* spent Christmas together. Here Rusty was sacrificing her happiness for Agnes and Agnes didn't even appreciate it. Rusty was saving her grandmother from spending lonely holidays just like this one.

Except, Rusty was the one who was standing in front of the microwave with a glob of frozen Chinese leftovers on Christmas Eve, while Agnes cavorted on a Texas ranch with three bachelors.

Something wasn't right.

The phone rang. Rusty scrambled to answer it, conscious of the pathetically eager tone in her voice.

"Rusty?"

It was Trent. She should hang up.

"Yes?" She turned out the lights so she could talk to him in the dark.

"I know you wanted a clean break, but I love you. Do you love me?" he asked without preamble.

Silent tears rolled down her cheeks.

"Do you love me?"

"Yes," she whispered, and heard him exhale.

"Then everything else will work out. I promise."

Rusty wanted to believe him. "How?"

"Did you get your account?"

"Yes!" she wailed, then sniffed. "And you?"

"All signed, sealed and delivered."

"Congratulations." There was absolutely no enthusiasm in her voice, but she couldn't fake it just now.

"Okay," Trent said. "We both have jobs to do, so we'll see each other on weekends for a few months."

"But what then?"

"Then...I don't know. But, Rusty, I'm telling you—we *can* work this out."

She was letting herself in for heartache, she just knew it. On the other hand... "All right. I don't suppose I could feel any worse than I feel now."

"I feel great! What's the matter with you?"

"It's Christmas Eve and I'm all alone!" she blubbered.

She heard a deep chuckle. "Then I'll fly up there or you can fly down here. It'll work."

"Are you nuts? There isn't going to be a seat available on any airline."

"There will be a way. We will find it. I'm hanging up now. I'm going to call the airlines. You do the same and we'll see what happens."

He sounded so sure. Halfheartedly, Rusty turned on the lights and grabbed the telephone book. The best she could hope for would be to get put on a standby list.

She'd start with the largest airlines first.

"Merry Christmas, this is reservations. How may I help you?"

As Rusty'd expected, she was put on a very lengthy standby list.

"Your name?"

"Rusty Romero." Rusty could hear the woman typing. There was a silence. "Ms. Romero, you're already booked first-class on Flight 476 nonstop to Dallas."

"What?"

"As well as flights 271, which is already boarding, 582, 1156 and 2558. You were also ticketed on Flight 121, but it departed earlier today." There was a pause. "Though the tickets are waiting for you at reservations, if you do not plan to use them, I would ask that you consider others who are currently on our standby list."

"I—I...okay." Dazed, Rusty hung up the telephone.

How was this possible?

If you change your mind, you can come back anytime. Harvey. Dear, sweet, dangerous-with-a-credit-card Harvey.

Dancing to the kitchen, Rusty shoved the Chinese food back into the freezer.

"DO YOU THINK they'll be surprised to see us?" Rusty asked as she and Trent snuck into the ranch house at dawn on Christmas morning. It was a white Christmas—but only on the Triple D front yard.

"Who knows with them?" Trent whispered.

They crept inside and hung up fuzzy stockings with glittered names that Rusty had bought at the airport.

Trent plugged in the Christmas tree lights and they put their presents under the tree.

"I suppose I could start breakfast," Rusty said, doubtfully.

"Uh, no." There was no doubt whatsoever in Trent's voice.

"Then—" Rusty bent down and handed Trent her Christmas present to him "—open this."

He looked from the flat package in his hands to her, then retrieved one in an identical size from beneath the tree.

They stared at each other, then tore open their gifts.

"'*Roaming Romeos. Keeping Long-Distance Love Alive,*'" he read.

"It's going to be hard, so I want to be prepared." She looked at him anxiously.

"Finish opening yours," he said softly.

Rusty did and stared at a book by the same author—the book she'd nearly bought for Trent. *The Commuter Marriage: How To Make It Work*. "Marriage? Trent?"

"Marriage."

"Well, if things work—"

"Marriage," he repeated.

"Are you asking?"

"Insisting." He kissed her. "I've known I wanted to marry you ever since I found out you'd been sitting in the dark with your blouse off. I have a feeling life with you will be full of surprises." He grinned. "Noisy, too."

"I'm not altogether sure you should be allowed to get your own way in this," she said, feeling her face heat.

"So what do you plan to do about it?"

"You'll just have to marry me instead."

"If you insist."

They laughed and kissed, which is where Harvey found them when he tiptoed into the den.

"Oh, oh." He clapped when he saw them. "So you're getting married?"

When they nodded, he turned to alert the others, then caught sight of the stockings by the fireplace. "Oh, look! My name!"

Rusty saw him quiver in delight. How a man could be so wise, yet so innocent at the same time was something she marveled at and was grateful for. She shared a smile with Trent just as the others appeared.

"Trent, my boy, I'm glad to see that you're the man I thought you were." Clarence clasped them both on the shoulders.

Trent smiled down at Rusty. "Only because I found the right woman."

"Oh, Rusty, you came back!" Agnes hugged her. "I'm so glad. You see, I have news."

"What news?"

Her grandmother left her and went to stand beside the silent Doc, who put his arm around her. Her cheeks pinkening attractively, Agnes smiled up at the man next to her.

"Gran?"

Agnes Romero held out her hand.

Rusty clutched Trent's arm as she caught sight of a diamond matching the twinkle in Doc's eye.

"Your grandmother and I are getting married," Doc said to a stunned Rusty.

"And that's not a cubic zirconia, either," announced Harvey. "I have the appraisal certificate."

After a round of congratulations, Rusty, still stunned, still unable to believe that her grandmother was actually marrying one of Trent's uncles, asked, "So you're staying here—for good?"

"For better or worse," replied her grandmother with an adoring look at Doc.

"I told you things would work out," Trent murmured next to Rusty's ear.

"Did you know?"

He shook his head just as Clarence cleared his throat. "All right everyone, time to eat breakfast and change into the costumes!" he ordered.

"What costumes?" Trent and Rusty asked in unison.

The others looked at them in surprise. "The Santa costumes for when we deliver the presents," Harvey said. "They're out in the barn."

"The barn is full of presents?"

"Oh, yes. Lots and lots of presents." Harvey retrieved

one of his ubiquitous notebooks. "I have the inventory right here. The tractor for the high school and the ultra-sound machine for the veterans home are the big ones this year." He stopped and looked at Trent. "But you two saw it all, didn't you?"

"I..." Trent looked down at Rusty and she smiled, knowing he was relieved to have an explanation for all the merchandise his uncles had stockpiled.

"Yes," he said. "Yes, we did." Turning back to Harvey, he asked, "Are you renting a truck? How are you getting all that stuff loaded and delivered?"

"Don't be silly, Trent!" Laughing, Harvey waved his hands and followed Doc, Agnes and Clarence out of the room. "That's what the elves are for."

"Elves?" Rusty and Trent looked at each other.

"I wonder where he ordered them from," she said.

"I wonder how much they cost," he said.

"I don't know, but they probably get time-and-a-half for working on Christmas Day."

"Double if they're wearing tights and pointy shoes."

Laughing, they started for the kitchen. "Hey, wait a minute." Trent stopped her and took her into his arms. "I skimmed that commuter marriage book while I was standing in line and one of the tips was to make each moment you have alone count." He looked around and whispered, "We're alone."

Rusty pulled his head to hers. "So start making it count."

He sure looked good holding a baby...

THE TRUTH ABOUT COWBOYS
Margot Early

"History is a vast early warning system."

—Norman Cousins

1

Reno, Nevada
June

NO COWBOYS, vowed Erin Mackenzie.

But the bullfighter clown, the greasepaint matador of the rodeo, had already helped himself to the vacant seat beside her. The clown's face was painted like a dog's, with a black splotch around one eye, and his baggy Wrangler cutoffs brushed the legs of her own not-at-all-baggy jeans as he gazed at her with a look of spellbound adoration. His thick-lashed green-gray eyes were made for pantomime—and unmeant seduction. Erin studied his suntanned knees and the stripes on his athletic socks and the dust on his cleats. Bandannas—red, yellow, orange and shocking pink—dangled from his baggies, fanning out to touch her, too.

Over the public-address system, the announcer said, "Found you a girlfriend, Abe?"

The rodeo clown jerked his chin up and down. Backing from Erin just a little, he shyly offered her some invisible flowers.

Erin took them.

The eye contact was long and awkward.

As though overcome by his feelings, he sprang to his feet and darted away. Seconds later, he settled beside a Nashville-haired blonde in the next section and regarded her hopefully.

"Now, Abe..." said the announcer.

Erin steadied her breath. Just part of his act. But when he back-flipped over one fence and vaulted over another into the night-lit arena, she admired his agility, the way he moved. Earlier, he'd made her laugh with the antics of his Australian shepherd and with a bareback act on a chestnut gelding. Few of his jokes were new; she'd heard them at rodeos before, but *he* had that rare gift. He was funny.

And according to the program, he hailed from Alta, Colorado.

Erin couldn't ignore that. Couldn't forget it.

His patchwork shirt and suspenders with sunflowers on them transfixed her as he wandered toward the barrel in the center of the arena. When he peered inside, the barrelman, another clown, popped up like a jack-in-the-box and shouted at him. The bullfighter ran away and the crowd laughed. But the mood changed as the man at the microphone promised, "Folks, you are about to see some of the rankest bulls on the rodeo circuit..."

Bull riding. Erin sat up, watching the chutes. The Reno Rodeo was a huge event, with a $175,000 purse. It was unlikely she would run into Abe the Babe—her bullfighter clown—again.

"No cowboys," she whispered into her beer.

Erin was a candidate for the Dumped by Cowboys Hall of Fame. Sometimes she thought her life was a case study in rejection by bull riders and ropers in too-tight Wranglers, with rodeo belt buckles the size of dinner plates and small closed minds. Erin had a broad educated mind. She prided herself on clear thinking, on commitment to all things rational.

So what was she doing at the rodeo?

Partaking of an ancient rite, she told herself, a rite as old as the domestication of animals. Hadn't Theseus ridden into the city of Athens astride a bull? Weren't bulls always considered symbols of virility and cattle a measure of wealth? Wasn't Erin herself descended from people who raised cows, from cowboys?

Nothing, not even an almost completed doctorate in History of the American West from the University of Nevada at Reno, not even her own history of cowboys, could destroy her childhood dreams of snagging a rodeo champion like Ty Murray. She imagined growing old with a millionaire Gold Buckle winner who would never walk right again. He'd raise Herefords; she'd grow prizewinning vegetables for the county fair.

A bullfighter clown would do just as well. A bullfighter from Alta...

As the first bull, a brindle monster as big as a car, plunged out of the chute, bucking and spinning and raising plumes of dust, the clown in the patchwork shirt and his partner danced just out of hoof's range, ready to help the cowboy.

When the bull jettisoned his cargo, Abe withdrew a red bandanna from one oversize pocket. With a mime's grace and a matador's speed and skill, he flourished the handkerchief like a cape. The bull swung its head away from the fallen rider. While the cowboy scrambled over the fence like startled wildlife, the clown crouched on all fours and pawed the ground.

Erin leaned forward.

"I'm not sure that's such a good idea, Abe," said the announcer.

The bull charged. Grasping its horns, the bullfighter vaulted over the animal's muscular bulk—a feat depicted on a wall painting in Crete dated 2000 B.C. Abe landed on his feet, and the bull spun to meet him.

"Abe, you've made him mad now. You just leave that bull alone."

The clown was done for. The brindle beast chased him, its lowered head committed to the seat of those baggies. Abe the Babe stood to get freight-trained by two thousand pounds of Brahma bull.

As the crowd salivated, the bullfighter swung toward the bull's shoulder, running in a small circle, forcing the bull to turn, too. Breathing deeply, Erin inhaled the rodeo smells— dust and manure and animals, beer and popcorn and hot dogs—all mingling in the dry hot Reno night. It was the modern equivalent of an evening at the Roman Coliseum.

Outmaneuvered, the bull grew bored with his quarry. Spotting the open gate and other animals, he lifted his head and trotted out of the arena, and Abe made a production of dusting off the seat of his pants and twisting around to blow on them, as though they were too hot.

"No cowboys," Erin repeated into her beer.

No cowboy from Alta.

JUST HOURS LATER, she changed her mind. On the grounds that he was a thread to her history, she'd brought him home. Granted, she would never follow the thread to its end, see where it led. But she could wrap herself in this bit of it for the night and try to stay warm.

In his sun-faded red Dodge pickup, he'd followed her to Reno's north side, to the neighborhood of houses all the same. The neighborhood that, for Erin and her mother, represented Success. Triumph over poverty. Security.

The glass patio doors were open. The swamp cooler was

broken, and the ninety-degree night was as stubborn as it was rare. Outside, in the compact grass-and-concrete yard, the bullfighter's Australian shepherd sniffed at Erin's mother's cocker spaniel, Taffy. Then, the two dogs wagged tails and sniffed some more and trotted together along the board-and-batten fence.

The cowboy on the plaid sofa gaped at the shoe-box yard as though he couldn't conceive of such closed-in spaces. His greasepaint was gone and she saw now that his skin was a smooth light golden brown, his lips flushed and sensuous. He had the hard square jaw Erin associated with descendants of those who had settled the West. Too-long Wranglers were stacked over his boots, and his white straw hat shone clean and white, not stepped-on, rolled-in-manure, end-of-the-season battered.

He was *so* cute. The cropped dirt brown hair reminded her of a World War II pilot—or the Marlboro man. So far, she'd learned he was twenty-seven and an Aries. She was a Taurus, just turned twenty-five last month; her belated birthday present to herself was a cowboy and a national-finals chance to break her own rodeo record in Getting Left.

Erin prepared for another hit of Jack Daniel's. Sloppy pouring had left shot-glass rings on the metal-legged kitchen table where she and her mother had sat so many mornings, eating Cap'n Crunch or Shredded Wheat. Now Erin and Abe were passing the bottle.

As a motto, *No cowboys* had lost its effect. Erin had been thinking of the bullfighter from Alta, Colorado, when she came home and showered and dressed after the rodeo. She'd stepped out to the rodeo dance in red Wranglers, a blue-and-red fringed Western shirt and tricolored hand-tooled cowboy boots, looking like the child of the West she'd never quite managed to become, no matter how hard she'd begged her mother for a horse of her own.

Lessons, six weeks each summer, were all they'd been able to afford. They happened only if Erin got straight A's.

Erin had never gotten anything else—except in that life course entitled Resisting Cowboys.

She studied the bullfighter, Abe Cockburn—pronounced Coburn, he'd said, same as Bruce Cockburn, the musician.

What was he thinking?

That second, Abe's thoughts were only whiskey-deep. Reliving the eight-day rodeo, subtracting the money he'd lost in travel expenses and hotel bills from what he'd earned bullfighting. Between performances he worked for Guy Loren, the stock contractor. He'd never get rich this way. But he'd always get by.

A photo above the T.V. showed a girl in a prom dress, probably this woman in high school. How did she stand living here, with just a patch of brown grass for a yard? The two-story house was identical to every other house on the street and on the next street and the next. Long and narrow with vertical cedar siding, it seemed flimsy enough to blow down in a good wind.

He blinked away drunken visions. Hotel rooms. The arena after the kids had gotten autographs and everyone had left—the trampled earth and the empty stands littered with beer cups and popcorn boxes. He imagined his truck on the road, hauling Buy Back in the trailer. Martha always rode in the cab, where Abe could sing Ian Tyson songs to her and she could put her head and paws in his lap while he drove.

The woman—Erin—took another drink. At the rodeo, he hadn't been able to decide if she was pretty or not, and he still couldn't. Her eyes were such a dark brown they seemed to make holes in her white skin, and her light reddish brown hair looked home-cut. The haircut suited her.

Her clothes did not.

He asked, "What do you do here?"

"I'm in grad school at UNR, and I work at the Museum of the American West. Also, I'm a valet." Parking cars at the hotel casinos was the best deal going for students, and Erin took pride in her work. Besides earning large tips, she'd discovered she had a way with small children abandoned in the parking lot by parents who were inside gambling. Like them, Erin understood abandonment. As they and she knew, it was often simply a case of being totally *forgotten*.

For days.

Or maybe for decades.

Now the cowboy would ask what she studied.

"You like rodeos?" he said.

"Of course."

When Abe had first spotted her, at the refreshment stand, she was rooting through a cracked and stained leather purse with dog-shredded fringe, hunting loose change. Seeing her, he'd felt like he'd walked into a post, and he'd been sure he'd never see her again. The rodeo was too big. But her seat was in the fourth row—accessible during the performance. He'd felt nervous, flirting with her. Only the greasepaint made it easy.

They'd met again at the rodeo party at the White Horse Hotel and Casino. Their eyes had caught—or rather, he had seen her staring at him, as though trying to figure out if she'd seen him before. He'd taken the bar stool next to hers and yawped at her just like he had at the rodeo, pretending he was still in his clown face. She'd recognized him then. And said, *Please go away. I don't like you.*

Soon they were two-stepping on a floor growing slick with spilled beer to country rock belted out by a band called the Spittoons.

Abe wished he wasn't leaving in the morning.

"Did you say you live with your mom?" he asked.

Erin nodded, thinking she was crazy to invite a stranger, any stranger, into her home this way. It wasn't safe. But Erin made a career of living dangerously. Hunting down gamblers in the casino to tell them when toddlers were hungry or needed their diapers changed. Frequenting rodeos, stock shows and the kind of cowboy bars famous for table-turning brawls, where people fell asleep in their drinks and no one had heard of line dancing. As a result, she had friends in low places and was often up to her ears in tears. This new friend had asked about her mother. "She's a croupier."

A blackjack dealer. Abe squinted at the croupier's daughter. Feeling romantic and wanting to *be* romantic, for her, he asked, "Who are you?"

Was he really curious? Erin thought so. As though he cared about her for more than this night. As though, even when he moved on in the morning, he would be thinking about her. As though he might be the one who stayed on— or came back. He would fall for her like Vince Gill for the "Oh Girl" girl. She'd be never alone anymore.

"What do you mean?"

He shrugged, a boyish half-embarrassed gesture, the kind of possibly false shyness she'd learned to distrust.

"I don't know. You seem different."

As his whiskey-glazed eyes searched hers, Erin decided this clown had used these lines before. "Who are *you*, Abe?"

She meant it to be ironic. It didn't work. Abe Cockburn's layers of manhood and cowboy pride were the real McCoy. Erin wondered who he was beneath them and knew she'd never know.

It made him fascinating.

He got up and drew out another chair at the dinette, to sit closer to her.

Erin offered the bottle, but he said, "I'm fine." Then, "Can I kiss you?"

It was inevitable. Why did she do this self-destructive thing?

Erin knew exactly why. She'd passed psychology, after all. "You could talk me into that."

Into feeling his fingers push back her hair. It was a soft kiss.

Afterward, he peered down at his chest. Slowly, he fished an imaginary object from his pocket—a key ring. Finding the key he wanted, he fit it into a lock in his chest, over the left front of his black-and-white-and-green Western shirt, and opened a door Erin could almost see. Removing an object, he blew some dust off it and held it up to his ear to check if it was still ticking.

Then he handed her his heart.

Erin received the imaginary heart, held it. *Boy, I bet this thing has been around.* She set the heart aside, on the table, and picked up the whiskey bottle.

He winced and sank in his chair, dying of rejection. An instant later, he tried to snatch back his heart, but Erin grabbed it from under his hand, and he caught her fingers and their eyes met.

She followed him upstairs to the bedroom he guessed was hers, maybe because of the posters of bull rider Lane Frost and rodeo-cowboy-turned-singer Chris LeDoux on the walls.

ABE TRANSFERRED a stuffed buffalo from the pillow to the desk, balancing it beside his hat on a stack of academic-looking books with thrill-a-minute titles like *The Territories of the United States: 1861-90*. The books wedged between two geodes at the back of the desk, beside her computer, were grim. *If I Die In a Combat Zone. Witness to War: Vietnam. The Battle for Saigon.*

What did she study, anyway? What were her dreams? Abe's own were gone. He did not ask hers.

Above her desk were signs of common ground. Breyer horses like his childhood playmate, Chaley, had collected. Erin Mackenzie was a grad student, but the room told her life story. It was the room of someone who loved horses and rodeo. Of someone who was herself loved. "What's your mom going to say when she comes home?"

"She won't say anything."

Though when it came to cowboys, no one's silence could be more vocal than Jayne's. And cowboys from Alta?

On the discount-house bed, in the glass-washed desert starlight and glow of far-off neon coming through her window, Abe kissed her again. He tasted like mint and whiskey. He smelled like horses, and she liked kissing him.

Don't think, Erin. Not about him leaving.

She'd stopped telling herself stories. He wouldn't love her.

He was scrutinizing her again, as though she mattered to him. Unbuttoning her shirt. A dog came into the room—his dog. Taffy, the cocker spaniel, needed her nails clipped. The Australian shepherd didn't.

"Martha, lie down," he said.

She did, and Erin knew how the dog must feel, that you wanted to please this man. You wanted him to love you.

They took off each other's clothes. She'd known his body would be this way—hard, his chest paler than his face and throat and forearms and hands.

He had his own condoms and was good at hugging, before, during and after sex. Muscle, hair and strength pressed to her, while the bed creaked and the headboard knocked the wall. But even excited, even coming, she stayed distant. She knew cowboys.

After she'd lain in his arms awhile, she pretended to hunt through the covers and drew out an imaginary key on a ring. She unlocked the door in his chest and put his heart away and locked it up again.

That made Abe want to do something funny, to make her laugh, to make himself laugh. But they both knew he would leave. *Maybe I'll see you next year*, really meant, *Goodbye*.

"I'm going to be in Twin Falls—Idaho—the first of August," he said, shocking himself. Even being in her bed surprised him. Picking up women after rodeos wasn't his way; usually he was busy helping Guy care for the stock. But he'd wanted to be with Erin. Because talking to her for five minutes at the White Horse, he'd found out she was smart. She'd made *him* laugh. And when the band played "My Heroes Have Always Been Cowboys," she'd said, in his arms, "It's my fatal flaw."

Abe was still thinking about that. "Do you think you could drive up?" he asked. To Twin Falls.

She looked starry-eyed and wary. "Is it a rodeo?"

"Just bull riding." Guy Loren was providing the stock. Working for the stock contractor was the best way Abe knew to guarantee work bullfighting.

Erin considered. He was from Alta. And she really liked him. Maybe... She lived on maybes.

"Okay. I guess."

He hugged her again, a long sleepy kind of hug like she'd never felt before.

"So—you're from Colorado?" she asked weakly.

"Yeah." The ranch was gone, had been for eleven years. Abe gave his address as Guy Loren's place in Alta, but he wasn't from anywhere anymore.

To Erin, his voice sounded rough. Husky. As though the land was someone he loved, someone he missed. "Do you have any brothers or sisters?"

"A little brother. His name's Lane."

The black shapes of the bull and bull rider on her poster swam in the dark. "Like Lane Frost?"

"Like, but not for. Rides in all the rough stock events, though. Junior rodeo. He's good." He paused. "My folks are divorced."

"So are mine. My dad lives in Colorado, too." It wasn't enough; she had to say more. "He's a cowboy. I've never met him."

That didn't make *any* sense to Abe. He loved his own daddy. Their relationship had its ups and downs and pissing contests, but Abe couldn't imagine life without him. Lloyd Cockburn had shaped who he was. "Why don't you look him up?"

Erin rolled onto her back. "Sometime I will."

"What kind of cowboy is he?"

Erin knew what he meant. There were rodeo cowboys and dime-store cowboys and urban cowboys and ranchers and... Well, there were real cowboys. Real, honest-to-God, home-on-the-range cowboys. Erin knew the answer that would satisfy Abe. She would tell him the work her father did, and he would form a picture that might be right or might be wrong.

But Erin was a little drunk, so she gave the answer she'd held in her heart all her life. So what if it was a mystery, like the truth about cowboys? As a doctoral candidate in History of the American West, she was entitled to an opinion.

"He's a real cowboy."

The night was cooling off. Abe drew her against him. But he wasn't thinking about sex, and he wasn't thinking of her father anymore. Or even how "My Heroes Have Always Been Cowboys" could be a fatal flaw.

He missed his own dad and the brother tagging along where he rode, where he walked. Lane, who looked up to him the way kids at the rodeo did, showing up with their faces painted like clowns.

Most of all, he missed the place that should have been his and the person he had always counted on being.

Erin didn't notice his wandering thoughts, only the way he was hugging her and how loose and sleepy her body felt. It wasn't usually easy to sleep with another person....

A WHILE LATER, she woke up with him, and the kisses and strokes resumed. It all seemed more intense than sex. Like those hugs, but more than that, too. As his penis nudged her, slid against her wetness, Erin knew it wasn't safe. Cowboys could have AIDS and make babies, same as other men. But it felt good to let him ease partway in and out of her, teasing until at last he sighed and turned to get a condom. This time, the headboard didn't hit the wall. Only their bodies shook.

Abe kissed her to sleep and couldn't sleep himself. But he lingered in her bed, thinking of Buy Back, his horse, in a stall at the livestock arena, thinking of the road heading east. It shouldn't have been hard to let a strange woman go; he would see her in a few weeks.

But his strings were unstrung and "pretty" would never matter again. She read war stories and had a cowboy father she'd never met. She was a graduate student, but Abe had never asked what was worth so much school.

He stole from her bed and dressed with Martha waiting. It was almost dawn, the day waking on a dimmer switch, and the view from her window was a hundred brown houses just like hers.

Abe folded his red bandanna into the shape of a heart and laid it on her desk on top of her opened notebook. On the blank page he wrote, "You can give it back to me in Twin Falls, August 1." He clapped on his hat.

Martha followed him from the room and down the stairs in the stillness. The cocker spaniel tore from the living room to the foyer just as a key turned in the lock. A woman in a black-and-white casino uniform froze in the half-opened doorway. Erin's face in an older portrait, with fewer angles and more curves. Sexy, like a showgirl.

Abe touched his hat. "Ma'am."

Looking suddenly weary, suddenly ten years older, the mother stepped inside and held the door in silent disapproval until he and his dog went through. The latch clicked behind him.

Two weeks later
Gunnison, Colorado

DUST.

The wind was up and they were all picking the dirt out of their teeth. Abe felt it catching in the paint on his face—the white base, the black spot around his right eye, his black dog's nose and mouth, and the brown-and-black spots on his cheeks. It had sifted into his cleats and through the weave of his tube socks and between his toes. The crowd hated the wind, especially with July heat, and it was his job to make them laugh about it, so he'd borrowed a duster owned by three-hundred-pound Marvelous Mark Friday, the announcer. In the center of the arena, Abe donned the coat and let it blow him like a sail on a boat.

He was barrelman this performance, leaving the bullfighting to Tug Holcomb and a rookie named Chad. Abe was sorry in a way. He loved clowning, and being the man in the can gave him the chance. But almost everyone he cared about was in the audience this afternoon. His father, Lloyd, sat in the stands with Abe's pretty and sharp-tongued childhood friend, Chaley Kay, and her father, Kip, who owned the last family-run ranch in Alta. And Lane, Abe's brother, was hanging out back of the chutes, checking out the stock; Lane was counting the months till he turned eighteen and became eligible to earn a Professional Rodeo Cowboys Association card.

For all four of those spectators but especially for his dad, who thought rodeo was play, Abe would have preferred to be bullfighting.

Saving cowboys.

There weren't many cowboys to save anymore. Old cowboys like his dad and Kip Kay were mostly gone. Soon the only ones left would be wannabes, like the movie stars and corporate bigwigs buying up all the land from Gunnison to Alta and line dancing at the I'm Okay, You're Okay Corral. Them—and rodeo cowboys.

Dark storm clouds tumbled overhead and Abe heard thunder. Yanking the duster over himself, he hurled his body to the ground in a timid quivering mass. Under the laughter of the audience, he peeked out and saw a bull rider wrapping his hand in the chute. *Left hand.* A bullfighter always needed to know which direction to turn the bull. Soon the cowboy would nod for the chute to be opened.

Abe jumped up, produced a whisk broom from his baggies and swept himself off.

"Now this next bull, Belligerence," said the announcer, "has killed a dozen clowns."

Still wearing the oversize duster, Abe ran for the barrel and climbed in, to sweat.

"In the can."

The crowd laughed.

Abe popped his head out, then ducked, jerking on his hat until the flapping crown popped up. As rain tapped the brim and wet his hair, he sprang up again, trying to close the crown. People were laughing, which was good. He was dying of heat and ready for the bull.

Guy Loren was the stock contractor for this rodeo—Gunnison was in his backyard—and Abe knew all the stock. Belligerence was the mean offspring of a Brahma and a Mexican fighting bull. Big brown patches ringed his eyes, and when he burst out of the chute, snorting bull slobber and standing on his head, Abe thought that if he ever saw death it might look like that. Chad, the rookie, tried to make the bull spin, but the rider was already launched.

Line him out. Belligerence had a reputation for charging downed riders, and it was the bullfighter's job to distract him.

The cowboy made it to the fence, and Abe took a bow as though he'd had something to do with it. The bull charged the can.

As Belligerence came, Abe crouched in the furnace of the can, bracing himself for the impact. His barrel was reinforced with steel and old automobile tire casings and painted with the sponsor's logo. One of the bullfighters rolled the barrel onto its side, and then the force came, a hard hit, and Abe was on the worst carnival ride of his life, not rolling on the ground, but spinning through the air with a horn in his shoulder and a bull's bad breath in his face, bracing his body against the sides of the barrel. Pain ripped his body, and the bull tossed free the can.

There was no landing right and lots of ways to land wrong, and later Tug said he heard the crack from outside the can.

Twin Falls, Idaho
August

A HIGH-SCHOOL STUDENT waved Erin to a space in the dirt parking lot. Signs throughout town had advertised the bull-riding event, and Erin had found the rodeo grounds easily. But when she arrived, her instincts said to hit the road again.

That would be futile. No matter how far she drove, this cowboy would be with her.

Anyhow, *he* had suggested the rendezvous. Erin was hopeful enough to wear her favorite black Wranglers and fringed black shirt and her favorite boots, black lace-up ropers, a two-year-old birthday present from her mother. Though Jayne didn't approve of cowboys, she did appreciate Western wear.

Erin had even worn a big silver belt buckle with her name on it—in case he couldn't remember. She didn't *need* a belt. Not now.

It was hot and almost muggy. As she shut the door of her mother's baby blue 1969 Mustang convertible, borrowed for the weekend, a half-ton pickup powered past, and the resulting dust cloud coated her clothing. Blinking and nauseous, Erin groped in her purse for her sunglasses, then headed for the entrance with the regret of those who wear black on August afternoons.

Where was he? As she paid admission—ten dollars—she caught sight of a bullfighter with a green wig and striped shirt. Not Abe. She followed the crowd into the rodeo grounds and past the refreshment booth. *He'll be near the chutes.*

Skirting the track that circled the arena, Erin scanned the bodies. She ignored bull riders in bright chaps, fringe waving with every step, and hunted for clowns. One rolled a barrel into the arena, but he was too short to be Abe—and wearing the wrong costume. Another bullfighter lazed against a rail near the chutes with a grizzled rancher type.

Where was Abe?

The bullfighter inside the fence was tantalizingly close. She could get his attention. Erin contemplated the back of his companion, the rancher. The white shirt stretched across his shoulders was damp under the armpits. His walnut-shell face and weatherbeaten boots marked him as a real cowboy.

Wondering if her father looked like that, if maybe this was her father—it always *could* be—Erin approached the fence. "Excuse me."

Neither man heard at first, and she felt stupid, especially when three passing bull riders smirked at her. *They think I'm a buckle bunny, trying to pick up a man at the rodeo.*

Red-faced, Erin said more loudly, "Excuse me."

The bullfighter turned. A moon-white wig framed his makeup. "Yes, ma'am?"

She hung on to the hot fence. "I'm looking for Abe Cockburn. Is he here?"

The old cowboy ignored her, though he'd shifted so that now she could see his weathered face. He wasn't her father. She had a twenty-five-year-old picture of her father, and this wasn't him.

"I don't know him," said the clown. "Is he riding bulls today? You might ask back in the chutes, but I think those cowboys are all thinking about the performance right now."

"He's a bullfighter. He's supposed to be working here."

"Oh..." His star-painted eyes squinted. "Cockburn. Yeah, he canceled. I don't know why. I live over in Preston. Stock contractor phoned and asked me to fill in. Maybe you want to talk to him. He might be able to tell you something."

Erin was afraid she'd throw up. "That's okay. Thank you."

"Sure." He tipped his hat. "Enjoy the bull riding."

"Thanks."

The stands seemed miles away. As the announcer welcomed fans to the professional bull-riding competition, Erin pushed toward the exit. Heat hung in her clothing.

Being Dumped by a Cowboy was nothing new. She was an expert in the field. But she'd never known till now that it felt even worse to be dumped by a cowboy when you were pregnant with his child.

"Cowboys hide the truth beneath their hats."

—Erin Mackenzie,
"Cattle and Cowboys: The Ancient
Currency of a Modern Enigma"

2

Reno, Nevada
March, twenty months since Erin was Dumped by a Clown

PENCIL HOLDERS. Seven days before Maeve's first birthday,
Erin was called for jury duty and took her daughter to day
care. She was dismissed before noon, and when she picked
up Maeve, the older kids were making pencil holders from
juice cans.

Driving home, Erin tried to forget this. But some things a
person couldn't forget—like the juice-can pencil holder in
her own past.

When she reached the house, *Prorodeo Sports News* was in
the mailbox, and *he* had the cover.

At six o'clock, still thinking of pencil holders, she picked
up the phone.

Her grip on the receiver was like a bull rider's suicide
wrap; she'd gotten on, and the only way off was through.
Cowboy up and ride. The now cut-up copy of *Prorodeo
Sports News* covered the table in the same room where she
and Abe Cockburn had drunk whiskey one fateful summer
night. On the paper sat a manila envelope stuffed with

clippings. Erin had removed a tiny cut-out want ad from the envelope—for reference. He still lived in Alta.

Where a phone was ringing. Not at Guy Loren's ranch, Abe's address, but at a neighboring place. The ranch of Missing Past. The ranch that kept Erin's grail, which was the truth about cowboys.

Between rings, someone picked up with a clatter. "Kays'."

A man.

Maeve sat in her playpen in the living room. While her daughter tried to stuff a square block through a round hole, Erin said, "Hi. I'm interested in coming to visit your ranch. I have a brochure." She supposed that was what she should call the tri-fold black-and-white leaflet.

"When were you thinking of coming?"

"Next week." The contract on the house was pending; she wouldn't hear on any of her applications before the following week was up; the kennel would board Taffy. The timing was perfect.

"We have room," he said, and he sounded like a cowboy, like his voice had been in the wind that day. "It's cold here, though, and we're calving. How many in your party?"

"Just me and my daughter. She's eleven months old." Outside, the sky had darkened from Baskin-Robbins pink to deep gray. Erin stretched the phone cord as she went to draw the curtains. It was seven months since she'd enjoyed a starry night through the glass patio doors. Seven months since she'd felt comfortable leaving Maeve even one room away. Now she shut all the curtains at night and carried Maeve with her everywhere in the house.

There was no reply. Had they been disconnected?

"Hello?" asked Erin.

"We don't have child-care services. You have a baby,

you'd best come in June. We'll have a barbecue and a dance after branding's done."

June? If she didn't come now, she'd lose her nerve. The house would sell, she would receive a job offer and move somewhere safer and more wholesome than Reno. The crucial would seem inessential, the matter of juice-can pencil holders...maudlin.

"I'd prefer to come now."

"Well, I guess we can find something for you to do. Make sure you bring warm clothes. It's twenty below out."

The man of the gruff voice might or might not own the Kay Ranch of Alta, Colorado. *Stop shaking, Erin.* "I'd like to make a reservation, then, for next week."

"We'll need a two-hundred-dollar deposit. But we don't take credit cards."

"I'll send a money order." It was what she'd planned. Because of his next, inevitable question.

"That'll be fine. What's your name?"

"Erin O'Neill." It was satisfying to lie to a cowboy for a change, instead of him lying to her.

"Address and phone?"

Erin told him her post-office box and phone number. They agreed that she would arrive on Saturday, March fifteenth, and stay through the twenty-first.

"You'll want to fly into Grand Junction, or Gunnison if you can get a decent fare," he said. "Either way, we'll meet you."

"Thank you."

"You're welcome. We'll be glad to have you."

The sign of warmth let her ask, "And who am I talking to?"

"This is Kip Kay," he said. "Owner."

HAUNTED BY A NAME, by the name *Erin*, Kip returned to the supper table. Only three others were eating tonight—

Beulah Ann, Lloyd and Lane. Kip's niece Beulah Ann had come to the ranch the past summer to work as wrangler and cook. Lloyd Cockburn, once his neighbor, was now Kip's foreman. And Lloyd's youngest son, Lane, was biding his time; his future was rodeo, not ranching.

Kip told them, "We have a guest coming next week. She's bringing a baby."

"We're calving," Lloyd said.

"I pointed that out." Kip picked up his fork, glad that Lloyd, too, had seen the problem. Lately his foreman—who was in his seventies—seemed a little vague. And right now Kip needed every mind and every pair of hands.

Twenty-four-year-old Lucky, who came from Alta to help out, was living on a trust fund and cowboying for fun; Kip found him reliable but inexperienced. Another hand was studying for finals at the college in Gunnison and showed up when he could, which wasn't often enough. That left Wayne, Kip's top hand, who had just accepted a job in Telluride, at a ranch owned by movie people; he'd have his own house and health insurance and fourteen thousand a year. No way Kip could match that.

It was coming down to family. At this minute Chaley and Abe were in the barn with a sick heifer who'd just aborted her calf.

Kip found that thought reassuring—not the heifer's troubles, but Abe's being with Chaley. Their engagement still gave him anxious moments. In fact, he spent hours every day mulling over his future son-in-law.

The question that ate at him was: why hadn't Abe quit his job down the road with Guy Loren and come home to the Kay Ranch? The offer had been made. And what kind of fiancé didn't want to spend as many waking hours as possible with his betrothed?

Seventeen-year-old Lane pushed back his chair. "Good night," he said. When no one responded, he cleared away his plate. Cold came through the kitchen to the dining room as he banged outside, probably heading for the trailer he and his father shared.

"We're all talkative," remarked Beulah Ann, who was eighteen and, in Kip's estimation, an excellent person in all ways. She had her past, and Kip had taken a risk bringing her on, but so far he didn't regret it.

One day he'd overheard Lane tease her about her weight, which was substantial, and Beulah Ann had said, *So what? I could ride one of those bulls as good as you.* Next day she and Lane were down at Guy Loren's bucking pens, and Beulah Ann stayed on one of his Brangus bulls for eight seconds. So there. Kip still chuckled thinking of it.

Now he winked at his niece. "That's a sign of good cooking."

"Or grouchy men," grumbled Beulah Ann good-naturedly. "You can sure tell the difference when Chaley's here."

Kip felt the same. It had made all the difference to his daily happiness when his daughter, Chaley, had graduated from the university in Fort Collins and come home to the ranch. Chaley was here to stay, and this ranch would one day be hers. Hers and her children's.

And Abe's.

From one brooding notion came another, unrelated. That bitter day twenty-five years past. A day invoked by the speaking of a name, the name of Jayne's child. Kip turned his thoughts to cows.

They crept to mortality, instead.

Things happened suddenly on a ranch, like earlier that week when he'd fallen from the sleigh while hooking hay to the cows. Like when Yule, his horse, had rolled over him last winter. Like years before, when Lloyd's little girl had fallen between the wheels of his tractor.

Life on a ranch was whimsical and he could die at any time.

He could die without ever having known the child Jayne had borne, without ever having seen her face.

And frankly he just didn't care.

HANGING UP THE PHONE, Erin glanced again toward Maeve, then put away her clippings, including the new photo of a bullfighter jumping a whitish Brahma cross. She'd seen the same patchwork shirt and sunflower suspenders at the Reno rodeo and in other rodeo photos since; they were his costume. The caption read, "Bullfighter Abe Cockburn, making a comeback after a broken neck, jumps Big Ugly in Tuscon."

Erin knew about Abe's broken neck. She'd read about it the day before Maeve was born. Somehow, reading about Abe's solid legitimate excuse for standing her up in Twin Falls had made her feel better, had in fact given her permission to go into labor and finally have his baby, who was nine days late. A broken neck was the best excuse she'd ever heard for standing up a date.

Though he'd never bothered to get in touch, either. To explain.

It had left her in limbo, arguing with her mother about right and wrong. Jayne had felt that the existence of a child should supersede "petty grievances." As far as Erin was concerned, the man had shown he didn't care about the fate of his sperm by never trying to see her again.

But what happened to Jayne made her stop thinking about Abe and start thinking about Maeve and how a person with one parent could become a person with no parents.

Meanwhile, Abe had been barrelman for Cheyenne Frontier Days and was featured in *Prorodeo Sports News*. Although bullfighting had itself become a rodeo event— bullfighters spent from forty to seventy seconds in the ring with a fighting bull, smaller and more agile than the stock used for bull riding—Abe did not compete. "'I never wanted to be a competitor,' says Cockburn. 'I just like protecting cowboys—and making people laugh.'"

Erin tucked the photo into the manila envelope, then picked up the want ad. It was three months old; probably he didn't need to advertise much these days.

ABE COCKBURN, Clown, barrelman, bullfighter. Unforgettable acts. Excellent cowboy protection. Loved by children and dogs.

Then came his phone number and address. Guy Loren Rodeo Company, 10598 Skyway, Alta, CO. Guy Loren was a former National Finals Rodeo champion calf roper and bulldogger, and as a stock contractor he was still a big deal in rodeo.

In July Erin had called for a brochure from the Kay Ranch, also on Skyway in Alta.

And now...

I'm going there.

She closed the envelope. It belonged upstairs. Maeve was trying to put a plastic ring around a cone on a rocking base. The toy had been Erin's when she was a baby; Jayne had saved everything.

Erin scooped up the baby, and Maeve whimpered, reaching out with her ring. But Erin could not go upstairs and leave her daughter downstairs in this house. Balancing Maeve on her hip, Erin took the manila envelope to the second floor, switching on lights, glancing around corners, jumping at the jingling of dog tags as Taffy emerged from her mother's room. Taffy liked to sleep on the bed, as though waiting for Jayne to return.

"Mama," said Maeve, rubbing her eyes and putting a baby hand on Erin's nearest breast. With Maeve crying in her arms, Erin made another trip up and down the stairs, double-checking locks, peering behind coats in the closets, looking for shoes beneath the drapes. At last she carried the baby into her bedroom, to the bed where Maeve had been conceived.

Erin turned on the desk lamp each night to sleep and turned it off in the morning when she awoke. Nursing Maeve to sleep in its glow, Erin studied a faded color snapshot turned toward her in its plastic gilt frame. Behind the glass, everything was faintly green. Her father's skin and his uniform and the washed-out hills behind him. Erin understood the details. A silver bar meant lieutenant. The weapon was an M-16.

There were no Herefords in Vietnam.

Had he forgotten his wife was pregnant when she left him? Once, Erin had asked her mother, *If he wanted to find me, could he?*

Oh, yes. He knows right where you are.

It would have been better, Erin thought, if he'd never known. And maybe it would be better for Maeve if Abe didn't.

But Jayne had stood up for Abe.

Erin, you shouldn't judge Maeve's father by your own. You don't know your father, and you barely know this rodeo clown. You must tell him about his daughter. It's right and it's fair.

Fair. She'd never told Jayne about the pencil holder. It would have troubled her, which Erin had known even at eight years old.

Maeve stopped nursing; her eyes had long since shut and

now she slept. Erin rolled her onto her stomach and covered her with a blanket. A crib was too faraway in the night, in this house.

She recalled her mother holding Maeve in the rocking chair downstairs, playing peekaboo with her. Night was here, and Erin greeted again the foremost uncertainty of life, which was the certainty of death.

IN THE KAYS' BARN, the heifer was wheezing and Chaley was crying. "Dammit, Abe, what are you doing? I've listened to your bitterness—"

"I'm not bitter."

"—and your anger for more than ten years. My dad wants you here, and what are you doing?"

Why answer? He was going to a rodeo—weekend after next. Chaley knew that, just as Abe knew what her father was offering. He'd been a rancher's son himself, and there was nothing finer than knowing the land was his, that he would marry a staying woman and raise children who would love the land and feed cattle from it. Chaley had recovered his stolen dreams and returned them to him.

But they were worn-out, changed like he was.

The diamond on her hand gave off a guilty gleam, and Abe stroked Martha, who offered a cold wet nose and serious competition for the role of main female in his life. "Want to see my new act?" He got to his feet and hunted for a prop. His art was turning tears to laughter.

But Chaley laughed slow and sniped quick. She whipped back her blond braid. She was a lanky woman with strong hands, and could clear ditches and handle livestock. She spoke plain. "Your act is a disappearing act, and I don't like it. I need a husband I can count on, a man who'll help look after cows and mend fences and care about this ranch. This past year, I've thought it could be you. But you won't even quit Loren's place—"

"He and I have worked together a long time, Chaley."

"But you're *marrying* me, and you belong on *this* ranch. Anyone could understand that. Besides, your dad's here, and he's an old man."

"He's not that old."

"Seventy-two?"

"He looks great."

"He forgot to close a gate yesterday."

Abe swallowed. That was serious.

"Six cows got out onto the highway."

"Maybe someone else left the gate open."

Chaley didn't dignify that with a response. Except, "He needs you. And *you* need a twelve-step program. You've got a problem, and it's called rodeo."

Abe didn't appreciate her point of view, but all he said was, "Stop now, before I command Martha to lick you to death."

She didn't smile. "Someone else would save those bull riders if you weren't there. It costs money to drive all over the country and stay in hotels."

"Sometimes I sleep in my truck. Anyhow, I break even." He loved bullfighting, loved making people laugh, loved how the kids stared up at him when he walked past the stands because he was the bullfighter, the man who put his body between the bull and a fallen cowboy. Most of all, he loved hearing their laughter the way he loved water in the ditches in August; he loved hearing some small voice say, *Look at the clown, Mommy! He's so funny.*

Chaley filled a syringe with antibiotic and injected the heifer. Her eyes were tender. She cared about animals, all animals, and Abe admired her. Chaley's mother had died when she was seventeen, and Chaley had done a good job of going on.

"I hate rodeos," she said. "I can't stand all those buckle bunnies and barrel racers and dime-store cowboys. It's just a big pickup scene. It's as phony as the I'm Okay, You're Okay Corral."

He couldn't take that comparison. Rodeo was nothing like the new dance hall near Alta called the Okay Corral, where rich people from cities tried ranch dressing and line dancing and called themselves cowboys.

Abe stood up. "I've got to get back and check on Missy." One of Loren's mares was due to drop a champion bucking bronc into the world.

Chaley glowered.

Abe said, "Martha. Attack."

The Australian shepherd wagged her tail and slurped a kiss across Chaley's face, teasing a smile to the corners of her mouth. The kiss that followed—Abe's—fixed it there.

CHALEY'S PROBLEMS simmered on the back burner most of the next week. At Loren's place, they were calving and foaling, and Abe had his hands full with sharp-horned Mexican cows and Brahmas who thought cowboys were for hurting. The pleasure was horses. Besides broncs and bulls, the stock contractor was assembling some good roping horses. And work for Guy Loren had no uncomfortable strings attached.

The strings dangling from Kip Kay's standing job offer weren't something Abe spent time noticing, though he kept tripping on them as a result. He just wanted to do what he was doing and leave it at that and not think very hard about the June evening he and Chaley had ended up engaged.

Early Saturday, as he crossed Guy Loren's snowy yard

after pulling a calf, the phone rang in the disabled fifth wheel he and Martha shared. Abe sprinted for the door and blew in with the snow. The clock on the stove read four-thirty.

His dad...

Shivering from the sweat that had cooled on his body, he snatched up the receiver. "Hello?"

Martha came down from the sleeping area, wagging her tail, and Abe stroked her ears, let her sniff and lick at him.

"Abe, it's Chaley. We have a problem."

His heart wouldn't slow down. He waited for her to tell him something had happened to Lloyd.

"That woman's supposed to come today, and the Snowcat won't start. There's three feet of new snow on the road, and we can't get the trucks out, and nobody but Lucky showed up today. We're up to our necks in calves, and every single one of them needs warming up. It's too damned cold."

"I know." He and Guy and Terry, Guy's wife, and Pedro, their other hand, had been up all night. Kip Kay had more stock and, at the moment, no more hands. Abe didn't mention that he was covered in blood and manure and ready to drop in his tracks. A shower and a cup of coffee would fix him. "I'll ask Guy if I can go. Where'd you say she's coming in?"

Chaley gave him the flight information. "Her name's Erin O'Neill, and she's coming from Reno. No, wait, the flight's from Salt Lake."

Erin from Reno. Erin from Reno.

"Erin who?" He tried not to sound very interested.

"O'Neill. Do you need it *spelled?*"

From the indoor-outdoor carpet, Martha watched him with eyes far more patient and loving than the voice on the phone. "I got it," he said. Erin O'Neill.

Different Erin from Reno.

A few minutes later, stooping down to kiss and hug his best girl, Abe realized he was disappointed.

And what a bad sign that was for him and Chaley.

There were a lot of bad signs.

IT WAS SNOWING in Grand Junction five hours later, and through the terminal window, Abe watched passengers leave the plane and descend onto the tarmac. He saw no woman with a baby. Maybe she wouldn't show up....

That might not be a bad thing. What if the Kays' guest didn't appreciate the unconditional affection of the most beautiful and intelligent dog in the world? Well, Martha might have to ride in the back. That was what the camper shell was for, protecting his dog from the elements.

Oh, damn. A car seat. The baby would need a car seat.

We'll have to go buy one.

If she showed up.

As he began to plan what he'd do if Erin O'Neill didn't get off the plane, he saw her. She carried the baby in one arm and a bulging black tote in the other. She had dude written all over her, from Stetson to ropers, and looked like she might catch a toe on the hem of her duster. Abe hoped she wouldn't slip on the snowy tarmac lugging all that gear—and the baby.

The arrivals poured in through the glass door of the terminal, and around him people greeted loved ones. Then she passed through the gate with the baby, and he saw her face.

Erin.

Erin Mackenzie.

No, O'Neill.

And she was holding a baby, a baby with curly light red

hair and a floppy denim hat with a flower in it and brown eyes like two holes in her face, just like her mother's.

She had a baby.

Then Abe understood, the way a man understands he's been shot.

She had married someone and had a baby.

When she saw Abe, she blanched.

Of course.

Married now, she wouldn't want to be reminded of their one-night stand.

In fact, *he* should hurry up and forget it.

There was really only one thing to do, which was to set her at ease. Make her see that no word or reminder of the night they'd spent together would pass his lips. The incident would never be mentioned. Abe would conduct himself as though it hadn't happened. As though they'd never met before. It was the decent solution.

"You must be Erin," he said. "I'm Abe. I came to drive you back to the Kay ranch."

"Maeve asked MacRoth if he knew where she might acquire a bull finer than Ailill's. MacRoth told her of a magical bull, the Donn Cualigne, the Dark One of Cooley."

—The Cattle Raid of Cooley,
   Ancient Irish oral tradition, first
   recorded in the eighth century

3

ERIN DIDN'T NEED a Ph.D. in Cowboys to grasp the situation. It was Abe. He recognized her. He was pretending they'd never met.

He wants me to forget it. This is his way of saying it was just a one-night stand and it's over now. He has someone else.

Well, one night together almost two years before wasn't much on which to build a relationship. Only a candidate for the Dumped by Cowboys Hall of Fame would think it meant something.

Abe was acting like a stranger, and he seemed like one. His black hat and blanket-lined Carhartt made him look like a real cowboy. His eyelashes and mouth made him look like Maeve's father.

"Thank you for meeting me." Erin regrouped. "Do you work for the Kays?"

Abe explained, omitting Chaley. It seemed insulting to Erin to mention his engagement. Why should she care about his love life?

"But how will I get out to the ranch if they're snowed in?"

"My boss will take his Snowcat up and clear their road." Neighboring ranchers did things like that for each other, like driving home your cows if they got out. Guy Loren had bought his spread just fifteen years earlier with rodeo winnings, but from growing up on a ranch in Oklahoma he knew how things were done; he'd earned the respect and friendship of longtime local cattlemen like his father, Lloyd, and Kip Kay.

"Can I get that?" Indicating Erin's tote bag, Abe stole a glance at the baby. He'd met eyes like those in bed one June night. It took time to get the situation straight in his mind. Erin had been looking at some other man when this child was made.

"Did you check anything?" he asked.

"Yes. One bag."

"Let's get it."

With Maeve on her hip, Erin matched his strides through the airport and couldn't match his grace. The baby began to fret.

A baby, thought Abe. He couldn't get it out of his head that she'd had a baby with someone—so suddenly. But it was a while since he'd driven down the road singing along with Ian Tyson's "Old Corrals and Sagebrush" and thinking of laying his own eyes on Erin from Reno. Usually he sang to Martha, who thought all his songs were for her.

Where was Erin's husband, anyway?

Pieces of nylon webbing hung from the tote bag Abe carried, with toys for the baby tied on. He stopped while Erin untied a rubber pretzel. The baby put it in her mouth, then flung it on the ground and began to cry.

"Oh, sweetheart." Carefully holding the child, Erin stooped to pick up the pretzel.

Abe got it first. It was slobbery, like Martha's toys after they'd been in her mouth. Handing it to Erin, he tried to see her wedding ring.

She wore none.

The baby fussed as an escalator lowered them to the baggage-claim area. The luggage was already on a carousel.

"Do you see yours?"

"The blue duffel bag with black straps."

When Abe turned with the bag, he found her sitting in a corner. She opened her duster, pushed up her flannel shirt and gave the baby her breast. Abe almost tripped. He had grown up around cows suckling their calves. He'd tied the hides of stillborn calves to the bodies of orphaned calves, to trick the mothers of the dead calves into accepting the others as their own.

He remembered his own mouth on this woman's breasts.

He stared too long. At the curve of the baby's cheek around that denim hat as she suckled from a breast he couldn't see. At Erin. As she watched the face hidden from Abe, her expression was loving and sad.

Maybe her husband was dead.

When Abe brought the duffel bag, Erin murmured, "Thanks." She took a bottle of springwater from her tote and loosened the cap. Holding one of the baby's hands in one of hers, she drank.

Abe sat and studied the people milling about near the carousel. "It took five hours to get here from Alta this morning. I'll get you back there soon as I can, but the roads are bad."

Erin remembered his voice. What did Abe remember? The house in Reno? The woman he'd met on the way out at dawn?

This journey, Erin told herself, *is not a betrayal of Jayne.*

Jayne had wanted her to tell Abe.

The Kay Ranch was the problem.

"Also," Abe said, "I didn't think to round up a car seat for your baby. So we'll go buy one." He was solvent this week, had finally saved enough for a new saddle. Keith Springs in Gunnison was making it, and Abe had already paid half down.

"Oh. Thanks." Absently Erin switched Maeve to the other breast. The baby was limp, eyes shut, and Erin wished she'd changed her before nursing. Maeve shouldn't sit in a wet diaper for the car ride. To the Kay Ranch.

It's for Maeve, Mom. Everything I'm doing is for Maeve.

It was like telling her mother that she hadn't even *liked* Abe Cockburn, that she didn't *want* to see him again.

If Jayne were alive, she wouldn't believe this, either.

SHE HAD TO CHANGE the baby, so Abe went to get the truck. A half-inch of snow candy-coated the red Dodge pickup he'd bought used from an NFR bull rider. Martha stood guard in the driver's seat, and her tail whipped back and forth when she saw him.

"Hi, Martha. Did you miss me?" They exchanged kisses, and he rubbed her mottled blue-gray-and-black coat, stroked the red patches near her face. Martha was the only light in this day.

It wasn't that he hadn't wanted to see Erin again. He'd often thought of Twin Falls, the rendezvous he'd missed.

Maybe he should explain about that.

No. She's Mrs. O'Neill. You're engaged to Chaley.

And this was not a good day.

He thrust Ian Tyson's *Cowboyography* into the tape deck while he warmed up the engine. Whistling to "Summer Wages," he drove around to the arrivals area. She wasn't out front, and he double-checked the airline sign and

calculated how long it should take to change a baby.
Letting the truck idle, he sang four songs to Martha and
thought about Erin till he wondered what was keeping her.
He turned off the engine. "Stay, Martha. Good girl."

As he left the truck, Erin emerged from the terminal with
the baby and the tote bag. In her hat and duster, she
reminded him of a kid dressed up for make-believe.

When he took her tote bag, she slipped—maybe those
new boots. Abe caught her arm. "Okay?"

She nodded, holding her baby tighter.

"Erin..." Oh, shit. He'd thought about her a lot. This was
payment.

Her darker-than-earth eyes gazed at him.

"We'll go to Target," he tried at last, "and get a car seat.
Can you hold her in your lap across town?"

"Sure."

Abe unlocked the passenger door for her, and Martha
leaned forward to sniff the newcomers.

"Hi, Martha," Erin said.

No other words could have made Abe more interested in
why she didn't wear a wedding ring.

The baby said, "Da-dee."

"Yes, it's a doggy," Erin agreed.

"I'll put her in the back. Martha, come."

The dog jumped down and sniffed Erin's duster and her
boots. While Erin climbed into the passenger seat with her
sleepy baby, Abe called Martha around back, let her in the
camper shell and told her to stay off the bed.

When he got behind the wheel and started the engine,
Ian Tyson's voice filled the cab, singing about his own
heart's delight. Abe turned down the stereo. The baby
dozed in Erin's arms, dreaming in Hatland. All babies
should have hats like that. Red curls like that. "This okay?"

"It's fine."

He pulled away from the curb and joined the light traffic. Slowing at the parking kiosk, Abe eyed the baby again. "She's still suckling." Air. In her sleep.

"I think that's what she dreams about."

It was extremely difficult not to comment. Abe concentrated on digging quarters out of the drink well behind the stick shift. He waited in line, paid the attendant and thanked him, then drove out onto the road.

Silently Erin watched the landscape. Buttes stretched along the horizon, not unlike Nevada, but at their feet were countless adobe mounds, and the angle of the sun made them look like tents. This was a land of big sky, too, but no casinos, and she looked carefully, thinking about safe neighborhoods. Erin had never wanted any kind of neighborhood, had never liked the way she'd grown up. So she'd played make-believe in a real past she hadn't lived. With history books, she tried to close a hole that could only be filled by impossible childhood dreams.

Life on a ranch and a horse of her own. A cowboy father on-site.

"Is Alta like this?" Hotels and restaurants lined the four-lane thoroughfare.

"Not much. You're going to the prettiest place on earth." Belatedly Abe realized he was picturing *his* childhood home, not the Kays' place. He was picturing the land that used to be. Now expensive lodge-pole rails replaced his family's barbed wire, making the new owner the ridicule of every subsistence rancher for miles. Jack Draw called it the Soaring Eagle Ranch, his way of making sense of Charlie Cockburn's hundred-year-old triangle-E brand, chosen in honor of his wife, Elizabeth.

Busy had been named for that same Elizabeth.

Abe blotted out thoughts of that land, of chasing calves for his dad, of summers at cow camp. Chaley and the Kay

Ranch were no refuge, just wear and tear on his honor and his pride. He thought of bullfighting, instead.

Of saving cowboys, the noblest work left to him.

"How much does she weigh?" Abe read tags hanging from the display car seats.

"I don't know. She's healthy, so I don't take her to the doctor much. She's just gotten her immunizations, nothing else." *You're probably wondering why I'm telling you all this. And, Abe, if you're getting a funny tingling in your veins about standing in the aisles of Target picking out a car seat with me and this baby, well, I could explain it.*

She *was* going to explain it.

Just not yet.

Maeve's head turned to follow the progress of a woman passing with a shopping cart. Another baby sat in the cart.

"Let me guess." Maeve's weight. Abe reached for the baby. For his daughter.

Erin let him take her. A scar on one of his knuckles mesmerized her. His hands were as confident with new life as with cranky bulls and needy women. Strong and gentle and...indifferent. No, indifferent wasn't right.

Abe smelled baby shampoo and baby skin. The small warm body in his hands brought memories. Childhood memories of holding Lane. An earlier recollection of when his mother had let him hold Busy, the new baby. He must have been just four.

Erin's daughter stared right into his eyes. God, her eyes were her mother's. But those dimples...

"Those are some dimples. What's your name?"

"Maeve." Erin saw other dimples—his. "M-a-e-v-e." Again she overexplained. "Maeve is the central character in the oldest recorded legend in Irish history, *The Cattle Raid of Cooley*. She was a queen and a warrior and some say a goddess. She led her men into war to steal a magical bull so that her possessions would equal those of her consort."

"A rustler. I see." Abe tickled Maeve's tummy through her purple sweatshirt. She giggled at him.

You're a heartbreaker, aren't you? Must run in the family. Abe gave Maeve back to her mother. "Twenty pounds? Not twenty-five, anyhow." Exploring the boxes, he asked, "How old is she?"

"She'll be a year old Tuesday." Erin hoped math wasn't his strong subject.

"That's my little brother's birthday." And that day would be the last they saw of Lane. All but Abe. He and Lane would meet from time to time at rodeos.

Eighteenth birthday.

First birthdays were a big deal, too. He had rodeo friends with kids, and usually a first birthday was a three-ring circus, complete with video cameras. *Will your husband be joining you?* he wanted to ask Erin. *And what about your mom?* Surely that mom who'd kept Erin's room for her while she was in college was in love with her grandchild. *That's how grandparents are.* His dad would be tickled pink if he and Chaley...

His father's mortality invaded the Target store, followed by the unsettling thought of himself and Chaley having children.

"First birthday. Wow." He picked a car seat off the shelf. "Let's go."

In the checkout line, when he dug out his wallet, Erin said, "You'll get the ranch to reimburse you?"

He nodded, and their eyes locked. Counting cash for the car seat gave him something else to look at. He remembered to get a receipt for Kip.

But did you ask your future father-in-law to reimburse you?

Or did you acknowledge that one day his place would be yours anyhow, that you were all in it together?

Maeve blew a big raspberry and beamed, and the tug on Abe's heart separated today from yesterday, the way losing the ranch had divided his life into before and after.

He didn't want to think why.

THEY HEADED SOUTH on Highway 50 into the storm. Raw desert bordered each side of the road. To the east, toward the Rockies, snow spread like powdered sugar sprinkled over rolling adobe foothills. It was land without vegetation but with an alien beauty. Anyone could see it would yield no crops; still, this place that the pioneers would have shunned seemed desirable at a time when other people grew the food, when City Market was ten miles north. To the west, the rock became swirling humps of reddish sandstone carving out canyons that fell from sight.

"When it's clear," said Abe, "you drive south on this road and you can see the San Juans. They're the most rugged mountains in Colorado."

Near Montrose, more than an hour and a half after they'd left the airport, the storm let up but clouds still hid the mountains. And as they wound east toward Gunnison, up into foothills and snow-covered rangeland, the weather worsened again. Snowfall faded the sagebrush and junipers and the gullies full of bare-limbed trees. Rock outcroppings jutted from the land and were suddenly mountains. The deserted stock pens, isolated gas stations and empty campgrounds were civilization. Maeve woke up tearful and whiny, and Erin fed her applesauce while Abe crossed a bridge over a vast reservoir where steam grew up from the water like grass.

"Need me to stop?" he asked.

"Not unless I'm distracting you."

She was, but he worked at ignoring her and driving. Why had she brought a baby to the Kay Ranch in March? Kip Kay never even promoted his guest business, banking on word of mouth. "You know the Kays?"

"Uh...no."

Maeve gave up eating and turned full-time to complaining. Erin could still remember what it was like to hear a baby cry before she'd had one. It could make you leave a restaurant.

There was no leaving the pickup, and Abe might have been deaf. Except that he sang to Maeve, replacing the music he'd turned off miles before.

I ride an old paint and I lead an old dam,
I'm going to Montana for to throw the houlihan...

Erin rearranged Maeve in the car seat. The baby burped, then quieted, looking about to find the source of the voice.

Git along, you little dogies, git along there slow,
For the fiery and the snuffy are a-rarin' to go...

When he was done, Erin said, "I wrote a paper on the history of cowboy music."

Abe quit pretending they'd never met. "Did you ever get your master's?"

"Doctorate. Yes."

"When did you get married?"

The driver could feel a passenger staring.

"I'm not married."

She must have been, though. Remembering he was engaged to Chaley made Abe stop asking questions. He began counting the miles to Alta.

Erin confronted the problems of her alias. He'd thought

she was married. Leaving other men's wives alone was a good trait.

Beside her, Abe checked out fences and stock. "Look."

A bald eagle perched on a cottonwood limb. Erin had never known birds came so large.

"They like it by the reservoir and along the rivers in winter. In summer they head for the high country."

His nearer boot eased on the gas pedal as he slowed for a curve. The back hems of his jeans had faded in ragged half-moons from dragging on the ground against his boot heels. Cowboys wore their pants long so the legs wouldn't hitch up when they were in the saddle. Erin thought about the seat of his Wranglers and how the denim would stretch over his thighs when he rode. She thought about sex in Reno.

It took a while to get smart and ask, "So, you know Mr. Kay?"

"All my life. My daddy's his foreman."

Erin's throat dried up. She'd brought Abe home that June night because he was from Alta; she'd never known Alta was such a small world. It was a prairie-dog colony. Like a military leader gathering intelligence, she asked, "Are they a big family? The Kays?"

"No."

He didn't elaborate. Erin didn't ask. White flakes flew at the window, with a polka-dot field beyond. They hid the world the way other things she couldn't change had hidden what she wanted to know, and they were unfriendly, the way cold is.

"YOU NEED ANYTHING here?" Abe asked in Gunnison. He'd lived on the Kays' ranch, and he knew their guest business. "You'll be staying in a cabin with a refrigerator and a microwave. They serve meals three times a day in the big house, but if you need anything special... Diapers?"

"Thanks. Let's stop." At home Erin used cotton diapers and laundered them herself, but she'd bought disposables for this trip. Still, she could pick up some of Maeve's favorite foods.

He parked in the City Market lot, and inside, when Erin began to buckle Maeve into the cart, the recollection of the baby's soft body, like a sack of warmth, like the best of new animals, made him ask, "Want me to hold her?"

"Oh. Okay. Thanks."

Abe lifted the baby again, smelling her scent and remembering Busy and the lives that had changed when she died.

He and Erin explored the aisles, and people smiled at the young couple with the baby. Hiding beneath her hat brim, Erin chose soy milk and applesauce and bananas for Maeve and tampons for herself.

The cowboy ignored her selections and played with Maeve. He used her hat to cover her eyes, then let her see him again.

In the register line, a white-haired woman behind them fell for Maeve. "She's darling," she told Abe. "You have a beautiful family."

"Thanks." He didn't look at Erin. It was time to get this baby out of his arms.

But her little hands were touching his neck and the collar of his coat, and Abe wasn't eager to let her go. The tabloids and chewing gum and candy grew hazy. Maeve would be a year old on Tuesday.

Abe's mind was a rodeo calendar, and while Erin paid for her groceries, he reviewed the date of the Reno Rodeo. He was used to figuring gestation periods. Cows went 280 days, more or less. So did humans.

He did the math, anyway. Three times, three different ways, his heart pounding harder every minute.

THERE WAS a traffic accident at the main intersection in town. Abe was so preoccupied that seconds passed before he recognized the one-ton blue truck and the cowboy finger-pointing at the driver of a crunched Range Rover. The pickup had won this round. Sort of.

Oh, shit, Dad.

Abe nabbed a parking space outside a furniture store.

"What is it?"

"Please excuse the delay." He got out.

A cop was trying to calm Lloyd, and Abe welcomed a few minutes of not having to think about suddenly having a daughter.

She is. You know she's yours.

We used condoms.

Yeah, but remember the second time, Abe, when you were both just waking up? You actually thought it would be really great if you didn't have to use one, so you tried it out that way.

It *was* great.

And now he had a redheaded baby named for a cattle-taking Irish queen.

"He was driving too fast," Lloyd told the policeman as Abe approached. "Couldn't even see him coming. Going like a bullet."

"Takes a sharpshooter to hit a speeding bullet." The driver of the Range Rover wore a long duster, but you could still see those snakeskin boots. Especially with his jeans tucked inside.

The street was icy, snow coming down again.

Abe thought about Maeve's hands.

"Abe, did you see it?" demanded Lloyd. "I had the right of way. That light was still yellow—"

"Red," said the Ranger Rover's driver.

"Let's get out of the street," the police officer suggested, "and let the tow trucks move these vehicles."

"Mine still runs," said Lloyd. "I'm not paying a towing fee." But the crushed wheel well spoke for itself. The truck might run, but it wouldn't go.

Abe stuffed his hands in his pockets and recalled being inside Erin without a condom.

Come with me, Dad. I'll introduce you to your first grandchild.

Grumbling, Lloyd stalked to the curb and produced his driver's license.

"We'll need the vehicle registration and proof of insurance, too."

As Lloyd started for the truck, he ordered Abe, "You wait. You can drive me to the parts store and back to the ranch."

When his father returned and gave the papers to the cop, Abe explained, "I've got Kip's new guest and her baby in the truck."

"What guest? We're calving."

"Chaley called this morning and asked me to meet the lady at the airport." Outside a store across the street, an OPEN banner flapped in the snow-wet wind. Abe huddled in his coat, trying to close the gap between his turned-up collar and the brim of his hat.

"Well, she can come along," Lloyd muttered.

"The seat's all taken up. Look, you'll be busy here for a while. I'll run her up to the ranch, come back and get you."

"Waste of gasoline."

"According to this, your insurance has lapsed," said the cop.

Abe and Lloyd looked up.

"What?" Lloyd examined the card. "I must have another in the truck."

"Where will you be?" Abe asked. Lloyd's insurance would be current. His father never forgot bills, and he paid cash for everything. Same went for Abe. It was the family habit of people whose overextended credit had cost them the ranch.

"Stockman's." The Stockman's Grill was the only place in town Lloyd still ate. He believed a cup of coffee shouldn't cost more than fifty cents and shook his head at the espresso shops springing up all over Gunnison. What was the point? If you wanted high octane, put in more grounds.

"See you in a while," Abe said.

"WHAT WAS THAT ABOUT?" asked Erin when he returned.

"My dad had a fender bender."

He fastened his seat belt and started the truck. He looked like he wished the day was over, and Erin let him have his silence as they headed out of town.

North of Gunnison, the road met mountains. Snow smothered the meadows. Aspens wearing just the gold twigs of winter surrounded a log cabin. Everything was frosted and irresistible, the way Christmas should look, until she saw the deer someone had hit lying stiff on the side of the road.

A sign said Alta was fifteen miles away.

That was where she would learn the truth about cowboys, and if she looked at it that way, she would be all right. She tracked the slushy marks left by the Isuzu Trooper in front of them. There were skis on the roof. Skiers shared places like this with cowboys, but the two did not meet. Erin understood the first group; the second was a closed order.

"There's Guy Loren's place," said Abe. "See that brindle

with the big hump? That's Ah'll Gore, 1993 Bucking Bull of the Year."

Erin studied the meadows fenced with barbed wire, the Corriente rodeo steers eating hay, a tractor pulling a sled loaded with bales. This was where Abe worked.

The miles held homestead cabins with fallen roofs, trailers in empty country and the occasional rich man's castle. The snow was everywhere, dangerous, and chimney smoke meant safety.

To the east, evenly spaced pine rails bordered a ranch where cows stood in the snow. A massive stockade gate, like something out of "Bonanza," declared Soaring Eagle Ranch.

A hitch in his throat, Abe recited the sight-seeing information. "That's Jack Draw's ranch."

The television actor was the star of "Rodeo," cowboy culture's answer to "Northern Exposure." His name was a household word. "It's beautiful," said Erin. "Oh, look, he's got those shaggy Highland cows. They're so cute."

The silly-looking Scotch Highlanders were only one of the exotic breeds in the actor's herd. What was wrong with Herefords, anyhow? Abe didn't look—at the cows or the glossy cabins Draw had built for his hands. Draw's own home was over a rise, out of view of the highway, close to the national-forest border.

Abe knew his own privation.

He had a child. And no land and no cows.

"How big is it?"

Draw's ranch. The question felt more personal than it was. When he got over being taken aback, Abe said, "Fifteen thousand acres."

Beside him, a tiny hand touched the sleeve of the dirty Carhartt he'd shrugged off. The coat had fallen across Maeve's little legs in her turquoise pants. *Oh, baby.*

He downshifted and switched on his left turn signal. Chaley was coming across the Kays' pasture with the teams and the sleigh, and Lane and Kip were with her, feeding hay to the cows who fell in behind. Everyone's breath was white.

The simple wooden sign over the swing gate read Kay Ranch. Erin offered, "I'll get the gate."

"Thanks."

She opened the door, and the cold made her want to shut it again. Instead, she stepped down onto the crunchy snow. While the truck blew steam, the icy latch burned her fingers. Pulling her duster sleeves over them, she swung open the gate and held it as he drove through. *I never knew there were places this cold.* Securing the gate was another arctic ordeal; then she was back in the cab, cold-shocked.

The team and sleigh loaded with hay grew larger, raising clouds like Maeve's chariot on the road to Ulster.

"Let's stop and speak to these folks," said Abe.

A figure waded through the white. When he'd almost reached the truck, Erin rolled down her window, letting in the frigid air. The lean-faced rancher removed a leather work glove and held out his hand.

"Kip Kay. You must be Erin."

Her throat felt like there were cracks in it.

He stared at her face, no reaction on his. "Mears Cabin is ready for you and your child. You'll find the key inside on the table." He glanced at the baby as he said, "Thanks for your trouble, Abe."

"Glad to do it. I'll take her up to the cabin. Dad had a wreck in town. He's okay, but the truck's not."

"That right?"

Erin counted smells on Kip Kay's barn coat—hay and manure and the hair of livestock—as he rested an arm on her open window. Under his hat, his earmuffs were faded gray, the pile worn away in patches. She knew his face.

"Well," the rancher said, "Beulah Ann's gone up to the big house to get supper on. Join us, Abe?"

"I'm going to get Dad. He said something about the parts store."

"The Snowcat. Well, you'll be hungry when you get back. Dinner's at one."

Abe studied the dash.

The pause stretched.

Never noticing, Erin breathed the rancher's nearness. Lived the moment he was close enough to touch. "Could I help Beulah Ann in the kitchen?"

Kip Kay started and stepped backward. "If you like." With a nod that encompassed Erin, Abe and the baby, he turned, and his Wellingtons and the legs of his insulated coveralls disappeared as he trudged back through the thigh-deep snow to the sleigh.

A real cowboy.

The truck idled, pouring smoke and steam into the freezing air. Erin rolled up her window.

"Erin."

Across the cab, Abe's black hat shadowed his eyes, half his face.

"What?" Erin saw he was holding one of Maeve's little hands in one of his, while Maeve gazed at the dash. Why was he doing that?

"Is this my child?"

> *"My books are the brooks, my sermons the stones,*
> *My parson's the wolf on his big pile of bones,*
> *My books teach me ever consistence to prize,*
> *My sermons, that small things I should not despise."*
>
> —"The Cowboy,"
> Nineteenth-century western
> folk ballad

4

IS THIS MY CHILD?

Student teaching had taught her to think on her feet. Being Dumped by Cowboys had taught her to think in the cab of his red pickup. "That's why I came to Colorado. To tell you."

"Glad you got around to it." Abe let go of the soft tiny hand with its miniature fingers and grabbed the stick shift.

He had reason to be mad, and her ifs, ands and buts would sound pretty lame. *If you'd just called after Twin Falls. And showed you cared....* "How did you guess?"

"It makes sense." Of something that made no sense otherwise. In March, people came to Alta to ski.

Guiding the truck over the freshly plowed road, Abe tried to plan. His father had wrecked the pickup. Kip Kay wanted him to join the family for dinner. And Chaley had suddenly become more than an object of doubt to be dealt with at leisure. "I have to tell you," he said, with the uncomfortable suspicion that he wasn't being clever with words. "I'm engaged."

It should not have meant *anything*.

Erin told herself it didn't as Abe drove on, taking her deeper into the snow-swathed mountain valley. "That's okay. I didn't come here to get you to marry me or anything like that." *I didn't. I really didn't.*

"It would have been natural if you had."

His honesty made her eyes burn. Who had caught this cowboy and how?

Just when she thought the white road would never end, she spotted buildings and livestock. In the corral, horses shook their manes and blew pale steam against the black trees. Cows—Herefords, Angus and black baldies—huddled in distant pastures. Barns, sheds, a four-square house made of fieldstone, a long pale green trailer and a couple of cabins broke up the white wilderness of the mountain winter.

Abe veered right with the corral. Far past the barn, smoke puffed from a cabin chimney. He parked under the fir trees, released his seat belt and unfastened the harness protecting Maeve.

Nervously Erin watched him lift their daughter from her car seat.

Holding Maeve, Abe raised the brim of her hat to see her face. He cradled her closer, then hugged her against his left shoulder. He felt his own heart and his daughter's little body, and he wanted to ask Erin, *You're sure?*

But she was getting out. And he was sure. Maeve was his. Cold filled the cab as she gathered her tote bag and groceries. Leaving him with the baby, she shut the door and hiked up the shoveled path to the cabin.

Abe sat Maeve on the bottom of the steering wheel and looked at her eyelashes and nose and mouth and carrot-colored curls. He thought he saw family traits. God, she was pretty. She was so pretty.

Maeve peered about. "Mama?"

"Mama went inside. Let's go find her." Setting her in his lap, Abe shrugged on his coat. He used it to shield the baby from the cold as he opened the door. When he let Martha out of the back, Maeve said, "Da-dee."

With his free hand, Abe grabbed Erin's duffel bag, and he knew the why of that change-of-seasons feeling in Target. This mattered like the ranch, and the moment dividing before from after was right now.

THE CABIN WAS WARM, Erin found, thanks to the woodstove. The bedroom contained a maple crib and a metal-frame double bed. The kitchenette had a fridge, toaster and microwave. She put away groceries, welcoming the heat. Here, heat was safety. She could pretend the cold wasn't right outside, wasn't everywhere else in this place.

But Abe was engaged to someone else and the cold was coming in.

His boots thumped on the rough wood floor. He set down her duffel bag and gave her the baby.

His voice matched the dusky room and the tall dark shape he was. "What about you? Any guys around?"

"No." Why was he asking?

"I have to go get my dad in town. And then I have to go home. But I'll be back."

Cowboys who didn't care were all she knew, and she forgave Abe in advance and spun lies like wool. "You don't have to do anything. It doesn't matter. I just wanted you to know about her."

Had his solemn eyes ever been clown eyes, gazing at her in the Reno livestock arena like a dog hoping for a bone?

These eyes belonged to a man living in the promiseland
Willie Nelson had described.

"It matters." She smelled the earth smells of his coat, as
he repeated, "It matters."

Then he left.

Erin remained motionless, holding a new piece of the
puzzle that was the truth about cowboys. His promise to
return hadn't set her at ease. The clown had been
transformed into a man. A man capable of being a father to
Maeve. Or of ignoring her, as Erin had been ignored.

Even of trying to take her from Erin.

Ultimately, of getting his way.

You're so stubborn, Erin, Jayne always said. *You don't think
things through; you just charge, and no one can stop you.*

This was where her latest charge had brought her. The
logs snapping in the stove spread the heat of burning
aspen. She pictured Kip Kay's face—a photo turned alive
and then aged to reality.

She'd come for the truth. If she found it, could she make
herself look?

Yes. When the black came, there would still be Willie
Nelson and Garth Brooks, believing in dreams.

She'd said she would help Beulah Ann, whoever that
was, prepare the midday meal. Erin washed in the cabin's
bathroom and changed Maeve's diaper and her clothes,
which had applesauce on them. She dressed the baby in an
outfit Jayne had bought—red pull-on pants, a white top
with leg-of-mutton sleeves and ruffly hems trimmed in red.
On the front was a soft silk screen of a red house, and the
outfit came with a matching floppy corduroy hat.

Oh, Mom, she looks so cute.

Erin had never cried easily, and she had never cried
about her mother. She couldn't, except without tears. And
it was a lifetime since she'd laughed.

She went outside, carrying Maeve. Sparkling snow heaped the meadows and hills and the cragged peaks of the Alta Range, but as before, the frost penetrated her clothes and bit her skin. Evergreen trees, their needles almost black, broke the white of the mountains. The hay stacked under a shelter and the livestock in the pastures filled out a scene that must have changed little in a hundred years.

A scene that must have looked identical a quarter century ago.

A past Erin hadn't witnessed.

She approached the two-story fieldstone house. Two dogs, a border collie and a blue heeler, watched from the barn but kept their distance. She climbed stairs to a red-painted deck, where plastic shrouded a barbecue grill and folded lawn furniture and snow topped the deck railings. Before she could knock, a female voice called, "Come on in!"

The door opened into a mudroom; jars of preserves crammed the shelves. Juggling Maeve, Erin yanked off her boots.

The voice belonged to a husky blonde in tight jeans and a Harley Davidson T-shirt. She shoved a casserole into the oven and straightened, pushing wispy hairs, ponytail runaways, back from her face. "Hi, there. I'm Beulah Ann Ellis. Wrangler, cook and bull rider. And who's this?"

"This is Maeve. I'm Erin."

"It's nice to meet you. Even up the gender odds around this place. You're here for a week? Tell me where you're from. Tell me if I'm being too nosy, but this is my social life, you know?"

The wrangler/cook/bull rider looked only about seventeen or eighteen, which made Erin wonder how she'd gotten a job on the ranch. *Could I get a job here?* "I'm from Reno."

"Well, I'm from Baton Rouge. That Garth Brooks song 'Callin' Baton Rouge,' I want you to know he wrote it for me. Can I hold your baby?"

Erin surrendered Maeve. "You know how to make friends."

"Not everyone would agree, speaking of which—" Beulah Ann thrust a finger of her free hand toward the back of her throat as a cowboy about her own age tromped up the porch steps.

The window gave a good view. "I don't see anything to make you throw up."

"Just wait till he opens his mouth." As the temperature dropped with a frigid draft, Beulah Ann yelled, "Shut the door!"

"Yeah, yeah, maybe I'll just stay outside and *freeze*." The door shut and the draft stopped.

"You're so cute," Beulah Ann told Maeve.

The cowboy entered the kitchen and paused dramatically when he saw Erin.

"Meet the reincarnation of Lane Frost, Mr. Lane *Cock*-burn," introduced Beulah Ann. "He was too nice in his last life, so no one gave him a heart this time. Kind of like the Tin Woodsman? Lane, this is Erin. And this is Maeve, and she's too sweet to talk to you. You don't appreciate people who are plump and cute."

Erin kept her face straight, the way she had when a student asked if sex could improve his grade. Lane *Cock*-burn must be Abe's little brother. The fair skin was different, but Erin knew that mouth.

He glanced nervously at the baby and began sniffing around the kitchen in his sheepskin-lined denim jacket and the hat he hadn't taken off. "When do we eat? Boss has a calf he wants you to pull, Beulah Ann. You being such a big girl and all, he could sure use your help."

"No, thank *you*. I am not sticking my arm up inside some cow."

The place was crawling with Abe's relatives. *Maeve's* relatives. This was her uncle. Abe's dad was her grandfather. And Kip Kay—

Breathe, Erin. This is where you find the truth. "Can I help with dinner, Beulah Ann?"

"Well, you're so nice! Thank you, Erin. You want to make a salad?"

"Sure."

"Everything's in the big fridge in the pantry, except the dressing, which is in this one. Now, you just make yourself at home. Whenever you get hungry, help yourself to whatever you want to eat."

"Yeah, take a lesson from Beulah Ann."

"Shut up, loser. Erin, just make yourself at home."

A draft cooled the room again, the door banged shut, and a blond gazelle sailed inside. In sheepskin jacket, jeans, riding boots and a good beaver cowboy hat, she was all long legs and competence. She registered faces. "Where's Abe?"

Abe. Erin's heart turned hot and hurting, the Dumped by Cowboys way. *It's her.*

She saw Lane and Beulah Ann shrug and almost missed the glances they exchanged that no one else was supposed to see. The cowboy opened and closed the refrigerator, and Beulah Ann said, "Chaley, this is Erin, and this is Maeve. Look how cute she is. She has these little hands, don't you love them? God, I love babies."

"Pity no one'll ever have one with you," said Lane, his head in the refrigerator.

Chaley's heel shot up and struck his rear end.

"Ow!" The refrigerator door slammed.

"Why don't you get out with the cows, brat?" Chaley said. "Maybe one of them will have *you*."

"I don't think they will," Beulah Ann said frankly. "Him being so little and all."

Chaley tugged off her gloves, and Erin saw the diamond ring with its heirloom look.

Abe's fiancée was everything Erin herself could never be. And everything she wanted to be. Chaley was strawberry blond rather than true blond, with freckles and blue eyes and angular features. There was hay on her clothes, and her boots were worn. Who was she on the Kay Ranch?

The blue eyes swept over Erin and dismissed her— *Dudette, no threat.* "Abe brought you, didn't he?"

Chaley inspired attention and speedy answers. Erin explained about the traffic accident and the truck that wouldn't go.

"Is he coming back for dinner?"

"This meal," clarified Beulah, like a bright student helping a slower classmate.

"I don't think so," Erin said.

Chaley made a face, and Beulah and Lane exchanged another glance as the blonde snatched a cordless phone off the kitchen counter and went into the other room.

Whistling to himself, Lane moseyed toward the hallway to listen.

Beulah Ann handed Maeve to Erin. "I'll get back to you in a minute, Maeve. There's a fly I gotta kill." She plucked a flyswatter from a wall nail.

"Leave me alone, woman!" Lane darted for the mudroom. "Nice to meet you, Erin." The door slammed behind him.

Beulah Ann hung up the flyswatter. "I guess you've figured out he makes my knees weak."

That trait ran in the Cockburn family. Erin asked, "Where should I put Maeve?"

"I just mopped the floor. Here." Beulah Ann opened a cabinet and dragged out an old pot and a pie tin. Banging through a drawer, she found a deformed spatula, a wooden spoon and an egg beater. She piled them on the linoleum, and Erin sat the baby beside them.

"You can help cook, Maeve," said Beulah Ann. "Would you like that?"

Maeve crawled toward the egg beater.

Erin retrieved the vegetables from the pantry. On the floor, her daughter experimentally dipped the wooden spoon into the pot.

Chaley returned then. She eyed Maeve like a dog who wasn't allowed in the house. "Beulah Ann, if they pull up here in the truck, will you catch Abe and tell him I'm looking for him?"

"If I can."

"Thanks. Oh, see you later," she added to Erin, and went outside.

Beulah Ann ended the silence. "Chaley's nice. She's just in a mood. *Men.*" She squinted at Erin. "Guess it would be nosy to ask if you've got one in your life."

"I don't."

"Must be hard with a baby. How old is she?"

"She'll be one on Tuesday."

"That's Lane's birthday." Beulah Ann repeated what Erin had learned from Abe. "We should have a party. Lane's counting the hours. He'll be eighteen, and that boy would rather have his PRCA card than a million dollars. Wouldn't it be great to want something that uncomplicated?"

PRCA was the Professional Rodeo Cowboys Association. "What do you want that's complicated?"

"A different past. And a fast metabolism."

You couldn't ask a woman you'd just met what was wrong with her past. Or why she and Lane had exchanged those looks when Chaley asked about Abe. Erin helped herself to a cutting board. Outside the water-blotched window, Chaley ducked between the rails of the corral fence.

"Here's the knife you want," said Beulah Ann. "Thanks for doing this, Erin. You sure don't have to."

"Oh, I want to help out."

"Well, visiting a working ranch, you probably didn't think you'd be stuck in the kitchen."

Chaley caught an Appaloosa from the corral.

"I've ridden my whole life," said Beulah Ann, "but she's way better with horses. Of course, she grew up on them."

"Does she work here?"

"Oh, no. I mean, we all work. But she's Uncle Kip's daughter."

Erin's eyes saw the vegetables, but it was some time before she remembered what to do with them.

AS KIP KAY PUT UP the harness in the tack room, he searched the barn for chores so he could postpone facing the ranch's new guest.

Erin O'Neill.

Kip rejected the creeping intuition. This was just life playing a trick, by making her eyes and face so like Jayne's at that age. He'd probably imagined it, and he had other things to worry him, so why stew about it?

Leaving the barn, he paused at Rowdy's stall. He'd planned on their guest riding the bay gelding, but the last time he was on Rowdy, the nine-year-old had spooked at a tractor. He'd have to lease gentler horses for the summer guests; in the meantime, he'd borrow one. For a thousand dollars, the woman deserved to ride, to participate in ranch life. Beulah Ann and Chaley could help with the baby.

He gave the horse a pat and went outside. The border collie and the blue heeler, named Gus and Call by Chaley and known by other handles to everyone else, watched him from near the shed. They were working dogs earning their keep and seldom asked so much as a scratch behind the ears.

Chaley was saddling Mouse under snow clouds.

"Where are you going?"

"Oh." His daughter wrapped the latigo through the cinch ring. Once. Twice. "For a ride."

Kip knew where. Down the road toward Gunnison, so as not to miss that old red pickup. "Why don't you come in for dinner, take your ride later?"

"I'm not hungry."

A woman who'd spent the morning driving the team through three feet of snow and lifting hay bales? But she had energy left to chase a bullfighter who didn't want to be caught. Kip sighed. "Suit yourself." *They'll work it out.* Once upon a time, he'd thought Jayne was right for him, the angel who would root him in these mountains so that his mind couldn't wander back to steaming jungles of mind-horror and death. But Jayne had flown, and it was Lorraine, Chaley's mother, who had saved him. Who had helped him save himself.

Chaley swung into the saddle, sitting a horse better than any woman in the state. *They'll work it out.*

"Chaley?"

"Yes, Dad?"

"If you catch him—" he winced a little at the word choice "—ask if we can have Noon for a week, for...our guest." Erin. That was a name he didn't want to say.

"Sure." She smiled, like the sun. And Kip recalled that

Chaley had saved him, too. That Chaley, most of all, had saved him.

"DON'T STEP ON THE BABY!" Beulah Ann cautioned.

But Kip Kay was already crouching to speak to Maeve. "Well, aren't you the cat's meow?"

Erin had finished the salad and set the table. She noticed the rancher and her daughter, the only things in the room that mattered. *He likes babies. He likes Maeve.*

She stored the thought in a distant place.

He hung his coat and hat by the mudroom door. "Like your cabin?"

"Yes. Thanks. Everything's great." The span of the room felt like the emotional miles between them. This stranger had a daughter.

Chaley.

Abe's fiancée.

Stepping around Maeve, Kip glanced at Erin again. She thought he sighed. "Chaley's gone to see about getting you a horse to ride," he said. "We've never had a guest this time of year before."

His eyes challenged her, asking for the truth.

Erin felt her lips half-parted. He was the one with the truth.

"We'll try to make you feel a part of things," he concluded. Picking up the *Rocky Mountain News* from the table, he left the room.

Erin made it a point to feel nothing. But it was a nothing like the inside of an empty juice can, like the inside of a pencil holder that would never hold pencils.

THE FOOD—chicken-fried steak, mashed potatoes and fresh-baked bread—was almost ready when Lane came in, hauling a baby's high chair. "Thought we'd need this."

"Thank you," Erin said. It seemed a thoughtful gesture from an almost-eighteen-year-old.

"Look out for spiders," he warned. "It was in the shed."

Beulah Ann gave Erin a wet washcloth to wipe the chair. "I think we're ready." She went outside and rang the dinner bell.

Erin cleaned the high chair, then carried it and Maeve into the spotless formal dining room. She'd gotten to know the plates in the antique china cabinet and the silverware as she laid the table. Buckling Maeve in her chair, Erin heard more voices in the kitchen. Three ranch hands came in. The only name she remembered minutes later was Lucky. Anyone that young and cute, with round gold-rimmed glasses, ought to be lucky—if you didn't count the receding hairline.

When everyone had sat down, there were several chairs empty. Beulah Ann said, "Well, this is a crowd. Think we'll have enough?"

"Abe and Dad are probably eating at Stockman's. They don't want indigestion."

"Neither do I," growled Kip.

Afraid she herself couldn't eat, Erin spooned mashed potatoes to Maeve, but Maeve turned her head with a fussy noise.

No, thought Erin. *No, please be good.*

No one looked up but Lucky, who said kindly, "Kids are great."

Erin had poured some apple juice into a baby bottle. She gave it to Maeve, and Maeve hurled it to the floor and fretted, her volume rising.

"Wish I had one," said Lane.

"You probably do somewhere."

"Enough."

One word from the rancher silenced Beulah Ann and Lane.

Erin stood, her napkin falling to the floor. She unlatched the tray on the high chair and unfastened Maeve's harness. Crying now, the baby lifted her arms to be held.

"So Dad had a wreck." Lane made another attempt at conversation.

"So it seems."

"Excuse me." Erin took Maeve to the kitchen and sat down to nurse her. Minutes ticked by with Maeve whimpering and nursing, but it was peace. Her place in the world was with this child. They were extensions of each other, and Abe Cockburn was just a sperm donor, a careless cowboy, and Kip Kay was just the rancher king who kept the truth. The only person who knew...

It matters, Abe had said, about having a daughter.

Well, aren't you the cat's meow?

Footsteps paused in the door.

She started to move, but Kip said, "No, that's all right. You're fine." With a smile that avoided watching her but seemed to like women who nursed their babies, the rancher carried his plate to the sink, gathered his coat and his hat, and said, "Well...back to work."

Then he was gone, whistling as the door closed, leaving behind a mix of cold and warm air, along with something Erin had never had in her life before and didn't give a shit about, really didn't *care* about. So why should her eyes start watering? All she'd seen was part of the truth, and she wasn't that damned hungry for it, even if it was the approval of her father.

Her father, Kip Kay.

HOURS LATER and five miles down the road, Abe was stroking Guy Loren's newest foal, getting her used to him, when Chaley appeared outside the stall. She let herself in, squeezing cautiously around Maylights, the mare.

"Pretty foal. Guy named her yet?"

"No." Abe had to tell her. Immediately. Now that he'd seen Maeve and felt it sinking in minute by minute that she was his, now that he'd recognized himself in her tiny face, all he wanted was to be with her and renew his acquaintance with her mother. He had to tell Chaley.

A few things.

"Dad wants to know if we can borrow Noon for our lady dude."

Noon was the first horse Abe had ever owned, the first that wasn't his father's on paper. He and his mother had gone to the sale barn together and bought him. Noon had all the best qualities of a cow pony, and at twenty-four he was gentle, a good horse for Erin. "He needs shoes."

"Can you do it today?"

Abe hadn't slept for twenty-four hours, and on the trip back from Gunnison with Lloyd he'd learned the extent of their problems. Lloyd's insurance *had* lapsed, and he'd hit a fifty-thousand-dollar vehicle. How were they going to pay for the damage to the Range Rover?

When the clerk at the courthouse had set a date for Lloyd to meet with a police officer and arrange forty hours of community service, Abe had talked her out of it under the office noise. *Look, he's seventy-two years old; he just forgot to pay his insurance.* She was all ready to write off the community service when Lloyd had cut in. *What are you doing? I'll pay the penalty.*

Though the clerk put him off with a story about the police being too busy to schedule people for community service, she also said Lloyd had to take a driving test. And the fine was more than two hundred dollars.

Abe had paid it, and now he had six dollars to his name till payday.

Six dollars. And a baby.

"I'll bring Noon over tonight or in the morning," he told Chaley. Shoe the horse, get some sleep, see Erin again. At least Guy let him have unlimited gas for his truck. Abe gave the foal a few last strokes, then released her and let himself and Chaley out of the stall.

"Billings place must have sold," said Chaley. "New fence. White PVC."

The Billings family hadn't lived on the place for fifty years, but that was what everyone still called the ranch, which was north of Jack Draw's. Lately, new fences announced the sale of local property—barbed wire wasn't pretty enough for these owners. Abe had driven all over the West for rodeos, and he knew how fast the range was being bought up, sold out of the families who'd settled it. Soon celebrities and tycoons would be the only ranchers left.

Chaley's voice distracted him. "I got tickets for the Dwayne Redd concert in Gunnison."

Dwayne Redd was the latest name in real western music, out of the mainstream, like Ian Tyson, and Abe liked his songs, which were about cowboy life. "When is it?"

"April eleventh."

"Farmington."

Rodeo.

"*Abe.*"

"It's my job."

"It's not a job, it's a *hobby.*" Down the row of stalls, the barn door creaked, but Chaley turned a deaf ear. "You ought to have a job sometime so you know what it is."

Abe *had* heard the barn door. Guy was coming to check on the foal.

"How is she?" The stock contractor ignored whatever he'd overheard.

"Doing good," Abe reported. Taking Chaley's arm, he guided her out of the barn. Snow fell, March snow that would not quit. "I have a job, Chaley, and it's here."

"You should be working for my dad."

His throat swelled. Time to confess what he'd done back down the road. Maeve's face, her soft reddish curls, the feel of her small warm body, reached into his mind. He pictured Erin, playing dress-up in her Stetson and duster. Erin's dark brown eyes and white skin. Erin didn't know about fences; she'd admired Jack Draw's.

Abe shut his eyes.

"What?" said Chaley.

He opened his eyes, saw her waiting with an expression that meant, *When are you going to grow up and be the man I want?*

"Chaley. I have a child."

"They're full of manure."

—Beulah Ann Ellis,
when asked the truth about cowboys

5

CHALEY'S THROAT vibrated with each steaming breath. "When did you discover this?"

"Today. She's staying at your place."

"That baby."

She sounded annoyed and disgusted. Hoping for the best—that she would promptly return his grandmother's engagement ring—Abe said, "She's mine."

Chaley studied Mouse, tied nearby. "Well, I'll have to get to know—her? It's a girl, right?"

Tension wrapped around him like baling wire. Abe recalled the night they'd become engaged, how it had happened. Mistakes Made While Drinking and Dancing.

He turned his coat collar up around his freezing ears.

"Abe? I'd love any baby of yours. Maybe that woman will let me baby-sit. She can go riding, help Dad and Lane check on the calves."

That woman. I really like that woman, Chaley. I really wanted to see her again, but I broke my neck and couldn't. The next summer, I was dancing with you and dreaming of your dad's spread. Of making it my own. Now I see that woman, and it's just like before, like it's never been with you, Chaley.

He met her eyes. "Let me go."

She spun away, stalking through the snow and mud to get Mouse. Abe caught the Appaloosa's reins as she mounted.

Chaley averted her face. "I love you. I've loved you my whole life."

He'd been afraid that was the case. Abe dropped his cold hand from the reins and stroked Mouse's neck, reassured by the feel of a warm horse.

Chaley clucked to Mouse, and Abe opened the gate for her.

It wasn't over.

CHALEY WAS SMOTHERING Maeve with a pillow, only it was Abe who couldn't breathe. He pushed the pillow off his face, and Lane grinned down at him in the early-evening light. "You called?"

Groaning, Abe rolled onto his stomach. He was in the fifth wheel at Guy Loren's place. Home. Recollecting why he'd phoned his brother, asked him over, he sat up. "I need you to do something."

Lane sank onto the edge of the bed.

Abe sniffed the air. "What is that?"

"It's your place—don't ask me."

"No, what are you wearing?"

Lane thrust the pillow into Abe's bare chest. "Alicia likes it. She likes to smell it *all over* my body."

The world fell on Abe, the magnitude of what he'd done after the Reno Rodeo.

"I want you to baby-sit."

"What?"

"Tomorrow morning. Six. For Maeve. The baby at the ranch."

Lane covered his face. "No. Say it's not true. It cried

through two meals. It barfed on its mother. It did number two right there at the table, and then it smiled at everyone."

"She's your niece."

"Niece? Who had a baby? Oh, my— Oh, my— No, not mine. *Yours*." Lane pitched to the floor and sprawled immobile. "I'm related to it."

Abe sprang out of bed, pinned his brother and ringed his hands around his throat. "She's the most beautiful child you ever saw."

"She drools. Oh, all right. Uncle. Oh, I'm an uncle. Let up, all right? Yeah, she's okay, for someone short and fat." He gasped and choked. "All right, I'll learn to like her."

Abe released him, and Lane sat up, rubbing his neck. "Jeez. Does Dad know?"

"No. And I want to be the one to tell him."

"The boss?"

Kip. "I doubt it."

Lane's eyes lit up. "Does *Chaley* know?"

"Yes." Abe dragged himself to his feet. He hunted for clothes in the cheap built-in drawers and as he dressed, said, "Tomorrow I want you to baby-sit so Erin and I can go riding." Saying her name now felt physical. Thoughts of her made his blood hum, and sorting right from wrong was easy. Making things right would be trickier.

His brother still gawked. "Hey, can Alicia baby-sit, too?"

Lane's latest girlfriend lived in Alta and would be forgotten the day Lane got his PRCA card. "No. This is bad enough for Chaley without Alicia spreading it all over Alta."

"Does Chaley know about this ride you two are taking?"

"I'll tell her."

"I bet that's why she didn't show up for supper. Hey, tell me about Dad's wreck. He's in a humor."

Abe related the Range Rover calamity, but Lane's

attention jumped to the countdown till his birthday and from there to his first professional rodeo, in Laughlin, Nevada, the same rodeo Abe was scheduled to work the next weekend.

On the surface it looked like a great weekend to get out of town. But he'd held Maeve, and he'd heard Erin say, *I didn't come here to get you to marry me or anything like that.*

She talked like a woman used to letting men go.

AFTER LANE STOPPED BY to tell her about the ride and offer to baby-sit, Erin set the alarm in the cabin bedroom for five in the morning. She went to bed with Maeve, ignoring the crib, but she was too busy dreading the ride to make her nightly meeting with death.

Abe was in her mind. Before, her images of him were grainy rodeo news photos. It had been hard to remember details like the shape of his nose and the way his mouth moved when he spoke and his lazy nimbleness, a clown's mercurial grace in cowboy clothes.

Mothering was a good cure for wanting cowboys, but it was no cure for wanting Abe. He was engaged to Chaley, and the memory of making love with him made Erin imagine him with Chaley. He loved Chaley, and he'd never loved her, Erin.

Just like the first cowboy who had ever dumped Erin, a man who made a better cowboy when he was just a photo in a plastic gilt frame.

IN THE MORNING she bathed a cranky Maeve, dressed her in clean sleepers and put her down in the crib. Erin had picked out clothes for the ride the night before. Wool tights and sweater, her duster, hat and wool knit gloves with leather palms. She was ready except for her coat and hat when she heard feet on the porch, the low sound of male voices and a knock.

The dark shapes with cowboy hats and the landscape behind them were out of her dreams and made her want to be part of what they had and to know what they knew. They'd tied the saddled horses to Abe's two-horse trailer, under the firs. The morning was blue, and the blast from the door chilled Erin, but she didn't care. She hadn't ridden a horse in almost a decade, and when she saw the horses, that was all she could think about.

Abe closed the door. "Where's Maeve?" he asked, reminding her of what was permanent, what would still be there when Erin left this cowboy land.

"Sleeping."

They all trailed into the bedroom. Abe crouched beside the crib and reached between two rails to touch his daughter's small back. In response Maeve gave a small sleeping sigh. She slept on her stomach, with her legs tucked under her. Standing, Abe rearranged the pink baby blanket.

He likes her. He really likes her.

Some things were too black to think about, like tomorrow and the day after and all the years of her life that Abe would love Maeve and not her. She got down to business. "Lane, if she wakes up while we're gone, there's applesauce and some bottles of juice and soy milk in the fridge." Erin buttoned her duster, pulled on her gloves. "She likes bananas, too. Do you know how to change diapers?"

The teenager reddened. "I'll work it out."

"Thank you. If she starts shoving her fists in her mouth, it's because she's teething. I put some teething rings in the refrigerator."

"Dad used to give us whiskey," Lane suggested. "Knocked us right out."

Abe squeezed his brother's shoulder. "Thanks for watching her like she's your own."

"Yeah, yeah, I get it." They all returned to the spare rustic living room. "There's not even a TV in here."

"Don't leave her alone," said Abe. "If you go flirt with Beulah Ann, take Maeve."

"Beulah Ann! There's an idea. You know, I'm going to come back and marry Beulah Ann someday, when I'm as rich and famous as Ty Murray and can afford to send her to a diet spa."

"Beulah Ann is too good for you."

By miles, thought Erin. Last night at supper, Beulah Ann had been like a flashlight in a blackout. Abe's father was immersed in cows and auto insurance, and her own father...well, he'd been preoccupied. He'd scarcely spoken to Erin or looked at the baby. But people didn't come better than Beulah Ann.

Abe held the door for Erin.

"Have fun, kids." Lane went back into the bedroom, and Erin heard him lie down on the bed she'd made.

Was she crazy to leave Maeve with him?

"They'll be fine. Come on."

The cold was brutal, but it didn't matter.

"Ridden before?"

"Yes." Speaking seemed to crack her lips. The snow had a layer of ice on it, and the trailer was white with hoarfrost. "Not for years, though."

He led her around a dark bay quarter horse and untied the reins. "This is Noon. Why don't you get up, and we'll see how the stirrups fit?"

Behind her, his body radiated heat and a security she could never have. Hating him for that, Erin grasped the saddle horn and the cantle and slipped her left boot through the stirrup. Abe's hands in worn leather work gloves reached around and put the reins in her left hand. He moved her right hand to the horn.

"Thanks." She swung herself up. The day before, Chaley had saddled that Appaloosa and ridden away so naturally. Erin practiced forgetting.

"Stirrups look good. How do they feel?"

"Fine."

"You just lay the reins alongside his neck to turn him, like this." Abe demonstrated, the worn sleeves of his coat brushing her legs.

The touch seduced her. She didn't answer.

Abe stroked Noon's neck, then left him to untie Buy Back. Mounting up, he turned the chestnut. They'd head past the cabin, away from the house. His phone conversation with Chaley last night had ended in a stalemate. She wanted him, the way she used to want a stable for her Breyer horses. And he was caught.

Noon walked beside Buy Back, hooves pressing into the snow.

"We'll go up this road a ways and cross the highway," said Abe. "There's a back road leads down to Guy Loren's."

"Is that where we're going?"

"Guess Lane didn't tell you. Thought we'd have breakfast together."

"Oh." Erin wiggled her toes, trying to feel her feet. "Is this okay with your fiancée?"

"She knows."

Erin's dark eyes were on Noon's ears, and she gave him just enough rein. She looked cold.

Abe took off his earmuffs and passed them to her. "Try these."

"Thanks." The earmuffs still held the heat from his head, but they were just earmuffs. And he was Chaley's.

Up ahead in the morning dark, a man in a coat and hat cut a path through the snowy pasture. He waved to the riders as they neared, and Erin recognized Lloyd, Abe's father.

The border collie slunk under the barbed wire as Abe walked Buy Back to the fence.

"I need you," Lloyd said. "Twins. Cow's got a foot back on the second one. Damn, she's leaving."

"I see her." Abe opened the swing gate from horseback.

What was he seeing? Erin wondered. There were dozens of cows out there, and even with the dawn lighting one of the passes to the east, she couldn't make out details.

At his bidding, she rode Noon through the gate while Lloyd slogged toward a distant stand of piñon.

"What are we doing?"

"Helping my dad." Abe secured the gate. "You warm enough?"

"Yes." Noon's body helped. She wished she could ride forever.

They walked the horses over melted snow where the sleigh had dropped hay for the cattle.

Lloyd called, "You take the calf in. I'll get the cow."

"Can I help?" asked Erin.

"You can help bring that cow in. It's the Hereford over by the piñons."

"What do I do?"

"Try to make her go toward the gate. Keep the reins loose. When Noon figures out you want her, he'll do the rest."

Erin tapped Noon with her heels, and the bay zeroed in on the cow. She didn't mean to keep looking at Abe.

He's going to marry Chaley. There was no point in getting

stupid over the sound of his voice or the way he looked on horseback or the sight of his back as he reached down from the saddle to take the wet calf his father lifted up to him.

The white-faced red cow went deeper into the trees, and Erin led Noon in a wider circle. Erin glimpsed the cow's vulva; it looked like a giant pink balloon, and a calf's hoof, still in the sac, hung out of it.

Noon did what Abe had promised. He went after the cow, crowding right up to her, until she tried to get away, and then the border collie was there, too, herding. All Erin had to do was hang on. *Toward the gate. Come on.*

The cow went. Lloyd, from the back of a bay gelding, opened the gate, and the cow followed her calf, packed on Abe's saddle. The dog trotted behind.

Lloyd's horse tried to bite Noon. Swearing, Lloyd released the gate and it swung back to the fence.

"Close the gate, will you?" he said to Erin, bringing his horse under control. To Abe he grumbled, "I told Kip not to buy this animal."

Erin hesitated at the gate.

"Just get down," Lloyd called, before his horse shied.

Erin dismounted. Her legs wobbled under her, and the blood sped back to her feet, filling them with tingling hot-cold pain.

Gripping the reins, she staggered to the gate. She grasped it, and something rammed her so hard that the reins flew from her hand and the gate banged the fence. A black animal more monster than cow pressed on her legs, and Erin climbed up on the gate as a cow and her calf went through the opening.

Oh, shit. Oh, shit. How was she going to get to her horse? Noon had walked across the road.

The black Angus snorted steam and rolled her eyes at Erin.

Abe and Lloyd were already halfway to the barn. Only the border collie looked back. Erin jumped down in the snow, sliding on an icy patch as the Angus charged. She was sprinting for Noon when the cow hit her again, boosting her across the road. The horse sidestepped.

Hooves clattered softly on the hard snow and Erin heard reins snap and Abe's "Get out of there!"

She grabbed Noon's reins and scrambled into the saddle with a leg that would never be the same. While Abe and the dog chased the cows back into the pasture and shut the gate, Noon stood calmly, tolerating his trembling rider.

Turning Buy Back, Abe rode up beside Erin, facing her. "You okay?"

"Yes."

"Come with me, then. I've got to help my dad." With a slight laugh that could have meant anything, he clucked to Buy Back and led the way to the barn.

IT TOOK ERIN longer than Abe to tie her horse outside the barn, and the whole time she felt the two ranch dogs, now together, watching her from the shed. When she limped inside, the men already had a halter on the cow and were maneuvering her behind a gate, placing a chain across her rump to hold her there. Abe stroked the cow's head. "Just one more, sweetheart. You had that first baby just fine."

Erin approached warily, the pain in her leg dull and distant in the presence of the straining lowing cow, and a man who talked the same way to women in bed. Who'd talked to *her* that way. *You're all right. Shh.*

The new calf waited in a nearby pen, warm and dry. Mind-fogged, Erin stared at it while Abe and his father shed their coats and washed their arms in a white plastic bucket. In the animal smells of the barn, unfamiliar scents of new life and earth, she watched Lloyd reach into the cow's vulva while Abe pushed hard on the body. Both men were sweating, Lloyd's face grimacing as his arm disappeared in the cow. The cow bawled and dropped manure, and Erin's heart raced at this strange spectacle of midwifery.

She'd never seen men work so hard before. Time seemed to take the cow's pace, the unrushable pace of birth.

Abe grunted something to his father as Lloyd pulled a second hoof from the cow. Then the calf's head emerged, teeth and tongue showing, and blood and yellow fluid gushed over the men. Abe caught the slimy wet calf and lowered it onto the straw, where it breathed for the first time.

The veins stood out in his arms, and sweat darkened his shirt. Erin was in a black hole, like being in labor with Maeve. She tried to stop her feelings. She couldn't let herself care about the way he touched the calf, which was like the way he touched Maeve.

Jayne had seen Maeve first, emerging from Erin's body. *Oh, she's beautiful, Erin.*

Her eyes felt wet.

Oh, God, not here. She hadn't cried for seven months, and it wasn't going to happen in this barn with these two cowboys. Though she knew they'd let her be.

Abe caught her gaze as he carried the calf past her to a stall lined with fresh straw. There was blood on his clothes, and manure, and she'd never seen anyone she wanted more. Faces like Abe Cockburn's didn't show up in university lecture halls. It depressed Erin that one second of eye contact was intimacy for her and not for him, and she stood numb while Lloyd released the mother to follow the calf, to lick it dry and shaggy.

"HERE WE ARE." Abe swung down from Buy Back outside Loren's barn and watched Erin dismount, as well. Her legs vibrated like the foot on a sewing machine when she touched the ground, a sure sign of a dude, but he checked her face to see how she was feeling. Those moments in the barn had been intense. He'd wanted Lloyd to meet Maeve. He himself had missed Maeve's birth.

And Erin wasn't the same woman he'd slept with almost two years ago. She talked less. And didn't smile at all.

Abe tied the horses. "This way. I'll show you around after we eat." They walked in silence to the fifth wheel. "Hey, Martha. There you are."

The Australian shepherd emerged from under the rig wagging her tail. She sniffed them both, and Erin petted her while Abe opened the door and warmth rushed out. Inside, on the blue-green rug, he tugged off his boots. Erin sat on a love seat built into one wall and untied her ropers. Removing her hat, she shook out her hair and looked around.

The tiny woodstove had replaced a booth seat on one side of the kitchenette. While Martha flopped down in a threadbare spot by the stove, Abe hung his coat and hat on hooks by the door and took Erin's, too. "I'm going to clean up."

He disappeared up a step into the sleeping compartment. No door, so Erin turned her back as she heard him rummaging in drawers, heard water running.

He returned in a fresh canvas shirt and clean jeans. "Bacon and eggs?"

"That sounds great. Can I help?"

He nodded toward the table. "Come talk to me. You can tell me about Mr. O'Neill."

Erin squeezed past him to the remaining upholstered bench. She'd thought they'd already covered her assumed name. But now there would be questions she didn't want to answer.

"There's no Mr. O'Neill." She rushed out an explanation that wasn't. "I didn't know what to expect here. But now you know about Maeve, which is what I wanted. We'll be here till the end of the week—"

"Whoa whoa whoa."

"What?"

Abe dropped to the bench beside her. Cheap curtains in the windows darkened the interior, but Erin could still see the green in his eyes.

"Look, Erin…"

How could he finish? Briefly Abe felt concentrated hatred for Chaley.

He thought harder.

"You know," he said, "I've only been engaged since last June, and you've known about Maeve for much longer than that."

She'd heard that accusation the day before. "You didn't show up in Twin Falls. I sure didn't think you'd show up for your child's life." It was a bald truth that Abe couldn't understand, not the way she did. Erin simplified. "I didn't think you'd want her."

I'm not the only woman who's been Dumped by Cowboys. Cowboys had been leaving women since Theseus abandoned Ariadne; after she'd saved him from the bull-sired minotaur. *So this isn't about you, Abe.*

"I broke my neck. That's why I wasn't there."

"I know. I read about it the day Maeve was born."

Abe played with a newspaper on the table, *Prorodeo Sports News.* Sorry wasn't enough. For nine months—give or take a month—she'd believed he had stood her up. He slid out from the table. At the counter, he unwrapped the bacon, heated the skillet.

Erin slumped against the seat back. This changed nothing. Chaley was a cowboy's cowgirl, the kind who kept the men she caught.

"I need to understand you."

She started. He was looking at her again.

"I need to know," he said, "why you had Maeve. Why you kept her."

Some things a man shouldn't ask. "I love her."

"You didn't tell me."

She sat up. He was different from what she'd thought in Reno. She'd remembered him as more boy than man, more clown than cowboy. But he was a man—who cared enough about another woman to have promised his life to her. Now, he was angry like a man. Because Erin hadn't told him they had a child together.

His green-gray eyes demanded answers.

It took effort to push her hair back from her face. Her head felt like a bowling ball, and she breathed so her voice wouldn't shake. "We weren't careful enough with birth control. I knew it at the time, and I take responsibility for my actions. Anyhow, I wanted her."

He couldn't ask *why* about that. He faced the counter. "Tell me what your life is like in Reno."

The request sank into Erin.

Her life.

The museum, day care, coming home to check all the closets and under the beds and hear the latest report on her mother's estate and on the sale of the house. Losing her job. Nights with the lamp on the desk. "It's..."

Abe was throwing the cellophane from the bacon into the trash.

"I still live in the same house."

"With your mom?"

Erin shook her head.

He turned. "Erin?"

"She was murdered."

Fingers raked the inside of Abe's throat. He slid back into the booth.

She told the dingy fake-wood tabletop, "It was one of several...murders. The guy worked at the casino, and he found out when people were leaving with cash. My mother knew him. She'd gotten cash because she was going to an antique sale that weekend. He shot her in our house. They caught him in Montana, buying land."

There was nothing Abe could say. The way she sat refused touch, and he understood. It was like climbing out of the barrel and taking a bow with a broken neck.

Crying, she turned her head away and wiped her eyes with her hands. "I'm sorry. Do you have a tissue?"

Abe got up and raided the bathroom cubicle. He handed her some toilet paper.

Make breakfast, Abe.

There was a sound on the floor, four feet and metal tags. Martha jumped up, into the spot he'd vacated, breaking rules. She sat and watched Erin's face with concern.

Abe didn't order her to attack.

He said the most inadequate words in the world. "I'm sorry, Erin. I'm really sorry."

> *"The cowboy wants to be understood. Tragically, he speaks a foreign tongue."*
>
> —Erin Mackenzie,
> "Cattle and Cowboys: The Ancient
> Currency of a Modern Enigma"

6

SHE GAVE DETAILS during breakfast, between spells of tears. She had not cried, she said, till now.

Maeve was two months old at the time of the murder. Erin had been working at the museum in Reno, with the baby in day care. The killer left the door open, and a neighbor found Jayne Mackenzie's body.

Since then, the Museum of the American West had lost funding. Erin was laid off, waiting for response to job applications—museum work in other parts of the country. Were there any openings like that around Alta or Gunnison? Abe wondered. Incentive for her to move here?

His problems were like hay in September, and Chaley was stacking the bales.

"Want to see the stock?" he asked as they left the trailer. Guy Loren had some fine animals.

"Sure." Though early rays of sunlight danced in the yard, pretending at warmth, Erin shivered, freezing. Walking hurt.

"You had a wreck with that cow, didn't you?"

"I'm fine."

Martha padded after them in the icy snow. Beyond the nearest barbed-wire fence, five bulls watched the humans. Abe told her their names. Two had performed at National Finals Rodeo. One had never been ridden.

"That brown-and-white one over there—that's a fighting bull."

"You don't compete in bullfighting."

"No."

Two bulls lay at the feet of the other three. "They look so...docile." *Fathers*, thought Erin. These were the fathers of calves. They wore their virility, their authority, their dignity.

"How did you know I don't compete?"

She started. "Oh. *Prorodeo Sports News.* Why don't you?"

Abe shrugged. He'd never put it into words.

She waited.

"It used to be that the clown's job was making people laugh, and the cowboys looked out for themselves. Then clowns became bullfighters, too. Now, there are lots of bullfighters and not many clowns."

"So you want to be a traditional clown?"

"Something like that." He couldn't explain. When the new bullfighters were introduced before a performance, the way they walked said, *You can depend on me. I'm a hero.* Like them, Abe drank in the applause, lived on it. But bullfighting wasn't cowboying; it wasn't getting calves to market. It was just another way to feed your cowboy pride when your business wasn't cows. When maybe you worked behind a desk five days a week.

"I want to save cowboys," he said at last, and meant that he wanted to save things the way they used to be. Abe tried to explain about fences. "It's like rich people buying ranches. They tear down the barbed wire and put up lodge pole. They hire some cowboys and buy some cows, and they show up at their places a few times a year and ride horses and have a barbecue. But it's not ranching.

"Now, somebody like my dad or Kip Kay relies on the land, gets his living from it. If the Kays mess up, they lose everything."

Erin hid her feelings. "Of course," she pointed out, "the Kays could sell their land for a lot of money. Millions of dollars."

"That would be the easy thing."

"I'd trade places with them." The envy came through. Hearing herself, Erin ran for the shelter of academics. "Ranchers can't scream poverty and make anyone hear, because the symbol of cattle as wealth is so deeply ingrained in the human unconscious. It's prehistoric, as old as the domestication of animals. Livestock growers are part of an archaic culture that goes back to the earliest Mediterranean societies, thousands of years before the time of Christ." Erin made herself draw a breath, slow down. "Someone from the city can't see that when you ask a man the size of his spread you're asking his income. Yet instinctively those same city dwellers see cattle ownership as a sign of affluence. They always will."

A tree creaked in a stir of cold wind.

"You've given this some thought," Abe said.

"It was the subject of my doctoral thesis."

She was serious, almost defensive.

Abe was bewitched. "What's your Ph.D. in?" *What.* He wanted to ask why. He remembered her fatal flaw.

"History of the American West," she said as though it didn't matter. Almost to herself she asked, "Who doesn't want land? Who doesn't want to live close to the earth?"

Her words revived an ache in him the way cold weather brings on rheumatism.

I'd trade places with them.

So would Abe.

Erin's skin was white under the brim of her hat, her dark eyes thoughtful. Even Loren's bulls seemed smitten with her.

"I take it you do. Want to live...close to the land."

Erin wiggled her fingers inside her gloves. It would probably be convenient for him if she settled nearby. Maeve could have visitation with him and Chaley. "I've always wanted to live on a ranch."

Abe wished he had one.

"Let's look at the broncs," he said.

He named Loren's horses with their long manes and tails, muscular athletes breathing out clouds. In the barn, he introduced her to a buckskin roping horse and showed her Maylights and the new foal. There were other roping horses, too, and a chestnut quarter horse named Wish. "Guy traded a bull for her. She's an NFR barrel-racing horse."

Erin touched the neck Wish stretched over the stall. Stroking the satin hair with its coarse ends, she was twelve again. "I used to want to be a barrel-racer."

"It's not too late."

"Just too expensive." Jayne's legacy, what was left after taxes, would be enough to relocate her and Maeve wherever Erin's new job took them. No extras.

"You don't need that much horse." Wish was worth $100,000.

"Any horse is too much horse." She repeated what her mother had always said. "You have to feed them and shoe them and pay vet bills."

Feed for his horses was one of the perks of working for Guy Loren. Abe could shoe anything with hooves. And he did a lot of doctoring himself. He'd never not had a horse to ride, since he'd been big enough to sit on one.

"When you have horses," he said, "you sacrifice other things."

In the shadows of the barn her eyes widened. "You just don't get it, do you? I'm a single mother."

And you're the father, asshole.

A direct hit. Abe was glad of the darkness.

He thought before he spoke again. "Would you feel differently," he asked softly, "if you were married? Say you couldn't have some things you were used to. Say you couldn't have nice clothes. Or a real house. Or medical insurance. But you'd have horses, live in the country. You'd have...the good life."

Erin's heart pounded. This man wasn't standing in a dark barn with her, all the animals breathing around them, talking hypothetical. He was talking about living in the promiseland, as though there was such a place, with room for her.

Here, where he had described the country of her dreams, she could be honest. As honest as she'd been at twelve, begging Jayne for a horse. "If I was married to a good man who loved me and loved Maeve, there's nothing I couldn't stand."

Abe didn't ask what a good man was and Erin didn't define it. They both knew he was one.

Too good to linger where talk could lead to touch, to finding an empty stall filled with clean hay and remembering what it was to kiss each other. And more.

"Let's get you back to the Kays'."

They left the barn.

Abe was checking Noon's girth when a man strode toward them from a double-wide trailer beyond the corral. The lenses of his metal-rimmed glasses winked in the early-morning light. In his sheepskin vest, he reminded Erin of a bear.

Abe stepped around the horse. "Guy, this is Erin. Erin—Guy Loren. Erin's staying at the Kays'."

Guy had a gift for minding his own business. The stock contractor said he'd need Abe that afternoon. They made arrangements to load some bulls to take down the road to be tipped; the tips of a rodeo bull's horns could be no smaller than a fifty-cent piece, so the sharp ends had to be sawed off.

Before leaving, Guy remarked, "Jack Draw's listed his place."

Abe's head shot up. "Really. That's news. What's he asking?"

"Five thousand an acre. About makes you sick. Let's hope they don't subdivide." He sighed. "We'll be seeing you."

Guy departed, and Abe thought about what he'd said. The television star was selling his ranch. Five thousand times fifteen thousand acres.

Seventy-five million dollars.

A second passed before he remembered Erin. He asked, "Want to ride Buy Back?"

Almost at the barn, Guy missed a step.

Erin's eyes swept the sleek chestnut horse, Abe's rodeo companion, then came back to him. "Are you sure?"

"Yeah."

Spots of pink stained her bloodless cheeks. "Thanks."

Abe turned to adjust Buy Back's stirrups. He crooned "Old Corrals and Sagebrush," and Martha came around and sat looking at him, thinking it was for her.

"WE DIDN'T COME this way before."

"Yes, we did. You were so cold you didn't notice." They were plodding through Jack Draw's ranch.

"Isn't this private property?"

"Public road. Forest-service access." Across the meadow to the north, cows—Highlands, Normandies, British White and Pinzgaus, talk about obscure—followed hay dropped from a horse-drawn sleigh. "How do you like that horse?"

She smiled, the first real smile he'd seen since she'd come here. "I love him. Thanks for letting me ride him. I think he's got more go than Noon."

"That's a fact, so keep after him. He'll try to run on the downhill."

The original homestead was a black skeleton in the southern field. Old chutes and sheds poked through the snow in front of an ancient cabin with the roof collapsed. The road eased upward, through aspen, and Abe stopped Noon. Quakies were notorious for falling, but these had stood since the last century.

Erin walked Buy Back past Noon and peered into the trees. Someone had carved an inscription on white bark:

THANK YOU, GOD. I LOVE THIS RANCH. C. COCKBURN, 1897.

The history grabbed at her, sucked at her irresistibly. She grabbed back, her mind dating Colorado statehood—1876. By that year, four million beef cattle roamed Western land, and by 1885 the grasslands were overgrazed. From ecological catastrophe came economic disaster. The large ranches that survived the depression gave way to smaller cattle operations relying on irrigation. In that time, C. Cockburn had found his spot of high country. "Who was he?"

"Great-grandpa."

"Was this your ranch?"

"My dad's. We lost it twelve years ago."

Lloyd. The magician who could reach inside a cow and

pull out a calf had lived in another world, another time. He would have stories. Erin wanted them.

"We'd borrowed against the land, overextended. Interest rates went up, and that's all she wrote."

The new history of the American West.

And the history of Abe.

They rode on. As the trees fell away, wind bit Erin's face. A frozen creek divided a meadow crowned with mountains miles away. "So your dad started working for...the Kays?"

"Yes." Abe was ready to change the subject. If Jack Draw sold to a developer, old Charlie's aspen might fall. He was glad he'd shown it to Erin, to the mother of his child.

It killed him that the tree might be gone when Maeve was old enough to read. Erin said cows were a symbol of wealth. But they *weren't* wealth. Not anymore. Here, real estate was wealth, and poor men held their land by gossamer strings.

Abe could never take back this ranch.

"So you lived here till twelve years ago?"

Abe nodded.

And the Kays had been their neighbors. "You and Chaley must have been childhood sweethearts." Erin envisioned them galloping across wildflower meadows, making out in a hayloft. Buy Back moved smoothly beneath her, and she told herself it meant something that Abe had let her ride him.

Abe focused on Buy Back, too. And on Erin, so he wouldn't think of land. "You had some lessons?"

"Six weeks every summer." She knew how her mother had saved for them. Kip Kay had never offered help.

Jayne had never asked.

He was the absent father of Erin's childhood, and she

couldn't fix that now. She was seeking the truth about cowboys. It couldn't hurt her. Not now.

But Colorado seemed colder than ever, and the white of winter was a kind of death. And the breathing and footfalls of the horses were too honest for her lies.

THE PLAN WAS to leave Noon at the Kay Ranch for Erin to ride. When she and Abe reached the barn, Erin asked, "Can I take care of Noon? Put away the tack?"

"Sure. Then we'll go see how Lane got along."

Erin lugged the saddle and saddle blankets to the barn, and when she came out, Chaley was with Abe and the horses. Snow and mud darkened her scarred and faded boots. Her sheepskin coat was luxurious against her slender neck. Seeing Erin, she began to remove Noon's bridle, a gesture that said, *Run along. You'll just be in the way.*

Abe turned Buy Back loose in the corral. "I'll be over in a bit, Erin."

"Thanks for...everything."

Erin limped toward Mears Cabin. The back of her neck suddenly prickled, making her spin her head. Kip Kay stood on the porch of the big house with a cup of coffee. He nodded to her, then gazed toward the corral, at his daughter and Abe.

Erin knew herself for an interloper who had shown up with Abe's baby.

To spoil everything.

"ENJOY YOUR RIDE?" Chaley asked Abe.

She must have seen Erin on Buy Back but hadn't mentioned it. Abe knew she wouldn't. "Sure."

His mind was full of Maeve. He hadn't held her yet today. Hadn't smelled her skin.

This was Kip Kay's property, where his own father had

worked for twelve years, where his brother had grown. The land enlarged the insult of his words. "Chaley, I can't marry you."

"I knew you were going to say that."

Like, *I knew you'd be going to a rodeo that weekend.*

"Good grief, Abe. Obviously she's gotten along fine for the past year. If she's not making out on her own, the baby can come live with us."

Her blue eyes were willful, seeing only what they wanted.

"Why are you making this so hard?"

"Because I know you." Chaley leaned against the corral fence, confident as the sun that had gone away. "You need space. You've always been that way. You're doing this rodeo thing because you're too noble to allow yourself to be part of this ranch. In twelve years you've never accepted money from my dad for work, and it's easy to see why. You feel like you need to have some birthright to the land before it's yours."

Chaley, I don't love you. He itched to tell her. And avoid hearing her scary perceptions.

"In fact, you probably think you don't love me enough, Abe, but I know you, and I know why you think that way. It's because you love the land so much."

"Chaley, I don't want your father's ranch." He wanted his own.

"Of course you do. We talked about it the night you proposed."

The night *he* proposed?

She squirmed away from his gaze. "You can't raise a family just cowboying, Abe. You think *she's* going to put up with that?"

Abe was back in Guy Loren's barn, inches from Erin, who seemed so used to getting less than she wanted.

Chaley kept her profile to him, and the afternoon sun outlined her silhouette. Using her teeth, she tugged the glove off her left hand. She drew off his grandmother's engagement ring and gave it to him, and placing her hands on the corral fence, jumped over it and hurried toward the big house, her father's house.

Abe suppressed the feeling he was about to get told on.

He zipped the ring into an inside pocket of his coat to put away later. Freedom should have felt good, but Chaley's parting gesture had been to plant doubts. She'd done a good job.

HE GOT TO HOLD Maeve for only a few seconds when he stopped at Mears Cabin. Erin said Lane had been a great sitter, that he and Beulah Ann were playing with Maeve, trying to help her walk, when she came in.

Abe had to return to work, and it didn't seem like the moment to tell Erin about Chaley. There definitely wasn't time to take Maeve out to his father in the pasture and introduce her.

So he went back to Loren's and helped Guy load the bulls. They rode to the sale barn in Gunnison, where each bull was held in a hydraulic iron compartment while a man used a circular saw to tip the horns. The animals bellowed. Abe saw the bloody horns and smelled the smoke and went outside into the cold to breathe.

The place was familiar. He had a memory of being at a livestock sale when eye level was Lloyd's thighs. He'd gotten separated, and there was just a sea of jeans and coveralls and boots, till a lean-faced cowboy had crouched down and said, "Well, you're Lloyd's boy." Abe must have been crying, but all he remembered was being lifted up to ride on the man's shoulders, and then he could see hats, and the man found Lloyd.

The cowboy was Kip Kay, and it was Abe's first memory of him.

And now if he closed his eyes, he could hear the background ruckus of the animals and the auctioneer's voice and see the old men in the back row soundlessly making their bids, their expressions unchanging. In a few years, Abe thought, he would bring Maeve here for a sale.

You can't raise a family just cowboying.

Guy paid him five hundred dollars a month, and he picked up extra money here and there shoeing horses for neighbors. The fifth wheel was too cramped for three, but he and Erin could scare up a larger trailer.

It wasn't enough. A man should give his family more.

That ancient symbol of wealth Erin recognized. Cattle and land.

Listening to the bulls inside, Abe shivered. Since they'd lost the ranch, he hadn't let himself imagine having his own spread. Success was just the fact that Lloyd had never arranged a tractor accident to trade his life for the ranch, like a neighbor of theirs had that year.

But he couldn't buy land on Guy Loren's pay. And he couldn't raise a herd without land. To become a cattleman would mean giving up cowboying, taking a job in town to earn enough money for a down payment.

Either that—or selling out. There were ranches that paid hands a living wage. Jack Draw's, for instance.

Strange to be thinking this way. Before his engagement to Chaley he'd stopped believing that his future held more than rodeo, more than a drifter's life. With the promise of marrying her, he *saw* what could be his, the Kay Ranch, and seeing was believing. Now, however, he needed a leap of faith.

He had to make it. What other work was there for a man with a family than to raise cows on his own land?

THAT AFTERNOON, while Maeve napped, Erin soaked in the cabin's oversize claw-foot bathtub until the pain leached from her muscles and her bruised right leg.

Everything, she told herself, was fine. It couldn't be helped that Chaley was Kip Kay's daughter and Chaley was engaged to Abe. Or that Erin was the mother of Abe's baby. She *wasn't* an interloper. She was a ranch guest minding her own business, which was the pursuit of truth.

It didn't quite play. If the week at the ranch wasn't so expensive—and nonrefundable—she would take a hotel room in Alta, explore the historic mining town with Maeve. Relax and forget about her quest. Call it failure and say that was part of life.

In fact, since her inheritance was coming, since the house was under contract, why not do it, anyway?

A vehicle pulled up outside, the engine went off and a door slammed.

Abe.

Erin yanked the plug from the bathtub. She was dragging on jeans and an indigo blue long undershirt when he knocked. "Coming."

No time to comb her hair. Barefoot, she crossed the plank floor and opened the door. It was Abe, in his barn coat and hat. His green-gray eyes held feelings. There were cracks around his lips from the weather and a half-burned look to his skin.

She recalled he'd been moving bulls.

Abe was thinking about breasts and sex and nipples that showed under cotton T-shirts and the way her bed had creaked in Reno, how the headboard had banged the wall and he'd liked it. He'd bought a $3.99 City Market bouquet for her in Gunnison; while the cashier rang up the sale, he'd worked story problems: *If Abe has six dollars and he spends four on flowers, how many does he have left?*

He'd thrown the flowers in a field on the way to the Kays'. And he didn't know how to tell a Ph.D. in the subject that history meant Chaley Kay.

"Let me in," he said.

She did. "Maeve's asleep."

"I want to take her down the road, introduce her to my dad."

Erin used her fingers on her hair and chain mail on her heart. She couldn't afford to care how he looked on horseback with a new calf on his saddle or that he'd let her ride his favorite horse. Or that his dad had lost ten thousand times more than she'd ever had. "He's seen her."

"He'll see her better when I tell him she's mine." He went into the bedroom.

Erin pressed her spine to the doorjamb and watched him contemplate his sleeping daughter like a man in a church.

"I'm not going to marry Chaley," he said. "It's settled."

You couldn't tell much from a cowboy's face. Erin left him, walked to the kitchen. Taking the chair near the woodstove, a battered oak piece with fat cushions, she warmed her feet and worked out how to tell him that he didn't have to give up true love for some imagined duty to his child. This was a song with lots of verses, and she'd written it herself; she ought to be able to sing it for Abe.

When he joined her, she started in. "You don't have to break up with Chaley." Erin let her head fall back till she could see the beams in the ceiling. "I'm not one of those people who think biological parents have to be married to each other for the kids to grow up normal. You told me in Reno your folks are divorced."

"They were married most of the time I was growing up." It was Lane who'd been broadsided by their mother's leaving.

Erin turned to find his eyes alert, waiting for her. She

would do fine Jayne's way, she thought, raising Maeve alone. After all, *she'd* turned out all right, if you discounted the business about cowboys. Pencil holders *were* trivial. "Abe, what I'm trying to say is, if you love Chaley, you should marry her."

The green eyes darkened. "I don't love Chaley."

"Then why were you engaged?"

An ember exploded in the woodstove.

"It made sense when she asked me."

When the crib creaked, Abe jumped up and hurried into the bedroom. Erin heard him say, "Hello, Queen Maeve. Hm. Soggy. And fragrant."

Erin went in. Maeve had decorated his Carhartt. The man who'd helped pull a cow that morning seemed paralyzed.

She set the disposables in front of him. "Cowboy up, Abe."

He met her eyes and grinned.

While Erin brought him a washcloth, Maeve lay patiently on her changing mat, trying to put her foot in her mouth, spreading the mess. As Abe faced his ordeal with memorable expressions, Erin couldn't help giggling, and Maeve joined in.

"Enough," he said. "Both of you."

Maeve giggled again.

Erin hunted clothes for her. She handed Abe some purple pile overalls and a white turtleneck. "Is this okay? My mom bought it for her."

"They're cute." Her mom. The trees outside made longer shadows. Her mom was murdered. "Hey, where are you going?" Abe caught Maeve as she began crawling across the bed in her diaper and plastic pants. When he sat the baby back down, she laughed.

"Daddy," he said.

"Da-dee."

"That also means doggy."

"I'll answer to it." He pulled the white turtleneck over Maeve's red curls, drew her hands through the sleeves. "God, Erin."

"What?"

He shook his head and gazed at Maeve's face and saw all the ways she was his.

LUCKY, KIP'S TRUST-FUND ranch hand from Alta, waved as Abe approached the pasture with the baby. Lloyd was checking an Angus heifer. When he finished, he led his horse through the melted snow and stopped on the other side of the barbed wire to stare at his son holding Maeve.

"Dad." Abe neared the fence, trying to keep both of Maeve's hands warm in one of his.

Lloyd stepped closer, almost scraping the wire.

"This is my little girl."

His father cocked an ear, as though to catch words blowing by. Then, in slow movements, he handed Bo's reins to Abe, over the barbed wire. Abe whispered, "Maeve, this is your grandpa," and gave her across the fence to his father, to hold.

*"A working cowboy is no one.
A clown is no one in public."*

—Abe Cockburn

7

"ERIN, DOES YOUR FAMILY live in Reno?" Beulah Ann asked, serving mashed potatoes around the table that night.

Everyone was there—Kip, Chaley, Lloyd, Lane, Beulah Ann and the four ranch hands. Everyone but Abe, who wasn't part of the household. Who had headed for his truck at the sound of the dinner gong without saying when he'd be back.

"I don't have any family. Except Maeve." She added, "My mother died this year."

Silence.

A chair scraped back from the table. Leaving his plate, Kip Kay stood and walked out of the room.

Erin listened to the door open, then slam behind her father. The emptiness that followed had a still quality, like the inside of a temple, and everything was quiet inside her, too, because she was within a breath of the truth.

Kip Kay knew who she was. Knew who her mother was. And he cared that Jayne was dead.

MY MOTHER DIED *this year.*

Were his senses deceiving him? For two days Kip had

listened to her voice, caught her mannerisms, found them like Jayne's. And her name was *Erin*, like Jayne's child.

Jayne's, never his.

His boots crunched in the half-frozen mud outside Mears Cabin. Shielded by moonless twilight, he jangled his keys in his pocket, wondering what law he was about to violate and what the penalty was. But she was a guest at his ranch.

Kip made the laws here.

With no backward glance, he mounted the porch steps. If she saw him, found him out, so be it. His instincts were shouting. He was right and only wanted confirmation.

He received it, through the wallet she'd left in the top drawer of her dresser. It was worn gray leather, old and dirty and taped in one place with duct tape.

That surprised him. Almost stopped him, because Kip had always associated thrift with decency. He began to shut the drawer, leaving the wallet undisturbed. But an icy draft from the door made him colder than cold. In his heightened state of sensitivity, irrelevant morals lost to imperative justice. He had to know. Swiftly he unfastened the billfold and found her driver's license to read her name. Her date of birth.

Closing it, replacing it in the drawer, he saw himself facing her, saying, *Get out. Leave, and don't come back.*

But nothing could be that easy. He didn't know why she'd come. He doubted it was to tell him callously at the table that his first wife was dead. She was a single woman with a baby. *God knows what she intends.*

What she meant to take from him.

But what could he do without confronting her? And confronting her meant speaking the truth. A truth she might then make known to Beulah Ann or to Lane.

Or to Chaley.

She might tell them, anyway, but Kip sensed she

wouldn't. She might have come because of natural curiosity, to see her father. Guilt needled him. She didn't seem like a schemer.

Except that she'd lied about her name.

Kip decided. For five more days, the week she'd arranged to stay, he could tolerate her presence. Then she would leave, and that would be that.

He let himself out into winter, closed up the cabin as Erin had left it. When he turned, his daughter with her yellow braid and Stetson made a totem-pole shape at the foot of the porch steps. "What are you doing, Dad?"

In the night he could dissemble easily. "Checking the ashes in the stove." He came down the steps. Chaley was why he would not confront Erin. Chaley was why he could keep his distance from Jayne's daughter for five more days. Chaley was why he could let Erin Mackenzie walk through his life uninvited, unwelcome, and do nothing in response. He smiled at Chaley encouragingly, knowing the kind of hard day she'd had. Finally accepting that it was over with Abe. "Where are you headed, sweetheart?"

"Thought I'd look at the heifers." She didn't move. "Dad."

"Mm?"

The cutout portrait of her face watched the cabin.

Kip wanted to say something about Abe. There was nothing in the world Chaley wanted—and that he'd thought was good for her—that Kip hadn't found a way to give her. He liked Abe Cockburn far less this evening than he had in the morning.

You may as well know, Chaley had said bluntly, *Abe and I are no longer engaged.*

Ah.

There wasn't anything else to say.

Until Chaley admitted, "That baby inside is Abe's."

KIP WAS HALFWAY to Guy Loren's place when he realized he was ashamed that Chaley had told him. Ashamed *for* her, for telling on Abe, for telling something Abe might just have learned and be figuring out how to deal with himself.

He pulled his truck to the shoulder alongside his own south pasture, startling a coyote eating roadkill. Its shape loped across the highway and disappeared into the trees, ignoring the feast beyond the barbed wire, cows with new calves, tagged so the hands could keep each pair together. They were Kip's own cattle, but the coyote was a symbol that something was right in the world. He'd seen no more than scat for three years and a den on Alta Creek; he heard their song.

The last firearm he'd held was an M-16.

Oh, Chaley.

What would Lorraine say?

It was the question of his life, of every day since she'd died, giving out to a sudden liver ailment; he and Chaley had watched it kill her.

It was the question of their twenty-four-year marriage.

Kip had told his second wife that he'd been married before, told her the first ran out on him, that Jayne's desertion almost killed him. He'd told her that Jayne had reasons for leaving, that he drank too much, that there had been other women.

But his second wife was deeply moral—and not always just. He'd feared in those early days that she would never have him if she knew that Jayne Mackenzie left pregnant. When he'd known Lorraine better, when they'd been married longer, he was afraid she would never forgive the lie.

She'd died never knowing of his other child.

Erin's existence would be news to Chaley, too.

Headlights whipped by him on the road, outside his

windshield smeared with dried water drops and dust. His truck idled warmly, puffing exhaust into the night.

Was that baby at the ranch really Abe's?

The baby was biologically his own grandchild, but Kip dismissed that. He did not love the woman Erin or her child. Was not interested in knowing them or loving them. Only in keeping them away from Chaley before they could do more to hurt the daughter he did love.

A breath dragged through his lungs, and he contemplated whiskey and vices he'd abandoned twenty-four years ago, self-prescribed painkillers he'd traded for Lorraine's arms.

"Oh, Lorraine," he said to the glowing dash, "what would you think of me now?"

He didn't know why he'd been going to Guy Loren's place, what he'd planned to do when he found Abe. Throttle him, but why?

Native rages stewed with old horrors inside him, and Kip told himself his anger was on Chaley's behalf, because Abe had hurt her this way. Made another woman pregnant and couldn't marry Chaley, after all. Broke Chaley's heart.

But Lorraine's voice was a ghost in his ear, saying what she had in life. *You keep giving in to her, Kip, and it's not doing her any favors. It wouldn't hurt Chaley to know there's some things she just can't have, and that's part of life. If she has to wait till she's grown-up to find out, it'll be a rude awakening.*

"She's waking up now, Lorraine."

He checked traffic and spun the wheel, driving for his own gate. His cows were calving and would be throughout March. If he could do anything for Chaley now, it was build the ranch, make it stronger each year, so that someday she would have it for her children. There was nothing he could do about this other situation. One thing he couldn't give Chaley was Abe.

He'd sure as hell tried.

But Abe had a baby with Erin Mackenzie.

A coldness crept over Kip's heart, recollection of bleak days of abandonment, of desertion to the solitude he most feared. He wanted nothing so much as to get the reminder of that pain off his property and out of his sight.

HER MOTHER'S MURDER was with Erin that night. She'd said the words out loud at dinner, that Jayne had died, and now she couldn't put it out of her mind. When she turned in, Erin left the kitchen light burning.

She would keep it lit all night.

In her white flannel nightgown, she lay on the sheet beside her daughter. That awful night came back. She hadn't cried. Too numb.

And the tears never came, until this morning at Abe's.

Erin tried to think of something else, but thinking was an enemy when the truth was so near. His leaving supper like that, a message just for her, that he knew who she was. Other messages invited decoding, but Erin didn't want to read them yet. She tried other topics—the half sister who hated her, the cousin who didn't know they were cousins. A cowboy who couldn't be trusted. She could hear the wind in the stovepipe and the ice on the pine needles tapping the gutters.

She'd been at the Kay Ranch only two days.

It felt like a century.

Hooves clip-clopped outside. Someone was riding, and she considered pushing aside the curtain to see who. But the sound had come from the far side of the cabin, away from her window.

Erin heard the creak of saddle leather and soft whistling.

Abe?

It was ten-thirty.

Boots on the porch. Erin got out of bed. Orange glowed around the door of the woodstove. The dry heat crept through her nightgown to her bare skin as he knocked. "Who is it?"

"The clown in your life."

Erin opened the door. Snow clung to a misshapen black hat and his Carhartt and gloves. Oversize flakes fell in a backdrop behind him.

His face was painted, and he carried a battered tapestry satchel.

He'd come too late; death had arrived first for its nightly talk. She just stared at the clown.

"There's a rodeo this weekend," he said. "I have new tricks. I need you to tell me if I'm funny."

He wasn't, but his boots looked cute with his tights and baggies. She let him in.

"Thank you. Did I get you out of bed?"

She shut the door. "Yes."

The kitchen light was on, Abe noticed, had been on when he rode up. The kind of person who slept with lights on needed to be visited by a clown after dark. Feeling like a doctor arriving at the scene of an emergency, he shrugged out of his Carhartt and pulled off his boots, ready to work.

Chaley was wrong; it *was* a job.

There just wasn't any money in it. A fact to keep him awake, weighing what he would sacrifice for land and cows. And for Maeve.

Erin curled up in a corner of the couch and pulled a throw over her.

"Since you're not a rodeo announcer and may be unfamiliar with the finest selection of jokes, I've prepared some for you." Abe handed her a piece of notebook paper. On it was written in pencil: *I want to lick you.* "Oh, wait, that's not it. That's just a note my dog left me this morning." He handed her another sheet, yellow paper typed with recognizable rodeo jokes.

Erin wanted to suggest they skip the clowning and get down to the part where he licked her.

"You've been to rodeos, so you know how to fill in with patter, right?"

"I'll do my best." After a sigh he saw and didn't hear, she straightened in her seat and found an announcer voice. "Now, before I introduce this next cowboy... Abe. Abe. Where'd you get that watering can, Abe?"

Indeed, he'd produced a small watering can from the satchel.

"You found it *where?* No, wait, no. This is too stupid. No one will laugh at this, Abe."

What she'd said wasn't in the script—in fact, the joke *was* stupid—but Abe made a deal of starting to cry and letting his tears fall in the watering can, then watering the rag rug with them.

"Okay, okay. I'll read the joke."

It was hard to be a good rodeo announcer while imagining she was being licked by Abe, but Erin gave it her best shot.

At last Abe collapsed beside her on the couch.

"What?" Erin asked.

"You don't smile much."

"I'm grieving." She was also in heat. When he touched the hem of her nightgown, she thought they were getting somewhere.

"Want to go to the Laughlin rodeo?" he asked. "I leave Thursday. I thought you and Maeve could come."

Erin considered. She'd been toying with the idea of talking to her father. Saying in front of him what he must know, that she was his daughter. She could ask why he got up from the table so fast, and then maybe the truth would come, and it would be what she hoped. Not that he hadn't cared about Jayne's leaving him, but that he'd cared too much.

"I said I'd stay here for a week," she told Abe.

"They won't be heartbroken if you leave early." When she flinched, he said, "They're calving." *And there's the matter of Chaley, of Kip Kay's daughter, hating you for having my baby.* "If you come, you'll get to see my act with Marauder."

Erin tucked the throw around her legs. Abe didn't know she was related to the Kays. How would he react if she told him? She kept her secrets. "Who's Marauder?"

"A bull." Marauder had been retired from the arena for refusing to buck and was headed for hamburger. Only Abe could save him, by making him a vital part of his act, so vital that Loren would keep him around.

But Abe's rodeo career was on death row, too.

The years ahead stretched in front of him. In some versions he worked construction; in others he was a farrier; in others he signed on with Jack Draw or someone like him. He could barely see ahead to rewards—his own spread, somewhere land was cheap, somewhere colder than Alta or hotter than hell.

But one reward was close.

"What are you doing?" asked Erin.

He'd gathered her up, her nightgown against his patchwork shirt and suspenders. She was bare beneath it, Abe knew, and he wanted to lift up the hem and get his face under there. But he wouldn't for the same reason he'd thrown out the flowers.

He carried Erin to the bedroom, imagining her hand wrapped around him. There was sure something for her to hang on to, which he hoped she wouldn't notice and hoped she would. He hoped she would insist on having him, which didn't seem likely but was possible. "I'm tucking you in. Sleeping with the lights on is easier if a clown tucks you in."

Maeve slept on the bed, with the spread turned back. Abe remembered sleeping with his parents, too. He put Erin down beside Maeve and turned the covers over her.

Erin gazed up at him. The room was dark, and he was there, the masquerade man who'd haunted her bed in one form or another since he'd shared it. She loved his eyes. He was smart. And funny.

He was Maeve's father, though "father" was a word she didn't want to think tonight. She wanted Abe, for himself, but there was something she had to know first. "Why," she asked again, "were you engaged to Chaley?"

The ragged clown was a solemn statue and a cowboy. And a man. The wanting, Erin knew, went two ways.

"Guess."

At first Erin thought she'd heard wrong. But he'd given her the clues that morning on their ride.

"And what I said before was true," he added.

That it had seemed like a good idea when Chaley asked him.

To marry her for her father's land.

His eyes were deep as he stood over the bed. They didn't expect love or acceptance. "Good night." He reached across her to touch Maeve's back, but didn't touch Erin at all, just left—conspicuously free or not worth catching, she didn't know which.

Fabric rustled as he gathered his things. A boot thumped on the floor. She heard him zip his coat, singing a verse of "The Old Chisholm Trail."

With my foot in the stirrup and my hand on the horn,
I'm the best damn cowboy ever was born.

Come a ti yi youpy, yippy-yay, yippy-yay,
Come a ti yi youpy, yippy-yay, yippy-yay....

His song lingered after the door had shut behind him
and the sound of his horse's hooves had faded away. And
Erin bunched the sheets under her, remembering how
badly she could want a man.

TUESDAY AFTERNOON, while waiting in the Gunnison
Department of Motor Vehicles office for Lloyd to complete
his driving test, Abe reviewed Colorado traffic rules and
regulations. He was testing himself when Lloyd walked
through the glass door, followed by the testing officer. Abe
dropped the manual and got to his feet.

"Let's go," growled Lloyd.

Chewing on his lip, the officer meandered behind the
desk with his clipboard. Abe silently posed a question.

The officer shook his head.

Damn.

Outside, sunshine slanted on the Gunnison storefronts.
Abe's front truck tire kissed the curb over a patch of
blackened snow, while the back wheel sat a foot from the
concrete. *Looks all right to me, Dad.* Wondering where his
father had failed the test, Abe took the wheel. It was
awkward to turn to Lloyd. "I need the keys."

"Oh. Here."

How could his father be foreman for Kip Kay if he
couldn't drive? Tractors, trailers, trucks...

Abe started the engine. This had put a kink in his own
plans, too. He'd counted on Lloyd being in a good mood
after his driving test. *Well, to hell with it.* He had to ask,
anyway.

And while he was at it, he might as well broach another
difficult subject. A logging truck rolled past, and Abe

pulled into traffic. "So, what's the story with the Range Rover? What's the damage?"

"I have no idea. His insurance is going to pick it up, if you can believe that. Seven hundred dollars a month he pays on one vehicle."

"How did you find that out?"

"Bought me a cup of coffee at Stockman's while I waited for you that day."

Abe was touched by the kindness.

At the traffic light Lloyd stretched in his seat, readjusting the shoulder strap. "Lots of questions about horses. Nice enough fellow. But too much money and not enough sense."

Abe pictured the young driver of the Range Rover huddled over Stockman's thick brew with Lloyd, soaking up information about horses. He'd asked the right man.

Abe parallel parked in front of the coffeehouse and killed the engine.

"What are you doing?" said Lloyd.

"I need some money. I paid your fine, and I'm broke."

His father blinked. "What do you need money for?" When Abe didn't answer, Lloyd dug for his wallet, opened it with sun-spotted, knuckle-swollen hands and selected a twenty. "That enough?"

For Abe it was fair time again. Nights Lloyd had given him and Lane money for the Zipper and the shooting gallery. Even when they had the ranch, there'd never been much spare cash. But when the county fair rolled around, Lloyd had given what there was. And when they got bored at the sale barn, he'd dished out money for ice cream, and Abe and Lane had walked down the street and gone into the store. And he remembered how they'd looked through the glass at the flavors and seen their hats reflected there. *Yes, please, ma'am. Thank you.* Sugar cones dipped in chocolate making puddles on the concrete and in the dust back at the barn.

Now the silver-haired man, the generous father, seemed uncertain about the amount of his fine. What fine?

Abe couldn't bring himself to clear things up. Friday was payday. "That's plenty. Thanks, Dad." He took the twenty, and feeling like he was soaking the old man, got out of the truck.

Lloyd didn't move from the passenger seat.

Heading for a toy store two doors down, Abe tried not to hear the gong inside him. Its toll announced his father's old age; it warned of hard decisions to come. What would Kip Kay do when he learned Lloyd had failed his driving test?

And what would happen to Lloyd?

ABE PLANNED to park at Mears Cabin when he dropped his father at the Kay Ranch. It was Maeve's birthday. Lane's, too.

But Lloyd wanted out at the corral. "Stop," he ordered.

Beulah Ann was hustling down from the deck. As Lloyd got out, Abe lowered his window.

"Birthday party tonight!" she said. "It'll be for Lane and Maeve both. Chaley's gone to Fort Collins to see friends."

That was supposed to ease his mind. It failed. Chaley might be gone, but her father wasn't. "Did you mention this to Kip?"

"He said it's all right with him, but I thought we'd have it in the trailer."

Tactful, Beulah Ann.

"Oh, come on, Abe! It'll be you and me and Maeve and Erin and Lane, and the hands said they'd pop in for cake. It's a farewell party for Lane, too. He's going to that rodeo with you Thursday." It seemed like she had more to say, but she stopped there.

She was right. Lane had signed on for the Mountain States Prorodeo Circuit—Colorado and Wyoming—but he'd try to hit performances all over the country. Lane would not be returning to the Kay Ranch. Though he'd spent most of his life there, he'd never really considered it home.

Same as Abe.

"It's your daughter's birthday," said Beulah Ann.

Abe stared, and Beulah Ann looked so guilty he knew she wasn't covering for Erin. Lane was the culprit.

So, now it's out. Did Kip know?

"Where's Erin?"

"Inside, making icing for the cake."

A glare fired up the kitchen window; he couldn't see past it. Why hadn't she come out? But why would she after what he'd admitted about his engagement? About his love of land? She'd never even said she'd go to the rodeo.

He wanted to ask Beulah Ann if Erin knew he'd be at the party. But of course she knew. Funny how comfortable she seemed here, how cozy with Beulah Ann, how at home on the ranch. She was just a dude, a guest, but now Abe felt like the stranger, the disconnected one.

He'd earned that role.

He asked Beulah Ann, "What time?"

"Seven."

"Okay." He put the truck in gear. Kip was riding down the road in his winter overalls.

"Sorry." Beulah Ann scooted back from the cab.

"I'm not avoiding anybody."

She made for the house, and Abe edged the truck forward, but Kip dismounted and waited on the road.

When Abe pulled up beside him, the rancher asked, "Did he pass?"

Lloyd's test. Abe had forgotten. He shook his head.

Kip gazed south at the equipment shed, nestled among the pines. The forest rose to the west, and on every horizon mountains jutted skyward.

Country worth having. A man's pride.

Never looking back at Abe, the rancher gave a nod and walked on.

Chaley. Abe's gut twisted. Things weren't going to be the same between him and Kip Kay ever again. And the birthday party already looked like a mistake.

"The truth will set you free."

—the Bible, John 8:32

8

ABE ARRIVED at his dad's at six-thirty and parked beside the trailer, wishing Kip Kay didn't have to look at his truck all night. A horse would have been just as conspicuous. No help for it. It was his brother's eighteenth birthday.

And Maeve's first. Yes, Kip must know by now that the most beautiful red-haired baby anyone ever saw was Abe's daughter.

Lane was watching bull riding on ESPN when Abe carried in the canvas duffel bag that contained his clowning gear. Martha squeezed in after him, making a beeline for Lane's feet, a banquet of scent.

"Hi, Martha, ol' girl. My brother treating you right?"

Using his left hand, which held a bottle in a paper bag, Abe shut the door. "Where's Dad?"

"Calving." Lane slammed his feet to the floor and sent Martha leaping back. Leaning toward the TV set, he slapped his hand hard on his knee. "Did you see that?"

On the screen a bull rider was trying to get up after being trampled. Abe handed his brother the paper bag. "Happy birthday. Use some sense."

His attention captured, Lane eased the bottle of Jim Beam Rye from the sack. Eyes slowly lighting, he built his voice to a rising, "*Yeee*-hah! Get a glass, brother. No, wait, who needs a glass?"

Ten minutes later, in his father's room, Abe sat before a lighted makeup mirror he'd bought at a garage sale, while Garth Brooks rattled the walls of the trailer. Beulah Ann had arrived, looking special in a fringed shirt and black jeans, and now she and Lane were drinking Jim Beam, cranking the music and still watching rodeo.

Abe had a glass beside him, but he wasn't enjoying it as he applied white greasepaint to his face. Kip hadn't said anything about Lloyd, but it wasn't hard to read his mind. You couldn't have a foreman who couldn't drive. Added to that, the foreman should have the best lodgings on the place, next to the owner.

Lloyd might be out of a home, too. This trailer.

Abe had tried to talk to Lane about it, but his brother had just shrugged, never taking his eyes from the screen. *So he moves to the bunkhouse. You and I both know Kip's not going to fire him. He'll still let him cowboy.*

When your brother thought that way, you had to point out, *It's a demotion.*

He's a tough old man. I'm not going to worry about it. I'm outta here.

Like their mother, a long time ago. She'd had an excuse, if there was such a thing. Lane was just Lane.

Martha rested her head on Abe's knee as he painted a black patch around one eye, a black circle around the other, a dog's black nose and mouth, and the brown and black and gray spots on his cheeks. "I'll never be as pretty as you, Martha." When he'd finished with his face, he fished a dog biscuit from his bag and tossed it to her.

Behind him, the phone gave a staccato rattle that was someone's idea of ringing. They'd gotten the phone with the trailer.

Abe waited for his brother to answer it, but Lane and Beulah Ann were backing up Garth on "American Honky-Tonk Bar Association."

"Erin," Abe muttered as he made his way around the bed to get the phone, "I hope you'll still tolerate me after you see how my nearest and dearest relative behaves tonight."

The phone buzzed again and he lifted the receiver. "Cockburns'."

"Abe?"

The voice was Kentucky sweet, always familiar. Abe's stomach dropped a mile. "Mom. Mom. Hi, Mom."

"Hi, honey. How are you? Are you there for Lane's birthday?"

"Yes. Yes." He met his dog's eyes. "Martha. Shut the door."

With her head and one front paw, the Australian shepherd pushed shut the flimsy door separating the master bedroom from the rest of the trailer. The music volume hardly lessened.

"Good girl. Yes, you're a good girl." When she came to his side, Abe petted the dog, then stretched the phone cord across the bed as he reached for the glass on the dresser. "How are you, Mom?" The phone crashed to the floor. "Sorry. That was just the phone. It's all right, Martha."

His fingers found the glass. The glass found his lips. He drank deep, swallowed hard, and the whiskey's fire braced him. *Cowboy up, Abe.*

"I'm fine," said his mother, bringing to his mind a picture of her smooth shoulder-length light brown hair. Abe had seen her just a few months before, back in November, during the Louisville rodeo. He'd gone to her place, to the stable she co-owned. Annabelle did not attend rodeos, especially when her son was bullfighting. *If I*

wanted to see you get killed, I would never have left Colorado.
One of those things that probably shouldn't have been said;
he'd had to leave pretty quick afterward, once he'd
comforted his mother through her tears of regret. Now, the
incident in the past, she told him, "We've got the prettiest
new foal. And we just signed on the owners of Total
Eclipse, who won the Triple Crown?" Abe's mother and
her sister and brother-in-law trained racehorses.

"Mom. I have a baby." There. He'd said it. "I just found
out. She was, um..." He'd learned this word a few months
ago—the name of a barrel-racing horse. Time to impress his
mother. "...Serendipity." *Which, rodeo fans, means "a happy
accident." And Serendipity sure has been a happy accident for
this cowgirl....* "Her name is Maeve. Today's her birthday,
too. Her first birthday."

Annabelle was a lady to her core. After just long enough
to blink three times, she said, "Why, honey, that's
wonderful! When can I see her?"

Abe contemplated the empty bottom of his glass, set it
down and stroked Martha. "Well...I won't be back out your
way for a while. You could come here, though." Annabelle
hadn't been west of the Mississippi in thirteen years.

"Well, surely you'll be coming somewhere close."

He imagined traveling to the South with Maeve for a
rodeo. He wondered how best to acquire cows and land.
He mourned the dry glass and the fact that his rodeo days
and maybe his cowboying days were numbered. "I'll let
you know."

"I want to see her, Abe. If you can't come here, you tell
me, and...well, I'll go there."

Annabelle—in Colorado again? His heart pounded.
"That's great. That's really great." Complications
suggested themselves. That he'd known Maeve himself for
just four days. That only two had passed since he'd broken

up with Chaley. That nothing with Erin was *settled*. But he wasn't going to say anything to discourage his mother from visiting her only grandchild.

"Will you send me a picture right away?"

"Yes. Yes." He was afraid she'd back out, so he said, "Did you want to talk to Lane?"

There was a whisper of quiet before she said smoothly, "Yes. That's why I called. I love you, darling."

"I love you, Mom." He laid the phone on the old Navajo blanket that covered his father's bed and went out into the musical din to get Lane. The boom box balanced on the edge of the kitchen counter, and Abe turned down the volume before he addressed his brother, who was glued to the tube with Beulah Ann beside him. "It's Mom. On the phone."

Lane's mouth twisted down, and his eyes remained fixed on the set for another three seconds, until the end of the televised ride. Then he slowly stood and stretched and started to make his way past Abe. He looked surly.

"Be nice," said Abe. "She's your mom."

"And such a good one, always."

The sarcasm was black smoke spewing after him as he headed down the hallway. On the couch Beulah Ann somberly directed her eyes to the television screen. "Someone knocked."

It came louder and Abe opened the door. Erin stood on the wooden landing that served as a porch, pretty as a barrel racer who'd just won a buckle.

Maeve, in her arms, took one look at Abe and began to cry.

IT WAS FIFTEEN MINUTES before he made her laugh. The followed-by-shoes trick did it. Pieces of string ran from the toes of some oversize black shoes to Abe's running shoes—

no cleats in the house. Whenever he walked, the shoes followed him, and he kept checking over his shoulder to see who was there. Sitting on the floor with the small stuffed rabbit he'd given her, a birthday present that had helped win her trust again, Maeve watched his antics and giggled.

After a while he sat down on the rug, blew up a long balloon and twisted it into a poodle for her. Maeve giggled again. "Da-dee!"

She meant him of course. That balloon didn't really look like a dog.

As Abe picked her up and hugged her, Erin watched from the nearest chair, a tattered recliner that no longer reclined. Willie Nelson was cautioning mamas not to let their babies grow up to be cowboys, and Erin wondered if there was a song about not letting your daughter grow up to be dumped by cowboys. Well, she'd saved Maeve, maybe, by coming to Colorado. She'd *always* admitted that her own problem in that direction probably came from being ignored by her cowboy dad.

And Maeve had won her own dad's heart. On the floor Abe was letting her sit on his chest and try to eat one of the sunflowers off his suspenders.

I should feel some satisfaction in this.

Instead, she felt nothing. Last night he'd left. After admitting he would have married Chaley for the Kay Ranch.

And I still think he's sexy.

The bull riding ended and Lane switched off the television.

"Birthday-cake time," said Beulah Ann. "I'm going out to ring the bell so we can get the hands in for a piece."

Lane rearranged magazines on the coffee table, swept up his and Beulah Ann's glasses and set the whiskey bottle on the counter. Leaving Abe, Maeve grabbed on to the leg of a chair and pulled herself to her feet. She tried to walk, holding on to the chair, then the television, then the coffee table.

Beulah came back in, and Erin heard voices outside asking, "Where are they? In the trailer?"

Soon the living room was full of ranch hands.

"Where's Dad?" Abe asked Lucky, careful to sound unconcerned.

"He and Kip are working on a cow. They said they'd have some later. Hey, cool duds you got there."

After two renditions of "Happy Birthday," addressed both to Maeve and to Lane, everyone had some cake and whiskey or lemonade, and the four hands drifted out to the bunkhouse or the pastures.

Abe's mind was still on his father. When Maeve got sleepy, he'd walk Erin back to the cabin, then go find Lloyd.

But for now...

Lane, modeling a new pair of turquoise chaps sprouting fringe from every edge, danced lewdly on the sturdy pine coffee table. He sang along with Alan Jackson into an invisible microphone, encouraging Beulah Ann and Erin to join in.

The door of the trailer opened and Lloyd stood on the threshold.

Peering from the bull-riding pop star on the coffee table to the clown lounging against the kitchen table—his progeny—he muttered an oath and entered his home.

"Hi, Dad." Lane leaped down from the table. "Now, don't drink all that whiskey. It's mine."

"It's just what you need to go with that hole in your head. Where's this cake I keep hearing about?"

"I'll get you a piece." Erin rose, holding Maeve.

"Hello, Tumbleweed," Lloyd greeted the baby. "I'll take her off your hands, Erin."

As Erin handed Maeve to her grandfather, Abe breathed easier. If Kip had demoted Lloyd, he was taking it well. While Beulah Ann danced through the living room, Lloyd sampled the cake. "You make this?" he asked Erin.

"Beulah Ann and I did."

"You'll do." He slanted a look at Beulah Ann, twirling under Lane's arm. "Not so sure about them."

Lloyd's praise reminded Erin of the single time she'd felt her father's approval. It made her wonder, again, if the way to get at the truth was to tell Kip she was his daughter, so that they'd have to look each other in the eye and admit it. *Look. I have your nose.*

She didn't want to wreck the night thinking about it.

The foreman's boots were cracked with dried dirt, his insulated coveralls made for warmth at work rather than fashion. As he exchanged grins with his grandchild, he said, "How do you like March in Colorado?"

"It's cold."

"That's so." Lloyd was admiring Maeve's incoming front teeth, but he said, "We used to have woodstoves and firewood in the school buses."

History. Erin held on to it like a tick on a dog, and only a small part of her mind kept worrying at her own missing history. "You're kidding."

"No, I'm not. One winter I'll never forget. My daddy used to keep the cattle in a corral near the barn at night, and in the morning, we'd let 'em out to roam. Well, one morning he looked at the sky and said he thought he'd just keep 'em in, and in the afternoon he brought 'em into the barn." He smiled at Maeve, swung her feet with his free hand, then met Erin's eyes to give impact to his next words.

"That night came a blizzard so fierce we had to tie a rope

from the house to the barn. Horses we didn't know came and stood on the leeward side of our barn, rubbing against the building to keep warm. When the storm was over, that side of the barn was thick with hair."

Erin was riveted now, the other rancher almost gone from her thoughts.

"Every cow in the county died, except my daddy's."

Clouds traveled fast in the West. What kind of person could look into the morning's sky and see an evening's blizzard?

"You like history," said Lloyd, "you should visit the Alta museum."

"They have an historical museum?"

He only had time to nod before Abe interrupted. "You don't mind, do you, Dad?" While Lloyd shook his head and grinned at the baby, the clown caught Erin's hand and led her into the living room to dance. He wasn't to be outdone by his little brother.

Erin wondered if he noticed, like she did, that it was their first real touch since the night they'd made Maeve. Holding his hand.

In order to become a member of the Dumped by Cowboys Hall of Fame, one had to have been whirled around the floor by a few cowboys, and Erin had known her share. Abe was the best. As he spun her close to him and away, skillfully giving Beulah and Lane their space, Erin found herself laughing, the way dancing could make you laugh.

Abe grinned back from his clown face. The God-you're-pretty-I-could-love-you look in his eyes made her half-giddy. Across the room his father held their child, rocking her to the music and smiling at his sons. The idea that she had any claim on these people—or even this moment—was illusion, Erin realized, the kind a person sought when she visited a working ranch. The illusion that there was a place in this West where she could belong. And so what if Lorrie Morgan's "Heart over Mind" was the anthem of Dumped by Cowboys Anonymous?

The song ended the tape, and as the dancers separated, Lloyd hummed a few bars of an old cowboy tune. "Abe, how about some 'Red River Valley'?"

"Sure, Dad." He beckoned Erin to follow him. The glossy cherry-wood stereo cabinet had been made in the late 1950s. It had been his parents' wedding gift from his father's parents.

Erin knelt on the rug beside it as Abe popped open a door and flipped through some albums. He chose a tattered jacket with a Remington print on the front, *Music of the West*, and reverently removed the album from its sleeve.

"I love records," said Erin. "They sound warmer than CDs."

"Well, this is real cowboy music. And that's what we like." He placed the record on the turntable, and Erin glanced up to see Lane gallantly offer Beulah Ann his arms in a gesture of friendship. Abe was taking her own arm, guiding her to her feet.

Across the room, Lloyd whistled along as a cowboy singer began crooning "Red River Valley." He turned in a graceful circle with Maeve, resting the baby against his broad comfortable shoulder.

But Abe took Erin's attention, catching her left hand in his right. His heart beat strong against her breast as his arm drew her closer, and he taught her a gentle dance of the Old West.

Come and sit by my side if you love me.
Do not hasten to bid me adieu...

A blast of cold whisked into the room, carrying whorls of fresh snow. Abe lifted his eyes and met those of the man whose daughter's heart he'd just broken.

The dance fell apart. Erin saw him, too. Her father with snow on his hat and his coat. Shunning her eyes and Abe's, he cocked his eyebrows toward Beulah Ann and Lane. "Where's the cake?"

Erin shot out of Abe's arms so fast his head spun. He stared after her. Why was she so keen to wait on Kip?

Shutting the door, Kip wondered how he'd be able to choke down a piece of cake. Twylla, Chaley's cow, lay dead in the yard with the bodies of the calves they'd lost. Chaley had fled to Fort Collins so she wouldn't have to see what he was facing now, Abe falling in love with another woman. Lloyd's revoked license and Jayne's daughter cutting the birthday cake... Well, it was plenty.

Lloyd knew about the cow, had helped him try to save her. He shook his head at Kip in shared regret. For the cow. Maybe for a son who'd fathered a child on the rodeo road.

It's me who's sorry, old friend, Kip thought. He'd decided to hold off mentioning the driving test. Lloyd was losing one of his kids tonight, and Kip knew how that felt—like Chaley going off to college. He wasn't going to kick a man when he was down. Though Lloyd didn't seem down with that baby sleeping in his arms. Singing:

But remember the Red River Valley
and the cowboy who loves you so true....

Abe eased around the counter behind Erin, glad she couldn't see his eyes. He wasn't jealous—just bothered. Like there was something he was missing that he ought to be able to see. "I'll take another piece of cake, Erin."

You never talked to Chaley like that, thought Kip. *With love in your voice.* Royally angry—at Chaley's stubbornness as much as Abe's taste—Kip accepted the cake plate from Erin's shaking hand. The hand made him look at the eyes.

Jayne's face stared back, and with a tight sigh he turned away.

MAEVE FELL ASLEEP on Lloyd's shoulder. She lolled against her grandfather with her head tipped back and one hand on the cowboy's creased red-brown neck. Knowing it was time to go, Erin collected the gifts. Beulah Ann's plastic dog with wheels and blinking eyes and a tongue that stuck out. The bunny from Abe.

Abe took Maeve from his father and carefully rested her against his own shoulder. She sighed in her sleep.

Erin kept her sighs to herself. Kip had eaten his cake and teased his niece and Lane, then departed. That showed grace, considering the circumstances of Abe's breakup with Chaley. Considering Maeve, having her first birthday on Kip Kay's property. The minutes he spent in the trailer had twisted Erin's mood. She'd been ignored. But Maeve earned his smiles, the warmth of his eyes. He wasn't, Erin thought, a cold man.

With distance, she counted the ironies. Kip must feel Abe had wronged Chaley. But if he knew Erin's identity, the rancher showed no fatherly concern for the daughter who had borne Abe's child. Maybe he believed Abe intended to marry her; Erin half believed it herself.

Or maybe it was just more evidence that, in Kip Kay's eyes, she wasn't his. *The truth about cowboys,* she told herself. *That's all I want.*

The wooden steps outside the trailer were slippery. Erin's boots made wet-wood prints as she descended to the snow-blanketed yard. Flakes dampened her eyelashes and settled on Abe's hat as they rounded the corral, Abe carrying Maeve.

"That was fun," said Erin. "Thanks for being a clown."

"Can't help it."

But he was staring ahead and he wasn't with her.

He'd lent her his denim jacket for the walk to the cabin, and Erin turned up the sheepskin collar against the frosty night. Snowflakes wet her nose. "What's on your mind, Abe?"

He stopped walking for a second. *Why not?* The barn was dark, no hands near. "Oh, my dad." Briefly he told her about Lloyd's test and that a man without a license couldn't be a ranch foreman. But before she could answer, his eyes caught something in the hump of dark shapes behind the barn. The mound had collected snow, too, and was indistinct beyond the veil of falling crystals. Abe walked toward it.

Erin knew that was where the carcasses were, the bodies of cows and calves who had died, and she didn't go close. In an instant of paranoia, it had even occurred to her that Kip had told the hands to put them there, just so she'd have to walk past them every day and smell the death. "What is it?"

Abe came back. "Oh, it's Twylla. Chaley's dad gave her a cow when she was nine to start her own herd, to put herself through school. My dad did the same thing with me, would have with Lane, too, if he'd still had the ranch when Lane turned nine. Twylla was Chaley's first cow."

Poor Chaley. But her sympathy felt shallow.

Some things you tried not to think about. Like the way rancher fathers raised the daughters they raised. "What happened to your herd?"

"Lost with my dad's." If he was bitter, he didn't say.

"You never went to college, then?"

"No."

His battered clown hat shut any light from his face.

As their shoes broke up the snow, Erin began singing "My Heroes Have Always Been Cowboys," and Abe sang with her.

On the porch of Mears Cabin, he paused. "Why is that?"

"Why is what?"

"For a city woman, you take a strong interest in cows."

She hedged. "Reno's really just a cow town with casinos."

"Yeah, I know." He repositioned Maeve, took Erin's key and unlocked her door. Fingers of heat reached out to them. In the open doorway he said, "But you're not a cowgirl."

The clown was too savvy. A trickster.

"People like...what they like." Erin glided into the cabin, unaware that she'd tossed her hair, lifted her chin. And made him wonder what lie she'd told.

Abe flicked on the wall switch, and a lamp beside the couch sent out a soft glow. The edges of the room hid in shadow. Abe took Maeve into the bedroom and laid her on the cowboy-print spread to take off her coat. He settled her in the crib, then returned to Erin, who was arranging an aspen log in the stove.

He got her out of the way and stoked the fire himself, building it warm. When he turned, Erin sat on the rug behind him, resting on her hand.

"Don't want to tell me why you like cows," he said.

Erin heard, *You don't want to tell me the truth.* Abe had known Kip Kay his whole life. Erin hadn't. And she hadn't known Abe that long, either.

She shook her head.

It made Abe think of Lane, coming home from grade school after someone had said Annabelle ran off with a man—which was a lie—or after someone had described what happened to dead bodies, what Busy would be like decomposed. Erin reminded him of Lane. Shaking her head, not telling.

He wasn't satisfied. "Come to the rodeo with me Thursday."

An overnight trip. Would they sleep together? "Keep talking."

He lifted one shoulder. "We could get a room with a couple of beds."

Which meant they'd sleep together. Erin had changed since he'd stood her up in Twin Falls, when she was pregnant with Maeve. Not resisting cowboys was unacceptable now.

But this is different, she thought. "Okay."

He kissed her the way you kiss someone if you're wearing greasepaint. Erin heard the log in the stove split.

"I want you to tell me now," he said.

"I'll tell you sometime."

"You trusted me more in Reno."

"You're mistaken."

When he stood, she saw his running shoes and thought, *Cowboys don't always wear boots.* She didn't move as he left, and afterward she sat there in front of the stove knowing she hadn't changed, after all. She still couldn't say no to cowboys.

It took effort to go to bed.

Moonlight coming through the limbs of a pine tree cast spotted shadows on the bed where Maeve slept. Erin had never seen that sight in Reno, pine-tree shadows. Reno had its own beauty, and the high desert and the lights of the casino were tied up with the vivid painted beauty, the world-weary humor, of Jayne.

This, Erin thought, *is my other side*. The mountains were the other half of her roots.

When half your roots never grew right, you did lopsided things. When your father was a cowboy and didn't...didn't have a part in your life, you looked for other cowboys to fill the gaps.

I need the truth. She thought it in the dark, and she thought it in the language that was comfortable. *I need to know the truth about cowboys.* Until she did, she'd never be able to say no to cowboys, to the restless search that always left her alone, abandoned like a kid in a casino parking lot.

There was only one way to the truth, and that was to face her cowboy father and say, "I am your daughter."

Tomorrow she would.

A HELICOPTER FLEW over the ranch three times the next day. Erin didn't pay much attention to it—she was thinking about telling Kip Kay she was his daughter—but at lunch her father stood up from the table and said, "I've had enough." He meant he'd had enough of the chopper, and he went outside, as though he intended to do something about it.

Erin thought she understood. That helicopters must affect him; so would a heavy downpour. There must be lots of things like that. She'd read that an ice maker could mimic an AK-47. She wondered what ghost sounds there were on a ranch.

While she and Beulah Ann washed lunch dishes, the helicopter hovered against the distant range, and Beulah Ann stopped singing "Someday Soon" long enough to say, "It's developers, looking at Jack Draw's place."

This pulled Erin's thoughts from her father. "Really?"

"Yes. There's no conservation easement, so whoever buys it will probably subdivide."

Erin winced. Abe would hate that. *She* hated the idea, and Jack Draw's ranch had never been her home. It surprised her that the actor hadn't put a conservation easement on the property; deciding the land couldn't be subdivided would have reduced its resale value and, therefore, his taxes.

But here he was reselling; maybe it was what he'd planned all along.

Two small feet showed just outside the mudroom as Maeve crawled toward the back door. While Erin retrieved her and set her near her toys in the kitchen, Beulah Ann resumed singing. She was in an awfully good mood, considering that the person who made her knees weak was leaving forever on Thursday morning.

Before Erin could ask if she'd come to her senses regarding Lane, Beulah Ann stopped her song and said, "But you know, if that happens, maybe he'll sell the brand."

"Who? What brand?"

"Jack Draw. The Cockburns' brand. It's one of those real old brands—they were the first ones to have it. Abe's tried to buy it before, but Jack Draw wouldn't sell. Wouldn't even talk to him in person."

"You can buy a brand?" Everything Erin knew about brands was historical. Branding and earmarking of cattle were used in the British Isles and in Iberia before the seventeenth century, and British colonists in the New World used both techniques, as well.

"If it's not being used, you can," Beulah Ann explained. "An old brand like the Cockburns'—you see them for sale sometimes for three, four thousand dollars. Lane says it's a real family symbol. A symbol of when they were all together before Busy died."

Erin knew she'd missed something.

Holding a chair at the kitchen table, Maeve pulled herself up to stand. She gazed up at her mother, waiting for approval. "Look at you," said Erin, her mind still on Busy. "You're standing!"

"She's going to walk any day," predicted Beulah Ann, drying a serving bowl that didn't fit in the dishwasher.

"Who's Busy?" Erin asked.

WHEN ABE WAS FOURTEEN, his ten-year-old sister had fallen between the wheels of a tractor and been killed. Beulah Ann thought it was somehow related to the Cockburn parents' divorce, but she didn't know the whole story. And when she got that far, she seemed to feel like she was gossiping and stopped altogether.

"Horse," said Maeve as Erin carried her past the corral. She was pointing at Noon.

"Yes, that's Noon. He's a horse."

The helicopter came over, a shadow sweeping the road and disappearing beyond the near ridge. Slowly, its chatter left silence.

"Da-dee?" Maeve was still looking at the horse.

Erin wasn't sure what she meant, but she gave it her best shot. "He'll come get us tomorrow. We're all going to a rodeo."

And she had to tell her father they were leaving early.

She was going to tell him more.

Kip's pickup truck was dead ahead, a quarter mile up the road, parked beside the north pasture. Erin walked toward it with her daughter in her arms, trying to step in the snow, instead of the mud where the snow had melted. She passed the barn. She passed the carcasses, some of them skinned and raw and rotting beside the shed. She passed Mears Cabin.

Erin rehearsed as she walked. The cold air on her face

helped her nerve. It was honest, like the dead grass and the snow and the Rockies. She would be like that, too, and the truth couldn't hurt her.

He was alone in the pasture. Glancing up, he saw her coming and stood still. Erin kept moving her legs, kept marching toward him in the withering sunlight. Eventually he slogged through the snow and mud and old yellow grass, and they faced each other across the barbed-wire fence in the sunlight of a March afternoon.

"What can I do for you?" He was weary and matter-of-fact—slightly tense and plainly ambivalent. "Everything all right in the cabin?"

"Everything's been perfect. I've actually decided to leave early."

He lifted his eyebrows.

A breeze gusted through her like the truth.

"Before I go," said Erin, "I want you to know..."

His expression hardened almost imperceptibly, but she ignored the cue. She was a wind that couldn't be stopped, and she said, "I'm your daughter."

Then, as though the wind had died, came the wait. A calf bawled somewhere behind him, and Erin watched his face. But his features didn't shift, and the silence became ghastly, eternal. His eyes were pale blue, like Chaley's. Impassive.

"I have just one daughter, Erin."

Another soft breeze made sounds she didn't register. Things blowing.

His words went through her, and it wasn't a shock, though she flashed on an imagined scene of her mother facing a man with a gun, a man she knew, and realizing he was going to kill her.

Maeve sat quietly in Erin's arms, a leg dangling on each side of her mother's hip, watching cows. Pointing to a calf, she said, "Da-dee."

Dogie. Erin suppressed a wild impulse to laugh.

Keep it together. Keep it together. Be a cowboy, Erin.

Her voice shook some as she said, "Then I guess we just need to settle for my week here. I'll pay for the entire week, since I know you don't have a by-the-day rate."

"That's fine. You can give the check to Beulah Ann."

"I have cash. It's right here." Erin dipped into the pocket of her duster. Watching her fingers and the paper, she counted out hundred-dollar bills, the balance of what she owed. She passed the money over the barbed wire to her father, and as he took it with his work glove and pocketed it in his barn coat, Erin tried to think of the truth about cowboys.

His lie didn't change the truth. And she told herself that, told herself she was still as strong and honest as the dead grass. It did not hurt to be the grass. It did not hurt.

"Well, I'd say we're better than the next man."

—Lane Cockburn,
discussing the truth about cowboys

9

THE LIGHT on Abe's answering machine was blinking when he came in that afternoon. He'd earned two hundred dollars in Gunnison shoeing horses and he'd just returned to shoe Loren's, as well, for the rodeo.

As Martha danced around his feet, he pressed the button on the answering machine.

"Abe, this is Erin. I decided to check out of the ranch. I'm in Alta, at the Victorian Hotel, room 213. It's nice here. I just didn't want you to think I disappeared. So...I guess I'll see you here Thursday morning? Thanks. Bye."

The machine beeped, concluding the message.

She sounded nervous. But then, she'd never called him before.

Abe replayed the message and scrawled down her room number. Why had she left the ranch?

Probably the tension was too much for her. He couldn't fault her decision. It was good for him, at any rate. His father still lived and worked at the Kays', but after he picked up Noon, Abe could keep his distance. He'd hoped for a chance to talk to Kip about his dad, but maybe it was best left alone. The two men had known each other for decades. And Abe would be there for Lloyd when it was over.

Provided that *over* didn't happen this weekend, which it might. Abe had no solution to that. He'd made a commitment to Guy and another, unspoken, to Lane. Abe needed to see his brother's first professional bull ride. Because neither Lloyd nor Annabelle would.

Why had Erin left the ranch? Something was off, the way there'd been something off with her coming to stay at the Kays' in March. Her wanting to tell him about Maeve explained that, but still...

Something had happened.

He dragged out the phone directory, looked up the number of the Victorian Hotel and phoned Erin. The desk clerk put him through, and Erin answered on the first ring.

"Hello?"

"Hi. It's me. I got your message."

In the hotel room, Maeve was playing with a football-size plastic car on the four-poster bed. Erin watched her without seeing and clung to the voice on the phone. For the past two hours, ever since she'd checked in, she'd wanted to call Jayne, to tell her mother, *You were right. You were right about him.* About Kip Kay, father no more.

It wasn't any fun to want to call someone who was dead.

Abe said, "What happened?"

"I left." She was honest. She had become honest that afternoon, and she didn't need to know the truth about cowboys now that she had said the words she'd said.

It does not hurt.

"You could have come here."

To his trailer at Guy Loren's. Not a chance. She wasn't going to cry on anyone's shoulder about this. Why cry, when she'd been courageous, when she'd confronted her greatest bugaboo?

"Erin?"

"I didn't want to show up at your place without being invited."

"You're invited now."

"Well, I paid for tonight. And tomorrow we're leaving for the rodeo, right?"

"Have you had dinner?"

He sounded almost stern, like he knew something was wrong and suspected she wasn't taking care of herself. Till now, no man had ever talked to her that way.

"No," said Erin. "We haven't eaten." When had his voice become a friend? When had *he* become one?

"I'll be up there in a half hour," said Abe. "After I have a shower. We'll go to the North Forty. Good steaks."

No cowboys, Erin thought. "Okay," she said. *Hurry, Abe.*

ERIN ANSWERED the door in a purple shirt and matching jeans. She looked like nothing was wrong.

But she'd left the ranch. For some reason she had left.

The hotel room was furnished with Tiffany lamps and antique nightstands. The wallpaper was tiny flowers, like the flowers on Maeve's corduroy overalls, and his boots looked messy on the gray plush carpet.

On the bed, Maeve smiled. "Da-dee."

Abe lifted her to his side, met her eyes. "Hi, Maeve. How's my girl? Round up any cattle for me?"

Erin stood at the window chewing her nails. She didn't watch Abe and Maeve. She didn't want to think about Abe or rely on him. He was just someone to be near. Dinner would help. You didn't need anyone when you knew yourself—and knew you were honest. She really was perfectly fine.

"You look pretty."

"Oh, thanks." He hadn't taken off his denim jacket, so he must be hungry for dinner. "Let me get my things."

The tote bag was ready. She shrugged into her duster and picked up Maeve's parka. While Abe guided the baby's arms into the sleeves, fishing in the cuffs to pull her little hands through, Erin stared across dusky rooftops to the gray-white mountains. No stars, no moon. She couldn't see the lights of the ski village from here, but the hotel was full of skiers; it must be spring break.

"Why did you leave?"

She snapped her head around. "What?"

Maeve was stuffing the collar of his shirt into her mouth. Abe set her on her feet on the floor, and the baby clung to the bed and tried walking. "Why did you leave the Kays'?"

Why.

Of course he would ask.

"Did something happen?"

Erin remembered the mud on the road where she'd stood. The mountains that were what they appeared and nothing more and nothing less. Hadn't she promised to tell him sometime why her heroes had always been cowboys? She'd said the truth once today.

You're my friend, she thought. *You let me ride Buy Back.*

The striped sateen chair by the window was ready support. Erin folded herself into it, gripping the arms like an old woman beginning the story of her life. "Kip Kay is my father," she said, and time creaked by with the rhythm of a rocker till her next words. They poured out slowly. "My mother was his first wife. They were married fresh out of high school, and he was drafted. While he was in Vietnam, his father died, and when he came home on compassionate leave, he and my mother conceived me. He was home again, for good, three months later, but my mother said he was different from the man she'd married.

She said he was unfaithful and an alcoholic and...scary. So she left."

The rhythm of the words carried her on. Talking loosened rocks and debris inside her, old junk, but it scattered free in a steady flow, no avalanche. There was no rush to tell Abe; a man who waited for cows to calve didn't know hurry. So she took her time.

"I'd never seen him in my life," said Erin. "He'd never tried to see me. But...when my mother died, it became important to see him. Like I needed to find you, for Maeve.

"I never thought I'd tell him who I was. That wasn't the point. I thought I'd just see him, see who he was. But—" She stopped, not wanting to say why knowing the truth was so important. She didn't want Abe to know how many cowboys had dumped her. "Since I had to tell him I was leaving Thursday for the rodeo, I decided to tell him I was his daughter, too. So I went out to the pasture to see him. I told him I was his d-daughter. He said..." Erin told it. Repeated her father's words. When she felt the tears on her lashes and cheeks, she thought, *The grass cries, too, in the morning, when there's dew on it.*

It did not hurt.

Maeve's sudden tears brought her out of her trance. Erin came up from underwater, and Maeve was staring at her face and crying.

"It's all right, Maeve." Damn, her breasts were going to leak. Erin wiped her eyes with the back of her hand.

"Mama." Crying, Maeve let go of the bed and toddled four steps to her.

"Maeve! You walked!" Erin scooped her up. Maeve was so sensitive, so connected to her. "I love you," she whispered. Abe handed her a bandanna, and Erin wiped her eyes, comforted by a piece of cloth and by Maeve's bottom on her lap. "Mommy's okay, Maeve. You took your first steps. Aren't you proud of yourself?"

After a moment Maeve reached for her bunny, and Erin got up to set her on the spread. She dabbed at her eyes again and didn't give back the bandanna and didn't plan to. "Let's go to dinner, Abe. I'm really okay."

When she turned, she bumped into him. He caught her arm, and Erin studied his hand. His shirt cuffs weren't frayed, but new. He'd dressed up for her. The shirt had an Aztec design and black buttons, and where it was open, she could see his throat. His mouth and eyes held her for a long time.

"I want to sleep over." The rodeo belt buckle almost touching her was a force field.

"Why?"

Abe released her to hold the collar of her coat, to turn it up because it was cold outside, because it was going to snow again. "Because I think about you too much." *I see your eyes when other things are in front of me.* "I like you better than Martha."

She crossed her arms and Abe tightened his grip on her coat. His voice would only stay low. "And I want you how I wanted Buy Back after I sold him."

He held her by her coat and stifled the words he couldn't say about a man he'd known all his life. *And he hurt you! Dammit, how could he hurt you like that?*

THE NORTH FORTY was gone, the windows empty and painted with the words COMING NEXT WEEK: RUNNING DEER GALLERY.

His favorite restaurant was gone.

Embarrassed that he hadn't known, Abe said, "Well, let's go..." He cast his eyes across the snowy street, over the ski racks on the roofs of parked Jeep Cherokees and Saabs.

While people his age rode past on mountain bikes, he strained through the dark to read the shingles swaying over the sidewalk.

Alta had plenty of restaurants. Italian, vegetarian. Holding Maeve, Abe drew Erin back under the old North Forty's awning as a man and woman in matching leather coats and hats walked past.

When he was a kid, this was *town*. Now, he always went to Gunnison for supplies; no one could afford Alta's prices. Abe felt out of place, a century removed from the mountain bikers and snowboarders. Because he had to suggest a restaurant quickly, had to get Erin and Maeve out of the weather, he chose the only one he could think of that he'd been told served steaks. "I guess we'll go to the Okay Corral."

The route took them past a three-story stone building with a historical marker in front. A four-inch layer of snow was heaped on top of the sign, and Erin had to brush more snow away from the front to read the history of the old hospital. Now it housed the Alta museum.

Abe tugged Maeve's floppy-brimmed pile hat down around her ears, keeping her warm. "Think you could get a job here?"

Shivering, Erin eyed the closed door. "It's probably run by volunteers. These small local museums are usually run on a shoestring. But I'd love to go in when it's open."

"I'll take you sometime."

They walked on through the fluffy flakes.

The restaurant sat on the outskirts of Alta on a wide lot with plenty of parking. It was a grand cedar-sided barn, and signs at the entrance read, LINE DANCING EVERY NIGHT.

"Pretty building," Erin said as Abe held the door. He'd

put Maeve down, and the baby practiced her new skills, teetering into the restaurant on her own two feet.

A blond woman with a fringed leather jacket and matching miniskirt beamed at them on her way to the waitress station. "Be right with you." She noticed Maeve's wobbly walk and said, "Well, look at you!"

Maeve laughed up at her, then fell over sideways like a drunk stumbling off a curb. Abe crouched near the baby, and a smile lit Maeve's face again. "Da-dee."

"Maevey."

A lantern made from a tin can punched with holes lit their booth—a thick pine table and good vinyl-covered seat edged with brass tacks. The waitress brought Maeve a maple high chair, and the baby gazed, mesmerized, at the flame in the can.

"This is nice, Abe."

He thought so, too, though he wouldn't have said it where anyone could hear. The I'm Okay, You're Okay Corral was owned by one of the most rabid developers in the Alta area, who made his fortune converting family-owned ranches to subdivisions with houses every half acre.

Erin sensed what he didn't say, that this was the lair of the new cowboys. "Beulah Ann said that if Jack Draw sells, you might want to buy his brand?"

"Our brand."

Smiling, Erin wriggled her hand into the stuffed tote bag and drew out the plastic dog Beulah Ann had given Maeve for her birthday. Maeve reached for it with both hands, but Erin cleared a path on the table, instead. Setting the dog so it faced Maeve, she pressed a knob on its head. It shut its eyes and lifted one ear, then the other. Its eyes shot open, its tongue popped out, and it rolled slowly toward Maeve, who watched studiously.

Abe studied Erin in the candlelight, trying to see a resemblance to Kip. And to Chaley.

He saw some. Her nose and chin were just like her dad's. You thought you knew a man. Kip must be worried now; Chaley sure didn't know about Erin, and Erin held the cards. But Abe couldn't picture Erin making a scene.

She hadn't wanted him to see her cry.

Insight came like a pile driver out of the chute. Wranglers. Riding lessons. Rodeos. A doctorate in Cows.

Her heroes had always been cowboys, and he knew why. She loved cowboys. Because she loved her dad. Without even knowing him. She'd come here to Alta...

To Alta.

Keep your head, Abe.

He kept his thoughts, too. Kept them quiet.

The waitress came around and they ordered. Then Maeve began to fuss, refusing to drink from the bottle of juice Erin had brought. Erin took a receiving blanket from the tote bag, got Maeve out of her high chair and turned toward the wall to nurse. As Maeve latched onto her and the milk let down, Erin relived the first day she'd come to the Kay Ranch, nursing in the kitchen. The approval she thought she'd received from her father.

It doesn't hurt. You never cared, Erin.

Maeve jerked away, not really wanting to nurse, something that happened often lately. It was time to wean her. She began to cry, and Erin unfastened a teething ring from the tote bag.

Abe was thinking about Alta, about being a bullfighter clown from Alta. He stood and reached for Maeve. "I'll take her for a walk."

He lifted the baby and settled her against his shoulder, where Maeve laid her head sleepily, still sniffling. His jeans passed Erin's eyes as he carried their child toward the dark and deserted dance floor.

Good father.

I have just one daughter, Erin.

On the dance floor, Abe turned about with Maeve in his arms, singing to her. Erin craved a pint of Jack Daniel's.

She'd said she was his daughter. She should be cured of cowboys now. But Abe had asked to spend the night, and she'd agreed. Liking her more than his dog and wanting her more than Buy Back were lines she couldn't resist. *They're not lines.*

Yes, they are.

She still couldn't say no to cowboys.

She couldn't say no to Abe. Abe, revolving on the dance floor with Maeve, who was Daddy's girl and the light in his eyes.

So I can't say no to him. So what?

So, it would kill her if he dumped her. *Again.*

He never dumped you; he dumped Chaley.

That didn't comfort her. And *no cowboys* wasn't going to help, not now.

It never had.

Erin tipped back her head, eyeing the chandeliers made from wagon wheels. *No cowboys* wouldn't work. She needed something else.

When she righted her head, she peered through the darkness at the silhouette scene played against a backdrop of red velvet curtains. Cowboy hat and floppy baby's hat, Wrangler legs and boot heels. Maeve's baby hand reached up to touch the square jaw of a descendant of the people who'd settled the West.

Erin forged a tenacity that would put her half sister to shame.

"Cowboy," she said, "you're mine."

She made a vow, and she swore it on the barbed-wire fence where her father had totally and completely rejected her. Erin Mackenzie had been Dumped by Cowboys for the last time.

BEFORE THEY LEFT for dinner, Abe had asked for a crib to be brought up to the hotel room. When they returned, it was there, and Maeve was so sleepy she drifted off while Erin changed her for bed.

Erin wasn't grateful. Because it was down to the matter of sleeping with Abe again and not getting hurt. Not getting left.

Jayne would have suggested—in fact, on occasion *had* suggested—that a little hard-to-get wouldn't hurt.

Too late. There was a cowboy on the bed, with his boots and his hat off. She'd had his baby and he was spending the night.

Erin sat in the wing chair and bent over to untie the laces on her boots. "Your dad's amazing," she said so it wouldn't be quiet in the room. "He told me about your grandfather knowing the blizzard was coming."

"And the hair on the barn."

"Yes." No wonder Abe wanted their brand back. Erin wished he could get it. But the West had already been won, and from now on it could only be bought and sold. Not the hardy or the brave, but the highest bidder would win.

The bed creaked. Abe phoned for a wake-up call, then stood and stretched. Erin dared to meet his eyes.

When he sat down on the edge of the mattress, near her, Erin asked the knees of his jeans, "Does your dog really write you notes?"

She wouldn't look up, so Abe read her question, turned it over and looked at the other side. She was in the game but bidding low; they could joke about "licking." Abe sat motionless, stuck in his own hand. He knew how to bluff and win, but he'd never told a woman he cared.

If he did, it would have to be without words. He didn't know the right ones. What came out was, "I want to kill your father."

Erin laughed, flushing.

Somehow, he *had* said the right thing.

Her eyes were with him then. He could see twin reflections of the Tiffany lamp in her irises. Her graduate-student skin, so much paler and finer than a cowgirl's, got to him. So did her mouth and thinking about the glimpse he'd had of one erect enlarged nipple while Maeve was messing around, not nursing.

You're in trouble, Abe. You're over your head.

He said, "You used me."

Erin jerked her head up, and he was waiting, eyes unblinking. This was the part where she got dumped, and she didn't know why. She tossed her head, used a hand to hold her bangs out of her eyes. "No."

The clock whirred on the nightstand. "What do you mean?" She felt her lips shaking, as though she were lying. "Alta."

Nobody had ever talked to her like this. So straight that she knew what a single word meant. "I showed up in Twin Falls." When his eyes didn't change, she said, "I had your child. Let's not talk about 'used.'"

His eyes kept watching, and she watched back until it became a different kind of looking. Time moved in the slow beats of a Patsy Cline song. "You're Stronger than Me."

He was leaning toward her, and Erin's lips met his, and her eyes watered. His hands took her face.

In bed with her just a little while later, Abe still felt the stuck words, the hand he couldn't play. He kissed them into her mouth, not knowing what they were. This was not Reno. This was not sex as he'd known it.

The insides of her thighs were soft in his hands. He held her and opened her and kissed her.

Erin heard her own moans. "Abe..." The blackness she'd known earlier that day was just outside the circle of pleasure. She could almost not see it. His fingers opened her, slipped inside her and he stroked her with his tongue. "Abe." *I don't want you to know me.*

But this was different from Reno. Different from ever.

He was careful with the condom this time, but it took too long. Long enough for her to forget the way he'd looked at her. His entering her was a return to the graveyard where she'd buried all her hopes and dreams.

Seeing her face, her closed eyes, he knew where she was. The place where fathers rejected you and someone shot your mother. And cowboys didn't show up in Twin Falls.

"Erin."

Her beautiful dark eyes opened.

"Be with me."

The eyes cried.

"It's okay." He laid his body against hers and felt the breasts that nourished his child leak milk against him.

"It doesn't hurt, Abe. It didn't hurt at all."

Bull riders always said the same thing. "I know."

But her eyes still cried and her tears said, *I'll call.* They said, *Show your hand. Like my daddy showed his.*

She was too damned used to letting men go.

He's a son of a bitch, Erin. His arms tried to hold all of her, her breasts and arms and tears and the head that knew all about cowboys. That knew too much.

Erin couldn't stop crying, but it was okay. This friend was with her, and he was such a good friend she could ask him for the truth about cowboys. She could ask him what she couldn't ask a man with two daughters who said he had just one. She could ask him what she'd known never to ask Jayne.

And she was crying so hard it didn't matter, it didn't matter if she said it out loud, if she wept it to Abe and the words were incoherent. *"Why doesn't he want me?"*

"And my gal has gone away,
Left my shack and traveled away
With a son of a gun from Io-way
And left me a lone man, a lone man today."

—"Ten Thousand Cattle,"
Nineteenth-century cowboy song

10

"I MADE HIM a pencil holder in day camp for Father's Day. I didn't want to. I wanted to make something for my mom and pretend I had a dad to give it to. The counselor kept asking me what my father liked, so I said cows, and then I was cutting out pictures of cows. I pasted them on this orange-juice can. Then, the day we took it home, I threw it in the outside trash can where my mom wouldn't see it." The clock whirred in darkness. "I've never told anyone that."

And she told him about the older kids making juice-can pencil holders at Maeve's day care. And about his being on the cover of *Prorodeo Sports News* the same day. She told him about the manila envelope, and then she was naked.

Sometime after midnight he said, "I want you to move in with me. I want to drive to Reno after the rodeo and get your stuff."

His hands and body had heated her skin for hours. There was no pain anymore. Just a bliss so complete that Kip Kay was irrelevant. What Abe said wasn't, and she imagined packing up everything in her mother's house.

It had to happen, anyhow; the sale would close soon, and where would she go? Earlier that day, she'd checked her answering machine long-distance. No one calling to request an interview. "I don't have a job here."

"That's okay."

I'll have some money from the sale of the house. His engagement with Chaley, the fact that he might have married for land, nagged at her for one second, then went away.

"Okay," she said.

Abe didn't answer. Her head was against his chest, and she raised it to see if he'd fallen asleep. His mouth was a bleak line that changed only when he saw her notice. "Great. Thanks."

"What's wrong?"

"Nothing." Abe hugged her. Nothing was wrong, except that soon he'd be out of a job, too. Looking for a new one, to carry him high and fast to his goals.

He would reach them, whatever it took, and someday he'd have a ranch of his own, a ranch for Erin and Maeve. But when he imagined that time, he thought of the best cowboy he knew, who wouldn't drive a tractor or pull a horse trailer again. He saw Jack Draw's lodge-pole fence and developers coming and going in helicopters.

He saw a world that had become hostile to his dreams.

THEY ARRIVED at Guy Loren's place at five the next morning. While Erin went back to sleep with Maeve in the fifth wheel, Abe helped him load broncs and bulls into semi trucks for the drive to Nevada. Buy Back would travel with the other horses so that Abe could go to Reno with Erin to help her move. Martha would ride in the truck bed, under the camper shell.

"So you've got a family now," remarked the stock contractor, who never asked what had become of Chaley.

"Yes."

Loren must have seen the future in the clouds. "There's room here for a bigger trailer than that fifth wheel. Feel free to bring one in."

"Thanks." He needed more than a bigger home. Abe worked twelve-hour days for Loren, feeding the stock, helping with calving and foaling, mending fences, shoeing horses, trimming the bulls' hooves. "But I can't support a family on four hundred a month."

Steam from the trucks billowed around the stock contractor while he considered. "Five do you?"

Loren gave him gas, food for the horses, the fifth wheel and utilities. *We could get by*, thought Abe.

But he wanted more than that for Maeve.

And he wanted to give Erin what Kip Kay never would. *I've wanted to live on a ranch my whole life.*

"Well, you think on it," said Loren. "Let's put Buy Back in the big trailer with the ropers."

At six Lane showed up in his quarter-ton pickup, fired with energy, like a gun ready to go off.

When he could get in a word around Lane's running commentary on the bulls, Abe asked, "Kip or Dad hasn't said anything about the driver's license?" The rancher's name was a bad taste in his mouth.

"Nah. Dad was saddling Bo when I left."

"Did you remember to say goodbye?"

"I did. He said, 'Don't break your neck like your brother.'"

When they returned from Reno, Abe decided, he would go see his dad, even if it meant running into Kip Kay. He didn't believe the rancher would let Lloyd stay on as foreman with no license. And if he didn't...

Maybe we can all leave together. Get out of Colorado and try Wyoming or Montana. He didn't think about real-estate prices climbing in those states, too. About land values climbing all over the West. He'd find a way.

Because he never wanted Erin to have to see her father again. He never wanted Maeve to have to know him.

And it would kill Lloyd Cockburn to learn he was working for a man who wouldn't acknowledge their mutual grandchild.

ABE'S AND LANE'S PICKUPS led the semis down the road and soon lost them. Clear skies and dry pavement started the day, and when the sun came up, as they neared Delta, Colorado, the snow had disappeared.

He and Erin listened to music and talked. Abe asked about Maeve's birth and learned Jayne Mackenzie was there and that Maeve had been pink and pretty from the start. He learned Jayne had been shot in the chest with a .38. He learned Erin had had the living room repainted and the carpet replaced. She couldn't sell the house the way it was.

He learned it was hard to travel to a rodeo with a one-year-old baby.

All the way they startled magpies and ravens in the road, eating the unlucky. Raptors circled high over Utah's San Rafael Swell, so many that Abe wondered what was dead or dying there.

Heading south on I-15, Erin suddenly turned down the stereo. "Abe, Beulah Ann said you had a sister."

"Yeah. Busy. She fell between the wheels of the tractor while my dad was baling hay. She liked to ride with him."

"When did your folks get divorced?"

"Oh, you want the *whole* story." He told her about the

days after Busy died, about his mother's leaving. "My dad said that Mom didn't know where she'd be going, that she'd be looking for a job, that she couldn't take care of us for a while. I was a teenager and wanted to stay where I was. I loved the ranch. But Lane loved Mom. He used to ask me every day when she was coming to get us." His voice quit him then. Lane was two vehicles ahead in his silver-blue pickup. The eighteen-year-old Lane. At six he'd been sweet. He'd turned from hopeful to heartbroken to bitter to thoughtless.

Did Erin need to know more? The phone call on Lane's birthday was worth a mention. "She hasn't been to Colorado since she left us. It sounded like she really wanted to see Maeve. But I'm not going to hold my breath." A prairie dog ran between his wheels and lived.

"It's interesting," Erin said, "that your mother and my mother both left their husbands."

"And for about the same reasons, sounds like."

"What's that?" As best Erin could make out, Abe's mother had left because she couldn't stand the pain of living on the place where her child had died. Jayne had left Kip because—

"Fear."

Passing a truck, Abe caught sight of Lane's bumper stickers. I'M A LOVER, FIGHTER AND WILD BULL RIDER. COWBOYS DO IT ALL. The seal of the National Rifle Association stained his rear windshield.

Lane was pulling off at a diner and Abe flipped his turn signal. As he shut off the engine outside the restaurant, he saw Erin twisting gingerly to unbuckle Maeve. "What's wrong?"

"Oh. I'm engorged. I'm weaning her."

He winced. Cows were never happy in that state of

affairs; he doubted women liked it, either. "Is there anything you can do?"

She shrugged. "It should just last a few days. But she flinched again as she started to lift the waking Maeve from her seat.

"I've got her." But Abe leaned toward Erin first, knocking her brow with the brim of his hat before he managed to kiss her.

"WHAT ARE YOU telling me, Abe?" asked the announcer.

Erin shifted a restless Maeve in her lap. In the center of the Laughlin arena, Abe raised one hand and bounced, as though he was on the back of a bull.

"You want to be a *bull rider*?"

Nodding. Swagger. Abe rooted through his satchel and pulled out a pair of pink chaps with green fringe. They looked like they'd been made from a tablecloth.

"And you even have some new chaps."

"That's Daddy," Erin told Maeve. "Do you see Daddy?"

"Da-dee?" asked Maeve, not finding him nearby. "Da-dee?"

Oh, God, we're a family. It was relief and bliss at once. After letting Abe really see her last night and finding she was loved, anyhow, Erin had started on a full-speed gallop, and she was still riding, and she'd already forgotten what it was like to be thrown.

"Abe," the announcer was saying, "if you want to ride a bull, you need to go to the chutes. Go to the chutes, and they'll let you ride a bull. They said so. Why, Marauder is all ready for you."

But the clown argued, shaking his head.

Erin wanted to see better. She picked up her tote bag. "Let's go down to the fence, Maeve."

"All right, Abe, we'll let you do this your way. Now,

we're going to let Marauder into the ring. Are you ready to ride him?"

Abe was cool. Abe was ready to ride. Abe was making hundreds of people laugh. Their laughter exploded around Erin as she negotiated the wooden steps, picking her way over half-eaten hot dogs and strewn buns and mustard.

A gate opened and a gray bull with a Brahma-type hump trotted into the arena, spotted Abe and stopped. Abe tiptoed toward it and the bull trotted away.

"Abe, how do you expect to get on that bull when it won't hold still?"

Finding an empty seat in the front row, Erin set Maeve on her feet. The baby squatted in the dust and slowly lifted her plastic dog out of the tote bag. Erin marveled at Abe. Mixing athletic skill with a clown's clumsiness, he ran toward the bull in the most ridiculous way imaginable and sprang onto its back.

The crowd's breath was a drumbeat through the arena.

Marauder came to a dead stop.

"Abe, that bull's not bucking too good. Why don't you spur him some?"

Abe spurred.

The bull would not move. Laughter rolled over the stands.

Abe slid off the bull, then came around in front of it, drawing out a bandanna to use as a matador's cape.

Marauder's head shifted from side to side. Then lowered. As he charged, Abe vaulted over his head and landed on his back, facing the tail.

Surely, Erin thought, it wasn't supposed to happen this way. It was all going too fast, with Abe being bucked through the air off the back of that bull, tumbling onto the ground. Scrambling to his feet, he ran, with the bull chasing, and Erin tried to revive the feelings of the first night she'd watched him clown and bullfight. When it didn't matter if he tripped and fell.

Abe hit the fence and flipped over it, and only then did Erin notice that her jaw hurt, that she'd been clenching it.

"Well, Abe, you didn't make eight seconds, but what do you say, folks? Let's give this cowboy a hand." Even the announcer was chuckling.

Cowboys would be cowboys, from Theseus to Abe. Erin asked Maeve, "Isn't Daddy silly?"

Maeve raised her head, hunting for him. "Da-dee?"

"Now, let's introduce you to our next bull rider. This cowboy is from Alta, Colorado, and he's the brother of our bullfighter clown, Abe. Lane Cockburn is a rookie who went to the high-school national finals, and this is his first professional rodeo. Let's see if this cowboy can bring home some money on Lightning Rod."

Abe and another bullfighter waited near the chutes. When number three opened, a black-Angus cross sprang out, bucking and spinning. Abe danced near the bull, turning him, helping his brother's score. Lane's arm sailed high, his body hung loose, and his turquoise chaps flapped and shimmered with each movement of the bull. When the bell rang, he dismounted with a well-timed leap to the ground and landed on his feet.

Erin jumped up, cheering at the top of her lungs till Maeve lifted her eyes, bewildered.

Even the announcer raised his voice to be heard over the roar from the stands. "Ladies and gentlemen, that is how the cowboys do it! You have just seen some *buulll* riding!"

"*Yes*, Lane," whispered Erin as he hurled his hat in the air. Because superimposed on the eighteen-year-old athlete, she saw a six-year-old boy asking when his mother was coming to get him.

Lane's score was seventy-eight, and Erin was so excited

for him that she scarcely listened to the next rider's introduction. A Brahma bull leaped out of a chute, losing his rider on the second buck. The cowboy fell directly under the bull's head, and its horns tossed him like laundry in the dryer while a figure in a patchwork shirt and Wranglers pushed on the animal's head, shoving against him.

Abe.

"Mama. Da-dee." Maeve pointed at a puppy going past on a leash.

The bull knocked Abe over, and its weight-bearing back hooves came down on his shoulder. Erin understood about seeing things in slow motion. Seeing him scramble away. Seeing him run, holding his shoulder, to the edge of the arena.

Erin stuffed everything in the tote bag and scooped up Maeve. Her engorged breasts felt like hardwood, ready to break off if they were bumped. The announcer was talking about the brave bullfighters, assuring the audience that Abe was all right but was going to visit the paramedics. He thanked Justin Boots for their mobile sports-medicine program, which made emergency medical care available at professional rodeos.

Abe was sitting in the back of the ambulance, getting his shoulder wrapped, when Erin found him. Lane and Martha were with him, Lane still flying high after his ride. As Erin joined them, Abe winked at her and told Lane, "You'll have to beat seventy-eight if you want to impress Beulah Ann."

Maeve made a sound asking to get down, and when Erin let her stand in the dirt, she toddled toward Martha. "Da-dee."

"Beulah Ann's impressed," Lane said knowingly.

And Erin saw Beulah Ann drying dishes and singing "Someday Soon," and she knew the reason for the song.

Abe grew interested in watching the paramedic finish binding his shoulder. "Thanks."

As a mutt trotted past, Maeve earned Lane's disinterested glance by waddling after it. He was closest to her and didn't move. Erin took two steps to pick her up, but Martha beat her to the scene. The Australian shepherd froze in front of the baby, held her ground and herded her back to Abe and Erin. Maeve put her hands up to Martha's head and giggled at a tongue licking her face. Then she turned and toddled to Abe.

"Good dog," he told Martha, and asked the paramedic, "Isn't that the smartest dog you ever saw?"

"Just about."

Erin helped him with his shirt and his suspenders. Her fingers liked even the sweat-soaked cloth of his shirt. He was warm—and hers. "Think they'll give you a reride on Marauder?"

Nearby Lane sang Chris LeDoux's "Reride" and threw his hat in the air again. Abe didn't smile at what she'd said, and Erin wondered if he, too, was thinking about Lane and Beulah Ann.

IN ABE'S OPINION, nothing short of a bone sticking through his skin deserved an X ray. And nothing less than a broken neck could have kept him from bullfighting and clowning over the next days. Filing this information under the truth about cowboys, Erin enjoyed the rodeo. Abe looked after Maeve so Erin could ride Buy Back before the performances. He introduced her to the other bullfighters, who treated her like a lady and flirted with the baby. And Lane kept the lead four days running and finished out the rodeo with eight thousand dollars in cash.

Erin learned more about Abe.

That he'd always loved clowns and that he'd only been a

bulldogger two weeks before he decided he'd rather be a bull*fighter*. That, like every rodeo cowboy she'd ever met, he really wanted to raise cows—his own. That the loss of his father's ranch had colored his horizons the shade of futility. And that she might find a rose on her pillow from time to time.

If she'd had seventy-five million dollars, she would have given him back the ranch. Short of that, she created other dreams.

Sunday night, after the last performance, Erin and Abe drove to Reno, an eight-hour trek. They arrived at Erin's mother's house, the scene of Jayne's murder, at five in the morning. In Erin's room they set up Erin's old crib for Maeve, and when the baby was asleep, they made love in the bed where they'd conceived her.

In the morning Erin phoned her attorney, told him she was moving, and made arrangements to come by and give him power of attorney so that he could close on the house and finish settling her mother's estate. As Abe helped Maeve with her breakfast dish of applesauce at the kitchen table, Erin said, "We've got to pick up Taffy, too."

"Who's Taffy?"

"My mother's cocker spaniel."

Abe remembered Taffy. She would never make a decent cow dog. In fact, she was the kind of creature that gave dogs a bad name. "I'll get her when I pick up the U-Haul."

"Thank you."

"Want to come with me, Maeve? We can have a good time in Reno."

He spent the next few hours helping Erin pack boxes, but at eleven she caught him loafing in the bedroom with Maeve. The baby was pulling tissues out of a box one by one. Abe was reading her doctoral thesis.

Erin left them there, and Abe didn't say anything about it

when he came downstairs with Maeve. The two of them headed out to drop off some boxes and furniture they didn't want at the Salvation Army, rent the trailer and pick up the dog.

Even after he'd gone, the house felt safe. But Erin was glad to be leaving it.

She'd already sorted through her mother's closet, saving a few clothes and some jewelry, boxing the rest to give away. She planned to keep the cedar chest Jayne had kept at the end of her bed, but she should also go through the contents.

On the top layer inside was a patchwork quilt Erin had asked years before if she could have. *No, it was my grandmother's.* Jayne's family was all gone.

I could have had family from the Kays' side, thought Erin. Beulah. Chaley.

It wasn't worth contemplating.

The box beneath the quilt contained her mother's wedding dress, which Jayne had let her try on when she was in high school. Erin set it on the bed, then lifted the lids on the shoe and hat boxes beneath. Costume jewelry. Photos.

Letters from Vietnam.

Erin snatched up the shoe box, tearing one side of the flimsy cardboard. Hurrying, shaking, she made a place for herself on the bed. She'd found her mother's letters from her father.

And she was going to read them.

The paper crackled as she opened the first airmail envelope with its military address and foreign stamps. Vietnam had happened before she was born and had taught Erin that war was a call for peace. Movies showed gore and evil and brutality. The writings of veterans told more, and Erin had read them until she thought she grasped the war and its aftermath as well as she could any history she hadn't lived.

But Kip Kay had been there.

And he wasn't what she'd expected at all. He wasn't like her history professor, or the man who ran the dry cleaner she and her mother had used, or their mail carrier, or Dan in the wheelchair at the university library, or any of the other Vietnam vets Erin knew, slightly or otherwise. Those men wore their sensitivity in their eyes and their smiles. Even their joy, friendliness at seeing her, had an aching quality, as though they had become helpless channels for emotion. She thought their pain must fill their whole insides, pack every pore.

She found them beautiful.

But she could only see Kip Kay through the eyes of the daughter he did not want.

Erin unfolded a letter.

"ERIN?"

Taffy raced ahead of Abe into the house, sniffing corners, madly wagging her tail. While Martha demonstrated more reserve, Abe set down Maeve, who wanted to walk. She made straight for the nearest dog, who was Martha.

"Erin?" he repeated.

Then he saw her, outside in a chaise longue, her face pointed to the sun, dark glasses over her eyes. Abe crossed the room, slid open the door and went out. "Hi." He kept an eye on Maeve and grinned as Martha herded her toward him.

Erin's eyes shifted from his boots and jeans to Maeve, who paused before testing out the step at the door. She couldn't decide whether to ask Abe to read her father's letters or to keep them to herself. The earlier letters were a man's attempt to conceal ugliness from his loved ones. In later epistles he'd told things.

It was hard to be a cowboy in Quang Ngai Province in 1969. It was hard to be at all.

"You okay?" Abe crouched beside her chair. He wished he hadn't left her alone in the house where her mother was murdered. Alone with her memories.

"Yes. Hello, Maeve."

"Mama."

Erin lifted the baby into the chair. The sun felt too intense on her skin; she burned easily, and she knew they should go inside. "I found my father's letters to my mother. From when he was in Vietnam."

Abe backed up and sat in the other folding chair. His hat cast a shadow across Maeve's body.

"She shouldn't have left him, Abe. She said he was scary. But I bet he was just afraid. Intense. He needed her."

Abe didn't know what to say. Except, "That doesn't make up for what he did to you."

"It does." She lowered Maeve to the ground, got up and went inside. She'd packed the letters in her duffel bag in the living room. Now she brought one out to him. "Read that."

Not sure he wanted to, Abe opened the envelope and unfolded the sheet inside. He read the whole letter, then folded it and replaced it in the envelope. He handed it to Erin. "Nice thing to do to your mother."

"Don't be such a cowboy," she snapped, surprising them both.

"What is *that* supposed to mean?"

"He couldn't stand it anymore! Terrible things happened to him." Erin's voice was too high, too insistent, almost hysterical. "It was my mother's fault, too. She should have gotten help for him, and she just left."

"Yeah, it's pretty easy to help a six-foot cowboy getting

drunk and going bonkers on a ranch too faraway for the neighbors to hear you scream." "Scary" sounded definite to Abe—definitely not a good place for a baby. Baby Erin.

Kip Kay was an asshole.

"I don't care." Erin seemed to be gazing at the board-and-batten fence. The sunglasses hid her eyes. "Maybe she should've left, maybe not. But now I understand him. He *is* my father. And he's still my hero." Her lips trembled like they had when she'd told him her father said she wasn't his. "Just for walking around today, being sane. Just for raising Chaley to a functional adult. Just for raising cows. Just for waking up in the morning. He's my hero."

Abe had never heard anyone's voice shake like that. If he'd believed in premonition, he would have acknowledged the goose walking over his grave. Would have acknowledged that Erin's declaration meant something, some unfocused determination in her.

He didn't listen. Erin's sweet loyalty made him want to get his hands on Kip Kay's throat. So did the sight of his own daughter, with her soft red curls, lifting up her arms to him. "Da-dee."

WHEN THEY REACHED Guy Loren's place Tuesday afternoon with Abe driving the U-Haul and Erin following in her mother's car, Kip Kay's truck blocked the steps to the stock contractor's trailer. The rancher leaned against the cab while Guy Loren rested at the edge of his porch with his arms across his chest. In the truck bed, the border collie and blue heeler stood alert, watching the vehicles drive in, barking as they spotted Martha in the window of Abe's pickup. Taffy was crated in the Mustang.

Abe turned past the corral and barn. What was Kip doing here?

It took only a heartbeat to figure it out.

Kip had come to see *him*, to talk about Lloyd. About Lloyd's not being foreman anymore.

Little as Abe wanted to breathe the same air as Kip Kay, he had to face him on this. He had to find out about Lloyd so he could be there for his dad when the blow came. If it hadn't come already.

He shut off the engine, and the Mustang parked beside him. Martha was whimpering, and he let her out to go have a reunion with the Kay Ranch dogs. Erin was unbuckling Maeve. When she put the baby down on the gravel, Abe asked, "Why don't you two go on inside? Don't unload anything. I need to talk to Kip. I think he's here about my dad."

Erin's face was startlingly white, her eyes strange.

"His job," Abe explained. "His license."

"Oh."

"Hold on to Taffy. That blue dog will eat her."

He left his family and walked back toward Guy's double-wide. The snow on the road had partially melted, and mud grabbed at his boots. The dogs were out of the truck bed, making rounds with Martha. The men watched him and then Kip straightened up and came to meet him, his hat low over his eyes.

Abe felt dizzy and, when the cattleman neared him, told himself it was just the usual uneasiness that never came to anything. Kip Kay's blue eyes were sober and steady.

"Abe."

"Kip." *I hate your guts. I hate you for hurting Erin, but I'll talk to you for my daddy's sake.* "What's going on?"

"Abe, your daddy had a stroke last night. He died."

There was some kind of scream inside him. He was going to cry. Lloyd couldn't be dead.

Kip kept his eyes on him, looking like a man who had seen other men break down and knew what to do. His eyes radiated—reached out—with a compassion Abe couldn't take. He turned his back, ducked his head to keep his face in the shadow of his hat. To block the force of the afternoon sun, the spring day his father was dead.

Kip was still there, his shadow stretching beside Abe's.

Abe started to walk away, to escape the gray shape on the ground, the man who had cast it, but Kip said, "Beulah Ann took off to tell your brother. She felt, since you were on the road, that waiting till you got home would increase the chances of Lane learning it from someone else."

Half-turned, listening, Abe nodded. Lane would be coming home. He wished he could have been the one to tell him. But Lane had taken this risk in chasing rodeo.

Abe had taken it.

That his dad would be dead someday when he came back.

"In a while," said Kip, "when you're up to it, I have some business I'd like to talk with you."

"You can talk now."

The cattleman's eyes were calm. Their calm muted the impact of Abe's quick wrath. "Let's wait till your daddy's in the ground."

"You and I don't have any business we can do together when you say something to Erin like 'I have only one daughter.' Do you have grandchildren, Kip? Do you? Because I have a beautiful red-haired daughter, and I had her with your beautiful red-haired daughter. I think that makes you a grandfather, don't you?"

A gust of wind shivered through the cottonwoods. High overhead, the branches creaked. "Your daddy had wages coming." Kip unfastened a pocket of his barn coat and drew out a folded bundle of hundred-dollar bills. "One month's foreman's pay."

Money to bury Lloyd. *He knows I can't do it.* Abe watched his own hand take the bills.

"I loved your daddy." Kip's eyes were square on Abe's. "I'd like you to have his job."

He wanted to say *no*. And *I'd like you to acknowledge your daughter*.

But he had no leverage with Kip Kay. He was a good hand, but he was young, without experience in running a ranch. Only the experience of watching his own father. No one else would offer him the position of ranch foreman.

And after he'd hurt Chaley...

There wasn't anything to say. He couldn't think or fight or hate anymore. So he walked away without looking back. He walked to the corral to rest his arms on the fence and stare at Buy Back till his horse came to him, the light glinting on his shifting muscles, moving the shadows on his coat, his red mane blowing.

With Kip behind him, out of sight and mind, there was only one thought left, only one reality under the dreadful afternoon sun.

He wouldn't see Lloyd again. Not alive.

The last of the great cowboys was dead, and Abe hadn't been there to save him.

> *"Those who work the land control the food.*
> *Nature prevents their being tyrants."*

> —Erin Mackenzie,
> "Cattle and Cowboys: The Ancient
> Currency of a Modern Enigma"

11

WHEN HE ENTERED the trailer, Maeve's toys made an obstacle course on the floor, and the dogs ran it to get to him. Erin was on the love-seat bench, and Abe said it out loud to her eyes, trying to make it real. "My daddy had a stroke. He's dead."

Erin got up and held him. She pictured an old cowboy gracefully spinning in place, dancing with a baby in the kitchen of his trailer, heard him singing "Red River Valley." Now she would hear no more stories from the man who had ridden to school in a bus equipped with a woodstove. Whose father had predicted an afternoon blizzard by looking at a morning sky.

And Jayne was newly dead. Parents left like this, one by one. Or they left their children by choice, and death's pain came twice. Or they never arrived, like her father.

Maeve stood up, wobbled and tried walking toward Martha. "Da-gee."

"Does she know the stove is hot, Erin?"

His voice was different. Slower, like his voice was trying to go somewhere and death had caught it.

"I watch her."

Abe picked up the baby, set her near the stove and put her tiny hand against it.

"Abe!"

Maeve began to cry and pulled her hand away. She wailed, gazing up at Abe with a look that said he'd betrayed her.

Meeting her eyes, he said, "Hot." He carried her to the sink to put her hand under the cold water.

Erin had risen. "I can't believe you did that."

Maeve was still crying as Abe shut off the water.

"There's a woodstove in half the buildings in Alta. Now she knows the stove is hot. This way, she didn't get hurt."

There were names to call him. Old-fashioned, pigheaded, stupid, ignorant cowboy whose father had just died. Spreading his pain around.

Maeve cried, "Bah-bah!"

Erin took a bottle from the refrigerator and Abe reached for it. He sat down with the baby in his lap, and Maeve held the bottle and drank greedily, sniffing only occasionally. Then she threw down the bottle and cried again. Erin picked it up.

"Don't give it back," said Abe. "She can start learning not to do that right now." He let Maeve down to the floor.

Beneath the table, the baby gave the stove a look that said it, too, had betrayed her. Then she made tracks for Martha. "Da-gee."

Abe dropped the bills Kip had given him on the table. Lloyd's last pay. *Lloyd. Oh, God, Lloyd, he must be wrong.*

When would Lane hear the words that their father was dead? And Abe had to call Annabelle, had to call her right away.... His eyes were wet, stinging, as Erin slid into the booth beside him. Family had changed, and he and Erin were the head of it, and he was a child no more. He was the father. He held Erin, the mother, needing her. Her mother had been murdered, and she'd shown him how strong he could be.

When he released her, Erin saw the hundreds on the table. On the outermost bill, someone had drawn a peace sign in ballpoint pen.

They were the bills she'd given her father for her week at the ranch.

"What's that from?"

"My dad's last wages. Kip offered me his job."

The foreman's job? The foreman's job came with the foreman's trailer, on the Kay Ranch. She refused to analyze this. She had turned her back on the truth about cowboys. Or maybe she'd read it in her father's letters. He'd played dead and survived. He said the wounded cried for their mothers.

"I won't take it," said Abe. Maeve had returned to him and was holding on to his knee. "Not while he won't acknowledge his granddaughter." Lloyd's granddaughter. *Lloyd... Oh, Daddy.*

"Maybe this is his way of giving her what he can. Of giving both of us...all of us...what he can."

Abe stared. He'd held a weeping child in his arms Wednesday night. *All I wanted was the truth about cowboys.* Her words had made no sense, but she'd made plenty. He hadn't been able to tell her why her daddy didn't want her. And she'd found love letters and war letters, and on the patio of her murdered mother's house she'd said, *He's my hero.*

There were answers to that, and he could say them now, when she defiled Lloyd by pretending Kip was generous. "He's not a hero and this isn't giving. He's sick, and we'll all be better off where we can't catch it."

She was white, and her lips shook, and then she wouldn't look at him.

LANE WAS HOME the next morning, and in the afternoon Abe drove to the Kay Ranch to pick him up so they could go to the funeral home in Alta and see Lloyd.

Chaley's truck was parked by the big house. She must be back from Fort Collins, but Abe didn't see her and was glad.

Lane was waiting outside the trailer like he couldn't stand to be inside. To get in the cab, he had to scoot Martha and Taffy out of the way. "What's that?" he said of the cocker spaniel.

"Taffy." Abe opened the door to put both dogs in the back, and Taffy took off down the road, chasing a bird. "Taffy!"

She stopped, looked back and sprinted away. The blue heeler sleeping in the sun by the shed opened his eyes and lifted his head. He sat up.

"Leave her," said Lane. "Maybe something will eat her, or she'll wander in with the cows and they'll step on her."

Abe went after the cocker spaniel and found her behind the barn where George, one of the hands, had caught her. The blue heeler was wagging his tail and all but French-kissing her. The cowboy smirked as he handed over the dog.

"I didn't pick her out," Abe told him. You spent five years raising the smartest dog in the world, and God gave you this to keep her company.

George said, "Sorry about your daddy."

"Me, too."

When Abe had put both dogs in the bed of the pickup under the camper shell and joined his brother in the cab, Lane passed him a pint of Jack Daniel's. Abe took a swig, gave it back and started the truck. Nothing was going to ease this pain. He'd called Annabelle yesterday, and she had cried, too, and asked if there was anything she could do and where to send flowers.

To the same place they'd sent them for Busy. But Abe didn't say that. Only the name of the funeral home.

Annabelle did not mention coming to Colorado.

At the highway Lane got the gate. Back in the truck afterward he asked, "You ever seen a dead person?"

"Busy."

"No one offered to let me see her." He swallowed more whiskey.

It wasn't the kind of thing you showed a six-year-old. Abe wished he could make the world right for Lane. His brother's meanness was like an unripe patch on a peach. A lot of the fruit was fine, and the bitter part could be, too.

If Lane could forgive what their mother had done.

Abe had forgiven her long ago. But part of him doubted his brother ever would. And he didn't know the words to tell Lane that the resentment, if he kept it, would eat away and make him rotten inside, all the way through.

THE FUNERAL DIRECTOR, who was in shirtsleeves and jeans and boots, said, "Sure you don't want to wait till I fix him up?"

Abe shook his head without consulting Lane. He'd seen Busy before and after this same man worked on her. Dead people were dead. With makeup or without.

"Well, let me wheel him out of the lab at least."

The funeral director left them in the foyer. The whole place had a smell Abe couldn't name but remembered from Busy's death thirteen years ago. He and Lane passed the pint in silence before the mortician returned and opened the doors to the chapel.

Abe removed his hat and Lane snatched off his, too, and they went in. Their boots on the oak floorboards made church echoes. While the funeral director hung back, Abe led his brother toward the gurney where their father lay, covered with a sheet. Then it was real. He saw Lloyd's face, so different with his mouth sealed shut over his overbite and something like Vaseline on his eyelids. His bare shoulder with its freckles and moles showed above the sheet, and Abe touched it. The body was hard and cool. Room temperature. Totally unmoving.

Dead.

His hair was combed right, because the funeral director knew Lloyd.

Lane's sob choked into the dark chamber. "Daddy."

Abe gazed at his father's face that would not awaken.

I miss you. I'm going to miss you.

After a bit he sat on an oak bench in the front row, three yards from the body, to get to know his father in death. Lane followed, sticking beside him, the way he had when he was a kid. The pint was stowed. Lane leaned forward, his hands toying with his hat.

The shadowed profile of their father's death mask, the body under the sheets, was not obscene. It was just death, and Lloyd's spirit was there with his boys. Abe's lips moved, and he sang softly:

"From this valley they say you are going.
I will miss your bright eyes and sweet smile.
They say you are taking the sunshine
That has brightened our pathway a while."

Lane chimed in, low at first, then strong. They harmonized as they had around mountain campfires, summer nights. Each note fell true and on key. Every word, every verse, every beat honored the waltz that was Lloyd, and the serenade swelled to its end with a sweetness born of deepest loyalty and love.

"But remember the Red River Valley
and the cowboy who loves you so true."

"HE HAS A PLOT," the funeral director revealed later across the desk where business was conducted, "with his parents and his sister. And with Busy."

"Fine."

"You'll need to choose a casket."

Abe and Lane descended to the basement, where the satin-lined caskets were all opened. The funeral director told them the prices, and they were all too much. Abe and Lane exchanged looks. Lloyd would have a fit if he knew they paid so much for a box to bury him in. Abe said, "We'll make one."

"You know, arrangements can—"

"No. We'll build it." Oak. Lloyd would look fine in his black suit and bolo tie.

Upstairs the funeral director gave him the figures and discussed payment plans. The brothers' eyes met again. As one they said, "We'll pay cash up front."

Abe brought out the bills Kip had given him and money from his own paycheck. Lane produced his wallet, stuffed with Laughlin rodeo winnings, to make up the difference.

They paid for these rites of death and left to go to the lumberyard to buy wood for another.

"I'M NOT STAYING for the funeral," Lane said.

They'd almost reached the Kay Ranch. Abe nearly swerved.

"I'm leaving for Texas in the morning. Corpus Christi."

Thirty-thousand dollars. Rodeo.

Abe flicked on the turn signal.

"I've seen him. We said goodbye. It couldn't mean more than that. More than 'Red River Valley.' I'm at peace."

Abe supposed he shouldn't blame his brother for thinking the world spun on the axis of his own existence. He sure hadn't thought of Lane when he'd signed on with Guy Loren at eighteen, when he'd hit the rodeo road.

What goes around comes around.

"You know, that was Dad's favorite song," said Lane, "and it's all about a sweetheart leaving. Does that make sense to you?"

"Maybe." Lloyd forgave. Lloyd had forgiven a president and an economy that cost him his ranch. And Lloyd had forgiven his wife, his sweetheart, who couldn't stay where her child had died.

From this valley they say you are going...

When Abe pulled up beside his father's old trailer, Kip was in the corral inspecting the shoes on his horses. He patted the horse he'd just been checking and let himself out the gate.

"Want me to help you clean out the trailer?" Lane asked.

"Just get whatever you want." *And go rodeo.*

As Kip Kay made his way toward the truck, Lane fiddled with a thread on his jeans.

"I'll help you build the coffin."

"I'll do it."

Biting his lip, Lane climbed out of the truck to go inside.

Kip Kay stopped six feet from the front bumper, and Abe got out, went to lean against the hood. It was almost warm, a balmy spring day. A day when calves were born and a cowboy was tempted to buy a new hat.

Lloyd...

"Given it some thought?" asked the rancher.

The heat in Abe's chest was painful. It hurt to be calm, to be level, the way you knew Kip Kay expected you to be. Kip Kay had been a soldier and had written things to his wife that had kept Abe, a man, awake nights. "I don't," Abe answered slowly, "understand you." He measured his words, shaped them. "You know I'm going to marry Erin. You know she's the mother of my child. And you won't say she's your daughter."

"She knows better than to expect to have part of this ranch. But if you take this job, you can give her a chance to know the life."

"She doesn't want your ranch. She wants you. My father's *dead*. You'll live another twenty years. She just wants to be your daughter."

"Well, that's not going to happen. You get older, you'll see that you invest your life in certain quarters, and you protect those interests when they're threatened."

Abe couldn't see Kip's face well because of the sun. "Chaley?"

"Erin's got you, the one thing my daughter wanted more than anything. The only compensation I can give her is this land. And during my lifetime, you and Erin can earn your living from it, too. She won't be salaried, but I'll give you a living wage."

Abe had counted the bills Kip gave him the day before. Counted them out to the funeral director. Eight hundred dollars a month. That and the trailer and unlimited gasoline were the foreman's pay.

He wasn't going to do better—unless he went up the road to ask a movie-star rancher for a job. And maybe not then. The dream of his own spread came and went. "What makes you so sure Erin isn't going to tell Chaley the truth, tell her she's her sister?"

"That would be her right."

He knows Erin wouldn't do that.

Erin had come to Colorado to know her father. And so that Maeve would know Abe. *I've wanted to live on a ranch my whole life.*

Now she had the chance to live on this ranch, her family's ranch, and his honor, the price of living a lie, was the only cost.

Not sure that he wouldn't pay it, for her, Abe said, "I'm still thinking." And got back into his truck before he could give Maeve's grandpa the medicine he needed.

HE WORKED on the casket in Guy Loren's shop. It took him till nine at night to design it and to measure and cut the pieces, to join the sections for the bottom and top. Then, after kissing Erin and Maeve good-night in the too-small fifth wheel, where they would all share the bed, he headed back to the Kays' to see Lane.

His brother was gone.

Abe hunted the cabinets until he found half a bottle of Jack Daniel's in his father's nightstand, squirreled away from Lane.

He drank freely from the bottle. He looked in his father's closet and found his grandfather's bearskin chaps. His grandfather had shot the bear whose hide had made those woollies. Abe tried them on.

Have to clean out the trailer. Have to find a place for all this stuff.

The chaps were for subzero days, and he left them on the bed and went out to the front room. Even looking at the stereo cabinet was painful, so he just lay on the couch with the bottle, drinking till he passed out.

He had a dream involving Beulah Ann being kind to him, like an angel. When he awoke, a light burned in the kitchen, Taffy was sleeping against his arm, and Erin was on her hands and knees scrubbing the kitchen floor. Abe shut his eyes and let the world go away.

ERIN CLEANED the trailer till midnight, tackling Lloyd's room, as well. She found the woollies Abe had left on the bed and laid them on the dresser after she dusted it. She studied the framed photos of Abe's grandparents and maybe great-grandparents. In Lane's room, she found things that had obviously belonged to Abe, including photos of him and a girl at a high-school prom years before. His date was not Chaley.

She had put Maeve down for the night on the bed that must once have been Abe's, and when Erin felt her own edginess giving way to fatigue, she lay down with her daughter. Hours later she opened her eyes to Abe sitting on the side of the bed. He was shirtless and smelled of whiskey.

"How did you get here?" he asked.

"Beulah Ann called to say you were passed out drunk and she was worried about you. I drove the Mustang over."

"Oh." Abe held his head, thinking about Kip Kay's offer and his grandfather's woollies, about family tradition and about Lloyd being gone. Erin was Kip's oldest daughter, Maeve his grandchild. Someday this ranch should belong to Maeve.

People murdered for less.

Abe didn't want to work for a man he wanted to kill. Didn't want to remain on his land. "Let's go home."

"It's the middle of the night."

"Doesn't it bother you?"

"What?"

"Your father."

"No."

He saw that she'd take whatever crumbs Kip tossed her way. "Well, I've got pride."

And I don't? "If my pride threatened to kill me, I'd get rid of some of it."

The silhouette of his back and its muscles and ridges did not shift. Sometimes you could know a man was angry by the way the silence felt.

"It's my inheritance," he said. "I'll keep it, thanks."

The bed creaked and was light and empty where he'd been.

Abe went into the front room to find Martha. The cocker spaniel wanted his attention, too, and he told her, "Taffy, you make an awfully silly cow dog."

A few minutes later Erin came out, dressed, accepting that they would leave. It was four in the morning.

My pride's killing her, too.

His family would be comfortable on Kip's pay. Any extra money he made shoeing horses would go to savings. To their future. "Okay," he said. "We stay."

"We don't have to."

"Damned right."

Her jaw tensed. "Want some breakfast?"

She made him bacon and eggs from the stores in Lloyd's refrigerator, and he ate, then showered and brushed his teeth with the toothbrush Erin had brought.

At five-thirty, he went out into the mountain cold and walked toward the lights of the big house. Stopping halfway, he stood by the corral fence, remembering the night Kip had told Erin he had just one daughter. *She cried while I was inside her.*

Chaley's Appaloosa, Mouse, came over to the fence, begging for a stroke, and Abe rubbed her warm neck with gloved hands.

A ranch couldn't survive without loyalty. Lloyd had lost

his ranch and gone on to work another man's spread, tend another man's cows. At seventeen Abe had asked him how he could stand it.

Easy, Lloyd had said. *You wake up in the morning. You go out to the calves. They're warm and wet when they're born, and you figure out it doesn't matter whose they are.*

The man whose cows they were came outside to start his day. The door shut behind him, a morning sound. He stopped when he saw Abe.

Abe nodded, and Kip continued across the deck and down the steps. He had coffee with him in a big plastic travel mug, and when he reached Abe he lifted the cup. "There's more where this came from."

"Thanks."

"Throwing in with us?"

"My daughter is your granddaughter. How would you feel?"

The black shadow sipped his coffee. "I guess, like your daddy, I'd just be glad for the chance to cowboy."

"If he were me right now, he'd have you on the ground."

The man's brittle smile was darker than the blue morning. "That's not so easy to do, Abe."

This is about Chaley. She had cried, too, and Kip Kay was righting the scales, pretending love was worth land and land worth love. Abe could have told him that neither could replace the other.

But Chaley wouldn't like his being foreman, and Kip must know that.

This hadn't been a whim.

Abe prodded the sore tooth that was Jack Draw's land. Might-have-beens and couldn't-be's weren't worth reckoning. Just can-be and can-do. "I'll be your foreman," he said. "For my daughter. And yours."

Kip's face held no shame. "Fine. Settle with Loren and

start when you can. I imagine you'll want to move into the trailer right away."

Abe's next rodeo wasn't for two weeks. Guy would have no trouble finding a replacement. The foreman of a ranch couldn't rodeo on weekends. He was needed on-site every single day. *No more clowning around, Abe.*

His last performance was over.

Kip shifted his coffee cup to his left hand and offered his right to Abe, meeting his eyes.

Reaching out, Abe shook on the betrayal of his family, his father and everything he believed in. But as he clasped Kip Kay's evil and mug-warmed hand, he heard Lloyd talking in his stern-gentle way. *If you work for the man, ride for the brand.*

Kip Kay had shown an incredible and stupid trust.

And Abe would honor it.

It was what he'd been taught.

"Yes, your father is a real cowboy."

—Jayne Mackenzie on her daughter's
sixth birthday

12

THE DAY WAS PACKED. Abe drove to Guy Loren's first off, to tell the stock contractor the news. Loren said there was no need for two weeks' notice; with Lloyd's death, he'd anticipated Abe wouldn't be working much, anyway.

Abe used the rest of the day completing the casket—he finished it by ten in the morning—and moving boxes and furniture from Loren's place to the trailer. It was soon to be dealing with Lloyd's effects, but Abe saw no good reason to delay. The sooner he started work for the Kay Ranch the better, and maybe this way he could get all the pain over with at once.

But after moving the bed—loading the mattresses to take to the dump—he left his father's room for Erin; she'd said she would clean it when she was done sewing. She and Beulah Ann had made a trip to Gunnison and bought yards of silver-blue satin. Erin stitched up the lining on her mother's sewing machine, and the box was ready for Lloyd's viewing that night. As Lloyd's room was ready for them to sleep in.

The trailer was theirs.

Lane had left for his next rodeo.

Evening came. Abe stood tall near the door of the chapel

trying to be as Lloyd had taught him. Talking to people, saying the right things, while his dear father lay dead across the room. Everyone asked after Lane, and Abe said, "He's seen him." He didn't know what he'd say tomorrow at the funeral. *Lane had a rodeo. It's his way of closing with Dad.*

Erin and Maeve wore purple dresses. He called them his family and stared down the looks that meant something about Chaley. *What goes around comes around, Kip.* Though when Chaley and Kip showed up, he nodded to them both. Shook hands and met their eyes. Tried to be the cowboy Lloyd had been.

And when it was over and everyone was gone, his father lay in the casket Abe had made. And Lloyd was dead.

Abe went to look at his face a last time and tried not to cry, tried to believe everything was going to be all right.

Afterward, he found Erin in the back of the chapel, holding Maeve and reading the cards on the flowers. Maeve wore a floppy-brimmed purple hat with a silk flower on the band. She swung her feet in tiny black Mary Janes, kicking a steady rhythm, tired and trying to stay awake.

"Ready?"

"Yes."

They rode home in silence, in an icy snowfall, to the Kays' ranch. The taillights of the truck ahead of them made watery Christmas ribbons on the road, while Merle Haggard sang "Silver Wings" on the Gunnison station that was trying to reach them through the mountains. When all was said and done, people left in coffins, not on wings of any kind. Abe punched buttons, and the Mavericks said, "What a Crying Shame," and Mary Chapin Carpenter felt lucky, and Abe shut it off. "My daddy said Patsy Cline was the only good thing to come out of Nashville."

Erin thought it wasn't a good time to say Lloyd had been wrong.

At the trailer Abe took a sleeping Maeve out of her car seat, and she didn't wake as he and Erin trekked through the snow to the door.

Erin called the place home and paid no court to the owner, to the king of this land. There was room for a garden behind the trailer, between the trailer and the pasture bordered by the highway. Bulls were penned there now. In July and August, Abe said, they would be put in with the cows.

She opened the door and took the baby from Abe. "I'll put her down."

A small fluorescent bulb illuminated the kitchen, the same light Lloyd had always left on. Abe felt his father's absence, from the trailer and from his life, as Erin hurried away to put Maeve to bed.

He didn't notice time passing till Erin came back. Her dress was loose and soft, the color of an eggplant, and Abe grabbed for her as she neared the couch. The blackness was made tolerable by her heat, by her life touching him. She had laughed with Beulah Ann while they sewed the satin lining for the casket. Abe had heard their voices as he and Lucky moved furniture in and out of the trailer.

"Erin." He couldn't remember what it was like to kiss anyone else. His erection pressed against her, and Erin squeezed her body to his on the narrow couch, kissing him back. She was trying to help the way he'd wanted to when she'd told him about Jayne's murder.

He dragged up her dress as Erin lay over him, and she unfastened his belt buckle, opened the fly of the dress slacks he hadn't worn for years.

"Abe?" Her dark eyes above him talked sense.

Abe wanted to make up for Lloyd with Erin's children,

and he met her eyes and entered her naked, and she pressed harder against him.

KIP KAY WAS CHECKING cows at midnight when Chaley parked her 4x4 outside the fence, spread the barbed wire to step through and braved the flying snowfall to join him. She'd been away most of the day in Alta and had ridden to the viewing with Beulah Ann.

Kip figured she'd come out in a snowstorm for a conversation he'd been waiting for since six this morning.

Now she had to compete with the wind. "So Abe's the new foreman."

He'd guessed right. Chaley couldn't like it. But he was a fair man, and he was doing what was fair for his foreman's son. Moreover, he was doing what was right for the ranch, and *that* was best for Chaley, whether she could see it today or not.

More words blew toward him. "They're going to live here."

"When has the foreman of this ranch not lived here?"

She wouldn't stomp her foot and cry. That wasn't Chaley's way. A gray shape with her hat collecting snow, she huddled in her sheepskin coat, her back to the wind.

Continuing work, Kip trod on through the pasture and shone his flashlight on the cows. The beam reflected the glassy particles of snow, the same snow freezing his nose and cheeks.

Abe, I'm glad you said yes. Abe was smart, a hard worker and a good one. You could tell the kind of man he was by how he cared for his gear; he was Lloyd's son, all right. He'd figure out how to earn the respect of the hands—and if he didn't, he'd know to fire them and start with a new crew—and that was fine with Kip. Youth didn't have to be a disadvantage. On this cold night Kip wished he had it, too.

"I'm going to look for a job in town," said Chaley in the slurred voice of someone too cold. "Or maybe somewhere else."

Going for the jugular; Chaley's way of getting what she wanted. *If you keep them, you'll lose me.*

He didn't bother answering. He'd given Abe his word. Chaley knew that. What was she hoping to accomplish?

"Is my ex-fiancé the *only* cowboy you could find for this job?"

"Don't get sassy. He's Lloyd's son." Directing the beam on a black baldy, a Hereford-Angus cross, Kip ignored any other reasons he'd offered Abe the job. They had to do with justice, too. He didn't know if Erin and Abe were in love, but they were sweet with each other. If they were trying to make it work for the sake of their baby, well, Kip could respect that.

It sure wasn't what Jayne had done.

It was still early for Erin and Abe. The first year of marriage was hell, and these two weren't married yet. But more and more, he found himself rooting for them, instead of waiting for Erin to disappoint him.

"I just thought you'd consider my feelings."

His tall beautiful angel was small and shivering now.

"Chaley." Kip stood near enough to make sure she saw his eyes through the slanting silver snow. "I always consider your feelings."

She lowered her head, cutting the exposed space between her hat brim and her coat collar. Her lips trembled. "Then I should look for a job in town."

"Or stay here and grin and bear it and keep your pride." It might have been different if he'd even once come upon Chaley and Abe lying in a field or in his truck bed together.

It might have been different if he really believed Abe had ever laid a lovemaking hand on his daughter.

This daughter... He wouldn't hear it.

Abe was doing as he ought.

"My pride will do much better somewhere he isn't," said Chaley.

"Fine."

Her father trudged on, and Chaley trailed him through the snow, pointing at a Hereford. "There's one."

The cow was lying down, pushing out her calf. Kip and Chaley watched and waited, stomping their feet. The calf would need to be taken in, warmed up. Kip had some battery socks to keep his feet warm—Chaley had given them to him for Christmas—but the batteries were dead. He'd make do till someone went to town.

"Can I borrow some money to get an apartment?"

Someday she would have to face living on this ranch with Erin and Abe, seeing the two of them together with their child. But for now, should he give her money for an apartment, for a place to heal?

"You see what you can find sharing a place with someone and let me know. Then we'll talk."

They grew cold as the cow strained, pushing. Two front hooves.

"There you go, Mama," Kip encouraged.

Chaley said, "Thank you."

Sweet Chaley. She was going to make it. Kip's snow-crusted lashes cracked as he smiled. "You're still my best girl."

Minutes later the calf was born into the storm with a hot gush of fluids, and its mother turned to lick the sac away.

"Want to use my truck to take her in, Dad?"

"Thanks, Chaley." *I'm going to miss you.*

But his heart knew that what was happening was right. And that it would come to good.

IN THE TRAILER Abe added more logs to the woodstove. He wasn't ready to enter his father's room. To make it his and Erin's.

She had put on a long-sleeved PRCA T-shirt that hung around her thighs, and she was looking through a cookbook in the kitchen and making notes. The funeral would be in the morning, with a wake afterward in the big house. Neighbors had brought food, and Beulah Ann and Erin planned to get up at five and prepare all kinds of extra dishes.

One more day. Then he could stop talking to people about it. Stop answering for Lane.

He arranged another log in the stove, shut the door and adjusted the damper.

Of course, that other recurring incident had been just as awkward as Lane's absence. *And this is Maeve's mother.* Everyone must have wondered what exactly she was to *him.*

She might wonder.

She'd been getting left since before she was born.

On his way past the kitchen, Abe stopped to kiss her temple from over her shoulder. She squeezed his hand before he moved on, heading for the master bedroom. Lloyd's room.

Curious, Martha followed.

The room wasn't so bad. With Erin's discount-house bed it seemed completely changed, even in the dark. Especially with the guilty sound of Taffy's tags. "Get down from there," Abe said.

The cocker spaniel jumped to the floor.

Without turning on a light he opened the sticky sliding

doors of Lloyd's closet and dragged the black bag off the top shelf, the bag that held the person he used to be. He carried it to the bathroom, where he did use the light and let Martha slip inside with him before he shut the door.

Dropping his dress pants to the floor, he sang Martha's favorite song, which was "Stand by Your Man." He buttoned the patchwork shirt, stepped into the baggies, pulled up suspenders and athletic socks, and before the mirror he painted his face, ignoring the quivering in his heart that he wasn't a bullfighter anymore. Couldn't be.

"You probably wonder why I'm doing this, Martha," said Abe. "You *know* this won't change my feelings for you, don't you?" He sat down on the toilet-seat lid and stroked Martha's ears while she made eyes at him. "She even remembered your name after all that time...."

"WHAT ARE YOU DOING?" asked Erin.

In his athletic socks, Abe trooped to the stereo. While he knelt on the rug and selected an album, Erin shut off the kitchen light. The sight of Abe at the stereo, dressed as a clown, brought back the birthday party. But he didn't choose the album of cowboy songs this time.

Instead, it was an old Willie Nelson record. Erin crouched beside Abe to look at the faded jacket. The owner had scrawled his name in the upper left-hand corner. Kip Kay. "It's my father's."

"Was. He gave me a bunch of albums when we first moved here." *And this was his, so I'm playing it for you, Erin. I'll hope for you that he sees how special you are.* Abe eased the record over the spindle, guided it to the turntable. As the disc spun, he set the needle on the groove beside the most worn section of vinyl.

He drew her to her feet as the crackle of much-played vinyl came from the speakers. "Remember the night we met?" When she'd still had dreams, he thought, of knowing her father and having his love. She pretended it didn't hurt when a cowboy crushed her dreams; she told lies in riddles and poetry. It was better, he thought, that her heroes should always be cowboys. He'd try to keep things that way.

They slow-danced, hands clasped, clumsily kissing. With one arm holding her waist, Abe freed his right hand and fished in his shirt pocket. The invisible shape he pulled out was a box.

One-handed, he popped the lid and showed the treasure inside.

Erin's eyes watered. *This is it. This is the truth. This is what it's like when someone wants you.*

She savored it. "Oh, it's beautiful, Abe." Joyfully she held out her left hand. "Put it on me."

Abe took the imaginary ring from its box, then fumbled, almost dropping it out of nervousness. He slid it onto Erin's slender white ring finger, and she used her right hand to spin the ring, to test the fit. She stretched out her fingers, admiring the stone.

"Will you marry me?" he asked.

"Oh, yes." She was crying.

He had healed the lies of her father. The truth about cowboys was beautiful. And they danced in the faded night.

MUSIC FLOATED from the trailer as Kip left the barn. George and Lucky had come out to take the next watch on the cows. The world should have been asleep, but Ian and Sylvia were come back from the war years, singing folk songs from the trailer, casting Kip back in time.

Nowadays Ian Tyson was the favorite singer-songwriter of working cowboys across the continent. But Kip remembered when the singer was half of Ian and Sylvia, and he knew the cowboy folk song playing from the trailer, about a cowboy who loved rodeo as much as he loved his sweetheart. And the sweetheart's disapproving father, who'd known his own wild days. And banking on someday soon, when everything would be all right.

Behind the trailer curtains, a lamp lit two players, a man in a lumpy-looking hat and a woman. Good grief, Abe was clowning around in there, wearing his baggies.

No, not clowning. Slow-dancing with Erin, as Kip and Jayne had danced to the same song.

Somewhere inside, a red-haired baby slept.

Kip recalled a night of shattered glass, of pouring sweat. Tears and fear. Jayne huddled under the corner cabinets in the kitchen. She'd hidden under the table once, too. From him. With him. He'd clung to her, crying, he'd been so afraid she would leave.

Resting his arms on the top railing of the corral, Kip watched the black shadow-dancers holding each other gently. Kissing.

I couldn't be like that for your mother, Erin.

And the red-haired baby couldn't have slept peacefully in the night.

His heart pounded with the soft strains of the melody, and peace came, a peace the war had never bought. He couldn't have put it into words. But it eased him, made the world sweeter and better, that there was a cowboy and a pretty redhead with dark brown eyes, with her mother's face, slow-dancing in the trailer. With their child sleeping in the next room.

BEFORE THEY WENT to sleep, Abe stowed his clown costume and makeup and props in the black bag. "I wonder what to do with this stuff."

Erin heard no regret in his voice, but a cowboy wouldn't let it show. Abe had been a rodeo clown for ten years.

"Well, we've got to save it. It's tradition. Put it in the closet with the woollies." Erin couldn't see the old bearskin chaps without remembering about "our brand." In his grief over his father's death, Abe probably didn't even remember that Jack Draw's land was for sale.

She was wrong.

Certain facts became a property of the blood. Abe remembered, but seventy-five-million-dollar problems he could not fix. Quitting bullfighting he couldn't fix. Kip Kay he couldn't fix; he'd never met a human that broken. But he would fix what he could.

He was going to save cowboys in the way that really mattered. He was going to ride for the brand, like Lloyd. Like the greatest cowboy he'd ever known.

And someday, someday soon, he would win his own dreams.

He told Erin, "I'm going to wear those woollies if this weather holds. They're not history yet."

Yes, they are, thought Erin. Living history. She'd see it kept living. "Speaking of history, there's something I want to do."

Abe listened to her plan and believed in it. History was her passion. And he'd read her thesis; she could write.

"I just need to find out if there are adequate records."

"We have lots of stuff, Erin. The photo albums out in the living room, and there's boxes of stuff in the shed. Plus, Dad's given a ton of paper to the museum. Letters, that kind of thing. My mom could help you, too."

Erin grew drunk on her dreams and spun one she knew was grandiose. A dream of firmly reuniting Annabelle Cockburn with her sons. She focused on more manageable plans. "Well, I ought to be able to get access to the museum collections. I met one of the people tonight." At Lloyd's viewing. "The local DAR runs it."

"You should join."

"Can't. You have to have to be descended from someone who actively participated in the American Revolution."

"You are." Cold eyes belied his smile. "Chaley belongs. Your grandmother helped form the local chapter."

Erin's chest tightened. She already knew the truth; she'd read it in her father's letters, and she'd learned it from Abe tonight, and that was what the truth had to be. No need to look anymore. "Sounds like a good reason not to join. I don't have to belong to volunteer at the museum."

"You don't have to accept his terms, Erin."

"I do."

She was shaking, but he didn't touch her. He didn't want her to know that he'd noticed her emotion. Fear had never stopped the strong. "Why?"

The breath singed the insides of her nostrils, already made dry by the wood heat in the trailer. "His name is not on my birth certificate."

The spell of the night died, and Abe tried to forgive her mother, the mother someone had shot.

Beside him, his betrothed straightened her spine, stretched it, yawned. Shook off the tension and started clowning. *She* was a lover and a fighter.

"What are you doing?"

Erin was holding out her left hand, smiling at the backs of her spread fingers. "Admiring my ring."

Abe tossed the rodeo bag onto the floor.

To make room for him and Erin on the bed.

There, he told her about his grandmother's engagement ring, that Chaley had worn it.

If it wasn't for Chaley's feelings, Erin wouldn't have minded a used engagement ring. Because it was an heirloom—and because of the nature of Abe's first engagement. Abe had told her how it was and she believed him. Supposing she and Chaley were friends, as close as sisters could be—supposing Chaley was over Abe—the ring might even seem a link between them. That first day in the big house, Chaley had booted Lane in the butt for teasing Beulah Ann; he'd deserved it. If things were different...

"It wouldn't bother me," said Erin, "if it didn't bother her."

Abe said, "It would bother her."

"In that case, can I just keep the ring I have?"

He clasped her warmth in the deep sheets and blankets on that snowy night. "If you're sure it fits."

And after they'd made love again, Abe lay with his head against her breast, his mouth to her skin, and gave himself to her father's ranch.

*"Whoopee ti yi yo, git along little dogies,
It's your misfortune and none of my own."*

—"Git Along, Little Dogies,"
A trail song whose English
antecedent, "The Song," was first
published in 1661

13

SHE WAS DEEP in Cockburn family history before Jack Draw's ranch sold to a developer.

There were photos to keep her busy for months. The albums in the trailer held baby pictures of Lane and Abe, shots of their grandparents, pictures of the ranch and black-and-white images from the turn of the century—even a wedding photo of Maeve's great-great-grandfather, Charlie Cockburn, with his handlebar mustache, and his wife, Elizabeth.

Erin asked Abe for the stories Lloyd had told. Abe told them and sometimes cried for thinking of Lloyd. But a calf that didn't make it, a calf he couldn't save, made his eyes wet, too, and no one thought him less a man. He was mourning that he hadn't saved Lloyd.

He rose every day at four-thirty and went to bed at midnight. Erin made a habit of taking him his supper and sitting with him in the truck, listening to Ian Tyson while he ate. And in the evenings, when the weather was bad, she took Maeve's playpen out to the barn and warmed calves as the men brought them in.

Whenever she saw Kip, they both pretended they'd never spoken over the barbed wire that day. *But I have read your letters.* She knew him now.

Two weeks after Lloyd's funeral, she drove the Mustang up to Alta and visited the historical museum with Maeve. Using volunteer labor and local funding, the Daughters of the American Revolution had turned the upstairs rooms into a nineteenth-century hospital room, doctor's office, law office and general store. Downstairs honored Alta's mining history and earliest settlers.

But Erin imagined the addition of a children's room where kids could dress up in period costumes. Saturday workshops where they could try doing chores—washing clothes, cooking meals—the way Grandma had.

When she and Maeve had seen the whole museum, Erin asked the volunteer in charge about collections that weren't displayed.

"The documents are old and fragile, dear. They're not open to the public."

"I have a doctorate in history from the University of Nevada, and I'm planning a book on some of the history of the area."

"I can't help you," said the bulldog.

Making up her mind to call Ella Kelsey, a woman she'd met at Lloyd's viewing, and also to query some university presses, Erin stuffed a twenty-dollar bill in the donation box and left.

A week later Jack Draw's land sold.

"I WONDER WHERE Lane is."

Beulah Ann and Erin were using old windows and scrap lumber to throw together a cold frame for starting seedlings. The mid-April sun had melted much of the snow, and Maeve played nearby, trying to dig in the dirt with a hand-spade. Erin had been about to drive an extra nail into the box when Beulah Ann spoke. The remark made her lower the hammer and nail.

Tucking a blond lock back into her ponytail, Beulah Ann gazed down the road that led to the highway as though expecting to see Lane's pickup coming toward her.

But the only people expected were guests, three couples, college friends making a twenty-year reunion. Erin had helped Beulah Ann clean the cabins. Chaley used to do it, Beulah Ann had explained. Now Chaley answered the phone at a veterinarian's office in Gunnison.

"Farmington," said Erin. "He's in Farmington." Abe would have been working the same rodeo if he was still bullfighting.

As Erin prepared to bang on the cold frame some more, Beulah Ann asked, "Does Abe get *Prorodeo Sports News?*"

"Beulah Ann, maybe you and I need a ladies' night out." *So you can meet someone else and stop thinking about Lane!*

She wished she could tell Beulah Ann they were cousins. Beulah Ann's mother was Kip's sister, Beth, and Beulah Ann had three younger brothers and a little sister. Which meant one aunt and four more cousins to Erin.

Beulah Ann was frowning. "Have you and Abe set a date?"

"June twenty-first." The summer solstice. Branding would be done, and the snow should be gone from the high meadows.

"I know this is a personal question," Beulah Ann said, "so you don't have to answer. But do you think you'll have more kids?"

"Might. Maeve, what have you got there, sweetheart?"

It was a stick. In Maeve's opinion, good for eating.

Erin picked her up. Maeve needed a bath, and the cold frame was pretty well finished.

At a sound from the road, the baby broke into a smile. "Da-dee!"

Abe was riding Bo, his father's horse, down the road, helping Lucky drive heifers to the corral near the barn. The dogs were with them, helping or, in Taffy's case, getting in the way.

"That is one handsome man," said Beulah Ann.

"I'll keep him. Thanks for doing this with me, Beulah Ann. Tomorrow let's plant the seedlings." They'd bought potting soil in town the day before, after filling four grocery carts at City Market. Ranch shopping.

Erin helped Beulah Ann clean up, then took Maeve to the barn, where Abe was unsaddling Bo.

"Hi," he said, carrying the saddle inside. "I need to go shoe some horses for a man. Called and left a message with Kip. Want to come?"

She had ten minutes to bathe Maeve, and then they were off.

The horses were at the old Billings place, down a ranch road beside Jack Draw's land. White PVC fencing glowed against the landscape, degrading a beautiful turn-of-the-century Victorian farmhouse. Abe sang, "Home, home on the range..."

"It looks all right. Don't be such an elitist."

"Such a *what?*"

"An elitist. You are. You and your grandpa's woollies. You have something these people couldn't buy with all the money in the world."

She must mean family history. Erin thought history made up for everything. Even the inheritance she and their daughter would never get—the land that owned his sweat and whose fences cut wounds in his hands.

"I'll take the money, thanks," said Abe.

"They sent flowers to your dad's funeral."

Abe drove under a massive white sign: TANNER'S PAINT HORSES. No one he knew. "Couldn't have. My dad never met these people."

Up ahead a man strolled out onto the gravel drive.

"He met him." Erin had seen the duster and the snakeskin boots through the snowy windshield of Abe's truck when their owner stood in Gunnison's main intersection. "That's the man whose car he hit."

Abe saw. This man had bought Lloyd a cup of coffee at Stockman's and asked him about horses.

They all got out, and Erin set Maeve on the ground, let her try to keep up with Abe on the slushy snow and mud and gravel till he stopped and picked her up.

The owner stuck out his hand. "Josh Tanner." Shaking hands, he squinted at Abe. "Have we met?"

"My dad hit your truck."

"Oh. Hey, I'm sorry."

"Thanks for the flowers."

"I liked him very much. He gave me some good advice about foaling."

With Maeve in his arms, Abe scanned the pasture. Tanner's Paints were brown and white, with black and flaxen manes and tails. Showy horses, with good American quarter-horse conformation. Abe didn't know anyone who rode a Paint, but Lloyd had sung the cowboy songs about them.

Maeve swung her legs against him as he followed Tanner to his barn to find a good place to set up. There was a large open area where the stalls ended. "This'll do."

Erin took Maeve, and while he backed the truck to the door and opened the tailgate to get his tools, Josh Tanner started catching his horses and leading them in. While Abe trimmed hooves, the owner asked most of what there was to ask about horses' feet. Nearby with Maeve, Erin watched Abe's hands and heard his answers.

Maeve wanted to walk, so Erin followed her toddling steps into the barn, where the baby squatted down and heeded the call of nature. When Erin returned from changing her in the truck, Abe was saying, "You need to call the vet."

"What?"

"It's probably laminitis. See this swelling?"

Holding the horse's hoof, Abe moved his hand to an area above the bulbs of the heel, gently probing something. With a look that said he was certain of what he'd found, he set the hoof down, stroked the horse's fetlock and straightened up. "You have a vet?"

"I have a card someone gave me."

"Dave Roe's good. Call him, and I'll do what I can here." Abe rubbed the Paint's shoulder.

They were at Josh Tanner's place for two hours, and while Abe tended the lame horse, the owner spoke with Erin. Josh, who hadn't seen forty, had just retired as CEO of a computer-software company.

"What do you do?" he asked Erin.

She told him her background in history.

"Boy, there's history in this area."

"If you're looking for a cause," Erin told him, "the museum in Alta is a good one."

"I'll keep that in mind. You wish you could do something, you know." He nodded stiffly toward the south. "About that place, for instance."

Jack Draw's place. The old Cockburn ranch.

"What do you mean?"

"Subdivision going in. Skyline Ranches. Martin Pickett got approval last night."

It was like being kicked by a horse. That beautiful country where she and Abe had ridden the morning she'd cried about Jayne's murder. The aspen tree. "I didn't know it was sold."

"Happened fast."

While they were burying Lloyd.

"First thing I did with this place," said Josh, "was put a conservation easement on it...."

Erin and Maeve waited in the truck while Abe presented the bill. The owner settled right then, and when Abe slid behind the wheel, he was whistling.

It would kill him, Erin thought. Josh Tanner had said, *Groundbreaking's set for July.*

"Abe. They're going to subdivide Jack Draw's ranch."

He stared. "Where'd you hear that? It hasn't sold."

"Josh Tanner just told me. He said it *is* sold. It all sounded true. The subdivision will be called Skyline Ranches."

Abe hadn't seen a paper that day. He tried thinking of other things. What came to mind was Josh Tanner having a cup of coffee with Lloyd at Stockman's. Friend and foe became one thing, a thing called New People.

Erin thought of the money in Abe's wallet and the check she was expecting from her attorney—the balance of her mother's estate. It couldn't outbid any developer. *But I can help save cowboys, too.* "Abe, do you think Kip would let us buy some cows of our own and raise them on his land?"

Abe glanced at Jack Draw's lodge-pole fence bordering the road to the left. He answered Erin's innocence. "That's the difference between being Kip Kay's daughter and the wife of his foreman. As far as he's concerned, you're one of those things and not the other."

Stopping at the highway, he could see only the back of her head. Abe wished he'd phrased it differently.

"Erin." He reached across the cab to touch her cheek.

She faced him, dry-eyed, her smile trying to hide that her lips were trembling.

Abe lost his words. There was nothing to say.

Chaley had a herd of her own on the Kay Ranch. Erin never would.

And Abe was glad Lloyd Cockburn hadn't lived to see the land he'd loved become Skyline Ranches.

SINCE LLOYD'S DEATH, Erin had not missed a sunrise. When the alarm beeped at four-thirty each morning, she and Abe both got up. She showered and headed over to the big house to help Beulah Ann with breakfast. Abe got Maeve up and dressed, took her with him in the pickup when he drove out to see the cows and brought her back to the house for breakfast.

On the morning after Abe shod Josh Tanner's horses, Erin left the trailer in the frosty dark. No lights burned in the kitchen of the big house. Beulah Ann must have been late getting out of bed.

Inside the ranch house, she flicked on the kitchen light and heard water running through the pipes upstairs.

There she is. Just getting a late start. I'll get breakfast going.

That meant checking the day's menu, which Beulah Ann wrote out every night on a spiral steno notepad and left on the counter.

An envelope lay on top of the pad, with Erin's name on it in Beulah Ann's curly writing, and Erin knew how Abe's grandpa had scented a blizzard coming. She felt a storm ahead as she opened the envelope.

It was the kind of floral greeting card the Boy Scouts sold, with the inscription "Friends Forever" inside.

Dear Erin,
Don't worry. I didn't leave you to explain this to Uncle

Kip and everyone. He has his own letter stuck under his door. I'm pregnant, and I'm going back to Louisiana to have this baby, because you don't know how stupid I feel, and I can't bare to face everyone there, especially Uncle Kip. He's done so much for me.

What I'm asking you is this. I'm going to have my baby, and then I want you and Abe to take it and raise it like your own. I know what your thinking. That I'm good with babys and all. But I can't be a mother. So would you please take my baby? You can write to me in Louisiana and tell me.

Love,
Beulah Ann Ellis

"Well." Kip Kay sighed in the door to the hallway. "Need a hand with breakfast, Erin?"

Erin jumped. His eyes knew everything, and he hated wasted words like any other kind of waste.

"No. No, I can handle it. Let me just..." She stuffed the card in the envelope and thrust it into the pocket of the coat she'd hung by the door, then rushed into the pantry to drag a bag of potatoes off the shelf.

Kip put on the coffee himself, silently, then grabbed his coat and went outside. When Erin turned on the radio to keep her company, Garth Brooks was "Callin' Baton Rouge."

Abe came in a half hour later with Maeve, and Erin, spinning away from the hot skillet, snatched Beulah's card from her coat pocket and handed it to him.

Holding his daughter, Abe read the card. Lucky came in before he could say anything, so Abe returned the envelope to Erin's coat pocket.

"Ring the bell for me, Abe, will you?" she asked.

He did, with Maeve's help, clasping her hand in his around the cord. Her eyes widened at the sound of the bell, and she grinned. Back inside, while Erin hustled about the kitchen, carrying hot plates of bacon and eggs to the table, Abe read the top story in the *Alta Independent*. Subdivision approved. Below was an AP feature, "Can Earth feed the world?" and the words "overpopulation" and "food-growing" leaped out at him, and he knew that cattle took half the water in the West. The world was getting crowded, till it wasn't safe for cowboys.

And another baby was on the way.

George and Kip came in the door with Pete, a hand Abe had hired from Pueblo just two days before. They'd met through rodeo, and Pete played a harmonica to the cows and was teaching Abe how. The guests trailed in next, to eat before riding fence with Lucky.

Soon everyone was eating. Erin's mind was half on keeping the juice pitcher and coffeepot full, half on Beulah Ann.

When Abe had finished breakfast, he got up to hug Maeve, who was playing patty-cake with George. Erin cornered him in the mudroom. "What do you think?"

"Do you know who the father is?"

"I have a guess."

"Me, too."

"What do you think?" Erin asked again. There was no greater compliment than someone thinking you were the person to raise her child. But so far it was just talk. Once a child had grown inside you, everything was different. And if Lane was the father, Lane who made Beulah Ann's knees weak and apparently her head, as well... "What should we do?"

"I want to know why Beulah Ann thinks she can't be a mother."

404 _The Truth About Cowboys_

"She's just eighteen."

Abe didn't think much of that. His mom had married at eighteen. So had Erin's.

"What are you two hiding in the mudroom for?" In the kitchen, Kip clapped his hat on his head and zipped his coat over his winter coveralls.

"Your niece wants us to raise her child for her."

He lifted his eyebrows. "You look like people who could do that."

Abe's brows pulled together. "You don't think she should keep the baby?"

"I imagine," Kip said, "that Beulah Ann doesn't think so." He addressed Erin. "That was a good job you did this morning, everything on the table, everything hot. Would you like to do that three times a day for a salary?"

How easily Kip had accepted Beulah Ann's departure. But Erin guessed he needed to be businesslike. He had a crew to feed. She looked at Abe.

"Fine by me."

"All right." She asked Kip, "Can I vary the menu?"

"Erin," her father said, slipping past them to the door, "on a ranch, no one criticizes the cook."

She couldn't help the rush in her heart, couldn't help _feeling_. But she'd gotten used to feeling in Abe's arms, and it was honest. Like the land. As the door shut behind Kip she lifted her eyes to her lover's.

His were grave.

He kissed her and left, and later, when Erin was cleaning up and saw the newspaper, she thought she knew what had made him sad. But she was wrong.

IT SNOWED AGAIN that night, and a prolapsed heifer died before Abe's eyes, before he and Kip could do anything. They cut the calf out, and it was alive. Abe packed it onto

Noon and rode back into the barn. In the barn waited the mother of a calf who had died hours earlier. Abe warmed the calf, left it and went out to retrieve the body of the dead calf. He was in the shed beside the pile of carcasses, skinning this one, when Erin's shape blocked out the snow-fogged moonlight. Carrying Maeve, she slipped inside.

"Hi," said Abe.

Erin watched. "If you show me how, I could do that."

Blood stuck his fingers together, stuck them to the knife, made them slippery and sticky at once. Abe recalled the first time Erin had witnessed this particular trick. She'd blanched, then made herself look again. He'd told her the whys and wherefores, and together they'd watched it work.

Abe didn't believe that skinning a calf was a skill she really wanted. She wanted something she'd never admit to, and he wasn't going to let her skin a calf to prove herself to Kip.

"No. You can keep me company, though."

It took him just seconds to finish the job. He took the calf's body outside and carried the bloody skin to the barn, with his family following.

In the barn, he tied the skin onto the orphaned calf, over the shoulders and under the belly, making sure the tail and hindquarters were covered, because that was where the mother would sniff. Then Abe led the calf to the stall where the cow waited. She sniffed the skin and recognized the scent of her own calf. Soon the orphan was suckling.

Erin heard Abe's deep sigh.

"What is it?" she asked.

"What do you mean?"

"You sighed."

"Tired." That was true. To win the respect of the hands, he made it a point to work harder, longer and better than any of them. Now, no one questioned him. George didn't even snicker at Taffy but stopped to pet her when he wasn't on horseback. And Abe had money in the bank, from the work he'd done for Josh Tanner.

Just keep thinking of that. And work like an animal. Try to forget Kip Kay and don't let this land catch your eye the way Erin did. He thought of his father's ranch. "How's your research coming?"

"Ella Kelsey said I should come to the museum when she's there and she'll help me find what I need. Abe, what is it really? Is it my father?"

For a fact. "Why do you play his game?"

"Because I know the truth about cowboys. It's you."

He knew she would never mention that birth certificate again.

But Kip held everything she wanted and what she didn't dare to want, because she'd grown up in a brown house in a field of brown houses just like it as far as the eye could see. *Someday,* Abe promised, *you'll have your own place, Erin, to make up for this mountain land that should be yours. And Maeve's.*

Forgetting his hand was bloody until he touched her face, he looked hard into her eyes. And didn't say a word.

KIP KAY PAUSED just inside the barn and prepared to duck back out into the snow, leave them to themselves. But before he could move, Abe came around the corner of a stall and saw him.

The foreman stopped, then passed on, ignoring Kip.

Kip ventured deeper into the barn, to where Erin still stood, looking at the cow and her adopted calf.

Is it my father? she had asked.

My father. So she and Abe called him that to each other. *What did you think would happen, asking them here?*

The rancher recalled the night he'd used his key to get into Mears Cabin, the night he'd seen Erin's driver's license.

Her calling him "my father" opened a door he didn't realize he'd shut. It wasn't a door to acknowledging her; that wouldn't happen. But he was curious.

"How did Jayne die?"

Erin started. Backing away from him, she gauged his blue eyes. No anger there. No warmth, either. Not exactly.

But his interest was sober and true.

Which left the question. Sometimes she actually managed to forget about her mother's death for hours at a time, sometimes for a whole day. Not now. Now it was hard and real and present.

"She was murdered. By a man from work."

Kip's breath caught. Like he'd walked into the muzzle of an AK-47.

She kept talking, telling him the rest. In Erin's arms Maeve rubbed her eyes, made a fussy sound.

Kip reached for the baby, and Erin, quavering, gave her. Through his shock over Jayne, Kip knew quiet contentment as he held the child against his shoulder, patted her back. Like holding Chaley when she was small. Sometimes babies liked to be held by a man. Easier to fall asleep on a big shoulder.

Twisting slowly back and forth, rocking Erin's child, deliberately forming no attachment to the creature, Kip asked, "Where is this man now?"

"In prison, serving several consecutive life terms." She averted her eyes from Kip and Maeve.

His eyes were cloudy, but his cheek rested against Maeve's small soft body. "When did it happen?"

"Maeve was two months old."

Kip felt the baby relax against his shoulder. She'd drifted

off. Putting away what Erin had told him, he slowly moved the sleeping baby, handed her back to her mother, who trembled again.

It was like fear in a prisoner, and you ignored it.

As kindly as he could, Kip said, "You best get some sleep. We'll want breakfast in the morning."

Erin's disappointment was blinding, like headlights on a highway. She wondered what she'd wanted. The sadness scarcely eased when Kip's eyes smiled at her and her daughter. "She's a good little thing."

THE STORY OF Jayne's murder did not leave Kip that night. As he drove back out to the cows, he could think of nothing else.

He was changing. Hearing Jayne was dead had started the change. Seeing Erin's face when he told her he had just one daughter had changed him more.

Bitterness was idiocy. He had spent twenty-five years hating Jayne, and now a man had shot her. She had shown Erin some kind of love, and Erin's voice had wavered when she told the story of the murder.

Like her body had shaken when their hands exchanged her daughter.

As he parked and got out of the truck, blowing snow burned his face.

He'd made every concession to her and Abe and their child. Even let Chaley, in her dissatisfaction, leave the ranch.

He had given. He had paid.

It was enough.

Though nothing could be enough to assuage the unexpected anger inside him that someone had murdered Jayne, had murdered Erin's mother.

LATE THAT NIGHT, while Erin slept beside him, Abe's thoughts kept going although his body resisted movement. Kip Kay wasn't the only thing that kept sleep away. It was all the parallels.

It was Beulah Ann.

No.

It was Lane.

Surely, *surely*, his brother had not done what he had, tripped and fallen into fatherhood. That was part of why he'd asked Lane to baby-sit Maeve, so that he would see the reality of a baby.

He had to talk to Lane. But how could he get hold of him? As foreman, he couldn't leave the ranch to track down his brother at a rodeo in another state.

It's not your place to tell him, anyhow. It's up to Beulah Ann.

And if Beulah Ann chose to keep it to herself? It was no light thing to miss the first months of your child's life.

It was something you would always wish you'd known.

Abe wondered if it ever bothered Kip Kay that he'd missed a quarter century of Erin's life.

His mind played a midnight movie of bulldozers turning up soil and mountain meadows erased by homes. He pictured his daughter sitting at a table with the man she couldn't call Grandpa. On a ranch that should someday be hers.

The sheets seemed tangled around him and wouldn't let him loose, wouldn't let his muscles go slack and drowsy. He sat up and held his head in the dark, missing Lloyd, for one cowboy's death had so diminished the honor of his world.

"I went to the boss to have a little chat,
I slapped him in the face with my big slouch hat...."

—"The Old Chisholm Trail,"
undated cowboy ballad

14

NO ONE COMPLAINED about Erin's cooking—the oriental stir-fry with chicken or Greek turnovers stuffed with spinach and feta—as long as there was meat on the table every night and enough food to fill everyone. Kip gave her a cooking budget, and every week she went to Gunnison and loaded three carts at City Market and pushed them through the checkout like a train, with Maeve in the caboose. She repaired the ranch chicken coop and bought baby chicks and feed. And she guided Maeve's baby hands over the fuzzy chicks and over the fur of baby rabbits they didn't buy. It was spring, and Abe had her burning weeds and helping clear ditches. While Maeve napped, she read books about the history of the area and organized her material on the Cockburn ranch. And each afternoon she and Maeve walked a mile down the road to the mailbox.

Four letters arrived for her the last day of April. She opened them all at the box while a neighbor's tractor crawled past on the highway. Carrying Maeve to keep her from wandering in with the cows or the bulls, Erin read Beulah Ann's loopy writing on the way back to the house.

Dear Erin,

Your so nice, all the things you said in your letter. You are so sweet to ask me to be your maid of honor and pay my way back out there and everything, but it's just not possible.

To answer your question about why I can't be a mother, I don't tell everyone this, but I was just out of prison when Uncle Kip let me come to the ranch. It was part of a probation thing, and now I've screwed up that, too. I just keep making mistakes, and I can't keep this baby.

You asked who the father is and if he knows. Well, you can probably figure it out when I say the baby might even bare some family resemblance to Abe. I tracked him down right where you said to find him and told him about the baby and what I'd asked you, and he thought that was fine. So please consider it. I know you probably never thought of adopting, but I'd feel so much better if you would.

Love,
Beulah Ann

Abe was in the corral when Erin returned from the mailbox. She showed him the check from her mother's estate, which her attorney had sent.

"What shall we do? Buy land? Buy cows? Build a house?"

Thinking that forty-three thousand dollars made his savings look pretty paltry, Abe hopped the fence to join her. "That's your money, Erin. You could buy yourself a good saddle. You could even buy yourself a horse, if you're not happy with Noon."

But he saw from her face that she wouldn't, though she'd

given him a new Navajo saddle blanket for his birthday last week; she still thought a horse of her own was an extravagance.

When Taffy came sniffing around his feet, Abe picked her up. "Whoever said you were a dog, anyway?"

"I heard from some publishers, too."

"Yeah?"

"They said there's not enough there—that the history of one ranch from settlement to subdivision isn't enough."

Erin found herself and Maeve crushed against him, smelling his skin, smelling horses on his canvas work shirt. *He thinks I'm disappointed about the rejection.* Or maybe he was disappointed himself, that his family's history wouldn't be immortalized. That soon there would be houses on the hill.

When he let go, she said, "I'm going to continue the research, anyhow. Maybe I'll make a scrapbook. Or go to a subsidy publisher."

There was nothing else to say, so she gave him Beulah Ann's letter.

He read, his skin darkening, his jaw aging before her eyes. Finally, almost blindly, he thrust the letter toward Erin and touched Maeve's little hand briefly. "I have to go see that Paint at Tanner's."

He got in his truck, and Erin watched through the dusty windows as he put his head in his arms on the steering wheel in a posture of defeat.

ABE SANG "Jack o' Diamonds" while he reset the Paint's heart-bar shoes.

"Whiskey, you villain,
You've been my downfall,
You've kicked me, you've cuffed me,
But I love you for all."

When he'd finished with the horse, Josh Tanner said, "You know, this is going to add up by the time we're through. I don't suppose I could interest you in a trade?"

"For what?" *I have a brother...*

"A horse."

A week earlier Abe would have refused, wanting the cash to buy his own spread. Erin's check changed things the way Lane had. Pride was manure, and registered Paints weren't running cheap. "Keep talking."

"Well, I've got a ten-year-old gelding that was sold back to me. You trimmed his hooves the first time you came. Rado? His owner's moved to the city. He's been ridden some, but has some bad habits. Say you continue to treat Naomi for laminitis as long as she needs it, do those heart-bar resets. I'd trade you the horse."

"Papers?"

"Included."

Abe rested his hip against the pickup's wheel well. The horse was probably worth more than the cash he'd be paid—if it was a good horse. Not likely he could work cattle, but the gelding might make a good pleasure horse for Erin. And that was one thing she'd never buy for herself. "I'll look at him."

"Like to ride him?"

"That, too."

Before he left Tanner's, Abe agreed to the trade. He would work up a certificate for one year's worth of farrier service for the horse with laminitis. Tanner would get the papers in order, and Abe could pick up the horse the following week. The gelding had some bad habits, as Josh had said, but he also had some go and mostly needed to be ridden.

Abe drove from the Billings place to the Dry Gulch liquor

and antique store on the highway, intending to purchase a bottle of rye like he had on Lane's birthday. But the ranch, the Kay Ranch, sang to him, the sounds of bawling dogies and water in the ditches, which were the sounds of spring. He never went into the store, after all—just home to the ranch.

That night, he found reasons to stay outside. Hunting the mother of a calf lost in a gulch. Stitching up a prolapsed cow. Pulling a calf. He rode Buy Back under the stars, drinking coffee from a thermos Erin had filled for him. As he practiced what Pete had taught him on the harmonica he'd found in Lloyd's junk, he thought in unconnected waves.

What had Beulah Ann done to go to prison?

"Amazing Grace." It was sounding pretty. At least, Buy Back was putting up with it.

Lane thought it would be fine if Abe and Erin raised his child. That was what Beulah Ann's letter had said. *Just the way Kip thought it was fine to leave Erin's upbringing to her mother.*

Be nice to play "Home on the Range." Lloyd had always liked it.

How could he tell Lane to own up to his responsibility when he, Abe, was working for a man who'd never met his? When Lane had grown up on that man's ranch? Of course, Lane didn't know that Kip was Erin's father.

But Abe knew.

Buy Back picked his way over the trail the team and flatbed had used that morning to feed the cows. In the saddle Abe asked himself if he should go find his brother, try to straighten him out.

I can't go after him. I'm needed here.

So was Erin.

And Kip would not acknowledge his daughter and grandchild.

In that instant Abe made up his mind and thanked Lane's selfishness for helping him do it. He rode for home.

"WE'RE LEAVING."

"What?" Erin was still up. Unable to sleep, she'd begun sewing new curtains for the trailer, from sale fabric she'd bought in Gunnison.

The sewing machine was on the kitchen table, and Hank Williams, Sr., was moanin' the blues on the stereo. One of Kip's records, which he'd given Abe.

Abe pulled out a chair near Erin's. "I thought I could stand what your father's doing. Well, I can't. Now my brother's denying his baby."

"It didn't sound like he *denied* it."

If he answered that, he'd say too much. "I'll stay on till he finds a new foreman. That's it."

He couldn't be serious, Erin thought. This was her *home.* The trailer, the garden, her job. Researching the history of the Cockburn ranch—preserving it before the ground was altered forever. She'd already talked to Ella Kelsey about volunteering at the museum a few hours a week; she could even bring Maeve along.

"There's not a single day this has felt right, Erin. Every morning I get up and see that man's face and know…"

"Know what?"

"That I'm *taking* it. He twists my balls. He *knows* you're his daughter and Maeve is his grandchild. When he dies, this ranch should be yours. *Yours.* And I'm supposed to pretend I don't care, that I've forgotten about it. I don't forget. I remember. Every hour of every day. I could live with that before. But not when my brother…" He shut down.

Yours. Yours. The ranch should be hers. That he had those thoughts distracted her, and her words came out weak. "It's just pride, Abe."

"It is *not* just pride!" He slammed his hand on the table.

Erin jumped. The first time she'd heard him raise his voice. The first time she'd seen the pulse in his neck like that.

More quietly he said, "It's honor."

After holding still and silent for a moment, he stood and left the kitchen and turned down the hall to the bedroom.

"Abe?" Erin jumped up and went to the edge of the hall.

His eyes gazed back, white, from the shadows.

Don't ask him. Don't ask him. All that matters is Abe. Have you forgotten what it's like to be dumped by cowboys?

Abe started to leave, as though he'd concluded she had nothing to say.

"Abe, please." She came close enough to smell the horses and cows and his sweat. Close enough to see the familiar lines near his mouth and eyes, to see his long lashes.

"What?" Abe knew, suddenly, that she was going to cry. That she would use tears and maybe threats to get him to stay.

He knew, also, that he would not give in.

"Can we stay...can we stay till our wedding? It'll be after branding, and then...then, I can be married here."

With her father present.

It seemed little to ask, and it surprised him she *had* asked. She made a study of not caring what Kip did, if he lived or died or wished her good-morning.

"I have to tell him we're leaving, Erin. Once he knows, he may not want us to stay that long."

She hugged herself.

There was no more to say.

And when they lay down to sleep, they closed the night

with chaste kisses. Neither mentioned Beulah Ann's request. When their love felt like walking on a roof peak, neither wanted to talk about raising someone else's child.

AT BREAKFAST, Erin knew that Abe hadn't yet had time to talk to Kip. But he was the first one in for the midday meal. As Maeve banged an eggbeater on an empty pot, Abe crouched to greet her, and Erin asked, "Did you tell him?"

"Yes." Abe didn't bother looking up. When it came to her father, she was like Martha, begging for a scratch. But less honest. Maybe because a dog couldn't understand words like *I have just one daughter.* "After the wedding is fine with him."

He stood up and saw her pretending it didn't matter. Gazing into her eyes, Abe called her hand, the way she'd called his the first night he'd told her, "I love you." He pushed back a lank lock of red hair, touched her face.

"What?" She glanced sideways at the soup on the stove.

"I have an idea." He had his own reasons, hopes of seeing she got what wasn't his to give. Of Kip Kay's giving it. "Your book. Maybe publishers would like it better if you covered the history of two ranches. A subdivision's going in across the road. But this ranch has a past and a future."

Her eyes blinked, then glowed. The way the kids had looked at him when he twisted balloons for them at rodeos.

Abe felt his face getting hot, but he confessed, "I even thought of a title for you. *A Tale of Two Ranches.*"

Her arms strangled his neck, and Abe hugged her back. He knew, from Erin's trembling, that she must be asking herself the same thing he was.

When it came down to recording history, would Kip Kay tell the truth—or choose to keep his lies?

ERIN WAS WASHING the supper dishes that evening when Kip came in to refill his coffee thermos for the night shift.

He missed a beat when he saw her there, looking like Jayne, as always.

Well, it wouldn't be happening for too much longer, Kip told himself. Just till after branding, till after she married Abe in June. Then, Abe said, they would go.

Chaley had come by that afternoon. Seeing her, seeing that she wasn't really happy in Gunnison, that she was despondent and seemed to miss the ranch, had reassured Kip about his own decisions. He'd made concessions enough to Erin and her child. What he'd done was fair. If it wasn't enough for Abe, well...maybe it was best that they left. Maybe it was best.

Hearing a sound from the dining room, Kip peered around the corner. In her playpen, the baby fit rings over a cone.

The water went off. "Oh, Kip."

He spun.

Erin pushed back her bangs self-consciously in a gesture of Jayne's. "I wanted to ask you something. Actually, a couple of things."

"Yes?"

"I...studied history at the University of Nevada. Anyhow, I've been recording the history of the Cockburn ranch." Her eyes watched him like they were afraid of a BT, a booby trap. "I'm putting together a book, and I'd like to balance the history of a ranch that ends up as a subdivision with a picture of a working ranch that's surviving. So I wondered if you would be willing...to share the history of this ranch."

Strings of tension pulled tight through his body. The Kay Ranch had a history. It included a soldier coming home to bury his daddy and a wife who wouldn't stay. Erin hadn't just studied history; Beulah Ann had told him she had a doctorate. *She's so smart*, Beulah Ann had said, as though her own smarts didn't measure up. Damn that Lane.

Erin waited with those big Jayne-eyes, the way Jayne used to look when she was afraid of him. *You ought to be afraid, Erin. Because we both know how smart you are and just what you're doing.*

"No," he said. He didn't want to hurt her, just be firm, as he would with Chaley. Being careful to keep his voice kind, he asked, "Now, what else can I do for you?"

Her chin shook. Kip reminded himself that Chaley had looked the same way when she'd said she was leaving the ranch. *We all have wrecks, Erin.* And like Chaley, Erin was getting up. Standing tall. Talking.

To Erin it barely felt like talking. Just like making it to the next moment, which she hoped wouldn't be another pencil-holder moment. Obviously, he wanted to say yes to something, to make up for that no. "I have some money," she said, "from my mom's estate. If I wanted to buy some cows, is there any way I could work out leasing pasture or something like that? Just till we go, of course."

His eyebrows tried to form one line. "You don't want to buy cows and move them so soon. Trucking them will cost you money. You should wait till you and Abe settle somewhere."

The way her throat felt signified nothing. Being honest didn't mean crying. You cried when you were dumped, and she was wanted by the best damned cowboy ever was born. "They're a wedding present for Abe. I really want them..." Chaley had a herd of her own. Why shouldn't...

That was the difference between being Kip Kay's daughter and the wife of his foreman, Abe had said.

"Give them to him on paper. Then have them shipped where you go. That's the thing to do."

"Yes. You're right," Erin said, her eyes bright. "I didn't think of that."

He filled his thermos while she resumed washing dishes. As he turned to go, Kip saw her reflection in the window. Jayne's face wet with tears.

He steeled himself. *Nothing to do with me. She knew how it was when Abe took the job. Abe knew, too.*

He left the house, closing the door quietly behind him.

"What's happening?"

The voice startled Kip, coming out of nowhere that way.

It was Abe, who had been standing in the shadows of the deck. Doing what, Kip couldn't imagine. Except waiting.

Kip pushed his hat tighter on his head. "Number 618 was looking close half an hour ago. I'm going out to check her again."

In the dark Abe tried to read his boss's face. "Why is she crying? Why is the woman I love crying?"

It came out like a line from a bad movie, and Kip's long sigh was the finest of insults.

Abe's hands itched.

In the black corridor outside the rectangle of light from the window, the rancher walked past where he stood. Walked past and did not look back.

He's an old man. He's your sweetheart's father, your daughter's grandfather. Don't do it.

Abe followed him down the steps.

At their foot the rancher waited, facing him expectantly. *Do you have something else to say?*

"Maybe Erin and I shouldn't go. Maybe we should stay here and fill this ranch with your descendants until you can see right from wrong."

"Suit yourself."

"More of my father's grandchildren. Are you ashamed to

have the same grandchildren as my father? He was proud of Maeve."

"I know." Kip's pale eyes were eternally calm, like the eyes of some Buddhist monk. "And I know how casually you fathered that child. Just like your brother fathered Beulah Ann's."

With the same instinct that told him when to dodge a bull, when to vault, Abe knew just what to say. His heart clenched just a little as the words came out. "Erin sure was easy."

His back slammed against the edge of the deck, hard enough that he would have a long narrow bruise the next day, and hands grasped his throat. The hard breaths of his attacker, the pressure on his windpipe, scared him, and it took will not to resist, to keep his own muscles slack. It helped that saying the words had shocked him, made him sick. He could only gaze at Kip's eyes, and the rancher's were waiting for him, his face twisted. Abe stayed limp, just looking at those blue eyes.

They changed. From anger to a realization that was like fear.

Eyelids the shape of Chaley's came down, and the powerful hands that smelled like leather released Abe's neck. One slid to the shoulder of his Carhartt and rested there, like Kip was an old man catching his breath, leaning on someone younger. Abe could only see his hat, not his face, before the rancher withdrew his hand and walked away.

Abe waited, motionless, till the lights of the ranch truck went on and the vehicle drove past. The next seconds were like seeing an empty bottle of rye and realizing he'd drunk it all.

He'd been stupid and now he was sick.

Abe had wanted to make Kip Kay admit that he loved Erin, loved her like a daughter. He had wanted to win.

He'd won.

And he stood against the deck in the dark, seeing Erin's face and reliving the night they'd made precious Maeve, till Martha came around asking what was wrong.

ERIN WAS IN BED when Abe came in that night, but she wasn't asleep. "I've decided about Beulah Ann," she said.

Beulah Ann.

I know how casually you fathered that child. Just like your brother fathered Beulah Ann's.

Abe stripped off his clothes and eased between the sheets.

"We should say no," said Erin.

"Why's that?"

Erin couldn't tell him. He was Abe, who smelled like the animals. Abe, who knew her father had never wanted her. But she couldn't say she'd spent her life being dumped by Lane, and it had happened again that same night in the kitchen.

"Erin?"

There were other things to say on the subject. Erin picked one. "Okay, no one's ever paid me the compliment she has, and I would love to raise my cousin's baby." It was a naked truth, calling Beulah Ann her cousin out loud. The blushing silence was brief and perfect, and during it Abe's fingers threaded through hers. "But when it comes down to it, she'll want her baby, and she should have it, and I wouldn't take that from Beulah Ann."

"You can't know what she wants."

"Yes, I can. And your brother's not fit to look at her."

His hand released hers. "Watch what you say."

Erin remembered about Annabelle, and she remembered

her father's love letters to Jayne. And that dumped could be a two-way street and a busy one.

To Abe her quiet felt like the silence women used to make men feel knee-high to a grasshopper. Closing his eyes, he saw Lane's birthday bottle of rye. *Use some sense.* But sense hadn't mattered in Reno. It was using no sense that had made Maeve. God, Maeve. He had to see Lane, had to talk to him. Had to look into his eyes and...

He saw Kip Kay's blue eyes in their fury.

Shame spoiled the victory.

Lane would be the same story told a different way. Lane might be persuaded to go to the birth, might see the baby, might even fall in love with his offspring in his own way. Might marry Beulah Ann.

But in the end he would leave. As their mother had left him.

And there would be a baby....

He didn't want to think about Beulah Ann, who became mixed up with Erin, Erin who'd borne Maeve. Erin he'd called easy.

We have to get out of here.

It would be good to leave the place where he'd called her easy—and where there were more stars than anywhere else and where water ran in ditches the two of them had cleared. To leave these mountains and never look upon the Skyline Ranches subdivision.

He remembered Rado, his barter from Josh Tanner a lifetime ago. He was tempted to tell Erin the Paint was for her, to cheer both of them. But Rado would be her birthday present, a surprise. So he told her only about the trade, that he'd acquired a new horse, and then he ran out of other talk.

"Abe?"

"Yes."

"Are you going to tell your mom about Lane?"

His mom.

"No." That was for Lane to do.

"She might come to see him. If you called her. Say you just said, 'Lane needs you. He doesn't know it, but he really needs you. Could you please go to whatever rodeo and watch him and spend time with him?' Say you—"

"No." Her turnaround made his head spin. *You're a good woman, Erin.* Easy was Taffy, so eager to lick his feet that he tripped on her. Easy was Martha's brown eyes gazing up at him.

Easy was giving it all.

When he wouldn't go away, Erin had said, *Can you dance, or are you just a public nuisance?*

"You don't have to tell her what's going on."

Lane again. Still. "My mother doesn't go to rodeos. She explained to me one time in Kentucky. I didn't get it till last fall. You know why she left?" He propped himself up in the moonlight. "She left because after Busy died, she figured she could love her children less if she lived apart from them. And if she loved us less, she wouldn't have to be afraid of something happening to us. So she decided not to love us anymore."

"She said that to you?"

"In a nicer way. She apologized for it, said she regretted it now. Said she loves us both. But Lane got the first message loud and clear. And he can't hear the second."

"Maybe if she said it to his face, he'd hear. Gosh, Abe, they're both alive. Your dad and my mom are dead, but your mom is still alive. She and Lane could make their peace."

Abe didn't miss the echo. Erin was saying to him what he'd said to Kip. About Kip's relationship with her.

Kip hadn't listened.

Would Annabelle?

"Oh, I love these wildflowers in this dear land of ours,
The eagle I love to hear scream,
I love the red rocks and the antelope flocks,
That graze on the mountaintops green."

—"Home on the Range,"
written by Dr. Brewster Higley, 1873

15

IN THE MORNING, fresh storm clouds rolled in from the southwest, and Erin stood by the cold frames wondering whether to keep things alive or let them die. The chicks had to be fed of course. Just as Taffy had to be disciplined for killing one. But the seedlings just starting to pop up green...were they worth the effort?

"Do it. Save them. I'll lend you the warmer for my car."

It was Lucky, ambling past from the bunkhouse.

Erin laughed. "I think they'll weather the storm without it." No reason to confess that she'd actually been deciding whether or not to water. Whether to let the little green things shrivel up and die because she wouldn't be there in August to freeze or can the vegetables, to fill pitchers with cut flowers. "Maeve, where are you going?"

Maeve wobbled after Lucky. "Horse!"

Lucky had sat her on his horse a few days earlier, for just a minute, holding her in the saddle so she could get the view.

Picking up the baby, letting the hand go on to work, Erin

stared at the clouds reflected in the cold frame's glass, trying to see a crystal-ball future. Abe would find a job on another ranch. Probably not such a pretty one, surrounded by mountains and forest. But he would continue to cowboy and she would go with him. She imagined another trailer, set in a sagebrush landscape, maybe near those adobe foothills she'd seen between Grand Junction and Delta, a desert out of *Star Wars*. She saw a uranium-era house in Nevada or Utah. She saw saguaros in Texas, blizzards in North Dakota.

And the lanky cowboy, her Abe, was always there.

"Wa-wa," said Maeve, who wanted to help pour water onto the soil in the black plastic flats. Good enough reason to do it.

While Erin held Maeve and let the baby dump too much water onto the soil, dislodging seedlings, they heard horses' hooves and saw Abe coming back from the pasture, driving the Percherons and the flatbed that was used, in good weather, to haul hay for the cows.

"Horse!" Maeve wanted to get down, to run to the flatbed, but instead, Erin brushed off a crate near the cold frame and sat holding the toddler. Abe waved as he drove past.

"Wave to Daddy."

"Da-dee."

He stopped the team at the corral to the south, beside the hay shelter and the equipment shed. When he began to unhitch the horses, Taffy scurried around his feet until he yelled at her. Erin called the cocker spaniel, but she ran away, chasing birds.

Then the day froze. Kip came from the barn, striding toward the equipment shed to give Abe a hand with the horses.

He was the hoarder of history, but she'd been silly to cry

over not having cows for Abe on his wedding day. There were finer wedding gifts for a rancher's son.

"Let's go to the trailer, Maeve."

INSIDE, ERIN HUNTED the local telephone directory. What was Jack Draw's place called?

Soaring Eagle Ranch.

The number was listed and she dialed it.

"Hello?"

"Yes, this is Erin Mackenzie calling. I understand Mr. Draw sold his property, and I was wondering what's happened to the brand?

"The brand? I wouldn't know about that." The woman sighed. "Hang on a minute."

Coming back on the line, she said, "I have no idea. We don't have anything to do with that."

"Could you give me the number of someone who could help me?"

"Just a minute."

After another twenty minutes on the phone, Erin had spoken with three people, none of whom knew anything about the triangle-E brand. The last shot was the realtor, who wasn't in his office. Erin left her number and put down the phone just as Abe banged open the door. "Erin, I'm taking Kip to town. He just broke his leg."

He left as fast as he'd come, running back across the yard in his insulated work overalls, under the charcoal sky.

Grabbing Maeve, Erin rushed after him. He was moving his truck to the equipment shed. Leaving it idling, he leaped out and dashed to the other side to help Kip to his feet. When she reached the men, Erin saw that Abe had immobilized the injury using an old wooden snowshoe and nylon webbing from a frayed halter. Obviously no one had considered 911.

"What happened?"

"Cocker spaniel." Kip gritted his teeth, sweat gathering in the pockets beneath his eyes.

"Taffy got under Marty's legs, and he reared," Abe explained.

One of the Percherons. Taffy must have startled him.

The two men made their way to the truck, Kip leaning on Abe. Abe said, "Get the door, okay?"

Erin opened the passenger door of the vehicle. Shivering, she wished she'd stopped for a coat. She bundled Maeve close. "Where's Taffy?"

No one answered.

"Is she all right?"

"Ran off," said Kip as Abe helped him onto the seat. Eyes clouded with pain, he inched back on the seat till he bumped into Maeve's car seat.

"Erin, move that thing," said Abe.

Setting down the baby, she raced to the other side. As she unbuckled the car seat and dragged it out the driver's side, her father said, "Thank you, Abe. Ah. That's fine. There..." Abe supported his splinted leg, lifting it into the truck, and Erin stood breathing, holding the car seat in the cold.

As she caught Maeve up in her arms again, she told herself she'd been silly.

For thinking that somehow Abe would have caused her father to break his leg. That maybe he'd been trying for something worse.

STARTING DOWN THE ROAD, Abe fought the urge to take every bump at thirty-five.

"Go to Gunnison," the rancher ordered, eyes shut. "Cheaper."

"They have all those ski doctors in Alta," Abe pointed out. "If you break a leg, everyone says go to Alta." He thought they should go to Gunnison, too, but someone should play devil's advocate. Especially since they had so much time to decide, slowing down and steering around every bump on the road.

"Want some music?" Abe thought Lane had an old Metallica tape in the glove box.

Kip was shaking his head.

Too bad Martha wasn't along to share the cab. She would *try* not to crowd his leg, being such a smart dog, but she did get excited....

"Ow! Watch your driving."

"Sorry. I'm doing my best."

The time till they reached the highway was like time for reflection in church. Counting sins and four regrettable words. The first snowflakes hit the windshield.

At the highway Kip said, "Wonder what Jack Draw's going to do with those cattle."

So here's where we pretend it didn't happen, thought Abe, *like we pretend Erin's not your daughter.* He didn't want to answer. But what did Kip care about Jack Draw's cows? "Thinking of crossbreeding?" He was kidding. Kip Kay lived and breathed Herefords and Angus, like sensible men.

"I'd take those Normandies if the price was right." Kip winced as he said, "Think I'll pass on the hairy ones."

Abe didn't feel much like chuckling or he would have.

Conversation lapsed and the snow kept on.

In the fuzzy thinking of agony, Kip replayed the night before. Erin's requests—and her secret. Wanted to buy cows for Abe. That morning before breakfast, he'd caught her looking through sale books in the kitchen. Well, if she asked his help buying cows, he'd give her that much.

As for what had happened outside... Grabbing Abe

430   *The Truth About Cowboys*

Cockburn by the throat was something he'd wanted to do for a long time. But now that it was over, he felt sheepish.

No, worse than that.

Why is the woman I love crying?

Raising Chaley, living with Lorraine, Kip had learned that women often cried—well, just because they felt like it. Hormones. Erin had wanted cows to show Abe on their wedding day. Good grief, he would have made room for a few more head. But it made no sense to haul cows around when you didn't have to.

As for the ranch history, that was manipulation.

But Abe had said too much.

"Kip, what did Beulah Ann do to go to prison?"

Kip blinked alert. He breathed through the pain in his leg. Beulah Ann. "Well, that's up to her to say. She's paid the penalty."

Abe avoided a pothole on the road. Kip was right. Strange how Kip could do some things right—and be so wrong when it came to Erin.

They were nearing Guy Loren's place, which had been his home for eight years. He'd given up bullfighting to come work on Kip Kay's ranch.

He told you what to expect, Abe. You're the one who shook on a bad deal.

Except it wasn't. The foreman's job was sweet.

The bad deal was that the boss wouldn't admit he had a daughter named Erin or a granddaughter named Maeve.

The bad deal...

The fifth wheel grew closer, and it said, *This is the best you were, after your daddy lost his ranch. Till Kip Kay gave you a break.* Slowing to check out Loren's stock, Abe felt Kip watching. But neither spoke, then, or for the rest of the drive.

Snow lay two inches deep on all the cars in the hospital

parking lot. It had collected on the hood of Abe's truck, too. He parked at the emergency-room door and went in to tell them he had a man with a broken leg.

When Kip was loaded into a wheelchair, ready to be taken inside, Abe wanted to tell him that he was going to Stockman's and that Kip should call him when the surgery was done.

But you didn't do that to your fiancée's father.

Even if the father wouldn't admit that he was.

Instead, you sat in the waiting room and hoped he didn't die on the table. And you pretended you'd never considered one main reason the deal was bad. That no part of Kip Kay's thank-you-God-I-love-this-ranch spread would ever be yours.

KIP HATED to be laid up, and within twenty-four hours of breaking his leg, he thought he'd go mad. He couldn't even drive his truck. The best he could do was ride in the cab of Abe's while the foreman made his rounds. And after a morning of that, Abe said the horses needed exercise, and Kip was stuck in the house. With all the ice from snowfall the night before, he could barely negotiate the steps to the deck; he'd break something else if he wasn't careful.

And in the house...

Well, there was Erin. Cooking and cleaning downstairs, though she'd never once ventured upstairs. But thanks to his injury, Kip was stuck in the downstairs guest room.

On the evening of the day following his accident, he broke down and called Chaley at her apartment. She wasn't home, so he left a pathetic message mentioning that he'd broken his leg. Then he grabbed his crutches to make it out to the den. As he left his room, a small toddling personage came down the dark hall toward him. "Mama?"

"Hi, Maeve. I don't know where your mama is." Erin

never left the child alone that he'd noticed, and as soon as he spoke, Kip heard the door bang. She must have taken out the trash.

"Maeve?"

Turning her teetering body around, Maeve walked toward her mother's voice. "Mama?"

Kip's heart twisted strangely. What *would* be the harm in accepting Erin as his daughter? Having to give in somehow? To say that what Jayne did was all right? Having to own up to his own hurt pride at coming in from the cows and finding his wife gone?

Or just simply having to face Chaley.

Chaley, who was out somewhere tonight.

Well, there were other problems. This leg. It made him feel weak, and in weakness he had to rely on Abe to run the ranch. Abe had tried to twist his arm, planning to leave. Just yesterday morning, Abe had said, *I'm afraid, if that's how you feel, we need to leave.* That night, he'd insulted Erin.

A man did not give in to extortion.

"Do you need more coffee?" Erin asked someone in the kitchen. "I just put on a fresh pot."

Kip had scarcely moved from the doorway where he'd seen Maeve. He couldn't tell who was in the kitchen with Erin until Abe spoke.

"Thanks."

"Abe, is everything all right?"

At first Kip imagined a dead cow; it was snowing cats and dogs outside. Then he realized the question was personal. Were the two of them having problems? *Was* Abe bluffing the other night? Or was he capable of saying the kind of things to Erin that he'd said to Kip? *That's just what he wants you to wonder.*

"When are you quitting tonight?" Erin asked.

"Midnight."

"Are you staying warm?"

"Sure."

Kip thought he should creep back into his room, not eavesdrop, but the conversation troubled him. Especially when he heard the door shut again. Abe leaving. No kiss for Erin.

Chaley had always complained that Abe wouldn't give up rodeo. And Kip had seen the way he'd looked at Loren's stock the day before. Rodeos, they got in a man's blood. When Abe quit here, would he go back to bullfighting?

That would be bad for Erin and Maeve. A man couldn't make a living that way. And it was hard on marriages.

Maybe even engagements.

In two seconds Kip thought it through, then leaned on his crutches and started out to the kitchen. Erin was tossing Maeve's toys into a big bag she brought over to the house each day, while Maeve chewed on a stuffed bunny.

When she saw him, she immediately straightened. Her hair was still damp from being outside. "Oh. Hi. Can I get you anything?"

She was like that. Always thinking of others' needs. If she tried half as hard to please Abe, he should be the happiest man alive.

And she *was* trying, wasn't she? With that wedding gift.

Looking after his own herd could keep a man too busy for rodeo.

"I have an idea for your cows," said Kip.

Erin stood there, unmoving, and Maeve gazed up at her grandfather with big dark eyes.

Damned, he thought, if she wasn't about the most beautiful child he'd ever seen. Abe should thank his lucky stars for such a pretty little girl. *Maybe we should stay here and fill this ranch with your descendants until you can see right from wrong.*

Thinking his broken leg was making him soft and sentimental, Kip nonetheless said what he'd come to say. "You might look at Jack Draw's cows. He's sold his place to a developer. The cattle won't be going with it. If you bought some, we could just drive them over here. You wouldn't have to pay for trucking. If you'd like, I'll call his foreman, and you and I can go over and look at them."

Erin hated herself for feeling like he'd just shared the truth about cowboys, for feeling like he'd just handed her the damned grail. It was Abe who'd given her that. But her father was going to help her buy cows! Her father.

"Oh, thank you!" she exclaimed. "Thank you."

Kip smiled and nodded and turned away, and she listened to the whisper of his aluminum crutches as he blended with the shadows in the hall.

IN THE TRAILER at the same moment, Abe held the telephone in the bedroom to his ear, listening to it ring a thousand miles away. He'd planned it out while mending fences the day before, but tonight had decided him. *Abe, is everything all right?*

Everything might be all right in a world where fathers always claimed their babies. And a man never spoke out of turn.

"Hello?"

"Mom, it's Abe."

"Abe! Is everything all right?"

He heard that jump of fear in her voice. She knew it wasn't Lloyd this time. Which left him. And Lane. And Maeve, if she cared about a child she'd never seen. Abe still hadn't sent a picture.

Is everything all right?

Just like Erin.

"Everything's fine. Kind of." Taffy flopped down near

his feet. The delinquent had shown up the night of Kip's accident, slinking to the porch with her tail between her legs. "Erin and I are getting married in June. The twenty-first. Will you come?"

"There?"

"Yes. On...the Kays' place."

"Oh. Well, yes. Of course I will. The twenty-first? I'm writing it down."

What kind of woman had to think so hard about whether or not she would come to her son's wedding?

"You can see Maeve then, too. Why I'm calling is, I want Lane to be my best man, and he's on the road, and I can't go track him down. Kip broke his leg, and I can't leave."

"Well, why don't you write to him? Isn't there a rodeo secretary or something like that?"

Abe smiled at his mother's version of the rodeo secretary. It was true he could get mail to Lane one way or another. Even have it hand-delivered by Guy Loren. That wouldn't accomplish his goal.

"We had a little falling-out." Lane's disappearing for Lloyd's funeral qualified. "I don't want to ask him in a letter. And—" he tried to remember what Erin had suggested two nights before "—Lane's going through kind of a rough time. I think he needs you."

"What are you talking about?"

Martha came into the room and he reached down to pet her. The bedroom was dark, and he could pretend he wasn't there, doing this. He could pretend to his mother, too, that all of this was casual. "Seeing you is just what he needs. If you came here, went to one of his rodeos, spent some time with him—that would be the thing."

"Abe, I don't go to rodeos. You know that. I just can't."

Abe wondered how he could look into the eyes of a charging bull and jump over it, how Lane could climb on the bull's back and ride it, yet Annabelle couldn't go *watch* a rodeo. If he played music for a living, would she come hear his band? If he raised cows, like his daddy...

"What if I send him a plane ticket to come here?" she asked.

There had been plane tickets before. They had come too late.

"Lane is having a problem with selfishness," he said. "And something's happening where he needs to think about other people, and he's not doing it. So, I think you should set an example for him." Wincing, he pressed a hand to the bridge of his nose.

"Abe, just what has your brother done?"

Martha, look how you're looking at me. You're still in love with me, aren't you? "I have to get off the phone. I have to go back to work."

Annabelle sighed. "Do you even know where he *is*, Abe?"

Martha kissed his hand. He let her kiss his face. "I have his schedule. I can send it to you. I will. I'll send it to you. And—" he remembered his story "—the wedding won't be the same unless he's there."

"Don't put that on me, Abe. I didn't agree to anything. I have to think this through."

"Okay. I love you. Good night."

"Good night, Abe."

He hung up, and Erin was in the doorway.

"Is she going to do it?"

"No telling."

Erin came in and sat on the bed. "Why aren't we making love?"

Time to swallow the burden of what he'd said to her dad. And to remind himself that he'd fallen in love before he

knew her birthright was the Kay Ranch. *Cowboy up, Abe.*
"Where's Maeve?"

"Asleep."

She must have gotten her down quietly.

They touched. Lay on the bed together.

"Tell me what's wrong."

"Nothing's wrong. Feel this."

She touched him, made fast work of his sterling belt
buckle, unzipped his fly and opened it, releasing the
pressure. With her hands on him, he dragged her closer,
unbuttoning her shirt. "That night," he said. "I'd never
been in love before that night when I saw you."

"THERE HE IS," said Kip, leaning on his crutches at the
kitchen sink the following afternoon. He and Erin had been
waiting for Abe to come back in his truck so that they could
use Maeve's car seat when they drove over to Jack Draw's.

"Good. Oh, he must have gone to get that horse."
Slinging her tote bag and camera over her shoulder—she
planned to photograph the aspen at the ranch—Erin
reached down for Maeve's hand. "Walk?"

Maeve lifted her baby hand up to her mother's larger
one.

"What horse?" On crutches Kip made his way to the
door. While Maeve slowly toddled the length of the
mudroom, he clapped on his hat, zipped his coat.

Erin told him about Abe's trade with Josh Tanner.

Kip only grunted in answer.

After holding the door for her, Erin led their slow
progress across the deck. She'd shoveled a path first thing
that morning. With the way from the house cleared, Kip
had spent a good part of the day over by the corral and the
barn, giving advice to the hands.

By the time Erin, Kip and Maeve reached the bottom of

the stairs, Abe was unloading the Paint, who snorted and shied and generally gave him trouble. Taffy raced to Erin's feet and stood barking, then charged across the yard and behind the trailer.

"Maybe she'll go in with the bulls," Kip muttered. The two ranch dogs were watching her from beside the barn with what could only be described as dismay.

While Abe calmed the Paint and stood holding him, Kip limped closer, his crutches sinking in the mud and snow. "That's a showy animal. For Erin?" He couldn't think of another good reason Abe would have done the trade. For the money he would've made from Josh Tanner, Abe could have bought two decent cow ponies.

Abe's eyes went keen—in a way that made Kip nervous. An ace up his sleeve? Not likely.

"He's kind of snorty. Hasn't been ridden much." Abe smiled at Erin. "Erin likes Noon just fine."

Erin's eyes dropped a little, though Kip could see she was nodding, agreeing. It was the answer of a woman who wanted a horse of her own, and Abe was the man to give it to her. Under the circumstances, Kip was a little surprised Abe had acquired another horse for himself, especially one so green.

Ignoring both Kip and Erin, Abe led the Paint toward the barn.

Erin gazed after it. The Paint was beautiful; no wonder Abe had agreed to the trade. She and Maeve would visit the horse in the barn when they returned from Jack Draw's, she decided as she opened the passenger door of the truck to get the car seat.

"Shall we take this truck? I can get Abe to unhitch it."

"We'll take mine," Kip said. "You drive." He whistled to the dogs, and the border collie and blue heeler came running, eager for a ride.

Distantly Erin observed that it was one of those firsts in life that she'd never had. Driving her father's car.

They were all loaded in, and Erin was turning the truck when Abe came out of the barn and gave her a "What gives? Where are you going?" look.

"Tell him you're taking me to see some cows," Kip said.

Erin threw him a smile, and Maeve giggled, almost as though she understood the conspiracy.

"You like that, do you?" the rancher said.

Erin rolled down the window, and Abe came near.

"I'm taking my— I'm taking Kip to look at some cows."

It was one of those slips that everyone noticed. For a heartbeat, no one spoke. At last, half-turned away, Abe said, "Have fun." He headed back for the barn, undoubtedly to see to his new horse.

He's right about Noon, she thought. *Noon's plenty of horse for me.* Watching uneven spots in the road, Erin eased the truck forward.

"Noon's a good horse," said Kip.

"I really don't need a horse of my own. I don't ride enough. And I'm probably not a good enough rider to have a more spirited horse."

"Buy Back's got a good dose of Thoroughbred in him. You handle him fine."

It took a second to answer. What with driving. "Thank you."

Puffs of dust plumed from the road ahead. A silver-blue mini pickup came toward them.

"There's Chaley. Pull over."

She did and rolled down the window. As her pickup stopped alongside Kip's, Chaley did the same. Her hair was in one braid, and she tossed it as she gazed past Erin at her father. With a smile that was affectionate and miffed in equal parts, Chaley asked, "Forget I was coming?"

Kip ducked his head. "Afraid I did."

"Going into town?"

"Actually we're going to look at cows."

"Whose cows?"

Erin flattened herself against the driver's seat so Kip and Chaley could see each other better and talk over her. In seconds the conversation subtly changed. Chaley hinting that her father should abort the trip, reschedule for another day and visit with her, instead. Kip not offering to do so.

It was not about her.

"We won't be more than an hour," he said. "We're just running over to Jack Draw's." He added, "You could follow along."

Chaley's eyes settled on the third occupant of her father's pickup. Abe's daughter. "No, thanks. I just came by to see your leg, see how you're getting along. It looks like you have plenty of help, so I'll see you later."

With that, she put her truck in gear and drove off, leaving Kip in the silent aftermath of her bad manners. He felt Erin glance over at him. Even from the corner of his eye, it was hard not to notice how pale she looked. Pale as the ground outside, spring trying to get through the snow.

Suddenly exhausted, Kip said, "Keep driving."

Neither of them spoke till Jack Draw's, where Kip said, "This man's got more money in his fence than I've got in cows. Now they'll tear it all down."

Erin drove under the stockade gate. Afternoon clouds hid half the mountains to the east, but their gray couldn't hurt the Soaring Eagle Ranch. "It's sickening to think of this subdivided," she said. She should photograph the stockade gate, the fence, the new buildings, as well as the old.

"Glad Lloyd's not alive to see it." The next words fell over those, as though he was pretending the first hadn't been. "The foreman here said he'd meet us at his house. It's that ski-condo thing over there. Good God, what people will do. That foreman lives better than I do."

Jack Draw's foreman was older than Abe and dressed in a good canvas shirt, a new pair of jeans and good Justin ropers. His coat was all sheepskin, his hat one-hundred-percent beaver fur, custom-made. He introduced himself as Randy and said, "You want to talk cows. We'll be having a sale June thirteenth. Want to take a drive? And you wanted to take photos, you said."

Erin nodded. "Thank you."

The foreman's extended cab pickup made it possible for them to ride together. They stopped for Erin to photograph the aspen and the old homestead and Jack Draw's mansion. Twice Kip suggested places on the ranch she should capture on film. *Now, the view from this rise is right pretty. Randy, drive over there. Let's see if your boss has replaced that old sign by the forest-service fence.*

Several times Kip got out with his crutches and inspected some short-haired white cows with brown and yellow-red spots. The second time he returned to the vehicle, Erin, in the back seat with Maeve, asked, "What about the Scotch Highlanders?" She liked the shaggy cows best of all. Though *The Cattle Raid of Cooley* was an Irish legend, she'd always pictured the Donn Cualigne as large and furry. A Scotch Highlander bull would be worthy of Queen Maeve's raid.

Kip's head didn't move.

Randy said, "Yeah. He's selling those, too. Calves, after they're weaned, will probably go for about five hundred, the mamas seven."

When Erin had her photos, the foreman drove them back to the barn. Kip angled his crutches to get out the door. "Well, thank you, Randy. We'll be in touch." He maneuvered out of the cab, wedged his crutches under him and shut the door.

As the foreman started to open his door, Erin asked, "Randy, what happened to Jack Draw's brand? Did he sell it?"

The foreman turned around, met her eyes and nodded. "Yes, ma'am. He sold it to me."

"If you speak the truth, have a foot in the stirrup."

—Turkish proverb

16

WHEN KIP AND ERIN and Maeve left to see the cows, Abe returned to the barn. Kip had been easy to read today. He thought Erin should have a horse of her own. He wanted his kin well treated, though he wouldn't admit the kinship.

It made a man wonder, and while Abe wondered, he tried a few notes of "Home on the Range" on his harp. The Paint was receptive, calm about it.

There just weren't a lot of jobs in this area, and Abe couldn't move away while he owed Josh Tanner work. Anyhow, moving would cost money, and that would be the end of his savings and the start of debt.

Or taking money from his wife.

He stowed the harmonica and petted Rado. *I'm going to give you to the woman I love. And my love for her will always be pure, because her daddy will never give her part of this ranch.*

"My dad's sure taken to your new fiancée."

At the voice Abe jumped, startling the Paint. In slow movements he rubbed the horse's shoulder before he left the stall and joined Chaley. Martha, appearing at the opened barn door, trotted inside to say hello. Patting his leg for her to jump up so he could scratch her ears, Abe said, "Really?"

"Well, she's driving him around."

They must have gone to look at Jack Draw's Normandies. Abe didn't believe Kip would buy any—he was probably just killing time on that broken leg—but you never could tell.

Martha sniffed Chaley's boots and Chaley said unenthusiastically, "Hi, Martha."

Why had Chaley come around? They had nothing to say to each other. Except— "Your dad tell you we're leaving?"

"No."

"Well, we are." Abe started toward the barn doors, and Martha tagged after. He wanted to ride the Paint, but other things came first. He hadn't seen any of the hands since he'd returned from Josh Tanner's. They had guests now, three sisters from New York, and George had them out riding fence.

"Don't leave on my account," Chaley called after him.

Abe stopped walking. "We're not."

She caught up with him just outside. "Look, what I came to say is...all of this hurts. I really... I'm just admitting to myself that I... Well, it's my own fault. I got you drunk and dangled this ranch in front of you, and then I told my dad we were engaged and...I apologize. It was a bad thing to do to you. I've just...always really liked you. A...a crush, I guess. I'm trying to grow up and get over it. Obviously you have this thing with her."

"Erin," Abe prompted. *This thing* didn't cover Maeve or till-death-do-you-part, but he let it go.

Chaley's eyes darkened sullenly. Her arms crossed her chest, hands holding the opposite elbows. "I just wanted to say I'm sorry. And I've accepted that you don't love me, that you never loved me."

She was bringing back days he didn't want to think about. He'd been a different man the night she'd proposed.

Back then, nothing was for keeps, and he'd had no faith in his own power to turn dreams into cows and grass.

You still don't, Abe. What in hell are you going to do when you leave here?

A truck was coming down the drive, probably Kip returning with Erin. Martha stood alert, then headed away to greet it. Abe said, "I'm sorry, too. And I'm trying to grow up, too."

Chaley latched on to him, hugging him around his coat, and Abe waited a polite period before trying to step back.

As the truck's engine shut off, they both turned to glance at the occupants of the vehicle.

It was Lane.

"Well, look who's here," said Chaley. "The deadbeat dad." To Abe's dumbfounded expression, she explained, "Dad told me why Beulah Ann left—he didn't have to say who. I think I'll leave you two virile sires and go back to my little apartment."

That was Chaley. Abe was glad to see her saunter away, with only a brief wave for the man in the pickup. Lane made no move to open his door.

Let him get out. Let him come to you.

It was tempting to walk back into the barn. But if he did, his brother would wheel around and leave. End of story.

Slowly, as Chaley spun a U-turn and spewed gravel on the trailer and the bull pens, Abe approached the truck. Through the windshield, he saw his brother's eyes, first meeting his, then dropping.

Abe came over to the driver's side. It had just been a month, but Lane looked different. Less like a rookie, more like someone who'd ridden some bulls and won some money. He wore the look of a full-time drifter, like he was already gone, present just in body.

But manhood hadn't settled yet.

"Bet you're pissed."

Abe didn't know what to say. That was a first for him with Lane. "What are you doing in town?"

"There's bull riding in Delta. Professional Bull Riders Association."

Abe changed the angle of his hat, lowering the brim to keep the low-slanting sun out of his eyes. Martha had finished sniffing his brother's tires and sat down at Abe's feet to scratch.

"I also wondered," Lane said, "if you're going to do what Beulah Ann asked."

Rubbing his chin and his jaw, Abe couldn't even look at Lane. *He's a kid. He's still a kid.* For the first time it occurred to Abe that Lane really wasn't ready to raise a baby.

He fathered one. He better get ready.

"I don't know." Abe leaned on the driver's door. *Do you have anything to say for yourself, Lane?*

One of those questions adults ask children when there's no answer. Thinking it, Abe felt like an asshole. His brother wasn't a child, but he was in a mess. He found a better question. "Are you asking me to do that? Not Beulah Ann. You?"

Lane's jaw was jumping, his mouth pressed shut. His pale-lashed gray eyes stared away from his brother's face, then back. "Why do you have to be so perfect, Abe? How come, when you screw up, it all works out easy for you, and you come out smelling like a rose? Beulah Ann says Kip made you foreman."

Abe backed away from the truck.

"Yeah," Lane said. "I'm asking."

"And I'm thinking." Perfect. Smelling like a rose. *You don't know what's going on with me.* "And while I'm thinking, why don't you think, too? Why don't you think about someone besides yourself for a change? Change. There's an idea. Why don't you *change*, Lane. You can come out smelling like a rose, too. If you stop acting like a pig."

He saw the words hit Lane. Sink in. Then his brother's clenched jaw gave an almost audible scrape. Firing up the engine, Lane spun the vehicle back so fast that Abe was knocked away from it and almost fell. Knocked far enough away that when he heard the yelp, he also saw Martha's body tossed away from the truck. She convulsed, out of anyone's control, then lay still.

"WELL, I'M NOT SURPRISED," Kip said as Erin turned onto the highway, leaving Jack Draw's place. She had just told him about Randy's buying the triangle-E brand. "You could see that about him. People want the damnedest things. Now, Abe... I can see Abe or Lane wanting that brand bad enough to pay thousands of dollars for it. But someone else? If it's not your family brand, a brand is a brand. That was a sweet thing to want to do, though. Abe would have liked it."

Abe would have loved it.

"Charlie Cockburn picked out that brand for his wife, Elizabeth," Erin said. "She used to call everyone to dinner with a big iron triangle. It's hanging in the trailer."

"It's something," remarked Kip, "that your name starts with an *E*, too."

Outside, green shoots were trying to penetrate the snow.

Stretching in his seat, Kip said, "Well, old Jack Draw will have his sale, and you and I will go buy some cows, Erin. You and Abe can pick out your own brand together. Might mean more that way, anyhow."

Erin couldn't imagine that. One night when she'd been working on the ranch history, Abe had said the same thing about her name—the coincidence of its starting with an *E*.

ABE AND LANE drove into the ranch just before supper, and Lane went straight to the trailer. In the kitchen Abe told Erin that Lane had accidentally hit Martha. They'd taken her to the vet, where she'd undergone two hours of surgery for internal injuries. She had to spend the night at the animal hospital.

Lane would be staying at the trailer, although he begged off supper. Didn't want to see Kip, Abe figured, and didn't blame him.

That evening Abe didn't go back to work after supper, leaving the cows to the care of the hands. While Erin made chocolate-chip cookies, he played the harmonica for Lane, then entertained Maeve and talked with his brother. Like Kip, Lane wouldn't say why Beulah Ann had been sent to prison, and Abe liked him better for it.

While the cookies were baking, Maeve went into her room and came out pulling a waddling wooden goose that quacked.

"It's Mother Goose!" said Lane. "I remember her."

Erin and Abe were motionless as he sat down on the floor with his niece.

Seeing that someone had come to her level, Maeve walked unsteadily to the edge of the room and brought back a small wooden wagon with blocks in it. She dragged it to Lane, and soon he was building towers for her to knock over.

From the broken recliner near the TV, Erin could see Abe's face. He was watching Lane the way you looked at someone who didn't know he was dying.

"Lane," asked Erin, "where's Beulah Ann?"

He set an alphabet block on top of a stack of blue square blocks. "She's in East Texas with a girlfriend."

"Why isn't she with her family?"

"She and her mom don't get along too good."

That was news. And here was Lane in Colorado playing with blocks and preparing to ride bulls and broncs the next day.

On the other hand, maybe he was practicing entertaining a baby.

And rodeo was how he earned his living.

Lane stayed only through the night. He left in the morning before breakfast, and that afternoon, while Maeve was napping, Abe brought Martha home from the vet.

The Australian shepherd's rear leg had been broken and was now splinted, and her abdomen was shaved and bandaged. Abe had to lift her up the steps and into the trailer.

While Martha and Taffy curled up together on an old Boy Scout sleeping bag of Lane's and Taffy licked her friend's paws, Erin and Abe lay together on the couch, like spoons, and she asked him what he thought about Lane.

"I'm thinking hard about doing what they asked. He tries, Erin. But he wants to rodeo more than anything. I was never like that with bullfighting." His mother wouldn't even have had time yet to get the rodeo schedule and pictures of Maeve and Erin that he'd sent her. They'd taken a whole roll on a disposable camera purchased at City Market.

"That's fine for Lane. But what about Beulah Ann giving up her baby? Maybe Beulah Ann could come live with us. Then you could be a male role model for the baby."

"Thank you, Erin. I always wanted a harem."

"You better not."

He squeezed her, got up and sat on the floor to pet Martha. He sang "Old Corrals and Sagebrush," and it was all for Martha, who deserved better than him. Whenever he tried to walk, he kept falling, and he wondered how his brother could think he came up smelling like a rose. He'd apologized to Lane at the vet.

There was nothing he could say to Martha.

ABE WANTED to invite the Lorens and a few rodeo friends to the wedding, but that was all. Erin wrote to some friends in Reno but knew they wouldn't come. That left family and the hands on the Kay Ranch and Ella Kelsey from the museum—and Josh Tanner. Ella liked the idea of a children's room at the museum and of Erin's running afternoon workshops; together they schemed on Tanner. A mountain wedding was perfect for introductions, they decided, for chatting up money.

Her father would be there of course, watching like any other guest.

Erin reread his letters to her mother.

He only had to get up in the morning to be a hero.

And Jayne should not have left.

Almost every day Abe made certain she got out riding. She knew the sun lighting dewdrops on new spring leaves, the slant of the same sun through the needles of the evergreens. And it wasn't just in riding that she'd become part of the ranch. She knew the black roll of clouds past the kitchen window and would never forget the sound of the dinner bell, the feel of ringing it. Her seedlings crowded the glass of the cold frame, running out of room.

The truth about cowboys had vanished and become life, where Abe raised Herefords and she raised prize-winning vegetables for the county fair. Honesty was pouring her father coffee in the morning. Honesty was a blank line on her birth certificate.

When she and Abe took Martha to have her stitches out, Erin made him come shopping for wedding clothes. In a high-dollar Western-wear store, which at first he wouldn't enter, they bought him a thigh-length black coat, a satin waistcoat, a white shirt, a black string tie and a new black hat. The whole set reminded Erin of Charlie Cockburn's wedding suit, but as they left the store, Abe said, "I'm wearing my own jeans and my own boots, if you don't mind. If you want to spend all your mother's money on wedding clothes, you'll have to do it without my blessing."

"I have my wedding dress already."

But you didn't wear an artifact that could stir painful memories in the living. Not without asking.

Kip's cast had been replaced by a splint, and he was managing with just one crutch. When Erin suggested barbecue for dinner, he had volunteered to get the coals going. Sunshine hit the deck at four. Maeve was playing with blocks and boxes in her playpen on the deck, and Erin waved at Abe as he rode in on Rado.

To Erin, Kip remarked, "That Paint has shaped up into a good horse."

"Yes."

"You must have done some riding in Reno." The grill smoked—the breath of summer nights.

Erin told him about making A's and getting six weeks of riding lessons each summer. "It was a lot of money for my mom. She told me once that she gave up her cable subscription for my lessons."

"No great loss." He studied the coals, stirred them with a poker. Before Erin could remember how to get mad, he said, "Your mama still like Joni Mitchell?"

She knew he couldn't say, *Did she.* "Yes."

Her father became like an old man searching for a memory, and it was "Both Sides Now."

Erin knew every word, and they sang that song until Jayne was there on the deck with summer's keenest smell, picking up her granddaughter and rocking her. Smiling at Maeve's grandpa.

They could not look at each other, and Erin watched Abe, instead, carrying the Paint's saddle to the barn.

"I'm going to wear her wedding dress."

Kip's eyes darted up from the grill, as though he was hunting a cooking implement, but the poker was in his hand. It was Erin he found. When she looked, his eyes tilted in a too-bright smile, that look of spilling-over emotion Erin had seen in other men who'd been to that war and suffered in the jungles of a strange and seductive land. He was beautiful, too, like they were; he was one of the channels for the deepest feelings of humankind, as he said, "I think that would please her, Erin."

They heard Abe on the deck stairs. He went to Maeve in her playpen first thing and lifted her out.

"How's that Paint on cattle?" Kip asked.

"Fair to middling. What is it, Maeve?"

She wanted to show him her bunny, the birthday present he'd given her.

"Yes, that's your bunny." Kip sure had a thing about that horse.

Calves were calves, as Lloyd had said. And Kip had come near to killing him for calling Erin easy. So why were they leaving?

He'd never have a ranch of his own. The cattleman's life was packing its bags, moving to history. Kip had a June-twelfth hearing in court, to fight Denver for water. And now that summer was coming, the town of Alta was screaming about grazing rights again, trying to outbid the rancher for rights that were his. Someday the town would win. Money always did.

His dreams were fading with the light, but Erin kept hers. They were thin green plants she coaxed straight. They were curtains for the trailer. On her birthday he would make one of her dreams come true, and this place would be sweet, though it would never be his.

Once Erin had gone inside to cut vegetables for supper, Kip said, "I hope you won't feel I'm prying. But is there some reason you two can't afford rings?"

They had picked out bands in Gunnison. "Doesn't seem necessary." When Kip started looking like bad weather, Abe said, "You can't imagine what it would mean to Erin to know that you care so much about how I treat her."

The rancher hauled around from the grill, pointing a hot poker at Abe. "I *don't* want to hear it again. We've had this discussion."

Hit him again. Hit him again. "Fine. Tell Erin I can't stay for supper. I'm going to work." Abe left the deck and strode down to the corral and deliberately provoked Kip further by spending several minutes with the Paint. When it occurred to him, he went into the tack room and dug up one of the few currycombs on the ranch and went out to groom the horse.

Kip glowered from the deck and Abe was singing "Eighteen Inches of Rain" as he climbed into his truck to drive out to the north pasture. This wasn't calling Erin easy. It was just foolproof mischief, guaranteed to help Kip see what Erin meant to him.

But the land took away his fun. There was a pile of twigs clogging one of the ditches. Abe got out to clear it, and his eyes ached over the grass and a bluebird on the barbed wire.

"Old Paint's a good pony, he paces when he can,
Goodbye, old Paint, I'm a-leaving Cheyenne."

—"Goodbye, Old Paint,"
traditional cowboy song

17

ABE BAKED her birthday cake the night before, and even Martha was more herself and chewed on a rawhide bone he'd bought her. He and Erin played albums on the stereo, walking after midnight with Patsy Cline, sharing "XXX's and OOO's" with Trisha Yearwood, and they took turns dancing with Maeve and rocking her as Lloyd had on a long-ago night. When the baby had gone to sleep, Erin opened a bottle of Jack Daniel's, and she and Abe passed the bottle and danced some more and made love on the couch.

In the morning Kip would watch Maeve so that the two of them could ride in the mountains together. Abe hadn't told a soul he was giving Rado to Erin, but he had enlisted some help. During breakfast Lucky would saddle the Paint and Buy Back, putting the saddle Erin always used on the Paint. Maeve's gift was a new bridle. A new saddle would have to come later; Abe wanted Erin to choose it herself. At lunch when she opened the saddlebags he'd packed, she would find Rado's papers.

It was midnight before they went to bed. "This is the best birthday I've ever had, and it hasn't started yet."

"Well, this is all you get, so I hope you're satisfied."

Abe was almost asleep by the time she answered. "That's what he says. Without words."

It woke him up all the way.

The world had never seemed uglier. And suddenly leaving was a black-and-white matter again.

HER FATHER DIDN'T SAY, "Happy birthday" to Erin the next morning, just, "Morning, Erin," as she poured his coffee. Abe dried the breakfast dishes, and as they finished up, Kip hobbled in from outside. "All right," he said. "Where's my charge?"

Maeve was in the dining room in her playpen. Erin and Abe both hugged her and told her they'd be back later, and as they left, Kip was lifting her from the playpen, a children's book under one arm to read to her.

Abe helped Erin into her spring coat, a blanket-lined denim jacket. They put on hats and gloves and went out.

Lucky had tied the horses to the corral fence. Buy Back wore Abe's saddle. Beside him stood a polka-dot Appaloosa, cream-colored with brown spots, a horse Abe had never seen before. The tooled saddle on his back wore a large pink bow.

Erin gasped. "Abe!"

"Don't look at me."

She ran down the steps, then crept toward the horse as if she couldn't believe it.

That made two of them. Abe trailed after her.

Emerging from the barn, Lucky gave Abe a puzzled shrug. "Boss took over."

Which must have seemed odd to Lucky. Not to Abe. Kip had given her an Appaloosa. Same as he'd once given Chaley.

It was as good as saying Erin was his daughter.

The manila envelope with the papers stuck out of the saddlebag. Erin watched her hand reach for them, open the envelope. *This doesn't happen in my life. What happens in my life are riding lessons six weeks a year. It doesn't happen that a cowboy wants to marry me and my father gives me a horse. This is Walt Disney, this is a Kodak moment, and it's not true.*

A sheet of notebook paper was on top.

Happy Birthday, Erin.
Enjoy him.
    —Kip

She looked toward the house, and Kip stood in the kitchen window with Maeve, watching her. Her legs were water.

A few feet away Abe checked Buy Back's girth.

Erin read the papers.

His name was Wish.

Holding Buy Back's reins, Abe said, "That is about the best-looking horse I ever saw."

Erin touched the horse's neck. Living flesh. Her fingers threaded through its mane. A part of her thought, *Too late.*

Erin gave the papers to Abe and walked toward the house. The steps were long. *You missed the second-grade-class play, when I was Dorothy. I couldn't give you the pencil holder I made for Father's Day. I'm twenty-seven years old, and I've never had a dad.*

When she came inside he was in the den, reading to Maeve in his easy chair. *Green Eggs and Ham.*

Seeing her, he frowned, all bluff, teasing. "Aren't you supposed to be out riding with Abe?"

She had read his letters from Vietnam, and sitting there in that chair, he was a man with eyes that held too much emotion. This was who he was, and he'd given her Wish with the broken heart he had. In an instant she crossed to being his caretaker and protector, without his ever having been a father to her.

This was his moment, his kind of healing, his gesture of love.

She would not say what she'd come in to say—the times he hadn't been there. She would thank him and try to make him feel like it was Disney, like she was a mermaid and her father had given her legs. "I've always wanted a horse of my own," she said. "Thank you."

CHEER UP, ABE. *Kip didn't do this on purpose. It wasn't anybody's fault.*

Except, of course, Abe's own.

Erin's going inside gave him a chance to retrieve Rado's papers from one of their lunch bags. Abe wished he had left them loose in the saddlebag; he'd been afraid they would shift position during their ride and Erin wouldn't notice them. Unfortunately this way, Kip had missed them, too. If he'd seen them, he would have withheld his own gift.

No. It's better this way. Rado couldn't make her as happy as this gift from her dad.

An Appaloosa. The Paint didn't even come close. The more Abe thought about it, the more he was embarrassed by his own gift. A horse he'd happened on by accident. A horse he'd traded for.

Wasn't even paid for in labor yet.

It's her day, Abe. Just help make it special.

Wish was a seven-year-old gelding. Abe wanted to insist on riding him first, to make sure Erin could handle him. Kip sure hadn't ridden the animal with his broken leg. But he would have bought him from someone he trusted.

When Erin returned to his side, he said, "Let's see how

those stirrups look. Why don't you put them where you want them, and we'll check the fit?"

Her fingers combed the leather of the saddle again before she assessed the stirrups. "I think they're right. I'm going to try them."

Abe saw she wanted to do everything herself. She untied the reins and mounted up, then reached forward to stroke Wish's shoulder.

When she turned the horse, he responded easily and well, but Erin found she had to hold him, too, that he had some go. She was suddenly in heaven. This was her own horse. Dammit, she had a horse of her own.

She grinned at Abe, and he grinned back, tightly, but she chalked it up to his quick glance at the deck. Kip leaned on one crutch, holding Maeve in his free arm and watching.

Abe mounted up.

They walked the horses past the house, heading for a trail that led up into the national forest. The rancher waved.

Trying to improve his frame of mind, Abe held a silent conversation with Buy Back, full of profanity and well-expressed opinions about Kip Kay. And finally it came down to one word. *Shit.* He had no gift for Erin, just a Paint he never wanted to see again. Wish had come with complete tack, and even the bridle from Maeve was now useless.

If Abe didn't watch it, he could feel that way himself.

HE'D PLANNED that they follow the Alta Mine Trail up into the national forest, but there was no way he was going to take a young horse he didn't know up anything that steep. Instead, he chose the four-wheel-drive Alta Road. Wish behaved well, though Abe kept a distance between the two horses and advised Erin to do the same. When they'd gone a mile, they stopped to let the horses breathe.

Erin took off her hat, then reset it on her head and sighed as Wish nipped at grass near the tree where she'd tied him. "Want to ride him, Abe?"

He had to smile. "I'll take you up on that."

Abe wanted to satisfy his curiosity, and he did. The Appaloosa was a damn fine horse, so good Abe felt some envy. Kip Kay must have given Erin a horse he would have liked for himself. There was no more generous gift.

And Abe suppressed the thought that in Rado, he'd thought he'd chosen a horse that was right for Erin and would make her happy. That the Appaloosa was too much horse. But it was sour grapes. The truth was, beside Wish, the Paint could not measure up.

THEY HAD BIRTHDAY CAKE that night after supper and everyone sang "Happy Birthday" to Erin, and Kip winked at her across the table. When the time came to blow out the candles, she wished happiness and peace on Beulah Ann. It was only as she and Abe took Maeve back to the trailer that Lucky, yards behind them, cleared his throat and said, "Would someone please tell me what is going on?"

Abe snapped his head around.

Lucky bent nervously to scratch the blue heeler, who was probably after dinner scraps.

The starry night shone on the four of them, the family of three and Lucky, and Erin realized there were no answers. That she'd never be able to say that Kip Kay was her father.

"Erin's birthday," said Abe, and he put his hand on Erin's back and kept it there all across the yard. She was shaking, and his hand felt warm and good.

Inside he said, "Sit on the couch and close your eyes."

Ah. The gift. She'd had the certain feeling he planned to give it to her on their ride, but what had happened was sex on a Navajo blanket next to Alta Creek, sex on scratchy wool under a blue sky, with the sound of water beside them. She'd said, *I just lost my virginity, Abe. Thank you.*

He said he'd never made love outside, either.

Now, eyes shut, Erin heard him say, "Here, Maeve. Give it to Mommy. Go give it to your mama. That's a good girl."

A large lightweight box was set in her lap. Maeve's little fingers plucked at Erin's jeans. "Mama."

Erin lifted her up to the couch. "Will you help me unwrap it?"

While Martha stretched out at her feet, Abe took the seat on Erin's free side. It wasn't much of a gift, he knew, but a shopping trip to Alta had yielded nothing except a Lorrie Morgan CD he'd tucked under her pillow. Nothing could measure up to that horse. Everything he found smelled like last-minute purchase. This...well, it was something real, anyhow. Erin had said how she would feel about having it. And Chaley was facing what their engagement had been—and realizing that his relationship with Erin was much more.

And if Kip noticed it...he'd interpret it his own way. Which might be good. *He'll think I'm cheap. He'll think I'm mistreating her. He'll squirm over it. And maybe...*

It wasn't outside the realm of possibility. In fact, the gift of the horse was another sign that things were going in the right direction. If, for instance, the news reached Chaley that her father had given Erin a horse...Chaley would ask questions. Kip must know that.

Erin had unwrapped the red paper and lifted the lid from the box. She pulled out the tissue and newspaper he'd stuffed inside, and Abe saw her growing more puzzled.

She'll find it.

She did. Unearthing the black velvet-covered ring box, she said, "Mmm," with a speculative smile.

Maeve was tearing apart a piece of tissue paper.

Erin opened the box. The ring was shaped like a twisted branch, and the diamond was its fruit. She had seen the ring before, on Chaley's hand; now Chaley would see it on hers. The thought made her tense, but Abe laid his arm over her shoulder, drew her close.

"It belonged to my dad's mom. It's important to me. Like Grandpa's woollies." Softly he admitted, "I let Chaley wear it because I didn't have any money. I want you to wear it because I love you." He made himself look into her cavern eyes, and he touched her face, her white skin. Pretty didn't matter, but they didn't come prettier than her. "Erin, I'll understand whatever you decide. But I would feel honored if you and Maeve would take my name."

Her lips were curving, smiling, and he saw behind her eyes that she knew Cockburn family history, that she understood about the triangle-E brand. "I never thought of doing anything else."

She held the box out to him.

Taking the ring from it, Abe remembered their imaginary ring. Then he slipped on her finger the ring that Chaley had worn, too.

KIP NOTICED the ring the next morning at breakfast. He said nothing, but Abe knew the minute he saw it. His mouth tightened and Abe felt like a jerk.

Like a real clown.

He was going to get rid of the Paint the first chance he could. Return him to Josh Tanner, if Tanner would take him.

Abe could scarcely eat and left breakfast early, giving Maeve and Erin a quick kiss. He saddled Bo, his father's horse, and set out to mend fences. By noon it was warm, and he came back for his truck and a shovel and torch and spent the rest of the day working on the ditches so the water would flow as it should. He worked hard, and the work taught him who he was and who he wanted to be. It taught him what Lloyd hadn't been able to, with words or the example of his life.

Branding in two weeks. More dudes would be visiting. Chaley would probably come home to help, and she would ask about Erin's horse....

He was sweating at six-thirty when Erin rode up on Wish, bringing his supper in an old lunch pail that had been Lloyd's. She looked good on the horse, proud of herself, but Wish didn't stand as she dismounted. Abe caught the reins and held them.

He'd been right. The Appaloosa was more horse than was good for her. "Erin, be careful riding him. He's got some spirit."

She took his words seriously, which helped. For some reason she still saw him as the man who had the truth about cowboys. They tied Wish to the gate and sat in the truck together while Abe ate the fried chicken and rice pilaf.

"Give me some pointers," she said.

So they talked about riding and Wish. The weather changed as they sat in the truck, charcoal clouds banking over the mountains from the southwest. Watching their progress, Abe said, "Erin, when your daddy gave you that horse, he had to know Chaley would ask why. You know what this means, don't you?"

She twisted his grandmother's ring on her finger and saw the storm coming and the darkness chasing shadows from the pasture, everything disappearing in blue-gray. "I know what I think *you* mean. What are you getting at?"

Abe didn't know what he was getting at. His feelings changed as often as the weather. The night before her birthday, he was sure they had to leave. The horse made a difference. And in the past twenty-four hours, he'd learned something elemental, the kind of thing you learned when you'd hit bottom.

"I'm saying I love this country," he told her, "and I can put up with your dad if you can." There was more—things he'd tell Kip at some point. What he needed to tell Erin was different. "At first, when I found out about Maeve, I was set on our getting our own place, something to give to her. But maybe people won't be raising cows in twenty years. Even on this place, the water is a fight every season. It seems better—it seems more right—to stay and help your dad."

Erin stilled. The land. This land. Her father had given her Wish, and now Abe was reading the future. It didn't have to be awkward to say so. "You think he might give us part of the ranch someday?"

It was a fair question, thought Abe. She suspected him fairly. But there was no answer. He couldn't say that the pain of not being able to give her Rado had taught him to be a better man. That the pride of having his own spread wouldn't make him finer, the secret Lloyd had always known.

He opened his mouth to tell her he didn't care about her father's land. When he couldn't say it, he understood that wants burned away slowly, even after you knew what was right.

There was no shame in the truth.

"I love this land. I love you more."

They looked at each other and her eyes watered. "I'm sorry."

Abe gazed toward the weather. "My mom had this saying when we were growing up. 'Where there's heart room, there's house room.' I feel that way, Erin."

He'd shifted topics, but she followed. Next he was going to say that he would look out for his kin; it was right.

You're looking out for Lane, she thought. *What about Beulah Ann?*

"She should keep her baby," said Erin.

"If she doesn't?"

It was a request.

"Okay." Her lips pressed together.

Abe knew the way she loved Maeve, knew she was scared of loving Beulah Ann's baby that much and giving the child back to her mother someday. Because Erin would give her back, if Beulah asked.

"As a niece or nephew," she said. "No lies."

"No lies." They were holding hands.

"Shall I write Beulah Ann?"

"Lane's my brother. I think I'll ask your dad for a few days off." He squeezed her hand and released it. "You better get that horse back to the barn before we see some lightning."

Thunder rolled overhead, and Erin peered out the window at Wish's ears. "I think I'll lead him. In fact, Abe..."

The dark brown eyes asked, *Please?*

He kissed the cook, then tipped his hat to her. "Yes, ma'am." Climbing out of the truck, into the wind, he sang:

"Foot in the stirrup and hand on the horn,
I'm the best damned cowboy ever was born.
Com-a ti-yi youpy, yippy yay, yippy yay;
Com-a ti-yi youpy, yippy yay."

ERIN MADE IT BACK to the house first. Kip had brought Maeve outside. He stood at the foot of the steps, leaning on his crutch, keeping a sharp watch on the baby and eyeing the road.

When she slammed the truck door, he said, "Abe bringing Wish in?"

"Yes." Erin was embarrassed.

But Kip's nod was one of satisfaction as he saw the cowboy riding the Appaloosa down the road. Thunder rumbled. As Erin scooped up Maeve, who wore her red corduroy hat, Taffy emerged from around the corner of the house and stared at the approaching rider. When she recognized Abe, she took off toward him.

"That dog hasn't got the sense God gave little green apples." Rain plopped on the brim of Kip's hat. "You'd best get your baby inside."

"Thanks for watching her." Maeve was only wearing overalls and a T-shirt, and it was getting chilly, so Erin carried her toward the trailer, calling to Abe, "I'm taking Maeve in."

He nodded, then nearly tripped over Taffy. "Go!" he said to the dog. "Go on!"

Taffy put her tail between her legs and charged through the corral, past Bo and Buy Back and toward Erin's garden. The trailer door shut behind Erin.

On his crutch Kip hobbled a short distance to see around that trailer. The dog was not above harassing his bulls, and she was too dumb to look out for herself, especially without other dogs around; Lucky had taken the ranch dogs into town, and Martha must be nursing her aches in the trailer.

Thunder cracked overhead, and the rain wet his shirt. Abe had Wish's saddle and bridle off and let him into the corral.

Kip made his way over to Abe. "What do you think?"

Of the horse.

"You made Erin real happy." Abe stood holding the saddle and tack. He needed to talk to Kip. About going to find Lane. About coming back to stay.

"What's wrong with him?"

"Likes to do things his way. He'll get over it."

"What would you have put her on?"

We're not standing in the rain to have this conversation. He couldn't undo yesterday and no longer wanted to. "A horse you gave her."

A distant yelp distracted the rancher. "Where is that dog?"

"Getting what she deserves." Shaking his head, Abe turned for the barn.

Kip maneuvered through the corral rails, limped past the Paint and Bo, then ducked through the rails again, getting cold and wet. That long-eared cocker spaniel was just the kind of dog Jayne would have owned—an animal without sense. She'd owned a declawed Persian cat when they were married.

Jayne had been murdered. He couldn't right that wrong, and so he worried that this dumb animal would sooner or later be stepped on by something with hooves.

Erin's garden, behind the trailer, was edged by a fence of chicken wire, crates and scrap lumber, all stuff she'd found around the place. It was a good fence, and her rows were neat. She'd gotten her root crops in already, and he could see green poking through the dark earth spotted by rain.

Where was Taffy?

The bulls stood in the rain, two Angus in the closest pens, others penned beyond. And there was the dog, whimpering in a heap as Black Jack, the bigger of Kip's bulls, prepared to hook her right out of the pen.

Something had already happened to that muddy mass of golden fur, and Kip didn't think twice before he wedged himself between the rails of the pipe corral. Black Jack looked up, eyes caught by the familiar.

"Hi, Jack," Kip said. "I'll just take this nuisance out of

your way." He left his crutch, to make less stimulation for the bulls. The other Angus watched lazily as Kip limped through the mud to the whimpering dog.

He'd just picked up Taffy and saw her leg bent funny and the blood on her belly when his own sense returned. Thunder banged almost simultaneously with a lightning flash.

Black Jack lowered his head, and Kip knew he couldn't run fast enough. But he damned better try, and he did, knowing that breaking his leg again would beat dying. The suddenly pouring rain took him to other places, monsoon season under a triple canopy. His feet felt wet although they weren't. *And this is how I'm going to die—rescuing Jayne's dog from my favorite bull.*

His boots slipped on manure, and he went down and felt the bull coming as he sensed something flying through the air nearby. A pair of battered ropers landed feet away, spraying him with mud, and Kip was never so glad to see a crazy bullfighter.

"Hey, Black Jack! Come and get me. Let's play."

Heart pounding, still under the giant trees along the Nam Nim, Kip held the whimpering dog and tried to drag himself up with his screaming leg. He'd never been wounded, but he'd seen men crawl away for their lives. He had to crawl while Abe played with the bull in the rain.

White lightning blinded him, illuminating the Colorado mountains, home for a cowboy. He dragged himself through the mud and manure toward the fence. A short spiral of barbed wire, lying where it shouldn't, poked out of the mud beneath the lowest rail. A wreck waiting to happen. The wreck was in his mind. The wire. Some things never went away. He saw again what he'd found in the wire after the sappers came. Jayne's dog was warm soft fur in his hands, smelling comforting like a dog. Her big brown eyes made him think there were things to live for.

Mud clung to his eyelashes, hanging before one eye as Abe turned that bull, had Black Jack chasing him in the mud and manure. Boots, instead of cleats. Kip dragged himself for his life and rolled under the pipe rail, tangling in the barbed wire, and then Abe was out of there, springing over the fence and landing beside Erin's garden. Kip saw him coming around the corral while Black Jack slammed into the fence, shaking the rails, rolling his eyes and pissed off. Shaggy wet father of the herd. *You're a damned good bull*, thought Kip.

Trying to get his good leg under him, he hunted for something to grab. A post. If he could just balance... But he couldn't let go of Taffy.

A young man reached beneath his arms, lifting him, and gave him his crutch. Kip felt weak and mean as he gripped the crutch, holding the dog, knowing he was a step from sliding in the muck again. It was all over him.

He still had his hat, anyway.

Taffy's eyes went wide at the burst of white flashing all over the yard, and Abe put out his hands for the dog. "I'll take her to Dave." The vet. "Let's get you to the house."

"Take her now," growled Kip. He'd risked his life to get her this far.

With a breath Kip heard, Abe adjusted his hat and walked away, strong and able, carrying the dog. A truck started in the storm.

Aching, Kip made for the house. And on the way he saw the pretty Paint that would never be a great cow pony. Not like the Appaloosa.

A horse you gave her.

"Oh, shit," he whispered.

HE WAS IN THE LIBRARY with his leg up, drinking whiskey, when Abe returned from the after-hours visit to the vet. Erin and Maeve were in the trailer; he'd talked to Erin, told her his plans and kissed her good-night. She'd asked how Taffy was, and he'd wondered what Kip had told her.

Now Kip didn't say a word.

"She'll live to cause more trouble," said Abe.

Kip nodded, took a drink.

There was something off about the sight. Abe didn't think hard about it, just sat on the edge of a chair and said he wanted to find his brother.

No response but another slim nod.

Abe thought he'd wait before he said anything about staying on. He left.

HE KISSED ERIN AWAKE to tell her he was leaving, and they held each other for a long time in the dark.

"Drive carefully. I couldn't stand it if something happened to you."

"I'll come home." He promised Martha, too, and she wagged her tail and wanted to go with him. The trailer was quiet; a draft reached under the door and chilled him. "Take care of Erin and Maeve, okay?"

He'd never left Martha behind until now. He wasn't sure why he was doing it, except that he would be apart from his family for the night.

Outside he loaded the Paint. He'd called Josh Tanner while he waited at the vet, and Tanner was sorry they "didn't need" the horse. Just bring him by, put him in the barn. They'd go back to cash payment.

Abe sang "Goodbye, Old Paint," and rubbed Rado's withers.

Wish had been skittish in the rain. He'd have to spend

some time on that horse; Erin alone couldn't do what the Appaloosa needed.

"You're a good horse," he told Rado, loading him in the trailer. He secured the butt chain, backed out and closed up the trailer.

Abe climbed into the cab without ever seeing the figure on the deck, spying in the dark.

> "They say I drink whiskey; my money is my own,
> And them that don't like me can leave me alone.
> I'll eat when I'm hungry, I'll drink when I'm dry,
> And when I get thirsty I'll lay down and cry."
>
> —"Jack o' Diamonds,"
> Confederate drinking song

18

IN THE MORNING, Erin lugged a box of Cockburn-ranch research material to the big house. Today was baking day; while the bread rose, she'd work. Maybe a subsidy publisher was the answer for her book. Self-published books on Colorado history did well, and Ella Kelsey had encouraged her. She said they would sell the book in the museum gift shop.

As she crossed the yard with Maeve, the door of Mears Cabin opened, and a man stepped outside and waved to her. It was the judge from Denver; he and his wife were the ranch's only guests this weekend. *They get up early.* They'd want coffee, so the minute she was inside, Erin filled the coffeemaker. The kitchen light was on, and Kip's hat still hung on the hook, but all was quiet.

Maeve tottered into the dining room and lifted her arms to be put in the playpen with her toys. "Mama!" When Erin set her inside, the baby immediately picked up her cube that had holes of different shapes for putting blocks in.

Starting to leave, Erin saw something from the corner of her eye and jumped.

A man in pajamas cowered beside the far credenza. Erin smelled whiskey from where she stood. She'd never seen her father when he hadn't shaved.

Slowly she inched her arms back down to the playpen.

"Spider."

The word made her look. His face was crumpled in fear and horror; he was wide-eyed, seeing something Erin couldn't. Except that she knew Spider. Spider was the Master of Bingo, Spider wore a peace sign on his helmet... Spider was in her father's letters. There was a sound outside on the deck, and Kip started wildly and screamed, "Incoming!"

The shout froze her as he dashed, awkwardly dragging his bad leg, to the playpen and grabbed Maeve, held her and dropped to the floor.

Heart pounding, Erin reached down for Maeve's soft body in her little overalls and turtleneck. Words wouldn't come. "Give me..."

Guests entered the kitchen and Kip's eyes darted toward the noise. He scrambled to his feet, clinging to the oak table, but still had Maeve, who was startled but quiet. Someone said, "I wonder if we can talk Erin into an early cup of coffee."

Her father beckoned with life-or-death urgency and held tight to Maeve. Limping silently, he stole across the dining room and down the hallway leading away from the kitchen. Erin rushed after him and her baby, unable to utter a sound, unsure what sound was right.

The ranch office held filing cabinets. There was a military orderliness to it. A desk. A picture of Chaley. A university degree on the wall. Erin had dusted the room. It was the ranch office, for her.

For him it was someplace else, and he shut the door behind her. The alcohol smell of his body blended with his sweat, a person unwashed. He was the only scent in the room.

"Get down!" he whispered. "Dammit, get down!"

"Maamaa." Maeve reached for Erin and kicked her feet, trying to escape. She was going to cry.

Erin held out her arms for the baby, and her father seemed to see her for the first time. His face changed, the lines going slack, and he all but furrowed his brow.

"Jayne?"

He was scary, Erin. I couldn't control him.

But he let her take Maeve, and her daughter's body was soft against her shoulder, soft and safe, and Maeve's cries subsided.

Erin felt her mother's presence in the room. A wave of Jayne.

Mom, help me. Help him.

The voices in the kitchen were muffled, faraway. Erin almost opened the door and yelled to them. But the guests shouldn't see the ranch owner like this. *He won't hurt us, will he, Mom?*

As the back door closed, Kip squinted at the sound. Slick perspiration coated his face and forehead, even his ears. He glanced down, and when he saw his own bare feet on the oak floorboards, when he saw the fabric of his striped pajamas, the panic left his face. He looked almost himself.

Erin tried to hold him in this world. "Dad." The deliberate choice felt accidental and natural. And good. "Want some coffee?"

His head shot up, and his window to the here and now had shut. "Jayne." His eyes fixed on Maeve. "Let me hold her, Jayne. Please."

"She'll cry."

"She won't." He stood, tall and newly confident in some other, younger persona.

Erin held her daughter, held one of her tiny hands in one of hers. *We're going to be fine.* "Can I call Chaley, Kip?"

"I just want to hold her! Please."

He was angry. Too intense. Afraid of what he might do if she didn't let him, Erin said, "Here's your grandpa, Maeve."

His hands shook the way hers had the first time she'd handed him Maeve, in the barn. He acted like a man with his firstborn, afraid of dropping her.

A place behind her eyes was suddenly too hot, as though a blinding light shone there.

"Look at you," he said to Maeve. His forehead creased, his mouth half-open, he lifted her to his shoulder and rested his cheek against Maeve's soft curls. "She's beautiful, Jayne. She looks just like you."

The tears seeped from Erin's eyes and hit her cheeks. *Stop! Stop. Please.* She was in the presence of the grail, and it shone too bright. It was the truth about cowboys, and it resided where darkness met light and became love, and now she was here, and it was stronger than she'd ever known. The truth was too strong.

She tried to make it go away.

"Kip. I'm Erin, your and Jayne's daughter. That's Maeve, your granddaughter."

He seemed not to hear.

"Kip, she's hungry. And I need to make breakfast. There are a lot of people who need breakfast." God, she shook, like him. "Here, Maeve."

Erin reached for the baby.

Kip hugged the child a moment more, with his eyes shut, then relinquished her. Holding Maeve tightly, Erin opened the door and went out into the hall. On rubbery legs she walked through the dining room toward the sunshine coming through the kitchen window, streaming in the doorway like a white glow at the end of a tunnel.

ABE FOUND LANE in Cortez, where he was supposed to be. His brother was sleeping under a new camper shell in the bed of his pickup at the campground near the rodeo arena. Abe parked and bedded down in his own truck. Long before dawn his eyes opened wide, and he saw Kip as he'd last seen him.

In the cold night, he banged on the back window of Lane's shell. His brother got up, and they drank coffee in the dark at a picnic table and pretended it was normal that Abe had shown up.

There's no hurry; this shouldn't be rushed. He shifted his feet in the sand and tried to see the desert. Somewhere coyotes yipped. He was five hours from home.

He pictured Kip.

Lane said that the Cortez rodeo wasn't big, not that much money. He was chewing, and he spit a stream of tobacco juice into the sagebrush.

"Trying to keep women away?" Abe asked.

"Right. Have to fight 'em off."

The summer constellations twinkled above. Morning stars. *Say it and go.* "Lane, if you and Beulah Ann both want it when the time comes, I will be a father to your child."

Lane removed the plug from his mouth, discarded it and leaned back on his hands, staring at the bumper of his truck.

After a minute he said, "Thank you."

There was no need to rush off, Abe told himself again. Martha was at home with them. Still, he shifted on the edge of the bench, wanting to be gone, as he asked Lane, "You ever seen Kip drink?"

SHE COLLIDED with Lucky in the mudroom and thrust Maeve into his arms. "Kip's been drinking and is having war flashbacks. Take Maeve to the trailer and call Chaley and tell her to come. And just watch Maeve, okay? I'm going to get breakfast on."

The hand peered past her. "What's Chaley's number?"

Erin didn't know. It must be coded on the kitchen phone, the ranch phone. "I'll call her. You watch Maeve. And try to keep the guests out of here till breakfast is ready. I'll try to do something about him."

As Lucky took the baby outside, Erin grabbed the telephone receiver and read the list of frequently called numbers. *Lloyd* had been changed to *Abe*. She found *Chaley-H*, Chaley at home. She pushed 3, and the number was dialed. The phone rang until an answering machine came on.

What could she say to an answering machine?

She hung up and tried 4. *Chaley-W*. An answering machine for the vet's clinic. *Saturday*. They were closed. Where was Chaley?

The house was quiet. She went through the dining-room door, and the sunlight from the kitchen window surrounded her and reached beyond her, making a tall black paper doll for her to follow.

Erin didn't mean to creep. She didn't fear a man who held a child so gently, who was a good father to his own daughter, Chaley. It was for his sake that she walked silently, to give him peace in the morning.

She returned to the office with her giant's shadow.

Breath was the first thing she felt, his in her face, accompanying the crack of her head slamming against the wall of the hallway, jarring her eyes, bringing tears. "Dad," came out of her. Then, there was only pain and no way to breathe or scream with his hands squeezing her throat.

Sweat ran in the sun cracks around his wide and staring eyes, and the stench of whiskey filled her nose and mouth as her arms flailed upward, grabbing his hands.

His eyes blinked, and the pressure on her throat lessened minutely. She tried to pull his hands away, tried to draw breath.

The back door banged. "Erin!"

She hadn't heard the truck.

"Erin!"

She pried Kip's fingers from her throat, and as they went away, her breath burned and her windpipe felt bruised, and she knew she would never be the same. The truth had many shades and she hadn't been there, she hadn't been there till this minute.

A cowboy cast a long shadow.

Erin watched her father study the new shape, the man and the hat outlined on the oak floor where it met wainscoting.

The shadow moved, and it was the only time Erin had heard boots in that house.

Abe said, "Everything all right?"

The unshaven man in sweat-drenched pajamas turned, saw him and was suddenly present. And defeated. Dragging a hand up the damp skin of his face, Kip said two words.

"The Paint."

ABE HELPED HIM bathe. Kip had broken his leg again yesterday in the bull pen and didn't know it. *I've had worse hurts.*

They didn't talk, besides that, for many minutes. Abe passed him towels in silence, gave him his crutch. Pretended there was no weakness, as he would want Kip to do for him.

When he was half-dressed, Kip sank onto the edge of the bed. "Did you find your brother?"

"Yes."

Abe stood near the dresser in the guest room while the rancher buttoned his shirt. *Those hands tried to choke Erin.* You couldn't hurt a man for mistaking his daughter for the enemy. You couldn't lose control yourself, the way Abe thought he might. He tried to see Kip as he would a temperamental horse, like that gelding Rowdy, an animal who couldn't help being what he was.

When Erin knocked and said she'd brought them breakfast, Abe opened the door. There were bruises on her throat. "All right?" he said, taking the tray.

She nodded. "Everyone's eaten." Her voice was hoarse. "I'm going to the trailer." Looking past him at Kip, she said, "Chaley's coming. She should be here any minute."

Abe set the tray on the dresser. There was a small folding table against the wall, and he opened it, set it in front of Kip and arranged Kip's breakfast and coffee on it. Then silverware.

When he looked up, Erin was gone.

Without lifting his eyes, Kip picked up a piece of French toast. There were two thoughts in his mind. Erin. And the Paint. The horse had set him drinking. Abe was a fox and a devil. That damned Paint.

Well, he'd had his moment of weakness. Now it was time to cowboy up and make things right again.

If he could.

The pictures came, the pictures of Spider and of other things, and he remembered that Abe was there in the room, Abe in his hat. He stared until he could see Abe's ropers. It was a trick he'd been using this past hour to take the images out of his mind.

Abe saw him wipe his hand across his face.

"Dad," said Chaley, in the doorway. She came to her father's side and bent over and hugged him.

He hugged her back, his eyes unfocused. When she straightened up, he said, "Abe, why don't you go see how...she's doing. Chaley will help me pack and take me into town. I'll be gone a few days."

"I'll take you," Abe said. "Send Chaley to the trailer when you're ready."

Too tired to fight him, Kip watched the foreman collect his plate and go. He listened to Abe's footsteps reach the kitchen. It was a long time before the back door shut.

Immediately Chaley asked, "Are you going to the VA?"

"Yes. But there's something I have to tell you first, Chaley. Sit down, honey."

She took a seat in the room's one armchair, one of those chairs none of them ever used, the guest-room chair. She looked as tired as he felt, and he saw that she had no inkling. She had always been the sun of her own universe. And of his.

It was his job to teach her to see beyond her own light.

"Chaley..." Ah, this burden, this secret could leave him now; the truth could come out. He took a breath. He saw Spider. He blinked and saw her eyes. "Chaley, you have a half sister. Her name is Erin."

ABE FOUND HER on the floor playing blocks with Maeve or, rather, pretending to play. Just an hour ago her father had half choked her. Since then, she'd fed the crew and cleaned up afterward. Now she was trembling. But the first words out of her mouth, in that same rasping voice, were, "Where's the Paint?"

He shut the door of the trailer and crouched to get a kiss from Martha, to pet her. "I'm so glad to see your tail wagging again."

Strands of red hair fell across the side of Erin's face as Abe sat beside her, put his arm around her.

Knocking over a tower of blocks, Maeve giggled. "Daddy."

"Hi, Maeve. I gave the Paint back to Tanner. Thought we could use the money, instead."

She didn't seem to hear. "I forgive her," Erin said. "I forgive her now."

Her mother. Abe didn't ask about her father, if she forgave him, too. He touched her throat and pressed her head against his chest. A lump rose from the back of her skull, and he asked her about it.

"He threw me against the wall." Hoarse shaking voice.

If he'd seen it, Kip would be dead. "Do you still want to stay here?"

She shook her head. "I want my horse. I want the Paint."

He held her away from him and saw she'd been crying while he held her. The bruises on her throat left no room for why. Why she wanted to leave. But everything had changed for him, too, that morning. It had to do with helping her father bathe and the fact that Kip Kay had a broken leg and hadn't noticed. The fact that he could mistake Erin for the enemy—and that Denver wanted his water and Alta wanted his grazing rights.

And that he was her father.

Abe kept quiet. If she wanted to go, they would. But where?

AFTER HE TOOK KIP to the hospital, Abe went to Josh Tanner's. He brought home the Paint, and Erin saddled Rado with the saddle Kip had given her. While Abe watched Maeve, she rode toward the north pasture, past the heifers. The Paint was gentle; she felt none of the anxiousness she had with Wish, none of the sense that she was not in charge. With the Paint, she could concentrate on her riding, and her eyes memorized the shades of his coat, the patch of black in his mane.

Here was none of the needy feeling, the desperation of something given too late, that she'd experienced from her father's gift. The Paint was like Abe's love for her, secure and dependable.

She breathed the mountains through her aching throat, tried to ignore the throbbing from the back of her head. Bluebirds, magpies, sparrow hawks, meadowlarks, red-winged blackbirds...they flew over the fields, landed on the barbed wire. To the west she spotted a pair of red-tailed hawks soaring. Rocky Mountain irises edged the road, and crimson and blue columbine grew beneath the fences. The cool air smelled of evergreen.

Her father would have wanted her had Jayne stayed. He would have adored her, as he'd adored Maeve in those moments of confusion, when he'd mixed everyone up. As he loved Chaley.

Do you want to stay? Abe had asked.

It didn't matter. She had received the thing for which she had come. She had gotten all of it, and after the wedding she and Abe could take their cows and go.

And Kip, she thought, would not drink again, would not be driven mad by the presence of someone who carried him back where he shouldn't have to go.

Pete was in the north pasture, and the sound of his harmonica reached Erin before she saw him. He was sitting under a tree playing "Amazing Grace." She listened hard, tucking the moment, like the smells and the land and the lowing of a cow, into her memory. She would collect these memories to take with her when she left, and the pencil holder would be full.

KIP RETURNED from the hospital five days later. Chaley brought him home in the afternoon, but when she opened the mudroom door for him and saw Erin she said, "I'll see you later, Dad."

"Thank you, honey."

From the kitchen table, where she sat polishing silver, Erin heard him kiss her half sister and heard Chaley say, "I love you. Call if you need anything."

Erin trained her eyes on the paper that lay on the table, the second chapter of her book about the Cockburn ranch. Maeve was playing on the floor, trying to fit the halves of plastic Easter eggs together.

Remembering the eggs when she saw her father's crutches and his new cast, Erin got up. "Let's make a path, Maevey, so he can get through."

The lie hurt her tongue.

He.

We will leave, she thought, *to end the telling of lies. The use of pronouns to avoid specific words, like "your grandfather."*

"She's fine," said Kip. "I'll be careful. What have you got there?" Still in his coat and hat, he leaned over the table, and Erin let him read. After a moment he stepped back, with his crutches, watching out for Maeve. Balancing on one crutch, then the other, he shed his coat and hat and hung them up.

He made his way around the baby, and Erin ignored his progress down the hall. She tried to concentrate on words. They swam before her. Rubbing hard with the rag, she hurried to finish the silver.

Footsteps creaked overhead. The sound of a drawer.

What was he doing upstairs on that twice-broken leg?

Erin rolled her eyes. "Cowboys," she said to Maeve. She put the silver away, twisted the lid on the polish, glanced at the clock. An hour to weed in the garden before she had to start supper.

The stairs, down the back hall by the den, creaked. Well, he was her father. He was a veteran, and he'd been wounded rescuing Taffy from a bull, and she would take care of him. She left Maeve and walked down the hall. As she rounded the corner, she saw him struggling down the last six steps, carrying a boot box and a cigar box and his crutches, clinging to the railing.

"There you are," he said. "Get this stuff, will you?"

She came to take the boxes, to help him situate his crutches. Slowly he descended the last steps.

"In your room?" she asked.

"Oh, let's go out in the kitchen."

The boxes. What was in them?

Her heart raced, and she wished it wouldn't. It was like when he'd given her Wish; she hated it that she cared so much. She pressed a hand to her forehead. Was there anything to say?

He was cheerful.

Erin walked ahead of him to the kitchen, set the boxes on the table and picked up Maeve, pretending the boxes didn't matter. One had once held Justin Boots, the other Havana cigars. She carried Maeve to the window to look out. "Do you see Daddy?" There was Abe, back from riding fence with three guests.

She watched one of the guests try to tip him. He shook his head.

The crutches made their muted sounds behind her. Kip was lifting the lid off the boot box. As though satisfied that it contained what he thought, he replaced the lid and said, "You're welcome to this stuff. Look it over and use what you can."

Maeve wanted down, and Erin let her squat to find an

egg that had rolled under the edge of the counter. She approached the table and opened the lid on the boot box. Photos and letters and news clippings. The one on top was about him coming home from the war.

She shut the box as though it was Pandora's. This was his way of saying she could write the history of the Kay Ranch, and it was just like Wish. It was everything except someone to give a pencil holder to. "Thank you," she said. "I'll enjoy looking through that. And I'll let you read whatever I do."

His callused brown fingers—the fingers that had choked her—had lifted the lid on the cigar box and were digging through trinkets.

He pulled one out and leaned on his crutches to face her. The crutches helped his balance as his workingman's fingers plucked the cape yoke of her Western blouse and prodded the pin through.

"I never knew you were decorated."

His look was like when he'd told her he had just one daughter, like nothing mattered. He'd finished with the pin and grabbed the hand grips of his crutches again.

He's going to say something—he's going to say something that will make everything right and end the lies.

"Now, you are." Kip closed up the cigar box and tucked it between his forearm and the crutch. Then he wheeled around Maeve again and hobbled down the hall to his room.

IN THE BARN, Abe touched the Silver Star. "Does it change anything?"

"We're not leaving because I'm afraid of him. I'm not afraid."

So she thought her father had acknowledged her valor. Maybe he had. Abe thought it more likely he'd apologized the best he could.

Maeve waddled toward the blue heeler, who had seen her, too, and was fleeing. Martha herded the toddler back to her parents.

"You changed your mind about staying the day he attacked you. I thought you were afraid. Or angry."

She shook her head. "I called him Dad. It changed... everything."

"You can call him that."

"I can't!"

Her shout startled Martha and made Maeve cry. Abe understood the reason for it—and that it was something he couldn't fix. Because of what her father had said to her and never taken back. That he had just one daughter.

As she gazed absently toward some hay bales, her hand against the medal on her shirt, he picked up Maeve. "Erin, it's going to be hard to find another place this good. You don't have to stay here and spend your life putting up with Kip. But if you want me to talk to him, I will."

"It won't help." Her face was white, her eyes two dark holes. "It has to come from him, and it never will."

He couldn't stop himself. "What happened to his being your hero?"

She shoved his chest with both hands and left the barn crying. He had to chase her to the trailer, carrying Maeve. Inside it was dark, and he put Maeve in her crib with some toys.

When he lay on the bed with Erin, not taking off his boots, she said, "Don't make me feel small. Before, I thought it was enough. But he tried to kill me, and he can't say the words 'I'm sorry.' Maybe he's not. I can't stay here."

Kip's hands had been around Abe's throat, too. *He tried to kill me, on your behalf.* He and Erin were strong enough together that she could hear it; she knew how he felt about her. He held her tight against him, so tight she wouldn't be able to see his face. "I need to tell you something that happened between him and me."

He crushed her in his arms while he told her that he'd just wanted to get her father's goat, that he'd just wanted to win. And what he had said and what Kip had done. Only then did he let her go, and her eyes weren't the same.

It was like the first time. It wasn't worth it.

"I didn't mean it," he whispered. "I fell in love with you the night we met. I had to have you."

She kissed him and got out of bed, like it didn't matter.

And the last thing he saw before he went back to work was Erin at the trailer's kitchen table, looking through the box of things her father had shared. Her fingers touched his Silver Star, pinned to her shirt, as though to make sure it was still there.

ERIN HAD NO MAID of honor.

She'd hoped for Beulah Ann, but Beulah Ann had not responded to her letters, sent to the Texas address Erin had gotten from Lane. At least Abe's mother had said she'd be there on the twenty-first without fail; they'd reserved Mears Cabin for her.

By branding time, the weekend before Jack Draw's cattle sale, Erin had nearly settled on Ella Kelsey as a matron of honor. Erin had spent a few afternoons volunteering at the museum. They liked each other. Surely Ella would agree.

But she'd also wonder why Erin didn't have someone closer to her.

Because of Maeve, Erin couldn't participate in the roundup and branding. So she watched from outside the corral, with the heat and smoke from the fire stinging her eyes, mingling in her nose with the scent of burning cowhide and manure.

Abe roped the calves from the saddle, and Lucky and

Pete dragged the animals to the fire. There, the calves bawled and dropped manure as they were branded, inoculated and castrated. They had all been treated with dehorning paste after birth to prevent horn growth.

Twenty calves had been branded and cut when Chaley's silver-blue pickup pulled into the yard.

Erin saw her father notice the truck. From his position just inside the corral, he gazed over the fence rails. But when Lucky and Pete dragged over another calf, he focused on that.

As Abe roped another calf, Erin took Maeve off the top rail where she'd had been holding her and set her on her feet to walk toward the trailer. Chaley was part of the lies. If Erin didn't see her, she didn't have to live them.

Chaley headed for the corral, leggy and athletic in her cowboy hat and jeans, and Erin coaxed Maeve around to the garden behind the trailer. The root crops and beans were bushy, the peas almost ready to pick.

While Maeve found her spade and pail, Erin attacked the bindweed, in a peace removed from the corral. The bawling calves and the men laughing and shouting to one another seemed faraway.

"Hi."

Chaley had let herself in the chicken-wire gate. The sinking sun cast part of the garden in shadow, and Erin's own shadow ran into Chaley's form.

"Hi," Erin said.

Her half sister crouched farther down the row from Erin and absently pulled a few weeds. "Be sure to watch the weather every night," she said. "The surprise frosts will really get you up here."

Erin knelt in the soil and sat back on her heels.

Chaley's eyes were just like Kip's. Blue, with heavy, almost serpentine lids. "Dad told me."

Maeve dumped dirt onto a carrot top, burying it.

A calf bawled, protesting his fate.

This is it, then. He told Chaley I'm his daughter. He said I'm his daughter.

It was flat, with something missing. There was only this strange distance between her and Chaley, and nothing to say.

But her half sister didn't seem to notice the absence of a reply. She was staring at something. Erin didn't know what until Chaley said, "Did Abe mention that ring's kind of been around?"

"Of course. It doesn't bother me. I just tell myself..." Why did she always have to be the nervous one, always the one afraid of getting hurt, of being a fool, of being the intruder? She finished, anyhow. "That my sister wore it."

Chaley's look was ironic.

I hate this. I'm going to leave. I'm going to pick up Maeve and walk away. Why did I ever want to get married on this ranch? Why did I ever say we should stay this long?

"He's changed," Chaley said suddenly. "I always wanted him to settle down and be like he is now. But he wouldn't. He must really love you."

Standing, Erin brushed off her jeans. Nothing could get worse with Chaley. This woman hated her, and Erin had nothing to lose except a dingy pride that had been beaten down to a pebble. "Chaley, are you going to come to our wedding?"

"My father would never let me forget it if I didn't."

My father...

Erin breathed through it.

"Since you're going to be there, anyway, would you consider being my maid of honor?"

Her half sister choked. Dragging her fingers through the

soil, she made a sound of exasperation. Still squatting, she stared off at the bull pens, then over at Maeve.

Erin waited for her to say something worse than no.

Chaley pushed herself to her feet and met Erin's eyes with no enthusiasm whatsoever. "If I can pick my own clothes."

Not sure whether to feel relief or misgiving, not sure this denouement was even a good thing, Erin said, "You can wear whatever you want."

"We never made love," said Chaley.

Erin answered, "I know."

*"We arrive at truth, not by reason alone,
but also by the heart."*

—Pascal, *Pensées*

19

THAT NIGHT, there was a barbecue and a dance on the narrow lawn alongside the house. The ranch had eight paying guests, and neighbors came, and Chaley stayed; Kip had hired a three-piece band from Alta. The hands had built a fire, and the guests stood near it, drinking beer when they weren't dancing.

When Maeve got sleepy, Erin kissed Abe and told him to have fun. She walked back to the trailer, thinking about Chaley, about her father confessing to Chaley. Abe knew, too; when Erin explained, he'd hardly reacted.

He'd already told her there was nothing to stop her from calling her father Dad again.

I can't. It's not enough.

She was a small girl walking home from summer camp, stuffing a pencil holder rolled in a paper bag into the outside trash can so Jayne would never see it. Jayne, who'd fled a man who mistook her for the enemy.

In the trailer she put Maeve to bed with her bunny, then set up at the kitchen table, to pore over the contents of the Justin Boots box, her treasure trove. She'd seen everything. Letters from her grandparents to various people. News articles about the ranch. Photos of relatives she'd never known she had.

Outside at the party Abe had smiled by the fire, laughed with the hands. He was happy here.

Erin opened the door of the trailer so she could look across the yard. He was coming up the steps, handsome in a red work shirt and new jeans and a new summer hat.

When she opened the screen, he grabbed her. "I missed you."

"Don't let the bugs in."

They shut the doors, shut themselves inside.

Erin opened her mouth to tell him they would stay.

And could not.

JACK DRAW'S CATTLE SALE was Friday the thirteenth, and on the twelfth Kip went to court to defend his water rights. When he returned that night for supper, he said, "Have to go back tomorrow." The kitchen was full—Lucky, Abe, Pete and Maeve were about—and he didn't catch Erin's eye or look at her.

She washed vegetables in the sink as though she hadn't heard.

So she had to go to the cattle sale alone. Her father's situation was unavoidable; this wasn't his fault. He had to defend the ranch's water rights.

At dinner food had no taste.

I'll go alone. And I'll talk to that foreman about the brand. Everyone has a price.

But the foreman, Randy, had been making good money with Jack Draw. His price might be more than she could afford. Or he might just refuse to sell.

After dinner, while Maeve played on the floor, Abe helped her with the dishes. These June nights he spent with her, quitting work early. Tonight, though, Erin wanted to talk to her father without Abe, to get advice about the sale.

Unfortunately Kip retired to the den and Abe didn't leave. When the dishes were dried, he poured a cup of coffee. "We need to tell your dad when we're going. He said Chaley's moving home. But he needs to fill two jobs, yours and mine. And, Erin, I haven't found anything. We have to stay in this area till I finish working on that Paint of Tanner's. And we haven't heard from Lane or Beulah Ann. If they want us to take their baby... We could do worse than stay here, Erin."

The door to the den was down the hall and around the corner. Was it open? Could her father hear?

As Abe watched her over the rim of his coffee cup, she felt like hiding. It had happened a lot lately.

Leaning against the counter beside him, she folded her arms across her chest. "What?"

He spoke close to her. "Maybe you should talk to him again."

Her chin shook. Abe scalded himself with the coffee and set it down. She was crying, and he held her.

"We can stay," she said. "We'll just stay, all right?"

Giving in, like he'd given in after Lloyd died.

"Fine," he said. "And what you call him is your business. But starting right now, to our daughter that man is Grandpa."

"All right." She tore away from him, ripped a paper towel from the roll by the sink.

When Abe turned, Kip Kay stood in the doorway.

He came in on his crutches and helped himself to a coffee mug from one of the hooks. Erin kept her back to him, wiping her eyes.

"We're staying," said Abe. "If you don't mind."

The rancher rested on his crutches to pour his coffee. "I don't. Be glad to have you."

Abe crossed one ankle over the other. "And I'm sure you agree that it wouldn't be respectful for Maeve to call you anything but Grandpa."

"You're her parents. I'm sure you know best." Kip took a drink and glanced at Erin, then set down the mug. "Erin, would you give me a hand with this? I'm going back to the den."

Abe smiled a little. He wasn't wanted, which was good. Maeve had wandered into the dining room and was crawling after a ball under the table; he went to get her as Erin carried her father's coffee down the hall.

"I'M SORRY about tomorrow," was the first thing Kip said as he settled into his easy chair. Through the open door Erin heard Abe talking to Maeve in the kitchen. "You should ask one of the hands to go with you. Pete or George."

"All right." Abe had told him they were staying. Now was the moment to be true and honest. To call her father Dad again, now, when he was in his right mind. She could not. She said, "Good luck in court tomorrow."

"Need plenty of that." Nodding, he said, almost to himself, "I'm glad you're staying. Chaley's coming back, too."

And Erin knew he was thinking about the ranch. That he needed Abe.

She left him drinking his coffee.

THE NEXT DAY at noon she saddled Wish. She'd begged Abe to baby-sit so she could "take a ride."

While Erin mounted up outside the corral, he said, "I wish you'd ride the Paint if you're going far." He grabbed Maeve, swinging her up onto his shoulder before she could wander in with the horses. The sun had brought out freckles on his nose. In the heat, the ranch smelled like dust and pine sap.

"I won't learn to handle Wish any better by not riding him." Today she would ride the horse her father had given her. Because they were staying and she needed to convince herself of his caring.

She slapped at a fly on her neck.

"Be careful." Abe stepped closer and lifted his face for a kiss, and she bent over and kissed Maeve, then him. Leaving her family, she wheeled Wish around and started down the road to Jack Draw's.

Chaley's truck was coming at her, raising sun-filtered dust clouds for a quarter mile behind. Erin turned Wish toward the side of the road and held his reins, made him stand although he wanted to go.

The pickup slowed and stopped. "Dad around?"

"He's in court again."

Her half sister's eyes studied the horse. "Where are you going?"

"To Jack Draw's cattle sale. I'm buying cows for Abe for a wedding present."

"You're kidding." Chaley smiled, as though Erin had done something endearing.

Wish shifted under her and lowered his head to try to eat. Erin kept his head up. "It's a secret." *Oh, hell, why not?* "Want to come?"

Chaley pondered it for two seconds. "Sure. Let me go get Mouse."

Erin trotted Wish on the road while she waited for Chaley, and soon she saw her half sister riding toward her on Mouse. She was wearing a white hat. Her braid flapped behind her and her horse kicked up dust as she rode.

The two Appaloosas walked side by side in the noon heat.

"How many head?" asked Chaley.

"I think about forty." She chewed her lip. "I want the Scotch Highlanders."

Her half sister stared straight ahead over the dusty washboard road, then laughed.

"What?"

Chaley shrugged. "People say they have a lean beef. That's good."

I'm glad I asked her to come.

But Erin didn't tell her about the brand.

Not then.

The road lay clear as far as they could see. Chaley asked, "Want to lope?"

Erin applied a gentle leg pressure to Wish's sides, and he broke into a trot, then a lope. No joy could compare to this; it was unique. This horse was hers, and she could ride him tomorrow, too. Later, as she and Chaley rode up to Jack Draw's barn, where numerous pickups were parked, the cowboys stared at their horses.

They dismounted and loosened the horses' girths and went to look at the penned stock and at Draw's remuda. Inside, the auctioneer's voice was already going, and soon they ventured through the doors into the place filled with men in cowboy hats.

It was Erin who made the bids, but Chaley coached her, and together they bought forty heifer calves. Randy, the foreman, was busy with sales, and Erin wouldn't get a chance to talk to him about the brand unless she stuck around. She dawdled outside with Chaley, discussing the calves. "I want to have them brought over the day before the wedding. Maybe send Abe to town or something."

"Is Dad in on this?"

"Yes."

"Let him take care of it," said Chaley. "He likes shenanigans."

There was a break and people streamed out of the barn. They would be selling the horses next, and Chaley said, "Let's get out of here."

Erin saw Randy and waved to him.

"Oh, did you have to do that?" Chaley muttered.

The foreman was making a beeline for Chaley, but he stopped a few feet away and stared at Wish. "Not for sale, is he?"

"No," snapped Chaley, untying Mouse.

Erin said, "Maybe."

"THE GUY TOOK A HORSE?" Kip asked, when she explained that night. While she washed dishes, Abe had taken Maeve out to the barn to look at some new kittens. Kip had spent a good day in court; the ranch's water was safe this time. He was eyeing a seat on the water board now. He and Abe and Chaley would have to talk about it, divide up the civic duties. Erin could do her share, too. That was quite a coup she'd pulled off today. "Well, I'll be damned."

He rubbed his jaw and faced the kitchen window, and Erin wondered if she'd hurt him. But he turned and smiled with a watery-eyed brightness and said, "That was a nice thing to do. Now let's see how we're going to move your herd."

Relief freed her tongue. "I cried riding him home." And Chaley had said, *I can't believe you did that.* Erin and Randy had shaken on the deal. He would do the paperwork and they would make the trade on Friday.

"Well, I think your Rado is a fine horse. Let's talk about those cows." Kip said he would send Abe to Grand Junction on Friday, and he'd have the hands move the cows then. The guests could help, too. "You can drive me over so I can see what you got. We'll help get 'em across the highway."

Erin had spent the day riding on the land. It had made her feel strong. She wanted to bloom, brave as the starry columbines. She could imagine Abe's arms around her, and if her father hurt her feelings, she could walk out to the barn and Abe would hold her.

But her voice wouldn't go above a whisper. "Thank you, Dad."

He winked at her, his eyes beautiful, like the eyes of someone who felt too much. The kitchen clock ticked, measuring the patient moment.

When she moved he asked, "What do you hear from Beulah Ann?"

"Not a thing. I've written her four times."

Kip went back to gazing out the window, which really meant seeing his own reflection, because it was dark. "That was a good trade you made. I'm glad you did it." He laughed and said, "Good for you."

SUNDAY WAS Father's Day. Chaley came for breakfast and brought doughnuts from City Market and a sterling silver bolo tie for her father. Erin gave him an unsentimental card—*Happy Father's Day*—signed only *Erin*. He said, "Thank you," and took it with him to his room.

With Erin's help, Maeve gave Abe a card with her handprints on it. He put it on their dresser. But from the way he smiled, not quite with his eyes, Erin knew he was thinking of Lloyd. When she brought him his supper in the south pasture, his eyes were red.

They sat in the truck bed to eat, and a cranky cow who thought they were threatening her calf tried to climb in with them. When they moved into the cab to escape her,

Abe said, "I didn't get him anything last year, and neither did Lane."

Maeve, in the car seat between them, touched Abe's hand. "Daddy," she said and lifted her arms. "Up!"

ON THE NIGHT before his wedding, Abe took his other girl with him to Grand Junction to buy a new lawn mower. He asked Martha repeatedly why Kip Kay had to have a new lawn mower today; the rancher had insisted he wanted Lucky to mow the lawn in the morning. "And why not Gunnison? Why couldn't I buy a lawn mower in Gunnison? Sometimes, Martha, I feel just like a slave."

It was ten when Abe got home, and finally dark, if you could call a full-moon night dark. Tomorrow would be the longest day of the year. Following habit, he did not park until taking a turn through the ranch to see if anything had changed in his absence. He trawled past the corral and the barn and the guest cabins.

It was time to go up to cow camp, in the high country. He would play the harmonica there, nights around the fire, and love Erin and Maeve, love having his family with him. But Lloyd would be missing from the circle.

Cows grazed in the pasture behind the guest cabins, and he slowed to see the stock in the full-moon light. It illuminated the barbed wire and everything beyond.

He braked.

Stared.

Leaving the truck idling, Abe got out and let Martha out, too. He spread the barbed wire and stepped through. With an eye on the cows and their calves, he headed for two shapes different from the rest.

No, there weren't just two. Ten...twenty...thirty?

They weren't keen on his coming near, either, and he

wondered how a person was supposed to read a brand on the things.

But the calves had been recently branded.

With a triangle E.

A heifer calf peered at him from under shaggy bangs. "You're not a cow at all." Good grief. He headed for the pickup to drive the rest of the fields, then back to the barn, to see the horses.

Wish was gone.

Not in his stall. Not in the corral.

"Come on, Martha," he said. "Let's go find Erin."

HE EXPECTED to find her waiting up, but only the light over the stove was on, and she didn't come out of the bedroom to greet him. Only Taffy showed up, wagging her tail and jumping on him like he was the only man in her life. "Yeah, I know who you love best," said Abe.

Kip had even been known to let her in the house.

Papers sat on the kitchen counter, held down by an unopened bottle of Jack Daniel's. The setup seemed like an invitation, addressed to him, and Abe stopped to read.

Then he opened the bottle of Jack Daniel's and took three long swallows.

Erin. Oh, Erin, sweetheart, you did good.

Mostly. Lord, had Kip had anything to do with this?

No, Kip wouldn't have let her do it.

On the way to the bedroom Abe stopped in Lane's old room.

Maeve slept on her tummy in the crib, her bottom sticking up in the air. She'd lost all her covers, and Abe put them over her and put her bunny right next to her tiny hand.

When he stepped into their bedroom, the room that had ceased to feel like Lloyd's, he thought he could smell Erin's skin. He could also smell faintly the scent of sex, of when they'd last made love.

Abe sat on the foot of the bed to tug off his boots and she sat up, the covers falling around her white chemise. He said, "Hi."

Erin studied him in the dark. He was smiling. When he came to her, naked, she smelled the Jack Daniel's.

"Is it all right?" she asked. Her father's chin had fallen to his knees that afternoon when he'd seen the calves. *You bought Highlands?*

Chaley had said innocently, *They have a lean beef. This ranch needs some innovation.*

Pete and George had smirked as they moved the herd.

"What? Getting our brand back?" Abe hugged her, messed with the sheets, figured out how to get on the same layer. Ah. There she was. *Oh, Erin.*

"The calves."

"You mean," he said against her skin, "do I mind being the sole owner of forty baby heifers of unusual breed?"

"Yes."

The Jack Daniel's had helped him adjust to the notion. Her body was also helping him adjust. "I love them. They're the cutest cows I ever saw."

"George laughed. He said they looked like walking wigs."

Abe had to take a breath. "No one around here," he said when he could talk, "is going to make fun of my herd." *Or my wife.*

She would be his wife tomorrow.

"How did you get the brand?"

"It's your wedding gift, Abe. It's not polite for you to ask how much it cost."

Wish's stall had been empty. "How does Kip feel about it?"

"I think," she said, "he's proud of me."

"So am I. I also have an attraction to you that will not quit." He went about showing her what he meant.

Much later Erin was almost asleep when he said her name.

"Hmm?" she answered.

"I really love my herd."

THE BEST MAN was absent.

The ceremony was scheduled for eleven in the morning, and by nine Lane still hadn't arrived. Abe loaded Buy Back and Rado into the trailer with the saddles and other equipment for the three days he and Erin planned to spend at the line cabin near the meadow where they would be married. There was a corral for the horses, and he and Lucky had brought feed for the animals and food for the people. Terry Loren, Guy's wife, and Ella Kelsey from the museum were handling the wedding refreshments. George would man the grill. When the horses were loaded, Abe and Lucky caravaned up to the meadow and set up the chairs and unloaded a big charcoal grill.

Once the chairs were arranged and the horses put in the corral, it was time to go home and change. If Lane didn't show, Abe decided, he'd ask Kip to stand up with him. Right now Erin's father was minding his granddaughter. And Erin was dressing in the big house, hiding out with Chaley.

Chaley. Abe hadn't got over gritting his teeth when he heard her name. Her smile at breakfast was Chaley-smug, and so was her self-defense. *It was Erin's idea. She said she wanted Scotch Highlanders. Anyhow, they've got good cold-weather tolerance. With all that hair.*

Back at the trailer, Abe stayed outside as long as he could, playing with Martha and watching the road. So far the people he was most counting on, most needing to see, were no-shows. Lane was working on a perfect track record of missing funerals and weddings.

And Beulah Ann...

Come on, Beulah Ann. Don't let me down.

But finally he had to go in and dress in the clothes he and Erin had picked out.

"Ah, Martha." Abe adjusted his string tie in the mirror over his father's old dresser. "I'm glad *you* could make it."

THE PERCHERONS' HOOVES made a soothing clip-clop on the graded road, but the borrowed buggy gave a bumpy ride. Chaley, at the reins, said, "Did you ever read those Laura Ingalls Wilder books? Didn't it sound so romantic when she and Almanzo would go riding in a buggy? But it felt like this."

Teeth-jarring.

"Well, the washboards on the road probably weren't so bad," Erin pointed out.

"But the roads were worse."

Chaley had dressed as a stage driver, in men's clothes with her hair in a long ponytail. Erin felt small beside this grand gesture of Chaley's, this buggy ride. She knew that it wasn't all generosity, that it was also Chaley's way of holding up her head. And maybe a way of apologizing for not steering her clear of shaggy cows.

There was dust on the road, so Erin clasped a lap robe around the tiered skirt of her mother's lacy dress. The country style, with a full sash and leg-of-mutton sleeves, had been popular when Jayne and Kip were married. Ella Kelsey had decorated Erin's ivory cowboy hat with flowers. And she'd worn sensible shoes, tan lace-up ropers, because she and Abe would be riding away after the ceremony.

She'd pinned her father's Silver Star to her dress, though she wasn't brave enough to ask for what she wanted or even to dream it. There were some things that meant nothing if you had to ask.

"There they are," said Chaley as the meadow came into view, filled with chairs and guests.

Abe, in his black coat and hat, held Maeve as he spoke with the minister. As Chaley drew the team to a halt, Kip walked toward the buggy. Coming over to Erin's side, he offered her his hand.

A lump in her throat, Erin took it, let him help her to the ground.

KIP JOINED ABE in front of the chairs in the shade of the trees. Like Abe, he watched the road, severely put out with Lane. If Lane didn't show, he'd have to stand up with Abe.

Oh, well, it would work.

Now Chaley was messing with the boom box, making sure the tape was set to the right place. He'd offered to hire live music, but Erin had said, *The hands want to play after the wedding.* George had a banjo and Pete would play his harmonica.

Kip had gone ahead and slipped money to Terry and Ella for the food.

Chaley checked her watch, said something to Pete and hurried to the area behind the chairs, back where the food was arranged, near the aspens.

The minister asked Abe, "Ready to start?"

Abe's eyes searched out Erin and he spotted her speaking with Chaley. Beautiful Erin, one of the aspens against the meadow grass. He'd thought she was a city girl when he met her. But Reno was a cow town with casinos, and she had a country heart.

No Lane anywhere.

Exchanging a look with Kip, he killed a mosquito on Maeve's arm. Bloodthirsty things were everywhere. "Maeve," said Abe, "it's time to go sit with Lucky."

"Mama."

"You'll get to see Mama in a minute. She's right back there."

"Mama."

Chaley came up the grassy aisle between the chairs. "I'll take her, Abe. We have someone to watch her."

Someone was blond and pretty and smiling big as Chaley brought Maeve over to her.

Beulah Ann.

Before he could go back and say hello, the music started. The minister said, "I guess this is it."

Where's my best man? Kip had left his side and gone to the back of the chairs, with the women.

Abe's heart knocked strangely.

Kip wasn't even looking toward the front but was staring at some latecomers. As the two figures made their way behind the last row of chairs, the rancher stepped aside to give them room.

They turned up the aisle.

The best man had arrived. On his arm was a beautiful woman with smooth light brown hair. She beamed at Abe.

Oh, Lane. Oh, Lane, you done good.

The best man, with the slow bow-legged stride of one who's ridden too many broncs and bulls, escorted the mother of the groom to her seat in the front row.

Then, to the tape-recorded "Wedding March," came Chaley in her stage-driver clothes, bearing a bouquet of wildflowers. Abe gazed past her, at Erin.

As SHE LISTENED to the music, Erin's heart and breath kept uneasy pace with the butterflies in her stomach. Chaley was already halfway to the minister and Abe. And Beulah Ann had taken Maeve around the seats and up to the front.

Erin moved toward the opening between the chairs. *Abe.* Close by, someone cleared his throat.

Erin had noticed him there earlier. She couldn't pretend she hadn't. This meadow was the most honest place she'd ever been, and she couldn't pretend, just bite her lips together hard.

Because he was still there, in his suit and vest and bolo tie, gazing down at her with eyes that felt too much, that brimmed with the deep feelings of the heart.

"I wasn't there for your first steps, honey, or your first words. But I'm sure as hell glad to be here today." Kip looked down at her face that was part his and part Jayne's, looked into her eyes just the way he did Chaley's to make sure she understood. "I hope you'll do your daddy the very great honor of letting him walk you down the aisle and give you to your husband."

Erin nodded.

Kip offered her his arm, and she took it, held it.

And they walked through the meadow grass toward Abe.

When they reached him, Kip put Erin's hand in Abe's, clasped the joined hands firmly together and stepped away.

And Erin, whole, looked into the gray-green eyes of the man she loved most. "Cowboy," she said, "you're mine."

"Anyone can see we may not be raising cattle here in twenty years, that the world might not let us. But these ranches weren't built on the prospect of defeat. And, one way or another, I hope my grandchildren will grow up working this land."

—Kip Kay, quoted in
A Tale of Two Ranches,
by Erin Cockburn

Epilogue

KIP HAD TOLD Beulah Ann he'd clean the line cabin after the honeymooners returned to their trailer. It wasn't from a sense of proprietorship—just a wanting to be back in that place, where he and Jayne had honeymooned, too.

Gus and Call, the ranch dogs, followed Rowdy up the road, running off to sniff trees and scrub oak. Damned blue heeler would probably end up with a nose full of porcupine quills.

A helicopter chugged overhead, and Kip lifted his eyes to the shape, spinning back, seeing a Huey. His knees hugged the horse, and he was grateful to be riding even a widow-maker like Rowdy. The shadow of his own hat on the ground reassured him, and soon he saw the cabin through the aspens. Rowdy picked his way over a fallen trunk, and Kip led him through the widest slots in the trees until he came staring-close to some newly stripped, newly carved bark. He reined in the horse.

"Well, I'll be damned."

When Kip had left the meadow at sunset on Saturday, the sound he'd heard as he departed was the mournful wail of a harmonica from the porch of the cabin, Abe playing "Home on the Range."

Ah, you'll be good to this land, thought Kip, reading the inscription in the broken tree bark, left for history:

THANK YOU, GOD. I LOVE MY WIFE. ABE COCKBURN, 1997.

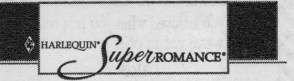

MORE PRAISE FOR
TO SPEAK FOR THE DEAD:

"Crackling in-and-out-of-courtroom suspense
from a welcome newcomer."
—*Kirkus Reviews*

"Paul Levine is guilty of master storytelling in
the first degree."
—Carl Hiaasen, author of *Skin Tight*

"A dazzler, extremely well-written and
featuring so many quotable passages . . .
you'll want someone handy to read them
aloud to."
—*Ellery Queen's Mystery Magazine*

"Levine keeps the plot spinning and the pages
turning. . . [Jake Lassiter is] a hero crafted
for the 1990s."
—United Press International

"If you decide to pick up *To Speak for the
Dead*, it's unlikely you'll be putting it down
anytime soon."
—*The Arkansas Gazette*

Bantam Books by Paul Levine

To Speak For the Dead
Night Vision
Coming soon: Slashback

TO
SPEAK
FOR THE
DEAD

Paul Levine

BANTAM BOOKS

NEW YORK · TORONTO · LONDON · SYDNEY · AUCKLAND

This novel is a work of fiction. Names, characters, places and incidents are either the product of the author's imagination or are used fictitiously. Any resemblance to actual persons, living or dead, events or locales is entirely coincidental.

TO SPEAK FOR THE DEAD

A Bantam Book
Bantam hardcover edition/August 1990
Bantam rack edition/October 1991

Grateful acknowledgment is made for permission to use an excerpt from "The Lawyers Know Too Much" from Smoke and Steel *by Carl Sandburg, copyright 1920 by Harcourt Brace Jovanovich, Inc., and renewed 1948 by Carl Sandburg, reprinted by permission of the publisher. "It's Still Rock and Roll To Me" by Billy Joel, copyright © 1980 by Impulsive Music. All rights controlled and administered by EMI April Music Inc. All rights reserved. International copyright secured. Used by permission.*

ISBN 0-553-29172-6

Published simultaneously in the United States and Canada

Bantam Books are published by Bantam Books, a division of Bantam Doubleday Dell Publishing Group, Inc. Its trademark, consisting of the words "Bantam Books" and the portrayal of a rooster, is Registered in U.S. Patent and Trademark Office and in other countries. Marca Registrada. Bantam Books, 666 Fifth Avenue, New York, New York 10103.

PRINTED IN THE UNITED STATES OF AMERICA

RAD   0 9 8 7 6 5 4 3 2 1

ACKNOWLEDGMENTS

I gratefully acknowledge the assistance of South Florida medical examiners Dr. Joseph Davis and Dr. Ronald Wright, orthopedic surgeon Dr. Joel Kallan, the great trial lawyers and friends Stuart Grossman, Edward Shohat and Philip Freidin, my indefatigable secretary Gayle Bouffard, my agent Bob Colgan and my editor Kate Miciak. The rest of you know who you are.

I also acknowledge the hellish paradise of Miami, a tropical Casablanca of sultry days and pastel sunsets, where buzzards endlessly circle the courthouse, some on wings and some in Porsches.

"The Coroner shall view the bodye and the woundes and the strokes, and the bodye shalbe buryed. And yf the Coroner fynde the bodye buried before his comminge, he shall not omitte to digge up the bodye.

"And when the inquest is sworne ye Coroner must inquire if ye person were slayne by felony or by misadventure. And after it shalbe enquired who were presente at the dede, and who be coulpable of the ayde, force, commandement, consent, or receite of suche felonies wittingly."

ANTHONY FITZHERBERT,
The New Book of Justice, 1545 A.D.

TO
SPEAK
FOR THE
DEAD

Prologue

TABLE DANCER

He would remember the sounds—the wailing sirens, the moans of the injured—and the smells, a smoky ashen stench that clung to hair and clothing. Late the first night, he slipped into the parking lot for some air, and he tasted the sky as the smoke rose above Miami's inner core. He heard the city scream, the popping of wood and plastic aflame, short bursts of gunfire followed by silence, then the crackle of police radios. Later he would remember slipping in a puddle of blood on the tile floor of the Emergency Room.

He would not leave the hospital for seventy-two hours, and by then, he had treated more gunshot wounds than most doctors see in a lifetime. Blacks against police, whites against blacks, savage violence in a ghetto hopelessly misnamed Liberty City. By the time the shooting stopped and the fires were out, an eerie silence hung over the area, an inner-city battle zone where neither side surrendered, but each put away its weapons and withdrew.

"That's a real poster ass, huh?"

Roger Salisbury shot a sideways glance at the man next to him. A working guy, heavy boots and a plaid shirt open at the neck. Thick hands, one on a pack of cigarettes, the other on his drink, elbows resting on the scarred bar. "Like to frame that ass, hang it in the den next to Bob Griese."

"Uh-huh," Salisbury mumbled. He didn't come here to talk, didn't know why he came. Maybe to lose himself in a place crammed with people and noise, to be alone amid clinking glasses, laughter, and the creaminess of women's bodies. He strained his neck to see her above him on the stage.

"Not that one," the man said, tapping the bar with a solid index finger. "Over there at the stairs, the on-deck circle. A real poster ass. Never saw a skinny girl with an ass like that. Eat my lunch offa that."

She wore a black G-string, a red bikini top, and red high-heeled shoes. If not for the outfit and the setting, she could have been a cheerleader with a mom, dad, and grandmom in Kansas. Good bone structure, fair complexion with freckles across a button nose, short wavy reddish-brown hair, wholesome as a wheat field. The face belonged in a high school yearbook; the body launched a thousand fantasies. Her thin waist accentuated a round bottom that arched skyward out of both sides of the tiny G-string. Her breasts were round and full. She was warming up, fastening a prefab smile into place, taking a few practice swings, tapping a sequined shoe in time to Billy Joel, who was turned up way too high:

> *What's the mat-ter with the clothes I'm wear-ing?*
> *Can't you tell that your tie's too wide?*
> *May-be I should buy some old tab col-lars.*
> *Wel-come back to the age of jive.*

The working guy was looking at Salisbury now, sizing him up. Looking at a blow-dry haircut that was a little too precise for a place like this. Clean shaven, skin still glistening like he'd just spanked his face with Aqua Velva at two A.M., as if the girls in a beat-your-meat joint really care. The hair was starting to show some early gray, the features pleasant, if not matinee idol stuff. A professor at Miami–Dade maybe, the working guy figured.

Salisbury knew the guy was looking at him, now at his hands, just as he had done. Funny how hands can tell you so much. Proud of his hands. Broad and strong. They could have swung a pick, except there were no calluses. He had washed off the blood, scrubbing as hard after surgery as he had before the endless night began. Seventy-two hours with only catnaps and stale sandwiches until the hospital cafeteria ran out. But he stood there the whole time, one of the leaders, the chief orthopedics resident, setting broken bones, picking glass and bullet fragments out of wounds, calming hysterical relatives.

After showering at the hospital, he had tossed the soiled lab coat into the trash and grabbed a blue blazer from his locker. Now he was nursing a beer and trying to forget the carnage. He could have gone home. Twenty-seventh Avenue was finally open after the three-day blockade. But too tired to sleep, he wound through unfamiliar streets and was finally lured out of the night by the neon sign of the Tangiers on West Dixie. He would think about it later, many times, why he stopped that night, what drew him to such a strange and threatening place. Pickup trucks and old Chevys jammed the parking lot. Music blared from outdoor loudspeakers, a rhythmic, pulsating beat intended to tempt men inside just as the singing of the Sirens drew Greek sailors onto the rocks. It might have been the flashing sign. The throbbing colors got right to the point——NUDE GIRLS 24 HOURS . . . NUDE GIRLS 24 HOURS——blinking on, blinking off, proof of bare flesh moment after moment after moment.

The working guy was talking to him: "I say let 'em burn colored town down to the ground if they want to, no skin offa my nose. I mean, the cops was wrong, killing one of the coloreds, had his hands cuffed behind his back, no need for that. But some of 'em just looking for excuses to behave like animals. They burned a poor Cuban alive in his car, heard it on the radio."

"We tried to save him," Salisbury said quietly.

The guy gave him a look. "Sure! You're a doctor. Should have known. Jesus, you musta seen it all. Wait a minute, Sweet Jesus, here comes Miss Poster Ass. She's worth a twenty-dollar dance, or I'm the Prince of Wales."

Roger Salisbury watched her walk toward them, an inviting smile aimed his way. The other men around the small stage hooted and slapped their thighs. Roger Salisbury lowered his eyes and studied his drink.

"Your first time?" the man asked. Silence. "Yeah, your first time. Loosen up. Here's the poop. First the girls dance out here on the bar stage. No big deal, they take it all off, you stick a dollar bill in their garter and maybe one'll kiss you. In the back, where it's darker, you got your table dances, twenty bucks. That's one-on-one and I may buy me an up-close-and-personal visit with Miss Poster Ass. Haven't been able to get here all week what with the jungle bunnies staging their block parties."

On stage now, grinding to the music, no longer the Kansas cheerleader. *Ev-ry-bod-y's talk-in' 'bout the new sound. Funny, but it's still rock and roll to me.* In a few moments, the bikini top was off, firm breasts bounding free. The G-string came next, and then she arched her back, bent over, and propped her hands on her knees looking away from the men. The poster ass wiggled clockwise as if on coasters, then stopped and wiggled counterclockwise. Salisbury stared as if hypnotized. The ass quivered once, fluttered twice with contractions that Roger Salisbury felt deep in his own loins, then stopped six inches from his face. His fatigue gone, the swirl of blood and bodies a dreamy fog, Roger Salisbury fantasized that the perfect ass wiggled only for him. He didn't see the other men, some laughing, some bantering, others conjuring up their own steamy visions. None of the others, though, seemed spellbound by an act as old as the species.

The dance done, the girl smiled at Roger Salisbury, an open interested smile, he thought. And though she smiled at each man, again he thought it was only for him. She sashayed from one end of the small stage to the other, collecting dollar bills in a black garter while propping a red,

7

high-heeled shoe on the rim between the stage and the bar. Other than the garter and the shoes, she was naked, but her face showed neither shame nor seduction. She could have been passing the collection plate at the First Lutheran Church of Topeka. Roger Salisbury slipped a five-dollar bill into her garter, removing it from his wallet with two fingers, never taking his eyes off the girl. A neat trick, but he could also tie knots in thread with a thumb and one finger inside a matchbox. Great hands. The strong, steady hands of a surgeon.

Her smile widened as she leaned close to him, her voice a moist whisper on his ear. "I'd like to dance for you. Just you." And he believed it.

Roger Salisbury believed everything she said that night. That she was a model down on her luck, that her name was Autumn Rain, that all she wanted was a good man and a family. They talked in the smoky shadows of a corner table and she danced for him alone. Twenty dollars and another twenty as a tip. He didn't lay a hand on her. At nearby tables men grasped tumbling breasts, and the girls stepped gingerly from their perches in four-inch spikes to sit on customers' laps, writhing on top of them, grinding down with bare asses onto the fully clothed groins of middle-aged men. "Didja come?" the heavy girl at the next table whispered to her customer, already reaching for a tip.

"I've never seen anything like this," Roger Salisbury said, shaking his head. "It's half prostitution and half masturbation." He gestured toward the overweight girl who was gathering her meager outfit and sneaking a peek at the president's face on the bill she had glommed from a guy in faded jeans. "You don't do that, do you?" Salisbury asked.

8

She smiled. *Of course not*, the look said.

He asked her out.

Against the rules, she said. Some guys, they think if you're an exotic dancer, it means for fifty bucks you give head or whatever.

But I'm different, Roger Salisbury said.

She cocked her head to one side and studied him. They all thought they were different, but she knew there were only two kinds of men, jerks and jerk-offs. Oh, some made more money and didn't get their fingernails dirty. She'd seen them, white shirts and yellow ties, slumming it, yukking it up. But either way, grease monkeys or stockbrokers, once those gates opened and the blood rushed in, turning their worms into stick shifts, they were either jerks or jerk-offs. The jerk-offs were mostly young, wise guys without a pot to piss in, spending all their bread on wheels and women, figuring everything in a skirt—or G-string—was a push-over. Jerks were saps, always falling in love and wanting to change you, make an honest woman out of you. Okay, put me in chains, if the price is right. This guy, jerk all the way.

I'm a doctor, he said.

Oh, she said, sounding impressed.

He told her how he had patched and mended those caught in the city's crossfire, how he wanted to help people and be a great doctor. She listened with wide eyes and nodded as if she knew what he felt deep inside and she smiled with practiced sincerity. A doctor, she figured, made lots of money, not realizing that a resident took home far less than an exotic dancer and got his hands just as dirty.

She looked directly into Roger Salisbury's eyes and softened her own. He looked into her eyes and thought he saw warmth and beauty of spirit.

Roger Salisbury, it turned out, was better at reading X rays than the looks in women's eyes.

DECEMBER 1988

1

THE RONGEUR

When the witness hesitated, I drummed my pen impatiently against my legal pad. Made a show of it. Not that I was in a hurry. I had all day, all week. The Doctors' Medical Insurance Trust pays by the hour and not minimum wage. Take your sweet time. The drum roll was only for effect, to remind the jury that the witness didn't seem too sure of himself. And to make him squirm a bit, to rattle him.

First the pen *clop-clop-clopping* against the legal pad. Then the slow, purposeful walk toward the witness stand, let him feel me there as he fans through his papers looking for a lost report. Then the stare, the high-voltage Jake Lassiter laser beam stare. Melt him down.

I unbuttoned my dark suitcoat and hooked a thumb into my belt. Then I stood there, 220 pounds of ex–football player, ex–public defender, ex–a-lot-of-things, leaning against the faded walnut rail of the witness stand, home to a million sweaty palms.

Only forty seconds since the question was asked, but I wanted it to seem like hours. Make the jury soak up the silence. The only sounds were the whine of the air conditioning and the paper shuffling of the witness. Young lawyers sometimes make the mistake of filling that black hole, of clarifying the question or rephrasing it, inadvertently breathing life into the dead air that hangs like a shroud over a hostile witness. What folly. The witness is zipped up because he's worried. He's thinking, not about his answer, but of the reason for the question, trying to outthink you, trying to anticipate the next question. Let him stew in his own juice.

Another twenty seconds of silence. One juror yawned. Another sighed.

Judge Raymond Leonard looked up from the *Daily Racing Form*, a startled expression as if he just discovered he was lost. I nodded silently, assuring him there was no objection awaiting the wisdom that got him through night classes at Stetson Law School. The judge was a large man in his fifties, bald and moon-faced and partial to maroon robes instead of traditional black. History would never link him with Justices Marshall or Cardozo, but he was honest and let lawyers try their cases with little interference from the bench.

Earlier, at a sidebar conference, the judge suggested we recess at two-thirty each day. He could study the written motions in the afternoon, he said with a straight face, practically dusting off his binoculars for the last three races at Hialeah. A note on the bench said, "Hot Enough, Rivera up, 5–1, ninth race." In truth, the judge was better at handicapping the horses than recognizing hearsay.

Another thirty seconds. Then a cleared throat, the sound of a train rumbling through a tunnel, and the white-haired witness spoke. "That depends," Dr. Harvey Watkins said with a gravity usually reserved for State of the Union messages.

The jurors turned toward me, expectant looks. I widened my eyes, all but shouting, "Bullshit." Then I worked up a small spider-to-the-fly smile and tried to figure out what the hell to ask next. What I wanted to say was, *Three hundred bucks an hour, and the best you can do is "that depends." One man is dead, my client is charged with malpractice, and you're giving us the old softshoe, "that depends."*

What I said was, "Let's try it this way." An exasperated tone, like a teacher trying to explain algebra to a chimpanzee. "When a surgeon is performing a laminectomy on the L3–L4 vertebrae, can he see what he's doing with the rongeur, or does he go by feel?"

"As I said before, that depends," Dr. Watkins said with excessive dignity. Like most hired guns, he could make a belch sound like a sonnet. White hair swept back, late sixties, retired chief of orthopedics at Orlando Presbyterian, he had been a good bone carpenter in his own right until he lost his nerves to an ice-filled river of Stolichnaya. Lately he talked for pay on the traveling malpractice circuit. Consultants, they call themselves. Whores, other doctors peg them. When I defended criminal cases, I thought my clients could win any lying contest at the county fair. Now I figure doctors run a dead heat with forgers and confidence men.

No use fighting it. Just suck it up and ask, "Depends on what?" Waiting for the worst now, asking an open-ended question on cross-examination.

"Depends on what point you're talking about. Before you enter the disc space, you can see quite clearly. Then, once you lower the rongeur into it to remove the nucleus pulposus, the view changes. The disc space is very small, so of course, the rongeur is blocking your view."

"Of course," I said impatiently, as if I'd been waiting for that answer since Ponce de León landed on the coast. "So at that point you're working blind?"

I wanted a *yes*. He knew that I wanted a *yes*. He'd rather face a hip replacement with a case of the shakes than give me a *yes*.

"I don't know if I'd characterize it exactly that way . . ."

"But the surgeon can't see what he's doing at that point, can he?" Booming now, trying to force a good old-fashioned one-word answer. Come on, Dr. Harvey Wallbanger, the sooner you get off the stand, the sooner you'll be in the air-conditioned shadows of Sally Russell's Lounge across the street, cool clear liquid sliding down the throat to cleanse your godforsaken soul.

"You're talking about a space maybe half a centimeter," the doctor responded, letting his basso profundo fill the courtroom, not backing down a bit. "Of course you don't have a clear view, but you keep your eye on the rongeur, to be aware of how far you insert it into the space. You feel for resistance at the back of the space and, of course, go no farther."

14

"My point exactly, doctor. You're watching the rongeur, you're feeling inside the disc space for resistance. You're operating blind, aren't you? You and Dr. Salisbury and every orthopedic surgeon who's ever removed a disc . . ."

"Objection! Argumentative and repetitious." Dan Cefalo, the plaintiff's lawyer, was on his feet now, hitching up his pants even as his shirttail flopped out. He fastened his third suitcoat button into the second hole. "Judge, Mr. Lassiter is making speeches again."

Judge Leonard looked up again, unhappy to have his handicapping interrupted. Three to one he didn't hear the objection, but a virtual lock that it would be sustained. The last objection was overruled, and Judge Leonard believed in the basic fairness of splitting the baby down the middle. It was easier to keep track if you just alternated your rulings, like a kid guessing on a true–false exam.

"Sustained," the judge said, nodding toward me and cocking his head with curiosity when he looked at Cefalo, now thoroughly misbuttoned and hunched over the plaintiff's table, a Quasimodo in plaid polyester. Then the judge handed a note to the court clerk, a young woman who sat poker-faced through tales of multiple homicides, scandalous divorces, and train wrecks. The clerk slipped the note to the bailiff, who left through the rear door that led to the judge's chambers. There, enveloped in the musty smell of old law books never read much less understood, he would give the note to the judge's secretary, who would call Blinky Blitstein and lay fifty across the board on Hot Enough.

"Your Honor, I'll rephrase the question," I said, as if I had a choice. "Doctor, I think you would agree that the rongeur blocks your view of the disc space, correct?"

"Substantially."

A twenty-five-cent word. What does it take to get a *yes* out of this guy? Dr. Watkins let his tongue dart over his lips. Getting a little dry, are we? Eyes just a bit cloudy and bloodshot. Cefalo put you up at the Sonesta Beach, I bet. Room service probably brought up a bottle of Russia's best. Maybe one of Finland's too. A Winter War in a tenth-floor suite overlooking the Atlantic.

I walked to the rear of the courtroom so that the jury was between the witness stand and me. I wanted all eyes on Dr. Watkins as I broke him like a rotten mast in a gale.

"Doctor, isn't it true that, because of the narrow disc space, any time a surgeon performs this kind of surgery, a known risk is that the rongeur will go too far, will pierce the aorta?"

"A risk? Of course, it's a risk, but . . ."

"And that's what happened here, the occurrence of that risk, that statistically will occur—"

"Objection! Your Honor, Mr. Lassiter refuses to permit the doctor to finish his answer. He's interrupting." This time Cefalo banged his knee on the plaintiff's table as he stood up and his tie flopped out of his misbuttoned coat like the tongue of a thirsty dog. Most days Cefalo dressed as well as the next guy, but in trial he figured he gained sympathy by looking like a vagrant. He'd drop his drawers if it would win one juror's vote. This day his suit was old and wrinkled and smelled like an overheated horse. But Dan Cefalo knew his stuff. Best to remember that or get blindsided when he transformed from Buddy Hackett to Gregory Peck in closing argument.

"Overruled," the judge said without looking up.

Thank you, Nathan Detroit.

I took a few giant steps toward the witness stand, feeling my oats. I wanted to finish with a flourish. Dr. Watkins had nailed us hard on direct examination. Now just trying to get even, or close to it. I walked to the clerk's table and picked up the stainless steel instrument that resembled a small, delicate pair of pliers. The clerk never looked up, leaving me staring into the top of her Afro. She was reading a paperback with a castle and a dark-eyed woman on the cover.

"Now, this rongeur, Plaintiff's Exhibit Five, is the perfect instrument for removing the herniated disc material, isn't it?"

"I don't know if it's perfect, but that's what's used."

They'll be examining his liver under a microscope before he'll give a defense lawyer a *yes*. I walked to the rear of the courtroom, the doctor's eyes tracking me, suspicion wrinkling his brow. He wouldn't trust me with the petty cash.

"But perfect as it is for one job, it poses a real and known danger to the aorta, doesn't it?"

Dr. Watkins smiled. The eyes seemed to clear. His chin thrust out and he shot a look at the jury, just to make sure they were paying attention.

"The rongeur poses no danger," he said in deep, senatorial tones. "The surgeon who is too hasty or too rough or loses track of where he is, that's the danger. A rongeur does not do the damage except in a most elementary way, the same way a gun kills, but it is the man pulling the trigger who is brought to justice. A surgeon who is negligent, that is the danger. It is professional negligence, or as you lawyers like to call it, malpractice, to damage the aorta while doing a laminectomy—"

"Your Honor!" I am much too loud, a wounded boar.
"The witness is not being responsive. He is the one who is
speech making for the benefit of the party that pays him
royally." Anything to distract the jury from my blood spilling across the floor. One question too many, the classic bozo
move on cross.

Judge Leonard swiveled in his cushioned chair. "Is that
an objection?"

I toted up the judge's prior rulings like a blackjack player
counting face cards. "Yes, Your Honor, I ask that the jury be
instructed to disregard the witness's self-serving soliloquy."

"Sustained. The jury will disregard the last statement of
the witness."

Fat chance, the jurors figuring that anything they're supposed to forget must be worth remembering. How to rescue
the moment? I caught sight of Cefalo. If his smile were any
wider, his uppers would fall out.

"No further questions are necessary, Your Honor," I said
with more than a touch of bravado. Then I swaggered to my
seat, as if I had just vanquished the witness. I doubted the
jury bought even a slice of it. *Lassiter, why didn't you shut up
when you had the chance?*

Ramrod straight, white hair in place, Dr. Watkins strode
from the witness stand, pausing to nod graciously at the jury,
a general admiring his troops. Then he walked by the plaintiff's table, bowed toward Dan Cefalo and tenderly patted
Mrs. Melanie Corrigan, the young widow, on the arm. As he
passed me, he shook his head, ever so slightly, a compassionate look, as if this poor wretch of a mouthpiece couldn't
help it if he was on the wrong side and an incompetent boob

to boot. What a pro. The jurors never took their eyes off him.

My eyes closed and behind them were visions of green hills and cool streams, where the courthouses were only for marriage licenses and real estate deeds. Then I wondered if it was too late to coach powder-puff football at a prep school in Vermont.

2

THE
GOOD GUYS

Roger Salisbury was pouring black bean soup over the rice, then carefully layering a row of chopped onions on top, building a little mound. Not a drop of the dark soup spilled. The Cuban crackers, which in my hands crumble into dust, he split down the middle with a thumb and index finger, a clean break like marble under a sculptor's chisel. The hands of a surgeon. Not hands that would have slipped, letting the rongeur puncture the aorta, leaving Philip Corrigan to die of internal bleeding and Melanie Corrigan to live as a young, beautiful, and very rich widow. Which is why Roger Salisbury was questioning my strategy in cross-examining the white-haired baron of bombast who nearly blew me out of the courtroom this very day.

"If our defense is that I didn't nick the aorta, why were you trying to get Watkins to admit that a surgeon can't see what he's doing in a laminectomy? It sounded like you were trying to excuse me for something I didn't do."

When a client thinks that you are letting him sink into the treacherous waters of the justice system, it is best to appear calm and knowledgeable, even when you are floundering about, looking for the nearest lifeboat yourself. This is easier to do when not distracted by two young women who are appraising you with large, luminous, and inviting eyes.

"It's called alternative pleading," I said with authority and a polite smile toward our observers, perched on barstools at the counter. When confronted with large, luminous, and inviting eyes, I am polite without fail. "We say to the jury, first, the good doctor didn't come within a country mile of the damn blood vessel. Second, even if he might have sideswiped it, that's not negligence. It's an accepted risk of this kind of surgery because of the small disc space and the proximity of the aorta."

"I get the feeling you don't believe me," Roger Salisbury said. He ladled more soup onto the rice with those sturdy hands, and I watched the steam rise, a pungent aroma enveloping us. One of the women was smiling now. At me, I thought. Or was it at Roger? He was handsome in a nondescript way. Medium height, medium build, medium features. The kind of guy who gives police artists fits. Nothing to work with, no missing teeth, bent nose, or jagged scars, nothing protruding, nothing receding.

I dug into my palomilla, a tough piece of flank steak marinated in oils and spices and likely left on the hood of a '59 Chevy in the Miami sun. I was talking with my hands, or rather my fork, which had speared a sweet fried plantain.

"It's a historic legal strategy. In olden times, a plaintiff might sue his neighbor and say, 'I lent him my kettle, and when he returned it, it was cracked.' The neighbor answers the lawsuit and says, 'I never borrowed the kettle, but if I did, it was cracked when he gave it to me.' "

Roger Salisbury shook his head. "Your profession is so uncertain, so full of contradictions. I'll never understand the law."

"Nor I, women." Their eyes were lighting up with magical, come-hither glints. I stayed put and Roger kept talking.

"Jake, I have a lot of faith in you, you know that."

Oh boy, I got fired once by a client who started off just like that. "Sure, and you should have," I said, showing the old confidence.

"But I can't say I'm happy with the way the trial's going."

"Listen, Roger. There's a psychological phenomenon every defendant goes through during the plaintiff's case. Try to remember it's still the top of the first inning. We haven't even been to bat yet. Wait'll old Charlie Riggs testifies for us. He's honest and savvy, and he'll make Wallbanger Watkins look like the whoring sawbones he is."

"Sure."

"You don't sound convinced."

"Riggs is on the verge of senile dementia, if not over it. He speaks Latin half the time. He's the friggin' coroner—or was until they retired him—not an orthopedic surgeon."

"Roger, trust me. We need a canoemaker, not a carpenter. Charlie Riggs is going to tell the jury why Philip Corrigan

23

died. It's a hole in their case, and I'm going to ride the U.S. Cavalry through it."

Finally the two women set sail for our table. One looked straight at me from under a pile of auburn hair that reached her shoulders and kept going toward Mexico. She had caramel skin and lustrous ebony eyes. The other had thick, jet black hair that only made her porcelain complexion seem even more delicate. She wore one earring shaped like a golden spermatozoan and another of ivory that could have been a miniature elephant tusk. Both women wore tourni-quet-tight slacks, high-heeled open-toed shoes, and oversized cotton sweatshirts, with spangles and shoulders from here to the Orange Bowl.

"May we join you for a moment?" Miss Caramel Skin asked. The *you* was a *chew*.

Roger Salisbury looked up and grinned. Even the punitive damage claim hadn't sent his hormones into hibernation. I could have used the distraction. My social life was as empty as a Miami Beach hotel in July. But I took inventory quickly, knowing I had several hours of work ahead. There is a time for dallying, but the middle of a trial is not such a time. I wanted to finish the postmortem on the day's events and prepare for tomorrow and the widow's testimony. Still, an old reflex, maybe eons old, had the mental computer figuring a sort of cost–benefit analysis—how long it would take—the flirting time, make-nice time, bone-jumping time, and call-you-again time. Too long.

They already were sitting down and Caramel Skin was chattering about her ex-boyfriend, a Colombian, and what a scumbag he was. *Skoombag.* She was Costa Rican, Miss Earrings Honduran.

I shouldn't have brought Roger to Bayside, a yuppie hangout with shops, restaurants, and bars strung along Biscayne Bay downtown. It was a pickup place, and these two probably assumed we were in the hunt—two decent-looking guys under forty in suits—when all we wanted was solitude and an early dinner. Outside the windows, the young male lawyers, accountants, and bankers headed for the nearby singles bars, suitcoats slung over shoulders, red suspenders holding up Brooks Brothers suit pants. They slouched against open-air bars waiting for their frozen margaritas to ooze out of chrome-plated machines that belong in Dairy Queens, not taverns. Nearby the young women—mirror images in business suits or no-nonsense below-the-knee dresses—their mouths fixed in go-to-hell looks, struggled with the degree of toughness and cool necessary to beat the men at their own game. Altogether, a smug clique of well-dressed boys and girls.

"Carlos had a Cigarette," Caramel Skin was saying. "Used to go like a son-of-a-bitch." *Sunavabeach.* "Liked the Cigarette more than he liked me. Now he's at FCI."

Salisbury wore a blank look. I said, "Federal Correctional Institution. Probably used the boat to bring in bags of the white stuff."

"*Sí. Hizo el tonto.* He played the fool for others. And, *como si esto fuera poco,* he used to beat me. Tie me up and spank me with a hairbrush. It was fun at first, but then . . ."

Roger Salisbury was into it now, asking Caramel Skin whether Carlos the Con used leather or plain old rope. Scientific study or kinky curiosity, I wondered. Miss Earrings was

25

telling me that they were fashion models—aren't they all?—
who really didn't have work permits. Came here on tourist
visas. Which meant they also were following the scent for
the Holy Grail, green cards. Bagging American husbands
would do the trick.

The earrings dangled near my face. Our knees touched
and her voice dropped to a whisper, a ploy to get me to lean
closer. Do they teach this stuff or is it in their genes? A long
fingernail traced the outline of my right ear. In the right time
and place, it could have been erotic. In a brightly lit restaurant with my mind on business, it itched.

"Thick hair, Mister Broad Shoulders," she said. *Theek
and Meester.* "Some of the Yankees, their hair is like, how
they say, *telaranas?*"

"Cobwebs," Caramel Skin said.

"*Sí*, cobwebs. But yours, *chico,* is thick like *cáñamo.* And
rubianco."

"Like hemp and almost blond," Caramel Skin said, helpfully. Her friend gave a tug on my theek *rubianco cáñamo,*
which did not help me get a fried plantain into my mouth.
"And *ojos azules,*" she said, giggling, looking into my eyes.

The women excused themselves to go to the restroom,
probably to divide up the spoils. Caramel Skin would get the
smaller guy with neat, salt-and-pepper hair who was practically smacking his lips over images of sweet bondage. Earrings was stuck with *Meester* Broad Shoulders, who at least
had neither cobwebs nor spiders in his mop but who seemed
distracted.

Salisbury lit a cigarette, dragged deeply, and sent a swirl
of smoke into the overhead fan. Doctors who smoke puzzle

26

me. You know they know better. Maybe lack of discipline and self-control. I couldn't imagine a personal injury lawyer riding a motorcycle, not after seeing those eight-by-ten glossies taken by the Highway Patrol. Need a shovel to scrape up body parts.

I wanted to draw Roger away from his Latin American fantasy and talk about tomorrow's testimony. But he was saying something about a doubleheader that had nothing to do with Yankee Stadium. I shook my head no, and he gave me that puzzled look. I'd seen the same expression the first time he walked into my office about eighteen months earlier.

"You must like representing doctors," he said that day, after we exchanged hellos.

"Yeah, it's a great honor."

He gave me that look and dropped the malpractice complaint on my desk as if it carried the plague. While I read it, he walked around my office, ostensibly admiring the view of the bay, but surreptitiously looking for merit badges on the walls. He couldn't find any. No diplomas, no awards from the Kiwanis. I hung my Supreme Court admission ticket above the toilet at home. Covers a crack in the plaster. He stopped in front of a photo of my college football team, one of those posed shots with a hundred twenty guys filling the bleachers.

"You played football," he said. Impressed. He couldn't be sure I ever graduated from law school, but he was happy I could hit a blocking sled.

"A lead-footed linebacker," I said. "Better at lawyering than covering the tight end over the middle."

"Been defending doctors long?"

"Not as long as I played games in the PD's office, keeping some very bad actors on the street."

"Why'd you leave?"

"It made me puke."

"Huh?"

"Realizing every client I ever had was guilty. Not always with what they're charged, but guilty of some crime, sometimes worse than the charge."

I told him how it felt to see some slimeball go free after a warrantless search, then pimp-roll back into the courtroom for pistol-whipping a sixty-year-old liquor store clerk. *Ja-cob, my man, they got no probable cause.*

Told him I quit and did plaintiff's PI. Half my clients were phonies. Phony injuries and phony doctors or real injuries and no insurance.

"So representing doctors is a step up," Roger Salisbury had said brightly.

"From the gutter to the curb."

That look again.

"I sold out, joined the high-rise set at rich, old Harman & Fox," I told him. "Ordinarily, the dark-wood-and-deep-carpet types wouldn't give a guy like me a second look. Afraid I'd spill the soup on my vest, if I owned one. But they woke up one day and figured they didn't have anybody who could try a case. They could shuffle papers and write memos, but they didn't know how to tap dance in front of a jury. So I won some cases, a few for very dangerous doctors."

Now his puzzled look changed to one of concern.

"Bottom line," I said, using a favorite expression of the corporate gazoonies who ruled the firm. "I've spent my entire career looking for the good guys and have yet to find them."

He was quiet a moment, probably wondering if I was incompetent. Good, we were even. I always assume the worst. Fewer surprises later.

Things improved after that. I checked up on him. His rep was okay. Board certified and no prior lawsuits. He probably checked me out, too. Found out I've never been disbarred, committed, or convicted of moral turpitude. And the only time I was arrested it was a case of mistaken identity—I didn't know the guy I hit was a cop.

So here we were, waiting for *dos chicas* to powder their noses or inhale something into them, and my mind was stuck on the mundane subject of the pending trial.

"Roger, let's talk about tomorrow. Cefalo will put the widow on first thing. Today I was watching you out of the corner of my eye and you were staring at her. I know she looks like a million bucks, but if I saw it while I was getting blindsided by Wallbanger Watkins, I'm sure the jurors did, too. It could be mistaken for a look of guilt, like you feel sorry you croaked her old man. That's worse than having the hots for her."

"Okay, didn't know I was doing it. Probably just staring into space."

"Yeah sure. The point is, she's likely to be a very good witness. The men in the jury all want in her pants, the women want to mother her."

"Okay already, I get the point."

"Good. I don't want to concern you, but the lovely widow is a real problem for us. She can make the jury forget all our

29

medical mumbo jumbo. That gray silk dress today with the strand of white pearls. Classy but not too flashy."

Salisbury laughed. "You ought to see her in a strapless cocktail dress."

"Uh-huh." *Uh-huh* is what I say when I don't know what to say. I would have liked Salisbury to fill me in here, but he didn't give me any help. After a moment I asked, "Since when are you Mrs. Corrigan's fashion consultant?"

"Oh that. I probably never told you. When Philip started seeing me for the back and leg pain, we became friendly. I wasn't dating anybody. They were just married. He started asking me over to their house in Gables Estates. Cocktail parties, dinners, sometimes just the three of us."

"So you know Mrs. Corrigan?"

"Melanie. Sure."

"Melanie, is it?"

He looked at me with a what's-the-big-deal look and I didn't have an answer so I polished off the palomilla and thought it over. No big deal. I just would have liked to have known about it sometime before trial.

In a moment our new friends cruised back, eyes a thousand watts brighter, ready to roll. I mumbled my apologies to Miss Earrings, who, with no apparent regret, shifted her electrified look to the blandly handsome doctor. I left them there, two women with a buzz on, and the man who had entrusted his career to me, the man who hadn't told me everything. What else, I wondered, had he left out?

I paused at the door to look back. The restaurant was filled now. Some of the yuppies were crowding the bar, making too much noise, pushing limes into their Mexican beer, a trendy brand aged about as long as their attention spans. If you have to put lime in your beer, you might as well drink Kool-Aid.

Back at the table, one woman sat on each side of Roger Salisbury. They all laughed. I left the three of them there, the mathematical possibilities of their union crowding Melanie Corrigan's testimony into a dusty recess of my mind.

3

THE WIDOW

"Mrs. Corrigan, do you love your husband?"

"I do." A pause, a catch in the throat, a quiver, the beginning of a tear, then like a lake swollen by a summer storm, an overflow cascading down sculpted cheekbones. "That is, I did. I loved him very much."

Blessed timing. They don't teach that in finishing school. Dan Cefalo continued his questioning. "Do you miss him?"

Another leading question, but only a dunce would incur the jury's wrath by interrupting the soap opera with a news bulletin.

"Very much. Every day. We shared so much. Sometimes,

when a car pulls into the driveway, I forget, and I think, well, maybe it's Phil."

And maybe it's the paperboy. God, could she lay it on thick. She looked toward the jury and then away as if the memory was too much to bear. A lace handkerchief appeared out of a navy leather clutch and the big, brown, wet eyes were dabbed dry. The pain radiated from her, but I was the one who was dying. Every question launched an arrow, and every answer pierced my heart. The widow was majestic, thick russet hair swept straight back to lay bare those chiseled lines, to expose her suffering. All for the glory of justice and a seven-figure award for mental anguish, loss of society, comfort, and consortium.

"Tell us about your husband, your late husband, Mrs. Corrigan. And I know it's a painful subject, so if you need a recess to gather yourself, please just say so." Cefalo extended his arms toward the widow and bowed from the waist, as if she were royalty. And she did look regal, white gloves setting off a navy and white double-breasted cardigan that covered a matching skirt. Maybe the gloves hid Racy Red nail polish, already slathered on for a night of romping through Coconut Grove clubs. Maybe on cross-examination I should order her to take off the gloves and bare her claws. Sure, or maybe I should just grab a sword and mutter a hari-kiri chant.

"I don't know where to begin, there's so much to say," she said, obviously knowing exactly where she would begin. I wanted her to say: *He was boffing half the stewardesses in town while his first wife lay dying; he made millions bribing county commissioners to grant zoning variances; and if it*

34

weren't for high-placed friends in Washington, he would have been indicted for tax evasion.

What she said was: "Phil was the most giving man I've ever known. The way he cared for his first wife when she was terminally ill, if you could have seen that, if you all could have seen it." Then she turned to the jury, an actress facing her adoring audience. "He never thought he could love again, but I brought something to his life. And to me, he was everything—a lover, a friend, even the father I never had. Then for him to die like this, in his prime."

Clever. Very clever. So well rehearsed it didn't look rehearsed. Explaining how a twenty-six-year-old woman marries a fifty-five-year-old man. A father, for crying out loud. No mention that the champagne corks were popping only six weeks after he buried his beloved first wife. And if I bring it out on cross, I'm a cad. It was a virtuoso performance. Even Judge Leonard was listening, practically a first. He had been in a fine mood at motion calendar in the morning, as well he should after Hot Touch paid $10.40, $5.40, and $4.80.

When Dan Cefalo turned to me and said, "Your witness," he was smiling so broadly I almost didn't notice that his fly was half undone and he had buttoned his shirt into his suitcoat.

The occasion called for brilliance. Roger Salisbury looked at me as if I were his last friend in the world. I approached the witness stand with a solicitous smile. I still hadn't made up my mind. Behind those tears I saw a flinty toughness that I would love to bring out. But make a mistake, reduce her to tears or hysterics, and the jury would lynch me and nail enough zeroes on the verdict to buy an aircraft carrier. She looked straight back at me. The full lips lost a bit of their

35

poutiness and set in a firm line. It's there somewhere, I knew. But my investigators couldn't find it in six months and my pretrial deposition came up empty. I couldn't risk it now.

I turned to the judge. "Your Honor," I said, as if seeking his approval, "I believe it would be unfair for us to keep Mrs. Corrigan on the stand to discuss this painful subject. We have no questions." Roger Salisbury sank into his chair looking hopeless and abandoned. Men on Death Row have brighter futures.

"Very well," Judge Leonard said, aiming a small smile in my direction. "Mr. Cefalo, call your next witness."

"The plaintiff rests," Dan Cefalo said, his goofy grin still lighting up the room.

"Any motions?" the judge asked. We approached the bench and the judge sent the jurors out to lunch.

"At this time, the defense moves for a directed verdict," I said without a great deal of conviction.

"On what ground, Mr. Lassiter?" the judge asked.

"On the ground that there's insufficient evidence of proximate cause, first that the surgery caused the aneurysm, and second that the aneurysm caused the death."

"Denied," the judge said before Cefalo even opened his mouth. "The plaintiff's expert testified to that. Whatsa matter, Jake, it's a jury question at least."

I knew that. Somewhere between his Bloody Marys and his White Russians, Dr. Watkins had stuck us on proximate cause, at least sufficiently to beat a directed verdict, but I was giving the judge a little preview of our defense. Oh Dr. Charles W. Riggs, I need you now.

The judge looked over the courtroom, which was emptying, and waved us closer to the bench. With a hand, he signaled the court stenographer to take a hike. "You boys talk settlement?"

A practical enough question. If he could clear us out of the courtroom, he could spend the rest of the week at the track.

"Judge, we offered the policy," I said apologetically. "A million dollars even, all we've got, no excess coverage. They oughta take it and spare the court all this time and effort."

Cefalo shook his head. "Our liquidated damages alone, lost net accumulations for the estate, are over three million. To say nothing of the widow's mental anguish and consortium claims."

The judge laughed. "Danny, your widow lady don't look like she'll be without consortium for long."

Good. I liked hearing that. Maybe the jurors will feel the same. Then we only get hit with three million, enough to wipe out the good doctor several times over.

The judge straightened. "All right, boys. Let's cut through the bullshit. Danny, how much will you take, bottom line?"

"Two-point-five. Today. No structured settlement. All cash."

The judge raised his eyebrows and ran a hand over his bald head. "Attaboy. I always figured you to bet the favorites to show, but you're no ribbon clerk, hey? Jake, whadaya got?"

I turned my pockets inside out and shook my head. "A million, judge, just the policy. Client's only been in private practice five, six years. Just finished paying off his debts. He's pulling down big income, but no assets yet. We can't pay it if we don't have it. Besides, he's simply not liable."

"Okay, Jake, but it's halftime, and you're getting your ass

kicked from here to Sopchoppy. You see what's coming, don't you?"

"Sure judge, but you haven't heard my halftime speech."

"Fine, we start with your first witness at one o'clock. Court's in recess." With that, he banged the gavel, and the hollow explosion echoed off the high, beamed ceiling. Roger Salisbury slumped onto the defense table as if felled by a rifle shot.

I headed into the corridor, nearly smashing into the lovely widow. She didn't notice. She was toe-to-toe with another young woman. Each was jawing at the other, faces inflamed, just a few inches apart like Billy Martin and an umpire. I didn't recognize the other woman. No makeup, short-cropped jet black hair, a turned-up nose and a deep tan, blue jeans and running shoes, maybe the last pretty woman in Miami with thick glasses. Tortoiseshell round frames, giving her a professorial look. Her language, though, was not destined to win tenure. "You're a conniving slut and a little whore, and when I get to the bottom of this, we'll see who's out in the cold!"

The widow's eyes had narrowed into slits. No tears now. Just sparks and flames. "Get away from me you ingrate, and clear your junk out of the house by six tonight or your ratty clothes will be floating in the bay."

Dan Cefalo stepped in and separated the two. "Miss Corrigan, I think you best leave."

Oh, Miss Corrigan. The one with the colorful vocabulary must be Philip Corrigan's daughter by his first marriage. I followed her down the corridor.

"May I be of assistance?" I asked politely. Trying not to

be your typical lawyer scavenging on the perimeter of misfortune.

She lowered the thick glasses and studied me with steaming eyes the color of a strong cup of coffee. The eyes had decided not to make any friends today. She looked me up and down, ending at my black wingtips. I could check for wounds later. Her nostrils flared as if I emitted noxious fumes.

"You're that doctor's lawyer, aren't you?" She made it sound like a capital crime.

"Guilty as charged. I saw you discussing a matter with Mrs. Corrigan and I just wondered if I might help . . ."

"Why? Are you fucking her or do you just want to?" She slid her glasses back up the slope of the ski-jump nose and headed toward the elevators.

"No and yes," I called after her.

4

THE
SPORTSWRITER

My desk was covered with little white telephone messages. Office confetti. You think the universe comes to a halt when you are locked into your own little world, but it doesn't. It goes on whether you're in trial or at war or under the surgeon's knife. Or dead. Dead rich like Philip Corrigan laid out on smooth satin in a mahogany box, or dead poor, a wino facedown in the bay.

Greeting me in my bayfront office was the clutter of messages that would not be answered—lawyers who wouldn't be called, clients who wouldn't be seen, motions that wouldn't be heard while my world was circumscribed by the four walls of Courtroom 6-1 in the Dade County Courthouse. Next to the phone messages were stacks of pleadings, letters and memos, carefully arranged in order of importance with numbers written on those little yellow squares of paper that have their own stickum on back. What did we do before those sticky doodads were invented? Or before the photocopier? Or the computer, the telecopier, and the car phone? It must have been a slower world. Before lawyers had offices fifty-two stories above Biscayne Bay with white-coated waiters serving afternoon tea, and before surgeons cleared four hundred thousand a year, easy, scraping out gristle from knees and squeezing bad discs out of spines.

Lawyers had become businessmen, leveraging their hourly rates by stacking offices with high-billing associates, forming "teams" for well-heeled clients, and raking in profits on the difference between associates' salaries and their billing rates. Doctors had become little industries themselves, creating huge pension plans, buying buildings and leasing them back, investing in labs and million-dollar scanning machines, getting depreciation and investment income that far outpaced patient fees.

Maybe doctors were too busy following the stock market to be much good at surgery anymore. Maybe the greed of lawyers and doctors equally contributed to the malpractice crisis. But maybe an occasional slip of the scalpel or a missed melanoma just couldn't be helped. What was it old Charlie Riggs said the first day he reviewed the charts in Salisbury's case? *Errare humanum est.* To err is human. Sure, but a jury seldom forgives.

I grabbed the first message on stack one. Granny Lassiter called. I hoped she hadn't been arrested again. Granny lived in Islamorada in the Florida Keys and taught me everything I know about fishing and most of what I know about decency and principle. She was one of the first to speak against unrestrained construction in the environmentally fragile Keys. When speaking didn't work, she got a Key West conch named Virgil Thigpen drunk as an Everglades skunk and commandeered his tank truck. The truck, not coincidentally, had just sucked up the contents of Granny's septic tank and that of half a dozen neighbors. Granny drove it smack into the champagne and caviar crowd at the grand opening of Pelican Point, a plug-ugly pink condo on salt-eaten concrete stilts that would soon sink into the dredged muck off Key Largo. While the bankers, lawyers, developers, and lobbyists stood gaping, and TV cameras whirred, Granny shouted, "Shit on all of you," then sloshed twelve hundred gallons of crud onto the canape table.

The judge gave her probation plus a hundred hours of community service, which she fulfilled by donating a good-sized portion of her homemade brew to the Naval Retirement Home in Marathon.

I returned the call. Granny just wanted to pass the time of day and give me a high-tide report. Next message, the unmistakably misshapen handwriting of Cindy, my secretary:

> *Across the River,*
> *A Voice to Shine,*
> Tempus Fugit, *Doc Speaks at Nine.*

What the hell? A headful of tight, burnt orange-brown curls popped through my door. To my eye, Cindy's hair seemed to clash with the fuchsia eye shadow but clearly matched her lipstick. If the lipstick were any brighter, you could use it for fluorescent highway markers.

"Cindy, what's this?"

"Haiku, *el jefe.*"

"Who?"

"I do."

"What you do?"

"I do haiku," she said, laughing. "Haiku is three-line Japanese poetry, no breaking hearts, just recording the author's observations of nature and the human experience."

"What's it mean?"

"C'mon boss. Get with it. Crazy old Charlie Riggs is set to testify at nine tomorrow morning. He'll tell one and all what killed filthy rich Philip Corrigan."

"Good, he's our best witness."

"I don't know," Cindy said, twirling a finger through a stiff curl. If a mosquito flew into her hair, it would be knocked cold. "I've got a bad feeling about this case. Your Dr. Salisbury has a weird look in his eye."

"All men look at you that way, Cindy. Try wearing a bra."

"I never thought *you* noticed."

"Hard to miss when the air conditioning turns this place into a meat locker. Now c'mon Cindy, help me out. We have anything on Corrigan's daughter by his first marriage?"

"Sure, a little." Cindy was not as ditsy as she looked. She could turn heads with her hyped-up looks, bouncy walk, and easy smile, but underneath were brains and street smarts, an unusual combination.

"Susan Corrigan," Cindy said, without consulting the file. "About thirty, undergrad work at UF, then a master's in journalism at Northwestern. Sportswriter at the *Herald.*"

"You're amazing," I said, meaning it.

"In many splendored ways unbeknownst to you."

I chose not to wade in those crowded waters.

"Wait a second," I said. "Of course. *Susan Corrigan.* I know the by-line, the first woman inside the Dolphins' locker room." I picked up yesterday's paper, which had been gathering dust in a wicker basket next to my desk. I found the story stripped across the top of the sports section under the headline, "Dolphin Hex? Injuries Vex Offensive Line."

BY SUSAN CORRIGAN
HERALD SPORTS WRITER

On a team where the quarterback is king, something wicked keeps happening to the palace guard.

And the palace tackles. And the palace center.

"It's scary the things that happened to our offensive line in the last three weeks," Dolphin Coach Don Shula said yesterday. "When injuries hit us, they come in bunches."

Sure, Susan Corrigan. Made a name for herself playing tennis against Martina, sprinting against Flo-Jo, then writing first-person pieces. I'd read her stuff. Tough and funny. Today I'd seen half of that.

"What's she have to do with Salisbury's case?" Cindy asked.

"Don't know. But there's more to the second Mrs. Corrigan than tears and white gloves, and Susan knows something."

"What's she look like, an Amazon warrior?"

"Hardly. Cute, not beautiful. Long legs, short dark hair

45

like Dorothy Hamill, wears glasses, wholesome as the Great Outdoors. No hint of scandal."

Cindy laughed. "Doesn't sound like your type."

"Did I mention foulmouthed?"

"We're getting warmer."

"Cindy, this is all business."

"Isn't it always?"

Practice was almost over and only a few players were still on the field. Natural grass warmed by the sun, a clean earthy smell in the late afternoon Florida air. It had been one of those days when it's a crime to be shackled to an office or courtroom. Winter in the tropics. Clear sky, mid-seventies, a light breeze from the northeast. On the small college campus where the Dolphins practice, the clean air and open spaces were a world away from Miami's guttersnipes and bottom feeders.

I spotted Susan Corrigan along the sideline. She wore gray cotton sweats and running shoes and seemed to be counting heads, seeing what linemen were still able to walk as they straggled back to the locker room. A reporter's notepad was jammed into the back of her sweatpants and a ballpoint pen jutted like a torpedo out of her black hair. All business. On the field in front of her only the quarterbacks and wide receivers were still going through their paces, a few more passes before the sun set. On an adjacent practice field, a ballboy shagged kick after kick from a solitary punter.

"Susan," I called from a few yards away.

She turned with an expectant smile. The sight of me washed it away. I asked if we could talk. She turned back to the field. I asked if she was waiting for somebody. She studied the yard markers. I asked who she liked in the AFC East. She didn't give me any tips. I just stood there, looking at her profile. It wasn't hard to take.

She turned toward me again, a studious yet annoyed look through thick glasses, as if an interesting insect had landed in her soup. "Why should I help you?"

"Because you're not real interested in helping Melanie Corrigan. Because you know things about her that could help an innocent doctor save his career. Because you like the way I comb my hair."

"You're dumber than you look," she hissed.

"Is there a compliment buried in that one?"

"You're hopeless."

I can take being put down. Judges do it all the time. So do important people like a maître d' in a Bal Harbour restaurant who insists that diners wear socks. But this was different. I looked at her, a fresh-faced young woman in cotton sweats that could not hide her athletic yet very womanly body. I gave her a hangdog look that sought mercy. She turned back to the field. Dan Marino was firing short outs to Mark Duper and Mark Clayton. Though each pass arrived with ferocious speed, there was no slap of leather onto skin at the receiving end.

"Soft hands," Susan Corrigan said, mostly to herself.

"These guys are good but Paul Warfield will always be my favorite," I said. "Had moves like Baryshnikov. Stopping him was like tackling the wind."

"Sounds like you know more about football than about your own client."

I gave her my blank look and she kept going. "You still don't get it. You still don't know the truth."

"Get what? Look, I'm defending a man accused of professional malpractice. I don't know what the truth is. I never know. I just take the facts—or as much of them as I can get from people biased on all sides—and throw them at the jurors. You never know what jurors hear or remember or care about. You never know why they rule the way they do. They can right terrible wrongs or do terrible wrongs. They can shatter lives and destroy careers, and that's what I'm worried about with Roger Salisbury."

"Bring out the violins."

Suddenly a shout from behind us: "Heads up!" I looked up in time to see a brown blur dropping from the sky. Susan Corrigan's hands shot out and she caught the ball with her fingertips. A cheer went up from the wide receivers, anonymous behind their face masks.

"Soft hands," I said, "and a lot of quick." I gave her my best smile. It had been good enough for several generations of University of Miami coeds, their brains fried from working on their tans. It had lowered the minimal resistance of stewardesses from half a dozen failing airlines. It did not dent the armor of Susan Corrigan.

"Sit on this," she said, lateraling the ball toward my gut.

I felt like popping her one. Instead I took my frustrations out on the funny-shaped ball. Fingertips across the laces, I heaved a hard, tight spiral to the punter half the field away. He took it chest high and nodded with approval. The toss surprised even me.

Susan Corrigan whistled. "You've played some ball."

Her tone had subtly changed. Good, maybe if I went a few rounds with Mike Tyson, she'd give me the time of day.

"A little," I said. I decided not to tell her my right arm

just lost all its feeling except for a prickly sensation where the wires had been frayed.

"Quarterback?"

"No, I decided early I'd rather be the hitter than the hittee. Linebacker with lousy lateral movement. Occasionally I'd hit people returning kickoffs if they came my way. Sometimes filled in when games were already won or lost and I'd smack fullbacks who trudged up the middle. Mostly I polished the pine, which is actually aluminum and can freeze your butt in places like South Bend and Ann Arbor in November. Gave me time to philosophize about cheerleaders' thighs."

"You look like you stay in shape."

"Used to windsurf a lot. Now I just hit the heavy bag a couple times a week and never miss a Wednesday night poker game."

"I can beat almost any man at almost any sport," she said. She didn't sound boastful. If you kin do it, it ain't braggin'.

"We should play ball sometime," I suggested.

She showed me the first hint of a smile. Her face didn't break. "Are you being a smartass now?" she asked, almost pleasantly.

"No. I just want to talk to you."

"I'll talk if you can beat me in a race."

"What?"

"The goal line," she said, pointing across the empty practice field. "Let's see who can score."

Only the punter was still on the field. He took his two-step approach and kicked the ball with a solid *thwack*. The same motion, time after time, a machine following the path designed for it on the drawing board. Like a surgeon clearing out the disc, the same motion, time after time. But the punter had shanked one off the side of his foot, and even Roger Salisbury could have booted one. There I go again, mind slipping out of gear.

"Yes or no?" she demanded. "I've got to interview Shula, and that's no day at the beach the way the Bills dropped buffalo shit all over them last Sunday."

"Okay," I said, taking off my Scotch brogue wing tips. "I suppose you want a head start." She laughed a wily laugh.

The sun was just dropping over the Everglades to the west and a pink glow spread across the sky, casting Susan Corrigan into soft focus. I stretched my hamstrings and concocted a plan. I'd run stride for stride with her without breathing hard, maybe make a crack or two, then shoot by her, and run backwards the last ten yards. I'd let her jump into my arms at the goal line if she were so inclined. Then, I'd be a gracious winner and take her out for some fresh pompano and a good white wine.

She dropped into sprinter's stance, shouted "Go," and flew across the field. I bolted after her, my tie flapping over my shoulder like a pennant at the big game. She was five yards ahead after the first two seconds. Her stride was effortless, her movements smooth. My eyes fixed on her firm, round bottom, now rolling rhythmically with each stride. Halfway there I was still in second place, the greyhound chasing the mechanical rabbit. So I picked it up, still three yards back with only thirty to go. So much for the plan. Chasing pride now. Longer strides, lifting the knees too high, some wasted motion, but letting the energy of each step power the next one. Two steps behind and she shot a quick glance over her shoulder. A mistake, but only ten yards to go, no way to catch her, so I lunged, grabbing at her waist, hand slipping down over a hip, tumbling her into the grass with me rolling on top and her glasses, notepad, and pen whirling this way and that.

We ended up near the goal line, her on the bottom looking up, moist warm breath tickling my nose. A lot of my body was touching a lot of her body, and she wasn't complaining.

"First and goal from the one," I whispered.

I looked straight into her eyes from a distance any quarterback could sneak. Was it my imagination or was the glacial ice melting? I was ready for her to get all dewy and there would be some serious sighing going on. But I had come up a yard short. She flipped me off her like a professional wrestler who doesn't want to be pinned, one of her knees slamming into my groin as she bounced up. She stood there squinting in the dusk, looking for her glasses while I sucked in some oxygen.

"You really don't know, do you?" she said, standing over me.

"Not only that, but I don't know what I don't know." My voice was pinched.

"Then listen, because you're only going to hear it once. Your client isn't guilty of medical malpractice."

"He's not?"

"No. He's guilty of murder. He killed my father. He planned it along with that slut who ought to get an Academy Award from what I saw in court today. I can't prove it, but I know it's true."

"I don't believe this."

"Believe it. Your client's a murderer. He should be fried or whatever they do these days. So pardon me if I don't get

51

all choked up over his career problems or insurance rates. He was planking the slut—something that doesn't exactly put him in an exclusive club—and they planned it together. The malpractice suit is just a cover."

"I still don't get it." I was starting to feel like a sap, something Susan Corrigan seemed to know the moment she met me.

"The lawsuit makes it look like the doctor and the widow are enemies. That's their cover. And the way I figure it, Lassiter, you're supposed to lose. Or at least it doesn't matter. If you lose, the insurance company will pay her, and she'll probably split the money with him. Or maybe he gets it all. She'll get more than she needs from the estate. And if she wins more than his insurance coverage, he doesn't have to worry because she won't try to collect."

I sat there with a look as intelligent as a vacant lot. "Murder and insurance fraud. You have no proof of that. And I just can't believe it."

"I can see that, now," she said. "You're not a bad guy, Lassiter. You're just not fast enough to be a linebacker, and you don't know shit from second base."

5

THE CORONER

Charlie Riggs took the stand with a smile on his face and a plastic model of the spine in his back pocket. I felt better just looking at him. Bushy gray moustache and beard, a brown tweedy jacket more at home in Ivy League libraries than art deco Miami, twinkling eyes full of experience. A trustworthy man. Like having Walter Cronkite on my side.

He'd testified hundreds of times for the state and was comfortable on the witness stand. He crossed his legs, revealing drooping socks and pale calves. He breathed on his eyeglasses and wiped them on his tie. He slipped the glasses onto his small nose that was almost buried by his beard. Then Charlie Riggs nodded. He was ready.

"Please state your name and profession for the jury," I instructed him.

"Charles W. Riggs, M.D., pathologist by training, medical examiner of Dade County for twenty-eight years, now happily retired."

"Tell us, Dr. Riggs, what are the duties of a medical examiner."

"Objection!" Dan Cefalo was on his feet. "Dr. Riggs is retired. He is incompetent to testify as to the current medical examiner's duties."

In the realm of petty objections, that one ranked pretty high, but it was the first one of the day, and you could flip a coin on it.

"Sustained," Judge Leonard said, unfolding the sports section, looking for the racetrack charts.

I had another idea. "Let's start this way, Dr. Riggs. What is a medical examiner?"

"Well, in merry old England, they were called coroners. You can trace coroners back to at least the year 1194. They were part of the justice system, part judge, part tax collector. The coroner was the *custos placitorum coronae*, the guardian of the pleas of the Crown. If a man was convicted of a crime, the coroner saw to it that his goods were forfeited to the Crown."

Cefalo looked bored, the judge was not listening as usual, but the jurors seemed fascinated by the bearded old doctor. It works that way. What's mundane to lawyers and judges enchants jurors.

"Later the coroner's duties included determining the

cause of death with the help of an inquest. The sheriff would empanel a jury, much as you have here." He smiled toward the jury box, and in unison, six faces smiled back. They liked him. That was half the battle.

"The jury had to determine whether death was *ex visitatione divina,* by the visitation of God, or whether man had a hand in it. Even if death was accidental, there was still a sort of criminal penalty. For example, if a cart ran over someone and killed him, the owner had to pay the Crown the equivalent value of the cart. That got to be quite a problem when steamships and trains began doing the killing."

The jurors nodded, flattered that this wise old man would take the time to give them a history lesson. "Still later, coroners began recording how many deaths were caused by particular diseases. Sometimes I spend my evenings with a glass of brandy and a collection of the Coroner's Rolls from the 1200s. You'd be surprised how much we can learn. At any rate, Counselor, the job of the coroner, or medical examiner, is to determine cause of death. Our credo is 'to speak for the dead, to protect the living.' "

"And how does a coroner determine cause of death?" I asked.

Charlie Riggs pushed his glasses back up his nose with a chubby thumb. "By physical and medical examination, various testing devices, gas chromatography, electron microscopes, the study of toxicology, pharmacology, radiology, pathology. Much is learned in the autopsy, of course."

"May we assume you have determined the cause of death in a number of cases?"

"Thousands. For over twenty years, I performed five hundred or more autopsies a year and supervised many more."

"Can you tell us about some of your methods, some of your memorable cases?"

A hand smacked the plaintiff's table and Dan Cefalo was on his feet, one pantleg sticking into the top of his right sock, the other pantleg dragging below the heel of the left shoe where the threads had unraveled from the cuff. "Objection," he said wearily. "This retired gentleman's life story is irrelevant here."

Taking a shot at Riggs's age. I hoped the two older jurors were listening. "Your Honor, I'm entitled to qualify Dr. Riggs as an expert."

Cefalo was ready for that. He didn't want to hear any more than he had to from Charlie Riggs. "We'll stipulate that Dr. Riggs was the medical examiner for a long time, that he's done plenty of autopsies, and that he's qualified to express an opinion on cause of death."

That should have been enough, but I still wanted Riggs to tell his stories. When you have a great witness, keep him up there. Let the jury absorb his presence.

"Objection overruled," Judge Leonard said. Good, my turn to win one.

"Dr. Riggs, you were about to tell us of your cases and methods of medical examination of the cause of death."

So Charlie Riggs unfolded his memories. There was the aging playboy who lived at Turnberry Isle, found dead of a single bullet wound to the forehead. Or so it seemed. The autopsy showed no bullet in the skull, no exit wound, just a round hole right between the eyes, as if from a small caliber shell.

"The police were stumped for a murder weapon," Charlie Riggs said. "Sometimes it's best to consider everyday items.

56

I searched the grounds and, in a dumpster near the marina, I found a woman's red shoe with blood on the metal spiked heel. The blood type matched the playboy's, the heel matched the wound, and the owner of a French shoe shop at Mayfair identified the woman who bought the six-hundred-dollar shoes two weeks earlier. The woman confessed to doing him in. A lover's spat, she didn't want to kill him, just brain him."

Then there was the mystery of the burned woman. She was sitting there, fully clothed, on her sofa, burned to death. Her clothes were not even singed. There was no smoke or evidence of fire in the apartment. The woman's boyfriend had found the body. He said she came home drunk, took a shower, and next thing he knew, she was sitting on the sofa dead.

"I took a pair of tweezers and probed the bathtub drain," Charlie Riggs told the jury. He paused. Several jurors exhaled in unison.

"It was just a hunch. Up came pieces of skin, and I knew the answer."

Charlie Riggs smiled a knowing smile and stroked his beard, everybody's favorite professor.

"Both had come home drunk, and she passed out. The boyfriend tried to revive her in the bathtub, but sailing three sheets to the wind, he turned on the hot water and left her there. The scalding water burned her to death. When the boyfriend sobered up, he panicked, so he dried her off, dressed her, put her on the sofa, and called the police."

The jury sat entranced. There's nothing like tales of death, well told. Riggs testified about matching tire treads to the marks on a hit-and-run victim's back, of fitting a defendant's teeth to bite marks on a rape–murder victim, of finding teeth in a drain under a house, the only proof of the *corpus delicti*, the body of a man dissolved in sulfuric acid by his roommate.

The litany of crime had its purpose, to shock the jury with deeds of true miscreants, to deliver a subtle message that the justice system should prosecute murderers, not decent surgeons, even if they might make mistakes. *Errare humanum est.* If that's what it was, an honest error.

I hadn't told Charlie Riggs about the conversation with Susan Corrigan. What would I tell him, that a dead man's daughter, poisoned with grief and hate, thinks my client is a murderer? She had no physical evidence, no proof, no nothing, except the allegation that Roger Salisbury and Melanie Corrigan were getting it on. I would talk to Salisbury about it, but not now.

While Charlie Riggs testified, I watched Roger. He kept shooting sideways glances at Melanie Corrigan's perfect profile. She watched the witness, oblivious to the attention. She was wearing a simple cotton dress that, to me, looked about two sizes too large, but I supposed was in style. A wide belt gathered it at the waist and it ended demurely below the knee. It was one of those deceiving things women wear, so simple it disguises the name of an Italian designer and a megabucks price tag.

I tried to read the look in Roger Salisbury's eyes but could not. Was there a chance that it was true? Not just that he might have been diddling his patient's wife. I didn't care about that. But that he might have killed Corrigan. That it was all a plot, that the malpractice trial was just a cover, or better yet, a way to pick up another million. If that's what it was, there'd be plenty of chances for Salisbury to tank it. He was scheduled to testify after Riggs.

I continued my direct examination: "Now Dr. Riggs, have you had an opportunity to examine the medical records compiled by the physicians and the hospital?"

"Yes."

"And based on the records, and your years of experience, do you have an opinion to a reasonable degree of medical probability what caused the death of Philip Corrigan?"

"I do."

The courtroom was silent except for the omnipresent hum of the air conditioning. Everyone knew the next question.

"And what was the cause of death?"

"A ruptured aorta. Internal bleeding, which in turn caused a lowering of blood pressure. In layman's terms, the heart, which is the pump in a closed circulatory system, didn't have enough fluid to pump, so it stopped."

"And what, sir, caused the aorta to rupture?"

"There is no way to answer that with absolute certainty. We can only exclude certain things."

"Such as?" Keep the questions short, let the doctor carry the ball.

"Well, Dr. Salisbury here certainly didn't do it with the rongeur. If he had, the rupture would be on the posterior side of the aorta. But as reported by the surgeon who tried the emergency repair of the aorta, the rupture is on the anterior side, the front. Naturally a surgeon making an incision in a man's back, working around the spine, is not going to puncture the front of the aorta, the part that faces the abdomen."

Dan Cefalo turned ashen. There aren't many surprises in

trials anymore. Pretrial discovery eliminates most of that. But Charlie Riggs gave his deposition before studying the report of the second surgery, the chaotic attempt to close the bursting aorta a dozen hours after the laminectomy. When he read the report, bells went off. Nobody else had paid any attention to where the rupture was, only that it existed.

For the next fifteen minutes, it went on like that, Charles W. Riggs, M.D., witness emeritus, showing the jury his plastic model of the spine with the blood vessels attached like strings of licorice. The report of the thoracic surgeon who tried unsuccessfully to save Corrigan's life came into evidence, and the jurors kept looking at Dr. Riggs and nodding.

It was time to slam the door. "If Dr. Salisbury did not puncture the aorta with the rongeur, could not have, as you have testified, what might have caused it to rupture?"

"We call it spontaneous aortic aneurysm. Of course, that's the effect, not the cause. The causes are many. Various illnesses or severe trauma to the abdomen can cause the aorta to burst. Arteriosclerosis can weaken the aorta and make it susceptible to aneurysm. So can high blood pressure. It could be a breakdown that medicine simply can't explain, as they said in the Middle Ages, *ex visitatione divina.*"

I smiled at Dr. Riggs. He smiled back at me. The jury smiled at both of us. One big happy family.

I was nearly through but had one more little surprise for Dan Cefalo. A nail in the coffin. I handed Riggs Plaintiff's Exhibit Three, a composite of Philip Corrigan's medical history. "Dr. Riggs, did Philip Corrigan have any prior medical abnormalities?"

Charlie Riggs scanned the document but already knew the

answer from our preparation sessions. "Yes, he was previously diagnosed by a cardiologist as having some degree of arteriosclerosis."

"And the effect of such a disease?"

"Weakening of the arteries, susceptibility to aneurysm. Men in their fifties or beyond commonly show signs of arterial disease. Blame the typical American diet of saturated fats, too much beef and butter. In that condition, Mr. Corrigan could have had an artery blow out at any time."

"At any time," I repeated, just in case they missed it.

"Yes, without a trauma, just watching TV, eating dinner, any time."

"Thank you, Doctor." I nodded toward the witness stand in deference to the wisdom that had filled the courtroom. Then I turned toward Dan Cefalo, and with the placid assurance of a man who has seen the future and owns a fine chunk of it, I gently advised him, "Your witness, Counselor."

Cefalo stood up and his suitcoat fell open, revealing a dark stain of red ink under his shirt pocket, the trail of an uncapped marking pen. Or a self-inflicted wound.

His cross-examination fell flat. He scored a meaningless point getting Riggs to admit that he was not an orthopedic surgeon and had never performed a laminectomy. "But I've done thousands of autopsies, and that's how you determine cause of death," Riggs quickly added.

"You testified that trauma could cause the rupture, did you not?" Cefalo asked.

"Yes, I can't tell you how many drivers I saw in the morgue in the days before seat belts. In a collision, the steering wheel can hit the chest and abdomen with such force as to rupture the aorta. That, of course, is trauma from the front."

"But a misguided rongeur could produce the kind of trauma to rupture the aorta?"

Hit me again, Cefalo seemed to plead.

"It could, but not in the front of the blood vessel when the surgeon is coming in from the back," Riggs said.

Cefalo wouldn't call it quits. "The thoracic surgeon was working under conditions of extreme emergency trying to do the repair, was he not?"

"I assume so," Riggs said.

"And in such conditions, he could have made a mistake as to the location of the rupture, could he not?"

Riggs smiled a gentle, fatherly smile. "Every piece of evidence ever adduced in a courtroom could be the product of a mistake. Your witnesses could all be wrong. Mr. Lassiter's witnesses could all be wrong. But it's all we've got, and there's nothing to indicate the rupture was anywhere but where the chest buster—excuse me, the thoracic surgeon—said, the anterior of the aorta."

Fine. Outstanding. I couldn't have said it better myself. Cefalo sat down without laying a glove on him. It was after one o'clock and we had not yet recessed for lunch. Judge Leonard was fidgeting.

"Noting the lateness of the hour, perhaps this is an opportune time to adjourn for the day," the judge said. Translation: *There's a stakes race at Hialeah and I've got a tip from a jockey who hasn't paid alimony since his divorce fell into my division last year.* "Hearing no objection, court stands adjourned until nine-thirty tomorrow morning."

Roger Salisbury was beaming. He didn't look like a man

who wanted to lose. It had been a fine morning of lawyering, and I was feeling pretty full of myself. In the back of the courtroom I caught a glimpse of Susan Corrigan wearing a Super Bowl XVI nylon jacket over a T-shirt. She eyed me as if I'd just spit in church.

I told Roger Salisbury I'd treat him to stone crabs, home fries, and cold beer for lunch. Time for a mini-celebration.

Time, too, for some questions I needed to ask.

6

THE VOYEUR

We walked from the dim light and dank air of the old courtroom into the sunshine of December in Miami. A glorious day. Not even the buzzards endlessly circling the wedding cake tiers of the courthouse could darken my mood. Souls of lawyers doing penance, a Cuban spiritualist told me. The huge black birds were as much a part of wintertime Miami as sunburned tourists, drug deals, and crooked cops. The buzzards congregated around the courthouse and on the upper ledges of the Southeast Financial Center, where for fifty dollars a square foot, the lawyers, accountants, and bankers expected a better view than birdshit two feet deep.

Building management installed sonar devices that supposedly made unfriendly bird sounds. Instead of being frightened, the buzzards were turned on; they tried mating with the sonar boxes.

The doctor gave me a second look when he got into my canary yellow Olds 442 convertible, vintage 1968. At home was my old Jeep, but it was rusted out from windsurfing gear, and my clients deserve the best. Having already passed through my respectable sedan phase when I temporarily decided to grow up, I had regressed to a simpler time of big engines and Beach Boys' songs.

We drove to a seafood restaurant in a new shopping arcade that the developer spent a bundle making look like an Italian villa, circa the Renaissance. It's full of boutiques instead of stores, places with two names that always start with *Le*, and women who'll spend a fortune for clothes so they'll look good shopping for more clothes. Notwithstanding the glitz of the surroundings, there's a decent fish house tucked away in back.

"The tide turned today, didn't it?" Salisbury asked.

"Right. We pulled even, which means we're actually ahead. The plaintiff has the burden of proof. Riggs negated Watkins's testimony about the rongeur. Back to square one. They'll have to call Watkins again on rebuttal and attack Riggs. They're stuck. They can't bring in a new expert now. Our strategy is to lay low. We don't want to get fancy, just hold our position."

"What about my testimony?"

"You'll do fine. What you say isn't as important as how you look, how the jury perceives you. If you're a nice guy and it's a close battle of the experts, they'll cut you a break.

If you're arrogant and a prick, they'll cut off your nuts and hand them to the widow."

He thought that over and I looked around for some service. We'd been there ten minutes before the waiter shuffled over to take our order. The kid needed a shave and was missing one earring, or is that the way they wear them?

"Whatcha want?" he asked, displaying the personality of a mollusk and half the energy. Service in restaurants now rivals that at gas stations for indifference and sloth.

I ordered for both of us. "Two portions of jumbo stoners, two Caesar salads, and two beers." Best to keep it simple.

"Kinda beers?" the waiter said. I figured him for a speech communications major at the UM.

"Grolsch. Sixteen-ouncers if you have them."

"Dunno. Got Bud, Miller, Coors Light, maybe."

"Any beer's okay with me," Salisbury said. Not hard to please. A lot of doctors are that way. They get used to hospital cafeteria food and pretty soon everything tastes alike. Not me. I'll start drinking American beer when it gets as good as its TV commercials.

The waiter shrugged and disappeared, probably to replenish his chemical stimulants. I was about to extol the glories of the Dutch brewmasters when Roger Salisbury asked, "Do you think I killed him, committed malpractice I mean?"

He wanted me to respect him. With most clients, winning is enough.

"Hey Roger, I checked around town. The med school has nice things to say about you. You've never been sued before, which in this town is an upset. Don't let my general cynicism get you down."

"Just so you believe me."

He had thrown me off stride. I wanted to ask questions, not answer them. "Roger, you know how important it is to tell your lawyer everything?"

"Sure thing. Soul mates."

"Right. Before you testify tomorrow, is there anything you want to tell me? Anything you left out?"

He cradled his chin in his hand. Something flickered behind his eyes but he blinked it away. "No, don't think so. I told you all about the surgery. No signs of an aneurysm, no drop in blood pressure. I didn't slip with the rongeur. I didn't do it."

"I know. Besides that. Anything personal with you and the Corrigans?"

"Like what?"

Oh shit. He wasn't going to help me out. Sometimes the best way to get through the chop is to trim the sail tight and just go. "Like were you screwing Melanie Corrigan?" At the next table, a couple of spiffed-up fiftyish women with fancy shopping bags exchanged disapproving whispers.

"At what point in time?" Roger asked.

My client, and he talks like Richard Nixon.

"Hey Roger, this is your lawyer here, not a grand jury." The waiter skulked by, his thumbs buried deep in the Caesar salad bowls. He wiped one hand on his apron, sucked some salad dressing off a thumb and brought us the beer, an anonymous American brand, devoid of calories, color, and taste. At least it was cold.

Roger took a small sip, a thinking-time sip, and said, "We were involved, sure."

"So why didn't you tell me?"

"Because it has nothing to do with the case."

My voice cranked up a few decibels. "How about letting me decide that? If it comes out, Cefalo would claim you had a motive for being a little careless, or worse, having criminal intent."

"I thought of that," he said casually, "but Melanie could never use that. It would hurt her case, wouldn't it, the unfaithful wife trying to profit from her husband's death."

"That's not the way it would play. You'd be the smooth seducer, or a madman obsessed with her, chopping up the husband so she'd be all yours."

Salisbury's fork stopped in mid-air. A look of concern crossed his face, but when he caught me studying him, he chased it away with a laugh. "A madman maybe," he said, smiling, "but when it comes to seduction, she's in a league by herself. Besides, I knew her before Corrigan did, and well . . . there's stuff you lawyers would call extenuating circumstances."

"I'm waiting."

"I'm not sure it's any of your business."

I drained my homogenized beer and tried to signal the brain-dead waiter to bring another. He looked right through me.

"Right now, my business is you, everything about you and the Corrigans," I said, waiting for him to fill me in.

Nothing.

The stone crabs arrived. Fresh, no black mottled spots, the meat tearing cleanly out of the shell, the mustard sauce tangy. I yelled for the second beer, and the waiter brought iced tea. It tasted like the beer.

I dug into the crabs two at a time, but Salisbury must have lost his appetite. He fidgeted in his chair and his eyes darted from side to side. Finally, he looked me straight on, took a breath and let it go. "Okay, here it is. I met Melanie eight or nine years ago. I was just finishing my residency, hadn't spent much time with women. You know how it is, premed in college, you bust your balls, then med school, internship, residency. Never any money or time. She was just a kid, mixed up, kind of an exotic dancer, but just for a while."

"Yeah, after that she probably was Deb of the Year."

"She wasn't bad or anything. Called herself Autumn Rain. Just used her body to make a buck. So I sort of fell for her. I started my practice, bought her a car, gave her things. It didn't last long. I found out other guys were doing the same. One guy paid for her apartment, another guy her clothes, another her trips."

"Sold shares in herself like IBM."

"Some guys can handle that. I couldn't. So I took off." He looked away. This wasn't a story he broadcast around town.

"Roger, it's nothing to be embarrassed about. It's an old story. You meet a pretty young thing who can suck a golf ball through a garden hose. You overlook the fact that she's collected enough hoses to water Joe Robbie Stadium. You'd be shocked how many guys fall for young hookers. Want to change them. Old male fantasy. Some guys lose their marriages over it. Not many doctors, though. Most are too scientific to get involved."

"She wasn't a hooker," he said indignantly and louder than necessary.

Now the two women were doing their best not to show that our conversation was more interesting than their own. I smiled in their direction. One recoiled as if I had exposed myself.

Roger Salisbury poked the ice in his tea. "Anyway, I hadn't seen her for probably five years when Philip Corrigan asked me over for dinner. He was seeing me for a cartilage problem in the knee. I scoped it. Then the disc started flaring up. We became friends. I had no idea he was married to Autumn . . . Melanie."

"So you started slipping out of the hospital a little early. Sneaking in nooners while old man Corrigan was littering the Keys with ugly condos on stilts."

He laughed a short, bitter laugh. "Hardly."

Then he clammed up again. I gave him a c'mon Roger look.

Finally he spoke in a whisper. "This is where it gets a little sticky."

"I'll bet."

They didn't have to sneak around, he told me over the watery tea.

Why not? I asked.

Philip wanted to watch, Roger said. Sometimes to take part, sometimes to videotape. On their boat, a custom Hatteras furnished like a Bal Harbour penthouse, in their mansion on a giant waterbed, in their swimming pool.

So Philip Corrigan was a peeper and an old letch. Probably got to an age where the money bored him, and his engine wouldn't start without some kinky provocation.

"Then, after doing a few lines of coke, we'd mix it up, *ménage à trois*," Roger said. He paused and gave me a sheepish look.

If the two women at the next table craned their necks any farther our way, they'd need a chiropractor.

Are you disappointed in me? he asked.

71

I don't make moral judgments about clients, I told him, because it interferes with my ability to give good advice.

Just the same I tallied a moral scorecard on the yellow pad of my mind. We all do that. We try to live and let live, but underneath it, we're left with a smug sense of superiority about ourselves and vague disgust for others who don't measure up. Roger Salisbury didn't measure up. He was doing drugs and a group grope like some kind of sleaze. But he was my sleaze, my client, and his bedroom—or swimming pool—activities didn't make him an incompetent doctor, much less a murderer.

After his *mea culpa*, I thought his morale could use a boost.

"Here's how I see it," I told him. "You got stuck in a little game with a tramp who slithered her way to Gables Estates and a guy who couldn't get his rocks off in the missionary position. That doesn't put you in a class with Charles Manson, but if it ever came out in court or the newspapers, that's all anybody would know about you. You might be donating half your time to charity cases and feeding homeless cats, but the world would know you only as a sex-crazed doctor who aced his girlfriend's husband. Makes good reading. Now do you see why I have to know about this? If I make an uninformed decision at some point, it could hurt you. Badly. Understand?"

"Understood."

"Is that all there is to it?"

"I guess so. Except that I'm still sort of under her spell."

Oh brother.

"In all these years," he said, "nobody's been able to turn me on like her. She knows things, does things. She's totally uninhibited and free with herself. She's a pleasure giver. Do you know how hard it is for me to give that up?"

Dr. Ruth, I'm not, but I took a stab at it anyway. "Roger, it sounds to me like Melanie Corrigan is a taker, not a giver, and you better stay the hell out of her hot tub."

"There is a certain side to her, a kind of danger," he said. "Maybe that's part of the appeal, I don't know." He just let it hang there, his mind working something over, not letting me in on it.

"Okay then, I've got it all, right? You played hide the weenie with the missus while the old man watched, videotaped, and once in a while jumped on the pile."

"That's it." He paused, looked side to side and added, "There is one more thing."

"There always is."

"She asked me to kill her husband," he said.

7

SQUOOSHY

Waiting. Like making a movie or going to war, there is more waiting than working in a trial. First the judge hears motions starting at eight-thirty. Twenty different cases, forty lawyers, crowding chambers, spilling into the corridor, milling around like chickens waiting to be fed.

Waiting, an army of minutes slogging through the mud. The judge makes several phone calls from his chambers. His bookie, his mistress, his campaign contributors, who knows? Then a clerk is late bringing up the evidence, or a juror's child is sick, or an expert witness, usually a doctor, has an emergency.

That's how it was the morning Roger Salisbury was to testify. The seconds ticked off slowly, dulling my edge. I studied the filthy acoustical tile that covered the walls. At shoulder level, countless pencils and fingernails left signatures there. The heavy, straight-backed pews in the gallery tested the mettle and the cushioning of the spectators, a few vagrants lured by the air-conditioning. The courtroom ceiling was thirty feet high. Together with the dark pews and the raised bench, it gave the courtroom the air of a cathedral. But where was His Holiness?

Just then the gleaming head of Judge Leonard poked through the door behind the bench that led directly to his chambers. He scowled and ducked back in. I unpacked my briefcase and found a note signed by Cindy:

Sportswriting Lady Buzzing Like Bee
Can't Get Number out of Me,
Maybe Has Pollen for You to See.

Apparently Susan Corrigan had been calling, maybe wanted to tell me what a schmuck I am, just in case I forgot. A few more minutes passed, and finally all the courtroom players were there, the judge, the clerk, the jurors, the lawyers, and the witnesses, all ready at the same time. Sometimes at this point, the electricity goes off or there's a bomb threat, but today, we started working.

Roger Salisbury came off well, just as I thought he would. I had told him not to overdress, and he was just right in gray slacks, a blue sportcoat, and tie. I had him wear a beeper on his belt to remind the jury that here was a man who responded to emergencies, who could be called at any moment to mend the injured. His salt-and-pepper hair was neatly trimmed and his face reflected confidence without being cocky. He looked like a skilled, compassionate surgeon who took the greatest care when working inside a man's spine. He spoke quietly, evenly, with no trace of the condescension that marks so many doctors in court.

I took him through the story. Philip Corrigan's office visits, fixing the bad knee, then complaints of back and leg pain. Even hurt when he coughed. All the usual tests, ankle jerk, knee jerk, straight leg raising. Salisbury found sensory deficits, a myelogram confirmed it. Finally the diagnosis, acute herniated disc at the L3–L4 vertebrae.

"Was there anything unusual about the surgery?" I asked.

"No, it was routine," Salisbury said.

I liked that. Here's a man who cuts into living flesh, fixes the problems inside, then puts it all back together again. And it's routine. No wonder we're in awe of doctors.

"I cut from approximately L1 to just above the sacrum," he said. "Nothing out of the ordinary. Down through subcutaneous tissue and adipose tissue. Bleeders were clamped and cauterized. I identified the L3–L4 interspace. I removed the ligamentum flavum and superior portion of L4 and inferior portion of L3 without incident."

I walked him through every step of it, sending the jurors messages that this doctor knew what he was doing. He was *there,* dammit. Dan Cefalo wasn't. Wallbanger Watkins wasn't. Now Salisbury was a teacher and the jurors, his students, listened to every word. Some might not have followed every move of the scalpel, but it didn't matter. Roger Salisbury knew his stuff, knew more than the jurors—a travel agent, two housewives, a student, two retired businessmen—

PAUL LEVINE

ever would. The impression I wanted to create was simple:
Who are we to judge this man?

"I removed the disc material, the nucleus pulposus."
Roger Salisbury pointed to a chart we blew up to poster size.
"In a herniated disc, it's like toothpaste that's been squeezed
out of the tube. It's pushed out of the disc space and there's
no putting it back."

Good imagery. It should have been. We practiced it for
months.

"Then what did you do?" I asked.

"I removed the degenerative disc material with the
rongeur."

"Was there anything unusual up to this point?"

"Nothing up to then or later," he said evenly. "The procedure was without incident."

"What were the patient's vital signs?"

"All normal. Blood pressure, pulse rate, breathing."

The anesthesiologist would confirm this when we read his
deposition to the jury.

"You heard Dr. Watkins's testimony about the rongeur?"

"I did."

"Did anything unusual happen with the rongeur?"

"No, it never went through the disc space, certainly not
around to the front of the aorta. In all respects the patient
tolerated the surgery normally."

"When was the last time you saw Philip Corrigan?"

"I checked him in the recovery room and once later in his
private room."

"And his condition?"

"Normal. No evidence of a mass in his abdomen, normal

78

blood pressure, hemoglobin, and hematocrit. No sign of hemorrhage or aortic aneurysm."

I kept him up there a few minutes longer to say how surprised he was the next morning when he learned that Corrigan's aorta ruptured during the night. And, sounding sincere, he expressed regret at the death of his patient. I nodded gravely with my own look of sincerity, a look that took three years of law school, a dozen years of practice, and a couple Jimmy Stewart movies to perfect. Then I sat down, and Dan Cefalo stood up.

Cefalo was in a box. He had deposed everyone in the OR, and they all corroborated Salisbury's testimony concerning Corrigan's vital signs. The aneurysm had not happened simultaneously with the surgery. Cefalo needed to convince the jury that Salisbury nicked the front of the aorta, causing it to rupture ten hours later. No use asking Salisbury whether that happened. He'd get a big fat *no*. He needed Watkins back for rebuttal testimony. But that would come later. Now, the jurors watched Cefalo, waiting to see if he could counter-punch.

Cefalo looked even worse than usual today. All the courthouse regulars knew that his trial wardrobe was a hoax, the result of a case he tried upstate years ago. In the wilds of Okeechobee County he had worn a sharkskin suit when defending a man accused of stealing fruit from an orange grove, a felony akin to cattle rustling in the Old West. The prosecutor was a good old boy and in closing argument told the jury that they could listen to him or they could listen to that *Mia-muh* lawyer in the shiny suit. They listened to the good old boy.

Dan Cefalo learned his lesson. He stripped off the Rolex

and the pinky ring and left the silk ties at home. He wore a selection of suits that the Salvation Army couldn't give away. As he won bigger verdicts, his clothes became more decrepit.

Today, though, it wasn't the clothing. Cefalo was pale and nervous. He came to court with a jagged square of toilet paper sticking to his chin. A spot of blood shone through. *Hands shaky this morning, my man?* He kept huddling with a young lawyer and two paralegals from his office. I picked up only three words of their conversation. "He here yet?" Cefalo asked. The young lawyer shook his head.

Cefalo started his cross-examination by asking whether it might be possible to pierce the aorta and not be aware of it.

"Not likely," Salisbury replied. "You watch how far you insert the rongeur and when you meet resistance, you stop."

I sneaked a look at Melanie Corrigan, who sat with legs demurely crossed at the ankles. She wore a simple black linen dress, probably to signify her continuing grief. I wanted to see, close up, what kind of woman plots to kill her husband. An actress, I thought. A fooler of men ripe to be fooled.

I turned her down, Roger had assured me last night. *Philip was my friend. I would never kill him.*

Did she take no for an answer?

Roger shrugged. Said she knew some guys who'd kill Philip and never blink.

I'll bet she did. A woman can't tiptoe through the gutter and keep her feet clean. If she'd been grinding in one of those jerk-off joints, she'd have run into pimps, dopers, dirty cops, confidence men, porno kings, and the other flotsam of the city. Plus, more than a few triggermen. Roger Salisbury was in over his head with that crowd. Of course, Philip

Corrigan didn't die from a bullet or knife or garrote. He died from an aneurysm twelve hours after my client operated on him.

Dan Cefalo kept after Salisbury for another twenty minutes but couldn't shake him. Then, tripping on his untied shoelaces, Cefalo called it quits and dropped into his chair. We tidied up some of the trial's loose ends, reading depositions into the record, admitting certain medical reports into evidence. I had no other ammo so I announced that the defense rested. We renewed our motions for a directed verdict, and Judge Leonard denied them, saying we had issues for the jury. Actually what he said was, "You boys got yourself a real horse race here."

Dan Cefalo said he had one rebuttal witness, and the judge figured we could breeze through that after lunch and he'd still have time to make it to Hialeah. The Widener Cup was Saturday, and, like football fans who go to practice, he visited the stalls and watched the horses eat their oats and crap in the paddock.

Another down time, waiting for the judge after lunch recess. While Cefalo paced, I made notes for tomorrow's closing argument, Roger Salisbury flipped the pages of a medical journal, and my secretary Cindy waltzed into the courtroom as inconspicuous as a shark in the wading pool. She wore a white miniskirt, black fishnet stockings, leather earrings with chrome studs, all topped by a new hairdo that was spiked, punked, and Day-Glo pinked. Her hair shot in various directions like hundreds of porcupine quills. It looked like she stuck her finger in an electrical outlet.

"*Qué pasa, el jefe?*"

81

"Do I know you?" I said.

"Not as well as some men I could name."

"Not enough time for that."

"You don't look so busy to me."

"We're waiting for the judge. At least *I'm* waiting for the judge. The grieving widow is waiting for Probate Court to release the estate funds. And Cefalo's waiting for Wallbanger Watkins, his rebuttal witness."

"He's got a long wait," Cindy said.

"Huh?" That's my probing question technique.

Cindy sat down and propped her feet on the counsel table. "Got a long wait for the good doctor," she said matter-of-factly.

"What do you know that I don't, but should?"

"So many things. But I'm willing to teach."

"Cindy, this is serious. We're in trial."

She frowned. "Lighten up. I just have a sneaking suspicion that Watkins is AWOL, and Dan Cefalo is so shit out of luck he oughta buy a new suit."

"You didn't kidnap him, did you?" With Cindy you never could tell. Once in a sex discrimination case, a department store executive denied that he ever hit on my client, his young female assistant. Said he'd never been unfaithful to his wife, never even made a pass at another woman. Cindy tracked the guy to his favorite watering hole, ran an inviting toe inside his pantleg, and took him home. Luis (Long Lens) Morales, a convicted counterfeiter and part-time divorce photographer, leapt from her closet in time to shoot some grainy black-and-whites of the executive slipping out of his boxers.

"Kidnap him?" she asked, feigning indignation and arching her eyebrows, striped brown and orange like a Bengal

82

tiger. "Do you think that's the only way I could get a man to buy me a drink?"

"You bagged Watkins in some bar?"

"How crude," she protested. "Last night, by utter coincidence, me and Margarita—the girl, not the drink—cruise into the lounge at the Sonesta Beach. And who do we run into but this nice older man with white hair and a silly seersucker suit. He's drinking vodka gimlets but leaving out the lime juice and telling us what a great doctor he is, and Margarita says she's got this back problem, and he says, come up to the room and he'll do a quick exam, so off we go, and meanwhile Harv orders three bottles of Finlandia from room service."

"Harv?"

"That's what he asked us to call him."

"Not very professional," I said.

"Neither was his treatment of Margarita. Unless all orthopods do pelvic exams. Not that Margarita cared. I'm not saying she's dumb, but she thinks the Silicon Valley is the space between her tits."

I closed my eyes and massaged my forehead. "Cindy, I can't wait to get a summons from the Florida Bar. It's just like stashing a witness."

"What? To have a drink with a nice man?"

We were interrupted by the banging of the courtroom door. In lurched Dr. Harvey Watkins, collar turned up on a seersucker suitcoat that looked like it had just cleaned all the windshields in the Baja road race. His tie was at half mast, his shirt unbuttoned nearly to the waist. He leaned back against the door as if the courthouse were plowing through rough seas. His hair was plastered against his scalp.

Bluish veins popped through his pink skin. Dan Cefalo was a step behind, trying to steady his witness. Watkins angrily shook the hand off his elbow. As bad as the doctor looked, he was doing better than Cefalo, who had turned an unhealthy gray.

At that moment the bailiff burst through the rear door, shouting, "All rise! Court of the Eleventh Judicial Circuit in and for Dade County Florida is now in session!" Everyone in the courtroom obeyed, except Dr. Harvey Watkins, who sagged heavily into one of the church pews, his legs jammed at odd angles into the aisle, his ankles bare of socks.

"Bailiff, bring in the jury, and Mr. Cefalo, call your witness." Judge Leonard wasn't going to waste any time. He might miss someone brushing the mane of Crême Fraiche or taking Personal Flag's rectal temperature.

Cefalo was about to hyperventilate. "Your Honor, may we have one moment?"

"A moment! You've just had ninety minutes for lunch. Now, do you have rebuttal testimony or not? If not, we'll recess and you can both close in the morning."

In a trial you must make immediate decisions. Object or not, ask a question when you don't know the answer or not, move for mistrial or let it go. Dan Cefalo had to decide whether to put on Wallbanger Watkins without even a chance to shave the white stubble from his chin or determine if the good—and drunk—doctor remembered his name. If he didn't call him, Cefalo would close the book on the case without rebutting Charlie Riggs's testimony that Salisbury couldn't have nicked the front of the aorta. Either way, a roll of the dice.

Cefalo took a deep breath and said, "At this time, the plaintiff re-calls Dr. Harvey Watkins."

Watkins tugged his necktie toward his Adam's apple, jutted his patrician chin forward, and, with the excessive dignity that the intoxicated muster in time of great need, walked almost steadily to the witness stand. He would have made it, too, had he noticed the six-inch step. He toppled forward into the walnut railing, which bounced him sideways until he fell, facedown, into the lap of the court reporter, a young black woman who didn't know if she should record the event on her stenograph.

"Beggar pardon," Watkins mumbled, and Cefalo leapt forward to help him.

A moment later the doctor was safely seated, gripping the rail of the witness stand and staring blankly out to sea. His shirttail hung over his belt and his tie was askew. He made Dan Cefalo look like the cover of *GQ*.

"Dr. Watkins, you are still under oath," Cefalo began.

"Oath?" Watkins ran a tongue over dry lips. Finally a light came on. "Of course. Years ago, I took the *hick*-ocratic oath. That is, of course, the *hick* . . ." A case of the hiccups was now distracting him and the clerk brought a glass of water. Watkins nodded a formal thank you.

Cefalo plunged ahead. "Dr. Watkins, you testified that, based on the medical records in this case, you could determine to a reasonable degree of medical certainty that Dr. Salisbury punctured the aorta with the rongeur, is that correct?"

"Objection! Leading and an inaccurate summary of the testimony." I didn't need to win that one, just to figure out what the next ruling would be.

"Overruled," Judge Leonard said. He started packing, dropping a cap and sunglasses into a briefcase.

"Is that correct?" Cefalo repeated.

Watkins nodded. Either he was saying yes, or he was falling asleep.

"Doctor, you must speak audibly for the court reporter to record your answer."

Watkins again nodded silently.

Cefalo pushed forward. "Now, to speed this up, let me tell you that another witness has testified that the rupture in the aorta was on its anterior side, in the front, and that a surgeon entering from the back could not have made the rupture there."

"Zat so?" Watkins asked, eyebrows arched in surprise.

"My question, Doctor, is whether it is possible for a surgeon performing a laminectomy to perforate the front of the aorta?"

Watkins stared into space.

Sweat broke out on Cefalo's forehead. "You may remember our discussing this yesterday morning . . ."

I was on my feet. "Objection! Leading. Your Honor, really, there is certain latitude, but this is too much."

"Sustained. Move it along, Mr. Cefalo."

Cefalo tried again. "The fact that the perforation was in front. What, if anything, does that tell you?"

Watkins mumbled something, his eyes half closed. The jurors were shooting each other sideways glances. *Get a load of this.* Somewhere a trillion miles away, some intergalactic god of luck was shining on Roger Salisbury.

"Doctor?"

"Squooshy," Dr. Watkins said.

"Squooshy?" Cefalo asked, his eyes widening.

A momentary brightness came to Dr. Watkins's face. "It's all squooshy in there. You might think it's like all these pretty pictures in the books, the vascular system here, the muscles there, the bones over there. Hah! Phooey!" The *phooey* shot a wad of expectorant toward the court reporter.

"It's all squooshed up. And it moves. The son-of-a-bitch keeps breathing while you're cutting him up. It's all squooshing around and moving. Front, back, in between. Who the fuck can tell the difference?"

Even Judge Leonard heard that. He aimed a murderous look at Dan Cefalo, who hastily advised that Dr. Watkins was now my witness. I didn't want him. The judge banged his gavel louder than usual and crisply ordered us adjourned. Then he shot off the bench, his maroon robes flying behind him.

Roger Salisbury was pumping my hand as if we'd already won. I told him to wait until tomorrow. You can never tell with juries. He said he felt like celebrating, maybe carousing, how about our finding a couple *chicas*. I didn't ask if they were both for him, just declined, saying I had to gather my thoughts for tomorrow. Then I asked him a question.

"What about it? If you go in from the back, could you tear the aorta in front?"

He smiled. "Our witness said no."

"Right. And Watkins said everything's squooshy. What do you say?"

He smiled again. "I say they're both right. Riggs is right in what he does. When a body is dead, it's inert. If you did a laminectomy on a corpse, you probably couldn't hit the front of the aorta with the rongeur. But Watkins was right that with a living, breathing body, there's movement. It's a mess in there, things can happen. If you pushed the rongeur too far, it's possible that on the way back, it could nick the front of the aorta. It's possible."

"But unlikely," I suggested.

"Unless you were trying," Roger Salisbury said.

8

THE
LATE SHOW

This is how I prepare my closing argument. I toss the files into the trunk of the 442 convertible and head home. Home is in the old part of Coconut Grove between Kumquat Avenue and Poinciana. You can't see the house from the street thanks to the jacaranda, live oak, and chinaberry trees that crowd the small lot. So little sun reaches the front yard that the lawn wouldn't support a hungry billy goat. The trees also shade the house, a 1920s coral rock pillbox that would be the last building standing after a direct hit by Alice, Bruce, Celia, or David. Granny Lassiter lived in the house when the Grove was full of artists and barnacled types, when there were saloons instead of boutiques. After the area became chic, Granny grabbed her fishing gear and headed for the Keys.

I leave the files in the trunk and head into the kitchen. There is a refrigerator, a microwave, some cabinets, and enough room for two very good friends to stand. The house is two stories but barely more than a cottage. It will never grace the pages of *Architectural Digest* but is perfect for someone who does not want to entertain or rub shoulders with society.

I turn on all the ceiling fans. I don't like air-conditioning. It dries out the air and shuts you off from the natural sounds of birds, crickets, and neighborhood burglars.

My porch looks into a jungle of overgrown shrubs and weeds that, like the battlement of a castle, shelters my tiny backyard. Because the neighborhood is secluded, drug dealers have been moving in. They are good neighbors for the most part, never noisy, never nosy. The ones who process the cocaine, however, are a problem. On Loquat Street last year, a house blew up when a barrel of ether ignited. Nothing left of the house or three Colombians. Charred pieces of greenbacks wafted over Coconut Grove, tiny embers blinking like fireflies in the nighttime sky. A portrait of U.S. Grant, his beard scorched, landed in my hammock.

I put on the eight-ounce gloves and hit the heavy bag that hangs on the porch. It doesn't hit back. It doesn't say ouch. I go four rounds and win them all. I think about the case, the high points, what to emphasize, what to shrug off. It all comes back, witness by witness. I don't need the files or my notes. Each jab is a scrap of testimony to push, each hook a point to drive home.

I lie on my back and do stomach crunches. When a man gets to a certain age, he has to work the stomach hard. If not, it starts to merge with the chest. The whole torso becomes one amorphous mass. I work my stomach hard.

I finish with push-ups. First regular push-ups, then elevated, with feet propped up on the porch, hands on the ground, lowering myself into the overgrowth of the yard until the weeds tickle my nose.

Then I check the refrigerator. Everything I need, starting with smoked amberjack. I find some mayo that hasn't quite turned green, some Muenster that has, a jar of Pommery mustard, half a lemon. There are fresh tomatoes on the counter, part of the Florida winter crop, pale and tough, the hide of tennis balls. I've brought home a fresh loaf of French bread. I stack some of the amberjack on the bread, slather on the mayo, layer three leathery tomato slices on top, and cover it with the cheese and mustard. Dinner is served. Life in the fast lane.

Back at the refrigerator, I buy myself a beer. The choice, a sixteen-ounce Grolsch with the porcelain stopper or Anchor Steam, my one exception to the American beer boycott. I study them both. My biggest decision of the day, other than deciding whether to get sucked into a discussion of damages, or throw all my weight into shouting, "no liability." Cefalo will have to argue both, first that Salisbury is liable for professional negligence, second that the damages should be roughly equal to Brazil's foreign debt. I have to argue there is no liability. Sometimes, if you think you're going to lose that one, you slip into the alternative argument, *but if you find the defendant liable, damages should not exceed*

91

the cost of a Dolphins' season ticket. Problem is, that weakens your liability case.

Now about that beer, the mind still cranking away. Anchor Steam has a deep amber color. Knew a girl with eyes like that once. Every time I looked at her, I got thirsty. I go for the Grolsch.

The files were still in the trunk, an emptied four-pack of Grolsch was in the trash, and I was in the hammock, letting the mind run through it all, visualizing tomorrow. I didn't hear the phone until the third ring. Realized I wasn't visualizing at all. Dozing.

"I need to see you," a woman's voice said. "Are you busy?"

It took a moment, then I placed it. Susan Corrigan. "I'm hard at work trying to find justice in an imperfect world."

"Do you know where Lagoon Road is?" she asked.

"Sure, Gables Estates."

"That's where I live, nine-ten Lagoon Road."

"The newspaper must be paying handsomely these days."

"It's Dad's house. Please come over. Now. It's important."

Of course, Dad's house. Which means, it's now stepmommy's house.

"I don't know if that's such a good idea. Ethically, I'm not permitted to speak to Mrs. Corrigan without her lawyer present."

Not that I toe the line somebody else draws. Guys from big law firms in three-piece suits sit around hotel ballrooms at ABA conventions thinking up lots of rules. Their idea of ethics is to give the side with the most money the upper

92

hand. My ethical standards are simple. I never lie to the court or knowingly let a client do it. Other than that I like to shoot the opposition in the kneecaps.

"She's not here," Susan Corrigan said. "Just come around back to the cabana by the pool. This involves your client."

Oh. A little bit of me knew that's what it was about. Another little bit of me hoped it was something else again. I stored a few megabytes of closing argument somewhere between my ears. Then I showered. I put on faded blue jeans that worked hard to get that way, a blue and orange rugby shirt, and a pair of well-worn running shoes in case I had to chase her again. I never got the 442 out of third gear going down Old Cutler, a two-lane, winding road heading south out of Coconut Grove. Huge banyan trees stood on each side of the road, their tangled trunks like giant snakes erupting from the ground. The thick branches met overhead, forming a dark umbrella that blocked out the moonlight. Briny smells of saltwater hammocks oozed from the bay side of the road. I turned left onto Arvida and headed down Millionaire's Row, lushly landscaped homes backed up onto canals with clear access to Biscayne Bay and the Atlantic beyond.

The Corrigan house sat on a cul-de-sac lined with royal palms a hundred feet high. You could get a crick in your neck looking up at the trees. The house, too. The first thing you notice is its height. You look up to see the ground floor. Though Lagoon Road is only five feet above sea level, if you add forty feet of fill and top it with a heap of landscaping, you have a Florida mountain. Then the sound, a waterfall tumbling through huge coral boulders.

You could look at the Corrigan house and be overwhelmed with its size or its styling, rough-hewn cedar flanking stone walls, sun decks overlooking the water. But I thought of only one word, electricity. How much juice did it take to run four separate central air-conditioning systems, to power the pump that ran the waterfall that cascaded down the man-made mountain, to illuminate with colored spotlights the palm trees and blooming poinsettias and impatiens? How much more electricity for the hot tub and the front gate and TV cameras? The Corrigan house was a one-family oil shortage.

The front gate was open and I pulled into the brick drive-way and sat there a moment. No other cars, no signs of life, the four-car garage buttoned up tight. A flagstone walk ran around the house. It was bordered with three-foot-high pine posts, each topped by a tiny lamp. Heavy hemp lines were strung post to post to form a path, like queues in a theater.

Behind the house, a wooden deck led to a swimming pool. Fifty yards long but only twelve feet wide, a serious pool for laps. It smelled of salt water, not chlorine, probably a pipe right to the bay. Beyond the pool was a concrete dock, a boathouse, and a private lagoon that opened onto Biscayne Bay. Tied to the dock was a yacht that in time of war would be impounded for transporting troops.

The cabana was an architect's idea of Tahiti. Whatever the building was made of was disguised by a bamboo front and topped, chikee style, with a palm frond roof. Half a dozen coconuts sat in primitive bowls on the front porch. A machete was wedged into one of the husks. I could hear the swish of a paddle fan through the open front door. I knocked on the bamboo.

"Lassiter, come in and make yourself a drink. There's some Gatorade in the fridge."

My potassium level seemed okay so I demurred on the

Gatorade. I nosed around. Her voice was coming from what had to be the bedroom. The rest of the place was one room, a galley kitchen that opened into a small living room with TV, stereo, and VCR. A bookshelf with some sports reference books, some poetry anthologies—maybe a woman's heart lurked beneath the sweats—and a survival manual for Miami, a Spanish/English dictionary.

Rustling noises women make when dressing were coming from the bedroom. She could have been changing into something sheer and flimsy and dabbing sweet essence behind her ears. But she emerged with a freshly scrubbed face, *sans* makeup, the faint aroma of Ivory soap in the air. Cut-off jeans revealed strong legs, calves that flexed with each step. Her short black hair was even shorter in a ponytail tied with a rubber band. She wore a Miami Dolphins' jersey that still had room for me inside.

"You like my place?" she asked.

"Sure. When you called, I didn't realize you *lived* in the cabana. Thought you were inviting me to a pool party. Have you been banished from the castle by the wicked stepmother?"

She shook her head. "I lived in the house until Dad married that . . . woman. Then I decided to give them some privacy. I do my mile in the pool every night. This is all I need."

"I like it. It's one of the few houses in Miami smaller than mine."

"Until yesterday I kept some things in the main house. My skis, scuba equipment, some clothes. She tossed everything out on the patio after we exchanged words in the courthouse."

"I heard some of those words. You can exchange them with the best. Mind telling me what you were arguing about?"

She was silent. I was sitting on a rattan loveseat and she sat facing me, legs crossed, enveloped in a peacock chair. She smiled. That made two smiles if you counted one on the football field.

She was doing something with her hands, buying a little time to get into whatever it was that prompted her to call me. She started slowly. "You finish the case tomorrow, don't you?"

"That's right."

"You think you're going to win."

That might have been a question. "I have my hopes."

"Would you feel badly if you get off a guilty man?"

"*Guilty* is a criminal law word. In civil practice, there's no such thing. I'm hoping for a no-liability verdict. But civil liability is a gray area. So I can't respond to the question as phrased."

"A real lawyer's answer," she said contemptuously.

"You don't care much for my profession, or is it just me?"

She laughed and put some rhythm in her voice:

> *Why is there always a secret singing*
> *When a lawyer cashes in?*
> *Why does a hearse horse snicker*
> *Hauling a lawyer away?*

"I don't know," I said. "It wasn't on the bar exam."

She grimaced and gave me another stanza.

Singers of songs and dreamers of plays
Build a house no wind blows over.
The lawyers—tell me why a hearse horse snickers
hauling a lawyer's bones.

"Do I win a new refrigerator with a correct answer, go on to the next round? Robert Frost, maybe."

She grimaced. "Carl Sandburg."

"Funny, he admired a pretty fair trial lawyer named Lincoln. And I was hoping your taste in poetry ran more to Grecian urns than lawyers' bones."

She steered the conversation back where she wanted it. "Murder is part of criminal law, isn't it?"

That didn't stir me so she kept going. "You said the other day I had no proof. Maybe you should look at something."

She hopped up and pushed a button on the VCR and another on the small Sony TV. She sat down again and turned away. The set blinked on, a typical home movie, jerky camera, panning too quickly through a lushly appointed room. It looked like a Beverly Hills hotel suite, piano bar, Lucite furniture, starlight ceiling. No people visible, just modern, expensive furniture, some lighted artwork, and a nighttime sky indoors.

"That's the main salon of the *Cory*," Susan Corrigan said.

"The *Cory*?"

"Didn't you see the boat outside?"

"Oh that. I thought it was the *Nimitz*, four thousand sailors on shore leave."

"Wouldn't that make her happy?" she asked, icily, gesturing toward the house. "The *Cory* is a custom-made Hatteras, about eighty-two feet. One of Dad's toys."

The picture broke up, some snow, then Melanie Corrigan in a bikini on the screen, cocking a hip at the camera, pouting a come-hither look to stage left. The screen went to black for a second as a shoulder blocked the camera, a man walking into view. He was medium size, wearing swim trunks and a T-shirt, and he turned self-consciously to the camera. Roger Salisbury. If it was supposed to surprise me, it didn't.

"That's the main stateroom," Susan said.

A king-size waterbed sat on a floor of black and white tile and was illuminated from below with neon tubes. The headboard was the skyline of Miami, etched into black glass. Rock music played in the background. Roger Salisbury stood awkwardly at the foot of the bed and Melanie Corrigan began doing a striptease, if that's what you call it when you're starting out with only a black bikini that must have been made during a spandex shortage. The top was a strap slightly wider than dental floss, the bottom no bigger than your average Band-Aid. She was grinding to the music, rather expertly, some very fluid hip movements. She motioned for Roger to sit on the bed and he did, obedient little puppy.

She unhooked the halter top and squeezed her high firm breasts together, taking a deep breath as if the tiny scrap of fabric had been crushing her poor lungs to death. Acting right out of a high school play or a porno flick made on the cheap in Lauderdale. She tossed the halter at Roger. It landed on his head and slid over his nose and mouth. He could have robbed a bank in a B Western.

Next the bottom came off, and she wiggled her can in Roger's face in time with the music. She wiggled left and wiggled right, wiggled fast and wiggled slow. I had a feeling this was not her maiden cruise.

It took a minute more and then they were at it. A moment later the photographer discovered the electric zoom. First the long shot of two bodies writhing beneath the etched glass Miami skyline. Then the bodies got larger until only one body part, or two parts joined, filled the screen. Finally the camera zoomed back to show us the writhing bodies.

Susan Corrigan looked at me, her back to the screen. I was half embarrassed for her, half bored for me. Like an ex-jock in the bleachers, I'd rather play than watch. It went on for a while, then a cut and roll 'em again. The scene might have been shot another day or later the same day. If there was any dialogue, it was lost in the music laid over the action. Now Roger Salisbury was wearing a stethoscope and nothing else. Compared to Melanie Corrigan, however, he was overdressed.

Roger looked down her throat.

She said something. Ahhh.

Playing doctor. A little pantomime.

Open wide.

She did.

He took her pulse. Then she inhaled and jutted her breasts out, and he tapped her chest and listened to her lungs through the stethoscope. They seemed to pass the test.

She turned over and gave Salisbury a view of a perfectly rounded bottom. He laid his right hand on her ass and tapped it slowly with his thumb. A medical procedure I'd never seen, more like checking a melon's ripeness. Whatever its purpose, Melanie thought it hilarious. Laughing, she turned over and the camera jiggled, some jollies from the photographer, too. Then Roger felt her forehead as if the poor child was fevered, and just to be sure, he took her temperature. With something too big to have been a thermometer.

The picture broke up, came back on and went to black as someone walked by the lens. I figured it was Philip Corrigan, dealing himself in, having put the camera on a tripod. But it wasn't Corrigan. It was Hercules, albeit a short one. He reminded me of the bulldog on the hood of a Mack truck, only not as cute. One of those sides of beef you see in the gym, a body builder, slabs on top of slabs of muscle, a thick neck and sloping shoulders, a tattoo of a lightning bolt on one arm. Dark complexion, a flat, broad, mean face, drooping black moustache. His arms hung out from his sides, pushed there by his overdeveloped lats. And he was naked, revealing one part of his body not pumped up to Schwarzeneggerian proportions. So now I was watching two naked men and one naked woman. There were arms and legs entwined, a couple of glances toward the camera, and much thrusting of loins.

A quick cut and the camera angle was different. I was trying to figure out how the photographer got over the bed, looking down at the goings-on like a dance number in an old Busby Berkeley musical. Then I saw the photographer on the screen, a neat trick. He was at the foot of the bed, aiming the camera up, a man in his fifties, thinning hair and pot belly, lying on his side, stark naked, shooting a trick shot at a mirror on the ceiling over the bed. Philip Corrigan. I consulted my scorecard: three men and a woman. Again, the zoom, and Philip Corrigan disappeared from view. The screen filled with the body builder's shoulders. Covered with pimples, the telltale sign of an anabolic steroid user.

It went on for a few more minutes, then the screen faded to black and then to snow. It stayed that way.

"Well, what do you think now?" Susan Corrigan asked softly.

"I think the hand-held camera technique is more suitable to documentaries. The lighting is too harsh, the plot a mite thin. The bit with the mirror is cute, but frankly, I prefer *The Lady from Shanghai.*"

"Is everything a joke to you?"

"Not everything, not even this. Susan, let it go. Every family has its dirty little secrets that are best left in the closet."

"My father wasn't like that. Not before her and Roger Salisbury."

"Okay. So she corrupted him. Maybe Roger's no angel, either. But what can be gained now?"

Her eyes blazed at me. "What about catching his killers?"

That again. "I still haven't seen any proof he was killed, much less that Roger Salisbury did it. What about Mr. Universe there? What about a dozen other guys you don't even know about?"

"More lawyer's games. Your beloved client is the only one who cut Dad open the day before he died. And as far as I know, he's the only one who carried poison around in his little leather case."

"What are you talking about?"

"This." She reached into a drawer, came up with something and tossed it at me. A small leather valise, a man's pocketbook if you're the kind of guy who carries that sort of

101

thing. A gold monogram, "R.A.S." Roger Allen Salisbury. I unzipped it. Two hypodermic needles, a clear small vial of colorless liquid, half empty. No labels, no instructions.

A nasty little package. I felt a chill. "What is it?"

"Succinylcholine, a drug used in anesthesia. It paralyzes the limbs, the lungs, too. In anesthesia, a respirator breathes for you. Without a respirator, you would just lie there and watch yourself die."

"How do you know all this? Where did this come from?"

"One question at a time, Counselor. First, I found it in Melanie's room. Hidden in a drawer with thirty pairs of black panties, which is an awful lot for someone who seldom wears any. I think she knows it's missing. Probably suspects me. That's why she changed the locks and tossed my things out. Second, I've done some research on it, had a lab test it. I'm a reporter, and I know a lot more than just box scores and yards-per-carry."

"Has this been in your possession continuously since discovering it?" Ever the lawyer, Lassiter, already thinking about chain of custody.

"The lab at Jackson Memorial took about five cc's out of the bottle. Otherwise, it's intact."

"What's this have to do with Salisbury, assuming the stuff is his?"

"Of course it's his! Melanie was screwing him, must have gotten the drug from him. She hated my father, just used him. She couldn't divorce him. She'd get nothing because of an antenuptial agreement. But if he died while married to her, she got the house, the boat, plus thirty percent of the estate."

I nodded. "Items in joint name plus the marital share."

"Right."

"So she had the motive. But that's all you can prove. For a criminal case built on circumstantial evidence, you need a lot more. Your case against Melanie is weak and you don't have anything on Salisbury. For one thing, your father didn't die of poisoning. He died of an aneurysm."

She turned her head away and blinked back a tear. "That's why I need your help."

"For what?"

"To figure out how they did it."

"Did what?"

"Oh Jake, think about it."

It was the first time she called me by my given name. I liked the sound of it.

"How they killed Dad with succinylcholine and made it look like an aneurysm," she said softly, her armor turning to tin.

I didn't buy it. "A hospital's a pretty risky place to kill somebody, doctors and nurses all around."

"That's what made it work. Who would object if Dr. Salisbury came into Dad's room after the surgery? He could have given the injection then. And who would be looking for poison when the patient dies of an aneurysm? It's a classic misdirection play. Like the old Oklahoma fumblerooski, where the center and quarterback drop the ball. Everybody goes one way and the guard grabs the ball and walks in for the touchdown."

It was crazy. No evidence. Just an angry young woman searching for villains. Blaming others for her father's descent. The old fumblerooski, for crying out loud! I looked at her. A tear came to those dark eyes and then another. I looked at the hypodermics and the tiny bottle. And back at those wet, dark eyes.

"Where do we start?" I asked.

9

PROXIMATE CAUSE

I was cruising on autopilot. On a very rough flight. I hadn't slept or thought about closing argument since Susan Corrigan handed me the vial and told me it was a murder weapon. I still felt it in the palm of my hand, the glass cool and smooth to the touch. Succinylcholine, a laboratory name. Like the clear liquid itself, impersonal as death.

The vial added a new dimension to Susan's bald allegation that Roger Salisbury killed her father. She had an exhibit. How juries love exhibits. The murder weapon, something to take back into the jury room and fondle.

My mind bounced it back and forth. I looked at Roger

Salisbury sitting next to me. Salt-and-pepper hair well
groomed, an oval face that was nearly delicate, intelligent
eyes. Almost a scholarly appearance, an overall impression
of competence. He looked like what he was, a physician. A
healer, not a killer. But I had seen him stripped bare—
literally—and wondered if his taste in after-dark activities
could lead him to murder.

That's what Susan Corrigan wanted me to think. Maybe I
was playing the fool for an elaborate scheme, Susan Corrigan throwing me a curve. She could have had the mono-
grammed leather valise made up in any shopping center.
The liquid could have been water. She could be in cahoots
with Melanie Corrigan to get me to tank the case. Or at least
to distract me enough that I boot it. Hauling me over the
night before closing argument. And me leaping for the bait,
a wholesome dark-haired young woman, maybe underneath
the Ivory soap just as mendacious as Melanie Corrigan. But I
didn't have time to think about it. Dan Cefalo was clearing
his throat and approaching the lectern. He looked remark-
ably normal in a dark blue suit and a white shirt that stayed
inside his pants. He turned to Melanie Corrigan, gave her a
fatherly smile, then bowed in the direction of the judge.

"May it please the court," he began, "and ladies and
gentlemen of the jury. First I want to thank you all for
coming down here and spending a week listening to a bunch
of lawyers and doctors. I know it hasn't been easy, but without the aid of responsible citizens such as yourselves, we
wouldn't have a justice system."

This is the *thank you folks* part of closing argument. It's a
way to butter up the jurors, then get down to the nitty gritty:

asking them to spend several million dollars of someone else's money.

"So on behalf of Mrs. Corrigan here," Cefalo continued, nodding and drawing their eyes to the plaintiff's table, "and on behalf of all of us whose privilege it is to serve, we thank you. You had to leave your jobs and families but that's what makes our system great. I love it, the American system of justice. It's what separates us from the barbarians and Communists."

I was starting to feel very patriotic and wondering when he would get into it.

"Now the first thing to remember when I'm up here and when Mr. Lassiter gets up here, is that what we say is not evidence. This is just lawyer's talk, and you know the old expression, talk's cheap. They call this closing argument, but I'm not going to argue with Mr. Lassiter. Think of me as a guide. I'm going to guide you through the evidence so that when you go back into that jury room, you can decide the case on the evidence you heard from that witness stand and the law as Judge Leonard instructs you."

Two of the jurors nodded. Cefalo was starting with the low-key approach. *I'm your pal; let's think this through together.* It's the right tone. Don't lecture. Schmooze with them, gain their confidence, then rev up the heavy equipment and steamroller them. I knew what was coming even if they didn't.

"You folks might remember back in opening statement I told you that we had the burden of proof, to prove that Philip Corrigan died because of the negligence, the malpractice, of the defendant. Now, when the lawyers get through talkin' at you, the judge will tell you that all we need do is prove our case by a preponderance of the evidence. What does that mean? Well, if you put two boys on a teeter-totter and one weighs fifty-one pounds and the other forty-nine, the boy who weighs more tilts the scales. We just need to tilt the scale."

With that, Cefalo moved from behind the lectern and held his arms out, pretending to be a scale. He lowered his right arm one way, just a bit, to illustrate his point. "A wee little tilt and you must find for the plaintiff on liability," he reminded them. He would make the case as easy as first-grade recess.

"I also told you back in opening statement that a trial is like a book, and every witness is a chapter. Every book has a story and this one is a tragedy. It's about a vigorous, healthy man in the prime of his life, a family man, a businessman, a husband, a philanthropist . . ."

Again Cefalo turned to Melanie Corrigan. Six heads swiveled the same way. She gnawed her lower lip and fought back a tear. Her long hair was lassoed into a knot on top of her head and again she wore black. It emphasized her fair complexion, made her seem wan and helpless.

Cefalo got back into it, building momentum. "Philip Corrigan went into the hospital to have routine disc surgery. He put his trust in Roger Salisbury, who held himself out to be an expert orthopedic surgeon. Now his widow wakes up each morning, and there's always that moment, that split second, when she hopes he's still beside her."

It went on this way for a while, Cefalo painting with a broad brush. His strategy was to dance around the evidence and avoid the expert testimony until he had heated up their emotions.

108

"Now you folks heard from a lot of witnesses. But the two you probably remember best are Dr. Harvey Watkins, the former chief of orthopedics at a great hospital, and the defense witness, Charles Riggs, the elderly fellow who used to be the coroner. I think you should ask yourselves one question about these two. Who's done more laminectomies? Why, Dr. Watkins has done more disc jobs than a dog's got fleas. Old Charlie Riggs, he's never had a patient that lived."

A big smile; the jurors tittered. Roger Salisbury shifted uncomfortably in his chair.

"Matter of fact, Charlie Riggs never had a live patient in his entire career. His testimony was all hypothetical."

Cefalo dragged *hypo-thetical* across his tongue, the same way a Florida politician once accused an opposing candidate's wife of being a *prac-ticing thes-pian*.

"They might as well have brought Gino, my butcher, in here to describe back surgery. You know what they call coroners in the medical profession? Canoemakers. They just chop, chop, chop it up like hollowing out a log."

"Objection, Your Honor! That's not a legitimate comment on the evidence." I don't like to object during closing argument. It sometimes angers the jurors who like hearing lawyers beat their breasts, but I wanted Cefalo to know I hadn't fallen asleep.

"Overruled," Judge Leonard said.

"Canoemakers," Cefalo repeated, needling me. "Riggs has never done one laminectomy. Not one! Mr. Lassiter should be ashamed."

With that Cefalo turned and looked toward me. So did the jurors, looking peeved, wondering if I tried to bamboozle them. Good strategy, avoiding what Riggs had said, just attacking his credentials. Sooner or later, though, he'd have to address the testimony or risk giving that ball to me on an open field. Roger Salisbury was squirming so much his chair squeaked on the old tile floor. I patted his arm, a coach telling a player to calm down.

"You heard the real expert, Dr. Harvey Watkins, on the first day of trial. It was only a few days ago, but it seems like a lifetime, so let me go over it. He said that it's malpractice to pierce the aorta with the rongeur. And it was Philip Corrigan's aorta that burst later that night. No one disagrees about that. All Mr. Riggs—excuse me, Dr. Riggs—all he said was he didn't know how the aorta got torn in front. But did he tell you what caused the aneurysm? No! He had no answer. The way I figure it, Dr. Salisbury here was poking around so much, it's lucky the rongeur didn't come out the belly button."

Roger Salisbury groaned. I had nearly forgotten how Dan Cefalo could make hokum sound like the gospel. I also had forgotten to tell Roger Salisbury not to have a stroke during the plaintiff's closing. I still had a few things to say if the jury didn't draw and quarter my client first.

"I do regret one thing," Cefalo said, lowering his voice. "Unfortunately, Dr. Watkins was taken ill shortly before his rebuttal testimony. He was not as articulate as he might have been. But I'm sure you got the drift. It was Dr. Salisbury's negligence and that alone which caused the death of Philip Corrigan and left this young woman a grief-stricken widow."

On cue Melanie Corrigan dabbed her eyes. Cefalo was gearing for the transition into the damages phase of his argument. He moved closer to the jury box and looked each juror directly in the eyes, moving slowly from one to the other.

"So, in summary, there is no question about liability. No, ladies and gentlemen, this is not a case of 'who wins.' This is a case of 'how much.' And this is a very substantial case because Philip Corrigan was a very substantial man. He was a builder, a developer, a man who employed hundreds and brought commerce to thousands with the first chain of shopping centers ever built in the Florida Keys. Before Philip Corrigan, there was no Zippy Mart south of Homestead. Before Philip Corrigan, there were no condos built in the flood plain. They said it couldn't be done, but Philip Corrigan did it."

Two jurors nodded, impressed.

"In a few minutes, the judge will instruct you as to the elements of damages, and they are all very substantial. You heard the accountants testify as to the loss of net accumulations of the estate of Philip Corrigan because of his untimely and tragic death. You will take their written report into the jury room. You heard the widow, Mrs. Corrigan, testify as to her grief. God willing, you will carry that grief with you into your deliberations and relieve some of it with your verdict."

God on the plaintiff's side. I didn't like that one bit. The widow's tears were coming now. Melanie Corrigan turned away, leaving the jury with her sculpted profile.

"The judge will instruct you that Mrs. Corrigan is entitled to be compensated for her mental anguish and the lost companionship and protection of her husband. Mental anguish is something she will carry with her every day for the rest of her life. Every wedding anniversary and holiday, every time she sees something in the house that reminds her of him, every morning when she awakens and every night when she goes to sleep, she will think of him, struck down. Negligently, mercilessly, senselessly. And for that reason we ask you for a total verdict of five million dollars for Mrs. Corrigan and five million dollars for the estate, a total, ladies and gentlemen, of ten million dollars."

He let it sink in a moment, then continued, "And I don't apologize for asking for one dollar of it. You know, folks, they auctioned off a racehorse the other day for fifteen million dollars."

Judge Leonard's bald head popped up. He wouldn't mind five points of that investment.

"No apologies," Cefalo repeated. "I'm told some Japanese fellows paid forty million dollars for a picture by . . . what's the name of that painter fellow, Van Gogh? And our very own United States Air Force pays millions and millions of dollars for each jet fighter. But you know, they build an ejection seat into each plane, 'cause if there's any trouble, they want to save the pilot's life, let the plane go down in flames. A life is worth more than a twenty-million-dollar airplane. So, no sir, I'm not going to apologize for asking you folks for ten million dollars."

Dan Cefalo was just about done not apologizing. He seemed to be gathering his thoughts for a final assault. He walked toward the defense table, where Roger Salisbury had broken a sweat. Cefalo took a deep breath and said, "Philip Corrigan went into that hospital and said, 'Take good care of me, Doctor. Use all your training and expertise. Don't cut me open and let me bleed to death.' They put him to sleep and there he was, innocent as a baby, at this man's mercy, and this man chopped him up."

With that Cefalo turned and stabbed a finger at Roger

Salisbury. *J'accuse*. Then he walked to the rail of the jury box and leaned on it, a close friend of all six honest folks.

"You know, some fancy writer, I don't know his name, once wrote, 'For of all sad words of tongue or pen, the saddest are these, it might have been.' The saddest are these, it might have been. What might have been for Philip and Melanie Corrigan, we will never know. Perhaps children, other lives to share with their own total love. But Philip Corrigan, who trusted this man with his life, left this world all too soon. And now Melanie Corrigan trusts you with her life. She has only one chance. If she is unhappy with the result, she can't come back and try again. Next week this courtroom might have some fender-bender case or a dispute over a parking space at a condo. This case is here and now and it is a tragic one and a substantial one. Don't let Melanie Corrigan walk out of here and say, 'It might have been.' Thank you and God bless you."

God again. We now knew that Cefalo was for God and against communism. He sat down and Melanie Corrigan opened the faucets. She buried her head into Cefalo's shoulder. He patted her between the shoulder blades. None of the jurors even saw me stand up and approach the lectern. I felt my throat tighten. Roger Salisbury's face was frozen with panic. It was important to show him that Cefalo's stellar performance did not bother me. I did this by not tossing my breakfast into the jury box.

It was a very lonely walk, those half dozen steps to center stage. I paused and finally the jurors turned toward me, their eyes challenging. I thanked them for their attention without waving the flag in their faces. I told them I only had one chance to speak to them, and then Mr. Cefalo would get up for his rebuttal. They seemed to like that. I told them that he had a second chance because the plaintiff had the burden of proof. As the defendant, we didn't have to prove anything. And then I said, let's see what they had proved.

"A man has died, and Mr. Cefalo is right about one thing. That is a tragedy. It always is when a person is taken before his three score and ten. But the world is full of tragedies. They happen every day. And not every one, not this one, has someone to blame. Mr. Cefalo is right about something else. This is a substantial case, but not because a lot of money is involved. It is substantial because it involves the reputation and good name of a very fine surgeon, a man who has treated the poor and underprivileged in our public hospital, a man who spent years training and preparing himself in every way for life-and-death decisions."

I caught a glimpse of Dan Cefalo rolling his eyes. Give me a break, Dan. You're way ahead in the laying-it-on-thick department. What did he expect me to say, that my client spent years planning his pension fund, that orthopods are out of their league whenever they move north of ankles and knees?

I continued, "Philip Corrigan died of a ruptured aorta. We all know that. No one disputes it. Aortic aneurysms happen every day. You heard the testimony. They can occur from high blood pressure, trauma, arteriosclerosis, a host of things. It can be, as Dr. Riggs said, '*ex visitatione divina,*' a visitation from God."

I was not going to be outdone in the God department. I studied the six faces. Nothing. Not a hint. At least they seemed to be listening.

"Let me now tell you of the crucial flaw in the plaintiff's case, the weak link, the stumbling block where this house of cards comes tumbling down." No one will ever accuse me of leaving a cliché unturned.

"The weak link is proximate cause. Let me repeat that. It's not *ap-proximate cause*. It's *proximate cause*. When we sit down, Judge Leonard will read you the law of proximate cause."

I needed to make a point based on Riggs's testimony. I could have said, *here's what Riggs said*, but that might not work after Cefalo's hatchet job. The trick now was to put Riggs's testimony in the context of what the judge would tell them.

I picked up the book of standard jury instructions. I wanted to look official, the judge's helper. Then in deep tones, trying to make the causation instruction sound like the Magna Charta, I said, "Here is what the judge will instruct you: 'Negligence is the legal cause of death if it directly and in natural continuous sequences produces or contributes substantially to producing such death, so that it can reasonably be said that, but for the negligence, the death would not have occurred.' Remember, that is not Jake Lassiter talking, that is the judge, and that is the law."

The risk in discussing jury instructions is that the jurors won't have the foggiest idea what you're talking about. The instructions are complicated, and juries are noticeably light on Rhodes scholars. I needed to explain the gobbledygook. *" 'But for the negligence, the death would not have occurred.'* That is what you must determine if Roger Salisbury is to be found liable for professional negligence, for violating his oath, for that is what they have charged him with. When Roger Salisbury became a physician, he promised to adhere to the Hippocratic oath. He promised to do no harm. And they have charged him under Florida law with negligently causing the death of Philip Corrigan. First, you must ask yourselves, what is the evidence that Dr. Salisbury contributed substantially to the death and that, but for the negligence, the death would not have occurred."

I couldn't tell if it was getting across, but I plowed ahead. "That is the ultimate question of proximate cause, and on that question, the evidence is undisputed."

I paused again, this time for effect. "Ladies and gentlemen, think back over the testimony of Dr. Harvey Watkins. You can think from now until the Orange Bowl Parade, and you won't find Dr. Watkins saying that the aneurysm resulted from anything Dr. Salisbury did. You see, I agree with everything Dr. Watkins said. He said it would be negligence to allow the rongeur to pierce the aorta. Fine, but there's no evidence that happened here. That's the missing link. The surgery occurred in the morning. The aneurysm happened late that night back in the private room. No loss of blood pressure during surgery, no indication of internal bleeding. Mr. Cefalo wants you to pile inference on inference, that the rongeur struck the aorta despite no evidence of an aneurysm for another twelve hours. And what did Dr. Riggs tell us?"

I spread my feet wide and stood two feet from the rail of the jury box. There I stood motionless, a rock. I wanted them to see nothing but me, to hear nothing but my words.

"Dr. Riggs told us two things, first, that the blowout in the aorta was in front where the rongeur couldn't touch it, and second, that Philip Corrigan had arteriosclerosis, hardening of the arteries. Now, unlike the name, hardening of the arteries actually weakens the arteries. Philip Corrigan was fifty-seven years old. A lot of blood had gone through those veins, a lot of miles on his odometer. And I submit to you, ladies and gentlemen, that his time had come, *ex visitatione divina.*"

I tried to see how it was going. If they bought this, we win. If not, we get hammered. I had a decision to make. This was the point where I should move to the damages issue, register shock at the ten-million-dollar figure. Hit them with the bit about cashing in on death. But I decided to risk it.

"Ladies and gentlemen, now is when a defense lawyer ordinarily discusses damages. But I am so convinced that the evidence does not support a plaintiff's verdict on liability that I find that unnecessary. They simply haven't proved their case."

I needed a way to wrap it up. Take a risky swipe at the sympathy factor.

"Finally, one word about Mrs. Corrigan. She is a young woman and her grief will heal. Surely she knew when she married a man twice her age that at some point she would be a widow."

This was thin ice. Go too far here and risk offending the jury into a retaliatory verdict.

"Mr. Cefalo quoted you an old saw about what might have been. Another writer once said that grief is the most intense of all emotions and therefore the shortest lived. Time heals. Grief ends. Life goes on. It is natural for you to feel sympathy for Mrs. Corrigan, as I do, but it is not to enter into your deliberations. Judge Leonard will instruct you that you are not to be swayed by sympathy. Sentiment has no place here. Only the facts and the law, and they will convince you that there is no liability in this case. Thank you."

Melanie Corrigan's eyes burned a hole in my back as I

walked to the defense table. Roger Salisbury's face was a mixture of hope and fear. Dan Cefalo didn't waste any time. He had the last shot.

"Ladies and gentlemen, I rise now to speak one last time for Philip Corrigan, who cannot speak for himself."

Talk about *non sequiturs*. If Philip Corrigan could speak for himself, we wouldn't be here.

Cefalo raised his voice in lawyerly indignation. "They've put this woman through the death of her husband, a funeral, a trial, a world of loneliness, and now they say, it'll pass. Go home, Mrs. Corrigan, it'll pass. Let me tell you folks something. When we're done here today, I'll go home to my family. You folks will go home to yours. Mr. Lassiter will see his friends and there will be cheery talk and hors d'oeuvres and the tinkling of glasses."

That was news to me. I was planning to open a can of tuna.

"But the Corrigan house will be dark and empty when she turns the key in the lock tonight. It'll be that way tonight and tomorrow and the next night. So Mr. Lassiter would have you split hairs over this and that, but the fact is that a man went into the hospital for simple surgery and he didn't come out, and they have a bushelbasket full of reasons why, but you and I know the truth. So as you prepare to go into the jury room, I leave you and ask that you remember you are this woman's last and only hope. God speed."

A dangerous combination, I thought, as the jurors filed into their windowless room. The intellect of man, the speed of God.

10

WE HAVE,
YOUR HONOR

Waiting again, this time for a verdict. Waiting is not my strong suit. I never did the bit outside a hospital delivery room, but I know all the clichés, the pacing, the endless cigarettes, the furrowed brows. At least there, when it's over, you've got something to take home. I leave it all behind. Win, lose, or mistrial, I bury it. Winning is less joy than relief, removing the knife from the wound. Losing is not agony, just the fulfillment of promised pain.

Defending a case is particularly frustrating. If you win, you have broken even, restored the status quo. Your client wants to take you to dinner. He shows you his new bumper sticker, *My Lawyer Can Beat Your Lawyer.* If you lose, he questions what you should have done to win. And always finds something.

Roger Salisbury paced in the corridor. I sat with Cindy in the courtroom. While I read the latest *Windrider* magazine, she propped her bare feet on the defense table and painted her toenails a metallic silver that reminded me of a '71 Corvette. The bailiff came by and gave her a dirty look. She wiggled a burnished big toe at him.

Still waiting, two hundred minutes creeping along, life ticking away. Somewhere off the Canary Islands, tanned young men and women from France are sailing windsurfers at more than thirty knots. On a hundred slopes in the Rockies, skiers are whooping it up on fresh powder. Only a hundred miles away, bass fishermen are lazing across Lake Okeechobee. So why am I waiting, just waiting, in an old relic of a courthouse for six strangers to tell me if I'm worth a hot damn in my chosen field.

"Is it a good sign they're taking so long?" Roger Salisbury asked, coming in from the corridor.

"It could be," I said. Very insightful. In truth, it's meaningless. If the jury comes back with a verdict after twenty minutes, you can be sure it's for the defense. They haven't had time to order steaks at taxpayer expense, much less determine both liability and damages. After that, anything goes. They could have determined liability in the plaintiff's favor hours ago and only now be deciding how many zeroes to tack onto the verdict form.

I picked up a newspaper and turned to the sports page. There was Susan Corrigan's by-line above a story on the Dolphins game, a loss at Cleveland. The Dolphins never did play well in cold weather, losing 24 to 10 to the Browns and their defense known as the Dawgs:

> *CLEVELAND—When the game was still dicey and the field was turning icy, the Browns showed the Miami Dolphins what a Dawg Day afternoon is like on the shores of frozen Lake Erie.*

Cute. I wanted to see her. Maybe after the verdict, if she calms down about this murder business. My daydreaming was interrupted by The Knock. It's the knock that sets the adrenaline pumping, the knock from inside the jury room. It could mean anything, including the fact that the jurors are hungry. The bailiff hurried over, as best he could. He was a retired motorcycle cop with snow-white hair, a bow-legged walk, and a hacking cough. When he came out, he headed straight for the judge's chambers, a poker face all the way. Must have forgotten about the bottle of Jack Daniels I *schmear* him with every Christmas.

In a moment the judge flew through the rear door of the courtroom, still hooking his robe in front, its tail aflutter like a mainsail tacking. Things would happen fast now if there was a verdict. But the jury might have a question, not an answer. Usually baffling questions. *Could the court reporter read back the nurse's testimony about the patient's postsurgery constipation?* You can never tell what goes through their minds.

But no questions this time. The foreman was holding a piece of legal-size paper neatly folded at the middle. He was a retired accountant. No trace of a sense of humor or spontaneity when I questioned him on *voir dire*. I had asked him the last book he read. *"The Price Waterhouse Guide to the New Tax Law,"* he responded. Not the kind of a guy to have a beer with, but perfect for the defense in a personal injury or medical malpractice case. I tried to catch the foreman's eye. No soap. Looked at the rest of them. Still no luck. Legal folklore has it that they avoid your eyes when they've voted against you.

One of the women, a housewife, looked toward Melanie Corrigan and teared up. Now what the hell did that mean? The widow was through with her tears. She had dusted on some blush during the long break. A nice mixture of healthy and sultry, shedding her mourning widow image a mite early. Her lips were freshly painted in a pink liquid gloss, a wet look. Her hair now cascaded over her shoulders. She ran a hand through the reddish brown waves and tossed her head back, showing me a fine line of neck. A splendid pose for a shampoo ad.

Roger Salisbury could have been in an ad, too. For Plummer Funeral Home. When news of The Knock reached the corridor, he quit pacing and hastily joined me at the defense table, the color draining from his face. Now his complexion was the gray of a California seal. I wondered if he was too young for a coronary.

"Has the jury reached a verdict?" Judge Leonard asked in a grave tone suitable for an execution.

"We have, Your Honor," said the foreman, with no wasted breaths. He stood and handed the verdict form to the bailiff, who used it to shield a cough, then handed it to the judge. Judge Leonard took a thousand years to read it, and I strained with X-ray eyes to read it from fifty feet away. Not a trace of emotion crossed Judge Leonard's face as he handed the form to the clerk. Annoyed at having been interrupted, she reluctantly put down her new paperback, this one a survey of women's sexual fantasies.

"The clerk will publish the verdict," Judge Leonard said in the same stern voice.

The clerk stood up, lodged her chewing gum in the roof of her mouth, jammed a pencil into her Afro, and in a bored monotone, started reading:

"In the Eleventh Judicial Circuit, in and for Dade County, Florida, Case Number eight-seven, one-eight-three-seven-six, Melanie Corrigan, as Personal Representative of the Estate of Philip M. Corrigan, deceased, versus Roger A. Salisbury, M.D." She paused, cleared her throat, *ah-chem.* Oh get to it, already. "We, the jury, find for the defendant."

Boom. That was it. She sat down. Roger Salisbury slapped me on the back. Dan Cefalo winced once, recovered like the pro he was, and asked the judge to poll the jury. He did. Each one affirmed the verdict. Melanie Corrigan looked over at Roger Salisbury and gave him a small, bittersweet smile. Like it didn't matter. Like that's one for you. If that wasn't the damnedest thing.

Judge Leonard was doing his thank-yous to the jurors while his bailiff handed them certificates bearing a sketch of the judge that made his round face look like Abe Lincoln on Mount Rushmore. Good for a few votes in the next election.

Then it was over. The jurors picked up their things, the few spectators ambled down the corridor looking for more action. Roger Salisbury began babbling about how brilliant I was, how great Charlie Riggs was, how beautiful Cindy was. He wanted to treat me to dinner, champagne, wenching.

I was spent. I told him I would be poor company. In truth

Paul Levine

I was tired of his company. I had given him a piece of myself. The camaraderie that comes from the shared experience evaporates when the experience ends. Like war buddies, you drift apart when the conflict is over. Quickly.

So why did I feel that the case of Corrigan versus Salisbury was only just beginning?

11

THE WASP
AND THE
CATERPILLAR

Cindy headed back to the office and I aimed the 442 convertible west on Tamiami Trail toward the Everglades. No way I was going to return phone calls and compile expense account forms after coming out of trial. I wanted some open air. Tamiami Trail is *Calle Ocho* in Little Havana. I passed city parks where old Cuban men played dominoes, drinking espresso, cigars clenched in brown teeth, vowing to return to a *Cuba Libre*. They do not consider themselves *immigrantes*, a term that implies a voluntary move to a new home. They are *exilados*, refugees in exile. When their homeland is liberated from the Communist butcher, they will return.

The young Cubans, the teenagers born in Miami, look at matters differently. With their 280Z's, late nights in Coconut Grove discos, and weekends on Key Biscayne beaches, they have no desire to take up arms or swing machetes in the sugarcane fields. If they don battle fatigues, it is only because the look is fashionable this season at the Banana Republic boutique.

When hundreds of thousands of Cuban refugees flooded Miami in the 1960s, there were few directions to go. East was the small downtown and Biscayne Bay. South was pricey Coral Gables, and it would be years before most exiles could move there. North was Liberty City, officially the Central Negro District on old police reports, a place the Great Society passed by, the scorching pavement without the palm trees of the Gables or the pines of South Dade.

The only direction was west, and those who fled Castro pushed Miami that way, blowing the city out at the seams, bringing new food and music and clothing, and in a generation, they owned the gas stations and restaurants and auto dealerships and furniture stores and even banks. From the bay westward for one hundred forty blocks, onto the fringes of the Everglades, on both sides of Tamiami Trail, they lived and worked and prospered. In the middle of what was a sleepy Southern town another country grew, strange and forbidding—*Fantasias Ropas, Vistas Funeraria, Clinicas Quiropracticas*—its premises off-limits to English speakers.

The Anglo immigrants of a generation before came from Georgia and Alabama. They lived in small concrete block stucco houses with no garages, and in their front yards pickup trucks were hitched to airboats, ready for midnight frogging in the Glades. These whites—airline mechanics, truck drivers, power company linemen—already feared the mean street blacks and resented the Miami Beach Jews. Culture shock for these Southern Baptists was a Florida town turned upside down, where native-born whites got the hell out, bumper stickers pleading sarcastically, *WILL THE LAST ANGLO TO LEAVE MIAMI PLEASE TURN OFF THE LIGHTS.*

Traffic thinned after I passed the sprawling campus of Florida International University. Now it was a straight shot across the Trail, all the way to Naples if I wanted to air it out. At first I pretended not to know where I was headed. But I knew. I knew the little dirt road that came out of the Everglades near Shark Valley just this side of the phony Miccosukee village where a bored Indian wrestles a stoned gator, tourists clicking their Nikons.

I slid into the turn, sending up a swirl of dust and startling a dozen snowy egrets in the sawgrass. A great white heron with matchstick legs eyed me from the shallow water, then stutter-stepped away like a man on crutches. The high ground—barely two feet above the swamp—was a mile off the Trail, just a patch of dirt behind a stand of scraggly trees. The house was an old fishing cabin, weatherbeaten boards topped by a corrugated aluminum roof that caught the late afternoon sun. An old fishing cabin is what you're left with when your wife's lawyer is a B-52 bomber with a mouth like a nuclear warhead. A Spanish-style house with an orange barrel-tile roof on a shady Coral Gables street is what your wife gets when the mushroom cloud has lifted.

In a dilapidated lawn chair, bare feet propped on a milk carton, sat Charles W. Riggs, M.D., retired medical examiner of Dade County, Florida. He put down a dusty book and motioned me toward another plastic chair with frayed straps for a seat. I looked at the book. *Select Coroners' Rolls, 1265–1413, A.D.* Must have missed it on the bestseller list. Riggs wore khaki bush shorts that stopped just above his knobby knees. His legs were short and pale, the legs of a man with enough sense to stay out of the Florida sun. His faded T-shirt advertised an oyster bar in Key West and bulged at the middle. His graying beard needed trimming or at least combing. His half-glasses had tossed a screw and were mended with a bent fishhook. The glasses sat cockeyed on his small nose. Behind the lenses, his eyes—the color of sawgrass during a drought—took it all in and let only some of it out.

"You make a wrong turn heading for the beach?" he asked.

"No, just thought I'd be neighborly, drop by. *Qué pasa,* Doc?"

"Mosquitoes biting, fish ain't. What're you doing this far west?"

"Lately haven't known east from west, up from down."

"Sounds like one of those country ballads. You're not in love are you, Jake?"

I fiddled with the old book. "Not in love, though there's a woman. But this isn't about her, not exactly. It's Salisbury. We finished today, defense verdict."

"Congratulations. When I saw your face, I thought the

128

jury might have stuck it to you. Would have been a shame. That rongeur never got close to the aorta."

My white shirt, angelic for verdict day, was beginning to patch with sweat. No breeze cut through the great river of grass today. "I believed you about the rongeur," I said. "The jury believed you. There's a young woman, Corrigan's daughter, who says the malpractice case was just a cover, that Salisbury and the widow poisoned her father with a drug, succinylcholine."

Charlie Riggs didn't bat an eye. "What's the motive?"

"Money. Melanie wanted her husband's. Salisbury wanted Melanie, the money, too, I suppose."

"Radix omnium malorum est cupiditas."

"Easy for you to say."

"The love of money," Charlie Riggs explained, "is the root of all evil. Not money itself. There's nothing inherently evil about money, but the love of it, that's what does them in. Money never meant beans to me. Martha, my ex, was always yammering about money. Wanted me to go into private practice, form my own P.A., start a chain of labs, pay kickbacks to the internists, the whole lousy deal. Imagine me a businessman, or even worse, looking at slides all day, a bookkeeper in a white coat with a microscope."

I kept my mouth shut and let him think about it, a brilliant career of public service, a wrecked family life. He smiled sadly and said, "Loved the scent of money, she did, and hated the smell of formaldehyde."

I navigated the conversation back on course. "I'm having trouble believing it, murder I mean. But Susan Corrigan came up with a vial that supposedly has the drug, a couple of hypodermics, all in a leather valise belonging to Salisbury."

Charlie Riggs shook his head. "Succinylcholine, a lousy way to die. You'd be conscious, fully aware, but paralyzed until your lungs and heart gave out. Ugly. Somebody must have a lot of hunger for money to do that."

"That doesn't surprise you, does it, Charlie? Man is the cruelest animal."

He waggled a finger at me. "A common misconception. There are animals in nature capable of the cruelest torture. Take the ichneumons, a variety of wasps. The ichneumon injects its eggs right into a caterpillar's body after shooting it with a paralyzing toxin. Sort of a succinylcholine in nature. When the eggs hatch, the wasp larvae begin eating the caterpillar, slowly and painfully. They keep that poor caterpillar alive so the innards don't spoil, first eating the fat and the digestive organs, saving the heart for last. Finally nothing is left but the shell. Nature is just as cruel as man."

This was standard fare for Doc Riggs, a mix of Biology 101 and Basic Philosophy. I said, "Sure Charlie, but the icky-whachamacallit does it for food, for survival."

"Is that really an important distinction?"

Pulling the old Socratic method on me. "Sure it is," I said. "Killing for food is justifiable homicide in the animal kingdom. I've watched enough Marlin Perkins to know that. Man kills for money or out of anger or passion. I've tried enough criminal cases to know that."

He looked at me over the repaired glasses that hung lopsided on his nose. "Either way, the victim is just as innocent, the pain just as real, is it not?"

I didn't answer, just sat there and listened to the sound of the swamp, the water stirred by unseen animals. Overhead I heard the short, mellow whistle of an osprey, the Florida fish hawk, and imagined its sharp eyes on full alert for catfish, talons at the ready. Two mosquitoes buzzed around my left ear, debating who would dine first.

Finally Charlie Riggs said, mostly to himself, "Succinylcholine. Be hard to trace. Breaks down into succinic acid and choline and both substances are normally present in the body. A physician would know that. We could check for needle tracks, though."

"Isn't it a little late for that?"

He sprang from the chair and bounded into the cabin, banging the screen door behind him. "Read the book," he called out. "Right where the mark is. I'll fix us some limeade. Key limes, sour as my ex-wife's disposition."

I blew some dust off the book and it fell open to the year 1267. A crummy time to be alive unless you were handy with a sword. The book was in Latin on the left-hand pages and English on the right. Riggs had been reading the left side, making little notes. Never having gotten past *amo, amas, amat*, I opted for the English:

It happened in the vill of Goldington after vespers the eve of the feast of St. Dunstan that strife arose on the Green between William Read and John Barford concerning sheep. William received a wound on the head from which he seemed to recover. Then he died of ague and his wife raised the hue. The coroner found that William Read had already been buried and instructed that he be dug up. When he be dug up, the coroner said that William Read died of the wound, not the illness, and ordered John Barford attached.

Charlie Riggs toddled out of the cabin carrying two mason jars of limeade with no ice. I put down the book and asked, "You want to exhume Corrigan's body?"

He handed me one of the jars, dropped into his rickety chair, and studied the swamp. "You'd be surprised how well embalming preserves tissues. Might be hard to find needle tracks, though. The skin will be moldy, and if he's buried in damp ground, it's probably turned to adipocere, sort of a waxy gunk. And he isn't going to smell like Chanel No. 5."

He let that hang in the still air, then said, "If you're getting hungry, I'm about to put supper on. Fresh possum."

I passed on the invitation, thoughts of parasitic wasps and moldy corpses failing to whet the appetite. I took a swig of the warm limeade. It puckered me up; he had left out the sugar.

"Well how about it, Jake? You ready to rob graves?"

"I've done worse, but Salisbury is my client. I can't do anything against his interests."

Riggs scowled. "The case is over, Counselor."

"Not in the eyes of the Florida Bar. I can't use something I learned in the course of representing Salisbury in a way that may harm him. I try not to break more than two or three of the canons each week."

I must not have sounded convincing. I hadn't convinced Riggs, and I hadn't convinced myself.

Charlie Riggs downed his limeade in one gulp, gave me his teacher-to-student look, and said, "It's not as if you're going to the authorities. Just a little private investigation to answer some questions, settle your conscience. Besides, it'll give me something to do. And maybe your young lady friend will appreciate you searching for the truth, kind of set you apart from most members of your profession."

He knew how to push all the right buttons. "C'mon, Jake. To hell with your canons."

"Come to think of it," I said, "they're not mine."

"Good boy. Let's get to it. The grave is silent, *magis mutus quam piscis,* but you and I, Jake, we can speak for the dead."

12

KNIGHT ERRANT

The city swallowed up the Salisbury verdict just as it did everything else. A tiny morsel for the carnivorous media machines. Two paragraphs in the "Courthouse Roundup" section of the newspaper, no television or radio coverage at all. *60 Minutes* did not call me for an interview; young lawyers did not stop me on Flagler Street and ask for words of wisdom; my partners did not toast me with champagne or vote me a bonus.

If the jury had hit Salisbury with a ten-million-dollar verdict, headlines would have screamed the news from here to Tallahassee. But a defense verdict sinks into the muck of the day's events, a fallen twig barely stirring a ripple in the malevolent swamp.

I did receive a memo from Morris McGonigal, the senior partner, a guy with a gray flannel personality in a seersucker town. Or rather my secretary Cindy received a memo from his secretary. It said, "Please advise Mr. Lassiter that Mr. McGonigal congratulates him on his recent verdict."

The personal touch.

I wasn't complaining about the lack of notoriety. It probably was better for Salisbury. A doctor gets hit with a big verdict, the public thinks he's a butcher. The doctor gets off, the public thinks the jury fouled up. Besides, it was a heavy news day, even by Miami standards. Police arrested two Nicaraguans who had a dozen TOW missiles and an antitank rocket in their truck, the Miami version of a traffic violation. The Nicaraguans were planning to fight the Sandinistas, a holy mission hereabouts, and would probably get probation, if not a key to the city.

A few hours later, most Miami police were busy pumping bullets into the van of a 63-year-old Cuban plumber. They had good reason. He had fired five shots at an undercover cop. But then the plumber had good reason. The cop, dressed like a thug, was stuck in a monstrous traffic jam on *Calle Ocho*. The cop waved his gun at the plumber to get him to move his van. His *motherfucking Cuban van*, witnesses would later recall the officer screaming. There was a convenience store robbery coming down a block away, and the cop, his Firebird socked in by the van, was hollering in English, a language as foreign to the plumber as Sanskrit.

The plumber figured he was being robbed and opened fire. That drew seven police cars, a number of shotguns, and forty-seven holes in the van, three in the plumber, and one in his colostomy bag. The plumber survived, and the convenience store robbers got away with seventy-three dollars and a box of DoveBars.

I was mired in my typical psychological letdown after a trial, just puttering around the office, shuffling stacks of mail, trying to figure out where to go from here. I tried calling Susan Corrigan, but a bored voice on the copy desk said she was on the west coast, headed out early for pregame stories on the Dolphins' next opponent, their old nemesis, the Raiders. I wanted to see her, and not just to talk about digging up dear old Dad. I had a little buzz about Ms. Susan Corrigan. That happens sometimes when I get stiff-armed. Don't know why, maybe my ego needs bruising. Maybe too much easy flesh in the early years. Or maybe I had matured a notch or two until I finally appreciated a strong, savvy lady more than a lusty, dim one. Whatever the reason, the image of the suntanned and sharp-tongued sportswriter was hovering just below the surface of my consciousness.

I had just hung up with the newspaper when Cindy slipped me a note:

> *Widow Not Merry,*
> *Do Not Tarry;*
> *Commotion, Line Two.*

I punched the flashing button and heard shouting in the background, a man's voice and a woman's voice. I couldn't make out the words. I said hello a bunch of times. The phone must have been put down. Some women need two hands to argue. The voices came closer. "You owe me," the man's voice said, booming over the wire. Then the sound of a woman laughing. More yelling, then a woman's loud voice telling the man to get out. I thought I heard a door slam. Then silence.

"Hello." The woman's voice, under perfect control. "Mr. Lassiter?"

I told her it was.

She told me it was Mrs. Corrigan calling. I knew that.

She said there was trouble. I knew that, too.

Could you come over?

"If you have trouble, why not call the police?" I suggested.

"You wouldn't like that," she said, evenly. "Neither would your client."

It was coming into focus. "Is Roger there?"

"He is, and he's making quite a scene."

"Put him on."

"At the moment, he's pacing on the patio by the Jacuzzi. If it's just the same to you, I'd rather not have him in the house. He hit me. And I don't think he'll leave my property unless you come talk to him. Or should I just call the police and charge him with trespassing and assault?"

"I'll be there in twenty minutes."

She didn't ask if I knew the address and I didn't tell her I did. I just headed to the parking garage, and like a knight errant, saddled my steed and galloped south on Miami Avenue toward Coconut Grove and Gables Estates beyond. At the same time I wondered what Roger Salisbury was doing, screwing everything up. Why wasn't he sawing bones and scraping kneecaps? What was it he'd said? That he was still under her spell. Didn't he know she was poison?

The water still tumbled through its man-made waterfall and the house still sat, silent as a tomb, atop its man-made hill. But no cars in the driveway, no voices to break the gentle roar of the waterfall, and no Roger Salisbury. The winter sun, low in the afternoon sky, slanted narrow shadows from the royal palms, like jailhouse bars, across the Corrigan house. A chill was in the air, a cold front from the Midwest rustling the palm fronds with a crisp northwest breeze. I parked by the waterfall, patted the 442 on the rump and told it to stay put. Then, I walked up the front steps and rang the bell.

"He threatened to kill me," Melanie Corrigan said.

She had thrown open the double doors, a good trick in itself. Fifteen feet high, six inches thick, crossed-hatched by thick beams, a circus elephant could slip in sideways.

"Where is he?"

"He threatened to kill me," she repeated. There was a red splotch just below her left eye. A right-handed guy who doesn't know how to punch might have glanced one off there. "He left. Drove away like a madman. Cursing at me."

She led me into the foyer and closed the door. An electric bolt clicked into place like a bullet shoved into the chamber. The foyer had a marble floor and a cathedral ceiling. Not as big as Madison Square Garden, but you still could play basketball there. Full court. Between the foyer and the living room was a pond stocked with fat orange fish. A fountain poured water over an island where bronze flamingoes and alligators eyed each other between rocks and ferns. We walked past the pond and around a glass-enclosed elevator, crossing no more than two county lines. We tiptoed down three marble steps without disturbing an eight-foot Zulu warrior carved from teak, and we landed in an octagonal, sunken living room.

The living room was black and white, black furniture that looked plastic to me but must have cost a bundle when selected by a trendy designer, white tile that wouldn't stay clean a minute if I lived there, white walls covered with paintings of women's heads floating away from their bodies, an ebony grand piano that was probably for show. All in all, a starter home for the nouveau riche who want to make a personal statement: *We have more money than we know what to do with.*

Melanie Corrigan fit right in—she wore black. I knew it was silk, but I didn't know if it was a slip or a dress. I did know there was nothing between the silk and her satin skin. The silk thing was held up by two thin straps, was cut low at the breasts and high on the thighs and was sheer as a shadow. If it was a dress you wouldn't wear it to church. If it was a slip, where was her dress?

"Thank you for coming, Mr. Lassiter. May I call you Jake?"

"Of course, Melanie." I nodded in the direction of her décolletage. "Are you auditioning for *Cat on a Hot Tin Roof*?"

It only took her a second. "Do you think I'd be a good Maggie?"

"From what I hear, you'd get an Oscar, a Tony, and a Super Bowl ring."

"Your client talks too much." She narrowed her eyes. "He also made the mistake of underestimating me."

"And I'll bet he wasn't the first."

140

She looked at me straight on, sizing me up. Then a little smile like we shared some secret. "Would you like a drink?" she asked.

I said yes but she didn't ask what I wanted. She slid behind a bar, and I took a seat on a Lucite barstool that would throw your back into spasms if you stayed for more than two drinks. The designer obviously had not been in many bars where men sit and talk and drink. Melanie Corrigan bent down to get a bottle and let me see the tops of very white, very firm breasts.

I would have liked a beer. She reached for tequila and orange juice and poured some of each in a glass you could have used to put out a three-alarm fire. She dropped in some ice cubes and shook a dash of bitters on top. I don't care for a drink that needs ice and fruit juice.

"Tijuana Sunrise," she said.

"*Buenos días,*" I said.

She poured herself one, and we each took a sip. She didn't seem to be in a hurry. Her russet hair was tumbling free today, lightly brushing her shoulders where the tiny silk straps did their best to slide downhill.

"Roger is getting to be a problem," she said finally, touching her cheekbone where the bruise was already beginning to darken. She had long, graceful fingers, nails expensively done with lots of color. "He can't accept the fact that it's over."

She tugged at one of the slippery straps. I kept quiet.

"He apparently told you about us," she continued, fishing to find out what I knew.

"Every dirty little detail, the twosomes, the threesomes."

She didn't blink, just gave a little shrug that sent the strap

141

slithering off one shoulder. The black silk fell open, exposing a cinnamon nipple that acted like it enjoyed being watched.

"He thinks he still owns me, thinks I'm still a kid. You've got to keep him away from me or he's going to get hurt."

"That sounds like a threat."

"I could say things that wouldn't be good for his health."

"Such as?"

She studied me a moment, deciding how much to say. "He wanted to kill Philip, wanted me to do it. That's all he talked about for months. I refused, of course."

"Of course," I said with just a dash of sarcasm like the bitters in the silly drink.

"Screw you, Lassiter," she said. What happened to *Jake*?

She gave me a look with a below-zero wind chill and said, "I might not have been the world's greatest wife by your standards, but I did a lot for Philip. Whatever he asked. We had an arrangement. He got what he wanted from me, and I got what I wanted from him."

"His bank accounts and stock portfolio."

She wouldn't let me rile her. "The freedom that came with those things. Philip didn't care if I saw other men, maybe even liked it. For me things were great. I didn't depend on men's handouts anymore. Why would I kill him? There was no reason to."

"So why did you keep your mouth shut when your darling husband planned to go under the knife of the doctor who wanted him dead?"

"I was scared to death when Philip went in the hospital, but I thought, with all the nurses and other doctors around, Roger just couldn't . . ."

She let it hang there.

"He didn't," I said. "The jury found that Roger wasn't even negligent, much less a killer. Your husband died of a spontaneous aneurysm."

"He was poisoned," she said without a trace of emotion. "In his hospital room."

I took a long hit on the drink to think that one over. This conversation sounded familiar.

She kept going. "Roger had this liquid in a bottle, an anesthetic. He wanted me to use it on Philip. Get him drunk or stoned, then inject him in the buttocks. Said it couldn't be traced."

"He gave you the bottle?"

"No. I wouldn't take it then. After Philip died, I was at Roger's house. I was still seeing him until I filed the lawsuit. I knew he kept the bottle in a small refrigerator, so I took it. I wanted to turn it over to the authorities."

"Did you?"

She looked away. "No. I know I should have, but then everything would have come out in the newspapers. I've worked hard to earn respectability, and it would all be gone."

"But you sued him for malpractice."

"I didn't want to. I didn't want the attention. But I was afraid if I didn't sue Roger, it would raise suspicions. Philip's daughter, that tomboy bitch, would have thought Roger and I killed him."

Lights were flashing like a pinball machine. Susan Corrigan may have been right about Roger Salisbury but wrong about Melanie Corrigan. Melanie had to be telling the truth,

I thought. She couldn't risk telling me about the drug if she had been in on it.

"What was Roger doing here today?"

"I never really told him it was over. I didn't want to hurt him. When I filed the suit, I told him we'd get back together after the trial. Today I told him to stay away and he freaked."

"Show me the drug," I said, already knowing the response.

She gave me a helpless look that I hadn't seen on her before. "I can't," she said. "It's gone, stolen."

I decided there was nothing to be gained in telling Melanie Corrigan that her beloved stepdaughter had been poking around in her underwear drawer. "What do you want me to do?" I asked.

She half smiled and half sighed. Her eyes seemed to widen, to change from business to bedroom, a neat trick. Outside the floor-to-ceiling windows, the sun was setting, and inside, the room was bathed in pink. Melanie Corrigan's skin took on a soft glow, and it hadn't looked bad in the light. She glided around the bar to where I was planted on the hard-as-granite barstool. She pulled up the silky strap one more time and now her perky nipples poked at the flimsy fabric. Maybe they were standing at attention because of the cool evening air or maybe it had something to do with the full moon coming up over the bay. Or maybe it was the proximity of me. Or maybe, just maybe, I should have my head examined. Ready to drink that pretty poison, as big a fool as Roger Salisbury.

At that moment what I wanted most was knowledge of self. I would have liked to figure out that urge that started halfway between my knees and chest and threatened to spread northward until it flooded whatever brain cells still worked without a jump start. I would have liked to, but I didn't have time because she looked me right in the eyes, smiled, and then slapped me.

There are slaps that ring your ears and slaps that bring tears to your eyes. This one could do neither. Less sting than my aftershave. I smiled at her and stood up. She had on a funny look, watching me with pouting lips. She had a good pout.

Then she slapped me again. Harder. Not enough to take an eight-count, but probably enough to bring some color to my cheeks, as well as to hers. Especially hers. She was enjoying this, warming up around the eyes. A hot little smile now. And *crack*, another slap. I was getting used to it.

She threw her arms around my neck, pressed herself up against me, then rocked up and down on her tiptoes as if stretching her calves. What she was doing was rubbing parts of her against parts of me like a very friendly, very slinky cat. My hands slid down her back to her round, tight bottom. She was firm where a woman ought to be firm and soft where a woman ought to be soft.

I looked at her close up. She had tiny golden freckles across the bridge of her nose, and little smile lines creased the corners of her mouth. A look of innocence and mirth. But the eyes were something else, wet and wild. And her neck was fragrant with the sweetness of the tropical night. A provocative blend of the pure and the wanton.

"When your face gets red, your eyes are even bluer," she said.

"Wait'll I start bleeding. I'll be another Paul Newman."

"You like being slapped," she said. Telling me, not asking me.

"Not as much as some other things," I said.

"You could learn." She pulled me toward her, looking into my eyes from under long lashes, still standing on her toes, straining against me. "You're a big man," she said, running her hands across my back. "More man than Roger or Philip."

Then she decided to see if I could swallow her tongue.

I could.

Just then an ugly noise from outside filled the room. A shout in Japanese split the air like a police siren. It could have awakened the dead at Guadalcanal, and it nearly cost Melanie Corrigan the tip of her slippery tongue. I let her go, and she straightened her sliding strap and brushed a hand through her hair.

"Must be Sergio," she said, as if there was nothing unusual in a banzai yell interrupting a perfectly fine kiss. We retraced the path to the foyer without pausing for food or water. Then another bellow from outside, and the front door shuddered as if hit by a wrecking ball. "He probably saw your car outside. He's insanely jealous."

Yet another Oriental war whoop and again the door groaned in pain.

"Sergio?" I asked.

"Sergio Machado-Alvarez," she said, serenely. "My chauffeur, boat captain, and . . . friend. We'd better open the door or he'll just break it down."

She punched the code into the digital alarm and unleashed the deadbolt. The huge door swung open to reveal a swarthy, moustachioed block of concrete. Sneakers, sweat

146

pants, and a sleeveless muscle shirt, a tattoo of a lightning bolt on his tricep. He had plenty of beef to show, huge shoulders and chest, a fireplug of muscle and malice. Recently, I'd seen even more of him on videotape.

Sergio Machado-Alvarez stepped into the foyer and shot me a sideways smile, a mean little smile under the drooping moustache. He had big gray teeth like a double row of gravestones. He needed a shave and always would.

There was only one thing that detracted from his overall appearance as a menace to society. He was short. Like a lot of little guys he probably was working hard on the compensation factor. Building huge muscles, getting tough with karate, having something to show off. Stand at any gas station and study men and their cars in relation to their size. Check out how many short guys drive Sedan de Villes and Lincoln Town Cars. They need pillows to see over the steering wheel. Then come the big guys. They have to unfold a section at a time to get out of their Alfa Romeos and Corvettes.

"Do you know who I am?" he asked. A voice of practiced toughness, a faint Cuban accent.

"Something that escaped from the zoo."

"Hijo de puta," he snarled, "I'll dig you another asshole."

"Why not spare yourself the trouble and just lend me one of yours?" Even I didn't know what that meant, the mouth being quicker than the mind.

He took a few seconds to think it over, then dropped into the half-moon stance with legs spread, left foot forward, hands on hips. I needed this like I needed to be in traction, which I might be if either of us found it necessary to show off for the lady of the house. I had been hitting the heavy

147

bag at home. But the heavy bag doesn't know karate. And this guy looked like he intended to scatter my teeth.

"Hombre, you think you're tough?"

"No, I'm a pansy. You're tough."

He was trying to figure out if I was pulling his chain. He was the kind of guy who needed to take a thought and spread it on the kitchen table with the comics page. "I got *cojones grandes,* balls the size of grapefruit," he said slowly, as if he had memorized the phrase.

"You can take penicillin for that," I suggested.

His throat released a growl that a Doberman would be proud to own. Melanie shook a long fingernail and said, "Sergio, Mr. Lassiter is my guest. Please mind your manners. And don't you have a class to teach?"

The sinister little hulk looked at his watch, his lips moving slowly.

"Little hand on the six, big hand on the eleven," I said, helpfully. "You can figure it out."

His eyes flicked toward Melanie. "I got to train housewives to kick their husbands in the balls." Then he looked at me and made his face even uglier. He seemed to be all forehead and whiskers. "I'll see you another time, *cagado cabrón* asshole," he said.

"How's Wednesday for lunch? Have your girl call my girl."

This time the growl became a shriek. He bolted through the open doorway and bounded down the steps as fast as his chunky legs could move. *"Ushiro-keomi!"* His yell nearly drowned out the sound of the electric-powered waterfall tumbling over the landscaping. Then, in the driveway, he spun sideways and put out the left headlight on my 442 with a back-thrust kick. Glass scattered on the cobblestones. What kind of a man hurts an innocent old car?

"Shuto!" He brought his hand down like a sword across the hood, the sickening sound of metal giving way, caving in. Next, I figured, he would bite the tires and give me four flats. Instead, he jumped on his motorcycle, a loud Kawasaki, did a wheelie, and screamed off into the night, shouting unheard insults over his shoulder.

I surveyed the damage to the 442, then sat down on the front steps.

"Do you want to come back in?" Melanie Corrigan said, with a promise as large as a king-size waterbed. But the moment had passed. My brains had taken over. I didn't want her tequila and orange juice and didn't want any part of her. She was too available, too free with herself, but too expensive for her men. Look at the price Philip Corrigan paid, and Roger Salisbury, tangled up with lust and maybe murder. And Sergio, the muscle-bound half-wit, martial arts fueled by jealousy.

I wanted to see Susan Corrigan, wanted to tell her about Melanie's charges against Roger. I wanted some help in figuring it all out. But first, I wanted to go home and pound out the vicious dent in my wounded chariot.

13

GRAVEYARD
SHIFT

A great piece of luck, Charlie Riggs was saying. Philip
Corrigan entombed in a crypt aboveground, an ornate mausoleum with the design of Palmland, his largest shopping
center, molded into the concrete.

"A great piece of luck," he said again, "especially with
Corrigan dead two years. In Florida the ground is so damp,
the tissues break down fast. I hate to tell you what corpses
look like when you dig them up, mold on the outside, para-
sites and larvae on the inside. Mausoleum tombs are so rare
these days, so expensive. But I guess he could afford it."

"Judging from his house, the tomb will have a wine cellar, an elevator, and a butler," I said.

"Just so it's airtight, that's the ticket."

Riggs was nearly smacking his lips at the prospect of popping the top on Philip Corrigan's last resting place. I had pulled the funeral bills from the case file. In a wrongful death case the estate recovers funeral expenses, and I remembered a fifty-thousand-dollar number. Sure enough, there it was, a bill from Eternal Memories Mortuary and Mausoleum. When the first Mrs. Corrigan had died, her husband bought the choicest acre plot and ordered a mausoleum built for two, and not the compact efficiency model either. The perfect touch from the loving husband, a promise that his bones would one day rest beside hers. Just not so soon, Philip Corrigan would have hoped.

Eighty-five thousand for construction and services related to Mrs. Corrigan. Another fifty grand two years later for finishing Philip Corrigan's crypt put the whole shebang into six figures for the condo-like mausoleum. According to the specifications on the bill, it had a sitting room with a concrete bench so mourners could be shielded from the midday sun, a main room with matching concrete crypts on raised platforms of coral rock, and a foyer with the inscription, "Death Pays All Debts," a fitting eulogy for a guy who leveraged construction loans into his fortune.

Charlie Riggs and I were in my Olds 442, which sported a new headlight and pounded-out hood, and responded with a happy roar coming east on Tamiami Trail. I had told Riggs about the conversation with Melanie Corrigan, leaving out the details of the slinky body and lingering kiss. Her allegations against Salisbury fascinated him.

152

"Fits a little too nicely," he said, chewing on a cold pipe. His forehead was furrowed in thought, and the lights were on behind his straw-colored eyes.

"How's that?"

"First the daughter tells you the doctor used the drug to kill Corrigan. Then the widow tells you the doctor wanted her to do it with the drug. You don't even know if the liquid the daughter showed you is succinylcholine."

"What are you saying?"

"That the two women could be framing the good doctor."

"I can't buy it. Every crime needs a motive, as you constantly remind me. Melanie Corrigan might have one, just to get rid of Salisbury. He's a pest to her. But Susan Corrigan, what could she have against Salisbury?"

Riggs tried to light his pipe, no easy task with the top down and the 442 howling at seventy-five. "Maybe nothing, except they needed a fall guy for the murder of Philip Corrigan."

"What?" I nearly lost control, swerving to avoid a dead armadillo.

"How was the estate split?"

"Melanie got the house, the yacht, and thirty percent of the gross assets. Susan got the rest after estate taxes. Neither one's going hungry."

"So they each had a motive, hypothetically at least, for wanting Philip Corrigan dead."

"Hey Doc, we're talking about a girl and her father."

"As Plautus said, *lupus est homo homini.* Man is a wolf to man. It applies to women, too. Inhumanity is often at its worst inside the family. Men beat their wives or commit incest. Wives kill their husbands, sometimes in the most

153

bizarre manner. And daughters sometimes kill their fathers."

"That's sick, Charlie."

"So it is," he said, giving up on the pipe and blinking into the wind.

We followed the stone path around the house and found Susan Corrigan just getting out of the saltwater pool. She wore a dark blue, no-nonsense Lycra competition suit. It clung to every curve and crevice of her athletic body. She put on her tortoiseshell glasses, which immediately steamed up.

"Finished with two hundred yards of butterfly," she said, puffing a little. "Gets the blood flowing."

I introduced her to Charlie Riggs, and she gave him a respectful hello and asked why the distinguished former coroner would hang around with a second-string ex-jock turned shyster. On the off chance that was a joke, I laughed like a good sport. Then I handed her a towel, but she neglected to ask me to dry her back so I didn't. Plowing common ground, I said I had read her game story from LA. *The Dolphin receivers dropped everything but their paychecks Sunday.*

"Eight dropped passes," she said, "two in the end zone, they lose by three points. And the defense played great. Did you see Tyrone Washington? Four sacks."

Charlie Riggs cleared his throat. Small talk was not his forte. "Miss Corrigan, you know what we want to do."

"Yes," she said. "Jake told me on the phone. Did you bring the papers?"

"I prepared an affidavit," I said, "but it's not going to be much good. I asked Melanie to sign it, too, to get permission from both of you, but she refused."

Susan flung the towel onto the wet pool deck. Her eyes blazed. "You did what! She killed Dad or at least helped Salisbury do it. Why would you ask her?"

"As the surviving wife and the personal representative of the estate, she technically has the right to say yes or no," I said. "And you might be wrong about her." I recounted my meeting with the widow, again leaving out the snuggling stuff.

"So," I said, "both of you accuse Roger Salisbury of poisoning your father. But she won't give permission to exhume the body. Says to let it go, she doesn't want to be involved."

"And don't you find that suspicious?" Susan asked as if I were a simpleton.

"Maybe if she hadn't tipped me to Roger in the first place, it would be suspicious. But now, I don't know."

She fastened me with an angry look I was coming to know too well. "*I* tipped you to Roger Salisbury. And now I authorize you to do the autopsy. If you won't do it, I'll go to the state attorney. He can get a warrant or something, right?"

"Right," I said. "A court order. But then you lose control of the investigation. The coroner will do it. You and Charlie and I will be out in the cold. In fact, if you tell them that you've got the succinylcholine and traces are found in the body, you'll be suspect number one."

Her eyes were flaming behind the tortoiseshell glasses. "Then what do you propose we do?"

I looked at Charlie Riggs and he looked at me. We both were thinking the same thing. We looked at Susan Corrigan,

155

whose short black hair was dripping little puddles onto the patio. We didn't say a word but she caught on.

Great minds think alike. But maybe slightly addled ones, too.

"There are some things we'll need," I said.

"I have everything back in the Glades," Charlie Riggs said.

"Tonight?" Susan Corrigan asked.

Charlie and I both nodded.

I went home to change. A charcoal suit with burgundy pinstripes is fine for lawyering, but it wouldn't do at all for my new avocation.

The saw made a frightful noise. Powered by a small gas motor, it was biting through the concrete seam of the crypt, tossing dust everywhere and making a racket that jack-hammered off the marble walls. Susan Corrigan stood guard outside the mausoleum, keeping an eye out for the night watchman.

I had second thoughts about bringing Susan on such a grisly assignment, but she was the only one who could bring us right where we needed to be. Charlie and I shouldn't be stumbling over gravestones after midnight looking for the right tomb. That was Susan's argument, anyway. Now that we were here, I saw it would have been hard to miss. Built on the top of a small knoll, the Corrigan mausoleum commanded an impressive view of a lake and the Palmetto Expressway in the sprawling southwest suburbs. I should have figured it. Even in death, Philip Corrigan adhered to the three rules of real estate: location, location, location.

I was muscling the power saw through the concrete. Charlie Riggs held a portable lamp that threw our shadows across the marble floor and up a decorative wall into which were inscribed the names of all the Corrigan shopping centers and condo projects, even the ones that resulted in class action consumer lawsuits.

I put the saw down for a rest. "This place raises ostentatiousness to new levels."

"*De gustibus non est disputandum,*" Charlie said.

"*Gesundheit,*" I said.

Charlie shook his head and grimaced. "There's no accounting for taste. Or your abysmal lack of training in Latin. Didn't you learn anything in law school?"

"Only not to draw to an inside straight," I admitted.

We went back to work. Twenty minutes later we were still watching our shadows dance up the wall when Charlie said, "Help me with this. The top's ready to move."

I got my hands into the seam and tried to lift the top. No dice. It must have weighed five hundred pounds. I put my shoulder against it and tried sliding it off. It moved two inches and sent a grinding noise up my spine.

Suddenly I heard padded footsteps on the marble floor of the foyer. A whisper from behind me, "How's it going?"

"Okay, okay," I said. "Next time, Susan, call before you drop in."

"Ignore him," Charlie said. "He's a little spooked."

I kept pushing the top of the crypt, but no traction, my sneakers slipping on the marble floor. It was like trying to move a blocking sled on a rain-slicked field with John Matuszak and Hulk Hogan sitting on top. Another inch. Nothing more. Just that damn grinding sound that maybe wouldn't bother someone used to opening tombs after midnight with the wind whistling through the gravestones.

Charlie lent me a shoulder. Another two inches. Susan pitched in and we got it going and then couldn't stop it. The concrete lid crashed to the marble floor and broke into a thousand pieces. The explosion echoed in my ears. Clouds of dust covered us and rose toward the ceiling. Someone sneezed. I hoped it was Charlie or Susan. I shined the light inside the crypt. Charlie leaned over as far as he could and patted a wooden casket.

"Good, very good indeed," he said. "Dry as toast."

I looked at Susan. "Why don't you wait for us by Charlie's truck?" Why ask her to watch as you dig out her father's body, two years in the grave. She gave me a look that said she was just as tough as me and probably a good deal more so, but she left anyway. Charlie and I went back to work. Both of us leaned on a crowbar to open the casket, a task we did in the dark because the portable light was now on the floor. The body was three feet below the top of the crypt, and since I was taller and stronger than Charlie, I was appointed as the retriever.

I leaned over, the concrete crypt folding me at the waist. I reached for what I thought would be shoulders and came up with a handful of mush.

"Yuck."

"What's the matter?" Charlie asked.

"Feels like I just stuck my hands in a barrel of apple butter."

"Mold," Charlie said. "That'd be his face. Even in a dry tomb, that'd happen."

I wiped off my hands, reached lower, found some shoulders and lifted. Lighter than I thought. Charlie put the flash-light down and held open a zippered body bag, and in a minute we were traipsing across the dew-laden grass, Charlie Riggs toting his tools in a burlap sack, and me with a body bag slung over my shoulder. Transylvania's favorite couple.

"That LA detective was wrong," I said, as we neared the truck.

"How's that?" Charlie Riggs asked.

"Marlowe, Philip Marlowe. In one of the books, he said dead men are heavier than broken hearts."

"So?"

"The former Philip Corrigan is a bantamweight."

"Bodies lose weight after death," Charlie said, as if every-body knew that.

"The ultimate diet," I concluded.

Charlie mumbled something to himself and kept walking, his scientific mind still on duty after our all-nighter. We were ten yards from the truck when Charlie stopped in his tracks. Susan Corrigan was crouched on her haunches at the rear of the pickup waiting for us, alone with her thoughts.

"Let's ID the subject," Charlie said, sounding like a homicide detective.

He unzipped the bag and popped the light into it.

"Uh-oh," I said.

"What's wrong?" Susan asked, joining us, a tremble in her voice.

"Was your father buried in a yellow chiffon dress?"

"Oh God," she said. "That's Mom and the dress is pink, or at least, it was."

"How the hell!" I shouted, nearly dropping the bag.

"I'm sorry," Susan said, her voice tight. "It's my fault. I

told you the crypt on the left, but that's looking out, not in. I got turned around."

We sat down on the wet grass, as much to rest as to figure out what to do next. We used a flattened headstone for a conference table, and like a good lawyer, I called a meeting. Moonbeams were bouncing off the pale tombstones, casting a gauzy, soft focus over Susan's features. Mood lighting. I looked at her, wondering. How could she make that mistake? Did she really want us to dig up Dad? I was thinking about what Charlie had said, homicide in the family. But I looked at Susan Corrigan in that misty moonlight and thought I saw tears in her eyes.

Crazy. A night without sleep hauling ass through a graveyard and the mind starts playing tricks. Susan Corrigan could no more kill her father than, than . . .

"Not much time," Charlie Riggs said, gesturing toward the east, where pink slivers of sky were beginning to show.

"Right," I said. "Let's put Mom in the truck and get Dad."

Like most things in life, grave robbery is easier the second time around. If we kept up our two-a-day practices like the Dolphins in August, we'd be able to purloin a body in forty-five minutes flat. This time the corpse wore a dark suit and was heavier to tote. I had it over my shoulder and was just leaving the mausoleum when I heard something, a soft singing.

Esta tarde ví llover,
Vi gente correr,
y no estabas tu.

Leather soles were scraping the marble in the foyer. Charlie and I backtracked into the mausoleum just as a flashlight poked around the corner. The night security guard.

Charlie Riggs flattened himself against a back wall. I heard his rasping breaths and hoped he wasn't going into cardiac arrest. I ducked into a shadow behind the smashed crypt, but there wasn't room for my dead buddy. Crouching like a catcher behind the plate, I gripped the seat of Philip Corrigan's pants. He stood, shakily, leaning against me like a friendly drunk. The flashlight illuminated the floor, clouds of pulverized concrete still rising from it. The dust tickled my nose, and I fought off a sneeze.

The beam bounced off the walls, and I caught sight of the guard. Private security, over sixty and overweight, probably working for minimum wage on a twelve-hour shift. The graveyard shift. In a footrace he couldn't beat Philip Corrigan.

The flashlight beam struck Corrigan's black shoes and inched up his body, finally coming to rest on a waxy, moldy face, a nose that melted into soggy cheeks.

"Madre de Dios," the guard murmured.

I was holding my breath, then had to inhale. More dust, then without warning, "AH-CHOO!"

The sound came from me, but all the guard could see was Philip Corrigan, his head flopping forward as my grip loosened.

"Don't worry," I whispered from the darkness. "Dead men don't sneeze."

The guard took a step backward. *"Jesús Cristo!"*

I raised one of Corrigan's arms, stiffly pointed a rotting

hand at the waxy face and said, "No way José. *Yo soy el anti-Cristo.*"

The flashlight clattered to the floor and the guard took off. A moment later, so did we, Philip Corrigan draped over my shoulder, Charlie Riggs hustling behind me, chuckling. Whistling past the graveyard.

The black night had turned to silvery morning and the early commuters were heading north on the Palmetto, tiny shafts of headlights cutting through the mist. We loaded the truck and joined in but headed south. The expressway dumped us onto South Dixie Highway, U.S. 1, the road that starts in Maine and ends at Key West. We aimed that way, past a hundred gas stations and fast-food joints, chintzy strip shopping centers with pet stores and scuba shops, boarded-up small businesses, a thousand broken dreams. Down through Kendall and Perrine, past mango groves, strawberry fields, and packing houses, through Homestead by the Air Force base, over the Card Sound Bridge, through Key Largo and south some more.

None of us said a word, not the three of us jammed into the cab up front, and certainly not the two reunited in a zippered bag in the back. The Corrigans probably hadn't been this close since their honeymoon.

I handled the driving. Susan sat next to me, the closest she'd been since I tackled her on the practice field. Charlie Riggs was slumped against the passenger door, snoring peacefully. Near Tavernier, Susan's head dropped onto my shoulder, and I put my arm around her. This time, she didn't give me the boot. I thought she was sleeping, but a moment later she whispered, "Thank you, Jake."

162

I looked down at her, not knowing where she was headed.

"I was wrong to be so petulant when we first met," she said. "I was hurting so much. Losing Mom, then Dad marrying that woman, and Dad dying that way . . ."

"I understand," I said, feeling her soften under my arm.

"You've taken a big risk. I know you want to learn the truth about what happened, but I know you did it for me, too. And every time you try to get through to me, I put you off. I won't do that anymore."

I started to say something, but she put a finger to my lips. So I kissed the finger, steered with my left hand and tried not to put the truck into the Atlantic on the east side of the road or the Gulf on the west. Then I felt her face against my neck, and she nuzzled me with her upturned nose, looped her right arm around my chest and gave me a good squeeze. A fine and dandy squeeze.

The sun was well up in the eastern sky by the time we pulled into the dusty road on the Gulf of Mexico side of Islamorada. The shutters were open in the small wooden house and the aroma of strong coffee and sizzling bacon greeted us. We parked in the sand under a jacaranda tree that had lost its flowers for the winter. A royal tern sat in the tree, staring at us from under its black and white cap.

"Look what the cat drug in," Granny Lassiter said from the front porch. "Jake, you look like the loser in a mud rasslin' match." Granny sat in a pine rocking chair drinking coffee from an oversized mug. She wore khaki pants and a colorful Mexican serape. A high-crowned sombrero rested on her upper back, the drawstring tied under her chin. Her features were still strong, high cheekbones and a pugnacious chin. The hair that had been jet black when I was a boy was streaked down the middle with a bright white stripe like the center line on the highway locals call Useless 1. Granny's buddies called her "Skunky," but only after downing a good portion of her home brew.

I introduced Doc Riggs to Granny. He bowed formally, complimented her south-of-the-border outfit, and recounted one of his visits to the pyramids of the Yucatan with a graphic description of Mayan hieroglyphics and burial practices.

"It's a pleasure to have a man of learning and culture in my abode," she said, swiping at some loose strands of her hair. "Perhaps you could be a good influence on that wastrel mouthpiece kin of mine."

"Granny, please," I pleaded.

She ignored me and turned her attention to Susan Corrigan, whose dark eyes were puffy from a sleepless night but still fetching. "And you must be the gal Jacob's been telling me about. Uh-huh, I see why. You're a keeper."

"Granny!" I bellowed, warning her.

"Pay him no mind," she said. "Like most men, he don't know which end is up. After some breakfast, they'll do their work, and we'll drop a line in the Gulf and do some talking. Tell me, girl, you see anything in Jacob worth losing sleep over?"

"He's got potential," Susan allowed.

Granny laughed. "That boy's gonna grow old having potential."

I had heard enough. "Maybe we should get to work," I suggested.

"Sure 'nuff," Granny said. "The beer cellar's chilled

down all the way, just like you said. Plus I got this filled with ice."

She pointed at a fish box that came from her old Bertram. It could easily hold both bodies.

Charlie Riggs eyed the box. "Forty-seven degrees would be perfect. That's what we keep the coolers in the morgue. Too cold is no good. Can't let the tissues freeze."

"So let's get started," I suggested again.

"No hurry, Jake," Charlie Riggs said, beaming at Granny. "No hurry at all."

Granny straightened up the front porch, swiping leaves off the wicker chairs with a palm frond. Then she poured everyone coffee, starting with Charlie Riggs. "Say Doc, I recognized you right off from the TV. The case of the capsized dory. Off Saddlebunch Key. You haven't changed a bit."

"Twenty years ago," Charlie said, shaking his head.

"*Tempus fugit*," Granny said, and Charlie's eyes lit up as if he'd found a long lost friend.

We all sat on the porch and Granny made a fuss over Charlie, who sat there reminiscing with his feet propped on the fish box that now held the Corrigans. Told us about the man whose wife drowned when their dory overturned, striking her head. The water had been calm, and the husband was a strong swimmer.

"So why didn't he save her?" Susan asked, snatching the bait like a hungry grouper.

A sly smile and Charlie continued. "Maybe his lifeguard's carry was weighted down by the million-dollar double indemnity policy he just bought on the lady's life."

Aha, we all said.

"He let her drown," Susan offered.

Charlie shook his head. "Worse than that."

"How'd you prove it?"

Another smile. "I put one of those department store mannequins in the dory facing front, just where the wife had been sitting. Sat in the back where the husband had been, stood up and smacked the mannequin with the oar. Left a mark the exact size and location of the bruise on top the dead wife's head."

The man got ninety-nine years, Charlie a TV interview.

Granny put her arm around Susan and steered her into the house. I hauled the body bag into the darkened room Granny called her beer cellar. The room was actually on the first floor, it being hard to dig a cellar when your house is built three feet above sea level. Inside were vats and bottles and the odds and ends used to make the home brew Granny gave away to neighboring fishermen. Two old air-conditioning units were turned on full blast and water dripped down the walls.

I suggested we cut first, eat breakfast later. I couldn't imagine doing the job on a full stomach. Charlie said he understood, then grabbed an old brown satchel from the cab of the truck. He unbuckled the worn leather straps and looked lovingly at half a dozen scalpels glinting in the light of the midday sun.

14

DEAD MEN
DON'T BLEED

"The skin is macerated and there's mold on the face, but all things considered, not bad, not bad at all," Charlie Riggs said. He was washing off the body with a hose. The remains of Philip Corrigan were spread out on an old work table in Granny's beer cellar. "Before we do any cutting, let's examine the body."

He slipped on surgical gloves and started poking and pinching various parts of the corpse, squinting hard through his half-glasses. In formal tones he continued, "The subject is a well-developed white male, age indeterminate due to deterioration of the face. The head and neck appear to be symmetrical and exhibit no masses. The chest is symmetrical and the abdomen flat. The body is in an excellent state of preservation due to the embalming and a nearly dry tomb. There is evidence of two surgical procedures in close proximity to death, unhealed wounds from both back and abdominal surgery."

He went on that way for a while, as if the tape recorder with the microphone swinging from the ceiling was still there, as if he was still the medical examiner and as if homicide detectives still waited outside for his findings. A little sad, a man retired before his time, maybe a different kind of death.

Charlie brought a lamp closer to the body, illuminating a small area of skin at a time. "Now for a closer look." He started with the arms and worked down. I helped him flip the body onto its stomach. "Hullo! What's this, Jake? Right buttock, upper quadrant."

"Looks like a freckle."

"Come closer, my boy. *Mortui non mordent,* dead men don't bite."

"No, they smell." I moved close but it still looked like a freckle.

"A puncture wound," Charlie said triumphantly. "Pretty large gauge hypodermic, too."

"You sure?"

He didn't say yes and he didn't say no. He picked up a scalpel and swiftly dissected a piece of meat that used to be Philip Corrigan's flabby ass. In a moment Charlie held a cross section of the buttock, down through the fat, all the way into the muscle.

"There it is," he announced. I looked at a red streak,

maybe three inches long. "That's the needle track, just as fresh as when it was made. Had to be done *in articulo mortis*, or there'd be evidence of healing."

I wasn't convinced. "It could have been a routine injection in connection with the laminectomy or the emergency abdominal surgery."

"Could have been," Charlie said, "but it's not on the charts. No doctor or nurse recorded it."

"Maybe the puncture was made after death. Something the undertaker did, I don't know."

"No way. See the little trail alongside the track, that's the hemorrhage. He had to be alive when the needle was injected."

"Dead men don't bleed," I said.

"You're catching on, Jake."

"Okay, so *somebody* injected *something* into Philip Corrigan. Hard to make a case of that. What next?"

He wrinkled his forehead. "The tissues will have to be checked for succinic acid and choline. Your granny doesn't have a GCMS on the premises, I suppose."

"Not unless it's used for bonefishing or bootlegging."

Charlie held the slice of Corrigan's flesh up to the light. "Gas chromatographic spectrometer. Test for toxic substances. We'll need some brain and liver tissue, but first I'm going to do the work-up in the usual way."

The usual way. Like it was something he did every day. Which it was. Every working day for over thirty years. Thousands of bodies. So he did it without pausing, opening the neck just below the ear, making a long, smooth incision to the top of the chest and then to the other ear. He pulled up the flap of skin and exposed the inside of the neck. He deftly carved a slice straight down the chest over the sternum, avoiding the navel. He showed me where the embalming fluid had gone in, the spot being hard to miss, a thumb screw in the chest where the mortician inserted the trocar.

He peeled the skin flaps down over the chest, like pulling on an undersized sweater, exposing bright yellow fatty tissue and purple organs. He snapped the sternum in two with rib shears that looked like hedge clippers, probed into the abdomen, and made a dissection of the aorta. The punctured aneurysm was in the front, right where he had testified it was. He hummed under his breath as he worked. It sounded like "Born Free."

"Let's open the aorta and look for chalky deposits," he said brightly. "Give me some light over here, Jake."

I did what I was told and Charlie went about his business. Happy to be in control, to be taking things apart and figuring them out. Alive again. "Some evidence of sclerosis, but nothing unusual in a man of his age. Not enough to block the blood flow. Probably not enough to cause the aneurysm."

"So you hoodwinked the jury with that arteriosclerosis stuff."

"Didn't mean to. I figured the sclerosis was worse."

"So what killed him?" I asked.

"Something that caused the aneurysm, and if Roger Salisbury didn't do it and the sclerotic changes didn't do it, there's got to be something else."

I was confused. "What about the drug?"

He smiled, and his eyes crinkled, and behind them his computer was whirring, a lifetime of experience filtering the information. "It doesn't add up, not yet. Even if the tests are positive for the succinylcholine, the fact remains that he died of the aneurysm."

"I don't get it. If we find traces of the drug, that means Roger injected Corrigan—or somebody did—trying to kill him. If Corrigan was still alive when he was injected, which you say he had to be, it would have killed him. But you're saying he had the aneurysm after the injection. So what killed him and who killed him?"

Charlie caught himself before he stroked his beard with a gunked-up hand. "It's a puzzle, Jake, and we don't have enough pieces yet. But if we find the what, it'll lead us to the who. So if you'll stop talking and stand back, I'll finish the autopsy in the usual way."

The usual way again. He unpacked a portable scale, removed the heart, weighed it—four hundred fifty grams—poked around in more blood vessels, snipped here and clipped there, examining organs I didn't know existed. I was okay so far. I was okay when he cracked the ribs to get underneath. I was okay when he sliced off a piece of the liver and slipped it into a plastic lunch bag. I was okay when the band saw bit into the skull. But when he pulled the brain out, tut-tutting because it was shrunken and dehydrated, I wasn't okay. Things went a little gray, the beer cellar listed like a dinghy in rough chop, and the next thing I knew, Granny Lassiter was saying something and squeezing an ammonia-soaked rag under my nose.

I coughed and sputtered and got to my feet with Susan Corrigan's help and found I was on the front porch. Granny laughed and handed me a mason jar filled with home brew. "Drink this, Jacob. It'll put hair on your chest."

PAUL LEVINE

"I'm okay, I'm okay." I dusted myself off. Nothing like having two women fussing over your fallen body.

Susan Corrigan had on a funny half-smile and was holding on to my arm, propping me up. "I kind of like you this way. None of your macho bullshit."

"Great, I'll faint every chance I get. Promise you won't take advantage of me when I'm out?"

"No promises. Now just hush up. You need something to eat. Granny's making conch omelets with salsa."

In a few minutes Charlie joined us in the kitchen. He washed up and wrapped both hands around a mug of coffee, letting the steam rise through a steeple of fingers. After a while he briefed us. I watched Susan's face as Charlie talked about the puncture in the buttocks. It seemed to be what she wanted to hear, but she frowned when Charlie said there was nothing conclusive. Had to test the tissues and still figure out where the aneurysm fit in.

"The doctor and that bitch did it," Susan declared abruptly. "I just know it."

"We'll find out," Charlie promised. "I still have a couple friends on the toxicology staff at the ME's office. I can sneak in after-hours and use the equipment."

"Why not just bring Dr. MacKenzie in on it?" I suggested.

Charlie snorted. "That prick, excuse my English, wouldn't piss on me if I was on fire. I didn't recommend him for the ME's job when I retired, and now that he's got it, the Ivy League twit won't forgive me. Loves his computers and statistics and that damn new building with its creature comforts. Hell, they got air fresheners in the morgue now, you can't use your nose anymore to smell stomach contents. You

172

know one time I opened a John Doe, smelled a familiar barbecue sauce. Full of vinegar, a touch of beer. Knew right away it was that ribs place on South Dixie. Homicide went down there, a waiter remembered the decedent and the guy he was with. Got a confession when they tracked the guy down."

Charlie went on like that for a while, unhappy with Dr. Hilton MacKenzie, the new ME who didn't like getting his hands dirty. "They built him a new building, state-of-the-art morgue, full of offices, as many administrators as the Department of Public Works, a lobby looks like a Hyatt. I remember our first morgue, just an abandoned garage. Hell, we did twenty-five hundred autopsies a year in the little building on Northwest Nineteenth Street. Then, after the boatlift, between the *Marielitos* knifing everybody and the Colombian cowboys machine-gunning each other, we ran out of cooler space. No place to put the stiffs."

"What'd you do?" Susan asked, always the inquisitive journalist.

"Rented a Burger King refrigerated truck," Charlie said. "Talk about a meat wagon. We stacked the bodies inside, put the truck in a parking lot by Jackson Memorial. Next thing you know, somebody hijacks it. Probably thought there was forty grand worth of burgers inside. Would have loved to see their faces when they busted open the trailer."

Charlie Riggs was into his storytelling. Finally, as the day wore on, the activities of last night caught up with all of us. Charlie took a nap, dozing on the front porch, mouth open, wheezing like an old Chevy. I curled up on a couch in the Florida room. A cool breeze from the Gulf whispered through open shutters. Granny tucked me in with a homemade quilt, just like the old days. Maybe later she'd drive me to Little League practice. I was halfway to dreamland when a second body joined me under the quilt.

"I'm too tired to race you to the goal line," I murmured.

"No hurry," Susan Corrigan said. "Take your time."

She kissed me very gently and then rubbed my chin with her fingertips. "You need a shave," she said. She stroked the stubble against the grain and kissed my neck. She pulled up my polo shirt and started kissing my chest. Wait a second. When I grew up, it was the guy who did the tussling with the clothes, the discovering of body parts. But I was not about to object. It would have been overruled. And I was enjoying the attention. When I tried to take the offensive, she gently pushed me down, gave me a *just relax* order with her eyes, and went about her business.

I was on my back, my clothes on the floor when she slipped out of her things, her small breasts tracing circles on my chest. From nowhere she produced a condom, as indispensable as lipstick to the modern woman. She slipped it on me without either snapping it like a slingshot or gouging me with a fingernail. Then, strong legs astride me, she eased downward, taking me in, tightening onto me. She exhaled deep surging breaths, all the time raising and lowering herself like a lifter doing squats.

I was liking it, liking her. But all the time watching her, and not just the curve of the hips. Watching her face, thinking about her and Roger Salisbury and Melanie Corrigan. And very rich, very dead Philip Corrigan. And who did what to whom.

Always thinking, damn it! Instead of just feeling. Thinking about the hacked up body a few feet away. Why not just enjoy the thrusting and the swampy heat rising from amidships? Damn it to hell, Lassiter.

I slept some more and when I awoke it was dark in the little house. Susan Corrigan purred next to me, stretched a leg until the calf muscle peaked, then curled up again. I thought about her. Smart and sassy. Part of the new breed. Toughing it out in a man's world. Elbowing past male reporters to get the best quotes in a locker room. Ignoring the wiseguys—*what happened to sportswriters who pissed standing up?*—dishing it out as well as taking it. This was the Susan Corrigan I knew. Which only made me realize I didn't know her very well at all.

I got up without disturbing her and poked around in the dark. No sign of Charlie or Granny. I found some smoked mackerel in the refrigerator and, still disoriented, tried to remember if this was dinner or a late snack. The house was quiet, the only sounds the palm fronds outside, slapping against each other in the breeze from the Gulf. I padded around to Granny's bedroom. The door was open a crack, a hurricane lamp burning by the night table. I should check on her. As she checked on me a thousand nights. She was there, under her own tufted quilt, sleeping peacefully, breathing steadily, her arms wrapped around the happy, slumbering hulk of Charles W. Riggs, M.D.

15

THE CONCH
BRIGADE

No cops waited to arrest me at my little house off Kumquat Avenue; no reporters paced in the waiting room of my office. For a while, I thought The Great Graveyard Robbery might have been a dream. I was sitting at my desk Monday morning, sipping black coffee, peaceful as a monk, when I found the story on page 7 of the Local section:

> *Vandals destroyed a double gravesite and removed two bodies from the Eternal Memories Mortuary and Mausoleum over the weekend, Metro police reported yesterday. The bodies of Philip R. Corrigan and Sylvia Corri-*

gan, his wife, were taken from a private crypt at the southwest Dade cemetery, according to police spokesmen. Mr. Corrigan, who died in 1986, was a well-known builder whose projects often were opposed by environmental groups. His wife died two years earlier.

"This looks like the work of the Conch Brigade," said Metro Sgt. Joaquin Castillo, referring to the radical Keys group that advocates violence to stop construction in environmentally sensitive areas.

Because the Conch Brigade refuses to identify its members, no one with that organization could be reached for comment. Police estimate the damage to the crypt at $50,000.

Wacky. So far off that, weirdly, it was not far wrong. The Conch Brigade consisted of vicious terrorist Granny Lassiter, part-time septic tank cleaner Virgil Thigpen, and two unemployed shrimpers who could be found fishing for snook in Hell's Bay when not in jail for public drunkenness.

The newspaper made no mention of the recent malpractice trial and said nothing about the security guard seeing anything suspicious. I figured the cops made no connection with Salisbury, and the guard wasn't about to describe his close encounter with a moldy ghost. No suspects except a phantom group.

There wouldn't be much of an investigation. A penny-ante crime in Dade County, particularly on the weekend a DEA agent got hit in the head with two hundred pounds of twenty-dollar bills. Sent him to the hospital with a concussion and he couldn't even keep the money. It was evidence against a North Miami drug dealer named Guillermo Montalvo. When federal agents surrounded his house, Montalvo tossed the money—trussed up like a bale of hay—out a second story window. It glanced off the head of the agent, who wore a bulletproof vest but no hockey helmet. How much money is there in two hundred pounds of twenties? Exactly one million, eight hundred thousand, one hundred eighty dollars, according to the feds, who often weigh the take because counting it takes so much time.

The same day another federal agent got shot in the gun. Not the gut, the gun. After selling a kilo of cocaine in a sting operation, the agent drew his nine-millimeter SIG-Sauer semiautomatic handgun. The stingee, one Angel Morales, did the same thing. Morales shot his weapon first, and his bullet lodged in the agent's gun barrel. Morales had little time to enjoy his marksmanship. Four Hialeah cops who had been lurking in the bushes emptied twenty-two rounds into Morales, then kicked him in the groin for good measure.

So with everything going on, the police couldn't be expected to worry about a little old-fashioned grave robbing. I did wonder, though, if Roger had heard about it. And Melanie Corrigan. Surely the police would call her. Maybe we should put a tail on her, see if she and Roger have a tête-à-tête to talk it over. My musings were interrupted by Cindy, buzzing me.

"Some bimbo for you on two, *su majestad.*"

"She have a name?"

"Sure, and a voice like melted butter."

"Please, Cindy, I'm not in the mood for Twenty Questions. Been a hard weekend and a crummy day."

"Mis-sus Philip Corrigan, and she asked for *Jacob* Lassiter."

Uh-oh.

I decided not to be expecting the call, but not to be surprised either.

"Jake," she said when I gave her a flat-toned hello, "I'm afraid there's been some trouble."

She waited a moment. I let her wait some more, then said, "I saw the story in the paper. What's going on?"

"I don't know but it's tearing me apart. You can't imagine the pain. I just keep thinking about him desecrating Philip's tomb, stealing the body, it's so terrible."

"Him?"

"Roger, of course. Who else would do it, unless that little bitch daughter was involved."

Whoops. A tiny shiver went through me, an icicle dripping down my back. Let's find out what she knows.

"Why would Susan be involved? Why Roger? Why anybody?"

"I don't know, maybe they killed him together. Now they're disposing of the evidence."

"What about Sylvia Corrigan, why her body?"

Silence. Then, "Why don't you ask the good doctor?"

So many questions, so few answers. "Why are you calling me?"

"I thought I could hire you, retain you, as my lawyer."

Suddenly I'm in demand. The doctor, the daughter, the widow. "I don't think so. I'm not sure you need a lawyer, and anyway, my representation of Roger Salisbury disqualifies me."

"I'm sorry to hear that," she said, sounding very sorry indeed. "We could have worked well together."

There was a hint there, an unmistakably seductive hint, the striking of a tiny spark that could be fanned into a flame with a few more whispers or the friction of that firm, sleek body against mine. It was her petition for rehearing. I decided to let the ruling stand.

"I'm sorry, Mrs. Corrigan," I said, as proper as a councilman declining a bribe. "It just wouldn't work."

"Then I guess I'll just do what I have to without your advice or assistance."

I let it hang there and we said our good-byes. I gave my conscience a pat on the back, the vision of Melanie Corrigan's unsheathed body a shooting star across the black sky of my mind.

The appointment was for two o'clock but Roger Salisbury was ten minutes early. Unusual for a doctor. He wore a coat and tie. Unusual, too. Doctors hereabouts usually sport the open-collar look—white smock or lab coat—and scruffy sneakers. Not Roger. Blue blazer, gray slacks, penny loafers. A frat man look. He gave Cindy a big hello, peeked out the window at one of the cruise ships chugging out Government Cut, then settled in a cushioned chair next to a thirsty rubber plant.

Charlie Riggs trundled in twenty minutes later, apologizing for being late. Just came from his semiannual haircut and beard trim, a Miccosukee barber in the Everglades. You could hardly tell he used a sawtooth fishing knife, I told Charlie, and he thanked me. Then Charlie cleared his throat, stroked his newly pruned beard, and slid his warped glasses back up the bridge of his tiny nose. Which was a signal for me to start.

"Roger, this is awkward for Charlie and me."

Expressionless, Roger Salisbury looked at Charlie, then

back at me, and I continued, "I have a confession to make—"

Roger laughed. "That's what clients usually do to their lawyers, right?"

"Right, but this case is different in a lot of ways. You know somebody broke into Philip Corrigan's crypt, stole the body?"

"Saw the story in the paper. Pretty bizarre. Antidevelopment nuts in the Keys, maybe."

Doc Riggs cleared his throat again. I swallowed and said, "A couple of nuts, all right. Charlie and I did it."

He raised his eyebrows. "No. Why?"

"Susan Corrigan wanted the body tested, Melanie Corrigan didn't. We chose sides. But I wanted to tell you before we deliver tissue samples to the lab. And I wanted to ask you, is there anything you want to tell us?"

Roger shrugged. "What would I want to say?"

If he was faking it, he must have taken some acting courses along with biology and chemistry. "Okay, Roger, here it is. Melanie told me you tried to get her to inject her husband with succinylcholine, and when she wouldn't do it, you did, murdered Corrigan in his hospital room."

A cloud crossed his face. A look more of bewilderment than anger. "Do you believe her?"

I paused long enough for Charlie Riggs to light his pipe. It took three matches. "No. I don't believe her. Since that day you brought the malpractice complaint to me, I've gotten to know you, and I don't believe you could kill."

Roger Salisbury beamed. I continued, "But what's been gnawing at me is that nothing about Corrigan's death makes sense. You didn't cause the aneurysm and, apparently, the sclerosis didn't either. The hospital charts show no injections in the buttocks but Charlie found one. Then there's the succinylcholine . . ."

Salisbury turned to Charlie Riggs. "Succinylcholine wouldn't be traceable, would it? Doesn't it break down into succinic acid and choline?"

I studied Roger while Charlie tamped his pipe and answered. "Yes, but those substances are detectable in various tissues. If there's too great a quantity, a reasonable inference would be that succinylcholine was injected shortly prior to death."

No reaction. Absolute calm. "You're the expert," Salisbury said in a neutral voice. "And if you want to test the tissues, I don't have a problem."

I was feeling good about Roger Salisbury. Confident in his innocence. Then he said, "Melanie knows the truth, and if you really want to know, I mean if it matters to you, Jake, just get her to tell you."

"And how do I do that?"

"I could inject her with thiopental sodium."

"Huh?"

Charlie chimed in. "Sodium five-ethyl-five-one-methylbutyl-two-thiobarbiturate. More commonly known by its trade name, Pentothal."

"Truth serum?" I asked, louder than necessary.

"A misnomer," Charlie said, "but you get the idea. A central nervous system depressant. In the right quantities, it induces hypnosis and, yes, the patient will tell the truth about past events."

"I could stick her, and we could snatch her," Roger said blithely, as if assault and abduction were standard topics of discussion. "Bring her someplace safe, and you could cross-examine her. You're so good at that, Jake. Then you'd learn the truth. I want you to believe me."

I looked at Charlie Riggs. He looked at me. In ninety seconds, my client had gone from innocent physician to lunatic kidnapper.

"Roger, I don't think we could do that," I said, gently.

He shrugged and said okay, then offered to take me bonefishing in the Keys sometimes. I made a bad joke about an orthopod bonefishing, and he headed for Mercy Hospital to do a knee replacement.

I put my feet up on my cluttered desk, and Charlie Riggs stoked his pipe. He didn't look at me, and I didn't look at him. I wanted him to say something, but he wouldn't. So I did. "Is it my imagination, or is my client sailing without a rudder?"

Charlie stood up and walked to the window. He squinted into the brightness and looked due east over the ocean toward Bimini. "Fantasies. I think Roger Salisbury has difficulty distinguishing fantasy from reality. He wanted Melanie for himself and might have wished Philip dead. Maybe told Melanie so. But judging from his reaction today, I would say he didn't kill Philip Corrigan. And he wants you to know that. He respects you, Jake. He wants you to like him—"

"So we can be fishing buddies."

"Something like that. So he fantasizes about injecting her with Pentothal."

"All of which means he's a dreamer, not a killer."

Charlie Riggs sent me a swirl of cherry-flavored smoke. "Unless the fantasies take over. Unless they become reality. Then, *Deus misereatur*, may God have mercy . . ."

I read my mail, returned some calls, skipped a partners' meeting called to debate new artwork for the reception area—Andy Wyeth was a five-to-one favorite over Andy Warhol—and headed for *The Miami Herald*. Susan Corrigan was waiting for me on the bayfront walkway behind the building. She stood silently watching a barge unload huge rolls of newsprint onto the dock. The drawbridge on the MacArthur Causeway was up, two hundred motorists waiting for one rich guy in a gussied up Hinckley to putt-putt underneath at three knots. A stiff, warm breeze from the east crackled an American flag flying above the walkway, and the Miami sun beat hard against the concrete.

Susan wore her reporter's uniform, running shoes, faded jeans with a notepad sticking out the back pocket. Her glasses were propped on top of her short black hair. On the barge a forklift kept picking up the newsprint and rolling it down a ramp onto the dock.

"They killed a lot of trees just so you could write about some overgrown boys in plastic hats and knickers chasing a funny-shaped ball."

She jumped a half step. "Oh, you startled me. I was thinking."

"And not about me."

"About you a little," she said, honest to a fault. "More about Dad and everything that's happened. Have you heard from Charlie?"

"Not yet. Expect something tomorrow."

"What do we do then? I mean, if the report says the drug is in the brain and the liver."

"I don't know. I'm taking this one step at a time. Today,

Charlie and I told Roger that we had the body and were having it tested. He didn't seem to care. So far nothing makes sense."

She thought about it a moment. "You could get in trouble for this, couldn't you?"

"What, for trespassing, destruction of property, grave robbing, and turning in my own client? Nothing worse than disbarment plus a short stay at Avon Park as a first offender."

"So why do it?"

The Hinckley chugged by, a pot-bellied middle-aged guy and three smug teenagers waving at us. The drawbridge clanked into place, the groan of metal on metal as its fittings meshed. Finally I said, "I guess I'm still looking for the good guys."

"Good guys?"

"Something I told Roger Salisbury. That I keep looking for the good guys and never find them."

She leaned close and kissed me on the lips. "Am I a good guy?"

Funny, I'd been wondering the same thing myself. "I hope so, because I've joined your side, abandoned Roger. I've stopped caring about the rules of the game, just want to do what's right."

"Sounds noble."

"Stupid, maybe. Maybe I'm swayed by those deep, dark eyes and the way you snuggle under a quilt."

She stiffened. "If you believe that, maybe you should quit the game altogether. Hit the showers."

I didn't believe it. I smiled at her and she knew I didn't believe it. She had me pretty good, and she knew that, too.

She popped me a playful punch in the shoulder. Her playful punch could leave a dent.

"Take me home," she said. "Let's see how much room there is in my shower stall. Afterwards, I may even put on a skirt and let you buy me dinner."

The Olds 442 found the Corrigan home just as before. Buttoned up tight. Dark and quiet. Either the rich don't make any noise or Melanie Corrigan was entertaining under the sheets. No motorcycle out front either, so little chance of running into Hercules.

We walked around back to the cabana. Dark inside, but the front door was wide open, hanging loose on a hinge. There was the moment of disbelief, that if you blink once, the scene will change, but it didn't. I flicked on the lights. The place was torn up, and a pretty good job of it, drawers pulled out, books spilled onto the floor, clothing strewn about. Susan made a small noise, deep in her throat, then ran into the tiny bedroom and hauled a golf bag out of the closet. The clubs were scattered across the floor, a three-wood jammed angrily into a planter. She reached into the bag, fingers clawing at the leather, not finding what she wanted.

"Damn, damn," she cried, tears forming. "It's gone. They've got it. They've got the evidence."

I knew what was gone. A little leather bag with a vial of liquid and two hypodermics. I just didn't know who *they* were.

16

OH NO,
SOCOLOW

When you live outside the law, you forfeit certain privileges. Like calling the police when you need them. In these parts, drug dealers are frequently robbed. Sometimes by other drug dealers, sometimes by cops. It's a fact of life that dopers won't blow the whistle. Their cars get blown up, their houses riddled with automatic weapons, their drugs and cash stolen. They write off the losses as part of overhead.

So here we were, a couple of upstanding, taxpaying citizens, a journalist and a lawyer, unable to call the cops. A smart cop would ask too many questions. *You say this drug might have killed Philip Corrigan. Say, wasn't his body stolen over the weekend?* A dumb cop wouldn't do us any good.

We cleaned up the mess. Nothing else was missing. Even the X-rated tape was still on the shelf, tucked away in a stack of exercise videos and feature films.

I tried to put two and two together. I kept getting Melanie Corrigan. The drug came from Melanie's bedroom, but Susan found it more than a year after Philip Corrigan died. Why keep a murder weapon around?

To use it again.

Maybe, I told myself. But Charlie Riggs says succinylcholine will lose its potency unless it's kept cold. Maybe Melanie doesn't know that. Or maybe she doesn't care. Maybe Roger Salisbury had already used it to kill her husband.

Roger a killer? No way. Not even concerned that we've got the body. A trifle weird, maybe. Walking a little close to the border of Fantasyland, as Charlie Riggs suggested. But not a killer.

Okay, I try something else. When Melanie finally gets around to putting on some underwear, she notices the drug's gone. It must incriminate her, or she wouldn't care about it. She suspects Susan, her nemesis. She has to get back the evidence to get rid of it, so she has Sergio bust up the front door of the cabana to make it look like a two-bit B&E. Or what was it the Nixon White House called Watergate? A third-rate burglary.

But what if I'm wrong about Roger? Maybe he and Melanie snuffed the old man. She keeps the drug as insurance against him fingering her. When it's gone, she tells him to get it back or they're both looking at a Murder One.

I didn't buy it. Maybe there was no burglary. Maybe Susan Corrigan ruffled her own sheets, got rid of the drug for her own reasons. But looking at the tears in her eyes as she cradled the empty golf bag, that made no sense to me, none at all.

I didn't want Susan staying in the little cabana, not with the door split open, so we headed to Coconut Grove and my coral rock fortress. I told her to wait outside under a jacaranda tree. Then I opened the front door slowly, stepping into the stale air, seeing shapes in the darkness. Looking for a karate freak crouched behind the sofa, waiting for the hardwood floor to creak. But the shadows held only dust and the only sounds came from a dripping faucet.

I turned on the lights and Susan stepped in boldly, and with a look of amusement, examined the spare furnishings. Her eyes sized up my little house like a broker on commission. She might wear sweats and sneakers, but underneath, she was still a rich girl who knew Chippendale from flea market.

"What's a guy like you doing in a place like this?" she asked, a lilt to her voice.

"What's a girl like you doing with a guy like me?"

She just smiled and stripped off her jeans. The adrenaline rush had ebbed, but I had enough energy left to carry her up the narrow staircase.

This time she let me take the lead, maybe content that she had already established her strength and independence. Once, she whispered, "Never stop," and at the end, she gave a yelp usually reserved for overtime victories in playoff games, and I let go with a little *whoopee-ti-ti-yo* myself. She fell asleep in my arms, her face innocent as a Norman Rockwell bride. But I was wide awake. I tucked her in and went downstairs to think.

Sometimes the best tactic is to wade right into it, pour gasoline on the flames, and see what's left after the explosion. First though, I poured myself a Grolsch. Then I dialed Roger Salisbury's number. It was nearly midnight.

"Jake, old boy, great to hear your voice. Just talking about you." *Old boy*. That was a new one, maybe into a polo-playing phase. Wonder if he'll be as chipper after I accuse him of icing Philip Corrigan. But I never got the chance. He said, "There's somebody here who'd like to say hello."

There was a short pause, a woman's soft laugh, then a silken voice. "Jacob Lassiter, how nice of you to call. We're having some champagne and caviar and other edible things. You can join us if you like. Two's company, three's a party."

Another laugh and Roger Salisbury was back on the line. "Jake, I'm so damn happy. Just like the old days. And I'll be forever grateful to you. You're a real friend."

"Sure Roger. Sure."

A little giggling, two sweethearts pressed up to the phone, ear to ear. Roger breathed a long *whoosh* into the phone and said, "Melanie, that can wait, whoa! Hey Jake, I got a hard-on that could plant the flag on Iwo Jima."

"Semper Fi," I said, thinking these two are made for each other. She accuses him of murder; he wants to stick her with a needle. One day, he's punching her out; next day, she's running it up his flagpole.

I wished him well, hung up, and tried to sort it out. Now I believed more than ever in Roger's innocence. If Roger was in it with Melanie Corrigan, he wouldn't let me know she was there. The two of them would go through the ruse of hating each other, particularly if they sensed an investigation would start up after the body disappeared. Unless it was a double twist, the old trick from "The Purloined Letter," making the fruit of the crime so obvious that it's hard to see. Too complicated. I rejoined Susan and fell asleep thinking about it, hearing a woman's laughter—mocking me—in my dreams.

At mid-morning Susan and I drove back to her cabana to look around in the light of day. I heard a motor cranking up as we walked around the house, and we caught sight of a Boston Whaler Temptation, a twenty-two-foot outboard, pulling away from the dock. Handling the wheel was a chunk of muscle who looked familiar and stretched out on a cooler in front of the console was the bikini-clad body of Melanie Corrigan. The widow had covered a lot of territory in the last twenty-four hours.

We ducked behind a poinciana tree and watched them slowly cross the lagoon into open water.

"Gone fishin'," I said.

"Doubt it," Susan said. "I don't think that woman's ever been on the Whaler. It's really a tender for the yacht. The man is Sergio Machado-Alvarez."

"We've met. Where do you suppose they're going?"

Susan shaded her eyes against the sun and shrugged. The Whaler headed into the bay between the channel markers, lazing at low speed. Still within sight, it dropped anchor.

"Great. We may have enough time if they stay put," I said.

The ancient Olds resisted, but I peeled rubber like a teenage punk and we slid around curves on the winding road to the marina at Matheson Hammock barely two miles away. The dockmaster there was an old client, but not exactly blue chip.

Bluegill Ovelman was shirtless and barefoot. He had a belly like a rain barrel and hands like grappling hooks. He was an old salt, an ex—commercial fisherman who earned his *ex* the third time he was arrested by the Marine Patrol. I kept him out of jail each time the patrol found a mess of undersize Florida lobsters in his cooler. The last time I persuaded the jury that Bluegill measured his catch in centimeters instead of inches, and being a mite poor at algebra, got confused on the conversion tables. Tired of using his drinking money to post bond, he retired and now tended rich men's yachts at the marina.

"Ey Counselor!" Bluegill Ovelman grinned. His cheeks were redder than a broiled lobster, and the lines under his eyes could map the trails to the Jack Daniel's distillery. "Wanna take the little lady fishing?" He eyed Susan Corrigan, who gave him a smile that he wasn't likely to see on his best day.

"I hate fishing and you know it," I lied. "I like my seafood caught, cleaned, and cooked by someone else."

This was a necessary routine, a dance we'd done before. He called me a leather-shoed, high-rise, pickpocket shyster and I called him a no-count, whiskey-riddled, lobster-poaching bottom feeder. Then he gave me a hug and asked what I wanted. I wanted a boat and a sailboard and he gave me both, an old Chris Craft inboard he used as a tow boat and a banged-up Mistral windsurfing rig he tossed onto the deck. I borrowed an old pair of his swim trunks that had to be a size forty-four and kept hitching them up as we motored into the bay.

"I wouldn't do any swimming today," Bluegill Ovelman shouted as I leaned on the throttle. "Water's full of men-of-war. Big ones, too. Enough poison for a week's room and board at Jackson Memorial."

In fifteen minutes we were half a mile from the Whaler, trying to be inconspicuous. I dropped anchor and peered through binoculars. Melanie Corrigan was still soaking up rays. Sergio was bent over the starboard side, away from us. He had a gaff or a fishing rod or a net in his hand. Too far to be sure.

There was only one way to get closer without attracting attention. It was awkward, but I rigged a six-square-meter sail onto a sixteen-foot mast, nearly falling over the rub rail. I dropped the board over the side, jumped in, and jammed the mast into the universal joint while treading water. The water was warm and clear. Susan stayed in the boat and looked at me skeptically. "Do you know what you're doing?"

"Trust me. I've sailed from Key Biscayne to Bimini on one of these."

I uphauled the sail in a measly ten knots of wind, and tugging at my oversize drawers, I sailed closer to the Whaler. Out of my customary charcoal gray suit, standing in the shadow of the sail, I figured they wouldn't recognize me. Just another bozo sailing standing up.

I sailed cautiously, eyeing dozens of floating purple-blue sacs with poison-packed tails trailing underneath. Our waters are filled with biters, shockers, and stingers. Sharks, of course, are biters. You see them sometimes near Virginia

Key on Key Biscayne, feeding a mile or so offshore. They seldom bother anyone. There are Atlantic rays, some weighing as much as a good-sized running back, and their tails pack over two hundred volts of electricity. They can explode out of the water and scare the bejesus out of sailors and windsurfers alike. Then, each winter, we get the Portuguese men-of-war, prehistoric animals of unearthly beauty with their iridescent bluish-purple sacs and crests of orangish red. For those lured to the luminous sac, there is only betrayal. Underneath the water, hidden from view, are dozens of tentacles, undulating with the currents, straining to inject their poison into those seduced by the beauty.

I tipped the mast forward to head downwind and sailed off the stern of the Whaler. Sergio was still bent over the side, a net now visible in his hand. I saw a fishing rod jammed into a rod holder. Okay, maybe after some grouper. I wanted to get closer, so I jibed and came back the other way. About a hundred yards away, I trimmed the sail and tried to pick up a little speed. I wanted to pass by without taking too long to do it, not give them a good look at me. It would have worked, too, if I hadn't dropped my drawers. Trying not to draw attention to yourself is hard to do when your bare ass is staring at the people you would just as soon avoid.

Not wanting to make a further spectacle of myself, I headed back to our boat where Susan Corrigan was shaking her head. "Showing off for the widow?" she asked as I climbed aboard.

"Just distracting her," I replied. "A diversion from my adorable face."

"Maybe she recognizes both ends of you," Susan said without the hint of a smile.

"If that's a question, the answer is no."

She measured that one, believed me, and we took the Chris Craft back to the marina. Mission bungled. I still had no idea why Melanie was at Roger's house last night or on the bay with Sergio today. But I was starting to get the idea that the lady had a plan for everything and everybody. Inviting me to her house had to be part of the plan. I wished I knew what part.

Susan and I headed to Coconut Grove, the Olds 442 purring in third gear. I pulled into the shade of a gumbo-limbo tree in front of my house, and she turned to me.

"Jake, we have to talk."

"Uh-huh."

"About the other night."

"The other night?"

"Don't be dense! At your Granny's. And last night, in your shoebox there behind the weeds. Have you forgotten?"

I put the stick into neutral and turned off the ignition. The engine groaned and died. "I haven't forgotten. I remember every parry and thrust."

"That's not what I mean. Don't you think we should talk about how we feel about each other?"

Uh-oh. I should have known. Somehow I assumed that Susan Corrigan was different from other women. Which she was, of course, in certain respects. She cared less about clothes than whether to pass or run on third-and-four. But she was still a woman . . . and women want to talk about relationships. I went into my big, dumb guy routine. It comes naturally.

"I'm not too good at postcoital conversation," I said.

"I know," she said compassionately. "Like most men, you have trouble expressing your emotions."

"Not all of them. Anger I'm good at."

She scowled and waited. I had one hand on the door handle, but she wasn't stirring. Trapped.

"Jake, if it helps, I'm not too good at this either. But here goes. I want you to know I wouldn't have crawled into your bed unless I felt something for you. Something more than a physical attraction. I don't know how much or where it's going. But it's real, and I wanted you to know."

She waited some more.

I was silent. Overhead, a snowy egret headed toward the Everglades. Free to roam. I fidgeted, and the old leather upholstery squeaked underneath me.

"The ball is in your court, Counselor," Susan Corrigan said.

"I appreciate what you said. Thank you."

"Thank you? You big lummox! Are there any feelings inside that block of granite that sits on your shoulders? I am so tired of commitment-phobic men who panic when things get too good. Are you afraid of love, Jake? Is that it, are you one of those guys who sabotages a relationship when it gets too close?"

I looked down and noticed I was stomping on the brake pedal. My right hand had the gearshift in a death grip. The car seemed to shrink around me, caught in one of those machines that pulverizes a two-ton sedan into a block of scrap metal the size of a sofa. "Don't you think you're over-reacting to my limited ability to express myself?" I asked.

"Is that code for inaccessibility and lack of emotional depth?"

17

TELLING LIES

IN THE NAME AND BY THE
AUTHORITY OF THE STATE OF FLORIDA:

The Grand Jurors of the State of Florida, duly called, empaneled and sworn to inquire and true presentment make in and for the body of the County of Dade, upon their oaths, present that on the 14th day of October, 1986, within the County of Dade, State of Florida, ROGER A. SALISBURY did, unlawfully and feloniously, from a premeditated design to effect the death of PHILIP CORRIGAN, a human being, kill PHILIP CORRIGAN, by injecting him with a dangerous drug, in violation of Florida Statute Section 782.04(1)(a), to the evil example of all others in like cases offending and against the peace and dignity of the State of Florida.

The indictment was signed by the foreman of the grand jury and delivered to my house by a messenger from Abe Socolow's office. I telephoned Roger, regretful and apologetic.

"I'll understand if you file a complaint with the Bar," I said.

"Then who'd defend me? The phony malpractice case was bad enough. But a murder charge? It's crazy, and you're the only one I trust to beat it."

He made it sound easy, as if I could pull a few strings, get him a bye. I halfheartedly tried to talk him out of it. "I'm a little rusty in Criminal Court. There are some big gun criminal lawyers you could get."

"But you believe I'm innocent. None of them will."

He had me there. I *believed* he was innocent, but I wanted to know. He was surprised when I asked him to take a polygraph test. When he agreed, I believed him a little more.

"This machine is so primitive," Roger Salisbury said. "I don't trust it, not a bit."

He was squirming in a hard wooden chair, a blood pressure cuff wrapped around his right arm, pneumograph tubes circling his chest and abdomen, electrodes attached to two fingers of his left hand. He sat on an inflatable rubber bladder and leaned back against another one, trying to balance his weight.

He was right; the equipment was primitive. The polygraph hasn't changed much since a psychologist named William

Marston started fooling around with blood pressure deception tests seventy years ago. Dr. Roger Salisbury would have been more comfortable lashed to a shiny chrome device with microchips and digital readouts, not this Rube Goldberg contraption.

"Just try to relax," I said. "They used to throw people into wells to see if they were demons. The ones who drowned were found innocent. The ones who floated were obviously children of Satan deserving of death. We've progressed a bit."

The technician had spent an hour with Roger getting him prepared, gaining his confidence. And setting him up. That's what polygraph examiners do. Some small talk, convince the subject he has to tell the truth, then try to solicit a lie to an irrelevant question to measure the response against the relevant one: Did you steal the petty cash, do you smoke dope on the job, then . . . did you murder Philip Corrigan?

Roger Salisbury wouldn't know this. And he wouldn't know what every con learns while still in reform school—how to screw up the test with a nail in the shoe, a hard bite into the tongue, or other ways of jacking up blood pressure. Good. That's the way I wanted it. I wanted the truth about the death of Philip Corrigan. Not to determine whether to defend Roger. I could do that either way, guilty or innocent. Even if Roger told me he planned the murder for months and carried it out, I could still give him a defense, force the state to meet its burden of proof. That's our system. But I couldn't let him take the stand and lie. So I needed the knowledge for strategy purposes and for another reason, too. I just wanted to know. I had gotten too close to this one, nearly seduced by the widow, sleeping with the daughter, and now defending Roger Salisbury a second time.

Regardless of the test result, it would not be admissible in the murder trial. Although juries frequently hear witnesses whose powers of observation are impaired by booze, drugs, or lack of intellect, polygraph tests are barred as not meeting scientific standards of proof. The courts constantly struggle to determine who lies and who tells the truth. Some judges claim to be experts on body language. A witness who raises one heel from the floor, bites a lip, or shifts his eyes is considered untrustworthy. I tell my witnesses to ogle the lawyer asking the question and not to keep time to show tunes with their feet. And I carry ChapStick for the biters.

"Do you understand that you must answer every question truthfully?" The polygraph examiner, a retired cop named Tony Cuevas, twisted the dial on the galvanic skin monitor and waited for Roger's response. Before he went on pension, Cuevas had a more direct way of eliciting the truth. A nightstick smashed against an ankle. But that was Cuevas the cop. Cuevas the security consultant was a laid-back, soft-spoken forty-seven-year-old guy of average build and pleasant demeanor. He could have been an assistant vice president at a small town bank. Today Cuevas was relaxed and informal, wearing a short-sleeved white shirt and nondescript tie, fiddling with the balance on the cardio amplifier.

"Yes sir," Roger Salisbury answered. The five pens on the charts made their little hills.

"Do you live in Florida?" Cuevas asked. That is a neutral question. The blood pressure, respiration, and perspiration are recorded, setting the lower borders for the test.

"Yes."

"Did you ever take anything that didn't belong to you?"
A control question.

Salisbury paused, then a soft "Yes."

That one didn't work. The idea of a control question is to
get a false answer. Nearly everybody has stolen something, if
only a candy bar. If Salisbury had falsely denied it, his
physiological response to this irrelevant question would have
been compared to the response to the biggie: *Did you kill
Philip Corrigan?* If the reaction is greater to the irrelevant
control question than to the relevant question about the killing, chances are he's telling the truth. If the reaction is
greater to the relevant question, chances are he's more concerned about that answer, and it's a lie.

Tony Cuevas may have wanted to stomp on Roger Salisbury's instep to get a better answer, but he simply smiled
and asked, "Did you ever cheat in school, even once?"

Another short pause, then a soft "No." I couldn't see the
charts, but that was the answer Cuevas wanted. An almost
sure lie to an irrelevant question.

A pause for about thirty seconds to let the reactions die.

"Did you kill Philip Corrigan?"

A hasty, firm "No, sir."

"Is your name Roger?" Back to the neutral question to
start the sequence again.

"Yes."

"Did you ever wish anyone harm?" Again, a control question, eliciting the lie.

"No." It's amazing how many people refuse to admit the
truth to questions they believe are irrelevant. They're afraid
that if they admit to skullduggery or viciousness in the past,
it's an admission of guilt on the subject of the polygraph

test, and figuring the question isn't the one that's being tested, they lie about it.

The required pause, and then: "Did you inject succinylcholine or any other substance into Philip Corrigan in an attempt to kill him?"

"No."

"Were you born in May?"

"Yes."

"Have you ever told a lie to get out of trouble?"

Silence, then "Yes." Roger Salisbury was more honest than most, but he still denied two of the control questions, enough for Cuevas to evaluate the charts.

"One more question, Dr. Salisbury. Do you know who killed Philip Corrigan?"

"No sir," Roger Salisbury said.

Cuevas went through the same questions two more times. The answers stayed the same. The pens never stopped gliding up and down the moving paper. Tony Cuevas never changed his expression. When it was over, Roger Salisbury ran a hand through his neat, salt-and-pepper hair and gave me a wary look. His shirt was soaked and he seemed worn out. I told him that honest men sweat, too, and sent him home.

I used to think I was a good judge of character. Then I got burned a few times. Now I watched Roger Salisbury heading out the door. Good looking in that bland, undefined way. A mild, passive demeanor. Troubled now. He was either an honest man worried about the reliability of the strange contraption or a killer fearful that his mask was about to be peeled back.

Very perceptive, Lassiter. And you are either a brilliant

lawyer riding the crest of a dazzling career or a has-been ex-jock who should be selling hurricane shutters.

Cuevas kicked open a mini-refrigerator and offered me a beer. I was thirsty and he was sociable, so we polished off a six-pack while going over the charts. Cuevas measured the little lines, some forming the Appalachians, others the Rockies. He made notes, used a calculator, scratched his head with a pencil, and said, "I got a plus eight or better on two of the three relevant questions."

"Meaning?"

"Truthful. He didn't kill Philip Corrigan. Or more properly stated, his physiological responses lead me to conclude that he doesn't believe that he did."

"So what did he lie about?"

"Nothing for sure. The machine gives us three categories. Truthful, deceptive, and inconclusive. He got a minus four when I asked him if he knew who killed the guy. Minus six would be clearly deceptive. Minus four is close but still inconclusive. Here, look at this."

He pointed at some squiggly lines. They trailed off, becoming shorter, then taller, then shorter again.

"Looks like the Dow Jones," I said.

"That's called a staircase suppression. See, it's like a series of steps. It shows suppression of respiration just after I asked if he *knows* who killed Corrigan. That's one of the indications of deception."

"So does he know who did the killing?"

"A definite maybe. Sorry, best I can do is he didn't kill Corrigan but may know who did. If he clearly lied about not knowing, I'd be even more convinced he was innocent of the murder itself."

I must have looked puzzled because Cuevas continued, "It's this way, Lassiter. If the test shows clearly truthful to the denial of having committed the crime and clearly deceptive as to the denial of knowing who did, he's absolutely innocent. Money back, guaran-fucking-teed clean as a whistle. A killer will never show a stronger response to the question of who did it than whether he did it."

I fooled around with the blood pressure cuff, then turned to Cuevas: "He told me he doesn't know who killed Corrigan. I don't like it if he's lying to me."

"He might have had an itchy foot or a chest pain when he answered. Or he might know the killer and be protecting him."

"Or her," I said.

Cuevas nodded. "Or them. But your guy looks clean on the big questions, so you got what you want, an innocent lamb being led to the slaughter."

Which means someone is telling lies about Roger Salisbury. I remembered the line from Kafka: "Someone must have been telling lies about Joseph K. for without having done anything wrong he was arrested one fine morning." Which also meant we needed to prepare for The Trial.

The next morning I was at my desk at eight o'clock when the call came on my private line. "You gonna surrender that pervert murderer or should a couple boys from major crimes cuff him and bring him in the front door with all the TV assholes outside?"

Abe Socolow had such a folksy way of saying hello. He was delivering a message, just in case I missed it the day before. There would be no breaks, no special treatment because we used to break bread together. Now I was just another problem for him. After he brushed me aside, he could sweep up the scum he saw in front of him.

"You shouldn't skip breakfast, Abe. Affects your disposition."

He snorted at me. "I chew nails for breakfast."

"And spit out tacks," I said. "Roger will be there whenever you want. We aim to cooperate. But we'd like some cooperation from the state, too."

"Like what?" he asked, suspicion rising in him like steam in a kettle.

"Bond, reasonable bond for someone never before arrested, much less convicted of a crime."

"Hey, Jake, don't pee on my leg, okay. We're talking a capital crime here. No bond. You remember your criminal procedure, don't you, or is the money too good handling divorces and corporate mergers?"

Socolow was going to make my life miserable, and if I couldn't figure that out, he was telling me about it. He wanted me to grovel a little, so I did. It wouldn't help my client to insult the guy trying to fry him. "Abe, the court will grant him bond if the state stipulates to it. He's not going anywhere. He's got his medical practice here. He'll show up for arraignment, the preliminary, the trial, the whole works."

"And what if he splits for Argentina with some *bambina*? I'll look like a schmuck."

"Who'd notice the difference?" I said, without thinking. I pictured Socolow scowling at me at the other end of the line.

"Fuck him and the horse he rode in on. Let him sit in the can with all the other shitheads."

Stay in the prosecutor's office long enough, you get warped. You start thinking like a cop and talking like a cop. Cops are everywhere—homicide, vice, narcs—telling macho stories, hanging together in the paranoid world of Us against Them. Then in the corridors of the Justice Building, you rub up against the silk-suited shoulders of criminal lawyers and their depraved clients. No way you can stay sane. Not after eighteen years.

He always thought I was too flippant. Become a judge if you want to be a wiseguy, Socolow once told me. They get away with that shit.

"So what's it gonna be?" Socolow said finally.

"I'll bring him in, but I want an immediate bond hearing. You and I both know he shouldn't have to cool his heels in that hellhole across the street."

Socolow laughed. "Good enough for spicks and spades, but not for the saintly doctor. Bring him in, and I'll get you a bond hearing this afternoon. But you know your burden under *Arthur v. State.*"

I knew, I knew. Unlike a trial, where the state has the burden of proving guilt beyond a reasonable doubt, at a bond hearing in a capital case, the defendant must show that the state lacks sufficient evidence of guilt. But there was something in that for us, too. I could cross-examine Socolow's witnesses. One more time to put them under oath, a great advantage, because the best trick in the defense lawyer's trial bag is to elicit conflicting statements from prosecution witnesses. Jurors love that, even if the testimony is as innocuous as the color of the tie someone was wearing on the day of a murder. So the state's case would be unfolded in front of me, and the state's star witness, Mrs. Melanie Corrigan, would have to testify much sooner than she could have expected.

"I can't believe Melanie set me up," Roger Salisbury said as we looked for a parking space in front of the Justice Building. He squirmed in the bucket seat.

"Believe it," I said. "Hey, she sued you for malpractice, planted the drug in your house, and gave the State Attorney's Office an affidavit for the search warrant. What more does it take?"

He slammed a hand against the dashboard. "I'll believe it when I see her take the stand against me, not before."

"Fine," I said, pulling the old convertible into the meager shade of a thatch palm. "That should be right after lunch."

18

CIRCUS MAXIMUS

The Justice Building hadn't changed, except to become more crowded, dirtier, and more forbidding. When I started practicing law, six Criminal Court judges handled all felony cases in Dade County. But that was before Miami became the major port of entry for various grasses, powders, and pills from south of the border, and before Miami earned its civic bones as murder capital of the U.S. of A. Now Miami has the highest crime rate in the country. That's important. Americans have a passion for being number one. Like having the highest humidity, the murder rate is the source of a bizarre sense of pride among locals. It takes a tough *hombre* to battle

Miami's mosquitoes each summer and the criminals all year round.

The city *padres* can't do much about the weather, but they keep adding personnel to the justice system. Now, eighteen state judges churn through calendars stocked with up to sixty felonies each day, hurrying through arraignments, motions, bond hearings, reports, soundings, trials, and sentencings. A constant flow of humanity crowds the corridors— Liberty City blacks, Hispanics from a dozen countries, dirt-poor whites—calling out for their public defenders in a Babel of tongues, inner-city jive, machine-gun Spanish, back-country Southern drawl.

I was pacing the fourth floor, getting the feel of the place again, waiting for the bond hearing. The tile floors were filthy, the corridors dim with dead fluorescent bulbs. Acoustic tiles were missing from the ceiling, leaving gaps like missing teeth. Every thirty feet or so, huge twists of electrical wires dropped from overhead conduits, waiting for county electricians to install some new device, maybe TV cameras, escape alarms, or other technological marvels. The wires could have been there a week or a year. In the Justice Building, time is another dimension.

An ancient bailiff in a baggy blue uniform came out of a courtroom shouting, "Judge Snyder's calendar is now being called!" All aboard.

A young assistant state attorney with too much hair and an unkempt moustache sang out, "Teddy Figuero-a! Teddy Figuero-a!" A prosecutor's missing witness, a case about to go down the tubes.

A huge black woman slammed into me. She held her even larger son by the scruff of his T-shirt and horse collared him down the corridor. The son was about twenty, with shoulders like a water buffalo but a choreographer's hips.

"What day they say your trial be?" the mom demanded.

"February four, Momma."

"No. No. The ar-rangement be February four. The trial be when, March something . . ."

They trundled toward the escalators, still debating.

Shackled defendants crossed the corridor in twos, shuffling from one holding cell to another, eyes darting left and right, looking for girlfriends, mothers, lawyers, or bondsmen.

A sunburned redhead in her forties removed one high-heeled shoe and wiggled the toes of her right foot. Four toes, the little one missing. Maybe the evidence in a criminal case. Who knows? The performers are crazed at Circus Maximus.

I threaded my way to Judge Randolph Crane's courtroom, a spacious arena with thirty-foot ceilings, paneled walls on two sides, and a stained glass ornamental wall behind the bench into which was cut a door and through which the judge miraculously appeared from chambers. Under his raised bench of simulated walnut was a red panic button that summoned corrections officers in the event a deranged defendant (or lawyer) attacked him, and on a hidden shelf sat a loaded .357 Magnum in case the officers were all squeezing up against the young women clerks in the police liaison office.

I was waiting for the officers to bring Roger into the courtroom from the county jail next door where he had been booked two hours earlier. The prisoners came through an overpass that crossed the street and led directly into holding cells attached to the courtrooms. I had stayed with Roger as long as they let me in jail processing, and when they took him back through the huge steel door that clanged shut with a sound of malice and finality, he shot me a helpless look.

It hit me then, the load I carried, Roger Salisbury's life weighing a ton on my shoulders. The first rule of criminal cases and here I was emoting, instead of thinking, feeling anguish for him instead of masterminding a brilliant strategy to set him free. If any there be.

A dozen defendants sat in the jury box waiting for their cases to be called. Lawyers milled about in front of the bar, whispering to each other, poring through files, making deals, swapping stories. The courtroom resembled a basketball court before the game, players at both ends warming up, taking shots from all over the court, slapping each other on the back, a kind of camaraderie before the battle. At the same time, the judge kept calling his calendar, sometimes banging his gavel to bring the uproar to a manageable din.

Judge Randolph Crane was serving his fourth six-year term on the bench. He was tall and spare with a long, gloomy, gray face. His pale blue eyes had seen it all and not liked any of it. He spoke quickly as if he wanted to get it over with, sometimes thumbing through his calendar, shaking his head at the number of cases still to be heard.

"Rodolfo Milan," the judge called out. A pot-bellied man in a stained guayabera dragged himself out of the jury box. A public defender whispered in his ear. In a singsong voice, the judge began his mournful chant, "You're charged with aggravated assault, grand theft, breaking and entering, possession of a weapon in the commission of a felony. Rodolfo Milan, how do you plead?"

The defendant looked for his public defender, who now

was huddled with a young woman prosecutor in a black miniskirt and fishnet stockings.

"Have I got a plea for you?" She winked at the defense lawyer.

It went on like this for a while, arraignments and some guilty pleas, a few cases *nolle prossed* because the state had misplaced files or lost evidence or forgotten to subpoena witnesses or violated the speedy trial rule. With all the traps, with the rules of criminal procedure a minefield for the prosecution, it's a miracle anybody ever gets convicted. Except when they really want you. When they pay attention to you, throw their resources into it, when an Abe Socolow gets a burr under his saddle, makes it personal, then it's different. Then it's all turned around.

The judge kept calling cases, and every few minutes, corrections officers brought a new load of defendants from the holding cell to the jury box. Still no Roger Salisbury.

"Ivory Holloman," the judge sang out. "You're charged with grand theft, auto . . ."

Marvin Pollack, a skinny sixty-year-old defense lawyer with a matted toupee, pushed a young black man in a muscle shirt up against one wall of the courtroom. "Ivory, you got the money?" Pollack asked, patting the man's back pocket and not finding a wallet.

"Tomorrow, Mister Po-lock," Ivory Holloman said, terror in his eyes. If he wanted to, Ivory could pick up Marvin Pollack and use him for a walking stick. Ivory didn't want to. He wanted Marvin Pollack to keep him out of jail.

"Let's see what you got there," Pollack said, jamming his hand inside the man's tight jeans, fishing out some wrinkled currency. "Shit! A fin, nine singles, and a Lotto ticket."

Pollack smoothed the bills, pocketed them, straightened his tie, and prepared to negotiate a fourteen-dollar plea.

"Lazaro Arango, first degree arson . . ."

Abe Socolow strutted into the courtroom followed by his entourage. A couple of detectives from Metro, a young woman assistant state attorney, the medical examiner, a paralegal, and two clerks from the prosecutor's office. The state can always outnumber you. The detectives flanked Melanie Corrigan, who looked a trifle uneasy, but in a virgin-white cotton dress, her arrival still cut the decibel level in half as she walked to the first row of the gallery.

Socolow stood motionless and surveyed the courtroom as if counting the heifers on his ranch and coming up one short. Finally he spotted me and nodded formally. His assistant stood a half step behind. She was a good choice for the trial, a fragile blonde, small and pale with translucent skin. Give her a good squeeze and you'd leave bruises, but just what Abe Socolow needed. Sometimes, he comes on too strong. A little righteous indignation is okay for a prosecutor up to the point the jury senses he's mean-spirited and unfair. Then, for reasons psychologists can explain, jurors begin to feel sympathy for the defendant, no matter how heinous the charge. Abe sometimes treads dangerously close to the mark, his motor cranking at the red line.

A moment later, the guards led Salisbury through the holding cell door. His eyes desperately sought me, and I moved next to him.

"We have a couple minutes," I said. "Now, no matter what Melanie or any other witness says, you're not going to testify. This is our chance to find out what they've got, not reveal our case."

Judge Crane saw Socolow in the rear of the courtroom and pulled the freshly minted file of *State v. Salisbury* off the floor. He would call us out of turn, a courtesy to the chief of major crimes, not to me. Still, Socolow had kept his promise. An immediate bond hearing, and he hadn't called the papers or TV stations. Most prosecutors would salivate over the prospect of seeing their faces in the first block of the six o'clock news. Not Honest Abe. He didn't care about publicity, and instead of sucking up to the reporters the way most prosecutors did, he avoided them. We had a one-day reprieve on publicity.

"Roger Salisbury, murder in the first degree, defendant's motion to set bond," Judge Crane called out. He seemed a little more animated. Murder One beats the dickens out of auto theft for the adrenaline rush. "Is the defendant present and represented by counsel?"

I stepped forward, nodded, and said, "Jacob Lassiter for the defense. Let the record reflect that Dr. Salisbury is present in the courtroom, just as he will be at every hearing and the trial if reasonable bond is granted and he is released pending trial."

"Hold on Mr. Lassiter," the judge said, "let's get the introductions done before you start arguing. Say, haven't seen you around here lately. Getting bored with the bankers and big shots downtown?"

The players in the criminal justice system always give it to you when you've been manipulating money instead of lives.

"I wouldn't be here at all if the state had indicted the guilty party, instead of a respected physician, a lifelong resident of this county, and a man with no prior criminal rec-

223

ord." Might as well score a few points before the other side gets the ball.

"Still relentless," Judge Crane muttered, shaking his head. "Perhaps the state should announce its appearance before you make your closing argument."

Socolow strode to the podium, his angular body splitting the mass of young lawyers like a sword. Some color had crept into his sallow cheeks. He stood there silently a moment, his hawkish face a mask. "Abraham D. Socolow for the people of the state of Florida," he announced. He bowed to the judge and continued, "Also for the state, Jennifer Logan." He nodded toward the small blonde who was invisible next to Melanie Corrigan.

I took a good look at the widow. Not as confident as in the civil trial. A different society over here. Less civilized. Maybe once she would have fit in with the grifters, hard guys, and con men. But maybe the comforts of Gables Estates had taken the edge off, dulled the street smarts that served her so well until now. And maybe, too, she was just smart enough to know it.

The judge began the preliminaries. "Mr. Lassiter. This is a capital case. You know, of course, the burden you face in securing bond pending trial."

"I know, Your Honor. However, by examining the state's main witness, we intend to show that the proof is not great, and the presumption of guilt is not evident. I believe we will meet the standards of *Arthur v. State*. This is a case in which the state's entire case, including the evidence on which a search warrant was based, depends on the credibility of one witness. We are prepared to demonstrate the total lack of credibility of that witness."

I was prepared for no such thing. I was ready to wing it, to go with the flow, to get her to admit the old affair with Roger and ask if she didn't want him out of her life now, and didn't this seem like a swell way to do it. Time to go fishing. You never know what you'll catch until you drop a line into the water.

Again I looked at Melanie Corrigan. Edgy, tension showing around the mouth. Good. Finally getting to her. Socolow looked at her, too. Then he whispered something to Jennifer Logan, who shook her head, *no*, thin blonde strands swaying. Socolow turned to the judge. "Your Honor. Of course we vigorously disagree with the representations made by Mr. Lassiter concerning the state's case and its chief witness. However, we agree that this defendant is not likely to flee. We will stipulate to reasonable bond, perhaps two hundred fifty thousand dollars."

Just like that. Throwing in the towel.

Of course he had good reason. He hadn't had time to adequately prepare his witnesses, and his instincts told him that Melanie Corrigan wasn't ready. While Abe Socolow might take some perverse pleasure in keeping Roger Salisbury in jail for a few months prior to trial, he wouldn't risk blowing the case by having his star witness crack at a bond hearing. We took the offer, Roger putting up his pension funds as collateral for the bond.

So we left the Justice Building together. Just like the old days during the civil trial, Roger Salisbury telling me what a great lawyer I am. Then he asked what my strategy would be during the trial.

I didn't know.

Who are our witnesses?

I didn't know that.

He gave me a funny look. I told him not to worry. The state had to show us its evidence and its witness list. And the state's case was circumstantial. Nobody *saw* Roger Salisbury inject the drug into Philip Corrigan. And nobody except Melanie Corrigan could place the black valise in Roger's possession. I liked that—Melanie's testimony against Roger's—one-on-one. I just wondered how Abe Socolow planned to change the odds.

19

THE NURSE

Like fine wine, a criminal prosecution needs to age. First, a flurry of activity during the fermentation of the case, hearings, depositions, and an exchange of papers. Then, a quiet time, waiting for a trial date, files stored away in darkened cabinets, a time for brooding, waking at dawn with brilliant strategies, tossing them on the scrap heap of half-baked ideas by midday.

Judge Crane had set the trial for June, the beginning of Miami's unremitting summer. Those who can afford it are already getting away, escaping the blazing sun, ferocious humidity, and afternoon gully washers. By June the winds have shifted to the southeast—a wet, warm breath from the Caribbean—a time when each day begins with the same notion: no relief for six months. The calendar still says Spring, but in the tropics, it is not a time of renewal. It is the season of decay, streets steaming in afternoon storms that soak but do not cool, businessmen ducking from refrigerated cars to refrigerated offices while the poor, like desert dwellers, seek shade during the day, then roam free after dark, a time of short tempers and midnight shootings. And it would be our time of trial.

Six weeks after the indictment, we knew the state's case inside out. Abe Socolow detailed it for us in a bill of particulars, a witness list, and a carton of physical evidence. We knew who would testify and what they would say. No more trial by surprise, no last minute witnesses popping from the gallery.

We knew there was no wiretap evidence, no statements made by Salisbury to be used against him, and that the confidential informant, one Melanie Corrigan, would be the star witness. We learned the test results from the Medical Examiner's Office: evidence of succinic acid and choline in Corrigan's liver and brain, but strangely, none around the needle tracks in the buttocks. I would talk to Charlie Riggs about that.

On a warm, overcast day in April, I deposed Melanie Corrigan in Abe Socolow's office, staring hard at her when she took the oath. She stared right back and promised to tell the truth, the whole truth, and nothing but the truth. Once upon a time, she held a rich man's hand and promised to love and to cherish, to honor and obey.

Today she had no surprises. After her marriage, Roger

Salisbury kept pursuing her. Yes, she had dated him years ago, but that was ancient history, she was just a kid. No, she was not having an affair with him. Kept spurning his advances. He said he loved her, that Philip didn't appreciate her, didn't spend enough time with her. Roger showed her a little black valise with hypodermics and a glass vial, clear liquid inside, like a miniature vodka bottle they give you on a plane. He told her to get rid of Philip by injecting him with the drug. She was shocked, then laughed it off, thinking it was all talk. Roger always talked crazy. But when Philip died after surgery, she suspected Roger. She wanted proof. She thought something would come out in the civil trial, but nothing did.

So after the verdict, when Roger invited her over to his place, she went, and while he was fixing drinks, she looked through a desk in the study. *Voilà*, the black valise and two hypodermics. Nearby in a small refrigerator was the vial, this time with some of the fluid missing. She slipped everything into her purse and the next day called the State Attorney's Office. At about the same time, Dr. MacKenzie tipped Socolow to the brain and liver samples that came from Charlie Riggs. When both the tissue samples and the liquid tested positive for succinylcholine, the grand jury indicted Roger Salisbury for Murder One.

She told her story well. Socolow had several weeks to prepare her for deposition after almost botching it at the bond hearing. I couldn't shake her. She denied that the valise was ever in her possession, denied planting the drug at Roger's house. Nothing there for us, but at least we knew the state's case and knew we could not win unless we discredited Melanie Corrigan.

What about the valise and the drug, I had asked Roger. I wanted him to tell me that he had never seen the succinylcholine, that Melanie must have come up with it and then stolen his valise to frame him. If we could trace the drug to her, bull's-eye!

"It didn't happen that way," he said.

"No?"

"I borrowed the sucks—that's what we call it—from an anesthesiologist. Had an old Lab retriever, must have been close to twenty, comatose, but still breathing. Put him to sleep by paralyzing his lungs with the sucks. Kept the bottle in a refrigerator. Don't remember what happened to it."

"The valise?"

He shrugged. "Noticed it missing shortly after Philip died. Didn't think anything of it."

I checked it out. The anesthesiologist confirmed the story, the pet burial place, too. An unexpected bonus, it all happened two years before Corrigan died. *Ladies and gentlemen, you don't get your murder weapon and wait two years to do the job.*

One name on the state's witness list meant nothing to us. Rebecca Ingram, R.N., Mercy Hospital. I took her deposition with Abe Socolow sitting grimly at her side. Nurse Ingram was in her thirties, no makeup, close-cropped dishwater brown hair. Next to her name on the witness list was the innocuous description: *Responded to decedent's cardiac monitor alarm.*

"Did you see Dr. Salisbury the night of Mr. Corrigan's death?" I asked.

230

"Yes. I saw him leaving Room five-twelve, Mr. Corrigan's room, hurrying down the hall."

Okay, the state can place Roger in the hospital that night. No problem. Seeing patients, stopped in to check on Corrigan after surgery.

"And what time did this occur?"

She did not hesitate. "Ten o'clock. Almost exactly. I remember because I was checking Mr. Corrigan every half hour on the half hour."

Still no harm done. The aneurysm occurred at eleven fifteen.

"Is that all?" That's not much of a question, sort of asking the witness what the heck you're doing on the state's witness list.

"He was carrying a little leather valise. Black. With three gold initials on it, about yea-big." She held her hands about one foot apart, and I felt a knife, the same size, lodge in my gut. Nurse Rebecca Ingram shrugged and smiled a tiny, innocent smile. "That's all," she said.

Oh. That's all. I asked Socolow if he would be kind enough to find Exhibit C in his cardboard box.

"Similar to this valise?" I asked the nurse.

"Well, it looks like it. Yes. Either that one or one just like it."

I put my hand over the gold lettering. "What initials were on the valise you saw?"

She shook her head. "I don't know."

"And of course you couldn't see what was in the valise, correct?"

"No. I mean yes. I mean, correct, I couldn't see what was in there." Questions phrased in the negative always confuse.

"Did you ask Dr. Salisbury what was in the valise?"

"No. I said nothing to him, and as far as I know, he didn't even see me."

"And in your experience, is it unusual for a doctor to carry such a valise?"

"Oh no. Many physicians carry small instruments in them or keep their patient notes there."

"Was there anything unusual about seeing Dr. Salisbury on the floor in the evening?"

"No. He frequently checks on patients after surgery."

"So in summary, you saw Dr. Salisbury on his regular nighttime rounds more than an hour before Philip Corrigan suffered an aneurysm from unknown causes, and the doctor was carrying a rather ordinary valise that may or may not be the one I am holding, and you don't know what, if anything, was in it?"

"Yes, yes, that's right," she said, clearly relieved not to have buried the doctor any deeper.

I paused a moment and tried to get smarter in a hurry. At trial you worry about asking one question too many; in discovery, one too few. I couldn't seem to pump any extra voltage into my brain. Abe Socolow cracked the knuckles of his bony hands and said, "Any more questions, Counselor?"

We were sitting in his tiny office in the Justice Building, files and cardboard boxes everywhere, a flood of paper, the daily bread of lawyers. The three of us plus a court reporter taking everything down on her silent machine. Socolow seemed a little too anxious to end this one. I pretended to study the chart of his convicted and condemned killers. Buying time, I stood up and walked to the small window that overlooked the trestles of the nearby expressway. I looked for a signpost on the foggy road that runs through my mind.

"One more question," I said.

Abe Socolow sighed and shook his head in disgust. That trick might work with kids just out of law school. Pretending exasperation: *Why the fuck you wasting everybody's time here?*

I smiled at Nurse Rebecca Ingram, who sat quietly with her hands primly folded in her lap. "Did you see anybody else on the floor that night prior to eleven-fifteen?"

"Yes, as I told Mr. Socolow, sometime between ten-thirty and eleven, I can't remember exactly when, I was at the station by the elevators, and Mrs. Corrigan came up with a gentleman."

"Oh," I breathed, trying to keep still, inviting her to continue.

"Well, they must have come up the fire stairs because I didn't see them get off the elevator. But I looked down the hall and there they were."

"Did you speak to them?"

"Yes, I told Mrs. Corrigan they really shouldn't be up there then, but she said they'd just be a minute. Then they went into Mr. Corrigan's room."

"Alone, the two of them?"

"Yes, I returned to my station."

"Did you recognize the gentleman with Mrs. Corrigan?"

"No. He was very . . . very muscular looking. I could see that even though he was wearing one of those khaki jackets with all the pockets, like he was going on a safari . . ."

"A bush jacket," I helped out.

"Yes. Heavily muscled men have a distinctive way of

walking, kind of rolling side-to-side. And he was not too tall. Short, actually."

"Would you recognize him again?"

"I believe so. I believe he was Cuban, kind of swarthy, you know . . . but I don't know. He could have been Italian or something." She blushed.

What a splendid break, what a wonderful witness you have handed me, Abe Socolow. A buck would get you ten the muscular, not-too-tall guy was Sergio Machado-Alvarez, the karate instructor, boat captain, and steroid freak who made a cameo appearance on the group-grope videotape and who bruised my ancient Oldsmobile with brutal efficiency. I made a note to have Cindy subpoena Sergio for the trial.

I continued, "How long were they in the room?"

"I don't know. I didn't see them leave. They must have gone back down the stairs."

"You were on the fifth floor, correct?"

"Yes."

"Do many visitors walk up from the lobby?"

Abe Socolow was fidgeting. "Counselor, I must object to that question. It's speculative and irrelevant."

"Save it for trial," I barked. "This is discovery, and it's my deposition, and if you're sorry you listed this honest lady as a witness, tough."

Socolow banged a fist on his green metal desk, sending a Styrofoam coffee cup flying. "Damn it, Jake, you know better than that! I never try to hide anything. Let the chips fall where they may. I'm only interested in the truth, and you can create all the red herrings you want, but I don't care who was in that room, only one person poisoned Corrigan."

I ignored him and turned to Nurse Ingram.

"Just one more question," I promised.

Socolow hissed at me, "You said that fifteen minutes ago."

I proceeded as if Socolow weren't there. "Nurse Ingram, did you check on Philip Corrigan between the time you saw Mrs. Corrigan and the gentleman enter Room five-twelve and the time of the patient's distress due to the aneurysm?"

"No sir."

Whoa. I had expected a *yes*. Another pleasant surprise. She continued, "I'm sorry, but I missed the eleven o'clock check. I was filling out reports. Next thing I know, at eleven-fifteen, the cardiac monitor is going crazy. He'd had the aneurysm. I called in the Code Blue, and he was taken to surgery. But as you know . . ."

"So," I began, disregarding my one-question promise, "as far as you know, Mrs. Corrigan and the gentleman could have been in Mr. Corrigan's room from ten-thirty to eleven o'clock or even eleven-fourteen."

"I don't know. I suppose. But I don't know why they would be. Mr. Corrigan was sleeping all evening. He was sedated, of course, after surgery."

"And the last time you saw him was ten-thirty, and he was sleeping peacefully?"

"Yes."

"After Dr. Salisbury left?"

"Yes."

"Then you saw Mrs. Corrigan and the gentleman?"

"Yes."

"And the next time you saw Mr. Corrigan, he had suffered the aneurysm?"

"Yes, I said that."

"No further questions," I said, regretting only that a

judge, a jury, and a gallery of spectators were not there. "Your witness, Abe."

If Abe Socolow's skin were any more sallow, he'd be quarantined for hepatitis. He started in without pleasantries.

"Nurse Ingram, as far as you know, Mrs. Corrigan and her guest could have left the room at ten-thirty-one?"

"Yes, I suppose."

"And Roger Salisbury could have come back in at ten-thirty-two?"

I let out a well-planned laugh. "Sure, and maybe Santa Claus came down the chimney at eleven-ten."

Socolow ignored me. "Answer the question," he ordered the nurse.

"Well, I would have seen Dr. Salisbury if he came up the elevator. But he could have come through the stairwell, yes."

"Nothing further," Socolow said.

Abe Socolow had gambled, had rolled the dice. He wanted to place Salisbury in Philip Corrigan's room, black valise in hand. He risked our finding out that the widow and her friend were there, too. He lost. But now, how to use that knowledge. I knew where we wanted to go with it, if not exactly how to get there.

If the state intends to prove a homicide with circumstantial evidence, it had better show that the defendant had the motive, opportunity, and means to commit the crime. With Roger Salisbury the state had all three; his motive was to get Corrigan's money and wife; the opportunity was being alone in the hospital room with Corrigan; and the means were dangerous drugs and the ability to use them.

If you are defending an accused murderer who has the

motive, opportunity, and means to commit the crime, you'd better have another suspect to toss to the jury. He can't be a phantom. Shadowy figures, unknown assailants without the motive to kill, get you twenty-five years to life. Or worse. To beat the charge, you need a suspect with a name, face, and social security number.

I had my suspect: Sergio Machado-Alvarez. Now all I needed was some proof.

20

THE CONTRACT

The phone call came three days after we filed our discovery with the state. We listed our witnesses and physical evidence, including a certain "videotape portraying a prosecution witness, the decedent, the defendant, and an additional party." I wanted to see if it got a rise out of Socolow. I don't know if it did. But the widow surely noticed.

"Mr. Lassiter," she purred on the phone.

"Mrs. Corrigan," I said.

"You have something I would like very much."

"You want my 1954 Willie Mays baseball card?"

"Don't toy with me, Jake," she said, impatiently.

"So sorry, that's what I thought you wanted me to do."

"And don't flatter yourself."

"Okay, a business call, you want an appointment?"

"I want to tell you things that you will want to hear."

"Let me guess. My eyes remind you of the Mediterranean at sunset." My witty repartee will never get me a table at the Algonquin or a guest shot on Johnny Carson.

She was quiet a moment, probably deciding whether to tell me to screw off. But she was after something, so she kept going. "If you'd stop being such a smartass and listen, you'd know I'm trying to help your client."

"Like you helped him by planting the drug in his house."

"Maybe I was just returning it to the place I found it. I'll tell you everything. Just bring me the videotape."

"What if I've made copies? A year from now I could blackmail you."

She laughed softly. "You're not the type. Besides, we'll sign a contract. You draw it up, that you've turned over the only copy. If you're lying, you could be disbarred, right?"

Right. She'd thought of everything.

"Tell me," I said, giving it my best Cary Grant, "how does a girl like you get to be a girl like you?"

"Practice," she said.

And all this time I thought that's how you got to Carnegie Hall. "Okay," I said, "I'll bring the cassette. There's only one. You'll make a statement exonerating Salisbury. I'll call Socolow. We'll need him and a court reporter to take your statement."

"No! Just you. Bring a tape recorder if you want."

I thought about it. Socolow might muck it up, talk her out of it, delay until morning. She was giving me the case on a silver platter. Either that or handing me my head. "Okay, I'll be there in twenty minutes."

"Not here. I don't want you in the house. Sergio might come by. Someplace else. You know where Shark Valley is?"

"What, the Everglades? I'm not in the mood for mosquitoes. Besides, it'll be nearly dark by the time we get there."

"You're not afraid of me in the dark, are you?"

I didn't trust her at dawn, dusk, midnight, or any time in between. And she might bring friends. "It's just a strange place to execute a contract, that's all," I said.

"There'll be tourists around, just no one we'll know. Meet me there in two hours. You'll have to prepare the contract and get going. I'll be on top of the observation tower."

I said okay, but I didn't mean okay. It made no sense, a meeting at Shark Valley. And by the time we got there, the tourists would be back at their hotels sipping six-dollar piña coladas. But if she gave me a statement, admitted planting the evidence, Roger's case was over.

I was dusting off a briefcase when Cindy buzzed. "Hey boss, now the other Corrigan babe wants you."

"Say what?"

"*Mizz* Corrigan," Cindy said, dragging out the name.

"What line?"

"No line. Here. The waiting room. Just dropping by, in a sweatsuit and black Reeboks, so says our sharp-eyed receptionist."

"Bring her back," I commanded.

"Black Reeboks," Cindy repeated. "Bet they're hightops, too."

When the oak door closed behind her, Susan gave me a

peck on the cheek. I grabbed her by both shoulders and brought her close. The kiss was straight on, slow and soft, and Susan half gasped and half sighed at the end of it.

"You charge by the hour for that?" she whispered.

"For you, a straight contingency fee."

She feigned anger. "You only want a third of my kisses?"

"No, I only want to spend a third of our time kissing."

"The rest talking?"

"That, too. It's good to see you, but I'm on my way out." I told her about the call from Melanie Corrigan, and she leaned against the windowsill frowning. Then she paced back and forth, her sneakers silent on the thick carpeting. Cindy was right. Hightops.

Finally she turned. "Don't go, Jake. It's a set-up."

"Maybe. And maybe I'll get a statement that will exonerate my client. I really don't have a choice."

"Then at least take the police along."

"The police work for Socolow."

"You're not going to give her the videotape." It was both a question and a plea.

"Tell me more about the tape."

"You've seen it," she said. "Nothing more to tell."

"When was it shot?"

"I don't know exactly. About two years before Dad died."

"Two years! What was it, a honeymoon cruise?"

"Actually it was right before Dad married her. Mom had just died. Dad took the *Cory* to the islands with Sergio as the captain, Roger and Melanie the guests."

"So much for a decent interval of mourning."

She turned away, an old memory dragging up the pain. "It's hard for me to be objective about Dad. He always

242

cheated on Mom, and that last year or so, when she was sick and he took up with Melanie, it was very hard for her . . . how cruel he was at the end. I can never forgive him for that. Never."

I didn't expect that tone, the bitterness toward her father. But something else interrupted the thought, something that wasn't making sense. "Roger told me he first met your father after he married Melanie."

"No. Salisbury treated both Mom and Dad. He definitely knew Dad before he married that slut."

"Strange he would lie about that." I stored the knowledge for later use. My mind is a warehouse of information like that, bushels of scrap paper filled with notes.

I told Susan it was time to grab the mosquito spray and head for the Glades. She drifted toward the door, blocking my path like a linebacker filling the hole. "What about the tape?" she asked.

I looked around on my shelves and grabbed a small cardboard box. "Maybe Melanie would like to watch *Cross-Examining the Expert in a Product Liability Case*."

"And you think that when she discovers what you've given her she'll consider it a big joke? She's dangerous, totally amoral, and capable of anything. She could seduce you or kill you. To her, it wouldn't make the slightest difference."

"Melanie? She wouldn't hurt a fly."

"Maybe not one that's zipped up. Jake, don't be foolish. You could get hurt, or worse."

"Would a hearse horse snicker hauling this lawyer away?"

"Tell me you won't go," she pleaded.

I didn't want to go. But I couldn't not go. I put some cowboy in my voice. "A man's gotta do what a man's gotta do."

"Don't be a jerk. And that self-mockery doesn't sell with me. You really believe that tough-guy stuff."

"Just locker room bravado. Inside I'm quaking."

"There you go again. What do I have to say to you?"

"You could tell me how much you'd miss me if I end up sleeping with the alligators."

"I would miss you. I . . . I care for you."

"Care for me?"

Still blocking my path, she moved closer and gave me a wistful up-from-under look. I had to fight the urge to grab her. "I think I love you," she whispered. "Satisfied?"

"You bet."

She took a half step backwards. "Somehow I expected a more eloquent response."

"Haven't we had this conversation before? Haven't I already professed my . . . my you know."

"Jake Lassiter, how can a man be so articulate in a crowded courtroom and such a bungler one-on-one? Is it so hard to say you love me?"

"Well, I do."

"Do what?"

"Do what you said."

"Jake!"

I threw up my arms. "Do love you, okay already?"

"Not okay. I forced you into it. You still can't express your feelings, and you treat me like some bimbo whose opinions aren't worth listening to."

Now it was my turn. I moved back a yard. "Did I say

something wrong? I thought we were engaging in sweet talk, and all of a sudden, I'm not listening. What is it you want me to do?"

"It's what I don't want. I don't want you to prove how tough you are. And I don't want you to walk into a trap."

"Sorry. I have a duty to Roger."

"Why don't you respect me on this?"

"Hey Susan, I appreciate your opinion, but I can take care of myself. I've been around this town a long time before I ever met you, and nobody's stolen my marbles yet."

Some color had crept into her dark complexion. "Maybe you ought to keep traveling solo, you're so good at it." She turned away, looked out the window over the Atlantic. The *S. S. Norway* was lugging its way out Government Cut, a thousand tourists headed to the Virgin Islands. "You don't take me seriously, Jake. You're a big, dumb jock like all the rest of them. I don't know what I ever saw in you."

With that, she pivoted on her black hightops and stormed out of the office, muttering "macho jerk" two or three times. Through my open door, I saw loyal Cindy shrug, as if to say, "What else is new?"

21

SHARK VALLEY

There are no sharks in Shark Valley. No valley either. Just miles of sawgrass and countless animals living in their natural habitat. Bull alligators rule the Everglades, eating turtles, white-tailed deer, and any birds that venture too close to the reptiles' muddy homes. There are wood storks and egrets and great white herons that would now be extinct if women still wore feathery hats.

But no sharks and no valley. Misnamed though it is, Shark Valley is nature unrestrained. It is a vast flat slough, a slow-moving river of shallow water that has not changed in appearance for centuries. If Philip Corrigan had ever seen the place, he would have licked his chops and dreamed of draining and filling, building on stilts, and calling it "Heron Creek." Of course, then there would be no more herons and no more creek.

Black thunderheads were forming over the Glades, mountainous clouds picking up the moisture from the fifty-mile-wide river. Nearly dusk and the world was gray. It was seven miles down a narrow asphalt road to the observation tower. No cars allowed. I rented a bicycle from the chickee hut run by the Park Service and got a second look from the ranger who warned me about the weather and the closing time. He probably doesn't get many bird watchers wearing blue suits and burgundy ties. I put my suitcoat in the car, peeled off my tie, and felt only half as stupid. I went into the restroom, tossed some cold water on my face, and stared at the mirror. I hadn't gotten any better looking. I practiced my cocky look, worked up a crooked grin, and said to the mirror, "Sure I have the tape, but first I'll take your statement." Behind me, a toilet flushed, the stall door opened, and a middle-aged tourist wearing a Mickey Mouse T-shirt gave me a sideways look, then backed away, never stopping to wash his hands. I checked my gear—the videotape, the contract, and a portable tape recorder—all safe in a thin briefcase. Then I headed into the open air, hunched over the saddle of my government-issue, dollar-fifty-an-hour bicycle that was the right size for Pee Wee Herman.

The dark clouds were growing nearer and the wind kicking hard from the west as I pedaled south into the Glades, my knees under my chin. Some serious bird watchers were hurrying back on the path, their binoculars swinging, tripods in hand. One white-haired man with knobby knees sticking out of safari shorts was carrying on about having spotted "two crested caracaras, not one, but two . . ."

Blackish-green alligators slid into the water from the side of the road. Some were babies, two feet in length, looking like rubberized gags from a hotel gift shop. The bulls, ten or twelve feet, launched themselves into the water with powerful haunches. Some dug into the mud, forming gator holes to trap the water and keep cool. Stop to look, they hiss at you, blowing air out their nostrils. Keep going, they watch until you're gone.

One of the big bulls grabbed a tourist last year. A stockbroker from Cleveland had wandered into shallow water to get video footage of a blue heron feeding. Just like an Abbott and Costello movie, the log he stepped on opened its mouth. The alligator dragged him into deeper water, then with powerful jaws, crushed the man's chest and pierced his lungs. Official cause of death: drowning. Like saying the victims of Hiroshima died of sunburn.

It took only twenty minutes to pedal to the observation tower, a sleek concrete structure with a long, elevated ramp leading to a circular deck sixty feet above the sawgrass. Deserted except for the animals. Birds fed along the banks of a pond below, keeping a watch for the gators that dozed nearby. I leaned the bike against a strangler fig, grabbed the briefcase, and slowly walked up the ramp, listening for human sounds.

Bird chirps and little splashes came from the pond below. Nothing more.

At the top, I caught the glint of the sun, hidden by the clouds, preparing to drop into the Gulf of Mexico off the coast of Naples. A hawk kite flew by, carrying an apple snail. A small unseen animal rustled the sawgrass below. Then a scraping sound from above. A dozen white terns bolted from a Caribbean pine and veered away from the tower.

Another scraping sound.

I was standing on a round concrete slab, maybe thirty feet across. Above me, the roof of the tower was another slab, the same size. I looked up into solid concrete.

A voice, just a whisper, then another.

He swung down from the slab above, landing six feet in front of me, blocking the path down the ramp. Behind me, another one dropped onto the concrete. The one behind me was short, muscular, moustachioed, and mean. Sergio Machado-Alvarez. The one by the ramp was bigger, not as many ripples, but maybe six-two, two-twenty, a gut beginning to give way. He wanted to play baseball. At least he was holding a baseball bat. One of the aluminum models. They make a funny *clonk* when they hit the ball. I don't know the sound when they crush a skull.

Oh shit. You were right, Susan. I didn't need this. I didn't need to prove how tough I was. Coming here already proved how smart I was.

"Hola, asshole," Sergio hissed. He showed me his large, gray teeth. A psychopath's smile. "You've got something for me, *damelo,* gimme."

"Say please." I never learn.

Sergio curled a lip at me. *"Hijo de puta,* you're going to hurt real good. Orlando . . ."

Orlando was smacking his palm with the fat end of the Louisville Slugger. If they were trying to scare me, it was working. But I was thinking, too. Orlando looked slow. That was a plus. But strong. That was a minus. Sergio was unarmed. Another plus. But I knew he was no stranger to the *dojang*, and from what I saw with my dear old car, he wasn't faking it. Another minus. So far I was breaking even but still didn't have a way of getting off the tower with all my parts working.

A humorless smirk twisted Sergio's moustache. He was going to enjoy this. Orlando kept plopping the bat into a bare hand the size of an anvil. I took two steps backward until I was leaning against the railing. Floating below me were five-hundred-pound wallets with teeth.

I held my briefcase in front of me. "Where's Mrs. Corrigan? This is for her."

"Home finger-fucking herself," Sergio leered, taking a step toward me.

"Whoa there," I warned, holding the briefcase over the railing. "One more step and it's in the drink." Now that was some threat. After all, they wanted the tape to destroy it. That fact escaped Sergio, who kept inching toward me.

"Throw it over, you're gator bait, *mamalón*." He bunched his forehead into little wrinkles and dropped into the straddle-leg stance, feet wide apart facing front, knees slightly bent, hands on hips, an attack position.

My move, but what to do? If your life is circumscribed by the four walls of the courthouse, your conduct is regulated by a myriad of rules. You become, in a word, civilized. You are not accustomed to dealing with those whose only rules are their own. In the swamp there is no court of appeal, no petition for rehearing. You depend either on the mercy of the one wielding the biggest stick, or on your own wits and strength. Of course, if I had any brains, I'd have a gun, not a product liability video, stashed in the briefcase.

The briefcase.

"Take it," I offered, extending the thin case across my body. Sergio relaxed, reached for the handle, and I brought it around, a tight backhand swing with a full follow-through. Three hundred dollars of Schlesinger Brothers leather caught him flush on the nose. He yelped, and a torrent of red spurted over both of us.

Sergio fell back against the railing, stunned, blood streaming over his sleeveless muscle shirt, looking far worse than he probably was. I watched Orlando, waiting for his move. The big guy still blocked the ramp. A concrete pillar came through the center of the deck, supporting the slab above. If he rushed me, he would have to choose one side or the other. I would go around the pillar the other way and down the ramp. But he just stood there, not moving, holding his ground like a defensive end unwilling to be faked out on a misdirection play.

And here was Sergio, swiping at his nose, his eyes teary but just as mean. "Orlando. Fuck up his knees."

My knees were already fucked up. Two cartilage scrapings through the scope, one major-league scar thanks to a ligament tear.

Sergio leaned his head back, trying to stop the flow of blood. His voice was thick. "Fuck him up good, Orlando, then throw his ass to the gators."

Sometimes it is best to turn an apparent weakness into your strength. Here was Br'er Wolf threatening to throw me into the briar patch. I leaned over the railing, stretched high and let go with a hook shot, sliding the briefcase onto the deck above me. Then I hopped over the railing, took a breath, and dropped toward the malevolent swamp.

I don't know how long it takes to plummet sixty feet. Ask Newton or Galileo or one of those guys. But it's long enough to do a lot of thinking. If an alligator wants to have you for dinner, do you smack him in the snout? Or is that a shark? I thought of Susan Corrigan, the lovely tough-talking Susan Corrigan who cared for me and worried about me and now would be left without me. And then I felt the splash.

And went under.

Deep.

Never touched bottom, and a long way up.

Warm and mucky. Brown algae clung to my legs. Leaves stuck in my hair.

I was treading water, kicking off my wing tips, swiveling my head, picking up a thousand sounds, birds fluttering away, a splash on a far bank. Something bumped my leg and I jumped. Jumping is hard to do while treading water, but I popped up like a jack-in-the-box, then fell back against the branch that had impersonated an alligator.

I heard something. A hiss like the air brakes of a bus. Behind me, not six feet away, were two nostrils exhaling spray and two eyes exuding menace above a flat, broad snout. All that was visible. The flat eyes locked on mine. The hissing grew louder. He didn't like me in his territory. That made two of us.

I started doing the backstroke. Slow, smooth strokes with my head up so I could watch him. More like Esther Williams than Mark Spitz. When I was twenty yards away, I turned over, and did a wild Australian crawl until I got to the bank.

Shouts in Spanish, the sounds of leather on concrete clomping down the ramp.

The bank was muddy and I lost my balance, slipping back into the water, trying to remember to breathe again. As I reached for the stalk of a leather fern, a large, strong hand swallowed mine and dragged me out. Now what?

Wheezing, I looked up into the face of a huge black man who now had me by the arm.

"You the lawyer?" he asked.

"Why, you need one?"

"You must be. She said you make lousy jokes."

She. Another of the widow's henchmen.

Then I recognized him. Two hundred sixty-five pounds of coal jammed into blue jeans, narrow waist rising to shoulders the width of a two-car garage. Stand leeward of him, you'd stay dry in a hurricane. Unlike some football linemen, there was no trace of fat. Six thousand calories a day burned off on the practice field and the weight room. Huge, yet Tyrone Hambone Washington moved with the grace of a dancer. He could bull rush an offensive tackle onto his backside, or with that high arm motion, swim by him. Strength and speed.

The big man wiped his hands on his jeans. "The little lady sportswriter said you might need some help. So here I am. All her good pub got me AFC first team, so I owe her one."

"Susan? Susan Corrigan sent you!"

"She say, you play some defense out here, only you don't know whether they run or they pass. Hambone's good at reading defenses. You just watch."

Sergio was down the ramp first. He stood there with front

leg bent, back leg straight, left arm extended with fist up, right arm curled alongside his jaw, a little slab of evil. His nose had stopped bleeding, but his muscle shirt was splattered with red.

Washington looked at him and said, "Shee-it, every little fucker in this town thinks he's Chuck-frigging-Norris. But you, shitface, you look like chuck meat to me."

"Negro hijo de puta—"

Washington's forehead seemed to drop over his eyes like a knight securing his visor before the joust. "Whadid the little Cube say?"

"Something uncomplimentary about your mother," I interpreted helpfully. "Don't think he wants you to marry his sister, either."

"Shee-it. His *seester* pull the train for every brother in Liberty City. She crazy about USDA government inspected, prime cut, Grade-A African beef."

Sergio had forgotten all about the videotape and about me. Now it was personal. Orlando watched from his perch on the ramp. He was good at watching.

"Singao, I keel you now," Sergio spat at Tyrone, "with my bare hands."

"Anytime, you Cuboid fag, body-building steroid-sucking cornholing midget. And stop pickin' your nose with your elbow, it won't bleed so much."

"Filthy *Negro mamalón.*"

"You gotta choice, Jose. Either git the fuck outa here now, or I'll drop kick your ass back to Havana."

I wanted to tell Sergio not to get excited, that Tyrone Hambone Washington probably says worse things to offensive linemen every week. In some quarters, his banter would be considered good-natured locker room joshing. Apparently Sergio was not well versed in this form of humor. Though his mouth was closed, a guttural noise came gurgling up from deep within him, a garbage disposal trying to digest a kitchen fork.

Seconds ticked by. Behind us, I heard a gator slip back into the water. The sun had dropped beneath the horizon, and a faint orange glow provided our only light. In minutes, we would be enveloped by the blackness of the prehistoric slough.

Sergio tensed his arms, flexed his shoulders. Hambone Washington stood with feet spread, arms loosely at his sides. Finally, the eruption. With a banzai charge, Sergio launched himself into the air, a jumping side kick. As he did so, he yelled, *"Tobi yoko-geri!"* His right foot was five feet off the ground, aimed at Washington's Adam's apple. A chunky Baryshnikov sailing through the air.

Tyrone Hambone Washington was on the balls of his feet. At the last second, he stepped deftly to one side, a small step, and moved his head to the left, like the young Muhammad Ali dodging a punch. "Tofu Yoko Ono," he said.

Sergio flew by him with perfect form and landed in the muddy sawgrass. I didn't have time to watch the rest. As Sergio drew an eight-inch stiletto from the waistband of his pants, Orlando came at me with the baseball bat. I stood there, sopping wet and barefoot, watching the pinch hitter, and not possessed of any particularly bright ideas. When Orlando was thirty feet away, I stooped at the base of a coconut palm and grabbed a yellow coconut, still in its husk, big as a volleyball and lots harder.

I heaved the coconut at Orlando. He swung and caught a piece of it. Foul ball. Strike one.

He kept advancing, triceps flexing with each warm-up swing, belly jiggling. Unlike Sergio, he was expressionless. Cold, black eyes that were all business. The mud smacked under his leather boots as he advanced. I backed up slowly, letting him close a little of the distance. Twenty feet away I flung a high, hard one with another coconut. He ducked. High and away. Count even at one and one.

This time he stayed put and I had time to scoop up a smooth round one that fit nicely in my hand. Made a motion as if to throw, held up, then came at him with a submarine pitch, an upward trajectory that caught him right in the shin. A satisfying *crack*, but he didn't drop the bat. He leaned on it like a crutch, and I came at him. Four giant steps, then, out of a crouch, shoulders square, legs driving, I made the tackle. Picture perfect. Head up, arms wrapping him, running through him, my shoulder catching the point of his chin. He went down and lost three yards.

I turned around in time to see Tyrone tossing Sergio's knife into the pond. I hadn't seen how Tyrone had disarmed him, but Sergio's right arm was hanging at an unusual angle. Then Tyrone scooped up the smaller man by the seat of his pants and dragged him across the path.

Sergio was moaning, but Tyrone was short on sympathy. "Shee-it, just a little shoulder separation. When it happens to me, they jam it back into place, tape me up, and I don't miss but one series."

Sergio did not seem to be NFL material. As he hobbled away, he turned to me and said weakly, "I owe you one, *hombre.*"

"And I know you're good for it." I started up the ramp to retrieve my briefcase.

"Now git!" Tyrone ordered, and the two men took off, wobbling, limping, and cursing until they disappeared into the darkness.

Charlie Riggs was tending a fire and scalding peanut oil in an iron skillet when I pulled up at his fishing cabin just off Tamiami Trail a few miles east of Shark Valley. The old upholstery in the 442 was smeared with mud, and I made squishing sounds as I eased out and walked barefoot into the campsite.

"Jacob, where you been?" Charlie Riggs didn't sound alarmed. "Either I'm seeing things or you've got a water lily in your ear."

"Been up to my ass in alligators, Charlie."

"I do believe there's a story in this. You'll find a bucket, a towel, and some shorts on the porch. Then tell me."

I cleaned up and told him. As I did, Charlie fixed dinner. He bent over a slab of pine with a nail stuck through it. He jammed a Glades bullfrog onto the nail, piercing its belly, then made a quick incision with a knife, and with a pair of pliers, he pulled off the pants of the frog.

"You like frog legs?"

"Like eating them better than watching them prepared."

Charlie shrugged. "Thirty years in the ME's office, I don't get queasy about much."

He heated some fresh tomatoes in the skillet, poured milk over the frogs' legs, dragged them through seasoned flour, then sauteed the whole mess in a sauce fragrant with butter and garlic.

"Love that country cooking," I said.

"Country nothin'. This is *cuisse de grenouilles provençale*."

We ate and I talked, Charlie listening silently. Finally I asked him what to do.

"I suggest we visit Susan at once," he said. "This has taken on a whole new dimension. Those two thugs might have killed you. They were certainly going to hurt you."

"What's this have to do with Susan?"

"They must know she gave you the tape. For whatever reason, they seem to place great importance on getting it. Frankly, I don't know why."

"That's easy, Charlie. First, it's embarrassing to the widow, prancing around with three men. Second, it contradicts her sworn deposition. She denied having an affair with Roger."

Charlie licked his fingers, sticky with garlic butter. "You may be right, but I get the feeling there's something more to the videotape than that. Regardless, the widow apparently will do anything to get it. Maybe harm anyone who's seen it. Shall we leave?"

We shall, I said. Not really believing Susan was in danger. But making a mental note to watch the videotape again, to look for something. Something Melanie Corrigan didn't want us to see, something other than her swiveling bottom.

22

FOR WANT OF
A NAIL

We tried calling Susan Corrigan from a gas station on Tamiami Trail. No answer at the cabana. We roared toward town, an evening thunderstorm slanting gray torrents across the two-lane road. For a while we listened to the machine gun rhythm of the rain on our canvas top. Cement trucks lumbered along, tossing filthy spray over our windshield. Charlie was thinking so I kept quiet. Then we argued.

"Your strategy won't work," Charlie Riggs said. "You want the jury to believe that Melanie Corrigan and this martial arts thug killed Philip Corrigan, then framed Roger to cover it up, right?"

"Sure, if you can tell me how they did it, how whatever they did ended up looking like succinylcholine poisoning."

Charlie Riggs stroked his beard. "Who says it looks like succinylcholine?"

"The ME says, choline and succinic acid found in the brain and liver."

"But none around the needle track in the buttocks?"

"Right."

"Hmmm," Charlie Riggs said, tamping tobacco into a corncob pipe.

"Well?"

"Regardless whether the succinylcholine played a role in Philip Corrigan's death, your strategy is flawed. The timing is way off. What motive would they have for framing Salisbury now? It would only draw attention to themselves."

"Plenty of motive once we dug up the body. They knew something was going on, needed to plant the drug and get Roger charged."

Charlie concentrated on lighting his pipe. "Foolish. They'd be better off sitting it out."

I laughed. "You're too logical. You're smarter than they are, Charlie, but you're forgetting one thing. The malpractice suit was intended to blame Roger or at least focus attention on the aneurysm. It's what Susan called the old fumble-rooski."

"The what?"

"A misdirection play. A plaintiff's verdict would establish the aneurysm as the cause of death and close the case. Even the defense verdict was no problem for them because the evidence still showed an aneurysm killed Corrigan. The jury just didn't blame Roger Salisbury for it. But then we grab Corrigan's body, and all of a sudden, they need a fall guy in case the tests are positive for poisoning. They break into Susan's cabana to get the drug, then plant it and get the murder indictment against Roger. Everything's coming up roses until they learn a nurse can place both of them in the hospital room after Roger left. Plus they know we have the videotape."

Charlie's face was shadowed in the lights of oncoming traffic. "No good. The video establishes Roger's motive for the murder, his lust for Melanie."

"But it also shows Sergio was just as bewitched, bothered, and bewildered and therefore would have the same motive to kill Corrigan. The tape furnishes reasonable doubt as to which of Melanie's admirers did him in. It also shoots some sizable holes in Melanie's grieving widow routine."

Charlie shot me a new look, one within an inch or two of respect. "If you're right, Jake, they're panicking. They know you still have the videotape. And that you must have gotten it from Susan." He thought about it a moment. "You might step on it a bit."

I was already doing seventy-five, but we were still half an hour from Susan's place. The rain came in gusts, sweeping out of the Glades, washing across the blacktop. Airboats were tied up in canals along Tamiami Trail, the operators sitting on the bank under thatched roofs, waiting for a break in the weather to head out for nighttime frogging. The Olds 442 roared eastward, the wet pavement hissing under its tires. I took my eyes off the road long enough to turn toward Charlie. "What's their next step? What will they try? Put the data into that computer on top your shoulders and give me a printout."

Riggs shrugged and sucked on his pipe. "I haven't the foggiest."

"Not a clue?"

"Nothing besides mere guesses. What I do is figure out things that already have happened, the hows, whos, wheres, and whens of death. Not even the whys. And you want 'What happens next.' No can do. Look at this sudden storm. Science can't even accurately predict the weather past seventy-two hours. How can we predict what men and women, perhaps psychotic men and women, will do when we have so little information compared to the data we have about pressure systems, winds, moisture, temperatures?"

I was quiet again, and Charlie blew some cherry-flavored smoke at me. "If I had to guess," he said, "it's that you're in some danger. You're the one unraveling the web they've spun. But then again, if you lose the trial, they're home free. Why should they risk it all by going after you?"

"But I know they'll try something. Melanie won't let it rest. I can predict that with virtual certainty."

"Your intuition tells you that, but your data is woefully insufficient. There is no way you can know thousands of incidents in her life that make her what she is so as to predict what she'll do."

"Whatever they are, they've made her evil."

Riggs smiled. "Correct. *Nemo repente fuit turpissimus.* No one becomes wicked suddenly. But knowing the woman is evil adds little to the equation insofar as predicting her behavior. Take my analogy to the weather. You would think that with our satellites and computers and sensitive equipment, we could gather enough data to predict the weather. Well we can't because our instruments don't collect enough information. We'll leave something out, millions of somethings out, and our predictions will be catastrophically wrong even if we leave out only a minuscule bit of data. The scientific name for that is sensitive dependence on initial conditions."

"But theoretically," I mused, "if you had enough wind gauges and satellite pictures and electronic doodads, you'd know all there is to know about the weather, and if you knew it enough times, you could see what it did the last time conditions were just the same, and you could predict weather for all eternity. So if you knew enough background about a person, you could predict his future acts."

Charlie Riggs paused to relight his pipe, an academic's trick of buying time. "For a human being, there are far too many events and no way to record them objectively. Even with the weather, Jake, you would need to know everything, the size and location of every cloud, the measurement of every bird's flight, the beat of every butterfly's wings."

"Butterflies, too?"

"The flap of a butterfly's wings in Brazil can set off a tornado in Texas."

"Metaphorically speaking," I said.

"No. Literally. It's part of the basis for the new science called chaos."

"Butterflies and chaos?" I said doubtfully. "An infinitesimal action radically affects mammoth events."

Charlie Riggs smiled, the teacher happy when a slow student catches on. "That's right. Just like the poem:

For want of a nail, the shoe was lost;
For want of a shoe, the horse was lost;
For want of a horse, the rider was lost;

And so on."

"I remember," I told him. "The battle and then the kingdom. All lost."

"Indeed."

I looked out at the rainswept street. "Then I'd better find the damn nail."

Except for the spotlights and the gentle roar of the waterfall, the Corrigan house was dark and silent on its hill. The rain had stopped just east of the Turnpike. In Gables Estates, not a drop had fallen. We jogged around the lighted path to the cabana. The screen door was unlocked, lights on inside, but no Susan. I walked into the small bedroom. Pale blue shorts and a faded Northwestern T-shirt had been flung onto an unmade bed, running shoes and socks tossed into a corner. In the galley kitchen, the oven was on four-fifty, a frozen vegetable platter was defrosting on the counter. An open can of Diet Pepsi sat on the counter. Half-empty and still cool to the touch.

We hurried onto the patio. The *Cory* was tied to the dock, lines tight, cabins dark. The pool lights were on, blue water shimmering in the night air.

The pool.

I don't know why I ran. I don't know what I felt. I don't know how I knew, but I knew.

Susan Corrigan was floating near the far end, facedown, wearing a black racing suit. I ran along the side and dived in. The taste of salt water filled my mouth. In three strokes I was beside her. With one hand, I grabbed a shoulder and turned her over. In the eerie light reflected from the water, her face was an unearthly blue, her features plastic. Her eyes were open but lifeless.

I carried her up the steps, her head slumped limply on my shoulder. A thin layer of white foam covered her lips. I gently set her down on the pool deck, Charlie helping with his hands under her back. I tore off the goggles, and my left hand lifted her neck to clear the air passage. My right hand pinched her nostrils to keep the air from escaping. Then I took a deep breath and sealed my mouth over hers. I blew hard, emptying my lungs, filling hers. Several short bursts, then one breath every five seconds. I looked for signs of life and saw none. Her breathing might have been stopped for two minutes or two hours. I couldn't tell.

Charlie knelt alongside me, letting me know with his silence that I was doing the right thing. My movements were automatic. Acting without thinking, doing what could be done. A volcanic mixture of anger and desperation fueled me. "Don't die!" I shouted at her. "Don't you die on me."

I covered her cold lips again with my mouth. I blew into her mouth again and again, trying to infuse her with oxygen, to give her some of my life. I leaned my ear to her lips.

Nothing.

I tried to find a pulse.

Nothing.

I sat on my haunches, placed one hand on her chest, just above the sternum, and pushed down hard with the other hand, trying to kick-start the heart. I kept pushing, up-down, up-down.

Nothing.

My heart was hammering. Hers was still. I paused long enough to choke back the helplessness that rose inside me. Charlie had run inside the cabana to call Fire-Rescue. I prayed for any sign of life, for a spark I could light. Still nothing. I went back to the mouth-to-mouth but it didn't work, so again I worked on the chest. I pushed harder and two ribs cracked under my hands. It didn't matter. Dead women feel no pain.

When we both knew it was over, Charlie Riggs put an arm around me and guided me to a chaise lounge. He brought two blankets from the cabana, covered Susan with one and me with the other. A numbness hit me, nailing me to the spot.

My body unable to move, the mind took over, rocketing past a hundred scenes, a thousand regrets. I had never told her what she meant to me. Why hadn't I just said that I'd never met anyone like her, a woman who was smart and sassy and strong and who thought she loved me. And died thinking I was a macho jerk. Thinking right. Dying because of me.

The numbness turned to pain.

She had been right about everything and died without knowing it. She had fretted for me, big dumb lucky stiff me who goes into the swamp and comes out wet but whole. I could have told her how much I cared, could have looked into those dark eyes and said, "Susan Corrigan, I love you and cherish you and want to be with you, now and always." But I'd held it back. And now she would never know. A step too slow, Jake Lassiter, then and now.

Charlie Riggs found a switch and turned on a set of mercury vapor lamps. The patio was doused with a ghastly green light. He called Fire-Rescue again, this time canceling the ambulance, and asking for the police. While we waited, Charlie scoured the pool deck. He found her thick-lensed glasses on a table, neatly folded, waiting for her return. Those silly glasses. I turned them over in my hands, fondled them. Charlie started to say something about fingerprints, then backed away.

"I'll look around for evidence," he said. "You stay put."

Charlie examined a pink beach towel draped over a chair. He looked in the shrubs; he crawled on hands and knees around a fifty-yard perimeter; he reached into the skimmer of the pool and came up with a handful of dead leaves; and he sniffed and tasted the water from the pool.

I watched him, letting the sorrow build inside me. When two uniformed Coral Gables policemen arrived, Charlie Riggs gave them a step-by-step description, the time we arrived, our efforts to revive her, his inspection of the scene. I sat, still wet, still holding the glasses. Beginning to shiver.

"Is the ME sending someone?" Charlie asked.

The sergeant shook his head. "No sign of foul play. We try not to drag 'em out to the scene unless it's an apparent homicide."

"She didn't drown!" I heard myself shout across the patio. "She could swim the English Channel. I want an autopsy done, but only by Doc Riggs."

The sergeant looked at me, then asked his partner to check out the house. The younger cop shrugged and walked slowly toward the darkened fortress. No hurry, just a routine job, a drowning in a pool.

The sergeant sat down on the end of my chaise lounge. It

creaked under his weight. He had a sunken chest, a beer belly, and was close to retirement. Coral Gables cops aren't the hard guys you find downtown. In the Gables, cops fish too many cats out of trees to get that cold-eyed look. Expensive cats and expensive trees.

The sergeant patted my leg through the blanket. "We take the body to the morgue. We gotta do that under section four-oh-six-point-one-one."

Charlie Riggs nodded. "Subsection one-ay-one. Then the ME determines whether to do the autopsy."

The sergeant looked back at me. "I've known Doc Riggs for twenty years, and we won't write it up, but if you want, why don't we let him have a quick look right here?"

My eyes pleaded with Charlie, and he said okay. The sergeant held a three-foot Kel-Lite and Charlie examined the body. He cupped his hands on her head, felt her skull and neck. He checked underneath her fingernails. He looked at her legs and arms.

The younger cop headed back to the patrol car to call in. The sergeant lit a cigarette and walked toward the dock to admire the *Cory,* maybe comparing it to a seventeen-foot Whaler he'd like to share with three other cops.

"Jake, I'm going to have to take off her swimsuit," Charlie Riggs said. I nodded and walked away.

After a few minutes, I heard him say, "No stab wounds, no bullet holes, no apparent loss of blood. No contusions or marks of any kind. No injection punctures. Not even an indication of a struggle."

The sergeant had come back from the dock. "A drowning, Doc. Just a drowning."

I turned around. "Charlie, please keep looking."

The other cop returned from the patrol car and told the sergeant they had to check out a ringing burglar alarm on Old Cutler Road.

"If it's the old Spanish house at seventy-three hundred, there's no hurry," the sergeant said. "Goes off every time the humidity's up, which is every week." In a few minutes, they would be roaming the suburbs, pulling over cars with missing taillights. Susan Corrigan would be just another statistic. *Accidental death by drowning.* Happens all the time.

The minutes dragged by. I watched the big house and concocted a vicious fantasy to vent my rage. Breaking down a door. Looking for them, the widow and the karate thug. Hurting them, killing them. Nice and slow.

Charlie motioned to me. "Jake, come here a second. My old eyes are failing."

The flashlight was shining on Susan's left shoulder. "Do you see any discoloration there?" he asked.

I shook my head wearily. "Maybe a faint pink. Maybe just skin color under the tan. Hard to tell."

"Hmmm," Charlie Riggs mumbled. He went into the cabana and came out with a plastic sandwich bag. Then, with a pocket knife, he cut a little square of skin from the shoulder and put it in the bag. Deep inside me, I felt every tiny slash.

"Jake, how about here on the leg?"

Same thing. A little pinkness, nothing more. I shrugged helplessly, and Charlie did some more slicing.

At the edge of the pool, the water rippled and slid under the lights. I remembered the breeze from the Gulf slapping palm fronds against Granny's little house, the sweetness of Susan under the quilt. I wanted a second chance, to tell her what had stayed locked inside me. I stood and stared into the pool, motionless.

Charlie Riggs came over and gave me a fatherly hug. Then he looked down at the pool. "Salt water. You don't see many saltwater pools these days."

23

VOIR DIRE

·"Mrs. Goldfarb, do you believe that old expression, where there's smoke, there's fire?"

Reba Goldfarb eyed me suspiciously from her perch in the front row of the jury box. She hadn't gotten settled yet, was still patting her ice-blue hair, locking it into a 1950s pompadour. She looked toward the judge for help, shrugged, and said, "Maybe there's fire, maybe just a teapot blowing its lid."

"Exactly," I said. "Things are not always as they seem. And just because Dr. Roger Salisbury is charged by the state with a crime doesn't mean he's guilty, does it?"

"Goodness no," she agreed, smiling, picking up the rhythm.

"And this indictment," I said, holding the blue-bordered document at arm's length as if it smelled of rotten eggs, "this piece of paper, this scrap, is not proof of guilt, has no more dignity than a grocery list—"

"Objection!" Abe Socolow was on his feet.

"Sustained," Judge Crane declared without emotion. "This is *voir dire*, not argument, Mr. Lassiter."

During trial I will argue over *Good morning*.

"Your Honor, I'll rephrase the question. Mrs. Goldfarb, do you recognize that Roger Salisbury, as he sits here today, is as innocent as a newborn child?"

Ignoring the concept of original sin.

She nodded.

"That he is cloaked with a presumption of innocence, that he does not have to prove anything, that the burden of proving his guilt is on the government?"

"I heard that before," she conceded, nodding again. She had seen enough television to know this stuff. My kind of juror, willing to believe that intrigue and incompetence frequently nail the wrong guy.

I liked her. Roger Salisbury liked her. She visited doctors regularly, an internist, a podiatrist, a chiropractor, and a dentist. She was Jewish, and defense lawyers from Clarence Darrow on down liked that. An old saw. Put Mediterranean types on your jury if you're defending. Jews and Italians are more sympathetic. Minorities, too. Blacks are suspicious of the police and will cut you a break in a close case. Hispanics used to fall into that group, but in these parts, they're the majority and may have lost the feel for the underdog. Keep

Germans, Poles, and Swedes off the panel. Too harsh and rigid.

Anyway, that's what the book says. But nearly every defense lawyer shakes his head over a black social worker or schoolteacher who ended up leading the posse for the state. And nearly every prosecutor remembers a Teutonic male who probably once wore a Luger but carried the banner for the defense in the jury room. Go figure.

I needed Reba Goldfarb. I had lost Deborah Grossman, Dominick Russo, and Philip Freidin. All three had said that they wouldn't vote for the death penalty under any circumstances. Socolow challenged them for cause, saving his precious peremptory challenges while I spent seven of mine getting rid of guys who had blood in their eyes.

It isn't fair. Talking about the penalty phase of the case before the trial begins. Mocking the presumption of innocence. But it's legal.

"Are you in favor of capital punishment?" Abe Socolow now asked Earl Pottenger, an airline mechanic.

"Yes sir!"

Hoo boy. This guy's ready to pull the switch. Ayatollah Pottenger. Socolow smiled and moved on to a heavyset black woman.

"Mrs. Dickson, if you find the defendant guilty of murder in the first degree, and if the state convinces you that the crime is sufficiently heinous, could you recommend to Judge Crane that he impose the death penalty?"

"Ah don't rightly know," Clara Dickson said, squinting up at him.

"Do you have moral or religious objections to the death penalty?"

"It's against the preachin' ah believe in."

"Challenge for cause," Socolow said.

"Granted," Judge Crane ruled.

I stood. "Objection, Your Honor. Dr. Salisbury is being deprived of a jury of his peers. We won't have a cross section of the populace if the state systematically excludes those with moral or religious objections to the death penalty."

"Denied. The Supreme Court ruled on this in the Witt case. The state is entitled to a death-qualified jury."

I shot back. "What's Roger Salisbury entitled to, just death?"

Oh, that was dumb. Judge Crane's long, sad face sharpened and he motioned me to the bench with a tiny wave of his gavel. Socolow slid silently behind me, his invisible smile a knife in my back.

"Mr. Lassiter, I don't make the rules, I just apply them," the judge said. "Now, one more remark like that in the jury's presence and I'll hold you in contempt. *Verste?*"

"Understood, Your Honor."

We would have a bloodthirsty, gung-ho, hang-em-high jury because the law allowed it. But I wasn't doing Roger Salisbury any good whining about it. I would just try to keep some people on the panel who neither belonged to the National Rifle Association nor folded their bodies into tight balls when I asked my questions.

So here I was, bobbing and weaving, trying to seat twelve honest men and women without itchy trigger fingers. Not that I wanted to be picking a jury. I didn't want to be doing anything except feeling sorry for myself. The three weeks since her death had been a blur. Preparing for trial, arguing with Socolow, waiting for some word about Susan from Charlie Riggs. At night, when sleep came, it was filled with dreams. An expanse of water, iridescent blue, a calm seductive lagoon. But when I dived in, the water thickened into a gelatinous muck and I sank to the bottom, gasping for air. Anonymous hands rescued me and dragged me to the beach where a laughing Roger Salisbury bent over me, giant syringe in hand.

Waking at dawn, I drifted uneasily toward consciousness, vaguely aware of an undefined pain. As my eyes focused on the light, the pain took shape, a vision of Susan Corrigan. Pretty and smart and tough. And dead.

Charlie Riggs had pulled some strings, and the ME's office performed an autopsy. Salt water in the lungs. A pinkish foam in the airway. Absolute proof, Charlie said, that Susan was alive when she stepped into the pool. If she'd been killed and dumped there, the lungs wouldn't produce the foam. Death by drowning on the certificate. Nothing to dispute it.

It was murder, I told Abe Socolow. He didn't buy it, asked for proof. I told him about the cabana break-in, the theft of the drug, the widow clamoring for the videotape. Proof, he reminded me, consisted of witnesses and physical evidence. Then I told him of my run-in with Sergio and his pal with the baseball bat.

He laughed. "Ambush at Shark Valley. Sell it to Hollywood."

"Your star witness set me up."

"Not the way I heard it," Socolow said, poking a finger at me. "She says you tried to extort her. If she testifies, you play the tape. She doesn't testify, you give her the tape.

277

Gonna get your balls whacked, Jake, you don't watch out. Could bust you for obstruction right now."

But he wouldn't. Because I was his buddy, he said. He wanted a copy of the tape. Fine with me, I told him, because it's defense exhibit number one.

He laughed again. "What's its relevance, that Melanie Corrigan is a sword swallower?"

"Pure impeachment. Lying under oath. On deposition, she denied the affair with Roger."

He wasn't impressed. "Nice try. She denied banging the doc *after* her marriage to Corrigan. The videotape was premarriage, so no lie on deposition, no impeachment. I'm filing a motion *in limine* to keep it out."

Judge Crane reserved ruling on the motion. Said he wanted to see the videotape. A couple of times. So did the clerk, the bailiffs, the probation officers, and everybody else within ten blocks of the Justice Building.

Without the tape, what would I have? Charlie Riggs saying that Corrigan died of an aneurysm, not succinylcholine. But no suspect to feed to the jury in place of Roger Salisbury. It would come down to a swearing match, beautiful widow versus spurned lover. Who said what to whom? Where did the drug come from? Who did what in Philip Corrigan's hospital room? Would the jurors even listen to Charlie Rigg's technical explanation of a bursting aorta? Probably not. Not with a black valise, two hypodermics, and a deadly drug staring them in the face.

Socolow had a tight little smile on his hawkish face as Judge Crane gave the newly empaneled jurors their preliminary instructions. Don't discuss the case among yourselves or with family members and friends. Don't speak to the witnesses or lawyers. Don't read the newspapers or watch television reports about the case.

Do jurors have the willpower not to follow *their* cases in the press? In a bribery trial a few years ago, a local columnist complained in print that the male jurors looked like they were headed for a ball game, all polo shirts and guayaberas. Next day, they all wore coats and ties.

My mind was wandering as the judge did his stuff. We would be back in the morning for opening statements. Tonight I would see Charlie Riggs. Beside me sat Roger Salisbury. Worried, a little grayer around the temples than at the first trial. His future a black hole.

"It is your solemn responsibility to determine if the state has proved its accusation beyond a reasonable doubt against this defendant," the judge gravely intoned. "Your verdict must be based solely on evidence, or lack of evidence, and the law."

I walked out of the courthouse into the blast furnace of a Miami afternoon. The blinding sun bounced ferociously off the marble steps. Thick fumes from the buses fought to rise through the soggy air.

There is no industrial smog in Miami. No steel mills, no oil refineries. Heavy industry is cocaine processing; high technology is money laundering. But a million cars in the shimmering heat add their own color to the horizon. Most days a fine red haze sprouts from the expressways and hovers over the city, hugging the ribbons of I-95 from downtown Miami northward to Fort Lauderdale. Not a thick smog, just enough airborne particles to add a counterfeit glitter to the sky, a reddish breast on the feathery clouds drifting over backlit beaches. One good blow, a cold front from the northwest, and the muck would be shoved out to sea.

But no more cold fronts. Not for six months. Until then, just broiling days and steaming nights. Purgatory for those who inhabit the swamp. My own fire burned deep inside. A score to settle. A woman had died. A woman I loved. I made a vow. When I knew for sure the how and the who of it, someone else would die, too.

24

VENOM

It had taken Charlie Riggs two weeks, but he had figured it out. Just as I knew he would. He kept it from me another week, not wanting to disturb me during trial preparations. But I badgered him and finally he told me to meet him at the morgue.

By the time I finished preparing my opening statement for the morning, it was nearly midnight. Charlie was waiting for me in the parking lot outside the new brick and glass building that looked less like a morgue than a modern office complex for a computer software company.

He puffed his pipe and scratched at his beard. I recognized the look. Acute discomfort. He took off his patched-up glasses, wiped them on his short-sleeve white shirt, and put them back on where they rode askew like a sailboat heeling in a strong wind.

"This won't be easy for you."

"Let's get it over with," I said.

The morgue was quiet. Two sheriff's deputies were hanging around the waiting area, drinking coffee, filling out forms after bringing in two bodies, a middle-aged man and his wife. The man had carved her up with a kitchen knife, then jammed a shotgun under his own chin and pulled the trigger with his big toe.

"Least he done the right thing," one cop said to the other.

"Yeah, saved us a lot of crap, blowing himself away."

A skinny kid with long, greasy hair in a ponytail sat at the reception desk, working the overnight shift. He leaned back in a swivel chair with his feet on a modern oak desk flipping the pages on a porno magazine and giggling. He kept sticking his hand in a huge bag of French fries, rooting around and popping them into his mouth, three at a time. He wore a green hospital smock and the shit-eating grin of the yahoo young. His nametag read *Curly*.

Charlie Riggs cleared his throat. Curly didn't look up. Making sure the county got no bargains on his minimum wage.

I rapped my knuckles on the kid's desk.

"Yeah?" A tone of mild annoyance, a face that needed a prescription for Retin-A.

I would have said, *Whatever happened to may I help you?* Charlie is more circumspect. He said, "We're here to see some tissue samples Dr. Kallan left for us."

Curly scowled. "Gotta name?"

I figured him for about twenty-one. If they're still sullen and whiny when they pass nineteen, they probably always will be. Another half century of bitching and moaning about bosses and girlfriends and how the other guys got all the luck.

"Riggs. Charlie Riggs."

Curly dropped the skin magazine and looked at a clipboard. "No stiff name of Riggs. Got a Rawlings."

Charlie smiled. "No, I'm Riggs. Dr. Charles W. Riggs."

The name meant nothing to him. Probably never read a newspaper, didn't know the building had a plaque honoring his nighttime guest. The kid likely was one of the astounding number of young people who can't name the century in which the Civil War was fought, much less the battlefields. On geography tests, they list Montana as an island in the Pacific.

"The deceased is Susan Corrigan," Charlie Riggs said, far more politely than the kid deserved. "Dr. Kallan was kind enough to make some slides of skin tissue."

Curly looked back at the clipboard. The month's guest list.

"Corrigan," he said. "Sure, Number eight-nine-dash-two-fourteen. Third cooler, first row."

His vacant eyes brightened. "Hey. Black-haired bitch. Love a dark bush, myself. Best looking piece of meat we've had . . ."

Charlie had a lot of quick left in him. Stepped wordlessly between us. I brushed him aside with a gentle forearm. Then my left hand found its way to the kid's neck, covered his Adam's apple, and squeezed, lifting him out of the chair. I didn't tell the hand what to do. It just squeezed and lifted. At the same time, the right hand balled itself into a good-sized fist and started coming over the top toward his pointy chin. From a deep tunnel, I heard the faraway voice of Charlie Riggs, "No, Jake!"

The right fist stopped short, uncoiled itself and slapped the kid hard. Once, twice, three times, red splotches shooting across his face. Eyes wide and white now, a scared rabbit. His feet were six inches off the floor when the left hand let him go. His knees buckled, and he crumpled to the desk, clipboard clattering at my feet. Charlie helped him up, mumbling apologies.

I walked away, head down.

Big hero.

Big tough guy.

Slapping around a pimply punk with a noodle neck and a garbage mouth. Wrapped a little too tight, are we now?

The two cops had watched it all without moving. Where they come from, an assault doesn't mean much unless automatic weapons are involved. I paced in the reception area, trying to close the spigot on the adrenaline flow. One cop looked at me and shrugged. Midnight in Miami, the crazies out. Anyway, what harm could a guy do in the morgue? Wake the dead?

The cops resumed talking, bellyaching about arresting hookers with AIDS.

"Ain't gonna wear gloves," one said. "Don't help, they bite you in the ankle."

"I hear you can't get it from somebody giving you a blowjob."

The first cop laughed. "What cocksucker told you that?"

The kid hadn't moved, but his eyes followed me across the reception area. Charlie finished apologizing and led me through the doors into a huge, brightly lit, cool room with a faintly antiseptic smell. The walls were covered with blue tile. Steel dissecting tables on wheels were rolled up to sinks. Hoses were coiled at regular intervals along the walls, and the tile floor was marked with drains.

Charlie was poking around in a refrigerator loaded with body parts and various tissues and liquids. Along one wall were five huge coolers loaded with corpses.

"What now?" I asked.

"I saw something on the skin sample I made at the scene. But my microscope isn't powerful enough, so I couldn't be sure. Dr. Kallan was my assistant for fifteen years. He took some other samples from the shoulder area, and . . . here they are."

He pulled out half a dozen slides and walked me through the procedure. If he could make a positive ID through the scope, we wouldn't have to enter Cooler Three, Row One. If he couldn't find whatever it was, we'd have to bring Susan's body out and make new dissections. My mind conjured up her body, already butchered in the autopsy, the parts tucked back inside. I told myself it wasn't Susan in the cooler, just the package that had held her spirit.

Charlie led me to an adjoining lab, where he climbed on a high laboratory stool, took off his cockeyed glasses, and peered through the lens of a high-powered microscope. Seconds later, he shook his head. He tried another slide. Nothing.

"What did you see in the samples you made?" I asked.

"I don't know, Jake. Something microscopic that disintegrated in the heat on my slide. It could be something that proves it was just a drowning. I just hope I'm not creating something from nothing—*ex nihilo nihil fit*—maybe trying too hard to prove it was an accident, to give you some peace."

He loaded another slide, took a long look, then exhaled a deep breath until it was nearly a sigh. "I thought so. Take a look, Jake."

I did. But I didn't see much, a tiny hair particle or nearly invisible twig magnified thousands of times.

"So?" I asked.

"It killed Susan," he said softly.

I looked again. "The hell is it?"

"*Physalia physalis*, one of your coelenterates, or all that's left of the one that killed Susan."

"I still don't get it."

"What you're looking at is a nematocyst, a tiny dart. Plus the remains of the sac that held the toxin. Each dart is invisible to the naked eye. She would have been stung by thousands of them, hundreds of thousands, really. The toxin is similar to cobra venom. Just about as powerful. A bad enough sting, the person goes into shock and drowns. Lots of drownings off the coast are the result of these stings. If you look at the body, nothing. No marks. So it's listed as accidental drowning. Which it is, of course. But the cause is the venom of the *Physalia physalis*."

I looked back through the barrel of the microscope. A tiny speck, that's all. But if Charlie Riggs says it's an animal's deadly dart, it is. All these years in Florida, snorkeling, scuba diving, windsurfing, and I'd never heard of a *fil-sailya* . . .

Charlie was still lecturing. "I don't think anybody ever got stung in a swimming pool before. Best I can figure, the Corrigans keep the water circulating from the bay. We can check it, but I'll bet there's no screen on the intake pipe. The pipe sucked water in, brought a couple of these creatures along. Susan goes for a nighttime swim. Can't see worth a darn without her glasses and swims right into one. Happens in the ocean all the time. Why not a saltwater pool? Pool bottom is painted blue. Wouldn't see the *Physalia*'s big blue sac."

Something was scratching around in the back of my mind. "What blue sac?"

"The floating sac. It stays above water. The tentacles trail underneath. They contain the darts, and when they uncoil, they shoot the toxin into the victim. The pain is intense. Horrible, really. Paralyzing. It can cripple the respiratory system and throw the victim into shock."

"A blue sac. Charlie, that sounds like a Portuguese man-of-war."

"Same thing. Forgive me for using the Latin, but it's such a beautiful language. To my ear, *Physalia physalis* sounds so much better than man-of-war or blue bottle, as we sometimes call them. Close relative of the hydroids, jellyfish, stinging corals, sea anemones."

"Man-of-war," I repeated, digging up a memory.

Charlie patted my arm and said, "I hope it's better, knowing it wasn't a murder. As Virgil wrote, *felix qui potuit rerum cognoscere causas*. Happy is he who learns the causes of things. Even if it can't bring you happiness, Jake, maybe peace."

Charlie Riggs was right. And wrong.

The man-of-war may have killed her. But it was murder just the same. Now I knew the how and the who.

Charlie was still prattling on. I interrupted him. "Melanie and Sergio killed Susan," I said, evenly and calmly. Keeping the burning rock inside.

Charlie looked puzzled. "Jake, I just said a *Physalia*—"

"I know, I know. Listen. After the malpractice trial, the two of them took a Whaler into the bay. Susan and I followed. I got as close as I could on a sailboard. It looked like they were fishing. At least they had fishing rods and Sergio was bringing something aboard with a net. But I remember this. It was one of those days the bay was covered with men-of-war. We could look up the date, I'll bet the county closed the beaches. Melanie and Sergio must have brought back some of them, kept them alive, probably in a tank on the *Cory*, then when Susan went for a swim, they dumped two or three in the pool. At night without her glasses on, goggles steamed up, she never would have seen them. Even if she managed to get to the side of the pool, Sergio could have pushed her back into the water. Before we got there, he netted the damn things and tossed them into the bay."

Still sitting on the high laboratory stool, Charlie was silent a long moment. Sifting through it. Finally he said, "It's possible. No reason it couldn't have happened. But you can never prove it. Not beyond a reasonable doubt."

"I wasn't thinking of legal niceties."

Charlie stiffened. His glasses were still on the counter

next to the microscope, and he looked up at me through tired eyes. "Don't do anything foolish, Jake."

Why not? I thought. I've done lots of foolish things. Just never one that leaves you face-to-face with a death-qualified jury.

25

THE ROAD MAP

Three A.M. and wide awake. Mind buzzing, a dozen different departments tying up the lines, busy signals all round. Up front some brain cells readying for trial, still rehearsing, doing what ought to be done. Some neurons in the back running through it all, the experiences of a lifetime, roads not taken, and for now and forever, mourning the loss of Susan. Shrouding it all, a poisonous gray mist choking me with rage. Hot to inflict pain. The pain of a thousand sea creatures a thousandfold.

It was stifling in my little coral rock house in Coconut Grove. The ceiling fans were on but I was soaked. Sitting in the living room on an old sofa of Haitian cotton, more brown than its original off-white, watching rivulets of sweat track down my chest and into the top of my Jockeys. Three Grolschs didn't cool me off.

I pushed the videotape into the VCR. Same interior shots of the *Cory*. Same striptease by Melanie Corrigan, same ass-rolling act in Roger Salisbury's face. A cut, then Roger playing doctor, listening to Melanie's lungs. When she turns over, he slowly taps her ass with his thumb. Laughter all around. Then Sergio joins the party, and finally, the trick shot with Philip Corrigan shooting the scene in the overhead mirror.

Nothing there I hadn't seen before. If there was something Melanie didn't want me to see, she had little to worry about. I'd seen it all and couldn't put a handle on it. I watched it again. Nothing changed. I put my feet up on the sofa and slept for an hour. Maybe two. Then I showered, and headed to the Justice Building. Putting everything else aside, concentrating on the mission, saving a man from the electric chair.

"What I say this morning is not evidence," Abe Socolow was saying as if it were indeed evidence of momentous weight. "It is a road map, a guide as to where the evidence will go."

He was wearing a black suit. All black. No chalk stripes, no patterns. You don't see many black suits these days. Or all black ties. A white shirt. And of course, shiny black shoes. With his beakish look and sunken cheeks, Abe Socolow could have been a small-town undertaker. Or an executioner.

I wore light brown. I almost never wear it, kind of blends me into the woodwork, sandy hair and sandy suit against oak paneling. Trial lawyers always used to wear dark blues and grays, power colors. Afraid brown made them look like salesmen. Then psychologists told us we were salesmen, and brown is friendly. Ronald Reagan wore it when greeting heads of state—big cordial brown plaid or checks. For this trial, friendly brown it would be. Jake Lassiter, the jurors' pal.

Hangman or not, Abe Socolow began his opening statement in restrained and understated tones, slowly building the tempo. First he matter-of-factly described the testimony to come. He turned it up a notch when he talked about the relationship between Melanie and Roger. With motive crucial to his case, he needed the jury to believe that Roger was obsessed with Melanie and would do anything to have her.

"You will hear Mrs. Corrigan describe her long-ago relationship with the defendant," Abe Socolow said. "Yes, they had a physical relationship when she was barely out of her teens, and he already a practicing physician." Socolow shook his head knowingly. How loathsome this defendant must be. Cradle robber.

Several jurors leaned forward. Eating it up. Socolow continued, "The affair ended, and as frequently happens, their paths crossed again. The defendant tried to talk Mrs. Corrigan into leaving her husband, tried to rekindle the flame that still burned within him, but not her. She would have none of it. But his obsession, his lust, his depravity, overcame his reason . . ."

Judge Crane looked toward me expectantly. I could object here but I didn't. Socolow was arguing his case, not presenting a sterile preview of the expected evidence. The judge shrugged. If I wanted to behave like a potted plant, no problem for the court. But I had a reason. If the judge let me get the tape into evidence, Socolow had just dug himself into a hole.

She would have none of it?

Depravity?

It takes two. Or three in Melanie Corrigan's case. I would use Socolow's own words against him in closing argument.

"First, he worked his way into Mrs. Corrigan's confidence," Socolow continued. "As occurs in marriages, the Corrigans had problems. We all do. Mr. Corrigan was often away on business. She was lonely. She confided in the defendant, sought his guidance as a professional and a friend, not knowing the evil within him."

A bit melodramatic for my tastes. But no one was dozing. I could hear the gentle whir of the television camera placed at an angle behind the bar. The still camera from the newspaper clicked incessantly, despite the muffler designed to quiet it. The newsboys were scratching their notepads, soaking up the sexy stuff.

"And what did the defendant do? Suggest to Philip Corrigan that he spend more time with his wife? No! Recommend counseling? No! This defendant, who pretended to be a family friend, who pretended to mend and to cure, this Great Pretender, whispered to Melanie Corrigan time and again that she should kill her husband. *Murder* him!"

He let it hang there, knowing the silence burned his words into them. No one even coughed. It was as if jurors, spectators, and clerks all held their breaths, afraid to exhale.

"Murder him," Socolow repeated, softer this time. Juror

number three, a middle-aged secretary, gasped. If Socolow had paused two more beats, she might have suffocated.

"He showed her how to do it. With a dangerous drug. An anesthetic that paralyzes the muscles and leads to a horrible, painful death as the lungs stop working. Naturally, she was shocked. So shocked that she couldn't believe he was serious. When he finally dropped the subject, she thought it was just a sick joke, a game. But then her husband died after routine surgery performed by this defendant."

For the first time, Socolow acknowledged Roger Salisbury's presence, pointing at him. The jurors' eyes followed Socolow's bony finger.

"Died after routine back surgery," Socolow said again, drawing the jurors into a cadence of repeated phrases. "Mrs. Corrigan was grief stricken. And suspicious. She sued the defendant for malpractice. The civil jury did not have the facts you will have, and he was exonerated. Still, she persisted. The defendant made advances toward her. She pretended to be interested, went to his home, and discovered the drug and the implements, the hypodermics, which you will see in evidence. You will hear testimony that a puncture on Mr. Corrigan's buttocks matches perfectly the twenty-gauge hypodermic found in the defendant's possession. You will hear evidence that this defendant surreptitiously entered Philip Corrigan's hospital room barely an hour before he died. You will hear from expert witnesses that tissue samples from Mr. Corrigan's brain and liver contain concentrations of the drug's components . . ."

It was a fine performance. Except for reading the indictment, Abe Socolow never mentioned Roger Salisbury by name, never called him *doctor*. The state's trick is to dehumanize. My job is to breathe life into the *man* who sits next to me, an innocent caught in a web of incompetence and deceit.

When Abe sat down, I walked to a comfortable spot six feet in front of the jury box. I put on a friendly smile and told them about the state's burden of proof, the burden to demonstrate *beyond a reasonable doubt* that Dr. Roger Salisbury intentionally killed Philip Corrigan. I mentioned Charles W. Riggs, M.D., and two jurors nodded, recognizing the name. How he would testify that Philip Corrigan died of natural causes. And I characterized the entire state's case as *circumstantial evidence*, spitting out the words as if describing a particularly odious disease.

I talked about Roger Salisbury, the doctor, the man. I talked about the long years of education and training, of good service to the community. Told them they'd hear character witnesses say they could believe Roger Salisbury under oath. Other doctors, community leaders. I promised they'd hear from Dr. Salisbury himself.

"You will hear a different story than Mr. Socolow tells," I said. "Not of a man spurned by a beautiful young woman. But of an ambitious, restless woman bored with her husband, a woman seeking excitement elsewhere. A woman who stood to inherit a fortune if her husband died, but would receive nothing if they divorced. You will see Mr. Corrigan's will and his antenuptial contract with this woman."

The reporters kept scribbling; the jurors kept listening. But that was about as far as I could go to toss another suspect at them. Until the judge ruled on the videotape, I was hamstrung. Still, I could put Melanie Corrigan's integrity at issue.

"You heard Mr. Socolow describe his case. He spent most of his time talking about the testimony of Melanie Corrigan. Why? She *is* the state's case. It is your job to evaluate the credibility of the state's witnesses. If you don't believe Melanie Corrigan, the state's case crumbles."

"Objection! Argumentative." Socolow stood and leaned forward toward the bench, his lean frame a javelin stuck in the ground.

Judge Crane paused and tapped a pencil against his forehead. In heavily publicized trials, he relied on signals from the press gallery to determine objections. Helen Buchman, a veteran *Herald* reporter, was the dean of the courthouse crew. But she kept a poker face this time, and the judge fended for himself. "You had considerable latitude in your opening, Mr. Socolow. Denied."

Socolow pouted and sat down. Emboldened by the ruling, I decided to finish with a flourish. "Yes, Mr. Socolow told you all about Melanie Corrigan and what she will *say*. But what evidence doesn't he have. Eyewitnesses to this alleged crime? None. Fingerprints? None. Confession? None. Just one woman's story and a prosecutor's case built on supposition, conjecture, fantasy, and whim . . ."

"Your Honor!" Socolow was halfway across the courtroom.

"Is that an objection?" Judge Crane asked.

"Yes. Improper opening."

"Granted. The jury will disregard the last statement of the defense. Mr. Lassiter, you are familiar, are you not, with the bounds of opening—"

A shout from the gallery interrupted the judge. Then a banging door. Then a woman's voice, loud: "Your grimy

297

hands off me! I ain't walking through no gamma rays. You wanna strip-search me, fuzznuts, see if you're man enough. I'm with Jacob Lassiter."

Judge Crane banged his gavel and said, "Mr. Lassiter, is that lady associated with your office?"

The bailiff had her by the arm. I approached the bench. "That's no lady," I whispered to the judge. "That's my granny."

The judge looked skeptical. "Madam, are you related to Mr. Lassiter?"

"Is a frog's ass waterproof?" Granny replied, loud enough to call the hogs home.

The judge called a five-minute recess. They always last twenty. Granny Lassiter shook loose from the bailiff and smoothed her ruffled feathers. She wore a yellow print sundress, deck shoes, and a heavy Navy peacoat, a gift from a grateful sailor who once tended Harry Truman's place in Key West.

"I brought you a thermos of hot conch chowder," she told me. "Know how damned cold they keep these government buildings and don't want you getting the grippe. Hope I didn't interrupt anything important."

"Your timing was impeccable," I said. "The judge was chastising me. Why the big fuss?"

Granny balled a fist at the bailiff. "They wanted me to walk through some damn machine, see if I was carrying hand grenades. Told 'em to shove off. Might affect my unborn children, deplete the ozone layer, and curdle your chowder. You still like a dash of sherry in it?"

I allowed as how I did.

She pulled out a flask and shook in three drops that

wouldn't wet the whistle of a priest receiving communion. Then she tipped the flask to her lips, drained it, glared at Roger Salisbury, and asked, "You kill that rich son-of-a-bitch who built condos in estuaries?"

"No, ma'am," Roger Salisbury said.

"Why not?" she demanded. "No balls?"

26

THE TEST

The state called its first witness, and Abe Socolow stayed in his chair. Jennifer Logan, pale and frail, stood to ask Deputy Sheriff Jack Roundtree what he found in the home of Roger Salisbury. Clever strategy. Letting the young assistant handle the preliminary witnesses. Keep Socolow from exhausting the jury with his hundred-kilowatt intensity.

The courtroom was packed. Granny Lassiter sat in the front row, doing her best not to hiss Socolow and cheer me when we emerged from the judge's chambers. I could use the moral support. Judge Crane had granted Socolow's motion *in limine:* the videotape would not be admitted into evidence.

In his usual laconic fashion, the judge had merely said, "Mrs. Corrigan is not on trial here. Her escapades are not relevant to the issue of the defendant's guilt."

I had paced in his small chambers, musty with stacks of casebooks. I tossed my arms, argued, and made my objections for the record. The judge was unmoved. Socolow's face flickered with a vulture's smile.

Now Jennifer Logan peered at Deputy Roundtree from behind horn-rimmed glasses and asked about the black valise, the two hypodermics, and the vial of clear liquid. All were found in Roger Salisbury's study. In a desk drawer just where the affidavit of Melanie Corrigan said they would be.

My cross-examination was short.

"Deputy Roundtree, did Dr. Salisbury offer any resistance to your serving the warrant?"

"No."

"Was he polite?"

"Yes."

"When you pulled the valise from the drawer, what did he say?"

"Something like, 'What the hell?' "

"Anything else?"

"Best I remember, 'I can't believe she'd do this.' Something like that."

"Did he say who the *she* was?"

"Not that I recall."

Jennifer Logan called the lab technician who had tested the liquid in the vial. She asked for his findings.

"Sucks," he said.

She reddened. "Beg your pardon?"

"Sucks. Succinylcholine, a muscle relaxant used in surgery. Sodium pentothal puts the patient to sleep, succinylcholine relaxes the muscles and helps the anesthesiologist intubate the patient, get the tube down the trachea. The lungs stop working, the patient breathes on a respirator."

"And if there's no respirator?"

"The patient dies."

"A strong drug?"

"Very strong. Sort of synthetic curare. You know, the poison the Indians in South America make from plants. They dip their arrows in it. Ugly way to die."

"Your witness," Jennifer Logan said.

"No questions," I said, visions of poison-tipped arrows sailing across my mind.

"The state calls Dr. Hilton MacKenzie," Abe Socolow announced. The jurors straightened, Abe's appearance signifying an important witness.

Dr. MacKenzie was tall and ramrod straight with fine features and a forelock of straight black hair that fell into his eyes. He was not yet forty and gave the impression that he grew up with all the advantages of money, family, and education. He had a habit of jutting his fine patrician chin toward the heavens, looking down over his reading glasses, and speaking in a tone most of us reserve for pets not yet housebroken. He lacked nothing except humility.

Socolow ran through his credentials. Penn undergraduate, Harvard Medical School, internship at New York Hospital, residency at Mass General, fellowships in pathology, the whole bit. Into public service as an assistant ME in Miami, then chief canoemaker. My terminology, not his. I would ask him on cross who trained him. Charles W. Riggs, of course. Let their witness polish my witness's silverware.

"Dr. MacKenzie," Abe Socolow said, his voice heavy with respect, "let me show you what has been marked Plaintiff's Exhibit C for identification and ask you to identify it."

MacKenzie removed his reading glasses from a breast pocket, ceremoniously put them on, and studied the document. "It's our toxicology report on certain brain and liver samples from Philip Corrigan's body."

"Objection," I said, popping up, reminding the jury of my presence. "Improper predicate. No showing of chain of custody of the alleged samples."

Socolow looked perplexed. He asked if we could approach the bench. Judge Crane leaned to one side, away from the jury, and we huddled there, exchanging whispers.

"Judge," Socolow said, "I'd assumed Jake would stipulate to chain of custody to save one of his witnesses some embarrassment. These samples were in the possession of Dr. Charles Riggs, and my sense of propriety does not allow me to say on the record where he got them."

Judge Crane looked my way. I looked back. "This is a capital case, Judge, and I'm not going to stipulate to the kind of sandwiches you serve the jury. Doc Riggs will understand."

The judge shrugged. "Abe, you gotta call Riggs. I'll let you get this in now, subject to tying it up with Riggs's testimony."

That was okay with me. I wanted Charlie on the stand as much as possible. Make him their witness for purpose of chain of custody. Let the state vouch for his credibility before I call him.

Socolow went through it with MacKenzie, the finding of succinic acid and choline—two of the components of succinylcholine—in Corrigan's liver and brain. The buttock dissection showed a needle track. His expert opinion on cause of death, cardiac arrest following the injection of succinylcholine. The aneurysm? In the throes of death, quite possibly the stress on the system caused the aorta to rupture. But the instigating cause, succinylcholine, no doubt about it. The whole dance took ten minutes. Socolow moved to admit the toxicological report into evidence, and the judge accepted it, subject to Charlie Riggs tying up chain of custody. Then it was my turn.

I grabbed the report and pretended to read it, furrowing my brow.

"Now, Dr. Blumberg—"

"Dr. MacKenzie," he corrected me.

"Oh," I said, feigning surprise, "there must be some mistake. A Dr. Blumberg signed this report."

Hilton MacKenzie smeared me with his exasperated look. "Milton Blumberg is the toxicologist who analyzed the tissue samples."

"Oh," I said again, looking around the courtroom for the toxicologist.

"Blumberg works under my supervision and I am responsible for his actions," MacKenzie piped up, getting the drift.

I turned toward the judge. "Your Honor, I move to strike all of Dr. MacKenzie's direct testimony as hearsay. Further, he's not capable of responding to my cross-examination of the report, so it too must be stricken."

Before Socolow could rise and offer me Blumberg, a guy I didn't want, MacKenzie chimed in, "Your Honor, I am intimately familiar with toxicology methods and the preparation of this report based on the chromatography tests."

Ah, vanity.

"Very well," I said, "as long as we have the expert here, objection withdrawn."

He settled back into his chair. Before he could get too comfortable, I asked, "How much succinic acid was found in the brain?"

"How much?" he repeated.

"Yes, your report—Milton Blumberg's report—says there was succinic acid in the brain. How much?"

He seemed startled. "I don't know," he said.

"In the liver?"

"I don't know. It doesn't matter—"

"And how much choline?"

"Objection!" Socolow stomped toward the bench. "Judge, he's not letting the witness finish his answer."

The judge looked toward the press gallery. Helen Buchman from the *Herald* was nodding. Or maybe just chewing her gum. No matter. "Sustained. Doctor, you were saying . . ."

MacKenzie was silent. Gathering his thoughts. He shook his head, confused. "We didn't measure the amount."

My face registered shock. I spun on my heel in front of the jury box and waved the toxicology report at the witness, a toreador taunting the bull. "So it could have been ten milligrams, twenty milligrams, a quart, a gallon?"

"You don't understand," Dr. MacKenzie said, scowling. Exasperated.

"I'm sure I don't. That's why I ask questions. Now, how much choline was found in the brain tissue?"

"I don't know. Again, we didn't test for amount, only presence. It was a qualitative test, not a quantitative one."

Fancy doctor words.

"Then how did you differentiate the substances you allegedly found from the choline and succinic acid already there?"

The doctor stared at me.

I moved closer to the witness stand. "Those two substances are normally present in the body, correct?"

"Yes, of course."

"So your test may have picked up the succinic acid and choline normally found in the body, correct?"

He was silent a moment. He looked toward Socolow for help. None came. He stole a sideways glance at the jury, brushed the forelock of hair out of his eyes and said, somewhat testily, "There is insufficient choline and succinic acid normally in the body to show up in these tests."

"How much is there, normally?"

"A trace. Nothing more."

"And it doesn't show up on your tests?"

"No sir."

"Then how do you know it's there?"

"Because I know! That's all."

"Now, in your training as a chemist—"

"I never said I was a chemist," he whined. Defensive now, hunching his long, well-bred body into a corner of the witness stand.

"But you know how to do the gas chromatograph tests?"

"No." Then he added quickly, "I supervise."

"Ah," I said. I liked that. Jurors know all about supervisors, leaning against the side of the truck, drinking coffee while other guys dig the ditches.

"And of course you found succinic acid and choline near the needle track in the buttock?"

"No, I never said that. You know we didn't."

"What do you make of that?"

"I would have expected to find it, if that's what you mean."

I nodded with approval and paused to emphasize the point. "You expected to find succinic acid and choline near the needle track because the concentration of the drug should be greatest near the injection, correct?"

Again he looked toward Socolow. "Ordinarily."

"Then how do you explain the lack of the two substances near the track where the drug was supposedly injected?"

He paused. One beat, another beat. Then, very softly, a murmur barely above the whir of the air-conditioning, "Sometimes, in science, we don't have an explanation for everything."

"Quite so," I said, and sat down.

Abe Socolow had been around long enough to know how to rehabilitate a witness.

"Just a few questions on redirect," he said with perfect calm. Never let the jury sense your fear. "Now, Dr. MacKenzie. Besides looking for the presence of succinic acid and choline, what else did your tests do, and I direct your attention to page seven of the report."

MacKenzie warmed to the friendly face and followed the coaching. He flipped through Blumberg's report, got to page seven, and smiled. "We scanned for other toxins. Those tests were negative. The tests were positive only for the components of succinylcholine."

Socolow nodded. "To exclude the remote possibility of picking up traces of succinic acid and choline occurring naturally in the body, what did you do?"

Dr. MacKenzie read some more, his eyes brightening. "We tested three other bodies that recently arrived in the morgue. We performed the same chromatographic tests on brain and liver samples. None showed any evidence of succinic acid or choline."

Abe Socolow smiled too. His jury smile. To carry the message, no harm done, just clearing the confusion caused by that wily defense lawyer.

"No further questions," Socolow said, easing himself into his chair.

The judge was ready to bang his gavel and call it a day. But I had one or two more questions. Recross.

"Dr. MacKenzie, these three other bodies you tested. How many had died during or just after surgery?"

He didn't know where I was heading. But Abe Socolow did. He stood up. Tried to think of an objection but couldn't. The question was relevant and within the scope of his redirect.

"None," the doctor said, looking at the report. "Two were gunshot victims, one died in an auto accident. All DOA."

"So none had received succinylcholine within the last twelve hours before death?"

There was an inaudible mumble from the witness stand. He shook his head from side to side. Now he knew.

"You must speak up for the court reporter," I advised him.

"No, none received succinylcholine."

"You're familiar with the records of Philip Corrigan's back surgery on the day of his death?"

A quiet "Yes."

"And the anesthetics included, did they not, succinylcholine?"

"Fifty milligrams, IV drip," he said, softer than the rumble of voices from the gallery.

27

IKKEN HISSATSU

I told Roger not to start celebrating but he was slapping me on the back. Brilliant again.

"You destroyed MacKenzie." He was jubilant.

"Maybe," I told him. "But they still have time to test someone who dies during surgery and Charlie Riggs doesn't know what it'll show. Nobody seems to know."

"Still," Roger insisted, "we won the day."

"Sure," I said, "but tomorrow is Melanie Corrigan. And the jury will convict if they believe her, acquit if they don't. Expert witnesses are just icing on the cake."

That was hard for his scientific mind to accept. "Then the

trial is just showmanship," he complained, "if whoever has the best looking, most likable witness wins."

"It sometimes works like that," I said. "My job is to get the jury to dislike her or Sergio or both."

"How do you do that?"

I winked at him. Like it was a great secret. Which it was. Especially from me.

I slept well. I had prepared. I lowered my pace a bit. Tried to forget just who she was and what she had done to Susan. My first responsibility was to Roger Salisbury. Time for the rest later.

She still turned heads walking into a courtroom. Unlike the civil trial, she could not sit at counsel table. The witness rule was in effect. No witnesses present except when testifying. So the jurors hadn't seen Melanie Corrigan yet. It made her appearance more dramatic. She didn't let them down. Poised, confident, a beautiful walk to the witness stand.

Still in his black suit, the Grim Reaper asked when she first met Roger Salisbury.

She was well prepared. "I was just a kid, really. I looked up to him. He was a doctor, and I was training to be a professional dancer. We became involved. He pursued me. He was, in a way, obsessed with me. He wanted to possess me, and I gave in to him."

Then she blushed. Really blushed. It came out well, set off nicely by a navy blue, dress-for-success skirt-suit. She had the whole shtick, white silk blouse and frilly bow, hair tied back in a pony tail. Little Bo-peep. Where was the slinky temptress of the videotape? I shouldn't have been surprised. Usually, it's the defendants who do the changeovers. Street hoods shave their beards, shower, and cover their tattoos with discount store suits. A crack dealer shows up for trial looking like an investment banker. And here was Melanie Corrigan, ex-stripper, semi-pro hooker, up from the streets, blushing on cue, Abe Socolow leading off Day Two with his strength.

He took her through it all, just as he had promised in opening statement. Roger Salisbury chased her long after the relationship was over, showed her the drug, wanted her to kill her husband. She thought he was joking or half crazy, would never do it. Then Philip died, darling Philip. The beginning of a tear, tastefully done. No gushers that would interrupt the timing of the questions. After the malpractice trial, Roger asked her over, and she found the drug and the black valise in his house.

It took less time than I had anticipated. Socolow got her up there, fulfilled his prophecy, then sat down. I stood up. And the worst thing that could happen to my cross-examination happened.

Nothing.

It was uneventful.

Flat, dull.

I had worked so hard to stay in control, to bury the hatred inside of me that I buried everything else. No spark, no inspiration, no edge. Flabby questions, brief denials, no follow-up.

"Were you intimate with Roger Salisbury after your marriage?"

"No, of course not."

I had no way of disproving it. The tape was shot before the marriage, and Judge Crane wouldn't let it into evidence anyway. Roger would contradict her statement, of course, but there is something unchivalrous about that. The jury will not like him.

"Were you intimate with your employee, a Mr. Sergio Machado-Alvarez?"

"Objection," Socolow yelled out. "Irrelevant."

The judge's eyes darted across the gallery. Helen Buchman had gone to the restroom. He took a stab at it. "Granted. Same ruling as on Mr. Socolow's motion *in limine*. Mr. Lassiter, I remind you that Mrs. Corrigan is not on trial."

"Thank you, Your Honor," I said, to confuse the jury. "Mrs. Corrigan, the black valise you testified about, was it ever in your possession?"

"No."

Again, nothing to disprove her. If Susan were alive, she could ID the valise in Melanie's underwear drawer. Destroy her testimony. I needed Susan for this and a thousand other reasons. I blinked and saw her face, nuzzling me on the way to Granny's house. I blinked again, and she was facedown in the pool. I was reeling, losing control.

"What do you know about the break-in at Susan Corrigan's cabana?"

An inane question. A preordained answer. Floundering.

"Nothing. Poor thing, to die so young."

I choked on my own incompetence, unable to muster anger or rage. I caught sight of Roger at the defense table. Catatonic. He knew I was blowing it. I improvised.

"You thought Dr. Salisbury cold-bloodedly murdered your husband and yet you went to his house after the civil trial?"

"Yes."

"You weren't afraid of him?"

"No, but . . . maybe I should have been."

I am not a mind reader. I have trouble enough understanding what people mean when they *speak* their thoughts. If I had known where she was going, I would have shut up. Instead I chomped at the bait.

"And why should you have been?"

An open-ended *why* on cross, invitation to disaster.

"He attacked me earlier at my home. He struck me right here because I would not . . . I refused to make love with him."

She was pointing to a spot below her left eye. Two female jurors looked upset. The cad. Killing a guy may be okay. But hitting a woman?

I was quiet so she kept going. "I'm sure you remember, Mr. Lassiter. You were kind enough to come over when I called you. After Philip's death, I had no one to turn to. I thanked you then, and I thank you now."

Ouch. So gracious. So ladylike. Socolow beamed. Palpable pleasure. Roger moaned. It was true, of course. Like so many big lies, this one was constructed of little truths. Roger *had* hit her. I *had* come over to keep him out of trouble. She *had* thanked me with a slippery tongue and a promise of more. Now she was making fun of me. Humbling men was sport to her. I decided to shut up before the quicksand rose above my neck. She glided out of the courtroom, elegant in her grief.

There was no time to regroup.

"The state calls Dr. Charles W. Riggs," Abe Socolow proclaimed.

The bailiff opened the door to the corridor, and Charlie

bounded into the courtroom with rapid, short steps. His beard was still bushy, and his glasses still askew on his tiny nose. The bowl of a pipe jutted from the pocket of the old gray suitcoat he still kept for court appearances. He didn't need to be shown the way to the witness stand. He raised his right hand and promised to tell the truth even before the clerk asked him. He smiled at the jury and waited.

I figured Charlie wouldn't give Socolow any problems. All the state needed was chain of custody, a formality having nothing to do with Roger's guilt or innocence. Abe Socolow approached the witness stand warily. He was politic enough to skip the night in the cemetery. Just asked if Charlie had made dissections of Philip Corrigan's liver, brain, and buttock material and passed them on to the Medical Examiner's Office.

Charlie gave him the right answers and was ready to step down. Something passed behind Socolow's dark eyes. I saw the shadow of his thought. When the defense stepped to the plate, Socolow knew, Charlie would testify that Corrigan died of natural causes. Socolow wanted an extra turn at bat.

"Dr. Riggs, not to steal your thunder, but you're prepared to testify for the defense that Philip Corrigan died of a spontaneous aortic aneurysm, isn't that right?"

"Correct."

Socolow had Riggs tell the jury what that meant and Charlie took him through it, an encore of his testimony in the malpractice trial. Great. I didn't know where Socolow was headed, but if he wanted to hear my best testimony twice, fine. "Lots of things can cause an aneurysm, correct?"

"Sure. Hypertension, arteriosclerosis, syphilis, trauma."

"Trauma. How about a huge injection of succinylcholine,

not the steady drip of an IV tube as in surgery. Wouldn't that cause trauma to the heart, the kind of trauma that could cause an aneurysm?"

So that's where he was going. Worried about my cross of MacKenzie, trying to tie the injection to the aneurysm. Give the guy a boost of the drug, it blows out an artery. A long shot.

"You'd have to ask a cardiologist," Riggs said. "But I had a different kind of trauma in mind." He smiled at Socolow, a witness at ease with himself and his surroundings. He had testified for the state hundreds of times. If Socolow wanted to debate medicine, Charlie Riggs was happy to oblige.

"Right. You previously testified that a driver can suffer an aortic aneurysm if he hits the steering wheel following a crash, isn't that right?"

Abe had done his homework, had read the transcript of the malpractice trial.

"Yes. I've seen several of those."

"In such an accident, there's quite a shock to the system, isn't there?"

"Surely," Charlie Riggs agreed.

"And can you say conclusively that the aneurysm is caused by the impact of the steering wheel or could it be the shock to the system, to the heart?"

He was winging it now, trying to find a parallel between an injection of succinylcholine and an auto accident. It wasn't going anywhere. Not helping or hurting his case. Just one of those tangents lawyers sometimes take.

Charlie Riggs wouldn't bite. He shook his head, and several jurors did likewise. "My impression has been that it's the trauma, the impact that causes the blowout of the aorta.

It takes a serious blow, but a steering wheel, or a very well-thrown punch by a trained boxer could do it."

"Even a punch," Socolow repeated, apparently happy that so many things could cause an aneurysm.

"A punch, a kick, even a karate chop."

Socolow went on, detailing every cause of aneurysm known to man, monkeys, and little white rats. But my mind stayed right there.

A punch, a kick, even a karate chop.

I hadn't thought of it before. But I did now. Nurse Rebecca Ingram said Roger left the room at ten o'clock. Sometime between ten-thirty and eleven, Melanie Corrigan waltzed in with the little hunk of martial arts skills.

A karate chop.

I didn't know whether to risk it now or wait until I had Charlie on my part of the case.

Your witness, Abe Socolow said.

I plunged ahead. "Dr. Riggs, are you telling the jury that one karate punch to the abdomen could puncture the aorta?"

Charlie Riggs looked toward the jury and stroked his beard. Say *yes*, I prayed. Say *yes*, you hairy wizard.

"Yes. The concept is *ikken hissatsu*, to kill with one blow. Some of it is exaggerated to the point of myth, but it does happen. Martial arts assassins are quite capable of it. The essence of karate is *kime*, an explosive attack using maximum power over a short distance. Of course, it would be difficult to rupture the aorta of a well-trained athlete with strong abdominal muscles, particularly if he expected the blow."

I let out a breath, awed at the range of Charlie's knowledge. Time to set the scene. "After a laminectomy, how would a patient be lying in bed?"

"After back surgery, you put a patient on his back. The pressure helps prevent further bleeding."

"With stomach exposed?"

"Yes."

"Muscles relaxed."

"Quite. The patient would be sedated."

"And, assuming a man in his fifties not in the best of physical condition was lying on his back, sedated, stomach muscles slack, could a karate expert rupture his aorta with one blow?"

Socolow leapt up. "Objection! Assumes facts not in evidence, irrelevant, beyond scope of direct, beyond witness's expertise."

"Anything else?" the judge asked.

Socolow shook his head. Already he had protested too much.

"Denied," the judge said.

"Yes. A well-placed blow, a *shuto uchi*, the sword hand-strike, could burst the pipe, the aorta, that is. Perhaps even the *stoshi hiji-ate*, the downward elbow strike."

Charlie demonstrated the movement of each blow, smiling shyly toward the jury box. "I learned a little of this on Okinawa after the war," he added.

Oh bless you, Charlie Riggs, master of a thousand subjects, encyclopedia of the esoteric, bestower of life on the condemned.

"Nothing further," I said, easing into my heavy wooden chair as if it were a throne.

28

THE KARATE KING

The five of us sat on my tiny back porch swatting mosquitoes, drinking Granny Lassiter's home brew, and arguing how to use the gift imparted by Abe Socolow.

"Show a video of Sergio winning the Karate King title," said Cindy. Ever efficient, she already had fished around town and found the tape.

"Let him split your head open with a shoe-toe oochi-koochi," Granny said. "Show his mean streak."

"Drop it now while we're ahead on the point," Roger Salisbury argued. His face was drawn, and he looked like he hadn't been getting much sleep. Being a defendant in a first-degree murder trial can do that. "Socolow will be ready for anything more about the karate."

Charlie Riggs drained the dark, headless beer from a mug that was once a peanut butter jar. "Not a bad idea. That was all off the cuff today. No matter what, we can't prove Sergio struck the decedent."

I shook my head, both at Charlie and at Granny, who was offering me a refill. Too heavy with hops, like an English bitter. "You're forgetting something, Charlie. We don't have to prove anything. All we need is to create a reasonable doubt that Roger aced him."

Charlie nodded and helped Granny into the hammock where she had decided to spend the night. I didn't think there was room for two.

"But it must be a reasonable doubt," Charlie Riggs declared. "Not a possible doubt, a speculative, imaginary, or forced doubt."

I laughed. "Whoa, Charlie, when did you start memorizing jury instructions?"

"I been in trials before you got out of knickers."

"Used to wet his knickers till he was four," Granny called out from the hammock.

Roger Salisbury leapt to his feet from an aging lawn chair. "I didn't kill Philip Corrigan!" Silently, three heads turned toward him. His normally placid face was twisted with pain. "When you talk about strategy, you seem to be trying to hide something, to get off a guilty man. You all forget I didn't kill Philip! He's the one person I could never kill. He was my friend."

Salisbury sagged back into the chair and turned toward the sprawling hibiscus that threatened to overrun the porch.

Everyone quieted down for a while. I thought about Roger's little speech. Something vague and fuzzy bothered me, but I let it go. We weren't getting anywhere except mosquito-bitten and drunk.

I was nearly dozing when the phone hollered. Everybody I wanted to talk to was within spitting distance. By the sixth ring, I stirred just to stifle the noise. Usually at this time of night, it's a boiler room call, somebody selling frozen beef from Colorado or solar water heaters made in Taiwan. Usually it's not Abe Socolow.

Breakfast before court? Sure. Bay Club? Sure.

"What does he want?" Roger asked, a tremble in his voice.

"Don't know. Maybe just wants to do a Power Breakfast."

Granny Lassiter snorted. "Then why call you?"

The Bay Club sits on the thirty-fifth floor of a new office building overlooking Biscayne Bay and the Atlantic Ocean. The dining room is chrome and glass, white tile, and a blinding brightness. All the charm of an astronaut's space capsule. The club was designed by a young architect adept at stealing ideas about modern design and making them worse.

Socolow was late. I looked around. There was Fat Benny Richards, all three hundred pounds of him, wolfing French toast with county commissioner Bradley Shriver. Fat Benny wore a six-hundred-dollar silk suit but looked like a ton of shit in a gunny sack. His clients called Fat Benny a lobbyist, which was a more polite term than bagman. Politicians courted him because he collected campaign contributions the way a sewage plant draws flies.

Fat Benny had the beady red eyes of an overfed rat, and his eyes were his best feature. His breath could kill a manatee and his toupee threatened to slide into his Bloody Mary. I picked up pieces of the conversation between the commissioner and the fat man. Arguing for a builder client, Benny wanted a variance from the ordinance requiring a parking space for every four hundred square feet of office space. A customary request by rapacious builders since parking garages cost a bundle and the cash return is diddly-squat compared to office space.

Fewer parking spaces, larger buildings, less green space, billboards the size of cruise ships—zoning was a scandal. But why not? In a town where William Jennings Bryan once hawked vacant lots from a floating barge, the hustle was still king.

Abe Socolow slid silently into his chair, folding his body like a scythe. He looked haggard. Black circles under his eyes, sunken cheeks, skin the color of a newspaper left in the sun. A waiter in a white vest and gloves took our order. Gloves at seven-thirty in the morning.

"Just coffee," Socolow said. "Black."

Naturally.

I ordered a large orange juice, a basket of sweet rolls, and shredded wheat with whatever fruit didn't come in a can. Let Abe suffer, I was hungry.

"That was some happy horseshit yesterday about a karate chop busting the aorta," he began irritably.

"Glad you liked it."

"Liked the bit about MacKenzie not testing stiffs who died after surgery, too."

"You ask me to breakfast to compliment my trial skills. How kind."

"Whadaya doing, Jake, just throwing shit on the barn door, seeing what'll stick?"

"Your breakfast conversation is most appetizing."

I didn't know where he was heading. He drained the coffee, and the waiter materialized silently with more from a silver pot. At the next table Fat Benny was offering the commissioner preferred stock in a cable television franchise.

"Just thought you should know," Socolow said, "I been at the morgue all night with MacKenzie . . ."

"The way you look, you're lucky they let you out."

He ignored me. "We got two stiffs out of surgery yesterday. Both had succinylcholine IVs as part of the anesthesia, and guess what?"

I didn't have to guess. No traces of succinic acid or choline. I figured Socolow would bust his balls to recoup after MacKenzie's debacle. Just didn't think he could do it so fast. Now I pictured him dashing from hospital to hospital, praying for patients to die in the OR, maybe pulling the plug in the ICU.

"As a personal favor, in a spirit of fairness," he went on, "I'll tell you about my rebuttal witness, an internal medicine guy. Feingold, head of the department at Jackson. He says a karate chop can't bust the aorta. No way. Too much padding in the abdomen, what with the fat and the stomach and all those organs."

"Kind of you to share your strategy with me, Abe. But we both know you can get Irv Feingold to say anything. I been around the rosy with him in two malpractice cases. Now, you didn't bring me here to talk about how strong your case is. What's up?"

He squinted at me through tired eyes. I smeared a large glob of butter on a heated cinnamon roll. Nearby, Fat Benny was extolling the virtues of a garbage compacting plant located upstream of a drinking well field.

"Jake, you know I'm fair. Tough, sure. But fair."

"Uh-huh," I mumbled. No use insulting him. If he had an offer, I would listen. Then I could insult him.

"We may have overcharged Salisbury," he said softly.

"Go on," I said.

"You know how juries are. Anything can happen. Hell, they can come back with Murder One and recommend death. Puts Crane in a tough spot."

"To say nothing of my client."

"Or they could compromise and recommend life."

"Yeah, and they could come back with a big fat NG."

He shook his head. "I'm not going to argue with you, Jake. Here it is. He pleads now to Murder Two, we agree to ten years. He'll be out in thirty-nine months."

It didn't take long to think about it. "No deal. A felony conviction, he loses his ticket to practice. Besides, he's not guilty. I won't plead him to jaywalking."

Socolow's jaw muscles tightened. "Jake, you're between the dog and the fire hydrant. If it's Murder One, even if no-go on death, it's twenty-five years minimum mandatory, you know that."

I knew that. And I knew that Abe Socolow was right about juries. You can never tell. I would tell Roger about the plea offer and let him decide. But I knew his answer. *I didn't kill Philip Corrigan!* It was still ringing in my ears.

"Sorry, Abe. Just dismiss the case and go away. If not, we'll take a verdict from the jury box."

"I'll see you in court," he hissed.

"In about thirty minutes," I said.

"The state calls Mr. Sergio Machado-Alvarez."

Now there was a surprise, Socolow trying to catch me off guard. Bringing the Karate King in now, figuring we hadn't had much time to work on the karate chop angle. Figuring right.

Socolow's direct examination was brief, first describing Sergio's job as the family's driver and boat captain. Brought Mrs. Corrigan to the hospital the night of October 14 to check on her husband. Clever. Blunt the jury's surprise when I show he was there shortly before the fatal aneurysm.

Sergio went through it matter-of-factly. Mr. Corrigan was fine when they saw him, sleeping peacefully. No, he never saw the doctor in the room, must have come by later. Such a shame, *qué lástima*, the boss dead, a good man. Then he corroborated Melanie's testimony about being attacked by Roger after the malpractice trial. Pulling up on his chopper in front of the Corrigan home, he saw the defendant, tires screaming, tearing out of Gables Estates. The *senora* showed him the beginning of a bruise under the eye. She was wailing that the doc struck her.

"Objection, hearsay," I sang out. "Move to strike."

"Denied," the judge declared firmly, pleased he could handle that one solo. "Excited utterance exception to the hearsay rule."

Socolow went on. "Did you ever speak to the defendant about this assault?"

327

"*Nunca.* I wouldn't say nothing to him. I told the *senora,* I mess him up she want. She says, no. She too kind."

"Did the defendant ever say anything to you about Mr. Corrigan when he was still alive?"

"*Sí.* He tell me Mr. Corrigan not pay enough attention to his wife, he lose her, one way or another."

"Your witness," Abe Socolow said.

I stood up and moved close to the witness stand. I kept my back to the jury and gave Sergio my best mean-and-nasty look. If we were playing poker, he saw my mean-and-nasty and raised it to cruel-and-vicious. Good. Let the jury see a hard guy up close. Too bad he was wearing a suit, covering up those slabs of muscle and malice. His shirt collar was buttoned too tight, and he kept craning his neck toward the ceiling and pulling at the collar as if to let out the steam.

"Mr. Machado, have you ever been convicted of a crime?"

He shrugged his rhinoceros torso. "No big deal."

"May we assume that's a yes?"

"*Sí,* sure. A crime, if you want to call it that."

"What do you call possession of illegal drugs?"

He snorted a little laugh. "Steroids, man. *Solamente* steroids. Possession without a prescription. Everybody I know does steroids."

"I'm sure they do. But you were convicted, were you not?"

"Yeah, sure. But I got no joo-dification."

"How's that?"

"My first offense. They didn't joo-dify me."

"The court withheld adjudication?"

"*Sí,* what I say, I got probation. I got the half-a-david with me."

He had lost me. He drew a crumpled legal-size paper from his back pocket, and sure enough, there was an affidavit from the clerk of the criminal court attesting that one Sergio Machado-Alvarez had been placed on probation, adjudication withheld.

Socolow was reading it over my shoulder. "Objection! This is not proper impeachment. That's not a conviction under Section ninety point six-ten. Move to strike."

The son-of-a-gun knew his statute numbers. And he was right. You can attack the credibility of a witness by showing a prior criminal conviction, but without an adjudication of guilt, it doesn't count.

I treaded water. "Your Honor, this is not, strictly speaking, impeachment of credibility. Mr. Machado's familiarity with the implements of steroid abuse has a direct bearing on the guilt or innocence of Dr. Salisbury."

"Tie it up quickly, Mr. Lassiter," Judge Crane ordered, turning his profile to the television camera.

I moved even closer to the witness stand. "You freely acknowledge being a user of anabolic steroids, do you not?"

"Sure, makes me big."

"And smart, too," I cracked, trying to rile him.

Abe Socolow was having none of it. "Your Honor, please admonish Mr. Lassiter not to be argumentative."

"All right, both of you. Let's get on with it."

I walked to the rear of the jury box. Let them focus on Sergio, forget about me. "How long have you used steroids?"

"*No sé.* Five, six years."

"So, at the time Mr. Corrigan died, you were a regular user."

"Sure, I guess."

"You're familiar with the studies linking aggressive, irrational behavior with steroid abuse?"

"Says who?"

"An expert witness, but we'll save that for another day. Mr. Machado-Alvarez, how do you administer the steroids?"

"Huh?"

He didn't know where I was going. Abe Socolow would have prepared him for cross-examination about his karate skills. That would come. But first . . .

"How do you take the steroids? Pills, liquids? Do they come in little doggy biscuits?"

"You inject them, man."

He took his right hand and made a little plunging motion with his thumb. He did it twice, and somewhere deep inside me, a man was hitting a gong with a sledgehammer, trying to force some rundown brain cells to match distant thoughts with nearby ones. It would have to wait.

"So you use a hypodermic needle?"

"Sure."

I walked to the clerk's table and picked up State's Exhibit Six.

"Like this one?" I asked, holding that little devil three feet in front of the jury box.

He didn't answer. He was slow but not that slow.

"Like this one?" I repeated.

"I didn't kill no old man," he said. "He's the one did that. He's the needle man." Pointing now toward Roger Salisbury. But the jury was looking at Sergio Machado-Alvarez.

Good.

Very good.

So good I was ready to stop for a while. So was the judge. He knew the evening paper had an eleven-thirty A.M. deadline. *Gentlemen, this may be a propitious time to recess for lunch.* Fine with me. Let the jurors chew over Sergio Machado-Alvarez with their roast beef sandwiches.

I returned to court early. Lugging a trial bag filled with ceramic tiles. A clerk from the law firm pushed a dolly loaded with concrete blocks. I built four stacks of blocks, leaving them far enough apart to place twenty tiles on top, the edge of each block holding a corner of the bottom tile. The top of the pile was about waist high.

Abe Socolow walked in, took one look, and began barking orders that stampeded a herd of law clerks toward the library. Socolow raced for Judge Crane's chambers, a vein throbbing in his neck. I moseyed along behind him.

It was either indigestion or our presence, but the judge looked pained. In a corner of the room, by the bookcases, Jennifer Logan scratched through the cases searching for precedent on in-court demonstrations. Meanwhile Judge Crane belched and listened to Socolow's bleating.

"Show biz," Socolow said. "Histrionics for TV. Irrelevant blather designed to distract from the issues of the guilt of the accused."

"We've laid the predicate," I told the judge. "Dr. Riggs testified that a karate blow could have caused death. This witness is a karate expert. He was in the victim's hospital room shortly before the aneurysm. Let's see how hard the Karate King can hit."

"If the witness refuses to hit these things, I can't make

331

him," the judge said wearily. "Even if he's willing to do it, I'm inclined to keep it out. Ruling deferred for now. Let's see where the testimony goes, but Mr. Lassiter, I admonish you, no circus tricks."

Abe Socolow huddled in the corridor with his witness, instructing him, no doubt, to downplay his karate skills and to stay away from the stack of tiles. Jennifer Logan neatly refiled her research in color-coded folders. The bailiff brought the jury in, and I started earning my retainer.

I asked Sergio about his training and his trophies, his black belt and his favorite *dojang*.

"First place in Florida sports karate, we don't hurt nobody," he said, obviously adhering to Socolow's advice. "Second in Atlanta, regional competition. Training for fifteen years."

I had him tell the jury about his weightlifting, Chinese boxing, judo, and aikido.

"You're a pretty physical guy?" I asked.

"I'm okay."

Ever so humble.

"Pretty good at karate?"

"If you say so."

Evasive.

"See this stack of tiles, think you can break them all with one blow?"

"Who knows?"

"Well, on this videotape from the Florida championships, you break a stack of boards like they were toothpicks, should we take a look?"

Socolow leapt up, objecting again.

Judge Crane, more dolorous than usual, peered down at

us, unhappy we needed his intervention. He looked toward the press gallery, but no one told him how to rule, so he took a stab at it himself. "Mr. Socolow, this is a capital case, and I will not unduly limit the defense. But Mr. Lassiter, get to the point. Objection overruled."

I raised my voice. "The fact is, you're not good enough to break twenty tiles with one blow, are you?"

"Huh?" Sergio looked puzzled. It did not seem to be an expression entirely foreign to him.

"Maybe Shigeru Funakoshi could do it," I suggested. "Didn't he beat you in Atlanta?"

"Home cooking. Two Japs and a Korean for judges."

"But you really couldn't break all twenty of these, could you?"

"You kidding? With my hand, my foot, or my head. Kid's stuff."

Adieu, humility. Socolow was grimacing, sitting on the edge of his chair, itching to pop up.

I said, "Let's see you do it. Mess them up. Isn't that what you said you could do to Dr. Salisbury, mess him up?"

Socolow was up again. "Your Honor. He's badgering the witness. As Your Honor said, an unwilling witness cannot be forced to take part in a demonstration. Miss Logan has handed me several cases on courtroom demonstrations that I wish to present on this issue. If the court please, in *Mills v. State* . . ."

Socolow approached the bench but I stayed close to the witness stand. The judge was going to set me down. I took a risk. It might get me another broken nose, maybe straighten out the one I had. It might get me some harsh words from the judge, nothing novel there. Or it might get me an acquittal.

I leaned over and murmured in Sergio's ear, "Stick around, Shorty. I'm gonna play a videotape of you and your friends. No wonder that bitch needs three guys. You not only have the brains of a flea, you've got the *pinga* of one, too."

Socolow was still at it, quoting the Florida Supreme Court. He couldn't hear the guttural growl that stirred in Sergio's throat. The Karate King rocked in the chair, his hands gripping the rail, his knuckles bleaching out. But he didn't get up. I leaned even closer, my mouth inches from his ear. Improvisation.

"Big pecs," I whispered, *"pero pinga chiquita, no pinga grande."*

It's important to be bilingual in Miami.

Sergio's cruel little eyes opened as wide as his brain would let them. Incredulous that I would mock him, enraged that I could do it from a vantage point half a foot higher than he'd be in elevator heels. But I needed more, something that would cut deep into the tender meat of his machismo, something to inflame a guy who spends hours posing his bicep curls in front of a gym mirror.

"What surprises me," I breathed into his ear, "is that you're a switch hitter. A fruit. Roger tells me he could never bend over with you behind him."

He erupted. A primeval roar. Socolow turned, eyes wide, frozen. Sergio stood in the box and tore off his coat, throwing it to the floor. Short sleeves underneath, arms exploding against the fabric. He bounded out of the box toward me. I backpedaled like a cornerback on third and long. I wanted the stack of tiles between the two of us.

He looked at me. He looked at the tiles. He would have it all.

"Shuto!" He brought the sword handstrike down on the tiles. A thunderbolt, a thousand broken pieces, dust rising from the floor, an echo bouncing off the walls. A six on the Richter scale.

He barely paused. Two more steps and we were face-to-face. Blood streamed from his right hand, impaled by a ceramic sliver. I backed up until I was at the bar. He kept coming. Too fast. If he was ever to get good at hand-to-hand combat, he'd have to learn to control his emotions.

It would be better for Roger Salisbury if I let Sergio hit me. Just as Granny had said, let him show his mean streak. And I will do a lot for a client. I will stay up three nights in a row preparing witnesses or writing a brief. I will cajole and flatter judges with two-digit IQs. I will even cry in closing argument to win sympathy from the jury. But I will not let my head be split like a cataloupe by a tattooed, muscle-bound, hopped-up steroid freak.

He telegraphed a roundhouse kick, and as I ducked to the right, a whirling foot breezed by my ear, a rush of air like a train through the station. He tried hitting me in the chest with a flurry of fast punches with the left fist. Later, Charlie Riggs would tell me this was the *Dan-zuki.* I deflected some of them but caught a good one in the ribs. I would feel it for a week. He liked going for the body and used a lunge punch to get one into my gut. I felt it and dropped my guard. Somebody in the gallery screamed.

He tried to come high with a looping roundhouse right. *Mawashi-zuki,* Charlie would explain. He had plenty of hip behind it, but I had figured he'd go for the head. I leaned to my right and the punch glanced off my ear, burning it, but not connecting.

Then I ducked inside and brought my forearm up under his chin, hard. There was a lot of shoulder in it and a good explosion from the legs. The forearm caught some neck and some jaw and lifted him off the floor. It would have been good for fifteen yards, unnecessary roughness, clotheslining a guy. The shot straightened Sergio up, made him gasp for breath that wouldn't come. Then I brought the left hook around, aiming for the chin. It took a while to get there, my timing was rusty, but that was okay. He wasn't going anywhere. The punch landed and tossed him backward onto the clerk's table, which crumbled into splinters, trial exhibits flying. State-issued furniture.

The judge was banging his gavel. I hadn't heard it during the ruckus. But there he was, banging away. And in his other hand was the .357 Magnum from under the bench. Then dead quiet. The judge looked at the gavel and then at the gun. Sheepishly. Then his eyes darted from Channel 10's video camera to the *Herald*'s still camera, whirring and clicking away. Preserving the sight for eternity, or at least until the next election.

Straining to appear judicial, he turned toward the jury box. "The jurors shall disregard the last . . . uh . . . colloquy between the witness and defense counsel."

Might as well ask the residents of Pompeii to ignore the volcano.

Then, eyeballing me, Judge Randolph Crane did a slow burn. "The Court, *sua sponte*, grants a mistrial. The jury is excused. Mr. Socolow, I assume the state wishes to retry this defendant. If so, a new trial date will be set upon subsequent motion and notice of hearing. Mr. Lassiter . . ."

He paused. He thought. His perpetual glumness was replaced with anger. It seemed real, not just a pose for the editorial boards.

"Mr. Lassiter, I have never seen such a display in a courtroom. I don't know what you did to provoke that witness, but I do know you committed battery upon his person."

Again he paused, and the courtroom waited. He was running out of steam. He shot a surreptitious glance at the press. No help. He banged his gavel three times. When no one moved, he banged it again, then looked at me sternly and in his deepest tones announced, "You have fomented anarchy in a court of law." A good quote, and from the front row, Helen Buchman nodded approvingly, her gray bouffant bobbing. Encouraged, the judge worked some righteous indignation into his voice. "In sum, Mr. Lassiter, you have flaunted . . . that is flouted . . . and in other words, you have affronted and offended the authority of this court. You are hereby ordered and adjudged in contempt of court. Report tomorrow morning at nine for sentencing. I suggest you bring counsel. And your toothbrush."

The judge bolted through the rear door into his chambers and away from the madness. A corrections officer helped Sergio to his feet. Reporters swarmed over me. From the corridor, the cameramen and grips stormed in, knocking spectators aside. A mini-cam examined my right ear. A microphone poked at my eye. I'd be the lead story at six o'clock. Good story, too. Defendant goes free, at least for a while; his lawyer heads for the stockade.

My ribs ached and my left hand was beginning to swell.

Roger Salisbury hadn't moved. He sat at the defense table, probably trying to figure out if I was a great lawyer or just a guy with an adequate left hook.

Abe Socolow looked at me and said, "You went too far this time, Jake, old buddy."

"In a pig's ass!" Granny Lassiter had hurdled the bar separating the lions from the Christians, exposing gray wool socks beneath her sundress. She hugged me and narrowed her eyes at Abe Socolow. "My Jacob can whup any man in the house, and a couple weeks of county victuals never did no harm."

29

TWO OUT OF THREE

I was playing a wicked first base, stretching this way and that, digging low throws out of the dirt, trying to avoid pulling a hamstring. The shortstop was a check bouncer with a weak wing. The third baseman was a bunco artist who threw hard but wild. The second baseman was a veteran, three falls for DUI, but I didn't know much about his arm. Every grounder trickled through his legs and into right field.

Seven days in the Dade County Stockade. Like a vacation. No phones, no partners' meetings, no hearings with cantankerous judges and disagreeable clients. Almost as good as a week-long cruise to St. Thomas, although chipped beef on toast is seldom served on the *S. S. Norway*. The stockade is different from the county jail, that dungeon attached to the Justice Building. The jail is for your hard guys—robbers, killers, rapists, and multikilo dopers. Here, just a bunch of misdemeanants, including my own contemptuous self.

I had just done my best imitation of a Nureyev split, scooping up a shin buster in time to nab a three-hundred-pound grocer doing ninety days for selling pork loins as kosher lamb chops. The applause from my teammates did not break my eardrums. "Good grab, shyster," the second baseman declared for the group.

Then, a familiar voice behind me: "Did I hear something crack or you just fart?"

I turned around. Now coaching first base for the Stockade Short Timers, Abraham Socolow.

"Hey, Abe. What'd they get you for? Purloining state-owned paper clips?"

He didn't laugh. "Looks like you been working on your tan."

"Yeah, lifting, too," I said. "Gonna get strong again. Maybe even take up karate like your favorite witness."

"Funny you mention him," he said, as if it weren't funny at all. "Machado-Alvarez is in Mount Sinai, got some weird sickness."

"I'll send flowers."

"You'll do better than that. You'll go there with me while I take a statement."

"You deputizing me?" I asked, keeping an eye on the runner at second, a shoplifter who would steal anything, including third base, if given the chance.

"He was busting up some boards at a karate exhibition

340

over at Convention Hall, suddenly gets a fever, the shits, then he's paralyzed. One of the Beach cops working security ID'ed Salisbury hanging around the stage just before macho man did his stuff. I'll need to talk to Salisbury. Thought you'd want to be present. As usual, old buddy, I'm going out of my way to do you a favor."

Next time he does me a favor, I'll probably do a month in solitary. The pitcher, a pickpocket, called a conference on the mound. He slipped the ball to the shortstop, who hid it in his glove then tagged the runner leading off second. Time was called, the runner whimpered, and there ensued some plea bargaining with the umpire, a trusty.

"I can't leave," I told Socolow. "Got another three days to satisfy the judge."

"Let's go. I sprung you."

I put on my best Edward G. Robinson. "You sprung me? You dirty screw. I was going over the wall tonight with the boys. What'll they think?"

He didn't smile; he didn't scowl, just the same straight-faced look. Ten years and he has yet to laugh at one of my jokes.

With Socolow running interference, we sailed through the paperwork for my return to society. We headed east in his government Chrysler—four doors, blackwalls—toward Miami Beach. Abe wore a dark three-piece suit with his Phi Beta Kappa pin slung from a vest pocket. I wore a blue chambray shirt with a nine-digit number. If we went to a Coconut Grove club, I'd be considered highly trendy and he'd be stashed next to the kitchen with a busload of retirees from Century Village. We took the Julia Tuttle Causeway, which connects the mainland with Arthur Godfrey Road on

Miami Beach. It's a great drive, high above Biscayne Bay, sailboats swooping beneath the pillars of the bridge, a fine view of the white and pink buildings of Miami Beach. From the top of the causeway you appreciate the fragility of that long, skinny sandbar with the bay on one side, the vast ocean on the other.

On the way Socolow told me he'd asked Charlie Riggs to meet us there. I thought that over a second. "Why not the ME? He's the guy on your side."

Socolow was silent. Like a good soldier, he wouldn't squawk about intramural warfare. Then he surprised me. "Maybe too much on my side."

I let it go. But he didn't. "MacKenzie's a turd," he said stiffly.

I had noticed a certain scatological bent to Abe's patter lately, but this was not the time to question whether he had been toilet trained at the appropriate age.

"A turd?" I delicately inquired.

"I can't prove it, but I think he cooked those chromatographic tests that night in the morgue, the guys who died in surgery. He wouldn't let me near Blumberg all night."

Why was he telling me this?

"You're probably surprised I'm telling you this," he said. Mind reader.

"There won't be a new trial," Socolow continued. "The widow refuses to testify."

"You could lean on her," I suggested, hoping he'd already tried and failed. "You've done it before with reluctant witnesses."

"Not in a case like this," he said. "What's it mean, Jake,

if a woman won't testify against a man she swore killed her husband?"

I thought about it. "Different possibilities. That she knows the defendant didn't do it. Or the defendant did it and she helped him. Or she knows who did it and she's afraid a trial would bring that out."

Abe Socolow didn't say a word, just nodded to himself, watched the causeway straight ahead, and kept both hands on the wheel, at ten o'clock and two o'clock, just the way they teach you. Some guys play it strictly by the book.

Charlie Riggs was standing inside the double doors of the ICU talking to a young doctor in a white lab coat. The doctor was short and pale with a bushy, unkempt beard. Charlie stroked his own beard; the young doctor stroked his. Charlie barely noticed our arrival. No introductions, we just picked up listening.

"He went fast," the doctor said with a shrug. "Ambulance brought him in, eyes bulging, stomach pain, vomiting, diarrhea, stiff joints, then paralysis. We tried to stabilize him. Barely got the IV in. Bang! Liver and kidneys fail, goes into respiratory arrest."

"Classic indicia of food poisoning," Charlie said dispassionately. "We used to see two or three deaths a year, green beans at church picnics. Botulism."

The two doctors kept talking, ignoring us. There wasn't much two lawyers could add anyway.

"That's what we thought," the doctor said. "But we checked it out. Last two meals were banquet style for the karate convention. Three hundred people, no one else even burped."

Charlie scratched his beard. The young doctor did the same. I didn't have a beard, so I ran a hand through my shaggy hair. Socolow didn't have much hair, so he lit a cigarette, then ground it into the tile after a nurse wagged a finger at him.

"Have you checked the body for punctures, fresh injections?" Charlie asked.

"Sure did, after Mr. Socolow told us his suspicions. Nothing."

Charlie Riggs turned to Abe Socolow. They had worked together in the past, shared a mutual respect, even if Charlie thought Abe was a little sharp around the edges. "What was he doing just before he was stricken?"

"Best we can figure," Socolow said, "he just finished chopping up a stack of boards with his bare hands." Socolow looked at me. "Except nobody slugged him afterwards."

"I see," Charlie said. He was the only one who did. "I think I'll take a drive to Convention Hall."

I was sleeping in my own bed with two pillows for company when four headlights glared malevolently through my front windows, and two horns blared. I rolled over and looked at the clock. The green digital numbers flashed from 2:57 to 2:58 as my feet hit the floor. Downstairs, a flashing of high beams. Maybe the cops picking me up. Maybe I really did go over the wall.

I wrapped a towel around my waist and opened the front door. Granny Lassiter and Charlie Riggs.

"Sorry to disturb you, Jake," Charlie said, sounding not a bit sorry.

"Let me guess," I said groggily, "you want my permission to marry this woman. Forget it. Elope if you like."

"I'm game," Granny said. "Only fellow my age I know still got lead in his pencil."

"C'mon Jake," Charlie commanded, his face serious, no twinkle in his eye. "Let's take a ride and talk."

If Charlie wanted to talk, I wanted to listen. I slipped on an old pair of gym shorts, running shoes, and a gray T-shirt, stepped into the humid night, and slid into the front passenger seat of Granny's mammoth 1969 Cadillac. Over the bay, lightning flashed and distant thunder followed, a thunderstorm brewing in the southeast, headed our way. Granny had the engine running and Charlie was already in the back. Before I had dented the velour upholstery, the smell rolled over me.

"Granny, you leave a mess of last week's grouper under the seat?"

She didn't even look at me, just jerked a thumb toward the backseat and flicked on the overhead light. My gaze followed the thumb and left me staring into the waxy, dissolving face of the late Sylvia Corrigan.

"What the hell!"

"Relax, Jake," Charlie said. "Jane did us a great favor by bringing the body here tonight."

Everybody was doing me favors today. As for "Jane," the name still struck me funny, like calling Charlemagne, "Chuck."

"Weren't nothing," Granny said. "That old gal been taking up room in my cooler anyhow."

"What's going on?" I demanded.

"I found the boards Sergio had broken at Convention

345

Hall," Charlie explained. "Easy enough. He did the noon demonstration. Slabs of pine were in the trash, stacked in nearly the same order that he broke them. I thought it quite natural to assume that the one with the cleanest break would have been the top board."

"Quite natural," I agreed.

Granny pulled onto Douglas Road, then turned right at Dixie Highway heading downtown. You expect traffic to be light after three A.M., but it never is. You wonder who these people are, looking for a party or heading for their night shifts.

"On close inspection I could see the top board had been coated with something. I took it to Dr. Kallan at the lab, and he confirmed my suspicions. *Clostridium botulinum*, and quite a liberal dose of it."

"The stuff that causes food poisoning," I said.

"The very stuff," Charlie said.

"What'd Sergio do, eat the boards for breakfast?"

"No, he just hit one with a hand that he had cut on the tile in the courtroom. Even without the cut, the abrasion from the board probably would be sufficient to allow the toxin to enter the blood. With the wound still healing and Sergio not wanting to show weakness by wearing a bandage —I asked around—it was an open invitation to the toxin."

"And you think Roger Salisbury cooked this up?" I asked.

"Chemical companies sell the toxin to universities and laboratories for research. A doctor would have no trouble ordering some."

I shook my head. "I don't know, Charlie, a little smear on a board killing a guy."

"It's perhaps the most toxic substance we know. A thousand molecules of botulinum toxin can kill an ox. Do you know how small a molecule is?"

About the size of all the gray matter in my brain, I thought. I'm the guy who trusted Roger Salisbury. But I wasn't ready to throw him over, not yet.

"Maybe Roger's got an explanation," I suggested, sounding hollow even to myself.

"That's what we'll find out," Charlie said.

We were at the intersection of Dixie and Miami Avenue. Granny swung the aircraft carrier across three westbound lanes of Dixie and we headed north on Miami, passing under the overpass to Key Biscayne. Roger lived halfway up a long block on the right, his house surrounded by finely aged royal poinciana trees.

"What's your friend in back have to do with it?"

Charlie sighed. "If I showed you her right buttock, upper quadrant, you'd know."

"An injection?"

"Twenty-gauge needle, I'd say."

"Wait a second, Charlie. Slow down. She died in the hospital. That could have been a routine sedative, a painkiller, anything."

"Could have been. We don't have the records."

"And you've done no test for succinylcholine or any other drugs?"

"Correct."

"So you have no proof?"

"Correct again, Counselor. Your cross-examination was always your strong point."

347

"With no evidence, where do you get off accusing Roger of killing Sylvia Corrigan?"

"Calm down, Jake. I'm not ready to accuse. But I've been at this a long time. I have a hunch, that's all."

"A hunch! Charlie. You're a scientist. I'm a lawyer. You deal with medical probabilities, I deal with evidence. And you have us hauling a corpse around on a hunch. I don't believe it."

When I don't get my prescribed six hours of shut-eye, I can be ornery, even to friends.

"What we believe and what is true," Charlie said, "are often quite different. *Deceptio visus.* It's probably healthy up to a point, to believe in your client's cause. Beyond that point, it will blind you."

I turned around to face him, and Sylvia Corrigan toppled forward, brushing my arm with a forehead the consistency of sponge cake left in the rain. The rotten fish smell washed over me. "What do you expect me to do?" I demanded. "Even if he confessed to me, I couldn't go to Socolow. The attorney—client privilege prevents that."

"It prevents your telling the authorities about past crimes, sure. But if you had probable cause to believe he's about to kill again, there is a different obligation."

"Who's left to kill?"

"The person who first made him a killer, of course."

A flash of lightning lit the sky and a thunderclap followed almost instantly, the storm closing in. I laughed but there was no pleasure behind it. "You think Roger will kill Melanie Corrigan. If you're right, why should I lift a finger to stop him? Maybe I'll help him."

"No, you won't. I know you, Jake. I know your code. It

isn't written anywhere except all over your face. You're one of the last decent men. You're a guy who looks for broken wings to mend."

"Yeah, I'm an overgrown Boy Scout."

"You won't admit it. You've created this image of the indifferent, detached loner, but I know you better than you do."

I forced the same hollow laugh. "You're a great canoemaker, Charlie, but a lousy judge of character."

"All right. We're not here to protect Melanie Corrigan or anybody else, just to learn the truth. Will you help?"

Fat raindrops splattered the windshield, prelude to a downpour. Granny slowed, then hit the brakes hard, and the old Cadillac's bald tires slid to a stop in front of Roger's house. "Tell me what to do," I said with resignation.

"Be tough with him," Charlie ordered. "He's cracking. The murder of Sergio was an irrational, bizarre act. He's crying out, perhaps over guilt, shame, who knows? He wants to be caught. But his first reaction will be denial. He trusts and respects you. You're the one who has to do it."

The house was one of those modern jobs, six concrete cubes at odd angles, a wall of glass bricks shielding an interior courtyard and a roof full of skylights. I rang the doorbell and waited. Three-thirty A.M. In Miami an unexpected visitor late at night is an excuse to set loose the guard dogs or open up with automatic weapons.

It took a while, then the intercom crackled with a sleepy, cranky, "Yeah?"

"Roger, it's Jake. Sorry to wake you. But there's news. Socolow won't refile. It's over."

Silence. Then, "Great. Call me in the morning."

"Can't. There's more. Got to see you."

"Minute," he said.

It was more like five. A hot, dank night. In the yard a row of crimson tobacco jasmine flooded us with a steamy perfume, even as the rain splashed under the portico.

Finally Roger eyeballed me through the peephole. I ducked to one side. I didn't have to move fast. By the time he turned the locks, slid the bolts, unhooked the chains, and punched the code into the digital alarm, I could have been appointed to the bench. Roger Salisbury opened the heavy beamed door to find a visitor sitting in a wicker chair on his front stoop, her head slumped to a shoulder, eyeless face melting under the ghoulish glow of the yellow bug light. Overhead, lightning crackled.

I heard Roger gag, a choking sound. I watched him slump to the Mexican tile floor of his foyer. My own stomach tossed as he clutched his throat, gagged again, and vomited. He stayed there awhile, emptying himself while the three of us stepped around him and into the house. Sylvia Corrigan stayed put.

"Why do this to me, Jake?" he whimpered, getting to his feet. Charlie steered him to a rust-colored leather sofa. Granny found a kitchen towel and helped clean his face. He sat there in a black silk bathrobe, bare feet on the floor, looking at me with vacant eyes. That bland, handsome face was gray now. "Jake, you're my lawyer and my friend. Why?"

"I'm resigning from both positions."

"Jake . . ."

"Why did you kill Sylvia Corrigan?"

His head shrunk back into his shoulders. "Why would I kill her?"

"Easy. Because Melanie asked you to. She very nearly told me you did it. When I asked her why anyone would steal Sylvia Corrigan's body, she said to ask you. It didn't make sense then, but it does now."

He cackled. Half a laugh, half a cry, a barely human sound. "I'm not a killer. You said so yourself in the malpractice trial. God you were good. I'm a healer. I took an oath. To give no deadly drug, to do no harm."

"You violated the oath, Roger. You gave it up. For flesh. You killed Sylvia and Philip and Sergio."

"I didn't kill Philip," he said softly.

Where I come from, that's an admission. Two out of three. I remembered what he said the other night on my porch. *I didn't kill Philip. He's the one person I could never kill.*

He started rocking back and forth, his head between his knees, his forearms resting on his knees. When he looked up, his eyes darted back and forth and his mouth hung slack. He cocked his head to one side and looked at me or through me, his mind somewhere on the far side of Betelgeuse. The look chilled the room. It could have frightened Sylvia Corrigan.

Then his eyes cleared. A calm voice, the old Roger Salisbury, "Jake, you remember what you said to me that first day in your office?"

I remembered fine but I didn't feel like reminiscing. "Probably that I was a lousy linebacker."

"No, that you kept looking for the good guys and couldn't find them. I admired you, wanted you to like me, to be my friend. I wanted to be one of the good guys."

He said it with sadness, finality. Knowing it was over.

"I didn't kill Philip," he repeated. "You can't believe that pig Sergio." Then he slipped into his best Cuban handyman accent: "*E's* the needle man." And he pushed his thumb against an imaginary plunger of an imaginary hypodermic just as Sergio had done on the witness stand, and there it was, the missing piece. Where it had been all along, on the videotape. That puncture in Sylvia Corrigan's backside could have been a routine injection in the hospital just before she died, but it wasn't.

Oh Susan Corrigan, you were right the first time. I am dumber than I look.

I put my hands on my knees and leaned over, my face close to Roger's. Our own little huddle. I wanted to look him in the eye. The sour smell of sweat mixed with vomit clung to him.

"Roger, I know it all now. You lied to me about when you met Philip Corrigan. You said it was after his wife had died. You were blocking it out, her death, staying a mile away from any talk about her. But you told me the truth about the succinylcholine. You did have it for two years before Philip died. And you did put an old dog to sleep with it. Plus an old lady you forgot to mention. You killed Sylvia Corrigan, and before the flowers wilted, the four of you were living it up on the *Cory*. You, Philip, Melanie, and the karate kid. A celebration cruise. Philip played cameraman. You played doctor with Melanie. After the examination, you gave her a little pat on the ass. That's what it looked like on the tape because you weren't holding anything. But what you were doing was giving her a pretend injection in the ass. She thought it was hysterical. Philip Corrigan laughed so hard he almost dropped the camera. You were showing off, letting them know how you killed her."

He stared off into space, his face devoid of emotion, without joy or pain. Charlie nodded, a signal I was playing the cards right. Granny had discovered a crystal decanter of port and a huge goblet. She drowned a look of sorrow with a healthy chug.

"One thing I can't figure," I continued, "is whether you and Melanie had it all planned. Kill Sylvia, Melanie marries Philip. After a decent interval, you snuff him, too."

"I would never kill Philip," he whispered. "Philip was my friend. I never had many friends. Philip taught me to share Melanie, something I never thought I could do. But she wanted him . . ."

"Dead," I helped out, as he drifted away again. "She wanted Philip dead. You were torn. The woman you never refused, the friend you longed for. She told you to kill him. You said you would. Just like before. But you didn't want to do it."

"I couldn't do it," he muttered, his voice thick, as if his tongue had swollen from thirst. "Philip shared his most prized possession with me. I watched him lying there in the hospital, my friend, knowing what that woman wanted me to do, but I couldn't . . ."

He floated off again, riding some inner current. I filled in the gaps. "So you duck out of the room carrying the valise. Nurse Ingram sees you. You run down the stairs to the lobby. Your pals Sergio and Melanie are waiting for the good news. But you don't have any. Melanie is furious. Sergio probably calls you a chicken-shit *cobarde*. He loves it— you're in pain—he can be the hero. You hand him the valise, and he tucks it into his bush jacket. Melanie goes with him, gives him a cover story for being there if he's seen. But he's nervous. This isn't like injecting himself with steroids. This is murder and there's a nurse right down the hall. So he hurries and doesn't get the hypodermic filled. Or he fills it and squirts it everywhere but inside Philip Corrigan. He makes a puncture, but it's a dry hole. Lucky for him and unlucky for Philip Corrigan, there's more than one way to kill a guy flat on his back. *Ikken hissatsu.* He kills him with one punch, probably the sword handstrike. Melanie keeps the valise with the drug and the hypodermics. You don't want to see it again, and you don't until she plants it in your house."

He was silent. What is it Charlie would say? *Cum tacent clamant.* Silence is an admission of guilt. Not in a courtroom, of course, but in human experience. A tremor went through Roger's body, and he wrapped his arms around himself and hugged as if to keep from splitting in two. His eyes kept clouding over, then clearing, slipping in and out of a haze like a foggy shoreline viewed from the sea.

"You knew Sergio did it," I said. "Why didn't you tell me?"

His lips moved but nothing came out. He tried again. "Because they threatened to tell Socolow about Sylvia. After the mistrial, they thought I must have told you about the karate punch. How else could you have figured it out?"

Charlie smiled, but only a little.

"Why did you kill Sergio?" I asked.

"He kept threatening me. I'll tell the cops this, I'll tell them that, I'll bust your head."

He was sing-songing it, sounding like a child. Coming and going, different people now.

I grabbed him by both shoulders. "Who killed Susan?"

"Sergio. With a poison fish or something. Melanie had him do it. She told me, laughed about it."

He said it so matter-of-factly, one woman dead, another woman laughing. Watching Roger self-destruct, I had buried it, the burning rage. The how and the who. My vow to Susan. Sergio was already dead. Only Melanie's laugh to stifle now. Melanie Corrigan, the source of the evil. Three murders, two by Sergio with Melanie's encouragement. One by Roger, same provocateur.

I let Roger go and talked to Charlie. He would take Granny back to my place. I'd babysit, spend the night on Roger's sofa.

Roger turned to me, his eyes bottomless holes. "Will you help me, Jake? Like you did before. I'm always being falsely accused, you know."

I didn't know what to say. Charlie did. "We can get you help," he said. "A very good doctor I know. In the morning, I'll make the call."

Charlie and Granny left, hoisted Sylvia Corrigan into the trunk of the Cadillac, and drove off.

Roger looked at me. Barely comprehending. I told him I would put him to bed. He didn't agree or disagree, just stood when I helped him up and moved where I guided him. He looked shrunken. So feeble and spent. His bare feet shuffled across the tile. I sat in a chair at the foot of his bed and watched him until he fell asleep. I figured the poison was drained from him now. Just the shell of a man, without the will or the weapons. Able to do no harm.

30

GREAT HANDS

I awoke at five forty-five, same as always. Tired but alert. Aware of the strangeness of the room. There is a sixth sense that tells us something has changed. Someone has passed through our space, coming or going. Our sensors—keen as orbiting satellites—track the unseen movement.

I unfolded myself from the sofa and checked the master bedroom.

No Roger.

The sheets still warm. The rest of the house, empty. I checked the garage. No Porsche.

I called my house, woke Charlie, who must have been

sharing the cubbyhole bedroom with Granny. Calmly, he said, "I'll drive to the Corrigan house. You stay put in case he comes back."

I didn't think he'd be coming back. Didn't picture him running to the 7-Eleven to buy juice and eggs. Charlie called in twenty minutes from a pay phone. Nobody at the Corrigan house.

I called a cab. In Miami that's like playing the lottery. Cab drivers hail from various Caribbean islands with one coast road and one mountain road. They can never find residential addresses. I called Roger's office and got the answering service. I didn't expect to hear back, and I was right. No cab, no phone call. After twenty-five minutes, I took off.

Jogging down Miami Avenue toward the causeway to Key Biscayne, then a right turn to pick up Coral Way, the pavement still slick from last night's rain. Roger's office was on Giralda in the Gables. Five miles tops. I needed the exercise but didn't know if I had the time.

I looked for friendly drivers. Most swerved to avoid me, one or two to hit me. No takers for a big lug with a grim look and a sweaty gray T-shirt. I should have slowed that last two hundred yards, but I tried to pick it up. Sprinting. Not much left in the legs, heart going wild. Too old to run gassers, coach's delight.

Roger's black Porsche Turbo gleamed in his reserved spot in back, Melanie Corrigan's green Jaguar in the next space. Good. Melanie must have come voluntarily, Roger calling her from the house. Running here, the mind pounding with each footfall, I had pictured her in the trunk of his car. But maybe Charlie Riggs was wrong. Maybe Roger had no intention of killing Melanie, maybe he just wanted to play some more doctor games. Except Charlie had been right about everything else.

I put my hands on my hips and bent over, sucking for oxygen. It was like breathing through a wet beach towel. One of those soggy Miami mornings without air, no wind from the ocean until the sun heats up the land.

The office was a tiny one-story stucco house with an orange, barrel-tile roof. From the thirties. A lot of doctors and lawyers have gone that route, getting out of the skyscrapers downtown, building equity and taking depreciation. No other cars in the eight-space lot. And there wouldn't be, no office hours Saturday.

The back door was locked. Front door, too. On the side of the house, a brown air conditioner poked out of a blackened window. House too old for central air. I tried yanking it through the window. No go. I gave it a shoulder, braced with legs made of spaghetti, and pushed it inside where it landed on a work table with a thud. I waited a moment. No other sounds. I crawled through. The X-ray room. Dark.

I opened the interior door into a corridor that led to the examination rooms. Then I padded around to the other side of the building past Roger's office, a file room, the bookkeeper's cubicle, and finally, the casting room, where a light shone under the door. I moved close, listening to my own breathing, still heavy. An air conditioner whirred from inside, muffling voices. A man and a woman. Normal tones, no screams, no threats.

I silently let myself in. Roger wore a green gown that was splattered white. His arms were bare and splotched with plaster. He kept dipping a roll of gauze into a bowl of water. Immediately the gauze became gooey, the water mixing with the impregnated plaster. Carefully he wrapped the soggy gauze around the cotton cast padding that circled Melanie Corrigan's left arm. He smoothed out the gauze with those strong, steady hands, tucking it into place, erasing any folds or creases. Then he dipped another piece of gauze into the water and kept building.

She lay spread-eagle on an examining table, both legs already casted from ankle to hip, the right arm a heavy circle of plaster from wrist to shoulder. She was naked except for a tiny white bikini bottom. Her breasts rose and fell with each breath.

"Hello Jake," Roger said, barely looking up. "I didn't want to wake you. Melanie looks lovely in white, don't you think?"

She smiled at me luridly. Her russet hair was loose and fell over the front of one shoulder. The hair hadn't been brushed, Roger probably waking her for the early morning visit. Tiny freckles dotted her chest. She wore no makeup and looked, I imagined, much as she did a decade earlier when Roger first met her in the jerk-off joint.

"Wanna party?" Melanie said. She ran her tongue over her upper lip. "I love a sweaty man."

"Isn't she something?" Roger asked, a tone of pride. "I used to be jealous, you know. But Philip changed that. He taught me. What she gives to someone else doesn't take away from me. That's what he said. He was a great man."

Melanie Corrigan laughed, her chest rising from the table but her arms and legs staying put, weighted down by the casts. "Rog is the sentimental type," she said, derisively.

Roger kept scooping and dipping and molding the plaster. Patting it dry.

"Look at these casts," he instructed. "Smooth, eh?"

"Good workmanship," I agreed.

"Great hands," Melanie said. "He wants you to say, 'Great hands.'"

"You have great hands, Roger," I said.

"Thank you, Jake. You always had confidence in me. You knew I didn't let the rongeur slip. Not in a million years."

He leaned over a work table and picked up a small tool, stainless steel gleaming. The rongeur. He twirled it around in one hand, tossed it to the other, back and forth without looking. Great hands.

He replaced the rongeur in a tray with half a dozen others, all different sizes, from the tiny pituitary model to the bone rongeur that looked like a pair of household pliers. He patted the last of the plaster into place, pausing to wipe his hands.

"Hurry up," Melanie ordered. "Colder than a witch's tit here. Hey Lassiter, wanna go first?"

Roger dried his hands and said, "You can if you want, Jake." His eyes were focused on Mars.

"Rog, I swear I'm going to pee all over your table, you don't hurry up," Melanie said. "Are you hard or you need me to talk dirty? Bring that worm over here."

Roger untied her bikini bottom and folded it over a chair.

"That's better," she laughed. "Hurry the fuck up before my tits freeze solid. Hey Lassiter, that's a joke isn't it? Hurry the fuck up . . ."

Roger looked at me. "Jake, you're my friend, just like Philip. You can have her if you want."

"Maybe another time, Roger."

"There won't be another time," he said flatly.

A chill went through me. Maybe it was the blast of the air conditioner on my overheated body. But maybe it was because I knew. My face must have shown it. Melanie smiled seductively. "Don't worry, Lassiter. He always talks like that. We haven't fucked once the last two years, he doesn't threaten to off me."

"Only this time, it's real," Roger said.

She laughed. I didn't.

Melanie leered at me. "What's the matter, Lassiter? You afraid he'll kill me? He only kills little old ladies."

"Who do you kill?" I asked her.

"No one, smart guy. I got men friends always wanting to please me, do me favors."

"You're wrong about Roger," I told her. She looked puzzled. He hadn't told her. No wonder she was so calm. Thinking he was the same old Roger, her favorite lapdog. "Roger kills more than old ladies, and he's pretty good at dreaming up ways to do it. Painful ways."

She still didn't get it.

"Where's your pal, Sergio?" I asked, wanting her to know, wanting her to taste fear.

"Miami Beach, busting up some boards," she said, doubt creeping into her voice.

"Wrong. Dead wrong. The morgue's on this side of the bay."

Her eyes darted to Roger, who worked silently with the plaster. She looked back at me, seeking help. I hadn't moved. I could stop him any time. I was bigger and stronger than Roger, and his mind was diced into an asteroid belt of colliding rocks. He turned his back to me, oblivious. One shot to the kidneys and it would be over.

I could, but why should I? You are wrong about me, dear old Charlie Riggs. I want her dead. Stop Roger?

Why should I?

Roger stood there studying her, ignoring me, that glazed look fading in and out. He unrolled another length of gauze, dipped it into the water bowl, then slapped it into Melanie Corrigan's crotch.

"Hey, I don't need a chastity belt," she said, the voice a notch higher.

He slowly stretched out more gauze, soaked it, lifted her a few inches and wrapped it around the top of the left hip and through the crotch. He caressed it into place.

"She looks just like a little doll, doesn't she, Jake?" Another strip and then another and the two leg casts were joined. Melanie tried moving but could not, the weight was too much.

Then he pulled a white Dacron stocking out of a metal drawer, walked to the head of the table, brushed her hair back, and slipped the stocking over her head.

"Makes the plaster set more smoothly," he explained.

"Stop fuckin' around, Rog," she cried, each breath sucking the stocking into her mouth. "This ain't funny." Her voice rising, the beginning of fear.

He placed some padding over her mouth, but she shook her head and it dropped to the floor. He didn't seem to notice. He dipped another length of gauze into the water, waited a moment, and then began wrapping it around her mouth. Even through the stocking, her eyes reflected it.

The realization. The terror.

I studied that look, snapped it into place. I wanted to remember it. Susan was dead because of her, and now here

363

she was, knowing what was about to happen, the horror of knowing probably worse than the pain itself.

She spit and coughed. The sticky mess stayed put, covering half her mouth. She breathed greedily through her nose and yelled something, muffled through the gauze. "Laschta, hughme." *Lassiter, help me.*

This time, Roger fashioned a longer piece and swaddled it twice around her head, covering both mouth and nose. She bucked up and down, involuntary thrusts from the diaphragm lifting her, the lungs searching for air. In another minute she would lose consciousness. Three minutes after that, irreversible brain damage. Then . . .

She looked toward me, eyes pleading, mouth working, the words unintelligible, her fear filling the room.

Why should I?

I didn't know. I just reacted the way I do to most things. Moved without thinking it through, doing what seems right at the time, listening to some voice inside, a smarter guy than me, someone who didn't want me to scream myself awake, seeing Melanie Corrigan turn blue under all that white.

I came up behind Roger, grabbed him by the left arm, and spun him around. From the way his right shoulder pivoted, I saw the punch coming but not the rongeur, the large one, in his right hand. His arm came hard and fast. I was going to take his punch and give back one that would sit him down. What I took was a fistful of stainless steel. It caught me on the left temple. Solid.

In the movies, guys get hit on the head all the time. Usually with a gun. Their knees buckle, they say *oooh,* and they gently fall and go to sleep. It doesn't work that way. There's a thunderclap, a blaze of lights behind the eyes, and a shooting pain, a loss of equilibrium. Then a gray fog settling.

I didn't fall down. I stumbled across the room on shaky pins, a wounded buffalo, bouncing off cabinets. Roger was standing to my left, my right, and straight in front. I took a drunk's swing at the guy in front but it wasn't him. He pushed me to the floor. I hooked an arm behind his knee and brought him down on top of me. On a good day, I could bench press him twenty times, then throw him from short to first. This wasn't a good day. He was back up and I was on one knee like a fighter taking the eight-count.

Then I felt the jab in my upper arm. *Déjà vu*, his thumb pushing the plunger on a hypodermic. I swatted at it and missed. He emptied it into me and I tore away from him, the needle still stuck in me, the world's largest voodoo doll.

I came at him again and took a swing in slow motion, my arms bulky girders. I didn't hit him and he didn't hit me. I just sat down at the end of the punch, then rolled onto my side, my face resting on the cool, clean tile. Then, just like in the movies, I said, *oooh*, and went to sleep.

My mouth was dry and my head was filled with barking dogs. I was cold. My face was still on the tile. It could have been hours or days. It must have been hours. Roger was sitting in a swivel chair next to me, splotches of plaster in his hair, on his face, on his gown. From the floor, I could see only the bottoms of Melanie Corrigan's bare feet sticking out of the casts. Nice feet, finely arched, clean dainty lady feet.

The feet weren't moving. I didn't need to see the rest.

"I'll help you up," Roger said hoarsely. "Don't worry about the Pentothal. You'll just be groggy for a while."

I tried to stand but he had to boost me. If he wanted to, he could finish me right there. I finally looked toward the table. The face gone, wrapped from forehead to chin, a mummy. Only the ends of her hair stuck out from beneath the plaster.

I sagged against a metal cabinet. Roger said, "You didn't mean it last night, did you, Jake?"

"Mean what?" My voice was thick; my head weighed a ton.

"That you're no longer my lawyer or my friend."

"What difference does it make?"

He swiveled in the chair to face me, his eyes dancing to a silent tune.

"Because I need you, Jake."

"Now? You need me now. What for?"

"To prove it, Jake. That I'm one of the good guys."

ABOUT THE AUTHOR

PAUL LEVINE is a Miami trial lawyer and a widely known authority on the First Amendment, who has represented the news media in libel and privacy lawsuits, including cases in the Supreme Court of the United States. He has taught communications law at the University of Miami Law School and authored both a syndicated television show, *You and the Law*, and a nationally syndicated newspaper column, "What's Your Verdict?" *To Speak For the Dead* is his first novel. His second Jake Lassiter novel, *Night Vision*, is available now from Bantam. He is currently at work on *Slashback*, which Bantam will publish in the Fall of 1992.

A JAKE LASSITER NOVEL

Here are special advance preview chapters from NIGHT VISION, the new Jake Lassiter novel by Paul Levine, a Bantam hardcover now available at your local bookstore.

NIGHT VISION

Paul Levine

CHAPTER ONE
A Matter of Honor

If Marvin the Maven tells me not to yell in closing argument, I don't yell. Marvin knows. He's never tried a case, but he's seen more trials than most lawyers. Drifting from courtroom to courtroom in search of the best action, he glimpses eight or nine cases a day. Five days a week for the last seventeen years since he closed up his shoe store in Brooklyn and headed South.

Some lawyers don't listen to Marvin and his friends—Saul the Tailor and Max (Just Plain) Seltzer—and they pay the price. Me, I listen. The courthouse regulars can't read the fine print on the early-bird menus, but they can spot perjury from the third row of the gallery.

Marvin, Saul and Max already told me I botched jury selection. Not that lawyers *pick* jurors anyway. We *exclude* those we fear, at least until we run out of challenges.

"You're *meshuga*, you leave Number Four on," Marvin told me on the first day of trial.

"He's a hard-working butcher," I said defensively. "Knows the value of a dollar. Won't give the store away."

Marvin ran a liver-spotted hand over his toupee, fingering the part. "Lookit his eyes, *boychik*. Like pissholes in the snow. Plus, I betcha he lays his fat belly on the scale with the lamb chops. I wouldn't trust him as far as I could spit."

I told myself Marvin was wrong and that he hadn't intended to shower me with spittle to make his point.

Some lawyers hire psychologists to help with jury selection. They'll tell you that people who wear bright colors crave attention and feel for the underdog. Plaintiff's jurors. Dark colors are worn by introverts who don't care about people. Defendant's jurors. Hoop earrings and costume jewelry are good for the plaintiff, Rolex watches and three-carat diamonds for the defense. To me, that's a lot of malarkey. I pick jurors who smile when I smile and don't fold their bodies into tight balls when I stand close.

No second guessing, now. Closing argument. A time to sing the praises of freedom of the press, of the great newspaper that fulfills the constitutional function of *blah-blah-blah*. And Marvin said don't yell. No emotion. *The jury don't care about the Foist Amendment.* Besides, Nick Wolf is a great *schmoozer,* Marvin told me. The jurors love him. Number Five, a Cuban receptionist, keeps batting her three-inch eyelashes at him.

And I thought she had trouble with her contacts.

The four men on the jury are your real problem, Marvin said. One black, two Cubans, one Anglo, all men's men. Nick's kind of guys.

So what am I, chopped liver?

He gave me that knowing look. *Ey, Lassiter, it ain't your jury; it ain't your day.* And with that, the gang took off, a kidnapping trial down the hall drawing them away.

Nick Wolf's lawyer, H. T. Patterson, yelled in closing argument. Hell, he sang, chanted, ranted, rocked and roiled. A spellbinder and a stemwinder, H.T. worked the jurors like a holy roller. Which he was at the Liberty City Colored Baptist Church while attending law school at night in the days before Martin Luther King.

"They subjected Attorney General Nick Wolf to scorn and ridicule, to calumny and obloquy," Patterson now crooned in a seductive sing-song. "They lied and distorted. They defamed and defiled. They took his honorable name and soiled it. Besmirched, tainted and tarnished it! Debased, degraded and disparaged it! And what should a man do when they stain, sully and smear his good name?"

Change it, I thought.

"What should a man of honor do when those with pens sharp as daggers poison his reputation, not in whispers but in howls, five hundred three thousand, six hundred seventy-nine times?"

Five hundred three thousand, six hundred seventy-nine being the Sunday circulation of the *Miami Journal*, and Sunday being the day of choice for fifty megaton, rock'em-sock'em, take-no-prisoners journalism. Which is what the *Journal* is noted for, though I thought the offending story—"State Attorney Violated Campaign Laws"—lacked characteristic punch. Not sharing my opinion was Nicholas G. Wolf, bona fide local high school football star, decorated Vietnam war hero, former policeman and currently State's Attorney for the Seventeenth Judicial Circuit in and for Dade County, Florida. The article accused Wolf of various technical violations of the campaign contributions law plus one unfortunate reference to accepting money from a reputed drug dealer.

"The man should seek redress in a court of law," Patterson solemnly declared, answering his own question, as lawyers are inclined to do. "He should come before a jury of his peers, citizens of the community. So my friends and neighbors, ladies and gentlemen of this jury, it is time to pay the piper. . . ."

I didn't think the metaphor held up to scrutiny, but the jury didn't seem to notice. The men all nodded, and Number Five stopped fluttering her eyelashes and now stared mournfully at poor, defamed Nick Wolf.

". . . It is time to assess damages; it is judgment day, it is time to levy the penalty for these knowing, reckless lies. And I ask you, ladies and gentlemen, is it too much to ask that the *Miami Journal*, that behemoth on the bay, that monster of malediction, pay ten dollars for each time it lied, yes, ten dollars for each time it sent its message of malice into our midst. . . ."

I never did better than C's in math, but I know when a lawyer is asking for five million bucks from a jury. Meaning H. T. Patterson hoped for two million, and I was beginning to wonder if taking this case to trial was so damn smart after all.

"A letter of apology, a front page retraction and fifty grand might do it," I told the publisher six months earlier in his bayfront office.

Symington Foote *bristled.* "We don't pay extortion. A public official's life is open to scrutiny, and we had a *bona fide* tip that Wolf was taking dirty money."

"From a tipster who refuses to come forward and a reporter who won't even reveal his source," I reminded the publisher, trying to knock him off the soapbox.

"But we don't need to prove the story was true, do we, counselor?"

He had me there. As a public official, Nick Wolf could win his libel suit only if he proved that the newspaper knew the story was false or had recklessly disregarded the truth. A nice concept for judges. For jurors, it's the same as in most lawsuits. If they like the plaintiff's attitude and appearance more than the defendant's, the plaintiff wins. Simple as that.

The case had been cleanly tried. A few histrionics from Patterson, but his tricks were mostly subtle. When I stood to make an objection, he would move close, letting me tower above him. He was a bantam rooster in a white linen three-piece suit and alongside was a bruiser representing the unrestrained power of a billion-dollar company.

So here I was about to deliver my closing argument in the big barn of a courtroom on the sixth floor of the Dade County Courthouse, an aging tower of gray limestone where the elevators seldom work and neither do the judges if they can help it. Heavy drapes matted with dust covered the grimy windows. The walnut paneling had darkened over the decades, and an obsolete air-conditioning system rumbled noisily overhead.

Several years ago, the electorate was asked to approve many millions of dollars in bonds for capital projects around the county. The voters said *yea* to a new zoo and *nay* to a new courthouse, expressing greater regard for the animals of the jungle to the animals of Flagler Street. And who could blame them?

Now I stood and approached the jury box, all six-two, two-hundred-something pounds of me. I tried not to get too close, avoiding the jurors' horizontal space. I shot a glance at the familiar sign on the wall above the judge's bench: "WE WHO LABOR HERE SEEK ONLY THE TRUTH." There ought to be a footnote: ". . . *subject to truth being misstated by perjurious witnesses, obfuscated by sleazy lawyers, excluded by inept judges, and overlooked by lazy jurors.*"

Planting myself like an oak in front of the jury, I surveyed the courtroom. Symington Foote sat at the defense table next to the chair I had just abandoned. The publisher fingered his gold cufflinks and eyed me skeptically. Behind him in the row of imitation leather chairs just in front of the bar were two representatives of the newspaper's libel insurance company. Both men wore charcoal-gray three-piece suits. They flew in from Kansas City for the trial and had that corn-fed, pale-faced, short-haired, tight-assed look of insurance adjusters everywhere. I wouldn't have a drink with either one of them if stroking the client's pocketbook wasn't part of my job. In the front row of the gallery sat three of the senior partners of Harman & Fox, awaiting my performance with anxiety that approached hysteria. They were more nervous than I was, and I'm prone to both nausea and diarrhea just before closing argument. Neither Mr. Harman nor Mr. Fox was there, the former having died of a stroke in a Havana brothel in 1952, the latter living out his golden years in a Palm Beach estate—Chateau Renard—with his sixth wife, a twenty-three-year-old beautician from Barbados. We were an old-line law firm by Miami standards, our forebears having represented the railroads, phosphate manufacturers, citrus growers and assorted other robber barons and swindlers from Florida's checkered past. These days, we carried the banner of the First Amendment, a load lightened considerably by our enormous retainer and hefty hourly rates.

Much like a railroad, a newspaper is a great client because of the destruction it can inflict. Newspaper trucks crush pedestrians in the early morning darkness; obsolete presses mangle workmen's limbs; and the news accounts themselves—the paper's very *raison d'etre*, as H. T. Patterson had just put it in a lyrical moment—can poison as surely as the deadliest drug. All of it, fodder for the law firm. So the gallery was also filled with an impressive collection of downtown hired guns squirming in their seats with the fond hope that the jury would nail my hide to the courtroom door. When I analyzed it, my only true friend inside the hall of alleged justice was Marvin the Maven, and he couldn't help me now.

I began the usual way, thanking the jurors, stopping just short of slobbering my gratitude for their rapt attention. I didn't point out that Number

Two had slept through the second day and that Number Six was more interested in what he dug out of his nose than the exhibits marked into evidence. Then after the brief commercial for the flag, the judge and our gosh-darned best-in-the-world legal system, I paused to let them know that the important stuff was coming right up. Summoning the deep voice calculated to keep them still, I began explaining constitutional niceties as six men and women stared back at me with suspicion and enmity.

"Yes, it is true that the *Journal* did not offer testimony by the main source of its story. And it is true that there can be many explanations for the receipt of cash contributions and many reasons why State's Attorney Wolf chose to drop charges against three men considered major drug dealers by the DEA. But Judge Witherspoon will instruct you on the law of libel and the burden of the plaintiff in such a case. And he will tell you that the law gives the *Journal* the right to be wrong . . ."

I caught a glimpse of Nick Wolf, giving me that tough guy smile. He was a smart enough lawyer in his own right to know I had no ammunition and was floundering.

"And as for damages," I told the jury, "you have just heard some outrageous sums thrown about by Mr. Patterson. In this very courtroom, at that very plaintiff's table, there have sat persons horribly maimed and disfigured, there have sat others defrauded of huge sums of money, but look at the plaintiff here . . ."

They did, and he looked back with his politician's grin. Nick Wolf filled his chair and then some. All chest and shoulders. One of those guys who worked slinging bags of cement or chopping trees as a kid, and with the good genes, the bulk stayed hard and his Brahma Bull neck would strain against shirt collars for the rest of his life. On television, with the camera focused on a head shot, all you remembered was that neck.

". . . Has he been physically injured? No. Has he lost a dime because of this story? No. Has he even lost a moment's sleep? No. So even if you find the *Journal* liable . . ."

H. T. Patterson still had rebuttal, and I wondered if he would use the line from Ecclesiastes about a man's good name being more valuable than precious ointment or the one from *Othello* about reputation as the immortal part of self.

He used them both.

Then threw in one from *King Richard II* I'd never heard.

•   •   •

"You could have advised us to settle," Symington Foote said, standing on the courthouse steps, squinting into the low, vicious late afternoon sun.

Funny, I thought I had.

"Three hundred twenty-two thousand," I said. "Could have been worse."

"Where the hell did that number come from? Where do these jurors get their—"

"Probably a quotient verdict. Someone wanted to give him a million, someone else only a hundred thousand. They put the numbers on slips of paper, add 'em up and divide by six. They're not supposed to do it, but it happens . . ."

Foote sniffed the air, didn't like what he smelled, and snorted. "Maybe it's time for a hard look at the jury system. I'll talk to the editorial writers in the morning."

He stomped off without telling me how much he looked forward to using my services in the future.

They thought they could get away with murder...
They overlooked one thing.

BANNERMAN'S LAW
BY JOHN R. MAXIM
AUTHOR OF *THE BANNERMAN EFFECT*

Things were quiet behind Bannerman's Maginot line of safe
houses and front operations in Westport, Connecticut. His
elite group of contract agents was retired, getting on with
their lives, blending into the community as ordinary citizens.
Just the way it was supposed to be -- until a phone call brings
them out of hiding for their most disturbing assignment yet.

A serial murderer is loose in Los Angeles, and he's already
murdered and mutilated at least six young women. Now it
looks like a copycat killer is at work. The police have next to
nothing to go on. But they are about to get more help than
they could have ever expected -- or wanted -- because the
latest victim is the sister of one of Bannerman's best people.

Graduate student Lisa Benedict had stumbled onto something that no one was meant to see -- something big enough
to cost her life. It won't take long for Bannerman and his
deadly band of operatives to start finding answers in some
very unlikely places...answers that make some very important
people very nervous. No one -- not the LAPD, not the FBI,
and certainly not the State Department -- thinks that Paul
Bannerman left Westport just to attend a funeral. And
they're right. In fact, before he is done, he'll be the cause of
more than one funeral -- *maybe even his own.*

Bannerman's Law.
On sale wherever Bantam Books are sold.

AN342 -- 10/91

Three time Shamus Award winner Loren D. Estleman turns his sights on the darker side of America's recent history in the first two novels of his Detroit Trilogy.

WHISKEY RIVER

"Estleman's *Whiskey River* is gritty, turbulent, unsettling, violent....It also is superb...." -- *Chicago Sun-Times*

It all begins in 1928. Detroit is growing by leaps and bounds. From the Mob's swankiest speakeasies and whorehouses to their private burial grounds, newspaperman Connie Minor chronicles the rise and fall of a charismatic young gangster named Jack Dance. He swaps secrets and strikes bargains with gang lords and on-the-take cops. But in a town like Detroit, knowing too much can be bad for your health, and soon the tabloid scribe finds himself not just a witness, but a key player in a story that gets hotter by the minute -- a story that could make him famous if it doesn't kill him first.

MOTOWN

The year is 1966, and Detroit reigns supreme at the height of America's love affair with the automobile. Threatened by the specter of safety legislation, the city's biggest manufacturer hires ex-cop and fervent car lover Rick Amery to go undercover and put the brakes on creeping consumer advocacy. It proves to be more than Rick bargained for as tensions between the Mob, unions and the black community escalate to all out war. *Motown* is a motor-driven snapshot of Detroit at critical mass. And when Detroit blows, she's going in a mushroom cloud -- every blood-stained block, all at once.

Whiskey River and **Motown** by Loren D. Estleman. On sale wherever Bantam Books are sold.

AN305 -- 8/91

Elvis Cole is a literate Vietnam vet who quotes Jiminy Cricket, drinks from a Spider-Man mug, carries a Dan Wesson .38, and is determined never to grow up. We met him for the first time in the award-winning novel *The Monkey's Raincoat* and now he returns here in

STALKING THE ANGEL
by Robert Crais

The blonde who walked into Cole's office was the best-looking woman he had seen in weeks. She had a briefcase on one arm and an uptight corporate hotel magnate named Bradley Warren on the other.

Bradley Warren has lost something very valuable that belongs to someone else -- an eighteenth-century Japanese manuscript called the Hagakure. The book outlines proper behavior for a samurai. It is also worth three million bucks. Somebody took it from Warren's safe at his Beverly Hills mansion. Cole's job is simply to get it back.

Nothing's that simple, as Cole and his borderline sociopath partner Joe Pike soon discover. Full of deadly high jinks, secrets of the orient, sex, madness, and encounters with the Japanese mafia sect known as the *yakuza*, **Stalking the Angel** is a detective story with something for everyone.

On sale soon wherever Bantam Crime Line Books are sold.

AN343 -- 10/91